MI GIRLS

Lulu Taylor was b ntryside, educated at Oxfor over the world. Her novels, are sexy, dramatic and enthra society. She is married and l

Praise for Lulu Taylor's *Heiresses*

'Nothing lifts the winter blues quite like a glam bonkbuster, and *Heiresses* is one of the highest pedigree . . . Addictive, decadent and sexy, it'll easily see you through the depths of winter's most depressing month. *5 Stars*'
heat

'If wealth and glamour turn you on, then turning the pages of this epic blockbuster will brighten the credit crunch chill for you.'
Best

'Well-written and fresh.'
Mirror

'Dubbed, "the new Jilly Cooper" . . . Perfect to forget the credit crunch and with a cast of characters who will constantly surprise, *Heiresses* is a great winter under the duvet read.'
South London Newsquest

'Pure indulgence and perfect reading for a dull January evening.'
Sun

'Such great escapism it could work as well as a holiday.'
Daily Mail

Also by Lulu Taylor

Heiresses

MIDNIGHT GIRLS

Lulu Taylor

arrow books

Published by Arrow Books 2010

6 8 10 9 7 5

First published in Great Britain in 2010 by
Arrow Books
Random House, 20 Vauxhall Bridge Road,
London SW1V 2SA

www.rbooks.co.uk

Addresses for companies within The Random House Group Limited can be found at: www.randomhouse.co.uk/offices.htm

The Random House Group Limited Reg. No. 954009

A CIP catalogue record for this book
is available from the British Library

ISBN 9780099524922

Penguin Random House is committed to a sustainable future for our business, our readers and our planet. This book is made from Forest Stewardship Council® certified paper.

Typeset by SX Composing DTP, Rayleigh, Essex
Printed and bound in Great Britain by
Clays Ltd, Elcograf S.p.A

To Emily Hamilton
The most glamorous girl in any room

Prologue

London
2009

The car drew to a halt in front of the most glamorous nightclub in London.

The uniformed doorman, accustomed to expensive vehicles stopping beside the discreet entrance, stepped forward and opened the door. A slim foot in a champagne-satin stiletto emerged, followed by a young woman with a pale cashmere cloak wrapped tightly around her oyster satin ruched dress. Her hair was pulled back into a glossy chignon and, despite the late hour, she was wearing a large pair of sunglasses.

The doorman shut the car door. As the vehicle glided away, she paused on the pavement at the entrance to the covered stairway leading down to the club. Then, pulling her cloak a little tighter, she descended swiftly, turned to the left and entered a long hallway.

'Madam.' A man in a suit standing close to the entrance stepped forward. He glanced at her face. 'Are you with a member?' he asked.

She nodded. 'Mr White.'

'Ah yes. Mr White is in the bar . . .'

Without waiting to hear more, she walked past him, poised and confident despite her high heels. The bar was crammed with well-dressed men and beautiful women, sipping cocktails or champagne or spirits, sitting on bar stools, leaning against the bar counter and the walls, perched on the low sills between the vaulted arches or on the velvet banquettes and comfortable little chairs in the sitting area. Scanning the room through her dark glasses, she still didn't find the person she was looking for. She made her way through the crush to the dimly lit dining room.

'May I help you, madam?' asked the maître d', smart in his dark suit, standing at his lectern with the reservation book before him.

'Mr White,' she said crisply. 'He's expecting me. Does he have a table?'

The maître d' consulted his book and then said with the faintest tone of surprise, 'He has the private room. Please, this way.'

He led her through the velvety darkness of the dining room, where the tables were illuminated only by candles in Venetian glass holders, and over to the right, through a door and up a small staircase to another door. He knocked.

'Come in,' said a deep voice from within.

'Your guest, Mr White,' said the maître d', standing back to allow the woman to enter the room. She walked past him with slow, sure steps.

Mr White stood up.

'Are there any more guests I should be expecting, sir?'

'No. No, thank you.'

This time, the maître d' remembered his training and did not show any surprise at there being only two guests in a room designed for thirty. 'Very well, sir. I shall send up a waiter directly.'

'Give us fifteen minutes, please, Gennaro. We have business to discuss.'

The moment the door closed behind him, the woman

took off her dark glasses and cashmere wrap and let them fall to the floor. Then she moved quickly towards Mr White, who pulled her into his arms, sinking his mouth on hers in a passionate kiss.

After a moment, she pulled away, her eyes sparkling, and said, 'This is very dangerous. Are you sure we won't be seen?'

'They're not here. I'm certain of it. No one knows who we are.'

She laughed softly and they kissed again, more slowly and tenderly. This time, when they came apart, she sighed happily. 'You're here.'

'Of course. What did you expect?' He reached out and took her hand, and they sat down together at the table. He gazed at her yearningly in the soft candlelight. 'You're more beautiful than ever. Where did we last meet? Milan?'

'Yes, Milan. It's been so long,' she said, stroking his hand.

'Oh my God, too long! I've been burning up for you, I've hardly been able to stand it.'

'How much longer will we have to go on like this? Only seeing each other in secret.'

'Until we've done what we need to do. I promise the wait will be worth it.'

She looked around at the room. 'This is my first time in here, can you believe it? After all these years. Will it really belong to us?

'In time, it will – I guarantee it. Every last napkin, sweetheart.'

She laughed with delight. 'I can't wait. But I'll be patient, I promise. Six months, a year – how ever long is necessary. And, you know, I'm getting rather fond of our clandestine meetings,' she purred, stroking a finger down his cheek. 'Aren't you?'

'I love it, you know that. I love *this* –' he cupped one hand around the soft satin that encased her breast – 'and *this.*' He ran his hand down her thigh. 'But I want you all the time.' He pressed his mouth against hers again and she opened her lips to him, savouring the exquisite sensation of his tongue exploring her. He pulled away with a moan. 'My God! You're driving me wild . . .' Then he took possession of her mouth once more, moving his hands up and down her body, heedless of the extremely expensive gown she was wearing. When he pushed the satin ruching down to release her breasts and took a small rosebud nipple in his mouth, she sighed with pleasure and whispered, 'Oh, that's beautiful . . . don't stop, don't stop, my darling . . . I want more. I want everything you can give me.'

They made an odd couple as they burst, giggling, into the dark, dusty, plastic-hung foyer of the half-built hotel. He was a young workman in a T-shirt and grimy jeans, his hair streaked with dust from a day on the site. She was a beauty, fine-boned, with a mass of thick hair twisted up in a lazy arrangement at the back of her head, and expensively dressed in a black boat-necked jersey dress and black stilettos that laced up to her ankle.

'Are you sure this is all right?' asked the girl breathlessly.

'Yeah. My boss won't find out. Probably wouldn't care if he did,' declared the workman with a touch of bravado.

They stood still for a moment and looked at each other, suddenly aware that they were complete strangers who had met only an hour earlier in the nearby pub. Then the girl reached for him, hungrily pulling him to her, not caring about his dirty clothes against her costly black dress. He didn't resist – she was easily the most gorgeous creature he'd ever seen and he hadn't been able to believe his luck when she'd flirted so blatantly with him. Now she was all over him, kissing him wildly and running her hands under his T-shirt and over his torso.

'Right here,' she begged him, possessed with desperate desire. 'Right here on the floor. Now. Please . . .'

The physical sensations she was igniting in him were so overwhelming that he could barely think straight, but he managed to lead her to a plastic-swathed sofa where they could sink down together. The girl moaned and cried, imploring him to kiss her, to touch her, to fuck her. He rolled up her short black dress to discover that she was wearing no underwear and she wrapped her long legs around him, pulling open his grimy work jeans to release his bulging cock, urging him to push it into her with no heed for the consequences. Unable to resist, he entered her soft dark warmth, gasping with pleasure as she dug her nails into his back and forced him deep inside. The pints he had drunk slowed him down a little, but he was soon in the grip of the fierce ride to his climax, pounding into her while she shouted and cried out, begging him for more.

'Oh . . . *shite*!' he yelled, as his orgasm burst out of him, and he collapsed on top of her, panting hard.

Barely a moment later, she was wriggling out from underneath him, pulling a tissue from her purse to mop away his spending, standing up and straightening her dress. He was still dazed by the whole experience as she looked down at him. There was a strange expression in her eyes: gratitude mixed with something else. Was it . . . sadness?

'Thanks, darling, that was heavenly,' she said in her low, musical voice with its perfectly rounded vowels.

'No, thank *you*,' he said with a lazy smile. 'I've never enjoyed coming into work so much.'

'Coming being the operative word.' She flashed him a smile. ''Bye.'

And she scooped up her bag, ran a hand over her hair and walked casually away, disappearing into the night as quickly and mysteriously as she had arrived.

*

Only a mile away, in a hot Camden nightclub, a young man was watching a girl dancing. She was tossing her head with abandon, moving her arms and swinging her hips in time to the music, showing off her ripe curves and full breasts to their best advantage in an electric blue body-con dress.

He was drawn not just to her feminine shape, but to the energy and vigour that emanated from her: it was obvious that she wanted to be free, to dance, to feel alive. Her life force was irresistible. He made his way across the dance floor towards her, pushing his way through writhing bodies. The girl he was watching sang as she danced, smiling with pleasure as she moved sinuously to the beat.

When he reached her she was oblivious, continuing to dance alone. Then she opened her eyes and saw him. For a moment she carried on smiling, gazing at him as though sharing her joy with him, then she came to a sudden halt, frozen on the dance floor, her eyes wide. She blinked. She mouthed a single word. He couldn't hear it against the noise of the music, but he could see clearly what she had said. '*You.*'

He smiled at her, nodding slowly. Then he took her hand, leant forward, put his other hand behind her head and pulled her to him, pressing his mouth to hers.

She was too astonished to resist and then, as she appeared to realise what was happening, she relaxed under his touch and began to kiss him back. At first, their kiss was almost unbearably tender: slow, gentle and beautiful. Then it grew more passionate as they both felt the spark between them ignite into flame.

The man felt a tap on his back. He pulled out of the kiss and looked round. Someone yelled, 'Oi, get a room, mate!' though their voice was almost lost in the music.

He turned back to the girl. Her eyes were shining now,

her hands clutching his. He raised his eyebrows at her and cocked his head towards the door. She nodded eagerly and a moment later they were making their way through the crowd, her hand held tight in his so he couldn't lose her.

Outside the club, they stood on the pavement, taking no notice of the people milling about them.

'It's been a long time,' the man said, smiling at her.

'I can't believe it's you!' she said breathlessly. 'What are you doing here?'

He said slowly, 'I guess I was supposed to find you . . . I always had a feeling I would, you know.' Then he kissed her again, wrapping her tightly in his arms as though he was worried she would float away if he let go.

PART 1

Chapter 1

Westfield Boarding School for Girls
May 2000

'We really have to do something about that awful cow,' declared Allegra.

She sucked hard on her Marlboro Light and puffed the smoke out of the open attic window and into the warm spring night beyond.

The previous term Allegra had discovered the caretaker had the key to the attics and, with her fearless charm, had persuaded him to lend it to her, then had it copied and returned it. 'Now we've got our very own headquarters. Isn't it brilliant?' she'd said proudly. She'd insisted that they make the most of the unlimited access to their secret place, and almost every night led the expedition out of the dorms and up into the filthy attic with its mountain of junk – broken chairs, trunks, shabby old desks and boxes – where they could indulge in their favourite vice in private. 'We won't be able to do this next year when we move into the sixth-form boarding house,' she'd said, 'so we have to make the most of it while we can.'

Now she looked over at the other two. 'I mean it, she's totally doing my head in at the moment.'

Imogen knew exactly who was meant. She blew out a stream of smoke, pleased with the nonchalant ease with which she did it. No one would guess she'd only been smoking for a few months and that, the first time she'd tried it, she'd been violently sick. She seemed just as cool as the others now. 'But what on earth can we do?' she said.

Romily looked blank. 'What are you talking about?' she asked as she pulled a packet of Gauloises out of her pyjama pocket.

'I can't believe you smoke those things,' Imogen said, shaking her head. 'They're so strong! They make me feel queasy even when they're not lit.'

'I can't believe you waste your time on *those*,' Romily said, gesturing at Imogen's cigarette. 'They taste of nothing. You might as well not bother lighting them and just breathe in.'

'They'll do me fine, thanks very much. They're better for you anyway,' Imogen replied. She held out the white and gold packet. 'Lights, see?'

Romily snorted. 'If you believe that, you'll believe anything! I've heard there's fibreglass in the filters that goes straight into your lungs and cuts them to shreds. Give me an honest French brand any time.'

Allegra frowned. 'Aren't we getting a bit off the subject? I was talking about Sophie Harcourt.'

'Ah.' Romily took out a lighter, clicked it into life and sucked at her Gauloise, the strands of tobacco and cigarette paper flaring orange. She exhaled a long plume of smoke. 'That's better! I needed that. So . . . what's La Harcourt done now?'

Romily hadn't been in the lesson to witness the event; she had no need of French tuition and was allowed to do other revision while the others rehearsed their verbs, tenses and vocab ahead of the exams.

Allegra made a face and crossed one long slim leg over the other. She was sitting on an old box in her night clothes of flowered cotton shorts and a blue T-shirt, her cigarette clamped between her fingers. 'She threw ink-covered blobs of tissue at me on her ruler. You saw it, didn't you, Midge?'

'Yeah.' Imogen took a puff on her cigarette, which she held exactly as Allegra did hers. 'She tried to pretend it wasn't her, but I saw her giggling with Arabella Balmer.'

'I hate her,' spat Allegra. 'She covered my shirt with ink splats, and it won't come out. It's the one I got at Camden Market too. She knows how cool it is . . . that's why she wanted to wreck it.'

'She's *so* jealous,' Imogen declared, a little pleased that someone like Sophie felt that way about them.

Romily nodded. 'She hates the fact that we aren't frightened of her like everyone else is.'

Sophie Harcourt was a powerful force in the fifth form; her wit and forceful personality made her popular, but her ability to turn her gimlet gaze on some poor unfortunate and ruin their life also made her feared. She had a talent for finding the weak spot in others and then teasing and mocking and bullying them until their life became a misery. As a result, everyone tried to keep on her good side or else well out of her way. Except for Allegra's little group of three.

'I don't know why she doesn't just leave us alone!' Allegra said, frowning into the night beyond the attic window. 'What is there to be so jealous about anyway?'

Imogen knew the answer to that: Allegra couldn't help drawing all eyes to her, wherever she was and whatever she did. She was very naughty, constantly breaking rules and playing tricks – she had once been suspended for a fortnight for organising the biggest food fight the school had ever seen – but her naughtiness was without the personal malice of Sophie Harcourt's, and everyone loved her for it. Except the teaching staff, of course. But even when she was behaving herself, no one could ignore her for long. Charisma seemed to shimmer out of her, partly because of her beauty

– fine-boned features with porcelain-and-gold skin, navy-blue eyes, thick blonde hair, and a slender, graceful figure – and partly because of the incredible air of self-confidence that enveloped her. It was as though she knew she mattered, and took it for granted that everyone thought the same. It armoured her impenetrably against Sophie and her cohorts. And then there was the title . . .

'She's jealous now that you're Lady Allegra,' Imogen said wisely. 'Ever since she found out, she's been ten times worse than usual.'

Allegra sighed. 'Bother that bloody title! I wish I'd never got it. Everyone's been different with me since Grandpa died, even Miss Myers. She told me the other day that ladies didn't run in the corridors and that I had to set an example to the rest of the school. What bloody nonsense.'

Imogen nodded sympathetically, but in her heart she thought that having a title must be wonderful – so romantic, so old-fashioned, so pretty. When Allegra's grandfather had died, her father had succeeded to the earldom and Allegra had automatically gone from The Hon. Allegra McCorquodale (and no one cared about that, there were plenty of hons kicking about the school) to Lady Allegra, daughter of the Earl and Countess of Crachmore, sounding like the heroine of a Walter Scott novel. Suddenly, she was someone of importance and it had put certain noses out of joint.

'Sophie loathes us all, for different reasons,' Imogen said, taking another delicate puff of her cigarette. 'She hates the way I beat her in everything, especially English. And she's green about Romily's money.'

Romily nodded, tapping her ash into a jar lid kept handy for the purpose. 'I saw her listening in when I was telling you all about Paris, and she had a face like thunder. And I swear she was trying to get my pink cashmere jumper out of my bag the other day.'

'See?' Imogen spread out her hands. It was perfectly obvious to her. 'She feels threatened by us, and by our club. She can't rule over us like she does everyone else.'

'I wish she'd leave me alone,' Allegra grumbled. 'If she doesn't, she'll be sorry.'

Imogen knew that Allegra was too strong-willed to let Sophie victimise her, and was sure that Sophie would be making a bad mistake if she tried to take any of them on. But lately there had been some minor skirmishes – such as the inky missiles fired in French – and there was a feeling in the air that a big battle was not far off.

There was a loud bang from down below in the dormitories at that moment and the girls all froze, staring at each other with frightened eyes. Imogen's stomach plummeted with a sickening swoop, and her hands began to tremble. 'What was that?' she whispered, her heart racing.

They were breaking some of the strictest of school rules: they were out of bounds, at a time when they were forbidden to be out of their cubicles, and they were smoking. Any one of these was an offence worthy of expulsion; taken together, they would mean instant dismissal.

They all listened a moment more, Romily with her Gauloise poised ready to be stubbed out on the jam-jar lid.

'Oh,' Allegra said finally, relaxing, 'it was nothing. An old pipe banging or something. You know what this place is like.'

It's all right for you, Imogen thought, her heart still pounding. Allegra seemed cool and unfazed by the terrible risks they were taking, but then, her parents didn't give a damn what she did and wouldn't even care if she was sent away from Westfield in disgrace. Romily's family would no doubt consider the school rules very petty and bourgeois, and simply find an even grander school for her. But Imogen could hardly bear to think of her own parents' disappointment if she spoiled this chance for herself. She could see her mother's face now, and the look in her eyes if she discovered that Imogen had forfeited her precious and hard-won education for the sake of a stolen cigarette in the night.

Please don't let us be caught, she prayed. She knew how dangerous their nocturnal activities were but couldn't resist them or bear not to be included, even when she risked expulsion. They were a special club after all, with Allegra as their leader, and they did everything together. Allegra had dubbed them the Midnight Girls, because that was when they made their secret treks to the attic, and it made them sound even more special, like a pop group or something. She had led them into all sorts of trouble, from adorning the statue of their founder, Dame Mary Westfield, with a particularly enormous bra and comedy straw hat, to the instigation of the great sock rebellion of the previous year when all girls began to wear forbidden colours of sock and, worse still, around their ankles instead of pulled up to the knee. But this was by far the most serious of her pranks, and every time they made the trek to the attic Imogen was filled with fluttering nerves, though she did her best to hide it.

'Come on,' Allegra said, stubbing out her cigarette end, tossing it through the open window on to the roof and then pulling the window shut. 'We'd better get back to bed.'

The other two disposed of their cigarette ends and got up to make their way back to the dormitory.

Thank goodness for that, Imogen thought, relief beginning to creep through her. *Another Midnight Girls meeting over and safely done. I'll be glad to be back in bed.*

She happily followed Allegra down the attic stairs, padding softly after her, with Romily behind. When they reached the bottom Allegra pushed at the door. When it was still only open a crack, she gasped and stepped back, pulling it shut again.

'Fucking hell,' she whispered, looking round at the other two with wide, fearful eyes. 'I just saw Sophie Harcourt walking down the corridor towards us.'

Imogen supported herself against the wall, feeling her knees weaken under her. Her heart started pounding again, and her breathing quickened. Behind her, she heard Romily gasp with fright. If Sophie caught them, they would be reported to Myers before morning and probably expelled by the following lunchtime. *Oh, God, I* knew *something like this was going to happen! Why the hell have we been so stupid?* Imogen asked herself.

'What *is* she doing?' murmured Allegra under her breath. They waited, trembling, for three long minutes before Allegra finally said, 'She must have gone.'

'Be careful!' hissed Romily as Allegra slowly opened the door again.

'Is anyone there?' asked Imogen, her voice high and breathy with fright.

Allegra poked her head round the door and looked up and down the corridor. 'She's gone.'

'Are you sure it was her?' Romily asked as they crept out of the attic.

'Of course I am.' Allegra frowned and looked back down the corridor away from their dormitory. 'But where was she going?'

'Who cares?' Imogen whispered, desperate to get back to the safety of her cubie. 'Let's just get back to bed, for God's sake. If she's up and about she may disturb Myers, and then we'll all be caught.'

'She was heading towards Kat's,' muttered Allegra. 'Perhaps she's meeting someone there.'

The dormitories were named after saints, perhaps to inspire their occupants towards a life of purity and obedience. Allegra, Romily and Imogen were in St Helen's, known as Hell's. Down the corridor was Kat's, from St Katharine's. In the other wing of the school were Mag's and Ag's, after St Margaret and St Agnes.

'I'm going to take a look,' Allegra said determinedly.

'No!' exclaimed Imogen in a fierce whisper. 'We've got to get back!'

'But don't you see? If Sophie's up to something, we ought to know about it. That way we've got our ammunition ready if she finds out about us. She may already know.' Allegra shot the other two a determined look. 'Go back if you want to. I don't care.'

Imogen looked at Romily and saw her own fright and anxiety reflected in the other girl's eyes. She reached out involuntarily and clutched her friend's arm, her hand chilly on Romily's bare flesh.

Allegra ran lightly on tiptoe down the dark corridor towards Kat's.

'What shall we do?' Romily said quietly.

'We can't just stand here.' Imogen looked up and down the passageway, eerie in the darkness and without the usual scramble of rushing girls. She knew that she couldn't bear just waiting for whatever it was to happen – whether it was Sophie returning from her mysterious errand or Myers appearing in the corridor, wearing her night-time hairnet and with her hideous towelling robe tied tightly round her barrel-like stomach. 'Come on, let's go after Allegra.' She walked lightly down the hall, keeping to the shadows as though they might somehow protect her, while Romily followed behind.

They turned the corner and saw that Allegra had already opened the door to Kat's and disappeared into the darkness. Imogen gave a tiny gasp. This was getting stupidly dangerous. They were familiar with the routines of their own house mistress but they knew nothing about Miss Jennings, who guarded Kat's. She might be in the habit of striding about the dorms at night, making sure that all was well and that none of her charges was up and about when they were supposed to be asleep.

Romily and Imogen reached the open door and glanced at each other, worried and pale. Then Allegra loomed out of the darkness, looking shocked and yet gleeful.

'Oh my God,' she whispered, 'look at this! Be very quiet. Silent as the grave.'

She led them through the doorway and into the blackness of the corridor beyond. All the boarding houses were laid out the same way: dormitory bedrooms divided up into cubicles on one side, and the house mistress's room, a common room and other amenities on the other. Kat's common room was in the same position as Hell's, looking oddly familiar and yet strange at the same time. Allegra stopped at the doorway to it. She glanced round at the other two and held her finger up to her mouth to indicate absolute silence was required.

Imogen peered into the darkness. She could hear a curious rustling noise, and then the sound of heavy breathing and some short, high gasps. What was it? she wondered. Her eyes were becoming accustomed to the darkness and she could make out that two figures were lying together on the common-room sofa. Like Hell's, it was long and large, big enough for about eight girls to sit comfortably when they were watching television. The figures were intertwined and furiously active.

It took a few more seconds for Imogen to register what she was seeing, but then she knew without a doubt. Her mouth dropped open and she felt a strange mixture of embarrassment, disbelief and a kind of excitement. There was Sophie Harcourt, lying half-naked on the Kat's sofa, wrapped in the arms of Martha Young, and they were snogging furiously. Martha was wearing only a pair of knickers. One of her long legs was tucked over Sophie's hips, and one of her hands was thrust down Sophie's pyjama bottoms where it seemed to be moving. Her naked chest was pressed against Sophie's.

Of course the girls thought and talked about sex all the time but the whole place was boy-mad. Everyone seemed to be pining away for some pop star or film actor, or else a boy they had met through friends or family. Every girl was desperate to be kissed, to move to first base and beyond. They were sex crazy – but, without exception, opposite-sex crazy. No one talked about any other kind of activity, as though it didn't exist, and other girls were appraised only on their relative attractions for men.

Imogen's heart started racing and she jumped back into the corridor, pressing her hand to her mouth. She knew that she should not be witnessing whatever it was she had seen: it was deeply intimate and private. She felt immediately tainted and dirty, as though she was a voyeur, preferring to watch other people rather than do anything herself. But she could also feel a fizzing, treacherously sweet excitement, filling her belly and making her almost uncomfortably aware of herself. Whatever Sophie was feeling now, she, Imogen, had never felt anything like this, having just had a glimpse of what awaited her, perhaps not with another girl but with someone, sometime in the future. It looked terrifying and tempting at the same time: could she really abandon herself as Sophie was doing? Could sex really do that to you? Could it really create the pleasure that Sophie seemed to be feeling?

'Let's go,' she whispered to the other two. Romily looked pale and frightened, half horrified, while Allegra's eyes were dancing and she was grinning widely.

There was no argument. The other two followed her

quickly as Imogen led the way swiftly out of Kat's and back to the safety of their own dormitory. They didn't speak again as they made their way to their separate cubicles.

Imogen lay in her bed, staring into the darkness, unable to shake the image from her mind: all she could see was Sophie, pushing herself into Martha's embrace, thrusting her tongue into Martha's mouth, and Martha's hand at its mysterious work inside Sophie's pyjama bottoms.

'Oh, God,' she murmured to herself, hardly able to believe she was thinking it. 'Poor Sophie. Poor, poor Sophie.'

Chapter 2

Stanley's Restaurant
West Coast of America
2000

Mitch bent over his paperwork, laboriously filling in the answers to his homework. It didn't come naturally to him, all this writing, and it wasn't what he'd come into the catering industry for. He'd come because he wanted to cook, do things with his hands, taste things with his mouth, and make things he could see and feel. But he also knew that he needed an education to get on, so he was taking a night course in business and accounting at the local college. It was hard for him, especially when the only quiet time he had to study was after his late shift finished, at one o'clock in the morning, when he ought to be getting to bed, considering it was a six a.m. start the next day. But his blood was buzzing from service now even though the next day he'd be pole-axed with exhaustion, fit only for making stocks and prepping for at least four hours, with a break before the evening shift started all over again.

So here he was, still in his chef's trousers – baggy black pants that didn't show the spills – sitting in his boss's office at the desk under the chipped aluminium lamp, making himself think about profits and percentages, and keeping going with the aid of Diet Coke.

A noise made him look up. In the doorway stood a woman wearing tiny denim cut-offs and a little pink T-shirt that strained tight across her large breasts. She shook out her canary-yellow curls, ran her tongue over her lips and said breathily, 'Hi, Mitch. How ya doin'?'

Mitch felt apprehension creep along his veins. 'Hi there, Jo-Lynn. Where's Stanley? He here?'

She shook her head. 'Uh-uh. I've come on my own.'

Ah, Christ. I've been expecting something like this. Mitch had been noticing lately that his boss's wife was taking an interest in him, and he'd been doing his best to deflect it. Jo-Lynn was an attractive woman, there was no denying that. Those long brown legs that she showed off so nicely in her little shorts were enough to give him a hard-on on their own, let alone those tits of hers, but he knew better. Stanley would not take kindly to the prospect of his pretty young wife being boffed by his sous-chef, and he was a large man with a meaty pair of fists on him. So Mitch had taken to keeping out of Mrs Baker's way whenever she sashayed into the kitchen.

'Actually,' Jo-Lynn went on, 'he's asleep.'

Mitch just stared at her.

'Pretty sound asleep, if you wanna know. I crushed up a couple of my sleeping pills in his Bourbon. I don't think he'll be stirring till morning.'

Mitch put down his pen, feeling uncomfortable. A nervous sweat was breaking out on his upper lip. 'Why'd you do that?'

She looked at him coyly, acting a little shy and girlish. 'Oh, you know . . . so that I could have some time on my own. A little bit of peace and quiet. You know what Stanley's like. He ain't easy. Sometimes I need . . .' she sighed softly and smiled at him, lowering her lashes '. . . some relaxation.'

Mitch nearly jumped up in fright. 'OK! Er . . . er . . .' he stuttered. 'Well . . . I . . .'

Jo-Lynn giggled. She advanced into the room, pushing out her ample bosom and giving him a look of burning lust from her china-blue, baby-doll eyes. 'You're so cute,' she purred. 'D'you know that? I love those brown eyes of yours and those muscles . . . how did you get 'em? You work out or something? You don't get those slaving in a kitchen, or Stanley would be Mr fuckin' Universe.' She perched on the edge of the desk, gazing down at him. 'I'm sure we could have lots of fun together.' Leaning forward, she licked her lips again and whispered, 'Stanley doesn't have to know about it.'

'Jo-Lynn . . .' He tried to sound masterful instead of frightened but knew he was out of his depth with this temptress, who was not at all like the girls he remembered in high school or the waitresses in the diners he'd worked in.

'How old are ya, Mitch?'

He put his pen down. *I guess I'm not going to get much more work done*. 'I'm twenty-four.'

She smiled. 'Huh! You look younger, honey. But I don't mind.' She leant forward again, showing him the vast lane of cleavage that ran between her breasts. 'I like 'em young. Plenty of energy.' An expression of distaste passed over her face. 'Not like Stanley. He's got nothing left. Not that he had much to start with.'

Curiosity overcame Mitch's anxiety. He'd often wondered why a pretty thing like Jo-Lynn was married to an overweight, balding, sweating, two-bit chef like Stanley. 'So, why do you stay with him?'

She gazed down at the desk then flicked her eyes back towards him, sadness in their blue depths. 'It's not like I got so many options, you know? I needed Stanley to get out of my home town and away from my piece-of-crap family. But I want something else . . . Stanley says you're good, really good. You're the best cook in the place, and the smartest. He thinks you can go far.'

'Really?' Mitch couldn't help the pleasure welling up in him when he heard this. Stanley might be a shitty boss, but his praise was worth having. He thought Mitch might be able to cut it on his own – that meant something. After flunking high school he'd worked in cheap eating joints, flipping burgers and dipping fries in boiling oil, until he'd suddenly realised that maybe he'd found his way out. He'd begun to wonder if cooking – real cooking – was what he could do with his life, and if it could lead him somewhere else, into business perhaps, where he could really make his mark. . . It had taken him six years already but he'd worked his way up into a proper restaurant, and he was sure he could go further if he only applied himself.

Jo-Lynn nodded. 'So how about it, Mitch? You and me? Right here?' She cast a longing look at his groin.

'No . . . no way, Jo-Lynn, I can't do it . . .'

Her face hardened. 'I hope you're not gonna make a fool of me, Mitch,' she said, a note of warning in her voice. 'I've gone to a lot of trouble for this, you know.'

''Course not. But it's more than my job's worth, you know that.' He tried to sound jokey and nonchalant.

'You might find it's more than your job's worth not to.' She dropped her chin coquettishly on to her shoulder. 'If you're not nice to me, I can always tell Stanley that you came on to me, made a pass at me . . .'

He was shocked. 'You'd really do that, Jo-Lynn?'

'Sure.' Her blue eyes were suddenly flinty. 'If you don't play ball. Now, why don't you bring that handsome face of yours round here and kiss me?'

Mitch floundered. He couldn't believe he was turning down a gorgeous woman who was sitting there, inviting him to fuck her, but he couldn't do it. For one thing, she was terrifying the life out of him. And whatever she said, it was just too risky. If he gave in once, he was sure she'd come back for more – she was the type to enjoy the thrill of the illicit. She'd make him do whatever she wanted, and eventually Stanley would find out anyway. 'I'm sorry, I really am, but . . . I gotta study. I gotta do my homework.'

'What are ya? Some school kid? Don't fuck me around, Mitch, I'm warning you.'

He shook his head. 'I can't do it. I'm sorry.'

Her face turned stony. 'No one turns me down. No one. You're gonna regret it, Mitch. I promise you that.' She slid off the desk, turned her pert rear into his eye line, and looked over her shoulder at him. 'You better think of some other town you'd like to work in, honey, 'cos you ain't gonna be here much longer.'

Chapter 3

Westfield Boarding School for Girls
2000

The Midnight Girls didn't meet for a week after they discovered Sophie Harcourt's secret. It felt too dangerous, somehow: they'd come perilously close to being discovered themselves and it was best to hold off for a while until things had quietened down.

Imogen couldn't help staring at Sophie in lessons, astonished that the other girl looked exactly the same as she had before: utterly innocent and normal, working away at her French verbs and preparing for the exams as though nothing had changed. Imogen had half expected to see signs of depravity on her face or maybe a new look of sophistication and knowledge, the kind of expression that Eve must have had after eating the apple. After all, Sophie had taken steps into the secret world they all longed to explore: she had experienced things they could only imagine.

She watched carefully to see if Martha Young and Sophie went near each other, but they didn't. They were in different houses and different forms. The only time they were together was in the upper-fifth common room during any free or revision periods. Imogen saw them together when Sophie went to make a cup of tea and Martha was rinsing a mug in the sink: they appeared not to notice each other at all, but Imogen thought she saw the merest flicker of a glance between the two of them. She remembered them embracing in the darkness, their skin soft against the rough old wool of the well-worn sofa, and looked away, her face burning.

The day after the discovery, Allegra had been in high spirits.

'I can't believe it,' she'd said excitedly, as they walked around the games field during break. 'Sophie Harcourt's a lesbian! And with Martha Young. *Shit*. I wonder if Arabella knows about it? Bet she doesn't. God, when you think about how mean Sophie is . . . Do you remember when she and Arabella spent the whole time teasing Portia Clifford about being a lezzer – and all along Sophie was one herself! Martha had her hand down her pants, for Christ's sake. She must have been *fingering* her. What a fucking hypocrite!'

They all agreed that Sophie was a terrible hypocrite, but Imogen found it hard to share Allegra's elation; something about the discovery worried her, though she wasn't sure if it was the revelation about Sophie's sexuality or the power of the secret they now guarded. No matter how worldly wise and grown-up everyone pretended to be, they would still be shocked by a gay relationship – it would mark Sophie out, make her the target of gossip and secret jokes. Romily maintained her cool French exterior as always and didn't say much, but the glances she swapped with Imogen showed that she secretly shared the same misgivings.

When the games mistress nominated Allegra to help collect kit from the sports hall, Romily pulled Imogen to one side.

'What are we going to do about all this?' she said, her dark brown eyes worried. 'Look at Allegra, I haven't seen her so cheerful in ages.'

'I know.' Imogen gazed at the ground. 'It's because of

what we've found out. I think she wants to use it.'

'I don't think she should,' Romily said urgently.

'Nor do I.' Imogen couldn't help noticing that her friend wore even her games kit with her customary sense of fashion: her tartan kilt was a little more rakish and stylish than the others, her initials stitched on to it in flowing pink script.

'If Sophie gives Allegra any reason or provokes her, she'll use it to get her revenge,' said Romily. 'She won't be able to help herself. It's bound to get out somehow, and it's going to cause a terrible scandal. Poor Sophie. I know she's a bitch, but I can't help feeling sorry for her. It will be so, so embarrassing. How will she face everyone? It will ruin her life here. And Martha's too. They'll have to leave.'

They stared at each other.

'Can we stop Allegra?' asked Imogen at last.

'All we can do is try and persuade her to go easy,' Romily said. 'I'm sure she'll listen to us.' The games mistress returned then with Allegra, whose arms were piled high with bibs. 'Come on. We'd better go and warm up.'

It felt strange for Imogen to be sharing a confidence with Romily. Allegra had always been their leader, the other two her close lieutenants with their first loyalty to her rather than each other. And Imogen had been at Allegra's side even before they came to Westfield, two girls from Scotland anticipating their grand English boarding school, Imogen with nervousness and Allegra with unbridled excitement.

They had first met when Imogen was almost ten years old.

'What an amazing coincidence!' her mother had marvelled as she dressed Imogen in her smartest clothes.

'What is? Where are we going?' she'd asked while her mother brushed out her hair and tied it in a ribbon.

'My old school friend, Selina Garrett . . . all this time she's been living ten miles away and I never knew!' Imogen could sense her mother's excitement. 'Who would have thought it? I met her quite by accident in Edinburgh and it turns out that she's only gone and married Ivo McCorquodale, the eldest son of Lord Crachmore, and they live at Foughton, that magnificent old castle on the edge of the loch. I can't believe how many times I've driven past it, and all the time Selina's been living there! We were very best friends at school, though we lost touch afterwards when she went abroad. We're going to visit today, and you'll meet her daughter who is the same age as you are. I'm sure you're going to be friends, just as we were!'

They seemed to drive for ages, out of town and into the countryside, and finally down long, twisty, overgrown roads that led to a beautiful, crystal blue loch, with Foughton standing craggy and impressive at its side. It was amazing, like something from Imogen's favourite storybooks, a castle where gorgeous princesses danced in satin slippers and where good fairies and wicked witches flew among the grey stone turrets and battlements.

I would love to live here, she thought at once, her imagination alight. *It's so much more exciting than our boring house in our boring road . . .*

She watched as her mother fell, screaming with pleasure, into the arms of her old friend, followed dutifully as they were led through the endless dark corridors and listened as her mother said what an incredible place it was, but her friend said it was a bore to live in something so big and that it was freezing in the winter and how difficult it was to find people to work there – and all the other adult problems that seemed so dull. Who cared, if you could live in a castle like this? And then, they came out into an enormous sitting room and suddenly they were in the light again. Huge windows opened on to a stone terrace edged with what looked like battlements, and beyond that was the sparkling loch and nothing else to be seen for miles and miles except soft Scottish hills melting into the horizon. And there, sitting on the rug in front of an enormous hearth, was a pretty blonde girl, her skinny limbs emerging from a T-shirt and some denim shorts, playing with a grey kitten.

'This is Allegra,' her mother's friend said cheerfully. 'Allegra darling, get up and say hello to Imogen. She's just your age and I'm sure you're going to be great friends.'

Imogen stood awkwardly on the edge of the rug while Allegra got slowly to her feet, her face impassive and her dark-blue eyes watchful and cool.

'Take her up to the nursery, darling, and show her your things. I'm sure you'll have a lovely time together. Take Zaza with you.'

Allegra tucked the grey kitten against her chest and padded towards the door without giving Imogen another glance.

'Go on, Imogen,' said her mother, obviously eager to sit down for a good chat with her friend, 'off you go with Allegra.'

So she'd gone after her, following in her footsteps and feeling silly in the smart tartan pinafore and patent Mary Janes that her mother had put her in for the visit. Allegra's clothes, although they were nothing special, seemed a million times more stylish and desirable. On that first visit she barely said a word to Imogen for the first hour. Up in the nursery, she put a cassette tape into a player and they listened to rock music at top volume while Allegra played with Zaza the kitten and Imogen lost herself in the nursery bookcase, which was crammed with Enid Blytons that she hadn't yet added to her collection. After an hour or so they went back downstairs and Allegra took her to the kitchen where the housekeeper gave them each a glass of orange squash and some digestive biscuits.

'Do you like Nirvana?' Allegra said at last, as they munched their biscuits.

'Mmm, yes.' Imogen nodded. That must be what they'd been listening to. She'd never heard of them. They were certainly loud, and seemed very het up about things.

'I fucking adore them,' Allegra announced. Imogen's eyes widened with surprise at the extremely naughty word she had just heard. 'I'm going to marry Kurt Cobain when I grow up.' She stared at Imogen. 'Who are you going to marry?'

Imogen didn't know whether to tell the truth about who she wanted to marry, but she had been brought up to be honest and wanted to be like this glamorous girl, so she swallowed her biscuit and said in a quiet voice, 'Kevin fucking Costner.'

Allegra laughed so hard she squirted orange squash all over the table. Imogen started giggling too, and the next minute they were squealing hysterically, with Allegra rolling on the floor holding her stomach, until the housekeeper came to find out what on earth all the fuss was about.

After that, they were friends.

Back home, Imogen's mother couldn't stop talking excitedly about Selina's life, her marriage into the aristocracy, her beautiful children, and her amazing house.

'Who would have thought it?' she kept marvelling. 'Selina Garrett. Well, well, well. Of course, it can't all be a picnic. Ivo's been married twice before and poor Selina's got three stepchildren to cope with, as well as her own two, and her boy Xander won't inherit a thing. And her grim old father-in-law still rules the roost, but still . . . Perhaps it's not too high a price to pay for everything she's got.'

Imogen wondered if her mother was drawn to her old friend and her impressive home because it was a life that perhaps she herself could have had. After all, they had both started out in the same place, as schoolgirls at Westfield, but where Selina Garrett now had a title and a castle to live in, Jeannie Heath had ended up in an average suburban house, with a decent but ordinary husband who ran his own Edinburgh law practice, living an uneventful life.

No matter what Selina Garrett now had, she must have been lonely too because their visits to the castle became quite frequent. Every few weeks Imogen and her mother would get into the car to make the trip to that strange otherworldly place. And with each visit, Allegra and Imogen grew closer. Allegra would take Imogen to her bedroom and show her her prized collection of Hello Kitty bags and T-shirts, and her sparkly bangles, and they were soon putting each other's hair into bunches and plaits, talking about whether they preferred Whitney Houston or Mariah Carey. They talked about the boys they were in love with; Allegra liked actors like River Phoenix or else rock stars, the grungier the better. Imogen preferred nice, clean-cut boys like Tom Cruise and Take That.

'How many brothers and sisters have you got?' Allegra asked one day in her clipped English accent as they lay on the nursery floor doing cat's cradles with pieces of string.

'Oh, none. I'm an only child,' Imogen said placidly. Her soft Scottish accent, picked up at school, was shortening into an imitation of the way her new friend talked.

'Really? You're so lucky. I wish I was an only child. I get forgotten all the time.'

'Where are all your brothers and sisters?' Imogen had never seen anyone else about and had begun to assume that Allegra was an only child, like herself.

Allegra shrugged. 'Dad's been married three times. He's really old . . . much older than your dad, I expect. He's over sixty.'

'Sixty!' breathed Imogen, unable to imagine her father at such a great age.

'He's got two children from his first marriage, Rory and Tristan. Rory's going to inherit this place when Dad dies, and he's grown up and married. Then there's Miranda – she's my sister from Dad's second marriage. She's away at Sherbourne, and in the holidays she goes to stay with her mother most of the time. After that Dad married Mum and had me and my brother Xander who's at prep school in Oxford. He's going to Eton next year.'

'Gosh.' It seemed terribly complicated but also very glamorous. 'I wish I had all those brothers and sisters.' Imogen twirled her string into a new arrangement.

'I'd rather be like you,' Allegra said. 'At least you get noticed in a good way. I only get noticed when Dad . . . when he's angry.'

But Imogen couldn't imagine why Allegra would want to be like her. To her, Allegra's life was bordering on the fairytale and she was irresistibly drawn to the other girl whom she considered perfect in just about every way. And, like a princess stranded in a tower, Allegra also seemed lonely and hungry for friendship. It was a perfect fit. Soon they couldn't imagine life without each other.

'Selina has a terrible time,' Mrs Heath said grimly to her husband as they sat at the dinner table back at home. 'Ivo isn't easy . . .' She cast a glance over at Imogen, who had finished. 'You can get down, darling. Go and watch telly if you like.'

Television was rarely allowed, so Imogen guessed that there was something of interest to be heard. She got down obediently and lingered outside the dining-room door, listening to the adult conversation, catching clear snippets among the low buzz of her mother's voice, like a radio tuning in and out to good reception.

'He drinks! It's nearly a bottle of whisky a night apparently

. . . his rages are terrible to behold, Selina says . . .'

Imogen kept her ear close to the crack in the door.

'The children are terrified too, she says . . . he's turned on them once or twice . . . kicked his boy down the stairs once, can you believe it!'

'Well, why does she stay?' came her father's deep, audible voice, in his reasonable lawyer's tones. 'He sounds like a monster, Jeannie.'

'It's not so straightforward, darling. She loves him, I think . . .'

'Or loves that castle and her title.'

'How can you say that? Selina's not that type at all! I've met him, and he seemed like a love. You know what drink can do to a man . . .'

Imogen knew nothing of drink except that one or two glasses of his favourite red wine could make her father terribly sleepy, and she decided to look at Allegra's father carefully next time she saw him for signs of what it could do. But when she did see him, striding down a corridor at Foughton, he seemed so huge and old and frightening that she ducked down a passage and hid.

'Have you heard?' Allegra said with excitement, dragging Imogen to the nursery almost before she was through the door. 'We're going to school together!'

'We are?' she said, amazed. She'd assumed that she was going to the local secondary school, like everyone else in her class.

'I heard our mums talking about it! I'm going to Westfield, if I pass the entrance exams. They were saying how lovely it would be if we could go together! Wouldn't that be fantastic?'

It was a glorious prospect and, as soon as they were in the car on the way home, Imogen asked her mother if it was true.

Mrs Heath seemed a little flustered. 'Well, how did you hear about that? It's true Selina and I have discussed it, and I would be so happy if you went to Westfield, just as I did, and with Allegra too. But . . . it's terribly expensive. The only way would be if you could win a scholarship to pay some of the fees. I don't see why you couldn't – you're a bright girl, top of your class in some subjects. We'll talk to your father about it.'

It didn't take long for Imogen to realise that her father was not at all keen on the idea. Loitering behind doors and on the stairs, she heard him state his views very clearly.

'I don't like the idea at all, Jeannie! She's too young for that kind of pressure. What if she doesn't get a scholarship? She'll feel like a failure, and she's only ten years old.'

'Of course she'll get it. She's very clever.'

'She'll be up against lots of other clever but poor girls. And if she does get it, what then? Surrounded by rich pupils who can afford anything they want . . . it could ruin Imogen. She'll turn into one of those nasty types, obsessed with herself and her possessions, and permanently dissatisfied. It's not what I want for her.'

'I went to Westfield and I'm not like that!' cried her mother indignantly. 'It's not the social aspect I'm interested in – it's the fact that I want Imogen to have the very best opportunities. The academic results there are excellent.'

'If it's academic results you value, why can't she go to school here in Scotland? Why send her all the way to bloody England? I don't want her to leave home so young. I'll miss her.'

'We must think of what's best for her. It's a wonderful chance. We must let her take it. Besides, she's longing to go. She told me.'

Imogen knew who would win and, sure enough, a few weeks later she was told that they would be taking a trip with the McCorquodales to Westfield so that the girls could sit the exams: a straightforward entrance exam for Allegra and a scholarship exam for Imogen.

It was a prospect that was exhilarating and terrifying in equal measure.

What if I don't pass? Imogen wondered, as they took the train from Edinburgh to London where they would stay overnight at the McCorquodales' house in Onslow Square, South Kensington. Her mother had arranged some extra tuition from a dry old ex-schoolteacher. Miss McTavish came over every evening to drill Imogen in French grammar and vocabulary, and put her through some mathematics exercises.

'*Soyez soigneuse*, Imogen,' she had warned in her Scottish-tinged French accent. 'You'll need to think very hard in these exams . . . and remember to read the question three times before you answer it.'

She tried to forget how frightened she was in the excitement of their trip. It was Imogen's first visit to London, and in the taxi from the station to the house she was silent all the way, watching as the famous landmarks drifted by outside the windows. Then they reached their destination: a tall, white-fronted house with an imposing columned porch, set in an elegant square. Inside it was enormous, tastefully and very expensively decorated.

'What a beautiful house,' exclaimed Imogen's mother when they went inside. 'Selina, it's exquisite!'

'Oh, it's nothing to do with me,' she said airily, leading the way down a long hall with every inch of the walls hung with paintings. 'It's Ivo's brother, David. He did up this place for us, and you know what wonderful taste he has.'

The two mothers looked at each other meaningfully.

'Come on,' said Allegra, pulling Imogen by the hand. 'Let's go upstairs.'

The room they would be sharing was right at the top of the house, looking out at the back over the rooftops of Kensington. It was done up like a traditional girly room, with rose-printed curtains, and pink-and-white counterpanes on the beds, and white chests of drawers with little lamps on them. Imogen fell in love with it at once and wished that her bedroom at home looked just like this.

'My uncle David did it,' Allegra explained. 'He designed this 'specially for me.' She jumped on the bed and bounced on it a little. 'He's quite famous.'

'Is he?' Nothing about the McCorquodales surprised Imogen: their lives were unendingly fascinating, glamorous and impressive. 'Why?'

'He knows absolutely everyone. Goes to all the parties and is friends with them all. I mean, he knows the royal family and film stars and rock stars and . . . *everyone*.'

'Does he know Claudia Schiffer?' asked Imogen. Claudia was her definition of the most famous and beautiful woman in the world, and her favourite supermodel. Allegra preferred Linda Evangelista.

'I expect so. And Joan Collins. And Princess Diana.'

Imogen shook her head and breathed, 'Wow! Princess Diana! Do you think he knows her well?'

Allegra said, 'She phoned him once when I was there, and he said, "Hello, Diana darling, how are you? When are we having lunch?"'

They thought for a moment of what it must be like to know people as famous as that, to have them phone you and to go out for lunch with them.

'Why does he know them?' Imogen asked. She sat down on her bed and kicked off her shoes.

Allegra shrugged. 'Mummy said he's a style . . . *arbiter*. He has a private members club that he started up years ago, and it's very exclusive and expensive.'

'A club?' Imogen thought of the Secret Seven, which was her main idea of a club.

'A nightclub. You know, a place people go to late at night, to have dinner and cocktails and talk to each other. Perhaps dance a bit, probably to classical music.'

'It sounds quite fun,' Imogen said, though she wasn't entirely sure.

Allegra nodded. 'I really want him to take me there but he says I'm far too young and that I can go when I'm eighteen.' She made a face. 'But that's *ages* away. I'm sure I'll be able to make him take me before then.'

Then they were called downstairs for tea and cake.

The next day they all climbed into the big black Bentley and were driven to Westfield School. It was beautiful, like a palace, and they were shown all over it by a prefect, who looked sophisticated, adult, and just a touch bored despite her impeccable manners. *If I come here, I'll be like that,* Imogen thought longingly. *I'll be like Allegra, and all the other girls here. They're so clever and confident . . .*

The school was full of wonderful facilities, from the huge sports hall, acres of grass tennis courts and Olympic-sized swimming pool, to the library, computer room, theatre, and light, airy classrooms. But it was the boarding houses she loved the most: the dormitories with their rows of cubicles, each decorated to its owner's taste with posters, family photographs, books and ornaments. It was everything she'd dreamt a boarding school would be, and her heart contracted with a violent yearning to belong here.

Before lunch they sat their first paper. Allegra was shown into a classroom and whispered, 'Good luck!' as Imogen was led on down the hall to the room where the scholarship hopefuls were sitting their exams. A sick feeling seized her stomach. *Allegra only has to do well enough to get in,* she realised as she surveyed the other girls, who all looked frighteningly bright, *but I have to do better than all of these others to get my place.*

The pressure made her hands tremble and her throat dry.

She did her best. There was nothing too terrifying, although she couldn't be sure how much she'd got right in the maths paper.

'How did it go?' Allegra whispered as they ate their lunch in the refectory, surrounded by the girls lucky enough to be at the school already.

'All right, I think,' Imogen said, mainly relieved that her least favourite paper was out of the way. 'You?'

Allegra shrugged. 'Okay. We did Venn diagrams this term, so it wasn't too bad.'

After lunch they had the French paper and then English, which Imogen knew was her strongest suit. Last of all there was an interview with the Headmistress, which wasn't as frightening as she'd expected: a casual chat about the things she liked doing, her favourite books and her ambitions. Then it was time to go.

'Do you want to come here?' Allegra asked as they watched Westfield disappear through the windows of the Bentley.

Imogen nodded. She didn't trust herself to speak. She wanted to go there more than anything in the world.

'Imogen, you clever girl, you've won a place at Westfield!' her mother said, full of excitement as she clutched a letter with an embossed coat of arms at the top of it.

Imogen gasped, her insides burning with pleasure and surprise. A glowing future appeared in her mind, full of dorms and sports kit and toast and lessons and . . .

'But . . .' Her father took it from her mother's hand and scanned it quickly. Then he glanced up at his wife. 'This is a standard place. Not a scholarship.'

'The competition is terribly fierce,' her mother said quickly, her cheeks stained with red. 'And look what lovely things the Headmistress has said . . .'

Not a scholarship place? Dismay rushed through Imogen. *So am I going or not?*

'Look,' continued her mother, 'Miss Steele says that your English paper was outstanding. It was just the slight weakness in your other papers that meant you couldn't be offered the scholarship. But they hope you'll be able to take up your place anyway.'

Her father said, 'I don't see how, Jeannie. It's ten thousand a year.' His face was grim.

Imogen glanced between her parents, her eyes wide and pleading. She knew that her mother usually won arguments, but when it concerned money, her father's word was final. 'Please may I go, Daddy?' she asked in a small, tremulous voice. *Don't you realise my life will be over if I can't go?*

'We'll see, Imogen, we'll see,' he said in a solemn tone, and she knew that the big debate was going to happen when she was in bed. All she could do was await the outcome.

'Oh, Jeannie, what a shame!' Selina said, her face full of sympathy.

'I've begged and pleaded, but he won't be moved.' Jeannie Heath's eyes were red and puffy from all the weeping she'd done in an attempt to shift her husband's resolve. 'He says we can't afford it, and that's that. He's been against it from the start, and this has given him just the excuse he needed. Oh, if only Imogen had had a little more maths tuition, she would have won that scholarship place, I know she would. But he wouldn't pay, and now look!'

The girls sat silently on the sofa in the drawing room of

Foughton Castle, listening to Imogen's fate being discussed as they munched Battenberg and Jaffa cakes. Allegra had her place and would be going to Westfield. The thought that Imogen would not had filled their hearts with despair.

Selina leant towards her friend and pressed a hand over hers. 'If money is all it is . . . well, we'll take the wind out of his sails, that's all.' She turned to Imogen with a broad smile over her face. 'Would you like to go to Westfield with Allegra, darling?'

Imogen nodded, her mouth full of cake and her heart full of longing.

'Then you shall!' she declared.

'But, Selina . . .' Jeannie looked dubious. 'You shouldn't say such things . . . it's really not fair to lead her on. Gordon won't budge.'

Selina turned back to her friend with a satisfied expression. 'There's only one solution. *We'll* pay for Imogen to go to Westfield. Oh, don't worry, darling,' she said, seeing her friend's expression, 'you can pay us back, of course. When you've got the money. But, in the meantime, we'll be more than happy to meet the fees. I know I can speak for Ivo. We'd both feel so much better about Allegra going if we knew she had her little friend with her.'

Allegra's dark blue gaze slid over to meet Imogen's grey-green one. Their eyes sparkled and danced. Here was the solution. They continued munching and listening as hard as they could.

'But, Selina, we couldn't possibly . . .'

'Don't be silly! I won't hear another word about it. We'll pay and that's that. It will be wonderful, darling! Your daughter and mine, at our old school. It couldn't be more perfect. And as for Gordon . . . well, you'll just have to persuade him, won't you?'

*

It was only Imogen's own special pleading, when they'd gone out walking together one day, that swung the balance. Her father was still reluctant but when he'd seen how much she longed for it, he couldn't deny her, even though she could see in his eyes that he didn't want to lose her to her new English school.

When he'd finally said yes, she'd screamed with joy and hugged him with all her strength, until he'd laughed but not with joy. She was going to belong to Allegra's world at last, properly, and on her own account.

They'd gone to Westfield that September, full of anticipation, trepidation and excitement, secure only in their friendship but brimming with hope for the future.

Chapter 4

New York
2000

Mitch got off the Greyhound bus at Port Authority and instantly felt like the smallest, most meaningless speck in a city full to the brim with people who knew exactly what they should be doing. Even the drunken bearded man in a mass of rags panhandling in the subway exit seemed more sophisticated than he was.

He pulled his rucksack tighter over his shoulder and headed for the daylight.

Once above ground, he was assailed by noise and movement. Cars rushed past, yellow cabs wove in and out of less nimble traffic, silver buses rolled imperturbably alongside the sidewalk, all stopping to obey the instructions of the traffic lights as though following the steps of an intricate dance: now one stream moving, now another, ever flowing up and down and across the grid system of the city's streets.

He felt overwhelmed by the size and sound of the city, the vast glass-and-steel office blocks rearing up into the sky, dwarfing him as he stumbled past their revolving doors, and the bustle and rush of people as they strode determinedly on their way. The people themselves were extraordinary: all colours, shapes and sizes, in all manner of clothes. There were races he'd never seen in his backwater of a town:

Korean boys with fierce eyes and set mouths wearing rock-band T-shirts and jeans; Chinese women in dark trousers and shirts hurrying by about their business with armfuls of packages; graceful Somalian girls wafting along the kerb. He saw giant women in leopard-print coats and glittery high heels, with heavy make-up and unnaturally large hair – *They must be men,* Mitch thought incredulously. He'd heard of trans-sexuals but never seen any – and beautiful girls, more beautiful girls than he'd imagined possible in one place, along with loping young guys, shuffling old men, and the armies of middle-aged, middle-income office workers in their dark suits and leather shoes.

Where am I gonna go? What am I gonna do? he wondered. His only plan had been to get to New York and find some adventure. He had $250 in his pockets, the sum total of his life savings, and a backpack with his few possessions in it.

He hadn't believed she would do it but Jo-Lynn had been as good as her word. The very next day, when he'd been in the kitchen with the commis-chefs, overseeing their preparations for the day's service and sipping strong black coffee to wake himself up, Stanley had come bursting into the kitchen, his fat face puce and his fists clenched.

'Where's that sonofabitch?' he bawled, scattering porters and chefs as he hurled his meaty body along the narrow gangways of the kitchen. Rounding a corner, he found Mitch putting down his coffee cup and staring up at him in surprise.

'There you are!' yelled Stanley.

'Huh? What's the problem?' was all Mitch had time to say before his jacket was seized by the front and he found himself close to Stanley's jowly, sweating face, red-veined nose and pink, popping eyes.

'You think you can touch my wife, do ya, ya piece of shit?' he screamed.

'No way, I—'

'She told me all about it, you fuckin' jackal. How you asked her to come over last night, and then tried to get your stinking hands on her – in my fuckin' office!'

Mitch's mouth gaped open but he couldn't think what to say. The truth was impossible, as incendiary as the lie. He couldn't say, 'Your wife tried to seduce me, sir, but I refused' – all manner of fresh insults were tied up in that. All he could do was defuse this boiling anger somehow . . .

'There's been a misunderstanding,' he panted, aware of Stanley's white knuckles only inches from his face.

'Yeah?' His boss's brow creased and his mouth twisted. 'How do you misunderstand a man shoving his fuckin' hand up a woman's chest, and tellin' her he wants to fuck her? Huh?'

Mitch saw with sudden clarity that his boss had been wary of him for some time: no doubt he'd always feared that his brawny young employee would set his wife's pussy buzzing. His suspicions were mature, ready to ripen the minute Jo-Lynn gave them voice. *I just gotta get out of here, as soon as I can,* Mitch realised.

'OK, OK,' he said in as calm a voice as he could manage. 'I fucked up, Stanley. I was drunk and made a bad mistake.'

'I'll say you fuckin' did . . .'

'I'm outta here right now, sir.' He felt Stanley's grip loosen and pulled himself free. 'I'm gonna get my things and go.'

Stanley looked surprised, wrong-footed. Then his face darkened. If Mitch was giving in so fast, then it must all be true, there could be no doubt. Fresh rage seemed to boil up in him. 'You get out of here within the next twenty seconds or you'll be so damn' sorry, you'll be cursing your mother for ever squeezin' you out! And I want you out of this town too. Or I'm gonna come looking for you, I promise you that, you cunt-stealing piece of crap!'

Mitch ripped off his jacket and headed for his locker, aware of the watchful eyes of the other chefs. Heading out through the restaurant with his jacket and bag, he saw Jo-Lynn sitting in the front. She gave him a look as he went, something like triumph and something like despair. He ignored her, walked out on to the main street and headed to his place to pick up his belongings. He was on the evening bus out of town.

The man behind the reception desk at the hostel on West and Sixty-third had a kind of surly air about him. Mitch had been expecting a warmer welcome than this: maybe not quite singing and dancing, but a smile and perhaps some food.

'How many nights?' the man demanded.

'I don't know. Three?'

'That'll be fifteen dollars a night.'

Mitch nodded. He pulled out some notes.

'Just pay for tonight. And fill in this form.' The man handed him a clipboard with a sheet of paper attached. 'Got some ID?'

Mitch handed over his driver's licence. The man looked at it and nodded. 'Now, you know the rules here. No drink, no drugs, right? Give me your bag, I gotta search it.'

'Sure.' Mitch had never felt so respectable in all his life. He'd never touched drugs, not even pot in high school when everyone was smoking it, and he rarely drank much beyond a couple of beers after work or when he was watching baseball games.

The man took the shabby nylon rucksack and unzipped it. He put his hand in and began rummaging about, peering in to see what he could find. 'What's this?' He pulled out a cotton towel rolled up into a thick sausage of cloth.

'Oh, yeah,' Mitch said. 'That's . . .'

Before he could explain, the man unrolled the towel,

revealing a steel knife glinting with sharpness, riveted into its handle for extra strength. 'What the hell—?'

'That's my knife.'

'I can see it's your damn' knife!' The man stared up at him with horror in his eyes.

'It's not what you think,' Mitch said, seeing at once how it looked. 'I'm a chef. It's a tool of the trade. It's my *knife.*' He didn't know how to explain what a chef's knife meant to him, and how right it felt when you finally found the exact one, weighted just so and with the heft that exactly suited your hand and a blade so honed it could slice through anything with the merest pressure.

'You can't walk around carrying this thing,' the man said, shaking his head in astonishment. 'You wanna be arrested? I'm telling you, I oughta call the cops!'

'Don't do that, sir!' Mitch said swiftly. 'Like I said, I'm a chef. I don't mean any harm with it.'

'You can't stay here with that thing. Want my advice? Go drop it in the Hudson right now. You'll only get into trouble – bad trouble – with a knife like that in a place like this.'

Mitch stared at him, his spirits dropping. 'I gotta go?'

'You gotta go this minute. Or I mean it – I'll call the cops. That's a deadly weapon, boy.'

Mitch walked through the city, disconsolate and apprehensive. He walked all the way to the western side of Manhattan, and stared out across the blue waters of the Hudson. Night was coming on and he had nowhere to stay. Should he drop his knife into the river, like the reception guy had said? He didn't dare even take it out of his bag.

No, I can't do it. It's all I've got. I could never afford another one like this. Besides, he loved it. He'd left behind all his books, his papers, his attempt to get himself an education. All he had now was his knife, the one reminder that he could cook.

Cooking is what I do. That's how I'll get out of this mess.

He turned away from the river and headed back into the city, veering south. He would find restaurants and ask for work. Restaurants always needed chefs, he knew that. The workforce was always shifting and changing. He would go from kitchen to kitchen and find himself a job, and then he'd worry about where he was going to sleep.

He wandered into a district where there were more restaurants and started going round the back and knocking on the kitchen doors, asking if anyone wanted an extra pair of hands. But it was getting late and evening service was well under way. In the packed restaurants they yelled at him to come back tomorrow, couldn't he see they were fuckin' busy? And in the quiet ones, they shook their heads sorrowfully: there wasn't enough work for the staff they had, they didn't need more idle hands.

It was two in the morning and the kitchens were closing when he gave up. He was exhausted, desperate to sleep, and feeling more and more lost and confused in the big city. The night seemed full of threats: faces looming out of alleys, cars cruising by with music thudding from the open windows and shouts and taunts from the occupants, passersby giving him suspicious looks. Then at last he found a grubby hotel, the kind where he didn't think they'd search his bag, and handed over twenty-five of his precious dollars for a bed, but the place was alive all night with noise – thudding, screaming, gasping, fighting – and he rolled over, buried his head in the thin pillow and tried in vain to sleep.

The next day, he was even more tired than when he'd gone to bed, but he knew that today he had to find a job. More than that, he needed some food. Apart from a bagel he'd bought from a stand the day before, he hadn't had a proper meal for nearly two days.

He walked out on to the grey streets and wandered for a

block or so, then found a cafe, went in and ordered eggs and coffee, which he wolfed down and immediately felt better.

I can do this. I'm young, I've got talent and I'm in the centre of the restaurant world, with no ties and nothing to hold me back. I can make it here, I know it! He had tried to look at the whole sorry incident with Stanley as the kick up the ass he needed to get him out of small-town life and into the big city. He'd always dreamt of something special for himself. Now he was forcing himself to seek it out.

The kitchens were just coming to life when he started looking again. The porters were hauling out rubbish, the day's supplies were being delivered to the back doors, and the chefs were fortifying themselves for the day ahead, outside with coffee, cigarettes and bacon bagels.

'Hey,' Mitch said, going up to a couple of guys in baggy black chef's trousers and white T-shirts as they stood smoking at the back of an Italian joint. 'Any work going around here?'

The men looked at each other and said nothing for a moment as they eyed him.

'What you do?' asked one, who was young but whose face still looked ravaged by late nights, hard work, and a punishing regime of alcohol, junk food and nicotine.

'I can turn my hand to most things,' Mitch said with a shrug. 'All the basics.'

'You speak English – so, you legal?'

Mitch nodded.

The ravaged-looking one ran a hand through his curly hair and turned to his friend. 'Tony's looking for someone while Jerry's in hospital. Whaddya think?'

The other one shrugged. 'Guess so.'

'Hey!' The younger one looked at Mitch with a smile. 'You know what? You might be in luck. Our pal's in hospital for a day or two, maybe you could fill in for him. How about you come in and meet the boss? He'll be here in an hour or so.'

'Great,' Mitch said, happiness filling his heart. *This is my chance, I know it.*

'Can you do pasta?'

'Are you kidding?' Mitch made a face. 'Never do anything else.' *How hard is it to dunk spaghetti in hot water?*

'Good. I'm Herbie, by the way.' The young chef held out a hand.

'Mitch.' He took the hand and shook it hard.

'Cool. Good to meet you.' Herbie grinned. 'You'll like it here, I promise.'

Chapter 5

Westfield Boarding School for Girls
2000

Romily could tell that Allegra was more dissatisfied than ever and had the distinct impression that trouble was brewing, though what it might be exactly she couldn't say. Exams were about to begin and she hoped they would defuse the tension she could feel like a storm in the air, ready to break. Usual lessons had stopped and now it was revision and study periods, and then long hours spent in the sports hall, sitting their papers.

Today they'd already stuffed their heads with geography and history and needed a break.

'We have to get out of here,' Allegra moaned discontentedly. She was sitting on the edge of Romily's bed and staring out of the window while Imogen was cross-legged on the floor, rifling through Romily's capacious and expensive make-up bag. Allegra pointed out over the playing fields that stretched away into the distance and disappeared into hedges and woodland. 'We're in the middle of bloody nowhere! I'm going to die of boredom if I have to stay here much longer.'

'What's the hurry?' Romily said, carefully painting pearly clear polish on to her nails as she sat at her desk. Polish was forbidden, of course, but she got round that in her usual way: she did what she wanted, but subtly, so no one would notice. 'Besides, we can't make it go any faster, even if we want to.'

'You're so unromantic, Rom,' grumbled Allegra. 'Don't you want to get out? Get away from school bloody uniform and start living properly? We're completely sex-starved. It's just not natural.'

Romily shrugged. She refused to let frustration get the better of her, the way Allegra did. 'Maybe. But I can't see the point in letting it make you miserable.'

'It's all right for you. You get to live so glamorously when you're not at school. Come on, tell us what you're doing in the holidays.'

'Well, the first bit of July I'll be in Paris and there are some parties and things to go to. Then my mother is taking me on our usual tour: Venice, St Tropez, Cap d'Antibes and the Moncivellos' palace in Tuscany. Then we go to Chrypkos for the rest of the summer, and back to Paris for fittings and clothes shopping for the autumn.' Romily looked up at the other two, her big brown eyes candid. 'Nothing special. Just the usual.'

Allegra and Imogen looked at each other and burst out laughing.

'What?' demanded Romily, hurt. 'What's so funny?'

'Oh, Rom, only you can talk about a summer itinerary like that and call it nothing special!' spluttered Allegra.

'You've got a private island, for God's sake!' cried Imogen. 'How normal is that?'

Romily frowned at them and then gave in, rolled her eyes and smiled. 'All right, all right. I get it.'

It was partly because the other two teased her that she felt so comfortable with them. She'd arrived at Westfield two years after most of the girls and at first she'd been very lonely indeed. For one thing, she didn't look like any of the others. While they tried their best to scruff themselves up and break the uniform rules, Romily had been perfectly turned out every day, in the most expensive shoes, tights and uniform that could be bought. She had been told off for wearing real diamond studs in her ears – they had been taken away and put in the school safe – and for putting on mascara for her lessons, which was strictly forbidden. The other girls had laughed at her skincare routine, when the idea of not following it had seemed heretical to her.

She had been, she could see now, very French, and also very sheltered. Her family's wealth had kept her removed from the world and she'd found the life of an English girls' boarding school extremely strange. Just when she had thought she would never understand and couldn't bear it any longer, Allegra rescued her. She came to her cubie one afternoon and asked if Romily would draw a picture of Queen Victoria for her history project, because she was sure Romily would be brilliant at it. 'After all, your grandfather was a famous artist, wasn't he?'

Romily had laughed and explained that although her grandfather had indeed been a very famous artist, she was only capable of drawing stick men and cats. Nevertheless, she would try and draw Queen Victoria if that was what Allegra wanted. Her attempt was so bad that Allegra said she thought perhaps she would give it a go herself.

Romily had already noticed Allegra and Imogen, of course, partly because of Allegra's striking looks and mischievous nature – even Romily had laughed when Allegra had remained hidden under a pile of science overalls for an entire lesson while Mrs Crawford taught on, oblivious – and partly because they always seemed to be talking and laughing together, engrossed in each other's company. Theirs looked like the kind of friendship where you would never be bored. She'd never had any hope that she would be allowed to join in, but with the ice broken, Allegra had asked Romily if she wanted to sit with them in the refectory and, slowly, they'd accepted her as one of them.

Now, she was almost impossible to tell apart from the other girls in the school, except for a certain polish she couldn't help retaining: her clothes and shoes were so much more expensive than everybody else's. While they were looking for copies of things they saw in *Vogue* at Camden Market and Top Shop, Romily was ordering the real thing, and all the girls came to sigh and 'Aah' when a box arrived for her from Harrods. An audience would gather – even sixth-formers came to look – when she unwrapped the wonderful tissue-covered goodies: real Chanel sunglasses; Vivienne Westwood jeans; T-shirts from Miu Miu, Chloé and Comme des Garçons.

She loved her clothes but she was generous with them: she let Allegra and Imogen borrow whatever they liked.

Other boxes arrived from Paris, direct from Romily's mother. They were full of skincare products, some specially blended for her by expert dermatologists, and supplements to ensure her perfect health.

'Mama is a hypochondriac,' Romily explained, emptying out all the bottles and packets. 'She organises most of her life around all this stuff.'

The other two found it fascinating if rather crazy and she didn't try to explain to them. From her earliest childhood, Romily had listened to her mother's maxims. Madame de Lisle had one mantra: *elegance*. A woman must be elegant in all ways: in her mind, her manners, and, of course, her person. Romily had already learned lessons in self-presentation from her. At six, she was going to bed wearing little white cotton gloves, her hands inside slathered with cream, in imitation of her mother who never went to sleep without lashings of expensive moisturiser wherever expensive moisturiser could be put.

'Protect your skin!' her mother advised her solemnly. 'It must last your entire life. Look after it as though it were your most precious possession.'

Romily had taken the lessons to heart. She wore hats and shunned the sun. She took her supplements and drank her water. She fed her young skin with the richest creams her mother would allow her ('Your skin is still adolescent – nothing too rich, it will overpower you and clog your pores. Light, oil-free and not on your T-zone!') and exfoliated religiously, all over, every day. She was blessed with a light olive complexion that appeared smooth and almost poreless, and was never marked with a blemish – unlike Imogen and Allegra, with their pale Scottish skins that seemed to change like the weather, veering between pink and healthy or grey and heavy. Then there were the spots that were the bane of their lives, which they hid under great dollops of pink concealer. Romily had never experienced more than one or two spots in her life, and secretly she was convinced it was because of her dedication to vitamin pills, and her strict regime of face masks, moisturiser and sunscreens.

'What's this?' Imogen held up a gold tube with a pinkish brush at one end.

'That's Touche Eclat,' Romily said.

Imogen brushed the tube across her hand but nothing came out. 'It's not working. What is it?'

'Look.' Romily took it from her, clicked the top and smeared a line of pale pink creamy liquid along the back of Imogen's hand. 'You use it under your eyes to hide the bags.'

Imogen looked up at her dubiously. 'Bags? You don't have bags under your eyes.'

'It's not just a concealer, it's a highlighter too. It reflects light and makes you look fresher and younger.'

'I don't want to look younger,' Allegra said with a laugh.

'I'm trying to look older. Any younger and they'll be moving me back down a year.'

'You know what I mean.' Romily clicked the lid back on to her Touche Eclat. 'Let's put it away. I don't want you to waste it.'

Allegra got up and wandered about the cubie, picking up anything that interested her. 'What I don't understand, Romily, is how you can go on about looking after your bloody skin the entire time, and then smoke cigarettes.'

Romily shrugged. 'My vitamins counteract the effects of the smoke. Besides, it will be years before I need to worry about that. I'm going to give up before then.'

The other two nodded. They had agreed that they would give up smoking before they turned twenty-one, and that way they would avoid any nastiness associated with their favourite vice. Twenty-one was so far away that they hardly needed to think about it.

'What does your mother say?' Imogen asked. Romily had regaled them so often with tales of what her mother proscribed that they all thought of her as a kind of oracle on beauty and behaviour.

'She says it's acceptable to smoke in certain situations. No lady would ever smoke on the street, for example. But after dinner . . . of course. My mother smokes one filterless Gitane every day at eleven o'clock with a very strong black coffee, and one after dinner with a *digestif*.' Romily was proud of her beautiful, stylish mother. It was her ambition to be as graceful and decorative as she was.

'Do you think we'll ever be grown up?' Allegra sighed, leaning against the chest of drawers.

'Imagine being married!' Imogen said. There was a quiet moment as they all contemplated this; it seemed an extraordinary idea. 'At least you've both been kissed,' she added. 'I haven't even had that.'

Apart from a little casual experimentation with her cousin one summer holiday, Romily's experiences of sex were confined to being kissed very passionately after a ballroom dancing lesson in Paris by a handsome young count, her partner that day. It had been extremely enjoyable, and she fully intended to repeat it as soon as she could. Her plan was also to be seduced, preferably before she'd left school, so she could go out into the world unencumbered by her tiresome virginity; she was very curious to know what all the fuss was about, and, if her first forays were anything to go by, sex ought to be delightful.

Allegra had told them all how she'd managed to have a snog with the gardener's son one afternoon at Foughton Castle and another at a Christmas party.

'You will,' Allegra said stoutly. 'We'll make it our mission this summer to get Midge a snog. I want to get to Glastonbury this year, we should all go together, it'd be really cool.'

'That sounds great,' Imogen said eagerly. 'We can camp! Oh, wow.'

'I'd never be allowed,' Romily said sadly. 'Never, never, never. But maybe you could both come and see me.'

'Come to Paris?' Imogen looked excited. 'I've never been there.'

'I want to go to the Greek island,' Allegra declared. 'That sounds amazing.'

'But I don't know how likely you are to get a snog on our island, Midge, unless you like old fishermen.'

Imogen wrinkled her nose. 'No. I was thinking of someone a bit younger. Maybe eighteen or something.'

The lunch bell rang out over the school.

Allegra looked at her watch. 'About time too. But I've heard it's disgusting chicken fricassée for lunch. God, I *hate* this place!' Then she leaned towards the other two conspiratorially and said, 'MG meeting tonight. Are we all on for it?'

The other two nodded as they jumped up and hurried to stay ahead of the mad scramble to the refectory.

When they got up to the attic that night, Romily could tell that Allegra was in a rage.

'That's it!' she said in a furious whisper, blowing a plume of smoke out of the open window. 'I've had it up to here with that utter *bitch*.'

Romily glanced at Imogen. She knew they were both thinking the same thing. *Trouble.*

'Did you see her? Did you?' demanded Allegra, turning to Imogen.

Imogen nodded. She was wearing, at Romily's instigation, a thick coating of glutinous night cream that made her look strange and ghostly. 'I did. You're right. She is an utter bitch.'

Romily tried to quell the nervous feeling in her stomach and said slowly, 'She's a bully, we know that. We've always known it.'

'But didn't you see poor Vanessa Hardy in the common room this afternoon when Sophie and Arabella were being so vile? It's not her fault she's got that dreadful skin. She does absolutely everything she can – her mother's taken her to a Harley Street dermatologist, she's on a special diet and hormone tablets and everything . . . The poor girl suffers enough. It's just sheer cruelty to mock her for it!'

They had all been there: watching while Vanessa, scarlet and fighting back tears, had tried to ignore Sophie Harcourt and Arabella Balmer as they sat giggling, whispering and then calling teasing questions and nasty names across the common room. It had been agony – and yet no one had spoken up. No one had wanted to draw Sophie's fire, not when she was in the mood for torturing someone. Allegra had leapt to her feet, about to say something, but Romily had jumped up, put a hand on her arm and said an urgent, 'No!' Allegra had clearly wrestled with herself and then turned on her heel and stalked out, her face flaming and her mouth set with the effort of keeping quiet.

'I wanted to shout in her stupid face, tell everyone what a hypocrite she is,' Allegra said, staring out furiously into the night sky. 'That awful cow deserves it, you know she does.'

Romily looked over at Imogen and they swapped solemn glances. Imogen stared down hard at the floor and twisted her cigarette uneasily between her fingers.

Allegra turned back to the others and said tetchily, 'Well? Don't you think she deserves it?'

Romily took a drag on her Gauloise and released a long steady stream of heavy smoke, then said slowly, 'You know, in France, we don't much mind how people prefer to get their thrills as long as it's all consenting. If two girls want to go to bed with each other, that's fine.'

'Very *sophistiqué,*' retorted Allegra, flushing. 'I don't give a shit about that. She can fuck Myers with a giant purple dildo and whip her blue at the same time for all I care! The thing is, Romily, she's a hypocrite – if it were someone else, she'd be the first to rip it out of them. That's what I can't stand. Besides, it's against the rules.'

'Come on, Allegra,' Imogen said, in a light-hearted voice. 'As if you care about that! You don't take much notice of the rules.'

She looked at them both, stricken. 'What's wrong with you two?' she demanded. 'It sounds like you're against me. Are you on Sophie's side now or something?'

'No, no, of course not,' Imogen said hastily.

'What about you?' Allegra demanded, turning to Romily.

Romily met the navy blue gaze with her own. 'Of course

I'm with you,' she said gravely. 'We're best friends, aren't we? We'll always stick together. The thing is, though, I don't know if it's wise to use what we know about Sophie against her.'

'But can't you see how she treats other people? Why shouldn't she have a taste of it herself?'

Romily frowned, thinking hard. *After all, why shouldn't we just punish Sophie? Hand back a little of what she's been dishing out for years?* 'Because it's so serious,' she said at last. 'It's different, that's all. I just don't think we should tell anyone.'

'I wasn't going to!' Allegra fired back. 'I'm just talking about it, getting it off my chest, that's all.'

But Romily knew that it would be hard for her to keep such a secret. They still had two years at Westfield, and that was a long time to keep quiet, especially in the face of Sophie's constant provocation. Could Allegra really resist? And what if it came to the attention of the teachers, as things almost always did by the mysterious telegraph that connected pupils to staff? Would Sophie and Martha be expelled? It wasn't expressly forbidden, but it was obvious that it would be treated as a transgression. How could it not?

They were all silent for a while, smoking and not catching each other's eye. Then Imogen said, 'Well, as long as we're all agreed. We won't tell. No matter how much of a bitch Sophie is. After all, Martha isn't half as bad, and she's bound to get caught up in it if we do.'

'I wasn't going to tell!' protested Allegra again, looking sulky.

'Good. So there's no problem,' Romily said lightly. *I mustn't let Allegra think we're against her.* 'Who knows what the hell Martha sees in Sophie anyway?'

'I wonder how they got together.' Imogen grinned, obviously wanting to lift Allegra's mood. 'Maybe they had a revelation in the games cupboard or something.'

'Maybe she tickled her fancy during choir practice,' Romily put in.

'Oh, Martha, you're not quite hitting that top E – perhaps this finger in *here* would help?' joked Imogen, making Allegra smile, as she always could.

Allegra said, 'Maybe they had a *Ghost* moment in pottery – Martha's hands over Sophie's as they rubbed a nice greasy wadge of clay together.'

They all laughed.

Just then there was the unmistakable squeak of the door to the stairs opening. They froze, staring at each other in horror: they were all out of bounds, all holding cigarettes, there was no mistaking their guilt. They were making too much noise – they must have left the door ajar, and Myers, on patrol for once, had spotted it.

Oh, shit! thought Romily. Her skin prickled with horror. *This is it. We're going to be expelled.*

Light footsteps came up the stairs – too light for Myers', now she thought about it – and then a voice said, 'So this is what you all get up to! I knew there was something.'

Sophie Harcourt emerged from the stairwell.

Romily's stomach turned icy cold: the sight of their enemy appearing in front of them was terrifying. She felt so vulnerable, not only because of the cigarette she had in her hand but because Sophie looked like a predator in her dark pyjamas, the same ones she was wearing the night they saw her with Martha Young. It was impossible not to remember her as she was that night: turned on, hungry, greedy for sensation.

Sophie stood with one hand on her hip, her chin thrust out and her eyes mocking. She looked at each of them in turn. 'And smoking too! I'm surprised at you, Imogen. I always thought you were far too timid and goodie-goodie for that. But I suppose you're copying Allegra, as usual.

Word of advice, darling – try to get a personality of your own sometime.'

Imogen looked ill even under her coating of night cream, staring at Sophie, unable to say a word. Romily wanted to say something herself, something sensible and grown up that would defuse the tension that had just skyrocketed, but she could think of nothing. Then Allegra stood up, stubbing out her cigarette.

'And what are you doing out and about, Sophie?' Beneath her confident tone there was a nervous tremor in her voice.

Sophie blinked innocently. 'I heard talking. I came to see what was happening and . . . oh, dear. I seem to have stumbled on the school's favourite princesses all being very, very naughty!'

Romily saw with sudden awful clarity that she had to mollify Sophie, get her on side and stop her telling. And she had to do that before Allegra was tempted to try and frighten Sophie into silence with what she knew. *If Sophie gets any hint that Allegra has something on her, this will spiral quickly out of control and we'll be in the headmistress's office first thing, all landed in the shit.* She stood up as well, smiling. 'Yes, you've caught us. Thank goodness it was you, Sophie, and not Myers. I thought we were really in trouble there for a moment!'

Sophie frowned, disarmed by Romily's friendliness. Then she laughed. 'Well, this *is* a turn up for the books, isn't it? You're at my mercy now, aren't you? I could have you out of here by lunchtime tomorrow.' She bit her lip and looked mischievous. 'Gosh, it's tempting.'

'You won't tell on us, will you?' Romily said swiftly, still smiling. Out of the corner of her eye, she could see Allegra stiffening, responding to Sophie's challenge.

'How on earth could you make it worth my while not to?' She looked down her nose at Allegra and then Imogen.

You stupid girl, Romily thought fiercely. *Can't you see how pointless it is to take us on like this? No one can win. We need to find a way that we can get out of this situation.* But she kept her face serene and her voice calm. 'We don't have to turn this into a big deal, you know . . .'

Sophie turned back to her. 'OK. If you really want me to keep quiet . . . well, I can think of a few things that might help. I've always fancied those Prada trainers of yours, actually. And your Rouge Noir nail polish.'

Allegra frowned and started to speak, but Romily quietened her with a look and said, 'OK. They're yours.'

'You can't let her blackmail us like this!' hissed Allegra.

'It's fine, let it go.' Romily raised her eyebrows meaningfully.

'But she'll never be satisfied and anyway—' Allegra began, her dark blue eyes sparkling with fury on Romily's behalf.

'Allegra, no,' interrupted Imogen fearfully.

'What's going on?' Sophie demanded, eyes darting, noticing the tension between them.

Allegra took a step towards the other girl. 'I don't want Romily to give you her trainers and nail polish. There won't be any end to it if she does. You'll start demanding all her stuff.'

'So what? She can afford it.'

'That's not the point. It's blackmail.'

'It's put up with it or be expelled,' Sophie said airily, 'it all depends which you'd prefer, doesn't it?' Her eyes turned cold suddenly and her face hardened.

Don't do it, Sophie, Romily begged silently. *You don't know what you're starting.*

But Sophie went on regardless, her voice spiteful now. 'You think you're so great,' she spat at Allegra. 'With your title, and your castle, and your little tame pets.' She shot scornful glances at Imogen and Romily. 'The teachers think the sun shines out of your ladyship's aristocratic arse, don't they? Well, the rules are the rules and, if you break them, you pay like anyone else. Maybe you'll find out at last that your title and Frenchie's money and Mousie's A grades can't get you out of trouble after all.'

Imogen gasped and stared over at Romily, her expression appalled. They both knew that Sophie had thrown down the gauntlet. But she didn't realise it.

Allegra stepped forward, even closer to Sophie now. She seemed very calm and cool. 'You're only revealing your own jealousy, you know. And you ought to be very careful before you start all this. We're not the only ones breaking the rules, after all . . . are we?'

Sophie narrowed her eyes. 'What do you mean?' She laughed nastily. 'Jealous of you? I don't think so.'

'Well, how did you find us?'

'I told you.' She smirked. 'I heard voices and came to find out what was happening.'

'I don't believe you. I think you were on your way to one of your little assignations.'

There was a chilled silence after Allegra said these words.

It's out now, thought Romily. A dull horror enveloped her. *It's begun.* She looked over at Imogen whose eyes were staring and huge in her gleaming, cream-covered face. Neither of them could move to intervene, only watch in frozen fascination as the other two squared up to each other.

Sophie's mouth dropped open but she swiftly got control of herself. 'What do you mean?'

'You know very well.' Allegra lifted her chin and gazed unflinchingly at her. 'I mean your secret little meetings with Martha Young.'

The colour drained from Sophie's face. 'What?' she whispered. 'I don't know what you're talking about.'

'Yes, you do. You and Martha are *special* best friends –

Does Arabella know, by the way? – and you like to get together and do what *special* best friends do.'

'That's not true!' cried Sophie, her voice harsh. Colour flooded violently into her cheeks, staining them bright red.

'You can deny it all you like, but we've seen you. All of us.'

Sophie looked round at Imogen and Romily, who couldn't meet her eyes. That was much worse than if they had faced her off, it seemed. Sophie seemed to realise all at once that she really had been seen, at her most intimate, private moment, with all that it implied. She looked sick and then her face was transformed by fury. Her lips drew back in a snarl. 'How dare you spy on me, you horrible bitch!' She ran at Allegra, knocking her backwards so that they both flew towards the attic window, Allegra tripping as they went and falling back against the sill. Sophie sank her fingers into Allegra's thick blonde hair and began to pound her head against the sill. Allegra tried to escape, scrambling on to the box she'd been sitting on and flailing at Sophie with one arm while trying to dislodge the hand from her hair with the other.

Sophie began to push her backwards on to the window sill, climbing up on to the box next to her.

Romily took a step forward, thinking, *She's trying to push Allegra out of the window!* She could hardly believe it was happening and started over towards them, but she seemed to be moving at half speed and could only watch with horror as Allegra was pushed back on to the sill, her bottom perched on it, her back arching out of the window itself.

Imogen rose shakily to her feet. 'Stop them, Rom, stop them!' Her voice came out in a cracked whisper.

'Yes, we've got to stop them,' she said, as she saw Allegra struggling and wrestling with Sophie, whose anger seemed to have given her extraordinary strength. She moved quickly towards them, Imogen following close behind. Now she could see that Sophie had Allegra's arms in such a tight grip that the skin was dead white where her fingers were digging deep into the flesh, and she was forcing Allegra back over the sill, into the yawning blue-blackness beyond.

'Sophie, no!' she cried, and grabbed at the other girl's pyjama top, just as Imogen came up level with her and reached out too.

At that moment, awful things happened so fast that later they could barely remember in what order they'd occurred.

In the flurry, Sophie gave Allegra a huge shove, trying to send her weight over the edge of the sill. Allegra kicked out with her feet, knocking Sophie off balance and forcing her to release her arms. Then, and with all her strength, she grabbed Sophie's arm and pulled it, using the other girl's weight to counterbalance her as she hurled herself back into the attic. And as she vanished from under Sophie's outstretched hands, the other girl flew forward.

Romily saw what was happening and with a gasp made a desperate attempt to hold on to Sophie's top, scrabbling at the soft slippery cotton with her fingertips. She could see shock and amazement on the other girl's face and then, with the grisly realisation that there was no way to prevent herself from tumbling over the sill and out of the window, an awful fear covered it and her mouth opened in a scream.

She was gone. A moment later there was a ghastly thud.

Imogen and Romily stood frozen for an instant before turning to each other in horrified disbelief. Allegra scrambled to her feet and peered out of the window. The other two joined her and they all looked out. A body lay, white and crumpled, on the gravel far below. A dark stain was spreading over the ground by the head.

Imogen screamed, an awful, stifled sound, stuffing her hands in her mouth, her eyes wide with shock.

'Oh my God, oh my God,' Romily said, over and over, very fast, her heart racing. 'Oh my God, what shall we do, what shall we do . . .' She looked over at Allegra, usually in control, their leader, but she was dead white, unable to speak, her whole body trembling violently.

'Look,' cried Imogen. She pointed to a figure running along the driveway towards Sophie's prone body. 'Someone's coming.'

Romily's head was in a whirl, adrenaline and panic coursing through her. 'It's a security guard,' she said abruptly.

'How do you know?' Imogen asked.

'I just do. Quick. We have to get back downstairs. The guard will help her, there's nothing more we can do.'

'We have to tell someone, we have to raise the alarm!' Imogen said, her voice growing shriller with fear.

'They already know! There's nothing we can do! Look at Allegra . . .'

Allegra said nothing but began to shake harder, her teeth chattering in her head.

'Help me, Midge,' Romily said, taking control. 'Take Allegra's other arm. Let's get back to bed as fast as we can. We can decide what to do in the morning. But they mustn't find us here . . . they mustn't!'

Chapter 6

The dreams were terrible. They woke her in the night, clammy with cold sweat and gasping. It was the look in Sophie's eyes, begging, terrified, in the moment before she fell, that she couldn't stand. Sometimes the broken body beneath the window got mixed up with an image of Xander lying at the bottom of the stairs after their father had kicked him there. Allegra had woken the whole boarding house one night with her jagged screams.

'We have to tell,' she said desperately to the other two as they marched endlessly round the games field, unable to sit still, needing to keep on the move. 'I can't bear it!'

'We can't,' Imogen said starkly, her face pale and set. 'Don't you see? It's too late. We should have told at the time. But we didn't. We can't tell now.' She clutched her friend's hand and held it tightly. 'We didn't even tell when Steele did her thing.'

Romily nodded solemnly in agreement with Imogen.

Allegra screwed her eyes shut and breathed in sharply. The interview with Miss Steele had been surreal. The night that Sophie Harcourt fell was now an awful blur in her mind but she remembered the atmosphere of panic as the lights came on, people began hurrying urgently around and an ambulance roared up the driveway, its siren wailing. Its blue light flashed across the wall of Allegra's cubie over and over again as she lay under her duvet, shaking and wide-eyed.

Don't let her be dead, don't let her be dead, she begged, but she knew what a fall from that height had to mean. Besides, she had seen the still, broken body lying on the gravel.

The next morning there had been wild whispers. At a sombre gathering of the entire school, Miss Steele had announced that there had been a tragic accident in the night. Sophie Harcourt was dead. A horrified gasp passed over the rows of girls and then there was a small thump. Martha Young had fallen to the floor in a faint. She was picked up by two teachers and taken to the sanatorium.

Miss Steele had explained that school business would continue as usual, in terms of lessons and examinations, but that the annual garden party would be cancelled and a memorial service held in its place. 'And now, you are dismissed. Except for the fifth form. I would like you all to remain behind, please.'

Allegra had felt numb and light-headed, as though she was being deprived of oxygen, and she could tell from their white faces and frightened eyes that the other two felt the same.

Miss Steele had taken her time before she began to speak, eying each girl with a piercing gaze as though she could see the inner workings of her mind.

She knows, she knows, she knows, thought Allegra, nausea churning through her. It was like living in a waking nightmare. Any second now, heavy hands would fall on her shoulders and she'd be marched away to prison. *Allegra McCorquodale, you are charged that you did hereby murder Sophie Harcourt . . .*

Miss Steele began to speak, slowly and calmly. 'You girls think that we do not know the minutiae of what happens between you: who is friends with whom, what alliances have formed, what enmities. You are wrong. You would be most surprised to learn how much we know about your private lives – not because we are spying on you, but because you do not trouble to hide it from us.

'We are certain that Sophie's death was a tragic accident, but it is important that we know the truth. Sophie was a strong and charismatic figure in the school, and it is fair to say that she was not always well liked – though I am sure that some of you are regretting any unkindness towards her now that she is dead. Because of that, the staff and I will be interviewing each of you in turn, to ask what you know about the events of last night. You will remain here until prefects send you to whichever member of staff will see you. That is all.'

The girls sat down, a low hubbub filling the hall as they talked to each other in quiet voices. Allegra was glad to sit: her head was spinning. She, Romily and Imogen looked at each other; although they did not dare voice what was in their heads, they were all thinking the same thing. *We must say nothing. No one will believe us if we say it was an accident. They'll think we killed her. Everyone knows she hated us . . .*

The hall began to empty as the prefects summoned the fifth form one by one. The interviews were mostly rapid, girls called in quick succession. Imogen was summoned first, to see Myers. She went with fists tightly clenched and her face drawn and white. Then Allegra was called, to see Miss Steele. She left Romily still cross-legged on the floor of the hall, wishing her good luck with her gaze.

'Sit down, Allegra.' Miss Steele nodded at the chair in front of her desk. Allegra slid into it, grateful not to have to stand on her shaky legs. 'I will say to you first what I'm saying to everyone. This is a desperately sad matter, first for Sophie herself and secondly for her poor family who are on their way. It goes without saying that it is also deeply private. I'm sorry to say that reporters have already been on the phone this morning, demanding to know more. It is precisely the kind of event that interests those with low minds. My strict instruction is that no one, absolutely no one, should discuss this matter out of school or talk to the press. Is that clear?'

Allegra nodded, unable to speak.

Miss Steele softened. 'I can see you are shocked. I'm not surprised. Many girls have been crying this morning. Their grief and sympathy for Sophie do them credit. But I must ask everybody to tell me exactly what they know about last night. Where were you?'

'In bed,' Allegra croaked. 'In bed, Miss Steele.'

'Did you hear or see anything unusual?'

Allegra shook her head dumbly. She wanted to believe it so badly that she was almost able to remember events as she told them: a quiet, blameless night in her little cubicle bed.

'Did the lights and noise wake you up?'

'No. I didn't wake up.' *Is that believable? Should I say I woke up?* She felt stiff with guilt and fright.

'Allegra, do you know anything at all about how Sophie Harcourt died?'

She stared at the Headmistress. All she wanted to do was break down and sob, to tell everything and be comforted; but she knew she must not do it. Everything depended on her silence. She shook her head. 'No,' she whispered.

'Very well. You may go.'

In their interviews, Imogen and Romily said the same, and were each dismissed the same way. They were all in the clear.

But then the dreams began.

There was uproar in the few days after Sophie's death, not just inside the school but outside too: the press were fascinated by the story and it was given pages of coverage for almost a week. The inquest a few weeks later renewed interest in the story. The coroner heard that it was not known how Sophie had gained access to the roof, or why she had gone there. Witnesses, including her friend Arabella Balmer, said that it was inconceivable that she was suicidal, despite the pressure of the forthcoming exams. It was death by misadventure, ruled the coroner.

Allegra could not bear to look at the pictures of Sophie's grief-stricken parents coming out of the Coroner's Court. In fact, she could not bear for it to be mentioned at all and, by common consent, none of them ever spoke of it. There was no question of their going back to the attic. Allegra threw the key away in the farthest reaches of the games field. Instead, they were grateful for the diversion of the examinations. In the evening they could lose themselves in their revision, and in the day they spent long silent hours in the examination hall, answering questions in history, biology, physics, geography, English, French, maths . . . Never had they been so grateful for their workload.

When Allegra's last examination was over, she was summoned to see her house mistress.

'We've decided that it's best for you to go home, Allegra,' Miss Myers said gravely, gazing at her through the spectacles that perched on the end of her nose. 'The sad events of this term have obviously affected you deeply. I'm sorry that you'll miss the end of term, I know you girls like to let your hair down when the examinations are over, but we think it's for the best, under the circumstances.'

So Allegra found herself on the train back to Foughton the next day, with her things to be collected in due course.

'What the hell are you doing here?' were her father's opening words when she came through the front door.

'Ivo, I told you,' her mother said, throwing the car keys into a china dish on the hall table. 'They've sent her home early.'

'Why?' he demanded, his blue eyes turning arctic. 'You haven't been expelled, have you?'

'Ivo!' Selina put an arm around Allegra's shoulders. 'There's been a tragic accident at the school, don't you remember? I told you all about it. I showed you that piece about it in the *Telegraph*. Poor Allegra's been horribly upset by it, tormented with nightmares, so they've sent her back.'

'Oh.' He frowned at his daughter. 'Well, we weren't expecting you for another fortnight, so just keep quiet, understand? At least it means I won't have to go to another blasted prize-giving, I suppose.' He marched off down the hall towards the estate office.

She watched him go, her mouth tight. *I hate him. Selfish prick.*

Selina sighed. 'Sorry, darling, you know what he's like. Now, be an angel and go and find Brenda in the kitchen, will you? She'll get you something to eat. I'm so busy this afternoon. I didn't realise I'd have to come and get you from the station, and it's put my whole day out.'

It was still a relief to be home. Allegra curled up in front of the nursery fireplace, though there was no fire lit, and lay for ages soaking up the comfort of the familiar room, clutching her favourite old Teddy, although she hadn't needed him for years. Here she could pretend that all the terror at school had never happened. *I just have to forget, that's all. We all do. We have to put it out of our minds and keep it out.*

The nightmares began to subside and she enjoyed her first peaceful nights for weeks. She spent the days on her own, reading in the nursery, sitting on the window seat where she could look out over the loch, or in the garden when the weather was good. She went on long walks through the rangy heather and into the woods, or helped the gardener in the fruit patch, gathering peas and berries. Sometimes she persuaded her mother to drive her over to the stables so she could exercise the horses – she loved the liberating hours of riding. She kept out of her father's way, though she could sometimes hear his bellowing even from her bedroom, when he'd been drinking and was shouting about something. As long as he stayed well away from her, she didn't care.

She wondered what was happening at school. Post-examinations was a time all the girls looked forward to: no lessons, no work, just lazy days, with tennis and swimming and chat, like an endless weekend, until speech day and the end of term. What were Imogen and Romily doing? Were they keeping their promise of silence? She wished that Imogen was here, able to make her laugh and make her forget.

Then a postcard arrived:

Allegra darling,

School is no fun without you. Hope you are feeling better. We're playing tennis for hours every day, but only with each other because Imogen's so shit no one else will play with us. See you in September. Love, Romily xxx

Hi, Lollie, hope you are having a sexy time. I'll be home soon, so get ready. No news here except that Gina Harris broke her nose on the side of the swimming pool – improvement! Her nose, not pool. Midge x

P.S. MG 4 EVER

It sounded so delightfully normal. Perhaps the worst was over. Could life go back to being what it was before. Carefree? Amusing? Free from the terrible guilt?

God, I hope so. I really do.

Chapter 7

Back from Westfield at last, Imogen was restored by the warmth and comfort of home. She had longed desperately to be in her safe, secure little nest, away from the cold, stark awfulness of school where everything and everybody was haunted by that dreadful night. Her parents were delighted to have her home, and sympathetic about the terrible events of the previous term.

'It's a frightening lesson,' her father said, his expression grave. 'You never know what might happen. You have to live every day to the full.'

'That poor girl's mother! I can't bear to think about it,' Jeannie Heath said, her green eyes watery with tears, hugging Imogen to her. 'When I think about the agony of burying your own child . . . It's just not natural, it's against the scheme of things. Are you all right, dear? You've gone all white.'

'I'm fine,' Imogen said faintly, clinging to the security of her mother and feeling like a little girl again. She had done her best not to think about anything connected with that awful night, and was grateful that she'd been spared Allegra's nightmares. When her imagination took her up to the attic, she had learnt tricks to stop herself remembering. 'Allegra's asked if I can go to Foughton tomorrow. Can I?'

'Of course,' said her mother happily distracted. 'I can take you over and have coffee with Selina. She's all taken up with this wedding they're having in London – not that she has to do much, bar pick a hat, it's all being organised by the bride. But I'm dying to hear about it.'

'Don't spend too much time over there, will you, Imogen?' her father said, looking worried. 'I never see you. I want to spend some time with my girl in the holidays.'

'Yes, Daddy,' she said, though she knew she would do all she could to be with Allegra as much as possible. After all, her friend needed her now more than ever.

It was lovely to see Allegra again. She looked taller and more graceful, as though the suffering of the last few weeks had refined her. They ran straight up to the nursery where they could talk in peace. Imogen told her everything that had happened in the last days at school, making her laugh with imitations of Miss Steele giving out the prizes. It was good to see her happy again.

'What was the memorial service like?' she asked casually, not meeting Imogen's eye.

'Pretty bad. Sophie's family were there. I couldn't watch. Her mum was crying into a hankie the whole time.' Imogen moved her finger over a pattern on the rug, remembering. The guilt had been like something vile sitting in her stomach – she'd wanted to puke it up and had even tried to make herself sick afterwards, but couldn't. 'It felt . . . dreadful.'

There was a long silence and then Allegra said in a low voice, 'Midge – do you think I'm a murderer?'

Imogen sat up straight. 'No,' she said fervently, and meant it from her heart. 'It was an accident, and that's the truth.' She believed it but that venomous snake of guilt still twisted inside her. *We did it, even if we didn't mean to. We were there, and we didn't tell.* She could never confess it to anyone, not even Allegra.

'Tell me again about Miss Steele and Hatty Perkins's

prize?' Allegra said, changing the subject, and they did not raise it again.

Later, they went out to the temple, a pretty pink marble folly built in the far craggy wilderness of the grounds and looking somewhat incongruous with its pale pastel delicacy amid the grey granite, gorse, bracken and heather. They brought cosy cushions so they could sit comfortably on the stone floor and talk away while they smoked their cigarettes and ate chocolate biscuits.

'Everyone's in a terrible fuss,' Allegra said, tapping her ash out on one of the pink marble columns. 'My brother Tristan's getting married in London, so we're all going down there next week. It's a turnout of the whole tribe, which is absolutely massive, what with all the divorces and remarriages and aunts and uncles and cousins . . . But it'll be nice to see Xander. I've not seen him since last hols, and he's staying with a friend at the moment.'

Imogen thought of Xander, Allegra's elder brother. He was a skinny, impish thing with a mop of hair the same dark blond as Allegra's. He liked to play tricks on the girls, usually involving something wriggling and slimy he'd found in the garden. Other than that, he liked to race around on his mini-motorbike, zooming through the heather and whooping as he went, or else to sail and fish on the loch in his red dinghy. She liked him because he was always cheerful and laughing, but he was around only in the holidays and not always then because he was often staying with friends. In fact, she hadn't seen him since the previous Christmas.

'Why don't we ask if you can come too?' Allegra said suddenly.

Imogen blinked. 'What? Where?'

'To Tristan's wedding.'

'How can I come? I haven't been invited.'

'I'm sure they can squeeze in one more,' Allegra said with a shrug.

'God, I'd love to.' She felt excitement fizz through her. It would be wonderful to be around the McCorquodales at one of their family events, to see the whole glamorous clan in one place, and at a wedding too . . .

'I'll ask Mum. I'm sure it won't be a problem.'

The invitation on the mantelpiece was on thick cream card and engraved in flowing copperplate: Brigadier and Mrs Archibald Pilkington requested the pleasure of Imogen's company at the marriage of their daughter Elspeth Mary to The Hon. Tristan McCorquodale. As soon as the invitation had been replied to, Imogen's mother took her to Jenners in Edinburgh, and they bought her a new outfit for the smart London wedding.

'What will you wear?' Jeannie Heath said, fretting. 'So difficult with a girl of your age. A nice smart suit would do for me, but would it be too old for you?'

'Allegra's wearing a plain dress with a sparkly cardigan,' Imogen said quickly, keen to stop her mother from buying something unsuitable and embarrassing. 'So we should get something like that.'

'Yes, yes . . . you show me,' she said, relieved. 'Will you need a hat?'

Imogen shook her head. 'Allegra's not wearing one. She's got these cool bits of hair jewellery – you stud them in and they sit in your hair.'

'Really? How strange. But she must know what's acceptable . . .'

I feel caught between Allegra's world and my own, Imogen thought as they shopped. *I know more about it than Mummy does. She's listening to me. She thinks Allegra knows how to do things, even though she's only sixteen.* It was an odd feeling and, for the first time, she felt herself growing away from her parents and into a new and different world.

They bought her a blue and white floral dress, a blue pashmina to go with it, and some blue suede kitten heels. Imogen found a white feathered hairclip that she could use to clip back her long straight honey-brown hair.

'Are you sure that's suitable?' asked her mother, frowning. 'It doesn't look much. Where did you say the reception was?'

'It's in a gentlemen's club on Pall Mall.'

'Really? That sounds grand. Perhaps you should wear a proper hat. There's a nice one over there with a bit of white veil on it . . .'

Imogen reeled back in horror. 'No way, Mummy, that's not right at all. I'd look all wrong.'

Her mother surrendered. 'All right, dear. I suppose you must know best.'

The night before the wedding they stayed in the McCorquodales' house in South Kensington, but it was much less relaxed than the visit of five years before when they'd gone to Westfield for the first time. Allegra's father was there and the whole household seemed tense and nervous, poised on the edge of some terrifying storm that never quite broke.

The girls ate their supper in the kitchen and then scurried upstairs to Allegra's room, to watch the television and smoke out of the bedroom window.

'Is it always this scary around your dad?' Imogen asked, as they crammed shoulder to shoulder against the sill and blew streams of smoke out over the Kensington rooftops. Ivo Crachmore seemed a world removed from her own cosy, comfortable, affectionate father. Was this simply what earls were like?

Allegra nodded. 'He's a nightmare. He stalks around in a half fury all the time, and it only takes a little thing to set him off.'

'What's he like when he's in a proper rage?' Imogen asked, trying to imagine it. 'Does he really roar?'

Allegra looked out over the chimneys and nodded. 'That's not the half of it.' She glanced sideways at Imogen. 'He lashes out as well.'

'Really?' Imogen was horrified. Ivo was a big man, with huge hands and powerful arms. She imagined he could pack a strong punch with them. Then she remembered hearing her mother say that Ivo had kicked Xander downstairs once. 'But he doesn't lash out at you, does he?'

'Yes.' Allegra's face was stony. 'He has done. But not for a while.' Then she said quietly, 'Sometimes I worry that I'm like him. That I've got his madness in me. After what happened . . .'

Imogen felt sick. 'Of course you don't! You didn't do anything on purpose, it was an accident. You're not mad.'

Allegra laughed with a hollow sound. 'You're wrong there. We're all mad. Mum, Dad, Xander . . .'

'Where is Xander?' Imogen asked, wanting to stop Allegra thinking about the thing they must not mention.

'Getting pissed with Tristan, I expect. He's an usher, and they're all staying over at a hotel close to the church, so they can make sure they get him there on time no matter what. Come on.' Allegra stubbed out her fag. 'Fancy a game of cards before bed? I've got some vodka I sneaked up from the drinks tray.'

The wedding the next day was beautiful. It passed by in a haze of excitement and interest for Imogen. She felt pretty and grown up in her dress, and relieved that it seemed to pass muster with Allegra, who pronounced it 'brill'. Imogen wished in her heart that she had her friend's natural panache – her plain dark pink dress looked so simple on the hanger and yet on her it had effortless style – but overall she was happy with how she'd scrubbed up. Her white feather clip was just right, even if it lacked the sparkle of Allegra's magenta hair jewellery.

The big black family Bentley took them to the church. Selina looked as grand as a countess should in a navy blue silk suit, heels and a huge silk hat wreathed in feathers, though the grandeur really came from the amount of diamonds she was wearing: a huge brooch on one lapel, a bracelet on each wrist, earrings, and a pearl-and-diamond choker at her neck. Ivo looked every inch an earl in his morning coat, striped trousers and silk top hat, though Imogen felt a tremor of fear when she saw him. She tried to imagine him striking Allegra, but the idea was so awful she pushed it out of her mind.

The wedding was held in an ornate Gothic Revival church just behind Oxford Street, full of colour and glittering with gold. As they entered behind Lord and Lady Crachmore, a tall young man came up to them with a smile on his handsome face.

'Aisle or window?' he said in a loud whisper. 'Emergency exits here, here and here. Lifebelts under the pews.'

'Xander!' cried Allegra, throwing her arms around him.

'Careful,' he said, kissing her cheek. 'My hangover is a wondrous thing. One hard squeeze and you'll have last night's curry all over these lovely tiles.'

Is this Xander? Imogen was amazed. Last time she'd seen him, he'd been her height, baby-faced and intent on dropping wet pebbles down the back of her T-shirt. Now he was at least a foot taller, and broad with it, and his face was a young man's, with dark blue eyes sparkling under thick brows. He still had his mop of blond hair, just a shade or two darker than Allegra's, but otherwise he was completely unlike the boy she remembered. *Oh my God, he's gorgeous! How did that happen?*

'How's Tristan?' Allegra asked, taking an order of service.

Xander nodded to where their brother sat in the front pew, his shoulders bowed. 'White. Shaking. With a rather revolting whiff of chicken madras and stale Cobra. But I think he'll get through it. Hi, Imogen, how are you?'

'Fine.' She managed to smile at him, though she found it hard to meet his eyes and a flush began to creep up her neck. *What am I doing? I'm blushing! Talking to Xander! This is ridiculous.*

'You look very nice,' he said politely. 'Now, I'd better get you two into a pew or I'm not going to be popular. We've got a queue forming and the bride's due in ten minutes.'

The wedding was very High Church. Imogen found the whole thing spell-binding from the moment the bride came down the aisle to a swell of organ music, four tiny bridesmaids and pages in front of her. The service lasted an hour and a half, with a full Eucharistic Mass celebrated after the ceremony itself, but Imogen enjoyed every minute: the choir's magnificent soaring voices as they sang Mozart's Missa Brevis in C Major and the glorious anthems, the sight of the robed priest and countless servers in their white surplices, carrying candles and crosses, and the spicy aroma of rich incense burning in a silver censer.

Now this is a wedding! she thought, delighted by the colour and spectacle of it all. She was used to plain Church of Scotland services and this was a delicious and unexpected sensual assault. And all the time she could see Xander, sitting at the end of the pew, and marvel at the way his profile had suddenly become as strong and perfect as it was possible for a profile to be . . .

'And now,' Allegra said, as they closed their orders of

service and watched the happy couple parade back down the aisle, 'the reception.'

Taxis took them down Regent's Street to Piccadilly Circus and then Pall Mall where they disembarked in front of the great grey frontage of a gentlemen's club. Inside they were directed up a small staircase and through into a great room with red silk-covered walls, enormous brass chandeliers, and vast portraits of kings, generals and noblemen.

'Are we allowed one of these?' Imogen whispered to Allegra as they went past one of the staff holding a tray of champagne.

'Of course,' Allegra said, helping herself to a glass. Imogen followed suit, feeling very sophisticated. So far, her only experience of alcohol was stolen vodka and cans of smuggled lager.

She sipped at the fizzing liquid. *It's nice . . . I suppose,* she thought, as it sent bubbly tickles through her nose. She gazed around the guests: immaculate older women in their silks, satins and pearls, pretty young things in their tight, sparkly dresses and heels, and the men in their well-cut jackets and silk waistcoats, each with the obligatory undone button at the bottom. *Where's Xander?* She couldn't see him in the crush.

The girls ended up on the far side of the room where they could observe proceedings, sipping at their champagne as their heads went woozy.

'Hello, my darling angel,' said a jolly voice behind them.

Imogen turned to see a small man with a pair of sparkling blue eyes in a lightly tanned face. His grey hair was combed into a careful bouffant, and his clothes were immediately noticeable for their beautiful cut and unusual style. In a room full of discreet dark-striped trousers, this man was wearing houndstooth-check bags, and under his morning coat was a vivid violet waistcoat and a shocking pink silk tie, with a matching handkerchief spilling from his breast pocket.

'Uncle David!' Allegra darted into his arms and gave him a fierce hug.

'My favourite niece. How are you?' He released her and looked at her hard, while sweeping a low, elegant bow. 'Your *ladyship.* You've moved up a rung in *Burke's* now, haven't you, darling? Daughter of an earl, no less. Up you go on the precedence scale, while we boys get nothing.'

'Serves you right for being a younger son,' she retorted, smiling.

'All is made equal by that word "younger",' sighed David. 'Only a year younger, but better than any title, as far as I'm concerned. Now, who is this delicious rosebud?'

'I'm Imogen,' she said.

'Of course you are. Imogen, the delightful heroine of *Cymbeline*. If you have half her spirit, you'll be doing very well. Did you enjoy the wedding, girls? I'm rather cross with the bride, even if she was wearing her grandmother's wedding dress, which I think is terrifically stylish and *very* brave. But August is a terribly unfashionable time for a wedding . . . what on earth was she thinking? We've all had to make the trek back into town when anyone decent was safely in the country weeks ago. Quite appalling.'

Allegra rolled her eyes and laughed. 'You must know what you're going on about, but we don't.'

'The young of today!' he sighed. 'So depressing. Never mind, you're pretty enough to get away with your dreadful ignorance.' He stared a little closer at Allegra as though seeing her for the first time. 'You know, you really are turning into rather a little swan, aren't you? Both you and Xander seem to have got the best of the McCorquodale looks, and the fresh blood from your mother's side has given you a charm the others don't have, even Miranda. I thought you were a funny, gawky-looking little girl, but now I can see what you'll look like as a woman. You're going to be rather stunning. An asset to us all, my darling.'

Allegra didn't say anything but sipped at her champagne self-consciously and looked away.

Imogen gazed at David, entranced by his flamboyant style and funny, jokey way of talking, as though everything were an amusing game. It was typical of Allegra, of course, to have such an entertaining uncle. This was the man her friend had told her about – the one with the nightclub, who knew all the famous people.

'Now, you two, tell me all about yourselves. I heard there was rather a scandal at your school this summer, Allegra. Some poor girl killing herself. Do tell all.'

Imogen gasped as her friend's face flamed scarlet.

'There's nothing to tell,' Allegra said, sounding cool enough, though her burning cheeks seemed to tell a different story.

David stared at her for a moment and then said lightly, 'Well, there's always someone who takes life too seriously, isn't there? A shame, but there it is. I'm glad that I'm fundamentally a *happy* soul. I see beauty and rejoice. I see ugliness, and shudder, and think how lucky I am to be able to live the way I want. I don't have to face those low, nasty aspects of life that blight the existence of so many. I can indulge myself in all the things that make life worth living: art, music, antiques, intelligent and cultivated friends. And good food, of course. Speaking of which . . .' He eyed a tray of canapés: rolls of white bread stuffed with khaki-coloured asparagus spears. 'Aren't they *nasty?* I would never allow such things in Colette's.' He pulled a disgusted face and then sighed. 'I offered young Elspeth the club to have her reception in but her parents had their heart set on this frightful old place. As stuffy as a grandmother's mattress.

The Brigadier's been a member since birth, apparently. Such a duffer.'

Imogen was relieved that he had so gracefully changed the subject. 'Allegra told me you have your own club,' she said, emboldened by champagne. 'Is that Colette's?'

Allegra had recovered from her discomfort. 'Yes, Uncle David, when are we going to be allowed to visit?'

'Mmm.' David's eyes twinkled at her. 'How much do you know about it?'

'Just that you started it ages ago, and lots of famous people go there.'

'Well, that's true, I suppose. But they're all just chums to me, you see. That's what the club is all about – a lovely place to meet my friends. That was what I wanted and couldn't find, so I decided to open it myself. It's been rather successful, even if I do say so myself.'

'We're absolutely dying to see it – aren't we, Midge?'

Imogen couldn't think of anything more glamorous and exciting than to go to Colette's. 'Oh, yes,' she breathed. 'Could we?'

David gave her a wise glance. 'Not yet, my darlings. You're not quite ready. Remember little Liesl's song in *The Sound of Music*? How she is unprepared for a world of roués and cads? I think the same about you. You're still very young. Some of the beasts in there would be happy to tear you to pieces.'

Imogen was disappointed. They looked so grown up and here they were, sipping fine champagne. Were they really not ready?

Allegra made a face. 'It's just a club! How dangerous can it be?'

David pursed his lips and said quietly, 'You need to learn a little more about the world before you get there – otherwise it could be a painful surprise. And I don't want to have to answer to your parents if you're corrupted too young.'

Allegra giggled. 'No one will corrupt me!' she declared. 'I can do a perfectly good job of that on my own, thanks very much.'

'I've no doubt. But that doesn't mean I have to help you along the way. You'll get into Colette's all in good time, I promise you that. Now, girls.' He offered them an arm each. 'Shall we perambulate? Let's go and look at some of the fearfully nasty hats on show. Ten pounds to the spotter of the worst.'

Chapter 8

New York
Autumn 2000

Ah, this is it! This is what it's all about. Sex, drugs, cooking. It doesn't get much better than this. Living the dream, man, living the dream . . .

Mitch closed his eyes and let out a long sigh of appreciation as the cute waitress he'd hired only the night before sank to her knees in the alleyway and took his cock into her mouth.

He knew he'd enjoy the whole thing a lot more if he wasn't high and three-quarters drunk, and if he weren't clutching a box full of lettuces under one arm, but he wasn't one to turn down an opportunity like this. He'd known she was up for something since the moment she'd arrived, from the way she'd wagged her little derrière at him, and when she'd found out he had a stash of heroin that he might possibly share with her, he'd seen that eager hunger in her eyes and known she'd do anything to get some.

He grunted happily as she slid her warm wet lips up and down his shaft, and then tickled the top with her tongue. That felt good – hell, it felt more than good, it was delicious. *Sex is like eating,* he decided. *It answers some kind of need right in the centre of us. When it's done right, it's the ultimate physical satisfaction, it's the reason to be alive.*

The problem was, his nerves were so strained and his body so jaded from the rigours he submitted it to, it was hard to feel that peak of pleasure any longer.

I'm fucking tired, he thought to himself. The waitress had brought her hand into play, rubbing his cock in firm straight strokes while sucking hard on his glans. *So fucking tired.*

He could feel that circling tingle deep within his balls that meant a climax was not far off. *But it's like a slot machine. Put your money in, you get your game. Doesn't mean it's worth the price of the play.*

The waitress increased her pace, stroking him hard and tickling faster with her mouth. Mitch felt his orgasm begin; he looked down at her blonde head bobbing up and down on his cock and it gave him the push over the edge: he groaned as he felt himself spurt into her mouth. He throbbed three or four times, his face contorting with the sweet agony of coming, then the ejaculation subsided and he quickly pushed her away.

'Did you like that, Mitch?' the waitress asked, wiping her mouth.

'Yeah, baby, thanks.' He tucked his cock back into his pants as best he could with one hand, the other arm still occupied with the box of Romaine lettuces destined for that night's Caesar salads. 'Very nice, honey.'

'Have you . . . Can I have . . .?' Her high voice faded away and she blinked big, needy eyes at him.

'You want the junk? OK, no problem.' He pulled a small plastic bag of pale brown powder from his pocket. 'Here. Have it.'

Her eyes widened even further. 'All of it?'

'Sure.' *I'll regret that,* he thought. 'Take it all. Just don't fuck up on the job, OK? And you'd better show up for your shifts or I'll fire your ass so fast you won't know what happened. Smack is no excuse for not working, understand?'

She nodded happily, evidently itching to get her hands on the treat he was holding out to her. 'You got it.'

'Good. Now, that was nice. Maybe we can do it again some time.'

'Any time, Mitch, any time.'

He watched as she went happily off down the alleyway, her little reward stuffed into the pocket of her denim jacket. She'd go back to some dive she shared with a boyfriend, probably a cook too, someone who lived in the same strange world of crazy hours, intense work, heat and pressure, someone who also experienced the mad high of the post-shift euphoria and who craved the same release that drugs brought.

Was it really nearly a year since he'd come to New York? Mitch found it hard to remember that innocent young man who'd got off the bus at Port Authority then. That kid had never dreamt he'd get involved in this kind of world. He'd been a hard-working boy who wanted to make something of himself, clean-living, a young man whose only idea of a good time was downing a few beers and watching the baseball. His one vice was smoking – he was addicted to Camels. The only time he didn't have one hanging from his mouth was when he was cooking. That was the crazy thing: he could go for eight hours straight without even thinking about a cigarette but, the minute he stepped out of the kitchen, he felt like he'd die if he didn't have one of those babies within about ten seconds.

He'd never experienced physical hardship like working in a New York kitchen in a proper fancy restaurant. Working in diners out West was nothing compared to this. He started at seven o'clock in the evening when the first covers came in – rich men and women who knew good food and expected it on their plates when they were paying top New York prices – and then did not stop until almost two in the morning:

cooking, tasting, seasoning and plating up, producing the same dishes to the exact same standard of perfection over and over again, as the kitchen grew hotter and tenser and more and more like his idea of hell. He thrived on the atmosphere and the manic way time passed but, with his working hours flashing by, it was no surprise he began to feel the need to live intensely outside of work too. Half his life was being swallowed up by it. There had to be moments when he felt alive and engaged with the world beyond the kitchen.

But there was nowhere else he'd rather be. He'd fallen in love with New York, and he'd fallen hard. Once he'd learnt how the place worked, once he'd found Herbie, the wild-eyed pastry chef from New Jersey who'd taken him under his wing . . . well, things became a lot easier for Mitch. He grew up fast. His first job was tricky, having to master making pasta from scratch in an hour, but Herbie had helped him. Then, just as he'd started to get the hang of it, the restaurant suddenly went bust, and shut. This came as no surprise to the other commis-chefs: they shrugged their shoulders and moved on, giving friends a call and finding a new position sometimes within hours. This was how it worked apparently: restaurants opened, a team was assembled to work there – usually friends and associates of whoever was hired as head chef – and then the great scam began. The cooking and waiting staff knew this world well. They knew it better than their fresh-faced, eager bosses, usually pleasant enough people who'd decided it would be fun to run a restaurant and had sunk all their money into it, that this world was a tough one.

'No one can make money out of restaurants,' Herbie told him. He looked even crazier than most chefs, with his mad curly hair and a criss-cross of burn scars up and down his arms and all over his hands. 'Except for the lucky few.

They're the ones who give all the others the impression that this is somehow a sure-fire way to make bucks. But you know what? It's a sure-fire way to lose your house, and that's about it.'

While the new restaurant was still afloat, the staff were quick to make as much out of it as they could: over-ordering food and selling it on; walking out with hundreds of dollars worth of prime seafood or top-notch fillet steak concealed under their coats. They drank themselves stupid at the bar and stole bottles of wine, cutlery, linen, and anything else that wasn't nailed down. They worked hard, too, but often while drunk or stoned.

'These guys are going to go bust,' Mitch said to Herbie disbelievingly.

'Uh-huh. Then we'll all move on. I already heard about a new joint opening up in the Village, if you're interested.'

'But shouldn't we try and help them?'

Herbie made a face and said, 'Nah. They were stupid enough to open a French bistro when everyone's crazy for Italian, and to paint it this shade of puke green, and to have a menu that gives me the shits just reading it. They deserve it.' He saw the expression on Mitch's face. 'Aw, c'mon, man. Don't feel sorry for 'em. That's just the way it is. We gotta feed the beast. This place has gotta die so others might live. It's harsh, but there we are.'

It was Herbie who got Mitch a place in the next restaurant as soon as the one they were working in went down, just as he'd predicted. He also got Mitch a bed in the apartment he was renting, though it meant sleeping on a futon affair in the tiny sitting room and folding it away every day before heading off to the restaurant. It was Herbie who brought him into the underground world of the chefs, kitchen staff and waiters, who worked and partied together in the small hours when the city's respectable citizens were all asleep.

It was Herbie who introduced him to heroin.

By the time Mitch had been working in New York six months, he was on the brink of a nervous breakdown. He was frying steaks, broiling chops and roasting Beef Wellington at his meat station in the restaurant, and then doing it all over again in his sleep. It felt like there wasn't an hour of the day when he wasn't sweating over a roasting hot grill, or slicing bloody meat, or crisping off fat.

'You need to calm down, man,' Herbie had announced, looking at Mitch's red, tired eyes and trembling hands. 'Here, try some of this.' He'd tossed a small bag of brown powder towards him.

'Uh-uh.' Mitch shook his head. 'I'm not going there.' He had a healthy disregard for drugs: only the losers in his town had taken stuff like that. He may have left small towns behind him, but he still had their attitudes.

Herbie laughed. 'Don't worry, kid. Don't like injections, huh?'

Mitch shook his head again. He'd seen some of the other guys shooting up – even stumbled across one of the kitchen porters in the alley outside the kitchen, pulling a bit of tubing tight round his arm, holding one end with his teeth so he could stab a syringe into a vein with his free hand. It had looked sick, and so did the porter, with his grey face and desperate eyes.

'You don't have to slam it. You *smoke* it. It's not addictive that way – well, not much. And it sure helps to calm you down. It's like stepping into Nirvana for a little while. Everyone does it, honest. I'm tellin' ya, man, it's amazing, and you won't get hooked. Ever heard of junkies who don't inject?'

He never had. Smoking didn't sound too bad. Mitch loved to smoke, after all. He'd been at it since he was fourteen and hiding under the bleachers from the football coach.

'Here,' said Herbie. 'Lemme show you. Once ain't going to hurt.'

He had fetched a good-sized piece of aluminium foil and given Mitch a toilet roll tube to hold over the little pile of powder.

'I'm gonna heat the dope till it turns into vapour, OK? You inhale it through the tube. Nod your head when you've had enough and I'll stop burning. It'll smoke for another couple of seconds after that, so don't waste it.'

Am I really gonna try this stuff? he wondered, as Herbie assembled the gear. But he looked up to the other chef, who knew so much more about how the world worked. Herbie was too smart to fuck up, wasn't he? If he said it was OK, then it must be. And Mitch would love to feel good again, and shake this bone-crushing tiredness, just for a while. *Maybe once . . . it can't hurt, not just the once. So I can see what all the fuss is about.*

He had watched while Herbie clicked his cigarette lighter under the piece of foil, heard the crackle as it heated and the heroin glowed. He sucked in the smoke, held it deep within while it worked its magic, and then released it.

The minute he did, he knew that his pal had been lying to him. There was no way this was not addictive: the feeling of utter bliss and warmth that filled him to the top of his skull was the most beautiful sensation Mitch had ever had, and he wanted it again as quickly as possible.

'Nice, huh?'

Mitch nodded.

'See? What did I tell you?' Herbie grinned. 'Don't say I never do nothing for ya, man.'

Oh, wow. That hits the spot. It really hits the spot.

Chapter 9

Westfield Boarding School for Girls
Spring 2001

Imogen and Allegra were in Allegra's room, putting off finishing their evening prep and painting their toe nails instead. Life in the sixth form was much better than lower down in the school – they were finally in Warwick House, where they were treated more like adults and had their own private study bedrooms.

When they'd returned to Westfield the previous September, armed with their respectable GCSE results, they all seemed to have grown up over the holidays, as though the months away from school had allowed them to digest and accept what had happened the previous term. It had changed them, there was no doubt about that. They were quieter than before, and their group of three became more and more insular, trusting only each other.

The teachers understood that Sophie Harcourt's death had affected some of their pupils more deeply than they could know – after all, Martha Young had never returned to Westfield after the holidays – but even so, they were surprised that their most rebellious characters had mysteriously settled down and begun to apply themselves to their books.

'Imogen Heath has always been a good girl at heart,' they

said to each other in the staff room, 'but who would have expected that vain little package Romily de Lisle to start caring about something other than lipstick and fashion? And what about Allegra McCorquodale? We always knew she had a brain, but no one guessed she'd ever start using it . . .'

Gradually, as the girls began to recover from the shock of what had happened to Sophie, they looked towards their own futures. Allegra even had a boyfriend, Freddie, who was at Radley. They wrote each other chirpy, unromantic letters and met in pubs off Sloane Square during holidays and exeats, usually ending up at someone's house where they could kiss and grope each other. She kept the other two endlessly entertained with stories of how far she and Freddie were getting. Imogen was working hard and, urged by the English teacher to apply to Oxford, had decided she would try for Christ Church, one of the largest and grandest colleges. Allegra followed suit, although without quite as much encouragement as Imogen received, and said she planned to apply to Lincoln. 'It's where my family always goes,' she explained vaguely when asked. 'Xander's going there in the autumn.'

Imogen had had no idea that you could have a family college, where you would expect to follow in your relatives' footsteps, but apparently you could. Knowing that Xander was going to be at Oxford gave Imogen a tingling, excited feeling in her stomach. Ever since the wedding in London, she'd nurtured a secret crush on him, wondering when she would see him again, but he'd proved much more elusive than he used to. Not so long ago, she and Allegra had spent their time planning how they could get away from her irritating brother – now all she could think about was how their paths might cross; but Xander was always off staying with friends or travelling abroad on some adventure. She had caught a tantalising glimpse of him at Foughton over the Christmas holidays and he'd looked more handsome and grown up than ever, but she'd barely been able to exchange more than a few stammering words with him. Now she dreamed of seeing him at Oxford, and it sent her back to her studies, determined to win her place.

'Do you like this colour red?' Allegra said, showing her toe nails to Imogen as they sat on the bed.

'*Très chic,*' Imogen remarked. 'But this grey blue is sooo trendy . . . I totally love it. I'd wear it on my fingernails if I could get away with it, but someone's bound to notice and make me take it off.'

'You could pretend you trapped all your fingers in a door,' suggested Allegra.

'Ho-ho.' Imogen frowned at her favourite colour. 'Do you really think it looks like bruises?'

The door was flung open then and they both glanced up, startled, as Romily came in, tears streaming down her face.

'What is it, Rom?' Allegra asked, jumping off the bed, not caring that her scarlet nails were still wet. She rushed over and put her arms round the other girl, who started crying hard.

Romily raised her face, leaving a damp patch on Allegra's top. 'I've just been talking to my mother. She says she and my father have decided that I've got to leave Westfield.'

'What?' Imogen gasped, and jumped up as well.

Romily nodded, sniffing, her brown eyes full of tears. Her mascara left inky trails down her cheeks but she wiped them away with the cuff of her exquisite white shirt.

'But why?' demanded Allegra.

'They've just heard about . . .' Romily looked reluctant to say the words '. . . about you know what.'

They all swapped glances. They knew what she was referring to.

'But all the parents got a letter, didn't they?' Allegra said.

She sat down on the chair by her desk. 'And it was in the news, all over the papers, we all saw it . . . Christ, everyone saw it. Remember how we had the press outside the gates for weeks? How Miss Steele forbade us all to talk to them? How could your parents not have known?'

Romily turned her eyes up to heaven and said, 'Because they're not like other people! They live in their own little bubble, you know that. They're hardly ever in London. Maybe they were at the château, or on Chrypkos, or in New York or Switzerland – I don't know. They don't really care about things like this – they know what's going on in high society, or politics, or fashion, or art. They don't give a stuff about what happens at a girls' school out in the middle of nowhere.'

'Not even if you're there?' Imogen asked tentatively. She'd seen Romily's parents only once, when they attended a speech day. Usually nannies and personal assistants escorted her to and from school, along with the mandatory bodyguard. The de Lisles had been stunningly glamorous, like creatures from another world. They'd seemed more highly coloured and textured than the people around them, as glossy and polished as fine porcelain. Their clothes, their hair, everything about them had screamed money: not just a bit, but oodles and oodles of it. It had made the other Westfield parents – the bankers, stockbrockers, lawyers and businessmen – look a little bit dowdy by comparison. Even the richest British ones, even the most aristocratic, couldn't compete with the sheen of French sophistication and the utter glamour of their haute-European lifestyle. At least, that was how it had seemed to Imogen. 'And didn't they get the letter from Miss Steele?'

Romily shrugged. Suddenly, she looked very young and lonely. 'I shouldn't think they ever saw it. All correspondence goes to the office. The secretaries would have opened it. They read all of it – they even précis my reports into one paragraph so my parents don't have to waste too much time over them. They probably didn't think it was worth bothering them over something so minor. Or they put it in a file for someone's attention and it's only now that it's been noticed.'

'But why should they care now?' asked Allegra.

'Oh.' Romily shrugged. 'My mother has decided that the school is obviously a den of vice and the wrong sort of people go here. So I'm leaving at the end of term.' Her lip trembled. 'She wanted me out immediately! I said no, I wouldn't walk out. So we've compromised. I can stay till the end of term.'

'Oh, Romily!' They stared at each other, hardly able to believe that their little triumvirate was about to be irreparably shattered. 'But what are you going to do? Where will you go?'

Tears flowed down her cheeks. 'I don't know. Mama has suggested some other schools – French and Swiss, mostly. Or a kind of finishing school where I would learn cookery and that kind of thing. She doesn't seem to think I need to go to school at all. She said that education is often vulgarising, and that she knows plenty of intellectuals – a few hours of conversation a week with them and some reading is all I need, apparently. She's already asked her friend Professor Levy-Lande of the Sorbonne to make a list of everything I should read by the age of twenty-one – all the classics.'

'Shakespeare? Shelley? Keats? Dickens? That kind of thing?' asked Imogen, interested.

Romily frowned. 'Well . . . more like Racine, Molière, Proust, Voltaire . . . you know, the classics.'

Allegra looked envious. 'Oh my God, so you get to live in Paris? Go shopping? Have dinner parties with the cool people your parents know?'

They all knew that the de Lisles, with one foot in the world of art and the other in shipping and international business, mixed with the cream of world society: famous artists, esteemed writers, the leading politicians of the day, along with singers, actors, directors, and people who were famous simply for being beautiful, rich and carefree – they all dined at the de Lisles' magnificent Paris flat, stayed at the wonderful properties all over the world, holidayed on the de Lisles' yacht or on their private Greek island of Chrypkos.

'Do you really want to stay here instead?' asked Imogen, finding it hard to believe.

Romily looked agonised. 'Of course I do!' She sank down on to Allegra's pink leather pouffe and wrapped her arms round her bare knees. 'I know my life sounds fabulous – and I'm very lucky, I realise that. The stuff my grandfather left . . .' She trailed off. She didn't need to explain. Everyone knew that Vincent de Lisle's legacy of hundreds of canvases was worth millions. He was one of the most famous artists of the twentieth century, and his work continued to break records in sales-rooms all over the world. Romily had owned several pictures in her own right since she was born; that alone made her worth millions, even without her mother's shipping inheritance. 'But my family's life isn't like other people's. Wherever I go, I have to have bodyguards and protection if I'm not on private property. Before I was allowed to come here, my parents paid for perimeter fencing and cameras round the whole school, and a security lodge where everything is monitored by guards on duty twenty-four hours a day.'

'Really?' Allegra looked astonished. 'You never said anything!'

'It's all kept quiet,' Romily said unhappily. 'It was one of my guards who found Sophie that night. He knew we smoked up there – I had to tell him so they didn't report seeing smoke. Then I had to beg him not to pass on what we did in the attic to my family. I didn't want anyone here to know about the guards. I'd never have heard the end of it. The first thing I learnt in life was always to be discreet and not draw attention to myself unnecessarily. And that's what I love about being here – I get to be normal. Just like everyone else. No one really knows or cares who I am here. Once I'm out, I'll never hear the end of it. That's why I want to stay. I feel safe. To you it might be shabby and boring and the end of the world, but to me, it's just . . . home.'

Imogen went over, put her arms around her friend and hugged her. Romily was right: school was about what made them the same, not what made them different. Stuck inside this old place, she easily forgot that Romily came from another world. But how sad it was that, to her, this was home! No matter how much Imogen loved Westfield, to her it was nothing like home and her own room and her mother and father who cherished her. If school was better than Romily's home, what did that say about her family life?

Romily leant her head on Imogen's shoulder and sniffed loudly. Just then there was a knock and the senior house prefect put her head round the door. 'OK, guys! That's enough now. Back to studies for prep, please.'

'Midnight meeting tonight!' whispered Allegra as the other two got up to obey instructions. 'In Romily's room.'

The girls had not met at midnight for a long time now. The activities of the Midnight Girls seemed too closely bound up with the tragedy that had shaken the school, and none of them had wanted to recall that terrible night. They did all in their power to avoid remembering: not one of them had walked across the patch of ground where Sophie had fallen, or even looked at it.

The news that Romily would be leaving Westfield was

important enough to resurrect the habit, however. As the old clock in the hall ticked round to midnight, two pairs of feet ran lightly down the corridors and into Romily's room. It was definitely the nicest study in the whole boarding house, partly because Romily's mother had somehow secured permission for her own interior decorator to come to Westfield during the summer holidays and make it over. While the other girls had standard issue magnolia walls covered in posters and pages from magazines, mud-brown curtains and Formica-veneer desks, along with a well-trampled dark carpet that might once have been patterned, Romily had pale green walls, curtains in cream silk sprigged with tiny green and gold flowers, and delicate antique furniture. She slept in a single mahogany sleigh bed, with a lusciously downy silk duvet like a mound of whipped cream. Most important, though, was the built-in wardrobe that stretched along one entire wall, in which Romily's fantastic clothes were carefully stored.

'I wonder who'll get this when you're gone?' Allegra said, as they settled themselves down on the bed.

Romily shrugged. 'It's my legacy, I suppose. Maybe they'll let you have it, Allegra, if you want it.'

She shook her head. 'It would be too weird. Besides, it's everything about you that makes it so lovely: your furniture, your clothes, your style. Once you're gone, it won't be the same.'

'Papa wanted me to have one of Grandfather's paintings on the wall – just a small one. But Miss Steele wouldn't allow it. Too much of a security risk.'

'I'm not surprised!' exclaimed Imogen, laughing. It was hilarious to imagine a real Vincent de Lisle hanging in one of the sixth-form studies.

'Shhh!' Allegra gave her a warning look. 'I know it feels safe in here, but we never know who's creeping along the corridors.'

'I can't believe we're going to be separated,' Imogen whispered, serious now.

'It was going to happen anyway,' Romily said in a brave tone. 'Once A-levels are finished, you two will go to university here. My parents don't want that for me. My mother is determined to have me home so she can start preparing me for life beyond school. She thinks eighteen is plenty old enough to start getting on with the serious things in life.'

'Like what?' asked Allegra.

Romily shrugged. 'Social life, I suppose. Society, fashion, the seasons . . .'

The other two stared at her. It seemed strange to them that anyone could pretend such things were a serious pursuit, a worthy way to spend one's life. Society was simply frivolous fun, wasn't it? Parties were indulgences, not things to devote oneself to.

'But we thought we had another whole year,' Imogen said wistfully. 'Anything could have changed in that time. Now you'll definitely be leaving.'

'The thing is,' Allegra said in a low voice, giving the other two a solemn look, 'we need to make a promise between ourselves. About what happened.' She bit her lip and a troubled expression passed over her face. 'We're the only ones who know the truth about . . . about Sophie. We are the only witnesses. We have to make a solemn vow, that we'll never, never tell. We must promise on everything we hold sacred – on our *lives* – that it will stay a deadly secret, and that we'll stay friends forever.'

They were all quiet for a moment as they recalled the scene in the attic above the dormitory. It was almost a year ago already. They had only just begun to recover from the horror of it.

Allegra may have been the driving force behind what had

happened, but we were all guilty, thought Imogen. *We were all there. We could have stopped it. We could have done something. But we didn't.*

They stared around, each seeing her own feelings reflected in the gaze of the other two. Their shared secret bound them together, they all knew that.

Romily broke the silence. 'I promise I'll never tell. Never, ever. It will always be our secret.'

'I promise too,' Imogen said quietly, 'on my life. I'll never tell a living soul.'

'Me too. I promise as well.' Allegra put her hand on to the snow-white duvet. 'Put your hands here. Let's all swear we'll be friends for ever. Remember how we used to call ourselves the Midnight Girls? It was a bit babyish, but . . . well . . . we'll always be Midnight Girls now. Like the Musketeers – one for all and all for one. Agreed?'

Romily put her slim brown hand on top of Allegra's and smiled. 'Agreed.'

Imogen added hers. 'Agreed,' she echoed fervently.

'I feel much better,' Romily said, smiling. 'Now I know that we can always trust each other. That we'll always be friends. I don't feel so lonely. You must come and stay with me in Paris, OK? There's so much room in our house.'

'Paris? We'd love to!' Allegra muffled her squeals of excitement in a pillow and the three of them bounced silently about on the bed, overcome with anticipation of the life that awaited them beyond the grounds of Westfield.

Chapter 10

New York
Autumn 2001

Because he smoked heroin and avoided injecting, Mitch told himself that he wasn't really a user. He was one of the lucky ones who would be able to stay in control. To demonstrate this, he only allowed himself to smoke heroin occasionally, when he felt like he really deserved it. It gave him the sense of staying on top, and he needed that.

'I don't want to end up like junkie shit!' he told himself sternly. The longer he lived in New York, the more he saw it: people reduced to dope-addicted wrecks, their veins collapsed, their money all spent on heroin or crack or whatever their drug of choice was. People disappeared out of the world of restaurants and kitchens as quickly as they entered it, falling away and forgotten before the night was out. There was always someone to replace them. When Mitch was made second-in-command in his kitchen, he soon started avoiding giving jobs to anyone who looked like they were using. Drinking was OK as long as it was confined to the hours outside the kitchen – and, hell, they were all drunks as soon they stepped out of the door – but the druggies were totally unreliable and as dishonest as they came. Mitch found he preferred hiring immigrants, who had no interest in drugs at all. They expected to work hard and uncomplainingly for little money, and put their backs into their jobs. He knew their wages were supporting families or being sent back to wherever they came from, and that pleased him even if it made him a hypocrite for investing a sizeable portion of his own pay in bags of dope.

Little by little, his addiction began to grow. He found it harder and harder to resist the lure of a smoke after work, the delightful comedown that melted away all his tensions and removed every care he had in the world. He had a girlfriend for a while, a sweet, pretty girl called Vanna who was a student at NYCU, but as his dalliance with heroin grew ever more serious, her love for him waned.

'You're an asshole when you're using this shit,' she shouted at him. 'I hate you when you're doing this!'

She had just discovered that he'd emptied her purse of money because he needed some cash for a fix and couldn't wait a second longer.

'You stole it!' cried Vanna, her green eyes flashing with anger.

'I'll pay you back,' he said, affronted.

'Yeah, right! Anyway, it's not the point. You went through my purse and took my money.'

'Ah, fuck off,' Mitch drawled, happy when she'd slammed out of the apartment, knowing he could now be alone with the substance that was fast becoming the love of his life.

'Why do you do it, Mitch?' she'd asked later, when she'd come back and they'd made up with a short but intense fuck, and were lying in each other's arms on his futon. 'What's the appeal?'

'It's hard to explain. It's like . . . getting high is like having sex, great sex, while simultaneously soaking in a delicious hot bath and eating the most sublime food in the world,' Mitch had replied, but she'd just stared at him, uncomprehending. She was still a creature of the real world, a normal girl with a normal job, who preferred real sex to dopamine-induced ecstasy. But then, she wasn't part of the kitchen world, with its nocturnal rhythms and craving for escape.

When Vanna dumped him the following week, he didn't even worry about all the sex he'd be missing out on: his addiction was replacing any physical desire he'd once had.

He still loved to cook, though. That passion was the only thing that heroin didn't touch. He could do anything outside the kitchen: fuck the waitresses, buy shit from pushers, chase his little dragons all night long (one smoke wasn't enough now, it didn't produce the required effect any longer), but when he was back at his station or at the pass, running the kitchen when Chef was absent, he was wholly and entirely focused on creating wonderful food from his rack of ingredients. When he was in the kitchen his world shrank to the metre or so of stainless steel that was his bench, and the shelves with his carefully prepped tray of seasonings and ingredients, and his knife.

Mitch wasn't working on the day the Twin Towers fell. He was shaken awake by Herbie who was grey-faced and sweating.

'Huh? What is it?' grumbled Mitch, rolling back into his sheets. 'Why're you up so early?'

'I ain't been to bed. There's some crazy shit going on, man! A plane's smashed into the World Trade Centre! You gotta wake up.'

'What?' Mitch scrambled out of bed and they switched on the television. The screen showed the towers alight, great billows of grey smoke sailing up into the brilliant blue sky. 'Holy fuck!' he breathed, dazed. Was it real? He ran to the window of their apartment, and saw the huge columns of smoke to the south, climbing upwards, bigger, denser and blacker than they looked on the TV. The air around the towers was shimmering with the clouds of debris floating downwards, clouds of office paper fluttering like falling leaves. The gashes that had been torn into the towers glowed orange where the fires burned. Fear rushed through him. What did it mean? Was the whole city under attack?

'What should we do, man?' Herbie said, his hands shaking and his eyes wild.

'I dunno. Stay here, I guess.'

Herbie looked agonised. 'My pal Bobby's in the North tower. He's working at Windows on the World, and so's his wife, Maria. Look, the whole place is on fire right underneath them. How're they gonna get down?'

Mitch went back to the television. He could see people at the windows of the upper floors, waving desperately, pleading for help. Then he saw that some were falling or jumping, small black stick figures floating downwards. 'He'll be OK,' he said, his voice shaking. 'The whole city fire department is there, and the police. They'll get 'em all out, I know they will. Those guys know what they're doing. Oh, Christ. I can't believe it.'

'I wanna get out of here,' Herbie said, panicking. Sweat glistened all over his face. 'They're trying to fuckin' kill us!'

I gotta keep him calm. 'It's OK, it's OK. Hey, let's have a smoke and take the edge off this thing. There's nothing we can do.' Mitch went to a drawer and took out a pouch of powder and his drug gear.

'Yeah,' Herbie said, looking relieved, 'we'll have a smoke. That's what we'll do.'

By the time the first tower fell, they were so stoned they didn't even feel the ground shaking or the massive rumble as the hundreds of tons of concrete, steel and glass collapsed. As the second tower went, they were still anaesthetising, chasing another flame across the hot tin foil.

When they came to, it was to a strange deathly quiet and an apartment covered in thick grey dust. It was all over.

In the aftermath, Herbie and Mitch were both out of a job. Their restaurant closed, first because it was choked with filth and dust from the nearby site of destruction; then because, when the restaurants began to open again, no one wanted to eat out.

Herbie said he was going to leave, go home, move to the sea, just escape the ruptured city with its atmosphere of grief and mourning. He was shaken by the way Bobby and Maria had died, trapped at the top of the burning building with no way out, waiting for help that never came and then pulverised in the mighty collapse. But Mitch wasn't ready to give up on New York yet. *I'm gonna stick it out,* he decided. He felt in an obscure way that the city needed him to keep going, keep working, that he owed it to the place to stay focused and act as normal. He persuaded Herbie to stay on with him, they found some temporary work in the kitchens of a big hotel, and gradually the dust and debris were cleared away, and the city began to recover.

The restaurant trade started up again, and they moved to a new place and then another.

If we can survive this, we can survive anything, Mitch told himself. But he could only face it with the help of his little bags of medicine.

Chapter 11

Paris
July 2002

'Allegra, Allegra! Over here!'

Allegra turned and saw Romily pushing through the crowd towards her.

'What are you doing here? I was going to get a taxi.'

'Don't be stupid. I brought the car. The driver will take us home.' Romily hugged her friend, her eyes bright. 'Come on, we'd better get out of this place as soon as possible. You must be dying for a shower.'

'I am a bit.' It had been a long journey from Scotland the night before. She had taken the train to London, stayed in Kensington, and then taken the first Eurostar train from Waterloo to Paris. The journey from London had been relatively swift but she still felt tired and grubby. Romily looked entirely different, standing out like a beacon from the people around her. Her simple outfit of a blue skirt and white jacket over a blue and white striped T-shirt, teamed with white, navy-capped Chanel pumps, was so stylish and expensive, she looked like a princess visiting a rundown corner of a deprived city.

'I'm so excited you're here!' she cried, giggling. 'We're going to have so much fun. Come on, let's find the car.'

She led Allegra through the milling crowd of people to

the pavement outside, where a sleek black Mercedes purred quietly at the roadside. A uniformed driver got out and opened the door for the girls and they got in quickly. A moment later, the car was gliding through the Parisian streets, heading for the central arrondissements. Allegra and Romily chattered all the way, about Allegra's journey and everything that had happened since they'd last seen each other. Romily was eager to catch up on all the gossip from the year she had missed at school and to find out what had happened to their old classmates. Allegra filled her in on where everybody was going now that school was over.

'And you and Imogen both going to Oxford!' Romily said admiringly. 'You lucky things.'

'Mmm – if we get the right A-level grades. We'll know next month.'

'Is Imogen excited?'

'Oh my God, she's over the moon, and so are her parents. She definitely earned her place. I'm not so sure about me.'

'Why not? Of course you earned it – how else would you get in?'

Allegra stared out of the window and said nothing for a while. Then she sighed and said, 'Oh, ignore me. I don't know what I'm talking about.'

'And you're both going in September. Didn't you want to take gap years?'

Allegra shook her head. 'We both agreed we didn't want to waste any time.' She looked over at Romily with a meaningful look. 'We just wanted to get on with things, get away.'

Romily looked down at her lap, her fingers twisting on her skirt. 'Mmm,' she said quietly.

Allegra changed the subject, saying in a jolly voice, 'But you've been having a splendid time, we hear! No nasty A-levels for you.'

Romily had kept up a stream of letters and postcards to Westfield sent from grand private homes and large hotels all over Europe, telling the other two about her hectic social life. They had even begun to see her in glossy magazines, pictured attending parties and glamorous functions. She was captioned 'socialite' or 'heiress' or 'fashion-leader', and was snapped in Versace, Nina Ricci, Chanel, and a host of other designers.

'It's been so busy,' Romily said almost wistfully. 'I can't think where the last year has gone. It's just melted away.'

'But you've had fun?' Allegra glanced over at her friend. She seemed older, even more polished, a world away from the schoolgirl Allegra had known. But one look into those brown eyes and Allegra knew it was the same girl, still Romily: cool, confident and determined.

'Oh, yes, lots of fun.' She grinned. 'But I don't have any partners in crime! That's the only problem.'

'That's why I'm here. So, what have we got lined up?'

Romily looked excited. 'Well, first we're going back to my parents' house. Then we can relax and get dressed before dinner tonight. It's just the usual Friday night thing: not a big deal, about fifteen guests. Tomorrow we'll go shopping! On Sunday we'll see some sights, and then on Monday we'll go shopping again. Just fun and relaxation for the whole week. Maybe even longer.'

'I've got to catch the train back to London next Friday,' Allegra warned.

'Of course, of course, don't worry,' Romily said, shrugging. 'You'll be back in good time. Everything will be just fine.'

Allegra suspected that Romily didn't quite take her need to get the return train to London seriously, but she also had the feeling that in Romily's world everything ran smoothly and things adapted themselves to fit her needs, rather than the other way round. Little things like return tickets and timetables meant nothing to her.

She wasn't quite sure what she expected Romily's parents' house to look like, though she'd assumed it would be lavish. Nonetheless, she was still taken aback by the luxury of the huge white-painted house on the avenue Foch. Iron gates to a grand courtyard opened automatically as they approached. The Mercedes entered and pulled around a fountain with water gushing from the mouths of marble dolphins before coming to a halt before an enormous, ornately carved front door. The driver let the girls out and then brought Allegra's luggage – a rather tatty looking rucksack – to the door. It immediately opened and a butler stood there, waiting for them to enter.

'Leave it here,' Romily said casually as Allegra went to pick up her rucksack. 'It'll be sent up.'

'Where's the car going?' she asked as the driver returned to the Mercedes and began to turn it smoothly around towards the gates they had entered by.

'I don't know,' replied Romily vaguely. 'It goes off somewhere – to a garage nearby, I suppose. We ask for it when we need it and it comes back. Come on, let's go in.'

They walked into a huge, ornate, marble-floored entrance hall. A table stood in the middle, dominated by the largest vase of white roses Allegra had ever seen. A vast crystal chandelier was centred upon it on the ceiling above, and all the cornices and panel-mouldings were gilt-covered. It was very different from the faint shabbiness and undeniable gloom of Foughton Castle, which was well lived in and draughty: this was all light and gold and sparkling richness.

Beyond the entrance hall stood a maid in a demure grey uniform. Romily greeted her in rapid French and the maid nodded before disappearing down a long corridor.

'So this is your home,' Allegra said, looking around.

Romily nodded. 'One of them.'

Romily really was in a whole different league. Allegra smiled. She herself was used to large rooms in grand houses, but there was something about the extreme luxury surrounding them that felt wholly unfamiliar. This place, with its polished marble floor, perfectly matching eighteenth-century gilt mirrors and carefully placed works of art, all clearly of museum standard, had a sheen that was quite unlike any of the houses Allegra knew.

'This way!' called Romily, and they went down a long hallway, carpeted in thick pale wool, to a drawing room laid out with exquisite taste and absolutely perfectly tidy, as though it had been prepared for a glamorous *World of Interiors* photo shoot. There was masses of pretty antique furniture: pairs of Louis XIV gilt chairs upholstered in pale grey silk; sofas with carved lion's-claw feet, delicately gilded; matching cabinets with wonderful marquetry; beautiful lowboys with great crystal lamps on them; and more vast glass vases containing masses of white lilies.

'It's lovely!' Allegra murmured. Enormous grey silk curtains swathed every one of the six huge windows. 'Look at those!'

'Mmm. The glass is bullet-proof,' Romily remarked, frowning. 'I thought Mama would be here.'

At that moment, from another set of doors, a tall slim figure glided in. Allegra saw at once that this must be Romily's mother. This was where Romily got her perfect olive skin from, and those large dark eyes. She was dressed in a stylish silk dress and high heels, her dark hair carefully styled into a chignon and her make-up fresh, a necklace of big, gleaming pearls at her neck. She seemed lost in thought as she came into the room then looked up and saw the girls, coming to a halt as if surprised.

'Oh, Romily, you're back! And this must be your friend,

Lady Allegra.' Romily's mother came towards her, smiling. She appraised Allegra with one swift glance and, although her expression didn't change, except perhaps by the merest lifting of one of her eyebrows, Allegra sensed that the older woman was a little startled by her.

Suddenly shy, and rather overcome by the formality of the occasion, she murmured, 'How do you do, madame?'

Madame de Lisle immediately leant forward and touched her cheek to Allegra's, first the left, then the right, then the left again. 'Welcome, my dear. I'm delighted you are going to stay with us. Now, Romily, I can see your friend needs to refresh herself. Then perhaps some tea here? Shall we say thirty minutes?' Her English was perfect and almost unaccented. Madame de Lisle gave them both another kind smile. 'Do excuse me. I shall see you in half an hour.'

'I don't think she thought much of me,' Allegra said, looking down at her jeans, plimsolls and tatty T-shirt as she followed Romily to her bedroom.

'Don't be silly,' her friend replied. 'Mama is a bit old-fashioned – I don't think I've ever seen her without make-up and her hair done – but she understands that our generation is different.'

Allegra thought that Romily now seemed more like her mother than her old Westfield self: her friend had always taken her personal grooming seriously, but she'd been prepared to scrape her dark hair back with an elastic band if that was all there was to hand, and hadn't minded being as grungy as the rest of them when there was a craze for baggy black cardigans and tight, ripped jeans. That Romily seemed a million miles away from this hyper-feminine creature, with her barely-there but perfect make-up and immaculate hair.

They passed four Vincent de Lisle canvases, a series from his period of experimenting with bright primary colours. Allegra tried not to stare, but seeing famous paintings that she'd seen countless times in poster shops and on cards actually in front of her was rather strange.

Romily went on: 'Perhaps she thought that as you're an English lady, you might be a bit more . . . oh, I don't know . . . a bit more . . . turned out.'

'I've only just got off a train from London,' Allegra said defensively.

'Don't worry, she's not criticising you or anything. Really.' They stopped at a pair of double doors with polished brass handles. 'These are my rooms.' She pushed them open and led the way into a small, bright and pretty sitting room, furnished with two cosy sofas and an armchair, an escritoire, bookcases, and some occasional chairs and tables. 'Through here is my bedroom . . .' She opened another door and they went into a very girly boudoir, with a carved, silver-painted four-poster bed hung with pale blue organza bed curtains. A French antique mirror with an ornate ivory-coloured frame hung above the fireplace, and by the window was a silver dressing table with interesting-looking little pots and bottles on it. 'Over there is my bathroom, but come and see my favourite room . . .' She opened a door to the left of the bed and there was a large dressing room, lined with shelves and rails. Inside, another grey-uniformed maid was folding a cream cashmere jumper. She jumped when she saw the girls, cast her eyes down and murmured apologetically.

'*Non, non, Estelle, ça va. Continuez, s'il vous plaît. Nous visitons seulement pour un instant, c'est tout.*' Romily turned to Allegra. 'Estelle looks after my clothes.'

'Really?' She laughed. 'Your own personal wardrobe mistress?'

Romily looked a little hurt. 'Not exactly. She looks after Mama's clothes as well.'

'But that's all she does? Just looks after clothes?'

'Of course! It takes up a great deal of her time. All these clothes – they can't just be put in the washing machine, you know! They have to be properly cared for and stored. And the couture . . . well, you understand, that has to be very carefully looked after. Not all my gowns are haute couture, of course, but most are designer and still need special attention. And look . . .' Romily went to a rail of dresses, each swathed in a muslin robe tightly tied at the neck of the hanger with a pink silk ribbon. Dangling from the ribbon was a large paper label with handwriting on it. Lifting up a label, she said, 'Now, this is a Versace gown that I bought last year. I wore it to a party at Vaux-le-Vicomte given by the President. You see – here it says when the dress was worn and the accessories I put with it. So I won't make the mistake of wearing it to a similar party in the same way.'

Allegra looked at her friend with a new respect. 'I knew you were organised, Rom, but this is something else.'

'I expect you're laughing at me . . .'

'No, no! It's just so grown up. You know me, piles of clothes everywhere. The cleaner has a sort through once in a while, when it looks as though I might drown in my own stuff, but I've never dreamed anyone could be this sorted. Wow, look at these amazing clothes!' Allegra gazed at the rows of dresses. Even if the most precious and expensive were under muslin and not to be seen, what was on show was still dazzling, with luxurious fabrics, shimmering colours and intricate embroidery and beading. Everything else was also meticulously organised and categorised. On one shelf were pastel-coloured silk, wool and cashmere tops: pale pink vests with matching cardigans; scoop neck, V-neck, buttoned and plain in white, ivory and cream. There were lots and lots of black trousers and skirts, rows of flat shoes and boots of softest leather, with high heels – plain, bejewelled, silk, satin, suede, even chainmail – displayed on shelves behind. There was a rack full of jeans in different coloured denims, cuts and stages of distress. Coats and jackets, from full-length dark city coats to sporty little trenches and light summer linen jackets, filled another rail. There were shelves with rows of handbags, from neat little pocket purses to big squashy leather bags in rainbow colours, and of course several of the quilted Chanel 2.55 on gilt chains, in white, grey, red and classic black.

'I knew you were keen on clothes, Rom, but bloody hell!' Allegra said. She laughed again. 'I'm still kind of surprised by this. It must take up all your time, just deciding what to wear and when.'

Romily looked a little stung. 'Perhaps it does. But, you know, it is very time-consuming, looking one's best. It's what women must do, isn't it?'

'Is it?' Allegra gave her friend a quizzical look. Then a panicked expression crossed her face. 'God, I bet everyone we meet will be dressed like you! Did you say we were having a dinner party tonight?'

Romily nodded, frowning.

'But I've brought hardly anything smart! I've got a navy skirt and a white top in my rucksack, but that's it.'

'In your rucksack? Oh, shit, they'll be in a state. Go and get them, we'll give them to Estelle to iron.'

'I don't know if ironing them will be enough. They're not up to anything in here.' Allegra waved her hand at the wardrobe.

'In that case, we will just have to dress you up from my clothes,' Romily said. She smiled and her eyes sparkled with mischief. 'I'll enjoy that, actually. It'll be just like at school. And we're still more or less the same size – you're only a few centimetres taller than me. I'm sure we can kit you out for dinner.' She turned to the maid who was standing quietly at the entrance to the dressing room and told her what was required. The maid nodded and went quietly away.

'I wasn't that bad at French at school, but I didn't understand a word of that,' Allegra said.

'I just asked her to get your good clothes from your bag and iron them. You can have a shower in my bathroom and freshen up, then put them on for tea with Mama. Now come on.' Romily chivvied her friend out of the dressing room and towards the bathroom. 'We've only got twenty minutes or so. Hurry up.'

Standing under a stream of hot water and feeling her travel weariness melt away, Allegra revelled in the sense of luxury. At Foughton, hot water was available only in the early mornings or the evenings: daytime baths were unheard of, unless you liked them icy cold. Here it was like a grand hotel where steaming water was always at hand. The towels were white, thick and luscious. She wrapped herself in a giant one, feeling cosseted and happy.

Emerging into Romily's room, she saw her best clothes already lying on the bed, more crisp and pristine than she'd ever seen them before, along with fresh underwear and her flat ballet slippers. Whatever Estelle had done to her clothes had virtually transformed them. Allegra put them on quickly and brushed out her hair. Romily came in from the next-door sitting room.

'That's much better!' She inspected her friend's face. 'No make-up?'

'I only brought a mascara and a lip gloss. They're in my rucker.'

Romily shook her head and rolled her eyes. 'Honestly, Allegra! You're hopeless. You're lucky you're so naturally pretty that you hardly need anything. But let me put some of mine on you.'

A couple of deft swipes of mascara over Allegra's lashes, a quick brush of powder over her nose and a coating of pale pink lipstick were enough to give her the requisite polish, and then it was time to make their way back to the drawing room for tea.

It was some time since she'd been anywhere quite so formal, Allegra decided, as she perched on a gilt-legged sofa in the de Lisles' drawing room. Opposite her, Madame de Lisle, every inch of her polished and groomed, sipped delicately from a china cup. A porcelain cake-stand on the marble-topped low table contained miniature pastries: éclairs, strawberry tarts, millefeuilles and tiny cream-filled *réligieuses,* as well as little sandwiches: slivers of duck breast with caramelised onion marmalade on rye bread, smoked salmon and shredded cucumber in soft white mini-rolls. Allegra eyed them hungrily, but neither of the other women touched the plate and she couldn't quite bring herself to be the first.

'Is the tea to your taste, Lady Allegra?' Madame de Lisle asked. 'I requested Earl Grey so you'd feel at home, but I'm afraid my housekeeper isn't very familiar with making tea in the English fashion.'

'It's great, thanks,' Allegra said cheerfully. 'I usually drink builder's tea, to be honest, but this is fine. And, please, just call me Allegra.'

'Mmm.' Madame de Lisle nodded at her with a puzzled smile. 'I've not heard of builders. Do they have it in Harrods?'

'Oh – I just mean ordinary tea. PG Tips or something.'

Madame de Lisle still looked blank.

Romily cut in, 'It's fine, Mama. Now, who's coming tonight?'

'Just some close friends. We'll only be fifteen at dinner,

nothing too formal. Mariette has just returned from her latest face lift in Switzerland. She's been hiding out in the country while everything healed and now, word is, she is looking amazing! Like a thirty year old again. I can't wait to see it. Her surgeon is apparently miraculous and, you know, it's never too early to start putting the right names in your little book for when the time comes.' Athina de Lisle had become quite animated.

Allegra couldn't imagine why anyone who already looked so perfect would want to think about a face lift. She had no idea how old Romily's mother was but her skin looked unlined, her complexion like a soft, velvet peach, and every time she moved there was a delicious citrussy waft of scent. No wonder Romily felt under pressure to live up to this unutterably glamorous mother.

Athina de Lisle turned to her daughter and unleashed a rapid stream of French which Allegra couldn't follow at all. Romily replied and a conversation began while Allegra passed the time looking at the pictures and books and admiring the massive flower arrangements. She noticed that all the pollen-bearing stamens had been snipped out of the lilies.

'Do excuse us, Lady Allegra,' Athina de Lisle said at last. 'I'm just running over a few very tedious matters with Romily – family things. Too boring to bother you with. Now,' she put down her tea cup and stood up, smoothing down her silk skirt and giving a slight tilt of the head towards Allegra, 'I will see you both later at dinner. I have an appointment first. Romily will show you around the house, and to where you are staying.'

The moment she had left the room, the atmosphere relaxed.

'Come on,' Romily said, 'We'll do the tour.'

The two girls spent a happy afternoon with Romily

showing Allegra some of the grander rooms, and then taking her to the guest suite, which made her think again of a luxurious hotel. Her rucksack had already been unpacked and stowed away in a cupboard, her belongings arranged in drawers or carefully laid out on the desk.

'Now, let's go and find you some clothes,' Romily said, and they returned to her dressing room to rifle through the drawers, shelves and rails for suitable dinner clothes.

They emerged in time for drinks, Romily in a short sky blue pleated silk cocktail dress by Celine, and Allegra in a classic Givenchy long black dress with tight sleeves that looked demure but was actually very sexy, especially with her long blonde hair piled up loosely and fastened with a clip that looked like a large diamond butterfly.

'You look fantastic,' Romily said. 'Black suits your pale English skin and that fair hair. It can wash me out if I'm not careful, but you'll always look amazing in it.'

'I can't believe this dress!' Allegra marvelled. 'It looked like nothing on the hanger, but it feels wonderful. And it's so flattering!'

'That is *cut*, darling,' said Romily loftily. 'The magic of the proper dressmaker. Honestly, once you understand what good clothes can do . . .'

Allegra laughed. 'I'm just not going there, Rom. I can't afford to get a couture habit, or even a designer one. I'm strictly thrift shop and High Street, I'm afraid.'

'We'll see,' Romily said with a grin. 'Tomorrow, we go shopping.'

Madame de Lisle might have been disappointed to see a real English lady turning up in shabby jeans and a T-shirt, but she was clearly mollified by Allegra's appearance at dinner that evening. She looked approvingly at the way the black dress clung to her guest's long slender body, and the dark red lipstick Romily had painted on her mouth, and herself took Allegra round to introduce her to the guests who had gathered in the drawing room for an apéritif. Once again the atmosphere was more formal than at English dinner parties. Allegra had often peeked round doors at her parents while they were entertaining, and their parties seemed to be characterised by noise, chatter, hilarity, and many bottles of wine. This French gathering was quiet, calm and polite in the extreme: the young men she was introduced to were very smart in crisp shirts, ties, dark jackets and highly polished shoes, and they bowed to her when they were introduced. One tanned man with sparkling eyes and gleaming white teeth even bent and kissed her hand.

'Lady Allegra, may I introduce Prince Jean-Christophe du Condé de Villeneauve,' said Madame de Lisle.

Allegra nodded graciously, thinking, *Cripes, it's a bloody prince kissing my hand. What next? Will my glass coach suddenly wheel up at the door?*

She tried to imagine Xander kissing someone's hand when he was introduced to them and the idea seemed ludicrous, but it felt natural here. Even Romily's brother, Louis, who was only fourteen and should have looked weirdly grown up and preppy in his Ralph Lauren shirt, chinos and blazer in other surroundings, seemed normal. He was a miniature version of his father, Charles de Lisle, who gushed over Allegra for several minutes before returning to an important-looking businessman.

I feel ridiculously adult, she thought, clutching her glass in one hand and trying to look as though she spent every night of her life in such polished surroundings. *It's brilliant fun. Imogen would love it.*

Poor Imogen did not even know Allegra was in Paris and would be horribly jealous when she found out. But her friend had been taken off to visit her grandparents, and it was once Allegra was on her own, slouching round Foughton and trying to avoid her pile of reading, that she'd hatched the plan to get herself to Paris. Everybody else was away enjoying themselves – Xander was out in Argentina playing polo with some rich friend, and her parents were on a smart yacht somewhere – so why on earth shouldn't she? But she knew Imogen would be furious that she'd made the much-discussed trip to Paris without her.

Over dinner in the dining room, she felt guilty again that Imogen was missing this. The food was extraordinary and exquisite: the first course was creamed Breton sea urchins served with a quail's egg and caviar; after that there was pigeon served on a bed of beetroot, with truffled potatoes and miniature garlic carrots. *That's the nicest thing I've ever put in my mouth!* she thought. Salad followed, and then a magnificent cheese board, and last of all a fresh clementine sorbet of such exquisite flavour that Allegra couldn't speak, but only concentrate on the burst of sweetness over her tongue. A different wine accompanied each course, but by the time they were on the cheese she was feeling woozy and tired so drank only water until her head cleared. Conversation was mostly in French but occasionally, as a courtesy to her, in English.

'No, no, I don't think so. It's a matter of the head over the heart. Don't you think so, Lady Allegra?'

She looked up, startled. She had just been chasing the last crystals of sorbet round her bowl and now someone was talking to her and she hadn't a clue what they meant. She saw that the important-looking businessman Monsieur de Lisle had been talking to earlier was now fixing her with a dark-eyed gaze. She had been introduced to him but couldn't remember his name.

'Er . . .' she said, playing for time. He came quickly to her rescue.

'We are talking about love, of course,' he said in a thick French accent. 'What else would you expect in France? The prince here says the heart must win out. He is young and romantic. But I say – the heart is all very well, but it must be the head that governs such matters. What is your opinion?'

'Oh.' She glanced over at the prince, who was looking at her expectantly, and then back at the businessman with his heavy-jowled face, large nose and wide mouth. 'The heart, I suppose.'

'But of course.' He laughed and lifted his glass to her. 'You are young and beautiful. Naturally you can follow your heart and it will lead you somewhere amazing, I have no doubt. Perhaps you will think differently in a year or two when your heart has been broken.'

Allegra felt herself blush scarlet although she hardly knew why she was so embarrassed, and her gaze dropped to the table cloth. She wanted to look back at the prince, who was, she realised, very good-looking and attractive, but she couldn't.

'Come, Paul, enough teasing! You cannot expect girls to know their minds on this. Let them experience love first,' said one of the older women.

'Mariette . . .' began Madame de Lisle, frowning.

The other woman held up her hand. 'No, no, Athina, I know you must advise caution and being sensible . . . that is your job as a mother . . . but I need have no such scruples. They must experience passion – grand passion. Or what is the point of being alive?'

From under her lashes, Allegra shot a glance at Romily who seemed quite composed although there were two high spots of colour on her cheeks. She realised that the businessman, Paul, was still staring at her with an unashamedly direct gaze. *But he's so old and ugly*, she thought. *How can he look at me like that? It's as though he already knows exactly what I look like with my clothes off! I wish he'd stop. He's fat and revolting.*

'Passion is all very well, but it is perfectly possible to fall madly in love with the person who will also make the best husband,' said Athina de Lisle, drily. 'And now, I think, coffee and petits fours are next-door. Shall we go through?'

She rose to her feet and everyone followed.

'How hideously embarrassing!' Allegra hissed as she and Romily met at the door to the drawing room.

'Was it?' her friend said, looking mildly surprised. 'Don't worry, everyone talks like that here. Love, love, love. It's all they seem to care about. Come on, we can have a cigarette now, if you want one.'

'Really?'

'Yes. And a *digestif*, if you like.'

A few minutes later she and Romily were standing out on the terrace, looking out over the courtyard below and the twinkling lights of Paris beyond, fragrant cigarettes in their hands. Allegra exhaled a stream of smoke, feeling luxuriously full, just nicely drunk and utterly relaxed. *I'll sleep well tonight,* she thought.

The prince and Louis de Lisle came out to join them and the four of them stood together, chatting idly.

I think I fancy him, Allegra thought, watching the prince under her lashes as she smoked. He was not tall, but slim and graceful, and looked fresh from the ski slopes with his nut-brown tan and gold lights in his dark hair. He had carefully cultivated stubble, flashing white teeth and limpid brown eyes, and seemed very aware of his own attractiveness, although his flirting was rather formal. *Perhaps all French blokes are like this,* she thought, wondering what it would be like to kiss him. Would the stubble be tickly? Would he want to stuff his tongue into her mouth and thrash it around wildly, like Freddie used to? That romance had faded out a while ago and there hadn't been anyone since. She couldn't imagine the prince kissing like Freddie, not with his manners. He would probably advance slowly and carefully, in polite little stages, asking her permission in tones of greatest courtesy every step of the way. She giggled. *I must be a bit pissed. Maybe I could get him on his own somehow.* She looked over at Romily to see if she might be amenable to helping her get her hands on the prince, but she seemed unaware of what Allegra was thinking.

'Ah, so this is where you young ones are!' It was the businessman. What had Madame de Lisle's friend called him? Oh, yes, Paul. He squeezed out of the French window on to the terrace and stood beside them, seeming much bigger than anyone else. He turned immediately to Allegra. 'So, what are your plans while you are in Paris, my lady?'

'You don't have to call me that,' she said, embarrassed. 'I'm just Allegra.'

'Very well.' He smiled at her, and again she had the sense that he was looking right through her clothes. 'Are you seeing the sights?'

Allegra looked over at Romily who said, 'We're shopping tomorrow. Next week we'll look around.'

'I hope you'll allow me to accompany you to the Musée d'Orsay. I assume you're going?'

'We hadn't really planned anything yet, but I suppose we could go there.' Romily turned to Allegra. 'It's the museum with the Impressionists. It's quite nearby.'

'One of the most beautiful museums in the world,' Paul Antoine said. 'A converted railway station from the Belle Epoque. You must see it. Shall we say Thursday afternoon? I will send my car for you after lunch.'

The girls looked at each other. This wasn't how they'd intended to spend their time together, but it would be far too impolite to say no.

'Very well,' Romily said at last. 'Thank you, monsieur. We should like that very much.'

Chapter 12

Although she might not have succeeded in getting her hands on the prince, Allegra was still having a wonderful time. The days in Paris passed by in a delicious whirl of pampering. She did not have to lift a finger and anything she wanted was hers. From the moment she awakened in her enormous bedroom, her clothes were clean and folded, the water hot and plentiful, and she could laze for as long as she liked, ordering breakfast on a tray or having it with Romily in the small breakfast room while they flicked through the day's papers from across the world. The kitchen was like a five-star restaurant with a limitless menu. Anything she wanted appeared in moments, from freshly squeezed guava juice to bacon and eggs, properly done. Romily was surprised by her friend's appetite, especially first thing in the morning when she herself ate only some fruit and yoghurt, accompanied by strong black coffee.

The hours were theirs to fill as they pleased, and naturally there was one occupation that they enjoyed above all others: shopping. At first, Allegra was worried by the fact that she didn't have the money to spend that Romily had. Her allowance was generous by some standards but it had very little purchasing power in the kind of places Romily was taking her: exquisite boutiques that seemed to sell only a few items, but each breathtaking, both in substance and in price. Then there were the *grands magasins* along the boulevard

Haussmann, and the designer shops around avenue Montaigne, place Vendôme and rue St Honoré. Everything there was so covetable and, what was more, so necessary, at least according to Romily.

'But you must have at least three pairs of jeans, of course. No one can survive with fewer,' she explained. 'And, naturally, you must have key pieces – the white shirts, the black trousers, the perfect heels, the beautiful jacket . . . and then you will need dresses for smart luncheons, skirts and little tops for afternoon gatherings, cocktail dresses for the soirées . . .' It went on and on. Allegra's purse was drained after only one purchase: a pair of black trousers from Yves St Laurent Rive Gauche that were absurdly flattering and were the most expensive thing she'd ever bought.

'That's me done,' she declared, gathering up the silken ribbons of the stiff cardboard bag.

'After this, I'll pay,' Romily said matter-of-factly, as they wandered along one of the *grands boulevards*. 'Let's go to the little *passages* – I love the boutiques there. Galerie Vivienne is my favourite.'

'You can't pay for me.' Allegra was horrified. 'I've seen how much things cost here! You'd end up spending a fortune.'

Romily stood still and gazed into Allegra's eyes, her own velvet-brown ones sincere. 'Allegra, you've seen our house . . . the servants, the guards. You know who my grandfather was. You must have realised that we're rich. Very rich. Imagine how rich we are, and then double it – triple it – and you might be close. I don't want to go into details but my dress allowance alone is more than enough to buy us both anything we want. Last month, I had a couture shirt made for me by Valentino. It cost the equivalent of fifteen thousand pounds. When Mama buys me a couture ball gown, it can cost over a hundred thousand pounds.'

Allegra felt the blood drain from her face. She could hardly believe such sums of money. On a dress! What would her father do with a hundred thousand pounds? He was always moaning about how much the family cost him and how little cash they had. Imagine if they had that to spend on a dress! One dress!

Suddenly the muslin covers and the full-time maid whose sole duty was to care for Romily's clothes didn't seem so crazy. She literally had a fortune in that dressing room of hers.

Romily put one hand on her friend's arm. 'I'm not boasting. I don't think it makes me better than anyone else. I just don't want you to worry. We can buy anything we like, honestly. A couple of pairs of shoes or whatever we want isn't going to make a bit of difference, I promise.'

Allegra stared at her for a moment longer and then burst out laughing. 'Oh my God! Imogen is going to be absolutely bloody *green*. A limitless shopping trip in Paris? I can't believe she's missing out like this.'

'I wish she was here,' Romily said wistfully. 'The only thing more fun than us shopping together would be if it was the three of us.'

'Another time, definitely,' Allegra said as they turned to continue along the boulevard. 'Not that I'm suggesting you start funding Imogen and me on a regular basis or anything!'

They went to the *passages*, beautiful glass-roofed nineteenth-century arcades, full of quirky little shops and art dealers. Allegra knew, despite Romily's assurances, that she couldn't let her friend spend too much money on her. It was tempting but it was also wrong. She realised instinctively that her parents would strongly dislike the notion of her dipping into Romily's purse, no matter how much cash she had to spare. A gift or two was one thing. Freeloading was something else.

So she managed to keep Romily in check and prevent her from handing over her platinum credit card whenever Allegra so much as admired something. She did let her friend buy her a skirt in a silk leopard-skin print that she thought looked foxy and punky at the same time, a pair of pink suede shoes with chunky purple heels, and a black cashmere sweater.

When they were tired of shopping, they drank *crèmes* and Allegra ate delicious strawberry pastries at one of the smart cafés near the Louvre. Then it was back to the house for a lazy afternoon before changing for dinner.

How much nicer could life be? wondered Allegra, already wishing that she didn't have the return journey ahead of her on Friday. But there was plenty to enjoy before then.

On Thursday, Romily wasn't well. She became more sick as the day progressed.

'It's a nasty tummy bug or something,' she said, looking pale and ill. She couldn't eat any lunch and decided she'd spend the afternoon in her room. 'I ought to stay close to the bathroom,' she said wanly. 'Don't tell my mother or we'll have the place flooded with doctors within the hour and I'll be stuffed with twenty different medicines and not allowed out for a week.'

'Don't you think you should see a doctor, though?' Allegra asked.

'No, no. I will tomorrow if I'm no better, but I expect it's just one of those twenty-four-hour things.'

'We'd better cancel Monsieur whatever-his-name-is. He's coming to pick us up for our trip to the Musée d'Orsay in about half an hour.'

'Monsieur Antoine.' Romily gave her a pleading look. 'Would you mind going without me? If we cancel, he's bound to ask my mother about it and then I won't get a moment's peace. But if you go off, she'll assume we're both there and I'll be left alone. I'm sure he'll be an excellent guide to the museum. He's bound to know lots about art and the best things to see.'

'I'm not quite . . .'

'Please? It's nearby, it will only take an hour or two. It's worth seeing, I promise.

'All right then. If you'd like me to,' Allegra agreed reluctantly.

'Thanks, I owe you. I'm sure I'll be better later,' Romily said, her eyes grateful.

At two o'clock the message came that Monsieur Antoine was waiting outside. Allegra found him waiting in his navy blue Audi, sitting on the white leather back seat, the darkened window lowered so she could see him.

'Where is Romily?' he asked, surprised. The driver got out and opened a rear door so that Allegra could get in.

'She's sick. She can't come.'

He raised his eyebrows. 'What a shame. Never mind. We shall have a lovely time together nevertheless. Musée d'Orsay, please, Georges.'

Allegra felt uncomfortable for the first few minutes but then she began to relax. Paul Antoine was friendly and polite, and although she didn't like the way his stomach strained over the top of his trousers, he wasn't quite as ugly as she'd remembered. Nevertheless, he was no oil painting: he had deep-set black eyes and dark hair streaked thickly with grey, while more wiry dark hair emerged from under his shirt cuffs. He had a melodious voice, though, and an undeniable charm that soon put her at her ease.

They arrived at the Musée d'Orsay within twenty minutes. The driver ignored any traffic restrictions and brought the car to a standstill as near to the entrance as possible, then opened the doors so they could alight.

'Now, this is a wonderful treat,' said Monsieur Antoine, as he ushered Allegra through what appeared to be a priority door for those who didn't need to buy a ticket. He murmured something to the person on duty who jumped up and made a great show of welcome. Allegra could make out that her host was waving away the offer of a guide.

'They know me well here,' he said as he led the way into the museum. 'I donated a painting or two a while ago and they make a great fuss whenever I come. Now, let us see what we shall see.'

Allegra had learned about art from what she had seen on the walls at home, and from trips to the National Gallery and the Tate with Uncle David. She had little time for Old Masters or endless portraits of pasty-faced ancestors in ruffs and jewels and furs. At once she could tell that this was her kind of art gallery: the paintings, some over a hundred years old, still shone with life and buzzed with energy. The Impressionists, Post-Impressionists, Expressionists, Modernists: all were represented here by the finest artists of their time, portraying ordinary people – peasants working the fields, girls at their dancing class, a woman drinking in a café – with brilliance and luminosity. Allegra wandered from picture to picture, taking it all in, entranced by what she was seeing. Every room offered some new delight, from famous paintings such as Manet's *Le Déjeuner sur l'Herbe* or Renoir's *Bal du Moulin de la Galette* to many she had never seen reproduced but found just as stimulating and interesting. And, to her surprise, Monsieur Antoine proved to be an excellent guide.

He didn't push her in any direction but let her follow her own inclination. When she stopped to observe a painting, he gave her time to look at it before murmuring to her about the artist and the techniques used in this particular canvas. When she came to halt in front of a painting of three women bending over a harvested field, picking up dropped wheat, he said quietly, 'Millet was fascinated by this subject, and this picture of the gleaners took him ten years to research. These peasant women are caught in the midst of their back-breaking work, scavenging what they can from the fields while behind them we see abundance in the full haystacks. And yet their grace is redemptive, is it not? We don't feel lectured about the inequalities of society. We see beauty and stoicism and humanity.'

Allegra nodded, moved and feeling as though she had glimpsed something important.

So they went on. The museum was not huge, it was nothing like the National Gallery in London with its majestic galleries and several floors. This was more manageable, but the richness on offer – not only paintings but sculpture and decorative arts – meant that it would have taken hours to see everything.

'We have been here long enough,' her guide said finally, consulting the bulky Rolex on his wrist just at the moment that Allegra was beginning to feel tired. 'Come, Georges will be waiting.'

As they went to leave, this time by the main entrance, Allegra's eye was caught by a painting hanging alone on a great wall by the door, and she gasped. Was that what she thought it was? Yes . . . it was the lower torso of a woman, entirely exposed. She was lying on a bed, but everything above her breasts was hidden by a swathe of sheet and the picture ended at her ripe thighs.

'Ah, yes.' Monsieur Antoine was standing beside her, gazing at the same picture. He was short, she realised, perhaps even shorter than she was. '*The Origin of the World*. A stunning picture, is it not? The female sexual organs in all their beauty and power.'

Allegra felt paralysed by embarrassment. Her face was

flaming so much, she thought she might be about to explode. She couldn't see any beauty or power – just the anonymous glorification of *that place.* What was it that drove men wild about it? It looked unattractive to her: biological, intimate, faintly repulsive. *And if I had pubes like that, I'd kill myself.*

'Come along, we must go.' Monsieur Antoine touched her elbow and guided her towards the door. Allegra was glad to take her gaze away from the mortifying picture.

A moment later, she was climbing into the cool interior of the Audi and the car was gliding off through the streets of Paris.

'Where are we?' she asked after a while. The journey from Romily's apartment had not taken very long and they had already been driving for what seemed far longer. She was sure they were heading in a different direction from the avenue Foch.

'We have a little time. I thought you might like some tea.' Monsieur Antoine smiled at her. 'I've enjoyed our visit together, haven't you?'

'Yes,' Allegra agreed politely. She had enjoyed the gallery, it was true, but now she was keen to get back to familiar surroundings and see how her friend was. 'Where are we going?'

'Ah, we are here now.'

The car slid to a halt beside a smart apartment block and she was shown into a tiny wrought-iron lift which climbed to the fifth floor.

'I've been bold enough to bring you back *chez moi.* It is clear you have a soul that is touched by art. I thought you might like to see my own collection.'

He opened the front door and Allegra stepped inside, curious. This apartment was very different from the pastels, silks and gilt of the de Lisles' home: it was more masculine, with its dark wooden panelling, heavy furniture and forest green velvet curtains, though there were flowers everywhere in all manner of vases. But each square of panelling displayed another painting; the walls of the apartment were covered in them, of every period: twentieth-century abstract, nineteenth-century portraits, Renaissance religious art . . . anything she could think of was there.

And everywhere there were sculptures – ancient Greece, Rome, China and Japan were all represented – with every flat surface covered besides in beautiful things: carved boxes, marble lamp-stands, onyx heads of African animals. Leaning against one wall was a gigantic Egyptian sarcophagus in polished wood. Bookshelves were packed with antique tomes, and tiny Etruscan-looking terracotta figures were posed in front of them.

'How extraordinary,' breathed Allegra, unable to take it all in at once. She stared about her at the incredible collection.

Monsieur Antoine went to a table in the corner of the room and returned with a tumbler which he pressed into her hand. She took it and automatically sipped without thinking, then winced. It was neat brandy.

'These are the fruits of many years' dedicated collecting,' murmured her host, holding his own glass to his chest. He began to wander about the room, pointing out his most prized possessions – a Matisse cut out, an Ingres drawing, the cameo head of a Caesar carved from jasper. Allegra followed him, listening. Her stay in the de Lisles' apartment had begun to inure her to seeing the kind of paintings that ought to be in a museum on the walls of a private home – after all, Romily's house was crammed with Vincent de Lisle's work – but nevertheless, all of this was stunning. She followed him as he showed off his treasures, going from room to room, sipping at her brandy which became less difficult to drink the longer she did so. Then they reached a room decorated Empire-style with a majestic bed standing in the centre and a large desk by the window, everything swagged in dark green velvet or covered in burgundy leather.

'The bedroom, where I keep my favourite pieces,' said her host, and put his glass down carefully on a small table crammed with bibelots. He leaned over and took Allegra's glass from her hand, putting it down next to his. Then he came and stood close to her, and she smelled the brandy on his breath. 'But you, my dear, are a treasure yourself.' He put out his hand and stroked her hair. 'So young and beautiful. You are a prize, aren't you, for some lucky man?'

'I think I'd like to go home now,' she said, stiffening as he touched her hair, feeling a crawling sense of horror.

'Come on, you're not going anywhere. Why did you come home with me? Why agree if you didn't want what I'm about to give you?'

She saw his hand move to the front of his trousers. He seemed to stroke himself there, just for a fluttering instant. Then she realised she could see a great bulge like a truncheon at his fly, and fear clamped round her like an invisible corset. *Run away,* she told herself. But she couldn't move.

The next moment, he was making a strange noise in his throat and inching her towards the huge bed.

I know what's going to happen, she thought. Half her mind was gripped by fright, but the other half seemed to be extremely calm and removed from the whole event. *He's going to do it to me. I wonder what it will be like. I hope it doesn't hurt.*

Hundreds of thoughts flashed through her mind as the man pushed her down on the bed and lay down next to her, panting, holding her firmly with one hand as he began to tussle with her clothes. He seemed overcome with excitement and didn't appear to know what to do first, pushing her skirt up round her thighs and scrabbling towards her knickers at one moment, then fumbling with the buttons of her shirt the next, desperate to get his fat fingers on her breasts. *This isn't how it was supposed to be,* she thought, remembering all the ways she'd fantasised about losing her virginity.

'You like this, don't you?' he muttered. 'I knew what you wanted. You've been begging me for this, don't think I didn't understand . . .'

Then he pressed his mouth to hers, forcing her lips apart with his tongue. She became passive, letting him lever her jaws open so he could push himself into her mouth. She wanted to close her teeth on his tongue but she did nothing. *Why can't I move? Why can't I do anything?* But she seemed gripped by a strange sort of paralysis that meant she lay there and endured everything, with a calm little voice in her head offering her a running commentary all the time on what was happening to her.

How strange – he's actually a better kisser than Freddie. He's not thrashing about like a snake in a washing machine. And he doesn't taste as bad as I'd expected, which I suppose I should be grateful for. Perhaps it's because I've been drinking brandy too. Oh, he's got my buttons undone at last, so . . . what now? Oh, of course.

He left her mouth and pulled the cups of her bra down under her breasts so that they were pushed upwards, their soft pink nipples tilting towards him. She saw his eyes for a moment and understood for the first time how someone's eyes could actually be glazed – his seemed only to be half-focused. He was still making that strange sound, in between panting for breath, then she felt her right nipple taken into his mouth. *Is he going to bite it?* But he sucked and sucked on her instead, pulling the nipple up into a tight peak. He grazed at it, rolling the little bud against his teeth. Something tingled within her and she moved involuntarily.

Oh, no, no . . . I can't start to enjoy it. She shuddered with revulsion at herself, which made him grunt and murmur, 'Mmm, you like this, little girl, don't you?'

No, I hate it! she told herself, appalled at her own body which seemed to be reacting despite itself.

He moved on to her other breast, sucking at it while his hand crept back to her skirt, pushing up underneath it across her smooth thighs and sliding under the elastic of her knickers.

He released her nipple with a tiny popping sound and said hoarsely, 'I cannot resist you, you are so beautiful. I must taste you.'

He moved down the bed, pulled her knickers down and discarded them, then parted her legs and put himself between them. 'Ah, the great mystery,' he said, 'the garden of delights.' He nuzzled into her small patch of fair pubic hair, inhaling hard. Then she felt his warm tongue dart out and touch the very top of her quim, where her small hard clitoris nestled inside its fleshy home. It sent an electric jolt through her, and she jerked. That place was always so sensitive, sometimes she could hardly bear to touch it herself.

He laughed throatily. 'You see? You like it. Of course you do, it's what you were made for. So delicious . . .'

His tongue came out again and began to lap at her, first tickling her around that unbearably sensitive place, and then lapping at her entire mound, pushing up inside her and rolling towards her bud. She had never experienced anything like it and couldn't prevent her body responding to his skill. She didn't want to enjoy it but it felt good.

So this is cunnilingus, the calm voice in her head told her.

You wondered what this would be like and now you know. Freddie wanted to and you wouldn't let him – now you're getting it anyway.

Each time his tongue reached her clitoris, it was as though she had been jolted: her legs jerked around his beefy shoulders.

'Come on, little darling,' he muttered, 'I love the taste of your cunt. You English have good words for things, and, you see, I know them all . . .'

The feelings were too hard to resist. Even the little voice in her head was quiet, unable to speak against this torrent of physical sensation. It was rushing up over her like a wave rolling inexorably up a beach, an almost sick feeling of intensity that built and built until she wondered what on earth was going to happen next – when suddenly she was possessed by an extraordinary crash of pleasure that shook her violently: her head thrashed, she gasped and cried out and felt her body spasm with the force of whatever it was. It seemed to go on for a long time then subsided, leaving her breathless and confused. But at that very moment, something new happened.

She felt a crushing weight on her stomach and chest and realised that Monsieur Antoine was now lying on her. He'd freed his cock from his trousers, though she couldn't see it. All she could feel was its great head pushing between her legs.

'You're ready for me,' he whispered. 'Beautiful and ready . . . ah, yes! There we are! There we are!'

The orgasm had left her slippery and accessible. He pushed his cock up inside her. She felt herself stretch to accommodate him – *Oh my God, it's happening, he's doing it, he's doing it* – and then a resistance.

'Ah,' he crooned. '*Ma petite vierge.* Don't worry, darling, just one quick push . . .'

He thrust hard and suddenly the resistance gave way in a rush of pain. Allegra screamed and tears sprang into her eyes. 'Stop it!' she cried. 'Get off! Stop!'

Paying no attention, he started to increase his pace, pushing into her harder and harder, his eyes tightly closed and his breath coming hard and fast between pursed lips. It hurt horribly and she started to moan and cry, which only made him thrust harder until, with a little yelp, he withdrew suddenly and she felt something warm splatter across her stomach.

He rolled off her and they lay in silence for a moment. Then he sighed heavily and said in a satisfied voice, 'As wonderful as I had hoped, *ma chérie.* You were made for pleasure. Do not worry about having a baby, I made sure you will be quite all right. Was that not good of me?' Then he propped himself up and looked at her, his gaze smug. 'And we both know that this is what you wanted, don't we? I hope you're not going to make up any silly stories about it, pretending that you were somehow unwilling. After all, you should thank me for that delicious little emission you enjoyed. Now clean yourself up. It's time to go home.'

PART 2

Chapter 13

Oxford University
Autumn 2002

What would my life have been like if I'd been at Oxford without Allegra? wondered Imogen.

She was sitting on a chair in her friend's room in the Lincoln College buildings, not the gracious medieval quadrangle but a more modern 1930s house on Turl Street nearby that housed some of the first years, a mug of coffee in one hand, a cigarette in the other, watching a boy curled on the bed as he flipped through the pages of *Country Life* and remarked, 'It's so funny seeing one's friends' houses in here, isn't it?'

'If you say so, Roddy,' Allegra said with a laugh. She was flicking through a gossip magazine while chain-smoking her Marlboro Lights and feeding her hangover with sweet tea and chocolate.

It was a silly question, really, because Imogen could never know it any other way. *I'd never get to go to all these glamorous parties if I weren't with her,* she realised. Allegra's pigeon hole was always stuffed with invitations to all manner of exciting things and they went to everything together – safety in numbers. It meant that Imogen's social life took place almost entirely outside her own college: she was always in Lincoln with Allegra, or in a cocktail dress in one of the grander colleges, sipping sparkling white wine that aped champagne. The only person she knew in her own college was Nick, her tutorial partner, a soft-voiced, guitar-playing lad from Wales with a Kate Bush fixation. 'I love hearing all about your high life,' he'd say when she told him what she'd been up to the previous evening. 'You really are living the Oxford dream, aren't you?'

I suppose I must be, she thought. *I've got a beautiful room in Christ Church overlooking the meadow. I have tutorials in an ancient set of rooms in Tom Quad, where my tutor plies me with sherry and talks about Dickens as though he were still alive. I eat dinner wearing a black academic gown and surrounded by portraits of Tudor monarchs, after listening to a Latin grace. And I spend most of my time gallivanting about in evening dress and hanging out with glamorous girls and Old Etonians. It's just what they said it would be.*

And it was fun, there was no doubt about that. Allegra was her passport into a more rarefied part of Oxford life, a world away from sweaty JCR discos or table football and pints of beer in the bar. And it would be wonderful . . . if it weren't for the way Allegra seemed to have changed. Imogen had noticed it at once, from the first day they'd met up in Oxford, when Allegra had knocked on the door of her room in the Meadow Buildings. Imogen had arrived early so she could settle in, but Allegra had been too cool for that: she'd turned up at her college at the last possible minute, and then knew everything and everybody immediately.

She had appeared late on the first afternoon of term, looking even more stunning than usual in tight dark jeans, a long tunic-style top, and with her hair stuffed up under a slouchy purple cap. Her skin was tanned golden, which made her blue eyes seem even more vivid. 'Let's go to the pub,' she'd said, and they'd gone to an ancient low-ceilinged place in a side street behind the college.

Imogen had not been able to put her finger on exactly what was different about her: something a little abrupt, perhaps, and she seemed less ready to smile and giggle the way she once had. Something had come between them, but Imogen didn't have a clue what it might be. After all, surely the darkest days of two years before were well behind her now . . .

'Did you enjoy Paris?' she asked a little tentatively, as they sipped their pints of lager.

'What?' Allegra said sharply.

'Paris. Didn't you go and visit Romily?'

'How did you know about that?'

'She told me.'

'When did you talk to her?' Allegra demanded tetchily.

'I spoke to her a couple of times over the holidays.' Imogen frowned in surprise. 'She called just a few weeks ago and told me you'd been over to stay with her. She was asking after you.'

'What did she say?'

'Nothing really – just that you'd been over and you both had a lovely time but that you'd not been terribly well by the time you had to go home. Was that why you weren't at Foughton over the holidays?' In fact she'd been mystified by Allegra's absence. Her phone had gone unanswered for weeks, and texts seemed to vanish into the ether.

Allegra stared into her glass for a while then nodded. 'Yes, I was ill. It was a shame. It ruined the stay. I went to Cornwall afterwards, to stay with my aunt.'

'What was Paris like?' Imogen leaned forward. 'Does Romily live in unimaginable luxury?'

Allegra fixed her with a strange glance, something like anger sparking in the back of her eyes. Then she gave a short laugh. 'Oh, yes. It was quite mad. They're rich as Croesus, they really are. You should ask Rom if you can go and visit.

You won't be able to believe it.' She paused and then said abruptly, 'Actually, I think it's a bloody shame she's got so much. It means that she's going to become just another bimbo with too much cash and nothing to occupy her mind. You can see it already – she's more obsessed with clothes than ever, spending obscene amounts. It's disgusting.'

Imogen was surprised by her vehemence. Romily's wealthy background was no surprise to either of them and Allegra hardly came from poverty herself.

'If you ask me,' she went on, 'Romily should get away from there as soon as she can, and do something useful with herself. And there are some horrible people in Paris.'

Did something happen between Allegra and Romily? wondered Imogen, worried. *Surely Rom would have said if it had. It must have been her illness that ruined it for them.*

She didn't mention the Paris stay again.

Roddy, one of Allegra's new Oxford friends, seemed to like Imogen well enough but was always angling to get Allegra on her own, as though he wanted to manoeuvre Imogen away and bag her for himself.

Imogen had quickly learned to recognise Roddy and his ilk: they fluttered around Allegra, attracted by her title and connections. Some were cool, sulky-faced girls with long legs and outrageously posh voices who thought Allegra should be part of their social whirl; some were minor celebrities in their own right, sons and daughters of well-known people. Others were social climbers who had come to Oxford to live out their Brideshead fantasy and wanted to be friends with the daughter of an earl, or perhaps even marry her. Whoever they were, Allegra was always surrounded. At first, Imogen was jealous and possessive, fearing their friendship was going to be broken up, but Allegra soon put her mind at rest, laughing about the climbers but tolerating the ones she found amusing, and making friends with some of the haughty beauties and the society crowd. She insisted on Imogen being included in everything, though, and they went everywhere together, from college to library to pub to party.

'Oh, God, look,' Allegra said one day as they stood in Lincoln porter's lodge. She was holding out a navy blue card printed with a golden crest and Latin motto. 'It's the Commandoes. They want me to go to one of their parties. Hmm, not too sure about that.'

'Why not?' Imogen peered at the card. It looked very respectable. And it didn't request the usual payment to get in. In general, even the smartest societies asked for money on the door to cover the cocktails that were then 'free' inside.

'Haven't you heard of the Commandoes? They're a terrible bunch whose one aim in life is to get utterly trashed and screw as many girls as possible. A bit like the Bullingdon but less into smashing places up and strippers, more into seducing other students. They go through the matriculations photos from all the colleges and send invitations to the girls they fancy.' Allegra laughed. 'Not sure. I'll think about that. After all, Xander is one. Bit too close for comfort.'

'Is he?' Imogen was instantly filled with longing. It had been almost a whole term and she still hadn't seen Xander, even though she'd been looking out for him wherever they went. But he didn't live in college any more; as a second year, he now lived in a house with some friends, and when he'd come by to see Allegra, Imogen hadn't been there. She was beginning to worry that she'd never manage to see him.

'Yes. He's a very naughty boy.' Allegra turned serious for a moment. 'Maybe I should go to the Commandoes party. I need to keep an eye on him. He's enjoying partying a bit too much for his own good now he's living with James Barclay.'

'His friend from school?'

Allegra nodded. 'James is a wild one. Loads of money from his family's bank and he *loves* parties. There're four of them in that enormous house in St Margaret's Road and it's party central.'

'Really?'

'Mmm. A den of vice, my darling. We must be careful.'

But Imogen thought Allegra seemed quite attracted to the notion of a life of vice herself. She seemed keen to try out any new experience, in particular drinking the noxious cocktails that were served at every Freshers party and college bop they went to. Usually after dinner Imogen would make her way to Allegra's room where they would get ready to go out. Allegra would already know the coolest parties that night, and then off they would go. Wherever it was, Imogen could predict that the night would end in her helping a drunken Allegra back to college, hauling her up the stairs of the building in Turl Street where her bed-study was situated on the second floor, and putting her to bed with a bowl on the floor nearby in case she needed to be sick. Sometimes Imogen slept in the armchair, ready to get up and hold her friend's hair back from her face while she vomited. It was better than worrying that she would choke while she slept.

'Are you OK?' Imogen said one day, when they were recovering from another big night in a café on the High.

''Course I am.' Allegra sipped her latte then poured a pouch full of brown sugar into it. 'I need to beef this up a bit.'

'I mean . . . you're hitting the parties kind of hard.'

Allegra sent her a withering look. 'That's what we're *supposed* to do. We're first years, at Oxford. It's practically compulsory.'

'I just wondered . . . whether anything is bothering you . . .' Imogen hesitated over her words. She hated to say anything that might be construed as criticism. Despite the loyalty they had sworn towards each other she felt that strange gulf she'd sensed right from the start of term gradually widening between them. She and Allegra might be physically together almost constantly but she had the feeling that her friend was sliding away somewhere else without her, a darker, more hedonistic place. She was drinking heavily, smoking constantly, and had begun to accept some of the drugs that were offered to her at parties.

'No, of course not.' Allegra took another sip of coffee, then fired up a cigarette. Blowing out a stream of smoke, she said, 'Well . . . actually I'm in a bit of trouble with my tutor. Missing essays. Stuff like that.'

Imogen had wondered how she was coping with the workload. They were required to write two essays a week, and while Imogen spent the mornings on hers and only just managed to stay on top of things, she knew Allegra slept till well after noon on most days, managing only a few hours in the library a week. As for lectures . . . she was fairly sure that Allegra had not yet even visited the English Faculty.

'Don't worry, I'll catch up,' her friend announced. 'By the way, did I tell you? We're invited to a party at Xander's tonight.'

Imogen felt a warm buzz of excitement. 'Are we?' She spoke casually but inside she was jubilant. *My first chance to see Xander properly!* She had managed to turn him into a proper little crush over the last few years. Of course, there had been plenty of other boys she'd liked in the meantime, and she'd even managed several clumsy, drunken snogs and some exploratory activity, but no one else had given her that thrill Xander had when she'd seen him at the wedding in London. She couldn't help holding on to the dream of seeing him again, perhaps awakening him to her womanly charms, perhaps even kissing him . . .

'Yeah. Do you want to go?'

'Um . . .' Imogen took her time. She licked her spoon. *I don't want to seem too eager. The last thing I want is Allegra to think I fancy her brother. She'd die laughing for one thing, and then probably tell him. I couldn't face the embarrassment.* 'I suppose so. If you think it'll be fun.'

Allegra leant back in her chair. 'Fun is one thing those boys definitely know how to have.'

They got ready together after dinner in Allegra's room, with a bottle of wine open on the table, cigarettes burning in ashtrays and the CD player blaring out while they took turns with the hair dryer and the mirror.

'How do I look?' Imogen turned round to show off her outfit.

Allegra scrutinised her. 'Very nice. Like the black pencil skirt.'

Black was definitely their colour of choice at the moment. Imogen put a tight black cardigan over a vest top to go with her skirt, and pulled her hair back into a pony-tail that she hoped made her look sexy in a mysterious and slightly intellectual way. Like Allegra, she'd rimmed her eyes with lots of dark kohl and mascara, and glossed her lips with a pale pink shimmer.

Allegra was wearing a black strapless dress with a purple velvet Edwardian-style jacket and high lace-up boots, her long hair loose but scrunched on the very top and pierced with a chopstick, a look that she declared to be punky Edwardian geisha.

By the time they were ready it was getting on for ten o'clock and they were already half cut on the white wine they'd been sipping. They decided to walk to north Oxford, going up St Giles and then following the Woodstock Road to St Margaret's Road.

'Have you been there already?' Imogen asked, as they went past Little Clarendon Street.

'Yeah, it's bloody amazing compared to the way most students live. But then, James Barclay's dad is immensely rich. I mean, James is no brain of Britain. Apparently his dad built the college a whole new wing in order to get him in. He's always hanging around with wasters, so watch out.'

We seem to be wasters ourselves these days, Imogen thought but she didn't say anything. *I've got to fit in. I have to seem like this is all completely normal to me.*

They walked quietly together through the Oxford darkness, passing the shops and restaurants of St Giles. Then Allegra said suddenly, 'What about sex? Are you fixed up? Are you on the Pill? Or do you have condoms?'

Imogen shook her head, looking at her friend who stared straight ahead, her jaw firm. 'No, no . . . nothing like that. Should I?'

'You don't want to be a baby about it,' snapped Allegra almost crossly. 'You may have had a couple of snogs at parties but these boys are grown up. They expect more. And once you're drunk, it's easy to get carried away. You're bound to get laid sooner or later. Just make sure you can look after yourself.'

'Are *you* on the Pill?' Imogen ventured. She knew that Allegra had gone pretty far, but she'd thought neither of them had actually had sex yet.

'Not yet, but I'm getting myself sorted out. You can get them to come on the outside if you haven't got any protection. Condoms are best anyway, in case of infections.'

Imogen said slowly, 'So . . . you've had sex?'

''Course I have. Everyone has.' She laughed. 'Don't tell me you're the last virgin in Oxford!'

Imogen was stung. This wasn't like Allegra; they had always told each other all their secrets and shared every step of the journey on the way to becoming experienced – 'our sexperiences', Allegra used to call them. *How can she imply that I'm some frumpy old loser because I haven't got laid? I haven't got a boyfriend – who am I supposed to have sex with? One of the porters?* Imogen was hurt.

'Who did you go to bed with? Was it Freddie?' she ventured at last, in a small voice.

'No. It doesn't matter who. Just someone.'

'What was it like?'

Allegra shrugged. 'No big deal,' she said. 'You know. Just sex. Come on, this is St Margaret's Road.'

The house was a large Victorian pile with Gothic arched windows, the kind of place a prosperous family would live rather than a bunch of dissolute students. The doorbell was answered by a tall boy with dopey eyes and long brown hair.

'Hiya, ladies. Come on in. Drinks in the kitchen, help yourselves.' He nodded his head towards the back of the house.

As soon as they were inside, Imogen sensed the dissolute atmosphere; even though the party was still in its early stages, she had the impression that people were determined to let go as soon as they could. She felt wary and inexperienced, as though she needed to be careful. *But this is the kind of world I have to be in if I want to see Xander . . .*

They went into the kitchen and poured themselves tumblers full of wine from the open bottles on the counter. They were talking quietly, getting their party bearings, when the door to the garden opened and Xander came through it.

Oh my God, it's him, thought Imogen, clutching her tumbler with both hands. Seeing him again was like being struck with something. Her knees weakened and she felt dazed and dizzy, her pulse-rate speeding up. He was as gorgeous as she remembered him: long and lean with poetically sunken cheeks and a smattering of brown stubble, looking both boyish and manly at the same time. He was shabbily dressed in battered jeans, an over-large holey jumper and a scarf that looked as though it had come back with him off one of his travels, but he was still ineffably glamorous.

'Hey, sis!' he said, brightening up when he saw Allegra. 'You came!' He gave her a kiss, then saw Imogen. 'Hi, Midge. Glad you're here.' Before she could say anything, he put his arms around her and pressed a big kiss on her cheek. 'You're at Christ Church, aren't you? Lots of dickheads over that way, but I'll forgive you. Have you got drinks? Good. Come on, I'll introduce you to some people.'

Imogen didn't want to meet anyone else, but she followed after Allegra and Xander, her cheek burning where he'd kissed it. He led them into the sitting room where a couple of boys were squabbling over the CD player and which music they should put on. Then he introduced them to some of the people sitting on the sofa, and left them, wandering off to answer the door and direct people through the house.

Imogen watched him go with yearning. She didn't care about socialising, she just wanted to talk to Xander – but how on earth was she going to get him on his own? For a while she sat quietly on the edge of things, listening to Allegra chatting and sipping away at her wine until gradually her confidence grew and she began to feel reckless. *I've made all this effort, and I look good, I know I do. I'm going to find him.* She stood up. 'Just going to the loo,' she said breezily, grabbed her cigarettes and headed out towards the kitchen.

She found him in the garden, despite the cold night, sitting with a group of people at a table, passing a bong around. She lit a cigarette to give her confidence and wandered over. 'Hi,

Xander. How're things?' she said casually, hoping she wasn't giving away her fluttering insides.

He grinned at her. 'Midge, sit down.' There was nowhere to sit, so he pulled her down on to his lap. She felt his hard thighs through her skirt and a thrill of excitement ran through her. 'So, tell me, are you enjoying Oxford life?'

She tried to look sophisticated and knowing. 'Oh, you know . . . it's great. Loads of people, loads of parties . . .'

'Boyfriends?' he asked teasingly.

She felt her cheeks flush as she said breezily, 'Oh my God, tons. I'm fighting them off, if you must know.'

Xander grinned at her, his blue eyes mischievous. 'I bet you are. You're not the innocent twelve year old I remember any more, are you?' He raised his eyebrows and looked briefly at her chest, which was almost at his eye level. 'In fact, I don't know if it's quite proper for you to be on my knee now you're so grown up.' He took her hand and gave it a squeeze. 'You're definitely going to be *very* sought after. And if any of those Christ Church boys give you a hard time, just send them to me, OK? I'll sort them out for you.'

She looked at him from under her lashes, trying to be playful and flirtatious. 'I certainly will. But I'm holding out for someone special.'

'So you should, young Imogen. Don't throw your pearls before swine, that's what I say.'

She wished she could have stayed on his knee all night, soaking up the warmth of his body against the cold autumn night, sipping wine and flirting, but it couldn't last. He was summoned inside and the moment was gone. She comforted herself by drinking more and more of the bitter red wine until she was woozy and drunk.

Does he see me as a woman now? she wondered, as she stumbled through the house, looking for him. *Maybe there's still a chance that he'll notice me . . .*

The house was full, the dining room thudding with music and packed with people dancing. Allegra was in there, moving wildly, a cigarette hanging out of her mouth, her arms in the air. The party was now a noisy blur of music and faces, the rich aroma of cannabis smoke mixed with the yeasty smell of wine and beer.

Imogen started dancing as well. She had the distinct sense that there was another, more exclusive party going on somewhere else in the house: a room where other, naughtier things were going on. Perhaps that was where Xander was. Then, suddenly, the floor cleared and she saw him.

He was in the middle of the dining room, swaying gently despite the fierce beat of the music. He had his arms wrapped round a beautiful girl, tall, coltish on high heels, a river of dark hair flowing down her back, and he was kissing her passionately. Imogen froze, unable to tear her eyes away from them.

'There you are!' It was Allegra, her eyes wide and her pupils dilated. She must have taken something. 'Where've you been?'

'Around,' Imogen said. 'Who's that with Xander?' She pointed over and Allegra followed with her gaze.

'Oh, that's Temple. His girlfriend,' Allegra said. 'Shall we go outside and get some air? It's so stuffy in here.'

Of course he has a girlfriend, Imogen thought dully, as she nodded and followed Allegra out of the dining room. *I'm so stupid. Why on earth is he going to fancy me when he can have a girl like that?*

Chapter 14

New York
2003

'Herbie, keep the fuckin' noise down, will ya?' Mitch pounded on the paper-thin wall. He could hear Herbie and his girlfriend like they were next to him in the bed, with Linda gasping and shrieking as Herbie panted and groaned with the effort of banging her.

I gotta get some decent sleep, he thought blearily, but now he was awake, he couldn't fall back into oblivion. The sound of Linda's ecstatic orgasm gave him a rearing hard on, so he shuffled off a quick one for himself then lay back on his thin futon, trying not to worry about the restaurant.

It's all right for Herbie. He's so crazy, no one's ever gonna make him in charge of shit. But me . . . they keep giving me more and more to do.

Mitch had given up on his ambitions years ago, but they still kept coming back to haunt him via the chefs and restaurants where he worked. No matter how hard he played, how many hours he stayed up drinking and smoking, it seemed that his natural talent for cooking made people notice him. And then they realised that he was also good at running a kitchen: his staff liked him (particularly the waitresses, who were always ready to welcome him into their beds) and worked hard for him, and he grasped quickly and easily the mechanics of running a business. He knew how to squeeze every bit of value from the food, how to turn valuable scraps and leftovers into delicious – and cheap – daily specials, and how to keep his staff costs low. All of this meant that he could keep the narrow restaurant margins as healthy as possible, and his bosses liked him for it. They were always sorry when he decided to move on, which he did often, usually because Herbie was fired and Mitch, from some inexplicable sense of loyalty, went with him.

Then somehow, after three years of bumming around the New York restaurant scene, he'd got a job in a classy midtown joint called the Greywell Brasserie, where the head chef, Patrice, ruled by terror and the sonic pitch of his screams. He was a crazy guy, a bona fide psychotic Frenchman who yelled and spat during service if things didn't go his way, threatening his sous chefs with knives if he didn't like the way they worked. But he cooked like an angel – real, classical French stuff, a world away from the burgers that Mitch had started out flipping, or the fries he'd learned to turn out by the basket full back home. He felt his old enthusiasm, long dormant and kept that way by the shit he still liked to smoke, stir and awaken as he became excited by what Patrice could teach him.

'You gotta go to France, man,' the chef would drawl to him as he sucked down another glass full of the rich red wine he loved while they sat in their favourite late-night drinking dive after the restaurant was closed. His accent was a curious mix of French and New York slang. 'I'm telling you, Mitch, you can't cook until you've learned ze French way. You should go to Paris. I got friends zere, I can get you a place if you want one.'

'Maybe.' Mitch took a long toke on his Camel, sucking it in like a diver pulling on his oxygen tube. He puffed out, his knees jerking and his fingers tapping the counter. He still found it so hard to come down after seven hours in the kitchen. The whisky helped. He lifted his glass to his mouth and drank.

'You gotta do it, Mitch! You got talent, eet's true. But wizzout learning French cuisine . . .' Patrice gave a Gallic shrug. 'You can't make ze big time.'

'I don't have to go to France. I could go to catering school.'

'Uh-huh.' The chef laughed derisorily. '*Oui*. But you wanna learn to turn out avocado mousse, cut tomatoes into roses and cry when your fucking soufflés sink? Fuck zat sheet! Go to France and get your fucking 'ands dirty, man.'

Mitch stared at him, then shrugged. 'Maybe. We'll see.'

The truth was, he didn't want to go anywhere. He liked it in New York just fine, even if he was still sharing dives with Herbie and looking down the barrel of his thirtieth birthday – now only two years away – with no savings and no real idea of what he was going to do with his future. Maybe partying and living the single life would get boring in a while, but he was in no hurry to pack it in just yet.

Once he was up, there was no point in hanging around the apartment with Linda there. The place felt crowded with the three of them so Mitch decided to go for a walk uptown to Central Park, get some clean air in his lungs.

He felt like he was wandering into a strange country as he made his way up the broad sidewalks into the more expensive part of town. Did he really live in the same city as all these people? These were daytimers, who got up at normal hours and went to bed before midnight. Mitch felt grey and unhealthy as he wove his way through the tourists and the office workers, aware that he was looking jaded by his nocturnal, hard-drinking, hard-living lifestyle. He was dazed by the colour and noise of the outside world.

He stared into the shop windows as he passed: impossibly

slender mannequins modelled the latest fashions. *Who the hell really looks like that?* he wondered, but then he realised that there were girls climbing out of discreetly expensive cars and tottering into the boutiques who were just as slim and unreal-looking as the pretend ones. They had glossy curtains of highlighted hair, immaculate, velvety skin, and whiter-than-white eyes and teeth. Huge handbags in exotic leathers – snake, crocodile, ostrich – hung off their waif-like arms, and they balanced on the kind of shoes that no one who did anything sensible for a living could possibly wear.

Rich bitches, he thought darkly. He saw plenty of them in the restaurant: sleek little honeys who only ate the meat on their plate, or demanded food off the menu, or simply returned everything untouched. *Dried up harpies,* he told himself. *They're not real. You don't get to be that way by eating and drinking and acting like a normal human being.* Then he laughed at himself. *And how much of a normal human being am I?*

He walked on, eager for greenness and nature, resolutely turning his back on the Park Avenue princesses. They were nothing more to him than dolls.

But those slender legs and the smooth, golden skin must have stirred something in him because when he got to the restaurant that night, he pulled Willa, his favourite waitress, to their regular meeting place in the dry store and humped her hard up against the wall, while she dug her fingers into his back and rubbed herself against him until they both came fast and hard.

'Seemed like you needed that, Mitch,' she said, smiling, as she straightened her clothes afterwards.

He grinned at her. 'Maybe I did.'

'You know, we could always make this little arrangement more . . . permanent, if you like?' She spoke casually as she put her hand to her hair, making sure it was still neat.

'Uh-uh.' He shook his head. 'Believe me, sweetheart, I'm doing you a favour. You don't want to get mixed up with a dead beat like me. I'm no good for any woman – not in the long term, anyhow. You've just had the best of me, and that's the truth.'

Chapter 15

Paris
2003

The nobleman opposite dismissed the sommelier with a tiny nod of his head, and then raised his eyebrows and smiled at Romily.

'Have you tried this?' he asked, lifting his glass.

She picked up hers and sipped a little of the cold Puligny-Montrachet. 'Delicious,' she said.

'Yes. It has a fine, clean, mineral taste, has it not?' He smiled again.

He's so handsome, Romily thought admiringly, *even if he is old. And he has so much to teach me.* The marquis had grey hair shading into white, and his face, although lined and well-worn, was tanned a youthful golden-brown that made his eyes seem bright under his slightly too-bushy eyebrows. He was turned out in perfect smart dress-down clothes: Ralph Lauren trousers with a knife-edge crease, an Armani shirt, and a blue cashmere jumper slung round his shoulders. On his feet were Gucci loafers. Everything about him was discreetly expensive.

They had met at the Crillon Ball where Romily had made friends with his daughter. The girls had spent a happy afternoon together, preparing for the ball and comparing their ravishing gowns, and in the evening Clothilde had introduced Romily to her father. The marquis was charming, sophisticated and polished. He obviously found her delightful company. He had rung the next day and they had met for lunch, and soon they were lunching together most days. She had quickly guessed that he wished to introduce her to the arts of love. Then he had changed an afternoon engagement to an evening one, and she'd known for sure that she was being seduced.

Getting ready for the evening she had been extra careful, showering slowly and making up her face with more attention than usual. She'd gazed into her own brown eyes, thinking with nervous excitement that when she next saw herself like this, she would no longer be a virgin.

Now, facing him over their table in the Brasserie Lipp, she felt daring and ready, eager to be initiated.

He leaned towards her slightly. 'My dear, I have a question for you. I don't think it will come as a great surprise.'

'Yes?' She blinked innocently but inside she was jubilant.

'I will come straight to the point: I wish you to become my mistress. You are young, I know, but I'm sure we will have much to enjoy together.' He sounded as suave and relaxed as though he were simply asking her if she liked vanilla ice cream.

She tried to stay calm and cool. 'What a very . . . interesting . . . invitation. I take it your wife will have no objection?'

He laughed. 'Oh, no, none at all. She is very happy with her own lover. Several of them, I believe. Neither of us believes in denying the other the pleasures of life. A happy marriage depends on the fulfilment of both. What use is it if we both become bitter and dried up, denied the necessity of making love with whoever it is we are attracted to? No, we have a very civilised arrangement, as do most married couples.'

'Do they?' Romily was surprised, but now she considered it, perhaps it was a sensible arrangement, if old people no longer loved each other. It was not something she could imagine for herself, of course. Whoever she married would be the love of her life, her grand passion, and she would never tire of him. 'Well, that's good, I suppose.'

'So, what is your answer, Romily?'

She hovered on the brink and then said, 'Yes. I think I would like that very much.'

He took her to an exquisite little flat in St-Germain-des-Près, in a honey-coloured stone building shut away from the street behind enormous green doors with great brass lions' heads on the front.

'Have you had many mistresses here?' Romily asked, feeling nervous for the first time. It seemed the place was a shrine to love: antique erotic prints on the walls, small nude sculptures on the cabinets, daybeds, pillows and cushions everywhere.

The marquis smiled. 'Of course. But I was faithful to each one.'

He went to her and gazed into her eyes. 'You're very beautiful, my dear, do you know that? Not simply in your body. As soon as I saw you, I recognised your soul. You may be young, but you have a natural maturity and understanding. I knew at once we would be a perfect fit.' He bent his head and put his lips to hers. They were cool but then he opened his mouth and the next moment she was tasting his warm mouth, feeling his tongue turning around hers. He tasted male, with a faintly bitter edge. *Perhaps that's because he's so old,* she thought, and that was all she was able to think before her body's reactions became her only concern.

He took her into the tiny boudoir, a room that was almost

all bed, and slowly removed her clothes, kissing her all the time. Somehow he also managed to strip himself and then they were both naked, her soft ripe body with its small brown-tipped breasts pressed against his rangy lean one, with the grey thatch of hair spreading out over his chest. His erect penis was pressed against her thigh, distracting her with its radiating heat and purposeful hardness.

The marquis meanwhile was interested in nibbling her rose-brown nipples, grazing them with his teeth and sucking them hard, which was making her groin contract with excitement. His fingers were roaming around her pussy, touching and stroking, teasing her unbearably. She could feel that she was wet and swollen, everything in her preparing for the moment when he would enter her.

'Are you protected, my dear?' he muttered.

She shook her head, sighing and gasping as his thumb rolled over her bud. It had not occurred to her. Why hadn't she thought of it before? Did this mean they would have to stop?

'I thought not. That is something you must address. But today is for your pleasure, not mine, so I shall make the sacrifice.' He rolled over and took a foil packet from the ebony casket by the bed, and a moment later had deftly sheathed his penis in the condom. 'And now,' he whispered, 'I think it is time.'

She opened her legs to him and he rolled on top of her, finding his position. He brought the tip of his penis to her entrance and rubbed it there for a moment, making a growling noise in his throat as he looked down at her, her breasts and smooth belly, the small thatch of dark hair on her mound and the wet, open lips of her pussy. 'You do me a great honour,' he said, his eyes glistening darkly, 'and your beauty is overwhelming.'

She felt deliciously desirable and hungry for his cock

inside her. 'Now,' she whispered, with a touch of pleading in her voice. 'Please?'

She felt a pushing at her entrance, and let her legs open even wider for him. A few nudges and then he was in her, and she was stretching to accommodate him as he moved slowly upwards, pushing gently and filling her up with the most extraordinary and pleasurable feeling. She sighed, shut her eyes and lifted her chin, concentrating only on the sensation of his cock sliding up within her, making her replete.

The marquis opened his eyes and said with surprise, 'I'm fully in. Are you sure you're a virgin, my dear?'

'Yes,' she said, momentarily anxious in case there was something wrong with her.

He smiled. 'Then you were made for love. I've never known such a painless and unencumbered entry.' He began to move, pushing up inside her until she wondered how she could take him any further, but the sensation of his movements was delightful. Each upward thrust took her breath away and each small withdrawal caused a delicious friction. They moved like that together for a long time, Romily luxuriating in what she was feeling. *I never want to stop this*, she thought, high on the pleasure. Then the marquis began to pick up pace, thrusting harder into her, making her cry out as he hit his mark. He kissed her and nipped at her neck and earlobes as the power of his fucking began to overtake him, and then he groaned, shuddered, pushed into her again and stopped, his face contorting as he came. When it had passed, he lay down next to her.

She wrapped her arms around him as happiness surged through her. She had made him climax. She must have done it right. And, oh, it had been lovely.

He looked at her solemnly. 'I must apologise. I was

overtaken by my desire for you. You haven't tasted the fruits of love.'

'What do you mean, the fruits of love?' she said, laughing, although she liked his flowery language.

'I mean, you haven't made your sacrifice at Venus's altar.' He smiled at her. 'Can I be any clearer than that?'

'Perhaps a little.'

He neatly removed the condom from his prick and disposed of it by the bed. 'Have you ever had an orgasm, my dear?'

Despite everything they had done, she was embarrassed. She felt her cheeks burn. 'Only . . . only by myself.'

'Excellent.' He rubbed a fingertip over her nipple, where it was stiff and sensitive. 'Then you know what to do.'

She looked back at him, not understanding.

'Touch yourself,' he urged, his voice mellow and hypnotic.

She hesitated, feeling shy.

'Do it. Don't be embarrassed. It is utterly natural.'

Delicately, slowly, she pushed her fingertips on to her clitoris and massaged it lightly. It was already swollen from the recent activity, still pulsing with desire, and it responded with a quiver, sending small waves of pleasure through her.

'That's right. A little more. Relax, my love. You have nothing to be ashamed of, you are beautiful and everything you do to yourself is right. And . . .' his voice dropped even lower . . . 'you are exciting me greatly.'

This made her breathe harder, and rub a little faster, picking up the delicious nerve endings with each circle of her fingertips. She dipped downwards into the depths, oiling her fingers with her own juices, before returning to the bud.

'Yes.' His voice was low. 'Open to yourself, darling. Let me see you. God, you are amazing . . .'

She let her knees fall open, parting herself to his gaze. The pleasure was building in her, her breath coming faster. She began to move unconsciously, arching her back and twisting her head from side to side, responding to her own incessant touching. Then she couldn't resist it any longer, rubbing harder and harder and then crying out as the delightful shiver took hold of her, shuddering along her limbs. 'Oh! Oh . . .'

The marquis smiled, pleased with her, then took her hand and placed it on his stiff rod. It felt huge, smooth and warm under her hand, rearing up from its nest of coarse curly grey hair at the base. 'You've warmed me up again with that little performance. Now, my darling, a few strokes and I'll be able to join you in bliss.'

She rubbed the hot flesh, moving it up and down the shaft. 'Harder,' he whispered, and folded his large hand over hers, moving it up and down with firm, fast strokes. 'Yes . . . that's it, that's it . . .' He gasped, and his cock jerked under her hand. A small fountain of white fluid gushed from its tip and down over her knuckles.

The marquis was still for a moment, his eyes closed. Then he sighed and looked at her. 'Thank you, my dear.' He passed her a silk handkerchief. 'You have given me great pleasure. I hope we will be able to please each other like this many times.'

'So do I,' she said, thinking, *I've done it. Now I really am a woman.*

In the weeks that followed, she and the marquis spent many hours in his little flat as he tutored her in how to make love. He adored her body, and while he was happiest simply gazing at her and caressing her breasts and bottom, or lying between her slim thighs, his penis thrusting hard into her until he came, he also took his duties as teacher seriously. He taught her how to please him with her mouth, and did the same for her, showing her how to draw out her pleasure by slowing down her ascent. He made her bring him to the peak of orgasm and then allow it to fade away, so that when the climax came, it was all the stronger and more necessary for the delicious wait. 'Never hurry,' he insisted. 'That is the worst way to make love.' He would spend the first hour of their time together kissing, massaging and stroking her, sometimes bathing her or using aids to warm her up and open her to her erotic nature. Then they would use new techniques or practise what he had already taught her. She revelled in the luxuriousness of sex, and delighted in what she learned about her own body.

I don't know why anyone does anything else, she would always think as she crossed the Seine and headed home. *But I suppose not everybody has the luxury of time, the way we have.* And she remembered what the marquis had done that day with the pair of cold jade balls, and shivered with pleasure.

Romily sent a postcard to Imogen from the palazzo in Venice where she was staying in advance of a society wedding.

Dearest Midge,

You may be at Oxford – and having a wonderful time, I hope – but I am also expanding my education with the help of a lovely new friend. Can't wait to see you. Can you come and see me this summer? Please say yes. Now I have to have my hair done, such a bore. Tell Allegra I love her and miss her too.

Lots of love, R
P.S. MG4E

Chapter 16

Oxford
2003

When she woke up, the guy from the night before was still in her bed. In the narrow college single, Allegra was jammed between the cool wall and his smooth brown back which was emanating heat like a radiator, so that she was freezing on one side and boiling on the other.

Who is he? she wondered blearily as she realised she was desperately thirsty. The man's body had blocked her in, and her basin and water glass seemed unreachable. *Oh, yeah. It's Paddy.* Bits of the previous evening were coming back to her now. She'd met him in the college bar in Hertford, they'd flirted, got drunk, gone back to someone's room, drunk even more and ended up staggering back to her place, and of course she'd ended up shagging him. They'd writhed around the bed, doing all the actions, and after a while she'd let him push himself into her and they'd bounced around for a bit. Had he been wearing a condom? Yes . . . that's right, he'd had to go and get one from his jeans . . . then he'd finally come but she hadn't, and when he'd asked if she wanted him to help her, she'd pushed him away, laughing, and said, 'Don't worry, honey, I think I'm past it, to be honest,' and then they'd fallen asleep.

She'd slept with loads of guys and never had an orgasm

with any of them. Every time she started to enjoy herself, something clicked off and stopped her feeling anything.

She nudged him in the back. 'Wake up, Paddy!'

He stirred, then grunted, then rolled on his back and yawned, releasing a waft of stale breath. Turning to look at her, he blinked and smiled. 'Morning,' he said. 'What's the time?'

'I've no idea.' She poked his arm. 'Get up, can you? Let me out. I've got to get a drink.'

'Sure,' he said amiably. 'I'd better be on my way anyway. Got some rugby training today.' He got out of bed and started looking about for his clothes while she pulled on a T-shirt and gulped down a glass of water. When he was dressed he said, 'Thanks for last night by the way. Are you around tonight or tomorrow? We could always go to the King's Head, if you fancy a drink?'

'Oh, no . . . no, I think I'm busy. Really sorry and everything.'

'OK.' He shrugged as if to say that he wasn't bothered either way, it had only been a suggestion and not one he cared about. 'See you round.'

'Sure. 'Bye, Paddy.'

Allegra shut the door behind him with relief. She hated seeing them the next day: it was only worthwhile when she was drunk or high, and the guys seemed so intensely desirable, and the whole encounter full of drama and possibility. It was so simple: a boy, a girl, and the excitement of the game of seduction. In boring daylight and awful sobriety, it was all so much more complex, and she couldn't bear the thought of them seeing her as she really was. And she was always haunted by the knowledge of the sexual failure of the night before – no matter how much she was pretending to get off, she never could – and so she preferred it if the men were out of her life as quickly as possible.

*

She texted Imogen and they arranged to meet at a café near the library. It was supposed to be a study day, they had decided, to try and catch up somehow with the mountain of work.

Allegra coiled her hair back into a loose bun and put on a pair of dark glasses, hoping that her hangover wouldn't get worse. Today she simply had to get over it: it was important that she tackle this week's essay and try to get on top of her workload.

How does everyone else manage? she wondered, as she went out on to Turl Street and headed for the main road. *They must somehow. Is it only me who can't seem to find the time? But it's not as though I'm out raging on my own, is it?*

The problem was that examinations were beginning to loom large in their consciousness: at the end of the summer term, they would have to sit their Honour Moderations, and pass them, in order to return for their second year. The examinations would cover all the work they'd done in their first year, including the dreaded Anglo-Saxon that Allegra hated. That meant she'd have to memorise several of the set texts so that she could 'translate' them convincingly in the exam, gambling that the ones she'd learnt would come up.

But it was so difficult to knuckle down and work, with so many pleasant distractions everywhere. As the spring advanced into summer, Oxford had burst into bloom and the college gardens and university parks became alluring: rugs were brought out, games of croquet were played, punts were hired. The last thing she wanted to do was sit in a stuffy library, poring over pointless poems.

How hard can it be? Allegra thought. *I mean, who on earth revises for Mods? They won't be strict about it. No one expects first years to perform very well, with all the stress we've been through adjusting to life at Oxford.*

She was sure that if she bombed, she'd be able to talk her way out of it. After all, her tutor loved her. She'd seen him glance appreciatively at her legs more than once, so he was definitely on side. So she might as well carry on having a good time while she could.

Imogen frowned at her. 'Are you all right, Allegra? You look terrible.'

She pulled a dismissive face and took another bite of her bacon sandwich. 'I'm fine. God, I'm starving. This tastes bloody fantastic.' She was jigging her knee and her hands were trembling: her alcohol and cocaine hangover was kicking in, and she could feel her spirits swooping downwards into bleakness. The only possible remedy was plenty of sweet, filling food, to try and push her blood sugar back up and combat the depression. 'Do I really look rough?' She looked down at her jeans, scuffed Converse trainers, and the grey shirt she'd knotted at her waist.

Imogen stared at her for a while and then said gently, 'Yeah. You do. Are you OK, Allegra? Really?'

Allegra looked away and then laughed. ''Course I am. I'm just tired, that's all. It's so hectic at the moment.' She took another bite of her greasy, reinvigorating sandwich. 'How about you?'

'I'm not going out much at the moment. I'm trying to revise for Mods. My tutor's been putting the fear of God into me – apparently I'll be sent down without question if I fail.' Imogen looked worried. 'It's a bit nerve-wracking. I've just finished an essay on Yeats for tomorrow.'

'Really?' Allegra said, perking up. 'I was going to ask if I could borrow anything you've got on Yeats.'

Imogen frowned. 'Well, yeah, of course you can. It's just that . . .'

'What?'

'Well, you've been borrowing quite a lot lately – which is fine, I don't mind,' she said hastily. 'But . . .' She struggled, obviously trying to find the right words. 'Don't you think that it's worth doing a bit yourself? I know we've got different tutors and everything, but someone might notice that our work is identical. And you won't be able to borrow anything in the actual exams.'

'Oh,' Allegra said stiffly. Imogen was right, she knew that. She'd started cadging the odd page of notes the previous term, and then essays which at first she used as models for her own before eventually she began copying them out almost word for word. Now she relied on Imogen almost entirely to keep up with her work. She was secretly ashamed that she was using her friend so blatantly, and usually because she was simply too tired and hungover to do the work herself, but she didn't like to think of it that way. 'Well, don't you think that it's the least you can do? Considering how much you owe my family. I mean, you wouldn't have gone to Westfield at all if it weren't for my parents. Have your mother and father ever got round to paying back mine for the school fees?'

Imogen gasped, her eyes full of surprise and hurt. She flushed red. At once, Allegra felt guilty and mean. But couldn't Imogen see how rotten she was feeling? Besides, it was true that Imogen owed her: without Allegra, she wouldn't be going to the kind of glamorous, exciting parties she seemed to enjoy so much.

Imogen still seemed stunned by her last comment so Allegra said, 'Don't lend it to me if you don't want to. I don't care.'

'It's all right,' Imogen said quietly, looking down at the table. 'You can have it if you like. I'll need it back in time for my tute tomorrow afternoon, that's all.'

'OK.' Allegra wanted to make up for her spiteful remark

so she said, 'There's a big party tomorrow at that new cocktail place on Walton Street. Want to come?'

Imogen shook her head. 'No, I can't. I'm going out with someone.'

'What?' Allegra leaned forward, surprised. 'Who?'

'A guy from Magdalen. He's called Sam. I met him in college, he's friends with the bloke in the room next to mine.'

Allegra stared at her. She'd grown used to the idea that Imogen didn't have anything to distract her from being Allegra's wingman as they whirled through her social life. Of course Imogen had got off with boys, and been interested in people, but nothing had ever really come of it, and that was the way Allegra had expected it to continue as long as she needed her. It wasn't that Imogen held no attraction for men: she was very pretty in her own quiet way, with those big grey eyes that showed everything she was feeling, pink cheeks and ripe figure. She might not have the aristocratic ranginess that Allegra and her other friends had, or the shimmering blonde hair that seemed to draw men like an irresistible flame, but she had qualities of her own that perhaps she herself didn't realise. 'So who is he?' Allegra said at last. 'What's he like?'

'He's lovely.' Imogen couldn't help giving a broad smile and her eyes brightened. 'Nothing glamorous, quite ordinary really, but very kind and funny. That's important, isn't it?'

'Mmm. Of course.' Allegra really didn't have any idea. She chose her men on quite different criteria – mostly looks, availability, and how much they seemed to want her. There was no shortage of candidates after all. She was intelligent enough to realise that her good looks and pedigree explained why men paid her so much attention, flattered her, pampered her, and tried to give her whatever she wanted. It wasn't unusual for huge bouquets to be waiting for her in the porter's lodge, for men to arrive at her room bearing gifts, and for her pigeon hole to be stuffed with notes and invitations. If she'd wanted, she could have dined out every night, been taken to expensive restaurants and smart hotels whenever she felt like it, the bill paid with a Coutts card by whichever lucky man was her escort for the evening. And he would probably end up in her bed, as well, if she felt like it or got drunk enough.

'I don't think we're properly going out yet,' Imogen continued, 'but I think we're going to. He seems really keen. It's so exciting. He's got brown hair and hazelly eyes and he's quite tall and he loves cricket, he's mad about it . . .'

'Have you had sex?' demanded Allegra.

Imogen shook her head. 'No . . . not yet. But if everything goes well, I guess it won't be long. I hope so. I think Sam would be really sweet with me.'

Allegra put her sunglasses back on. 'Can't stand this light,' she muttered. She was ashamed of it, but somewhere in her heart, a rope of jealousy was uncoiling. Why should Imogen get a caring, affectionate lover – a proper boyfriend? Would this Sam person take her away? 'Can't wait to meet him,' she said at last, trying to resist the blanket of misery threatening to envelop her. *Why do I feel like this? I can have anyone I want.*

'Shall we go to the library?' she said, suddenly wanting to be somewhere where they couldn't talk about Sam. 'I've got tons to do.'

'OK,' Imogen said, giving her friend a quick look as though making sure that the nastiness of earlier had been forgotten. 'And I'll give you that Yeats essay, if you like.'

Chapter 17

'Did you enjoy the film?'

'Yes, it was good. I liked the ending, it made me quite teary.'

Sam took Imogen's hand as they wandered along Walton Street and she leaned her head on his shoulder. They'd been going out for only a fortnight but somehow it seemed much longer. Life at Oxford, with its eight week terms, could be so intense: plays were auditioned, cast and put on in a matter of three weeks; fashions appeared and disappeared in half a term; people were always dashing about, with an essay or two to write a week, on top of all the other things they had to occupy their time. Some people thrived and flourished under the pressure, others buckled. Most coasted as best they could, doing the work they had to do while devoting as much time as they could to their social life and everything else that Oxford could offer. Imogen liked the sense of busy activity and time rushing by. She feared she was naturally lazy and that only by being chivvied along by the relentless timetable would she get anything done.

'Shall we go back to yours?' Sam said casually. He hardly ever suggested going back to his shared house on the Banbury Road because there was little privacy there, so it wasn't unusual for them to go back to her room. But Imogen knew at once that this time he had something in mind. It was no surprise. They'd been getting ever closer to it. They were meeting almost every night – she'd been introduced to his circle of friends at Magdalen, and he'd been over to Christ Church – and each time they ended up getting just a little steamier. It was obvious what the next step was.

'OK,' she said. She'd already decided: Sam was the one she was going to sleep with. She was so fond of him that it was very close to being in love, even if she knew in her heart that this wasn't *it*. There was cosy affection, and pleasure in his touching and kissing her, but there was no grand passion. He didn't thrill her, excite and engage her imagination – he was lovely, but he wasn't romantic hero material and that was that. There was only one person who made her feel that intense yearning, and that was Xander. But it was her secret, something she would share with no one else because it was so impossible. No matter how hard she tried to get close to him, he was always so far away. And, besides, he had a beautiful girlfriend and would never, in a million years, look at her.

I know I could love Xander and understand him better than anyone else in the world. But I've got to face it – it's never going to happen. I'll just have to adore him from afar, that's all.

Imogen worried over it sometimes, feeling guilty for nurturing her secret crush. *Is it fair on Sam to go out with him when I feel like this about someone else?*

When she was with him, though, the reality of his warm body and tender affection was more appealing than her lonely, empty fantasy. He would never know the truth and perhaps, eventually, her feelings for Xander would fade away and be forgotten.

Sam squeezed her hand in response and they walked back to Christ Church, where Tom Tower stood huge and spiky against the dark night sky. Back in her room, she opened a bottle of wine that she'd put on the window-sill to chill and they drank it together, both suddenly a little nervous of what awaited them.

I know I want to. I'm eighteen years old and still never had sex! The truth was that Allegra's jibe about her being the last virgin in Oxford had struck home, and Imogen knew that she wanted to get rid of her virginity. She needed to grow up.

'You look tired,' Sam said. He put his empty glass on the coffee table. 'Shall I give you a massage?'

So that was the way it was going to start. She smiled and nodded. They dimmed the lights, put some Nick Drake on the CD player and went over to the bed. Lying down together, they started to kiss. He was a good kisser, she thought, patient and tender, and she liked the taste of him. The kissing relaxed her and she felt the tension ease out of her muscles as he rubbed her back and shoulders. She wasn't nervous now, only filled with a sense that she was about to understand one of the mysteries of existence.

'God, Imogen, you're lovely,' he murmured.

She laughed and said, 'Don't you mean fat?'

He pulled back and looked at her, surprised. 'Fat? What are you talking about?'

'My big bum. My thighs. My wobbly breasts.'

He shook his head. 'You girls. You're your own worst enemies. Do you think I'd like you if you had no bum, or thighs, or breasts? Those are the very things that turn me on, you idiot.' He ran his hands up her leg and over the curve of her hip, making an appreciative noise. 'Gorgeous. I love all this. And as for these beauties . . .' He touched her chest lightly, then smiled. 'What have you got to be ashamed of? I'd be obsessed with them if they were mine.'

He kissed her again, now with added vigour, and began to move against her, so she could feel his erection bulging through his trousers. She surrendered to the sensation, excitement building up in the pit of her stomach and sending out waves of pleasurable feeling to her groin.

They slowly undressed each other until they were lying together in their underwear, Sam's bare chest pressed against her. He fumbled a little with her bra and then sighed with appreciation when her breasts came free of it at last.

After a while, she pulled away to ask breathlessly, 'Do you have a condom?'

Sam nodded. 'You bet.' Then he looked into her eyes. 'Are you sure? You want to do this? I don't want to rush you if you're not ready.'

She nodded back. 'I'm sure. I'm really sure.'

'Oh, look.' Imogen pulled a card out of her pigeon hole. 'It's from Romily.'

'Who's Romily?' asked Sam. He was reading the *Daily Information* news-sheet while he waited for her to check her post.

'My friend from school. She was one of our gang of three – me, Allegra and Romily.'

Sam raised his eyebrows. 'And was Romily as much of a hell-raiser as Allegra?'

'Mmm, no, not really. She's very glamorous and rich and French. I think you'd like her.' Imogen was well aware that Sam didn't think much of Allegra. He never said anything but she knew he disapproved of her party lifestyle and all the drugs. It was no coincidence that since they'd been going out with each other, she'd seen less of her friend. Now she had the joys of coupledom – nights in together having lovely sex as often as they could – the endless round of parties was much less appealing. At a little distance, Imogen could see that the constant late nights and drinking had been exhausting and, after a while, a bit boring. Besides, exams were almost upon them and she had to concentrate on them.

Romily had written:

Oh, my Midge,

I miss you! I'm bored silly at the moment as my friend is away and I'm all alone at home. I'm thinking of exciting things I might do to keep myself interested and interesting . . . I will tell you more when I see you. SOON.
Romily xxx
MG4E

Midnight Girls forever. Imogen stared at the letters, nostalgia rushing through her. What had happened to the Midnight Girls and their vow of loyalty? They hadn't seen Romily for ages, and she and Allegra were drifting apart. More than that, she was worried about Allegra, who had been snappy and spiky with her for weeks now, ever since she'd got together with Sam.

She can't be jealous, can she? How could she be? She's got strings of boyfriends.

'I must see her soon,' Imogen murmured to herself.

'Who?' Sam had come up behind her. He nuzzled into her neck and slipped his arms round her waist.

She dropped a kiss on his cheek. 'Both of them. My schoolfriends. We're best friends.'

'Bound together by shared lipsticks and promises you'll always lend each other your clothes?'

She felt a tiny cold shiver as she remembered what did bind them together, then put it out of her mind. 'Something like that,' she said. 'Now, are we going to get some lunch or what?'

The door opened and Allegra stood there. She looked Imogen up and down.

'Who on earth are you?' she said.

'Very funny. Can I come in?'

'If you want.' Allegra stood back and let her into the room.

'Oh my God!' Imogen said, shocked by the sight that met her eyes. 'You've let things slide a bit, haven't you?'

Allegra looked at the mess and shrugged. 'My scout won't come in until I've tidied up but I never seem able to get round to it.'

The room smelled stale and heavy with old cigarette smoke, and overflowing ashtrays were everywhere. Butts floated in the bottom of mugs or had been stubbed out on the dirty plates that lay everywhere. The desk was piled high with books and folders and a mass of scribbled-on paper, and the floor was littered with more books, clothes, and all manner of rubbish and abandoned possessions. The curtains were closed, despite the bright day outside.

'Let's open a window.' Imogen stepped over the clutter to the sill. A gust of fresh air came in, along with the sunlight. 'That's better.' She turned back to Allegra, who looked terrible. She was pasty, her eyes dull and her hair lank. 'Are you OK?'

''Course I am. I'm fine. Do you want a cup of tea?' Allegra went over to her kettle and switched it on. 'How's lover boy? I'm surprised you managed to drag yourself out of his arms for long enough to drop by.'

Imogen sat down on a chair, brushing aside a pile of dirty clothes to make room. 'You don't really mean that, do you?' she said, worried.

'Well . . .' Allegra shrugged. 'You know, I don't see as much of you as I used to.'

'I know. I'm sorry. I've been neglecting you a bit. I got a postcard from Romily today. Have you had one?'

'Dunno. I've not checked my post for a while. What did she say?'

'Not much. But it reminded me how long it's been since

we've seen her, and I thought . . . how about we go to Paris and see her in the vac when the exams are over?'

'No,' Allegra said sharply.

Imogen was startled. She'd thought it sounded like a lovely idea.

Allegra glanced over at her and said, more gently, 'I mean, I don't want to go to Paris. Why doesn't Rom come here? Or else Scotland? Or we could meet her in London. But I don't want to go to Paris.'

'Allegra . . .' Imogen spoke slowly. 'Are you really OK? You haven't been the same since you came back from Paris. I know it was ages ago, but it just feels like you've never been yourself since then . . . you seem so unhappy.'

Allegra turned away to make the tea, and when she spoke again, her voice was gruff and thick. 'I'm fine, OK? I just don't much fancy Paris.'

'All right.' Imogen wanted to believe her, but Allegra seemed to be crumbling in front of her. The state of her room seemed to reflect her state of mind: chaotic and bleak and miserable. *Is it the drugs*? wondered Imogen. *Is she drinking too much?* She looked over at the desk. 'Have you been revising?'

'Kind of.' Allegra brought the mugs of tea over. 'I've had a warning from my tutor after I missed a few essays. But it's nothing I can't handle. I know it looks bad in here, but I'm doing all right at the moment.'

'That's good,' Imogen said, relieved. Perhaps it wasn't as bad as it looked. Allegra had probably just had another crazy night. 'Now, tell me exactly what you've been up to. I've missed all the gossip for ages.'

Chapter 18

Paris 2003

Life is so boring, Romily thought. She stared at her reflection and turned slowly in front of the mirror in the *chambre d'essayage,* while her mother and the seamstress looked on. *When did it get so boring?*

She was missing her marquis more than she'd expected. He'd gone away on a long trip and their delicious afternoons had come to an end. Without them, she had become rather depressed. Plenty of sex was obviously vital to one's physical health and sense of well-being.

I'll just have to look out for a new lover, that's all.

'Oh, yes,' said her mother to the seamstress. 'That's much better. A much better fit. Well done, madame.'

'Are you now satisfied, Madame de Lisle?' asked the atelier manager.

'What do you think, Romily?'

'A much better fit,' she said obediently. It was true: the dress now fitted her perfectly around her tiny waist, flowing out over her hips and coming to a narrow hem exactly on the knee.

'Just right for the races,' her mother said, satisfied. 'Now . . . the jacket.'

Oh, shit, don't tell me we have to do the jacket too? thought Romily, despairing. *I just want to go home.*

Although what she would do when she got there, she had no idea. She was feeling the lack of something to do with an intensity that shocked her. She'd even begun to lose interest in clothes, which was so out of character that it was simply not normal.

She had been out of school now for almost two years, and while at first the limitless leisure had seemed wonderful, it had quickly begun to pall. She had never before understood why her parents were always on the move, from Paris, to Italy, to Switzerland, to New York and on to Chrypkos, then back to Paris again, but now she was beginning to understand: they had to stay busy in order to keep that monster, boredom, at bay, and moving around was an effective way to fill in time. And then there was their social life, a slow-grinding eternal machine that never stopped, and it was always the same people who gathered together: she would see the same faces in St Moritz as she did in Venice. All of them kept moving in a flock, like birds flying in the same direction, swooping up and down in formation.

It was supposed to be entertaining: the travelling, the endless succession of gatherings and parties, always in the lap of luxury. And yet, for now, it wasn't. There was something enervating about it, as though the very fact that her heart's desire could be hers, as long as money could buy it, made life less interesting rather than more.

What I want is to have real *fun,* she thought longingly. *I want to be young and carefree. My social life is too full of grown ups, that's the problem.*

When she tried to say this to her mother, Athina de Lisle looked both hurt and puzzled. She looked up from the elegant bureau where she was writing letters in her firm clear hand.

'My dear child, you can have as much fun as you want. What would you like to do? Shall I telephone the Comtesse and see if Jeanne would like to go to the opera with you tonight? Or how about a trip to New York? The ballet is putting on *Coppélia*, I've heard it's fantastic, and dear Amy Randwick is one of their biggest donors and can certainly get us tickets.'

'No, no . . .' Romily drifted about the drawing room, fiddling with one diamond earring. 'That's not what I mean.'

'Then what do you want to do?' Athina de Lisle put down her Montblanc and looked worried.

'I want to do something with my life! Learn something, do something . . . I don't know.' Romily sighed. 'I'm only twenty. I can't go shopping for the next sixty years.'

'Of course not. That would be very wrong. You must certainly find some worthy ways to occupy your time. What about charity work?'

'Yes,' Romily said eagerly. She sat down in one of the little gilt chairs, leaning over the armrest towards her mother. 'I was wondering about volunteering for an overseas organisation. There are so many places I could go to learn something and be useful: Africa, Sri Lanka . . .'

Her mother looked shocked. 'Oh, no, *ma chérie*. I think committee work is much more appropriate. Fundraising. Promoting awareness. Lovely Françoise has made millions for the Red Cross by holding the most delightful parties. But you can't actually go to those places. They're dangerous!'

Romily sat back in her chair. It was exactly as she'd expected: her mother was happy for her to do something as long as it was within the prescribed limits of what a young lady of her status should do. 'I'm bored with parties. I want to do something interesting.'

'I arranged you those classes with the Professor. Aren't they stimulating your mind?'

'Not really. He's a bore. He likes the sound of his own voice, and whenever I try to start a discussion with him, he blinks at me and acts as if I said nothing at all, and simply drones on and on.'

'How strange,' murmured Athina de Lisle. 'He's so well regarded! His book won so many prizes. I haven't read it, of course, but others have said it's a masterpiece . . .'

'I do want to learn,' Romily said. 'But I'd also like to travel and see the world.'

'See the world?' Her mother laughed, a trilling, musical sound. 'My darling, you see the world all the time! You travel everywhere, all year round. Why, we're off to London next week for darling Jenny's little soirée, and we're going to Delhi later in the year for the Laksi wedding. That's going to be splendid.'

'Yes, yes, but . . .' Romily sighed. 'I won't really see anything in Delhi.'

'Well, I think a Maharaja's palace will be quite a sight myself . . .'

'Yes, I know.' She tried not to sound impatient. 'Of course it will, and I'm looking forward to it, but I won't get to see the place as others will. I won't get to see the poverty and colour and people and beggars . . .'

'Exactly – and you should be very thankful for it!'

'I am thankful, but I also want to know what else is out there, what life is like for people who haven't been born with everything I've got. Do you know what I'd like to do? I'd like to pack a rucksack, take a few hundred dollars and travel the world like any other student on a budget. I'd like to sleep in hostels, and eat from tins, and drink cheap wine from plastic bottles, hang out on beaches . . . just bum around for a year or so.'

'That sounds awful!' declared her mother, looking horrified. 'I can't imagine why on earth you would want that. Besides, the security implications are unthinkable. You would have to take a guard with you wherever you went. If you want a holiday, darling, just say and we'll arrange something. The Matthews have that estate in Zambia. I've heard it's magical. I'm sure you'd be able to get in touch with nature, or whatever it is you want to do, out there. And it's all very safe and fenced in.'

Romily shook her head impatiently. 'No, that's not it at all.'

Her mother looked cross and picked up her pen again. 'For goodness' sake, Romily, I never knew a girl who was so dissatisfied with her lot! What more could you possibly want? You are simply determined to be contrary. If you really want something to occupy your time, you should get married and have children. *That* will keep you busy!'

Romily was jealous of Allegra and Imogen, and the freedom they must be enjoying at Oxford. She was sure they would be having adventures, meeting hundreds of people and learning amazing things. That must be why she had lost touch with her friends recently, despite the postcards she often sent. Her emails to Allegra went unanswered – in fact, she'd heard almost nothing since her stay in Paris before going up to Oxford; Imogen was better, but even so, the occasional email and scribbled letter did nothing to tell her what life there was really like. Imogen was always so apologetic, explaining how busy it was at Oxford, and how her time was taken up with studying for exams. She'd written that she had a boyfriend now, but hardly anything else about him. Romily had been hoping for an invitation to visit, but it had yet to come.

Why didn't I force my parents to let me apply to university? I can't believe I let them take me away from Westfield. She regretted it now, but there seemed no way to reverse her decision. She had left school before her A-levels. There was no way she could go to university now, unless she took the

Baccalaureate. But the idea of going back to school was too depressing. *I want to get on! I've been left behind. I must get a job or something – that's the only answer.*

'Well, you know what you simply must do,' her friend Muffy Houghton Geller said while they were lunching together at the Ritz in the place Vendôme. 'You must come to Manhattan!'

'Really?' Romily was doubtful. Would anything change for her there?

'Yes!' Muffy was a sweet-natured American heiress who had moved in Romily's circle for years. They'd struck up a friendship in Venice one summer and now they were firm friends. Muffy's only ambition in life was to get married to as rich a man as possible, although she had certain conditions: it had to be old money, and he had to be Ivy League and a banker or financier. Apart from that, she wasn't fussy. 'Everyone would simply adore to see you. We'd *totally* spoil you. All the girls are dying to meet you since I told them about your amazing style.'

'Did you? I'm very flattered. I don't think my style is anything special, is it?'

'Are you kidding?' Muffy rolled her eyes and tossed her carefully low-lighted chestnut hair. 'You've got that amazing Parisian chic we all long for. It's not just your clothes, it's everything! I love your entire . . . *ambiance*. Is that the right word?'

'Well – not exactly, but I know what you mean. Thank you, Muffy.' *Perhaps it wouldn't be so bad to go to New York and be spoiled and fêted for a while.* She perked up a little. *Perhaps I could try an American lover. That might bring a bit of spice back into my life.*

Muffy suddenly gasped and dropped her fork into her salad. 'Oh my God, I've got it! I know what you can do. You know how Lily Handford is designing her own handbags for a Japanese luxury goods company, and has even created her own colour of lipstick for their make-up brand – called Lily Splash or something equally dumb – well, if people want to buy *her* style, imagine how much more they'll want to buy *yours*! Think about it: you're related to one of the most famous artists of all time, no one can doubt your artistic inheritance, and you're rich and gorgeous. Everyone would want to buy your life if they could.' Muffy looked solemn. 'I know I would.'

Romily was intrigued and flattered by this notion. 'You think I could sell my style? How?'

Muffy looked around for inspiration. 'I don't know. In a shop?'

Romily sat back in her chair, overcome by this new idea. 'Do you mean . . . clothes?'

'I mean everything!' Muffy waved her hands about. 'There's no limit! Clothes, furniture, jewellery, objets d'art . . . The whole damn' lot. Under the Romily de Lisle name.'

She felt a spark of excitement. 'Do you really think I could?'

'Of course. And you've got a place in the city, haven't you?'

Romily nodded. The palatial de Lisle apartment on Fifth Avenue was only used for a couple of weeks a year.

'Well then.' Muffy looked satisfied. 'I think you should come over as soon as you can, and see what you think. I'd just love you to meet all my girlfriends back home.'

Why not? What's keeping me here? I'm tired of Paris, Allegra and Imogen are about to do their exams so I can't visit them. I may as well see what New York has to offer.

Romily smiled at Muffy over the crisp white linen. 'You know, Muffy, I think you've just had a brainwave.'

Chapter 19

New York
2003

Mitch was in the office after service, looking at the orders for the rest of the week and adding a little extra here and there.

He'd been promoted to deputy head chef of the Greywell, which was nice, but it didn't exactly pay him much more and he was expected to do a hell of a lot more work for the paltry increase. But Patrice had got used to landing him with nearly all the paperwork which meant he had the chance to make a little extra on the side by ordering surplus ingredients – another crate of veal or a case of wine on top of his usual order – and selling it on. He'd seen it done in other places he'd worked and it was easy enough when he was in charge of the order sheet and the budgeting. All he had to do was sign off the supplies and whatever he wanted appeared at dawn the next morning in the tradesmen's vans.

The extra money he made selling it on went on his rent, his whisky, and, of course, his supply of heroin. He and Herbie had moved to a slightly bigger apartment, where the walls were a little thicker, but it was still bare and basic, furnished with odds and ends they found in skips and thrift stores. He didn't care much how the place looked: he was only alive when he was cooking or smoking his shit.

Herbie put his head round the door and said, 'Hey, Mitch. Boss wants to see you.'

'You mean Chef?' Mitch looked round for Patrice but he was nowhere in sight. Herbie shook his head.

'Nope. The boss. Mr Panciello. He's out front with Chef.' Herbie disappeared out of the kitchen.

Mitch wiped his hands on his apron. He had very rarely seen Mr Panciello up close. He knew that the owner often came in – a table was reserved for him every night and Mitch had seen him over in the shadows, with business associates or his wife and children, eating one of the special dishes he requested. It was a French brasserie but Mr Panciello liked Italian dishes and particularly pasta, so there was always some fresh linguine or new-made ravioli especially for him. Patrice often had meetings with Mr Panciello, to discuss menus, costs, staff and customers, and all the other minutiae of running a restaurant, and their relationship seemed cordial enough. Nevertheless, Mitch felt nervous. Why would Mr Panciello want to see him?

He made his way through the kitchen and out into the dining room. It had the curiously dead look it always had when there were no customers. There wasn't a place in the world so achingly in need of people as an empty restaurant, Mitch always thought. The room seemed echoing and forlorn without them. In the far corner, Mr Panciello was sitting at his special table. Patrice was sitting opposite him, his chef's hat laid respectfully in his lap. The two men were murmuring quietly to each other. Mr Panciello's gaze flicked up and registered Mitch's approach, and he said something to Patrice, who got up at once and turned on his heel to leave. He passed Mitch without meeting his eye or speaking, and hurried out to the kitchen.

What the fuck is this? he wondered, frowning. A small trail of nervousness crawled through his belly.

'Mitch?' Mr Panciello smiled at him. He had an unexpectedly smooth, deep voice. 'Come sit down.'

Mitch approached and took Patrice's empty seat. Mr Panciello was dressed in a dark, well-cut suit, with a scarlet-and-blue striped tie that looked as though it might be in the colours of some smart university or country club. His dark hair had receded, leaving a smooth pink dome to his head, and what was left was streaked with grey.

'How are you?' Mr Panciello asked, giving Mitch a warm look. He was tanned and his eyelids dropped down at the edges, lost in creases and wrinkles so that he looked like a tired but friendly old hound.

'Fine, thank you, sir,' Mitch said cautiously. He felt his knees begin to jiggle beneath the table. Out of the kitchen, he was suddenly seized by a violent desire for a smoke. It made him feel almost breathless and panicky, how much he wanted it.

'Good, good.' Mr Panciello clasped his hands together on the white linen table cloth and leaned towards Mitch. 'So, how long you been here now?' His accent was solid New York.

'Ah, about a year, sir.'

'You like it?'

'Uh-huh. It's good to work in a place with a reputation like this one. The last places I worked in all went bust. Couldn't get the customers in.' Mitch grinned. 'But your restaurant, sir, isn't like them. You got good people. Good food. A solid menu.'

'Glad you approve.' A small smile twitched about the other man's lips. 'You're right, you aren't going to see this place closing. That can't happen. Tell me a bit about yourself, Mitch. Where you from?'

'Small town in the West. Nowhere special. You know the kind of place – a thousand inhabitants, a school, a church and a diner, a row of shops you can put your arms round.'

'And you wanted to get out, did you? Wanted to come to the big city.'

Mitch nodded. 'Nothing to keep me there, sir. My parents and I don't get along. They weren't keen on me being a cook. They wanted me to go into the church – they're crazy keen church goers, sir – maybe become a priest. But that life wasn't for me, only they couldn't see it. I got myself a Saturday job at the local diner, started flipping burgers and found out I liked it, and was good at it. I got myself interested in cooking and started reading about it, getting books out of the school library. When I left school, I knew college wasn't for me. So I moved to the next biggest town and got myself a job at a bigger restaurant and off I went, moving along to something bigger each time until I got myself here.'

Mr Panciello nodded and seemed to be thinking hard. 'Well, that's an interesting story, Mitch. It makes a lot of sense to me, and I admire your determination and your drive. You're gonna make something of yourself, I'm sure of that. But, you see, there's a problem.'

The nervousness, which had been settling down, flared back into life in Mitch's belly. 'What's that, sir? You unhappy with my work?'

'Not with your cooking. I know what you can do. Patrice has told me how much you've improved lately. Your steaks are making this place famous. I value that. But there is something going on that I will not tolerate. I *cannot* tolerate.' Mr Panciello fixed him with a stern gaze, his previously warm brown eyes turning flinty. 'You know what I'm talking about, Mitch?'

He stared back. 'No, sir,' he said slowly, trying to sound honest.

'Hmmm.' Mr Panciello leant back in his chair and stared

up at the ceiling. 'OK. Let me tell you something you might not be aware of, young man. There are bad people in the world – very bad people. People who'd do anything to make money. Some of those people are just low-down criminals. Scum. The kind who mug old ladies and steal their purses for a couple of dollars. I don't have any time for those people and I'm sure you don't either. But there are other people who take a more sophisticated approach to breaking the law. You may have noticed that the restaurant world is full of these people.'

Mitch blinked at him, unsure if he was supposed to reply or not.

'For some reason, this business attracts criminals. Perhaps lawbreakers like a good party, because they sure seem to get themselves deep into anything to do with people having fun: restaurants, films, bars, clubs . . . you name it, they're swarming round it. Now, anytime your average joe opens a restaurant, he'll find that before too long he'll have some unexpected visitors.

'Some very polite guys will turn up and kindly explain to him that they control things in his area, and shed some light on how things are. First, they'll be supplying protection to his outfit, and he'll need to pay a little something for that. If he protests that he doesn't need protection, they'll make him see very clearly that he does. They'll also explain that one of their aunties, a very sweet old lady, runs an excellent laundry service and they'd greatly appreciate if Joe could send all his table linen and napkins there, for a very good rate, a rate for friends, understand? And one of their brothers has a fish business, and whaddya know, he sells the best fish in the city, for the best prices! So it will make sense for everyone if Joe uses this guy for all his fish. Why not? Let's keep our business between friends, huh?

'And so it goes on. Your meat, your vegetables, your salads, even the fucking floor cleaner. Someone has a cousin or a sister's husband or someone else who supplies this shit, and it's in Joe's best interests to buy it. Fuck, it's in everyone's interests!' Mr Panciello barked out a short, mirthless laugh. 'Do you see what I'm saying, Mitch?'

He nodded slowly.

'Now, this is the important part.' The restaurant owner leant in towards him again, clasping his hands and fixing him with an earnest stare. 'You ever seen any of those guys round here?'

Mitch shook his head. Actually, now he came to think of it, that was unusual. In previous restaurants he'd worked in, there had been unshakable relationships such as his boss had just described: suppliers who were never fired despite their poor produce, for example. And he distinctly remembered visits from heavies in suits that were almost comically Mafioso in style, with pinstripes and padded shoulders. What did it matter to a lowly commis-chef who spent all day peeling shallots, blanching tomatoes and chopping parsley? But all that was notable for its absence in this brasserie.

'Ever wonder why that was, Mitch?' Panciello said in a low voice.

He caught the hint of menace and felt cold. He shook his head again, still not daring to speak.

'Well, maybe you should have, my friend. Maybe you should have.' Panciello made an almost imperceptible gesture with his head and suddenly two burly men, one in dark glasses, the other with a face thick with stubble, appeared as if materialising from the shadows. 'It's come to my attention that you are stealing from me. Please don't insult us both by denying it. It's bad enough that you attempted to pretend otherwise earlier, but I'm prepared to overlook that for the moment. The fact is, you are the deputy head chef here. That's a position of trust. Am I right?'

'Yes, sir,' Mitch said, trying to control his breathing. He could feel his heart beginning to race. He was sure that things were about to turn very bad indeed. Panciello knew everything . . . and who were these thugs who'd just appeared from nowhere?

'You are abusing that trust,' continued Panciello. 'You are over-ordering supplies and making money for yourself by selling on, sometimes to rival establishments. I don't need to tell you what kind of a view I take of that. Now – are you wondering how I know about this?'

Mitch could feel beads of sweat breaking out across his nose and forehead. He nodded, not trusting himself to speak for a moment.

'The rival establishments have told me. They've told me because they are under contract to use suppliers designated only by me and my business associates.' Panciello smiled. 'Yes, I'm afraid *I* am that somewhat persistent visitor who insists on his friends making use of his services. And that is why my own establishment is remarkably free from those very gentlemen. In short, I am in charge of all the money making in this entire district.

'Now you will probably be feeling the soft warm trail of shit as it drips down your leg while you realise the extent of your error. You have made the mistake of fucking over the man who excels in fucking over, who specialises in it. Who *owns* fucking over.' Panciello's eyes, hard as two pebbles, glinted with something like amusement. 'I feel kinda sorry for you, kid. But you must see that there have to be consequences to your actions. Punishment. Ever heard of the French Foreign Legion?'

Mitch shook his head, confused by the sudden change of direction. 'No . . . no, sir.'

'They are one hard-assed outfit. They train the best, the toughest, soldiers in the world. You know what they used to do to deserters? It was so bad that when men were caught after deserting, they'd beg to have a bullet through their heads because it was preferable to what they'd have to go through. And they all had to go through it, in front of their comrades – it was the only way of showing the others what would happen if they tried the same trick. It made sure that anarchy was kept in check. Think about it. What if every soldier decided to mutiny, to rise up and destroy the few men who were ordering them about? They'd be an unstoppable force, they'd slaughter everything in their path, all control would be lost. The guys in charge cannot allow that to happen, can they? If one little piece of scum is allowed to get away with it, it would start a rush. So you'll see, I'm sure, why I cannot allow you to get away with stealing from me.'

Panciello spread his hands, as though seeking Mitch's sympathy. 'It could ruin my entire operation. One little fucking chef from Nowheresville fleeces Panciello's operation and suffers no consequences?' He shook his head. 'Nuh-uh. Can't happen. In a moment, I'm going to ask my pals here to take you outside and explain to you the extent of your mistake, but before that I have a word of advice for you, because I like you, Mitch. You won't believe me, but I really do, and it saddens me that you're not going to be around here any more.'

Panciello stared at him for a moment, raking his face with his hard gaze. 'Get off that shit you're smoking. Make something of yourself. Fuck making shitty little dollars on a crate of fucking lemons. Think big. Be someone. Understand? Be an owner. That's the only way not to get fucked. Stamp on everyone else before they stamp on you. Because the truth is, everyone's out to screw everyone else. Have I made myself clear, kid?'

Mitch nodded, feeling icy cold. *Are they gonna kill me? For the sake of some fucking food? Oh, man . . . Oh, man, I need a smoke like I've never fucking needed it before . . .*

Panciello stood up and offered his hand to Mitch, who took it, and they shook hands solemnly. 'Good luck, young man.'

Mitch watched him as the older man buttoned his suit jacket, gave a small nod to the burly men who stood silently on each side of Mitch's chair, and made to leave.

'Please, Mr Panciello . . .' His voice came out high and with a trembling edge, although he tried to conceal his fear. 'I apologise, most sincerely, I . . .'

The other man didn't turn round. 'Goodbye, Mitch. Take it like a man, huh?' And he was gone.

Mitch felt his stomach turn to water as two big meaty fists landed on him, one on each shoulder. *Ah, fuck!* he thought, as the nausea of fear swamped him. *Shit, man! What the fuck are they going to do to me?*

Chapter 20

Oxford 2003

The problem with having fun, Allegra decided, *is that it wears itself out.*

The thing that was the most enjoyable you could possibly imagine one day grew wearisome the next and needed something extra to enliven it. She could quite see how the rich needed more and more extravagance to tickle their jaded palates. If caviar and champagne became commonplace and mundane, then how about making fountains flow with the champagne and having the caviar served on solid gold platters mounted on the backs of baby elephants?

And if taking drugs and getting drunk or high meant that a party was more enjoyable, then how could a party be fun without those things? And surely, by extension, the more drink and drugs there were on offer, the more fun the party would be.

That's the trap, Allegra thought. *That's why it's so easy to fall into it, and once you're in, it's harder and harder to get out . . .*

She sensed it in herself. Ever since what had happened to her in Paris, she'd been possessed by a kind of nihilistic spirit that told her not to care about anything. She didn't know why exactly – it wasn't as though anything really bad had happened to her. She hadn't been beaten or badly hurt.

There was no way she could explain why it had somehow poisoned her, but it had. Deep inside her was a sense of shame about what had taken place: shame that she had let it happen, and shame that she had allowed that disgusting man to make her experience those feelings. It revolted her.

She never had an orgasm when she was conscious, but sometimes, in her sleep, she would be back in that apartment in Paris, with the awful man pushing his tongue into her and endlessly licking and licking until she would shudder, and wake up, feeling she had climaxed. When that happened, she sickened herself. It seemed that any pleasure she got from sex was bound up with the man she hated, and no matter how many others she slept with, they couldn't wipe his imprint from her.

So she'd found a kind of release from that shame by giving herself whatever she wanted, and seeking a numbness in sex and substances that would help her forget.

I want to party, she told herself. *What's wrong with that? I'm young, I'm free and I can do whatever I want. And look at Xander, he's having a fabulous time.*

Her brother always seemed to be having a ball. Every day, from the moment he woke up in the afternoon, he began again. He was at the heart of a circle of privileged young men who lived for the pleasures of the flesh and threw their plentiful money around. They treated five-star restaurants like cafés; they began to drink the finest vintages – often from their families' estates and vineyards – as soon as they got up. They were surrounded by fawners and hangers-on, keen to share in the spoils of wealth, and these people supplied their every want, whether it was drugs or willing girls or boys for sex. Debauchery was funny as far as they were concerned, and the pursuit of pleasure gave meaning to their lives. After all, these golden university days would be over before too long and then they'd have to clean themselves up, find something to do with themselves, and become responsible adults . . . wouldn't they? But all that was safely in the future. Until then, they were young, good-looking, rich and eager for a good time.

Xander didn't always want Allegra around him, though. Sometimes, when things at the house in St Margaret's Road were getting out of hand, he would tell her to go back to college. Usually so laidback and relaxed, he could get quite agitated if he thought she was witnessing something he didn't want her to see.

'Come on, Xander, I'm not a baby,' she complained, when he hustled her out of the house the night some of the boys ordered in two prostitutes and got them to start putting on a show. 'Other girls are staying, why can't I?'

'You're my baby sister, that's why. Now, I've ordered you a taxi – look, it's waiting outside. Go home and go to bed, OK?'

It frustrated Allegra, though she obeyed him. Why was it all right for him and not for her? He'd been cross when she'd emerged one morning from the bedroom of Dominic, one his housemates, and he'd bawled her out when he'd found her sniffing up a line of cocaine from a wrap Dominic had given her.

'Why can't I?' she'd yelled back. 'You take it by the bloody barrelful! You've put half of Columbia's crop up your nose, and so have James and Dominic and everyone here. Temple's out of her head half the time. What's so wrong with me having a line?'

Xander had snatched the wrap out of her hands and thrown it in the waste disposal, then said quietly, 'I don't know. It just is. I want you to be careful, OK? That's all. I don't want you to turn out a waster like me. You're only nineteen.'

'You're only twenty!' she flashed back.

Xander had sighed. 'I feel like I'm fucking forty-five. I need a break from all this.' And she'd noticed then how grey and unhappy he looked. But the same night, he and the gang went out to a pub in the countryside and trashed it almost beyond repair. Only some smooth talking and an enormous cheque for the landlord had got them out of serious trouble.

Xander couldn't seem to stop his party lifestyle. He spent the vacations at the homes of his rich friends and the terms were melting away in a series of parties and serious hangovers.

One day she had met him by chance in the Broad, and they'd bought a bottle of champagne even though it was only eleven o'clock and gone to the Parks to drink it. Xander had lain on his back with his eyes closed and told her how tired he was and how hopeless it all seemed.'But you look happy from the outside,' Allegra said, picking a blade of grass and slowly slicing it to ribbons with her fingernails.

'Do I?' He looked at her through one bloodshot eye. 'That's funny. So do you.'

She thought about this. 'I am . . . I mean, when I'm drunk and the music's playing and I feel young and excited and like anything's possible . . . then I'm happy.'

'You mean, when you've escaped from the bloodiness of daily life. When you've got enough chemicals to help you feel as though you're happy.'

'But why,' she said tentatively, 'is daily life so bloody for us? Why can't we be happy?'

Xander said nothing but, after a while, he sighed heavily.

'Do you think it's because of Dad?' she asked.

'I don't doubt it,' he replied. He looked at her, his eyes sad. 'We're just like him.'

'What?' Allegra was horrified. 'How can you say that? He's an awful, violent bully. We're nothing like him.'

'We might not beat people up or throw them downstairs, but we've got his strange personality, with its streak of black melancholy, running through us, haven't we? And we spent our childhoods living in fear of him. You know, last holidays, I tried to reach out to him. I wanted to see if he really cared as little as he's always seemed to. When I was leaving Foughton, I put my hand on his arm and said, "I love you, Dad. I mean it." And he stared me in the eye with the cold look of his and said, "Then you're a bloody fool."'

'That's awful.' Allegra felt shaky and tearful as she imagined it. She could hear her father's voice spitting out the words. 'It's an act. It must be. He can't mean it.'

'I'm not so sure. Look at his track record – three marriages, five kids, feuds with all his relatives. If he was any good at love, we'd know by now. No, he's fucked, and he's fucked us up too.'

'Has he? How?'

Xander shrugged. 'We're addicted to unhealthy relationships. I know Temple's no good for me but I can't break free from her. I always love what's bad for me, in just about every sphere.' He grinned at Allegra, lightening the mood. 'And you're working your way through the entire male student body by the looks of it.'

'Mmm. Well . . . not *all* of them.' Allegra grinned as well, running her fingertips through the cool grass. 'These damn' vacations keep getting in the way. Everyone goes home.'

He rolled over and looked at her. 'You are being careful, aren't you? I don't want you to get hurt.'

'Of course I am. If anyone's doing the hurting, it's me. I'm very cruel,' she said lightly, thinking, *It's too late for that. It's already happened.*

'So this is the English Faculty,' Allegra said, looking about in mock surprise. 'It was my ambition to avoid this place for the whole three years, but it looks like I'll have to surrender to it.'

Imogen smiled. 'This is the café. You'll need to work up to actually going into the library.'

'One step at a time, Midge, one step at a time.'

'Well . . . Mods are only three weeks away now.'

'Yes, but it's a bloody crime to be inside. Look at that weather!' Allegra nodded to the beautiful bright day outside. 'Revision weather,' she said gloomily. 'You can bet that when we've finished those bloody exams, it'll start raining. Now, how are you? How's Sam?'

'Fine. Yeah, he's good.'

Allegra ignored the No Smoking sign and lit up a cigarette. She held out the packet to Imogen. 'Want one?'

'No, thanks.'

'Have you given up?'

'Well, Sam doesn't, so . . .'

'Of course he doesn't.' Allegra puffed out some smoke and dropped the match on the table. 'Listen, we haven't been seeing much of each other lately.'

'I see you just about every day,' Imogen protested.

'Socially, I mean. Yeah, we meet up here or in the Radcliffe Camera or wherever, but we're not partying together like we used to.' Allegra fixed her with a direct gaze. 'So . . . why not?'

Imogen looked uncomfortable. 'Well, I suppose it's because of Sam. He's not a party animal really . . .'

'I noticed, love.'

'And your friends are all so rich and glamorous. He doesn't really get on with that scene.'

'You used to love it, though. You loved hanging out with me, and going to Xander's house, dropping into the Grid and all that . . .'

'Yes, I suppose I did.' Imogen thought for a minute and

then said, 'How is Xander, by the way? I haven't seen him for ages.'

'Actually, he's not that great.' Allegra tapped some ash on to the floor and then frowned. 'He's broken up with that silly bitch Temple.'

'Really?' Imogen looked interested. 'When?'

'Oh, a couple of weeks ago. She dumped him.'

Astonishment passed over Imogen's face. 'But *why*?'

'For someone better . . . at least, in Temple's book. She's going out with some baronet's son now, someone who'll actually inherit something rather than see his older brother move into the family house.' Allegra shook her head sadly. 'Some people are like that. He's far more cut up about it than I expected and he's necking even more drugs than usual. Those friends of his . . . it's terrible. They can all afford anything they like, and all they like is to get totally wasted. Last week, they went out to James Barclay's farm – you know his dad bought him a kind of small estate? – and all got out of their minds on coke, acid and speed.'

'Is Xander OK?'

'Yeah. But I'm worried about him. He needs someone to calm him down, and he won't listen to me. So I thought that – well, maybe *you* could have a word with him.'

'Me?' Imogen looked bewildered. 'Why on earth would he listen to me?'

'He's not going to pay any attention to me but he always thinks of you as that sweet, innocent girl from his childhood. So maybe he'll listen to you . . .'

'I'm not sure.' Imogen frowned. 'Even if I wanted to, how would I get to speak to him?'

'There's this big party coming up. The Piers Gaveston. Have you heard of it?'

Imogen shook her head.

'It's organised by the society crowd and it can get

somewhat debauched, so the venue is kept deadly secret until the last minute to prevent it being stopped by the authorities. The boys all go in drag and the girls go as wild as they like, and it gets kind of crazy. The thing is, you have to be invited so you know where to go. Xander is going to be there and I think he might let rip, get off his head and do something stupid. If we go, we might be able to keep an eye on him.'

'Or . . . I could just go round to his place, or meet him for a drink somewhere?'

'No, he'd never fall for that. He'd know I'd put you up to it. You've got to make it happen naturally.'

'OK. I don't think it sounds like Sam's sort of party, though . . .'

'Really?' Allegra tried to look innocent, but in fact her plan had been to separate Imogen from Sam anyway. She found it frustrating never to have Imogen to herself any more and couldn't relax with Sam around – his disapproval of her was too obvious and made her uncomfortable. What was worse, he was making Midge boring. They spent all their time together like an old married couple and it was beyond tedious. 'Oh, well . . . you'd better come without him, then. He won't mind, will he?'

'I suppose not.'

'Good. I'll get you an invitation then.'

'When is it?'

'It's Monday of Eighth Week.'

Imogen's expression changed and she looked horrified. 'But that's virtually the night before Mods begin! The first exam is on Wednesday morning.'

'I know. It's a bit of a pain, but you'll have all of Tuesday to recover.'

'Aren't you worried about going out to a party like that just before exams?'

Allegra shook her head. 'Nope. I'll just do my revision the week before. Besides, they say last-minute revising is pointless anyway.'

'Not in my experience.'

'Come on, Midge! You don't have to drink if you don't want to.'

'But it'll be an all nighter . . .'

'Are you a man or a mouse? Did we come to Oxford to have fun or not?' Allegra leaned forward and fixed her friend with a long stare. 'Please, Midge. It's really important to me – and to Xander. Will you do it?'

She could see that Imogen was torn. On the one hand, her common sense was evidently telling her not to be so stupid as to go to a party like the Piers Gaveston just before her vital exams. But on the other – an event like that was not to be missed. It was tempting.

'Please?' wheedled Allegra, sensing weakness in her friend. 'It's not just a favour to me. It's for Xander as well. I know you've got a soft spot for him . . .'

Imogen flushed and said quickly, 'No, I haven't! Except as a friend!'

'That's what I mean. He's like your big brother as well, isn't he?'

'Yes . . . that's right, he's like a brother . . .'

'Come on, Midge, you've already done tons of revision, you've really got nothing to worry about. Look at me, I've done virtually nothing.'

'Then perhaps we should both stay at home.'

Allegra sighed. 'OK, I see. Honestly, Imogen, I'm beginning to wonder about you.'

'What?' asked Imogen, with a hurt expression. 'Why?'

'I don't know if our friendship means anything to you any more . . .'

'Of course it does!'

'If you really mean it, then you'll come to the Piers Gaveston with me.'

Imogen bit her lip, obviously wrestling with her conscience.

'Well, there's my answer,' Allegra said caustically. 'So much for our eternal friendship.'

'All right then. All right, I'll come. But only to keep you company and talk to Xander, if he'll listen. I'm not going to drink anything or stay out late.'

'Great!' Allegra smiled broadly. 'That's settled then. Now all we need is to decide what we're going to wear.'

Chapter 21

New York
2003

Muffy had the most adorable jewel box of an apartment on the Upper West side that was now full of pretty young American girls, fluttering about like bright butterflies in their silk tea dresses and satin high heels. Romily was guest of honour, Muffy's glamorous European friend with the famous name and the vast fortune.

Some of the girls she already knew from skiing trips in Gstaad, Megève and Verbier: she kissed Carolyn Makeheart who was married to a press baron's son, and Annie Schaupman, whose father had made a fortune in Duty Free shops. The others were part of Muffy's circle, and she'd invited them because she was sure they'd all be fascinated by Romily's new venture.

The minute she'd arrived in New York, she'd felt enlivened and interested in life again. Perhaps it was the bustling crowds, the traffic, the way the place was always open for business, always buzzing. Perhaps it was that American girls seemed to have so much energy, and so much to do. Romily knew for a fact that Muffy got up at seven a.m. every morning to begin her regime: first, a swim in the pool followed by an hour's Pilates. Every other day she ran in Central Park and had an hour's yoga. Then it was time for the serious stuff of life – her masseur or facialist or manicurist would arrive for treatments, and last of all her hairdresser came to her to tend her locks. Then, at last, it would be time for breakfast – an omelette and some supplements, along with herbal tea and a wheatgrass concoction. Then Muffy was ready to begin her day.

While the dedication this required was impressive, it seemed like a lot of hard work to Romily, who preferred to feel a little more pampered. She was awakened at nine a.m. by her maid with a tray containing a tiny but delicious breakfast: a boiled egg and some warm brioche with strawberry conserve was a favourite; or rye toast with Marmite, a substance she had learnt to love at Westfield but that seemed to revolt everyone but the British. Then, while she breakfasted, she read several papers: *The Times*, *Le Monde* and the *New York Post*, checked her emails, read her letters, did some correspondence, made telephone calls and flicked through her diary, trying to keep on top of her busy life. There were always more invitations to accept or decline, more travel arrangements to make, endless appointments and shopping trips to fulfil.

She was lucky if she was out of bed by lunchtime, but felt as though she'd put in a morning at the office before she'd even got up. Then it was time for her constitutional: she preferred to get her exercise in a less prescribed way than Muffy, and liked to wander through the park or go skating rather than visit a gym or an exercise class. She was lucky – she never seemed to put on weight.

Perhaps that's because I avoid confections like these, she thought, regarding the pretty cake-stand piled high with cupcakes that Muffy had ordered in from a local bakery that was the social favourite of the moment. The cakes were smothered by huge pastel swirls of buttercream icing and topped with little jelly diamonds. *Why do American and*

British girls eat between meals? It's something I don't understand at all. The other girls were eyeing them greedily and denouncing Muffy for bringing such temptation into their orbits, when carbs and sugar were strictly forbidden, but nibbling away at them all the same.

When everyone was supplied with herbal tea or sparkling water, Muffy clapped her hands for quiet.

'Now, girls, I've asked you all here because I want to tell you about Romily's new idea. As you know, she's the granddaughter of Vincent de Lisle and she's inherited his artistic eye. As you can see by the gorgeous Chanel dress she has so cleverly teamed with those Prada sandals, Romily has impeccable style. And she's decided to open a boutique, right here in New York, bringing us all an exclusive taste of her Parisian chic. Isn't that wonderful?'

There was a general chorus of approval. Everyone knew how hard it was for well-brought up girls to find a suitable occupation. The cleverest and most ambitious ones went into law, finance or politics, but they were rarely seen because of their strenuous working hours. Others headed for the media world – high-class fashion magazines were an excellent choice: well-paid and giving the inside track to the latest designers, beauty products and best surgeons in town. More artistic society girls became painters, sculptors or interior designers. Others opened galleries or got jobs in the big, glamorous auction houses. And a few started their own clothing lines, which was considered respectable. A boutique would be perfect: someone else would do the hard work of designing and making the clothes. One could simply concentrate on the fun of stocking the shop and then having one's girlfriends come in and try everything on.

'Oh, how perfect,' sighed Annie Schaupman. She looked enviously at Romily's dress. 'I'd love to steal your style.'

'I'm flattered you're all so keen,' she said, delighted that her venture was being so warmly welcomed.

'It would be so cute!' cried Stella Al Rijan, a beautiful dark-skinned half-Egyptian girl who had recently started a jewellery designing business. 'Imagine what fun you'll have – *everyone* will come. Muffy will see to that. Perhaps you could stock my new topaz line.'

'Wonderful idea,' cried Muffy. 'I want you girls to be Romily's source of inspiration for the things we'd all like to buy.'

Everyone was hugely enthusiastic and a lively conversation ensued in which the boutique grew from a simple clothes shop to a vast emporium selling everything anyone could think of.

'Wait, wait!' cried Romily, laughing. 'I'll need a shop the size of Bloomingdales at this rate. We'll have to be more focused, that's all.'

'We'll all help,' declared Muffy. 'I'd just love to play shop! You'll do it, Romily, won't you? Say you will!'

'You know what? I think I will.'

At last there was something to occupy her time. Romily and Muffy went looking for suitable premises for their shop and found a place they both adored on a slightly ramshackle street on the Lower East Side. It was on one of the more run-down streets and most of the shops around them sold second-hand clothes, vintage trinkets, or cut-price electricals and junk, but the area was on the up. Not quite as trendy as the East Village but on its way.

'I love this!' cooed Muffy. 'It's so funky, isn't it?'

'It's cool,' agreed Romily, looking about. Across the street was a place selling artists' materials. 'I love the vibe. Is this the place?'

They looked at each other.

'Go for it,' said Muffy.

'I will.'

It didn't take much to persuade Charles de Lisle to allow Romily to invest in her shop; perhaps it was because her mother had reported their conversation about boredom, and her parents felt that some money invested in a boutique in New York was preferable to her hotfooting it off to the world's trouble spots to start clearing mines, or whatever it was she had in mind.

The family's attorneys organised all the boring paperwork. Romily went to their New York office, explained to them what she wanted and asked when her shop would be ready for her. A week later, she was taking a designer round the rundown old space and they were sharing their vision of what it should be like.

'Oh my Gaaahd, how fabulous!' cried Stefan, as they went round the shop together. It was a very basic layout – one large room at the front, a stock room, small kitchen and washroom at the back. Everything was grimy and shabby. 'I can see it now. We'll make it fresh and clean, with lots of light, lots of fantastic steel, chrome and concrete.'

'I like white,' Romily said. 'And mirrors.' She'd had lots of ideas for how she wanted it and had spent many happy hours flicking through design magazines and browsing in expensive shops, looking at fittings and colour schemes. 'I'm thinking of a minimalist/Baroque hybrid.'

'We can work that, we can *definitely* work that.' He made some quick sketches on the notebook he carried. 'Rails *here*. Display *here*. Fitting room *here*.'

Romily nodded. 'Oh, yes, that's exactly how it should be.' It all looked perfect so far. Stefan was obviously exactly right for the job – he shared her vision. 'How fast can we do it?'

He frowned and thought for a while. 'Well, there are first designs to be drawn up, consultation, costing, fitting . . . I guess we could be ready to go in six months, if we really hurry.'

'Six months! That's far too long. I want it done in three. Max.'

Stefan looked doubtful.

'Money no object,' Romily added.

The designer's face cleared. 'I'll see what I can do.'

Cherub opened three months later almost to the day, looking a little different from Stephan's original concept once Romily, Muffy and the others had all had their say. It was now a mix of modernist industrial, with a polished concrete floor and exposed pipework, plus more girly pink and gold touches. And now that it was called Cherub, the angelic motif had been worked into the shop wherever possible, from the golden angels flying across the walls to the hooks in the dressing rooms that were cute little pairs of wings.

Opening night was a glamorous affair, with all of New York's finest young socialites making an appearance, looking polished and glossy and altogether unlike anything seen in a rather down-at-heel street on the less salubrious side of the East Village.

Romily turned out for the evening in a wonderful Dior gown, in keeping with her angel theme: a long white flowing goddess dress that showed off her gleaming olive skin, graceful arms and silver sandals. Her brown hair was pulled back into a loose bun, clasped with a fabulous piece of wrought gold, an actual Roman antique, and she had gone for New York style nude simplicity in her make-up. The rest of the girls were dressed like Gwyneth Paltrow, who was their idol, with straight blonde hair and the crisp cool colours of Ralph Lauren and Donna Karan.

'Oh my God,' breathed Muffy, who was wearing a

Michael Kors maxi-dress with a scarf halter-neck, 'it's all so beautiful.'

It was. Romily had taken elements of everything she admired from her favourite Paris boutiques and put it all into one place. The effect, she decided, was unusual and very creative. Velvet pouffes in harlequin colours sat on the polished concrete. Plaster angels with trumpets and harps hung over unusual modern ceramics: vases bursting with fists, or plates with china thorns all over them. A collection of vintage lamps – something Romily had a particular passion for – stood on a shelf over a row of dresses, scraps of bright chiffon and silk from a designer friend of Annie's. On another modern chair was a pile of sweaters in cobweb-fine cashmere in a variety of styles and colours. Stella Al Rijan's jewellery was displayed in original butterfly-display cases that were once in the Natural History Museum in London. A row of hats sat on fairground clown heads, the kind with an open mouth for balls to be tossed inside.

The crowd wandered about, sipping their champagne and 'oooh'-ing over all the lovely things in the shop. Society reporters and photographers snapped the beautiful crowd and asked them for their thoughts on the new de Lisle incarnation.

Romily was delighted. She had loved the whole process of pulling the shop together. She'd never been so absorbed and happy. 'Now I understand why people work,' she said to Muffy. 'This is fun!' She had loved sitting down with Stefan to look over his designs and then going with him to warehouses and trade outlets, to look at fittings and swatches and tiling effects and all the other things she had to choose. She could understand now how her upbringing had affected her and influenced her taste and style: she had gravitated towards the most expensive of everything as though by instinct. Even the staff washroom was tiled in the most costly Milanese mosaic marble and featured a designer toilet that self-flushed.

When it came to stocking the shop, Romily had decided that several heads were better than one. Although she was able to stock one or two of her favourite young designers, she was not going to be able to sell her cherished haute-couture labels. The licensing arrangements did not permit it. That didn't matter – she would make a virtue of it and break new names. So she formed the Cherub Committee, on which all her friends had a place if they wanted, and took their advice as to what she should sell in the shop. After all, if her stylish, rich New York girlfriends liked it and wanted to buy it, it would surely fly off the shelves, like the little angels flitting above them.

'Do you like it, Mama?' Romily went over to where her mother, immaculate as usual in a Givenchy black and white suit and daintily heeled white pumps, was chatting to Muffy's mother.

'Darling, it's wonderful,' she said, kissing Romily on each cheek. 'You're so clever! I'm so proud of you.'

'Do you like what I'm selling?'

'Oh, yes!' cried her mother, looking about. 'It's all beautiful. But . . . what exactly are you selling? Are those sweaters for sale?'

'Yes. I think it's rather new and different to display them on a chair like that. That way, you can imagine them stacked on a chair in your bedroom.'

'I see now – yes, that's very clever. And is the chair for sale?'

'Of course. Just about everything's for sale! It's a kind of . . .' Romily frowned, looking for the right word. 'A kind of *lifestyle* shop. The things in here are all about taste and individuality.'

'Of course, of course.' Athina de Lisle nodded. 'There is

just one thing, my darling. The area is rather . . . well, rather *déclassé,* is it not?'

Romily rolled her eyes. 'Mama! You really don't know anything. This is a very chic part of town! Just a few blocks over there are new hotels opening, old buildings being developed into fabulous apartments. I promise you, this place is at the forefront of where everyone will be in just a few months.'

Her mother smiled. 'If you say so, my darling. But, I must admit, I shan't be sorry to get back to Fifth Avenue. I love your little pet project, though, it's adorable. And I think I must buy one of those sweet enamel brooches you have displayed so prettily in the goldfish bowl. They could almost be Chanel . . .'

The stylish, good-looking crowd spilled out on to the pavement where local residents and other shop owners eyed them suspiciously. Across the road, some young black kids gathered to observe the proceedings, in their street uniform of baggy jeans, baggier T-shirts, back-to-front baseball caps and trainers. Adults sat on the low walls or in stairwells, watching the chattering socialites with mild curiosity and casual disdain.

As night fell and cars began to draw up to collect their owners and convey them to the next party or launch or smart restaurant, the watchers began to whoop and whistle and call out comments.

Romily felt her first tingle of nervousness about the location. It was true that during the day, as she'd been putting out her stock, she had started to wonder who exactly was going to pop in and buy an $800 sweater or a vintage French chrome lamp for $550, let alone the dresses that started at $1,000. They were only a few streets away from the more sophisticated area north of Delaney Street, a few blocks from Orchard Street and its upmarket restaurants and boutiques.

Even if no one else comes, she told herself, *all my girlfriends will. They'll spread the word. I'm going to help this area come up in the world. Once Annie and Stella and everyone get to work, there'll be more than enough customers.*

She circulated again, quietly giving orders for glasses of champagne to be topped up, trays of canapés to be replenished, and stock to be tidied after guests had rifled through it. A couple of girls had even bought something: they'd sold a huge scented candle with six wicks that smelled of tuberose, and a silver wine bucket. Romily felt a surge of pride as she rang up her first sale.

It was after midnight when the last guests left and she could shut up the shop. She sighed happily as she looked around it, as proud as a mother of her new baby.

'Come on, Muffy!' she called out. 'My car will be here in a moment. Have you finished in the back?'

There was a muffled exclamation and then Muffy came rushing in, her face white and scared. 'Romily! Something awful is going on in the alley. Come and look!'

The girls hurried through to the back room where a barred window looked out over the side alley. Muffy had switched off the light so it was possible to see out clearly into the space outside, half illuminated by a streetlamp. Something violent was happening there: two huge dark shapes were scuffling round a smaller white one, thumping, punching and kicking.

'Oh my God!' whispered Romily, staring out in horror. 'Someone's being beaten up!'

'What shall we do?' squeaked Muffy, hiding her eyes behind her hands.

'We'd better call the police. Do you have your cellphone?'

'Somewhere, somewhere . . . It's in my purse, I think! Anyway, I don't know if I can call them on a cell. Is it 911 or do I need a dialling code . . .'

Romily hissed, 'Just hurry! Use the phone in the shop.' Outside, she could see that the white shape was becoming more and more limp as the other men continued their attack. 'Oh my God, they'll kill him. Quick, Muffy!'

Just then, the men in black threw their victim to the ground, aimed another couple of kicks at him, and then stopped their assault.

'Let that be a lesson to ya!' said one in a thick, deep voice, and then the two assailants turned and sauntered off, lighting cigarettes as they went.

Romily watched as the man on the ground groaned, rolled slightly as if trying to get up, and then lay still. A moment later she was unlocking the back door, which took some time because of the complicated locks and bolts all over it. As soon as she'd opened it, she darted out into the alley and over to the prone figure. The man's face was covered in blood but she could see that his nose was probably broken and his eyes and lips were hugely swollen. His clothes were also blood-stained, where the gush from his nose had covered them, but she could make out that he was wearing chef's whites and baggy checked trousers.

'Oh my God, are you OK?' she said helplessly.

He moaned and then winced in pain. 'My . . . my chest. I think they broke my ribs,' he said in croak.

Romily stared at him, wondering what on earth she could do. She put a hand on his arm. 'Don't worry,' she said, 'I'll get you some help.' She got up, ran back in and called to Muffy, 'Get an ambulance, I think he's badly hurt!' Then she grabbed the first-aid box and a cup of water, and ran back to the alley.

The beaten-up chef was still lying there – a pathetic, prone figure in the darkness. She felt sorry for him as she knelt down next to him, trying to push her white skirts off the dirty ground.

'Don't worry,' she said reassuringly. 'Help is coming. Now, let me see if I can staunch some of this bleeding . . .' She opened the first-aid box, took out a wadge of cotton wool, dipped it in the water and began to dab at his blood-covered face. The man groaned as the water touched his wounds and swollen skin, but she murmured soothingly and carried on. 'I don't think your nose is bleeding as badly as it was . . . look, I'm cleaning it all away and it's looking fine. I guess the doctor will have to fix it somehow. I don't know what happens with broken noses, but I suppose that if they can do nose jobs, they must be able to make original ones look like new.'

The man gazed at her through eyes that were just small slits in puffed red skin, but she seemed to see gratitude there.

He blinked and then rasped, 'Oh, no. Your beautiful dress.'

She looked down. The fine white silk had streaks of red blood and smears of pink on it by now. 'Oh never mind. It's only a dress. Blood comes out anyway, as long as you get to it fast enough.'

He stared at her from his foetal position, arms wrapped round his poor broken ribs. 'Thank you,' he said at last.

'Don't worry. I couldn't exactly leave you here. Why did those men beat you up? Were they robbing you?'

He shut his eyes. 'Not exactly.'

She looked down again at his stained work clothes. He hardly looked like a worthwhile target for a mugger – in fact, his attackers seemed to have been better dressed than he was.

'You can tell the police all about it when they come,' she said.

There was the sound of an ambulance siren approaching in the distance.

'Is that for me?' he said, looking anxious.

Romily nodded. 'I hope so. You need to be checked over.'

'Ah, shit.' The man groaned. 'I don't need it. The last thing I want is the police getting involved. I'm fine.'

'Don't be silly – you've been badly beaten. You might have internal injuries. You have to see a doctor.'

'I'm . . . I'm OK.' He tried to struggle up to sitting position. 'I'm going home.'

Romily watched as he made an effort to get up, but the pain on his face told the real story and he slumped back to the ground with a sigh. 'Don't worry, you're going to be fine,' she said, and looked towards the street where she could see flashing lights approaching. Just then Muffy came out of the back door of the shop.

'They're here,' she said breathlessly.

'Good,' Romily said. 'This man needs to see a doctor as fast as possible.'

Chapter 22

Oxford
Summer 2003

I really can't believe I let Allegra talk me into this.

Imogen walked through Peckwater Quad feeling self-conscious even though her outfit was covered with a trench coat. The directions had been for party-goers to meet in Oriel Square, which was just at the back of Christ Church, through Canterbury Gate. Allegra was going to meet her there.

Some second-year men, in a motley collection of drag outfits and made up in clownish colours, whooped through the gate, rushing past her into the square where more people had gathered in various stages of undress. Passers-by and tourists gaped at the sight as the undergraduates gathered, the males in dresses or women's underwear and the girls in the skimpiest of clothes, extreme make-up and outfits that looked as though they had come from fetish shops.

Imogen pulled her coat more tightly around herself despite the warm evening and looked about for Allegra.

'OK, guys!' shouted a man in an extraordinary blonde wig with glitter lipstick thickly smeared all over his lips. 'Can everyone bring their tickets, please? The buses are parked just down the road by Merton, so make your way there now.'

I can't go on my own! Imogen felt panicky. *Where the hell is Allegra*? For a moment she hoped that her friend had changed her mind. Then she could go back to her own room, put on some proper clothes and settle down to the piles of notes and books on her desk. The fact that Mods were now only a day away made her feel sick with nerves. She knew that she'd made a dangerous decision – and Sam had been so furious with her when she'd told him what she was planning that she'd eventually pretended that she'd changed her mind and wasn't going to the Gaveston at all, but would be spending a quiet night in her room revising. That was another reason why she was feeling so uncomfortable. What if Sam or one of his friends saw her?

Two more minutes then I'm going back to my room, she decided.

The problem was Xander. Allegra, whether she meant to or not, had dangled him in front of her like a piece of bait, and of course Imogen had been unable to resist it. The magic that surrounded him always reeled her in. She'd seen him several times over the last months and he was always so sweet to her, with that gentle and slightly flirtatious tone he'd always used and his protective attitude. 'You tell me if you run into any problems, Midge,' he'd say, 'and I'll sort them out for you.' She couldn't help what she felt for Xander: a dizzying passion that made her mouth dry, and her palms damp, and her whole being contract with longing at the very thought of him. Just the shortest moments of imagining what it might feel like to be in his arms made her feel faint – and that was something she never felt with Sam, no matter how sweet and kind he was. How could anyone resist the lure of that feeling? It was like a drug that once tried could never be refused: the pleasure it offered – or, at least, the intensity of emotion – was too extraordinary not to be taken.

The opportunity to spend the evening in Xander's company, and, more to the point, at a party where she'd specifically been asked to talk to him, and where recklessness was encouraged if not compulsory, was too much. She couldn't turn it down.

So here she was, standing in Oriel Square, surrounded by wild-looking people, wondering what she was doing risking her Oxford career for the sake of a few precious moments with Xander.

'Midge, Midge!' It was Allegra, waving at her and grinning broadly as she marched down towards the square in the company of some other girls. She looked astonishing in miniature gold hot pants and a pair of thigh-high black patent boots with five-inch heels that made her legs seem to go on forever. On top she wore a magenta silk bustier trimmed with sequins from which her breasts billowed upwards, her modesty only just preserved. Her blonde hair was hidden under a pink Afro that bounced round her head like a balloon of candyfloss and she wore gold-rimmed round sunglasses.

'I nearly didn't recognise you. You look amazing,' Imogen said as Allegra approached her.

'Thanks, honey.' Allegra slapped one hand with the riding crop she was carrying in the other. 'What are you wearing under there?'

'It looks pretty dull next to yours, I'm afraid.' Imogen opened her mac like a reluctant flasher to reveal a black silk negligee nipped in at the waist with a bondage-style leather corset-belt, covered in studs and buckles. The negligee ended at mid-thigh and below that were fishnets and her silver platform heels.

'Very nice! I don't know what you're talking about. Like the boudoir bondage look. It suits you.' Allegra grinned naughtily. 'Look at all these boys done up like women –

most of them very ugly women, I might add. And isn't everyone staring!'

She looked up at all the student faces peering out of the windows of Christ Church and Oriel at the colourful throng in the square, and shouted out, 'Come and join us! We're off to do some shagging!'

There was general laughter, and then they were chivvied out of the square to where three coaches were waiting.

'Where are we going?' Imogen asked, as she and Allegra climbed into their seats.

'Not sure, but I think Xander said it was James's farm – remember the one I told you about? Now . . .' Allegra opened a plastic bag she'd been carrying and pulled out a bottle of champagne. 'How about a little something for the journey? You obviously need a bit of warming up. Got to get you out of that coat somehow.'

The coaches crawled out of Oxford and then they were coasting down the motorway. No one paid much attention to where they were going, the atmosphere was too het up and excited for that, with drink being passed around, along with the odd spliff and a box of pills marked 'Eat Me'.

'Ecstasy, I should think,' Allegra remarked as they went past her. 'No, thanks, darling, never take a pill I didn't buy myself. Want one, Midge?'

Imogen shook her head. *Exams the day after tomorrow*, she reminded herself. *But a glass of champagne or two won't hurt.*

Before long, the coaches came off the motorway and began bumping along country lanes. It was almost an hour after they'd left Oxford when they turned up a long driveway and finally pulled to a halt in front of a farmhouse and a large barn, which had its doors wide open.

'This is James's place,' Allegra said as they disembarked. 'I think his dad gave it to him for his eighteenth.'

Imogen looked about. She'd got used to some of the

extravagant ways of the rich while still at school: there were the girls who drove up the day after their driving test in a brand new car; girls with their own credit cards and accounts at Coutts; girls who seemed to be constantly abroad, skiing, or cruising on luxury yachts, or soaking up the St Lucia sun. It was all so far from her own experience. Her parents didn't have that kind of money – there was no way they could afford to buy her a car or give her a lavish dress allowance. They had agreed she could have a certain amount of money to live on while she was at university but everything she needed above that was her own concern. Even Allegra, while she was certainly more flush than Imogen, didn't have mountains of cash at her disposal.

These rich boys, though . . . Imogen sighed. They just didn't seem to realise how lucky they were. Their wealth made them arrogant. James Barclay was average in so many ways, but his money meant he had an endless supply of friends ready to tell him how wonderful he was. And despite his ordinary looks, he had beautiful girls hanging off his arm, fawning all over him, desperate to get their hands on a little of that lovely cash. There he was now, driving his Porsche up to the barn, screeching it to a halt on the driveway. He turned the stereo up to full volume so it was pumping out dance music, opened both the doors and shouted, 'This'll have to do, lads, until we get the system working!'

He looks ridiculous, thought Imogen as they approached the barn. James was wearing a black leather mini-skirt, a black bra stuffed with a couple of fleshy rubber false breasts, and a black feather boa round his neck. On top of a curly dark wig, a black leather cap sat at a jaunty angle, and he stumbled around clumsily on his high heels.

The atmosphere was charged as everyone made their way to the barn where some early arrivals were already waiting, loitering by the long trestle table that would serve as a bar. The space inside was huge. In a far corner, amps, a sound system and turntables were being set up. Around the walls, bales of hay were stacked on top of each other reaching halfway up the walls, with a single layer of bales in front serving as seats.

'Look.' Allegra pointed up. 'Tasteful.'

Severed pig's heads, eyes closed and their pinkish cheeks waxy, with flaps of skin and dried gore at the neck, had been perched on the high bales, one every few feet around the room.

'Yuk!' Imogen made a face. 'What have they done that for?'

'To show us that anything goes . . .'

'Ladies, would you like a drink?' A boy in huge gold false eyelashes and a turquoise leotard came up to them. He was holding a stack of plastic cups in one hand and a green watering can in the other.

'What's in there?' asked Allegra, peering into the watering can.

'A cocktail.' He grinned at them.

'What kind of cocktail?'

He shrugged. 'Bit of pomegranate juice or something. Some vodka. Lemonade. Simple stuff. Pretty harmless. After all, we've got the whole night to get through.'

Allegra and Imogen swapped glances. 'May as well,' said Allegra.

'I'm only having one,' Imogen said. 'I can't afford to get too pissed, and we've already had champagne.'

'Come on, we had hardly any of that – it got passed around the entire coach.' Allegra helped herself to one of the plastic cups. 'I'll have some, please.'

'A wise decision. You won't regret it.' The boy poured some of the cocktail out into her glass. It was boiled-sweet pink. 'Some for you?'

Imogen took her own cup, let the bearer of the can fill it

and tasted it. 'It's quite nice. It tastes just like sugary fruit juice.'

'Have as much as you like, girls!' said the friendly boy. 'There's enough to last all night.'

Music was pounding away from the huge sound system, filling the barn with its thudding beat. Lights flashed, spinning up to the ceiling and back down again. On the concrete floor, hundreds of people were jumping up and down, dancing wildly to the music.

What time is it? wondered Imogen blearily. It must be late because it was dark outside, though the summer moon lightened the sky to inky navy and provided enough illumination to show the orchard's twiggy fingers, spreading out and reaching upwards. Time had become very slippery all of a sudden: it leapt and jumped about, disappearing entirely and then reappearing to slow right down. Imogen tried dancing for a while, but found the beat kept vanishing and then returning unexpectedly, making it very difficult to keep in time. So she stopped dancing and had a long and earnest conversation with one of the pig's heads that seemed particularly friendly, despite its closed eyes and the coarse lashes brushing its dead cheeks.

After a while, she thought she should find Allegra but when she tried to walk towards the dance floor, the lower half of her body developed a will of its own and walked off in a direction she had no desire to go. For a while, she was heading off blindly into the darkness, as she tried to cajole her legs to obey her. 'Turn round!' she shouted. 'Go back! I'll get lost if we go on like this.' Just as she was tottering on to a dirt lane, she managed to stop, regain control, and then stagger back towards the light and noise of the barn.

'That's better,' she gasped to herself. She found herself next to James's car, the doors now shut and the stereo off, so she leant on it, grateful for something to clutch on to for a while.

'Hey, Imogen, are you all right?'

She looked up and found Xander standing next to her. She'd seen him earlier in the evening, one of the few men who managed to look gorgeous even when he was dressed in drag. He'd had a long white dress on over a pair of jeans, and his dark blond hair had been pulled back into short pony-tail. His concession to make-up had been some red gloss that only made his lips look more desirable so far as Imogen was concerned. Even though her brief was to talk to him, she hadn't been able to pluck up the courage and, besides, he looked happy enough without her offering him any words of wisdom. He must have got over his break up – she'd seen him chatting with his friends, laughing and smiling like he didn't have a care in the world.

'Yes, yes, I'm fine,' she said breathlessly, gazing up at him. He was haloed in light from the strobes in the barn, his white dress glowing. *He's like an angel!*

'You look a bit funny. Sure you're all right?'

She nodded and stood up straight, swaying violently. 'It's my legs,' she explained. 'They're being very disobedient. Naughty, naughty legs. I shall have to smack them.'

He laughed. 'What've you been drinking?'

'Nothing!' She looked up at him solemnly. 'Nothing at all. Well . . . I had some cocktails. But that was ages ago.'

'Some of that pink stuff in the watering cans?' He shook his head. 'Never take the drink they offer. It's spiked, you little idiot.'

'Spiked? What with?'

'Speed or something. Come on, let's walk you around, get you some air.'

He took her arm and led her across the yard towards the orchard. She leant on him, feeling suddenly very tired and unable to focus well. For ten minutes they stumbled along together in the darkness, the noise from the barn fading away.

'Ah – I'm a bit pissed,' he said apologetically as he tripped over a branch on the ground.

'That's all right. Turns out I'm stoned!'

They both giggled. They were in darkness now, weaving their way between the trees with no particular destination in mind. Then Imogen felt her platforms slip under her and tumbled down, taking Xander with her, and the next moment they were lying on the cool grass, tangled up together. There was a startled pause and then she said, 'Whoops!'

Xander laughed. He propped himself up on one elbow so that he was staring down into her face, his nose only an inch from hers. His eyes looked almost black in the darkness, glittering a little. He smiled gently.

'Little Imogen. What are you doing here, in a place like this? You're not like this lot.'

'Yes, I am!' she declared, wanting to belong.

He shook his head. 'I remember you at Foughton – in your denim skirt and your Disneyland T-shirt, those big grey eyes of yours like saucers as you trotted about after Allegra. You'll always be that little kid to me. Don't turn into one of these girls – hard as nails. Brittle.'

'Like Temple?' she ventured.

Xander sighed. 'Yeah, like her. She's in there right now.' He darted his gaze towards the barn. 'Doing Christ knows what. Last time I saw her, she was dancing on a hay bale with her girlfriend, taking her clothes off. I don't know if she does it because she knows it hurts me or because she just doesn't care.'

'Poor Xander,' whispered Imogen, and touched his face softly. She didn't care about his ex at that moment. The whole world had shrunk to just the two of them and she felt bizarrely happy, as though nothing could separate them now, not even the dreaded Temple. In a second Xander would see her, *really* see her, feel the purity of her love coming out and embracing him. He would realise that they were meant to be together . . .

He smiled at her. 'Poor me? Why?'

'You're lost, I can see that. You're lonely. You're all alone.'

He looked startled, then puzzled. 'Is that what you think?'

'It's what I know. You don't need to take all those drugs and drink so much. I've been trying to find you, to tell you. You don't have to be lonely . . .'

His eyes grew tender. 'You want to look after me, don't you? You want to make everything all right.'

'I can, you know . . . I can do that.'

'Oh Imogen . . . sweet little Imogen . . . you really mean it, don't you? I wish you could.'

'Let me try, please.' The soft night breeze lifted her hair and whipped it lightly over his cheek. She turned her face to his, yearning for him, trying to convey her longing. He stared at her, his expression unreadable. She couldn't tell if he was sad, happy or angry. 'Xander . . .' she whispered. She trembled on the brink. She wanted to say 'I love you' and, as she gathered her courage and formed her lips to say the words, he suddenly put a finger on her mouth.

'Shhhh,' he said. 'Don't say anything. Oh, God. This is wrong, I know it is.'

She shook her head, her eyes filling with happiness. The next moment, to her astonishment, he was kissing her. His arms went round her, one hand behind her head, pulling her close to him, and then he had taken possession of her mouth. It was the sweetest kiss she could ever have imagined. She'd fantasised hundreds of times about kissing Xander but nothing prepared her for the reality: it was as though she'd met her perfect match. Their mouths fitted together like two halves of a whole, and the taste of him was the most wonderful thing she'd ever known. It felt as though her body were melting into his.

After what seemed like a long time, he pulled away, panting, his eyes surprised. 'Bloody hell, Imogen!' he stuttered out.

'Please don't stop!' she begged, and pulled him back to her. More than anything she didn't want to stop. She wanted more and more. She wanted to be completely joined to him, to be entirely one. The dream was coming true at last – and he could obviously sense how right it was as well. Why should they stop?

She lost herself in his kiss again, this time putting her hand down to feel for him, pushing back the skirt of the negligee he was wearing. It seemed so deliciously wanton and forward, to slip her hand down the front of his trousers and touch the silky smooth tip of his cock, but she needed him to know, without a doubt, that she wanted him, completely and entirely. He moaned lightly as she touched him.

Am I doing it right? she wondered, hoping that she wasn't hurting him somehow, but she carried on and the next moment had managed to undo the front of his trousers and release him. She ran her whole hand up and down his cock, glorying in its smooth warmth and solid heft.

'Christ, watch out, don't do too much of that,' he murmured.

She wrapped him in her hand, moved him gently towards her, shifting her thighs apart and pulling her knickers away so he had access to her.

He pressed himself against her entrance, then seemed to consider for a moment. She put her arms around him and pulled him closer. He didn't need any further urging and the next moment he was inside her, moving slowly.

She felt a great pool of happiness engulf her. It was not physical exactly – she still seemed too removed from her body to feel very much – but she felt drenched in the pleasure of being near him at last, as close to him as it was possible to be. It felt wonderful and right, even if she couldn't sense much else.

They moved together in an instinctive and natural rhythm for what seemed like ages. Then slowly they stopped. He pulled out of her and they lay together for a while in each other's arms. It didn't matter that there had been no climax for either of them, Imogen was sure of that. They were too numbed by drink and drugs to become aroused enough to see it through. But it had been gentle and beautiful, and this way she had showed him how much she loved him, cared for him and wanted to be close to him.

'Come on,' Xander said at last. 'We'd better get back to the party.'

He helped her up. She felt dizzy once up on her feet but that passed after a moment and then she enjoyed the glow that had enveloped her. *Oh my God, I made love with Xander* . . . She felt special, as though she'd been granted some precious boon. Surely now, for the rest of her life, she'd carry this sense of being blessed.

What about Sam? asked a tiny voice at the back of her head but she ignored it. All that was far away from her at the moment. She would think about it when she was forced to step back into her ordinary life. Right now, she was walking on air, ecstatic.

Just then someone came running out of the barn towards them, shouting, 'Xander, Xander, where are you?'

They were followed by a man holding a mobile phone to his ear and shouting the address of the farm into it.

'I'm here!' he shouted, letting go of Imogen's hand and hurrying forward. 'What is it?'

'You'd better come quickly, there's been an accident. We're calling an ambulance.'

'Is it Allegra?'

Imogen gasped and put her hands to her mouth.

'No, it's Temple. Come on!'

Xander ran for the inside of the barn, leaving Imogen standing in the deserted courtyard, watching as the flashing lights dimmed and the party was illuminated by harsh yellow industrial lamps, and the music faded to nothing.

Chapter 23

'Oh. Oh, *God.* Oh, *fuck.* What the . . . hell . . .'

There was a pounding on the door. It was loud but no louder than the racket inside Allegra's head. The two together were almost unbearable.

'OK, OK!' she shouted. 'Jesus Christ.'

She wasn't sure where she was but, opening her eyes, realised she was back in her rooms in Lincoln, although how she had got there, she had no idea. She rolled over and put her legs over the side of the bed to see if they would support her if she tried to stand up. They felt distinctly shaky.

There was another knocking on the door and then the sound of a voice calling, 'Allegra . . . Allegra, are you in there?'

'Yes!' she called back, but her voice was croaky and sore as though it had been overused recently. 'Just coming. Give me a moment, for Christ's sake.'

Getting some control of her limbs at last, she stumbled over to the door and opened it. Imogen was standing outside. Allegra looked her up and down through bleary eyes.

'Why the fuck are you dressed up like that?'

Imogen was wearing the university uniform of sub fusc: a black skirt and white shirt, with a black ribbon knotted at her neck and her gown over it. In her hand she clutched a black mortar board. Sub fusc was worn on formal occasions, such as matriculation and . . . exams.

Allegra felt a small flicker of panic, and the expression of alarm on Imogen's face didn't help. 'What time is it?'

'It's half-past twelve!' she exclaimed.

Relief flooded her. 'Half-past twelve? No wonder I feel like shit. I only got to bed about an hour ago. Why are you waking me up like this? I need at least another four hours. And why are you wearing sub fusc now? It's a bit eager, isn't it?'

'No, no! It's half-past twelve on *Wednesday*.'

Allegra blinked at her friend's anxious face as the information sank in.

'But . . . but that means . . .'

'Yes!' Imogen nodded frantically. 'We started exams this morning. Hasn't anyone come for you? I thought they came to college to get you if you didn't show up. We've already sat one paper, the next one starts at two. Come on, you have to get dressed right away.' The expression on her face told Allegra all she needed to know about how she must look.

Clammy horror chilled her all over. 'Oh, *fuck*. I'm completely screwed.'

'No, you're not! Quick, get dressed and get down to Schools. Tell them you were ill this morning and that you haven't seen anyone who has taken the exam already. They might let you stay in the building and sit it this afternoon, once the essay paper is finished. Quick, quick . . .'

'Look at me!' Allegra croaked. They both stood still for a moment and took in her state: her filthy clothes, her lank greasy hair, the stench of booze and chemicals that was seeping out her skin. She looked terrible. 'I can't do an exam like this. I'll throw up halfway through.'

'But you've got to try!' cried Imogen. 'You can't just flunk it like this! How did you manage to lose a whole day?'

'I don't know.' Allegra felt on the verge of losing it entirely – either bursting into tears or becoming furiously angry. 'I don't fucking know, all right?'

Imogen grabbed her arm and spoke fast. 'Look, there's time, all right? Go and get into the shower, be as quick as you can. I'll run to the JCR and get you some food – a ham roll and some Coke and chocolate. That will give you a boost. You get dressed, then look over your translations of *The Seafarer, The Dream of the Rood,* and *The Wife's Lament*. They all came up in the paper. We can do all that in an hour, easily. Then get yourself down to Schools before the afternoon paper starts.'

'And when am I going to find the time to revise *that* one?' Allegra demanded.

Imogen blinked at her. 'Haven't you done any revision at all?'

'What do you think?'

'Then you'll just have to wing it. I've hardly done anything myself.'

'Oh, don't give me that,' sneered Allegra. 'You've been swotting away all term, pretending you're not.' She knew she shouldn't be turning on her friend, who had just risked her own university career by telling her the contents of the Anglo-Saxon paper, but she was frightened, and angry, and couldn't believe the mess she'd found herself in.

Imogen stood looking at her helplessly for a moment and then said quietly, 'Well, I don't know what else to suggest.'

Allegra went over to her bed and sat down on it, her back hunched.

'What happened?' asked Imogen, coming into the room.

'I don't know.' Allegra stared down at her hands. 'I think I remember coming back in someone's car some time – it was daylight, I know that. I've got the vague idea that I ended up in a house – Park Town, I think. But I thought there was loads of time. I can't remember really.' She saw flashes of events: a glass bowl of cocaine on a table and lines being chopped on the top of it; bottles of vodka and champagne being passed around; mad dancing in a grand drawing room somewhere. *Did I have sex?* It was a distinct possibility. She had a fleeting vision of writhing bodies. Had she been a part of it, or just witnessed it? She simply didn't know.

How the hell am I supposed to get to Schools and write a paper on T. S. Eliot and the deeper meaning of The Wasteland*? I feel like I'm in the fucking Wasteland myself.*

She glanced up at Imogen who was watching her silently. 'I guess you got back all right?'

Imogen nodded. 'After what happened to Temple, I didn't feel much like partying. So I got a lift back. I was home before dawn.'

'Temple . . .'

'Don't you remember?'

Allegra frowned. She had a snatch of memory of the girl lying on the floor of the barn, some people coming to take her away, and then the party resuming. 'Is she OK?'

'I don't know. I thought you might have heard something. Apparently she was climbing the wall of bales, and got quite high up – then they collapsed and she fell straight on to that concrete floor. The paramedics strapped her into one of those special stretchers and had a neck brace on her. It looked serious.'

'Oh, fuck. No, I don't know anything. Shit. Poor Temple.' Allegra laughed almost sorrowfully. 'And we all kept on partying.'

'Some people did. Most of us went home.'

'Just the hardcore, huh? What about Xander?'

'He insisted on going in the ambulance with her. They didn't want to let him but he said he was the closest she had to next-of-kin right then, so they gave in.' There was a pause and then Imogen said softly, 'If you don't need me, I'll go. I have to look over my notes before the exam.'

Allegra took a deep shuddering breath. Her eyes stung.

'I've really fucked up, haven't I?'

Imogen rushed forward and knelt down next to her. 'It's not too late, Allegra, you've still got a chance! But you'll have to act fast.'

'Do you really think I can?'

'You must try. What have you got to lose?'

Allegra slumped for a moment, her shoulders drooping as though she really were defeated and couldn't summon another ounce of strength. Imogen grasped her hand and squeezed it hard. 'You can do it,' she whispered. 'I know you can. Don't give in now.'

Allegra lifted her head and stared into her friend's eyes. Imogen's clear grey gaze looked back. *Imogen's so lucky. The world is so clear-cut for her. She knows her good from her bad, and she wants to be good. I wish it could be like that for me.*

'All right,' she said in a small voice. 'I may as well try.'

She didn't know how she'd managed to convince the officials to let her sit the Anglo-Saxon exam after that afternoon's paper. Her performance must have been stellar but her appearance probably backed up her story. *I must look like I'm at death's door*, she thought as she explained that she'd crawled from her sick bed to take the exams and pleaded to be allowed to sit the paper.

While the other students streamed out of Schools after the afternoon session, Allegra was put into isolation with a chaperone, accompanied to the loo or when she went to get a glass of water, but she was given an hour's recovery time before she sat the translation paper and that gave her the chance to read over her notes and refresh her memory.

When she was finally released from the building, she walked out into the summer evening, switched on her mobile and sent a text to Imogen.

*I can't f*g believe it. Success. Wife's Lament a breeze. Thx so much for yr help. Back to revision now! See u tomorrow. Love, A x*

The final paper was on Friday morning, and when it was over, the first-year undergraduates spilled out of Schools on to the High Street in a burst of wild relief, keen to shake off the stress and anxiety of exams.

'Do you think you passed?' Imogen asked as she and Allegra made their way down the steps of the building, buffeted and bashed by the students heading for the pub.

Allegra shrugged as she fished about in her pockets for her cigarettes. 'This bloody gown! I can't wait to get this nonsense off.' She had interpreted sub fusc in her own particular way, wearing black flared trousers, shabby plimsolls and a white vintage Victorian lace blouse with a broad black grosgrain ribbon tied in a bow at the neck. Her commoner's gown fell off one shoulder.

'It's bound to be all right – they let you sit that paper after all.'

Allegra smiled at her friend. 'Yeah. Thanks for making me do it. I would never have had the imagination or the balls otherwise.'

Imogen grinned back at her. 'It was the least I could do. I was so worried when you didn't show up for the exam. I thought you'd been kidnapped or something!'

'No,' Allegra said fervently. 'I really owe you, Midge. None of my other so-called friends turned up to find me, and I know what you risked for me.' She put a hand on her friend's arm. 'Thanks.'

'You're very welcome.'

'And now . . .' Allegra put a cigarette in her mouth, lit it with her silver lighter, and exhaled in a joyous puff. 'Party time!'

Chapter 24

New York

The shop was a terrible mess: everything had been ripped from the hangers or swept from the shelves; mirrors had been smashed, furniture overturned, and all the pretty things torn and stamped on.

Romily put her head in her hands for a moment and sighed deeply. Then she gathered herself and looked around at the chaos. 'I just don't know how long I can carry on like this. This is the third time we've been broken into. Don't they understand? We don't keep any money here at night! And the things they take . . . Anything electronic disappears, no matter how worthless it is. The sound system has gone again – it's worth about eighty dollars. They ignore the things that actually count for something, or just destroy them for the hell of it. It breaks my heart!' Angry tears sprang to her eyes.

'It's a terrible shame,' agreed Muffy, looking about, her expression gloomy. 'I can't believe we're gonna have to clear this all up again.'

Cherub was not going well. The neighbourhood, it turned out, had been a big mistake. It was not up and coming at all but seemed to be staying much the same, and Cherub, with its glossy, expensive frontage and pricy, eclectic stock, stood out painfully on the rundown street. It attracted attention all right, but not the kind that Romily had been hoping for.

Where were all the rich girls whom she knew browsed the designer boutiques only a few blocks away?

In the first few weeks they'd come by all the time. Romily kept a constant supply of very good coffee, more of those princessy cup cakes and plates of pale Ladurée macaroons in her favourite pistachio and strawberry flavours, and the girls arrived just before their lunch dates or before they went to their beautician or manicurist, to pick up something to wear for a party or give as a gift, have a coffee, nibble on a cake and gossip with Muffy and Romily.

The shop took several thousand dollars in the first week. Romily proudly totted up her takings and recorded them in her accounts, thinking to herself that this was easy and fun. Why didn't everybody have a shop? It was just the best thing in the world.

Then came the first break-in.

Perhaps she should have worried more about crime in the area when she found that poor man in the alley on the opening night, but it had been easy to dismiss that as a one-off. She just hoped he'd recovered, whoever he was. Still, she'd been careful to keep her eyes open for anything suspicious. Her alleyway already seemed to be popular with drug users and pushers. She often saw furtive transactions taking place there when she went back to the stock room or kitchen, and she'd found abandoned scraps of foil, burnt patches on the ground and the inevitable abandoned syringes out there.

'It's just awful!' she told Muffy as she carefully cleaned everything away while wearing industrial-strength protective gloves. 'Dogs or children could so easily step on these vile things! It's so selfish, isn't it?'

'Incredibly,' agreed Muffy. 'Why can't they just do their horrid drugs at home, like everyone else? The last place I'd want to get high is some filthy alley.'

Then Romily discovered that local prostitutes were using it as a handy place to service their customers when she went to put out some rubbish and found a beautiful black girl on her knees, her hands wrapped round the shaft of a throbbing cock, its large head filling her mouth while its owner cried, 'Yeah, baby! Oh, yeah, baby,' and pushed it deeper down her throat.

Romily ran back inside feeling sick and appalled. After that, she seemed to see them all the time: girls of all shapes and colours, but mostly in the usual mini-skirt, high heels and jacket, sucking off men or letting them pump into them as they leant against the wall, one leg curled round the client's back to help his efforts along. Often they would stare Romily straight in the eye, their expression cool and uninterested, as they waited for their client to finish.

'It's disgusting,' she said, outraged. 'Those girls don't care that they're having sex in the street!'

'Totally,' agreed Muffy solemnly.

'I had no idea this kind of thing went on in real life. I mean, you expect these things in the movies or on the TV, but outside my own shop . . . In the daylight!'

Looking back, she could see it was only a matter of time before Cherub was robbed, but it had still come as a shock. She'd wept bitterly over the broken and ruined things, and mourned everything that had been lost: the electric till and card reader had gone, so had the phone, the stereo, and even the tiny microwave oven from the kitchen.

'At least we can replace those,' she said tearfully. 'But my lamps!'

Beautiful vintage pieces had been wilfully wrecked. The police had little interest in the case, giving her the distinct impression that they thought she was foolish for placing such temptation in the way of people who could hardly be expected to do otherwise than help themselves.

Then, she had to go away: she had to get back to Paris for various social events and there was the Laksi wedding in Delhi to attend. Her mother was getting tetchy about the fact that Romily had been away for so long. She asked Muffy to run the shop in her absence and hired a girl to be the sales assistant but, without Romily to oversee everything, it turned into a disaster. Muffy kept forgetting to open the shop at all, and when she did it would be for a few hours in the afternoon, when she could fit it into her hectic social life. Sales plummeted and the stock looked old, dusty and neglected.

'I don't understand it!' Romily exclaimed when she got back and looked over the books. 'We've made nothing at all . . . we've hardly sold anything. In the first few weeks, we made thousands. Now we're making nothing. How can that be?'

Muffy looked gloomy. 'No one's coming in, darling. It's deserted. The girls have all done their duty – they all came by at the start and bought something. Now they're busy with other things.'

'Don't we have any other customers apart from our friends?' demanded Romily.

'It doesn't look like it,' Muffy replied, glancing at her manicure. 'And to be honest, honey, I don't know how much longer I can help out. I'm so busy! And I'm off to Mustique for three weeks. Maybe we'd better count me out from now on.'

Romily couldn't blame her. Muffy had only been helping out on a temporary basis. She could hardly be expected to devote herself to Cherub's success. So Romily soldiered on alone. Every day, her driver brought her down town from the Fifth Avenue apartment and she opened the shop, sat around, made phone calls, ordered in her lunch, sat around, then closed up the shop and was taken back uptown by her driver. Occasionally a customer came in, wandered around and then left. Once in a while, someone bought something, but it was a rare occurrence.

I don't understand it, she told herself, glancing round at all the lovely things. *It's all so stylish and so covetable, and reasonably priced as well. People come in, look at the stock and then leave! Why aren't they buying?*

Then the shop had been robbed for a second time, and now here they were again, picking their way through the wreckage. She had called Muffy because she hadn't known who else to ring, and her friend had come down right away.

'I'm beginning to wonder if this is worth all the effort,' Romily sighed. 'It's just heartbreaking. Don't people round here have any respect for other people's property?'

'Maybe you should have gone more uptown,' remarked Muffy, dipping her dark glasses so she could inspect the mess more closely. 'After all, people prefer class in the end.'

'Perhaps you're right.' Romily put her hands on her hips and looked about. 'Well, we'd better get on with clearing up.'

'Are you going to call the police?' Muffy asked.

'There doesn't seem any point. They didn't care much the last two times and I don't think it's going to be any different now. I guess I'll have to, though, so I can talk to the insurers again. They're not going to be happy.'

Muffy picked up a bag of rubbish. 'I'll put this out.'

'OK.' Romily retrieved a torn silk dress from the floor and gazed at it, wondering whether it could be mended or if it was now only good for cutting up for scarves. A moment later she heard a small crash from the back room, followed by a squeak. 'Muffy?' she called. 'What's up?'

She went back through to the stock room. The back door was open and standing in it was a wild-eyed white boy, with terrible spotty skin and a crew cut that had left ginger stubble all over his skull. He looked filthy and frightened in an overlarge baseball jacket and baggy jeans. His hand was trembling so hard that the gun he was pointing at Muffy was veering to right and left.

Romily gasped and the boy jumped, swinging the gun over so that it was aimed at her, and then pulled it back towards Muffy again.

'OK,' he said in a high voice. 'You gotta gimme your money.'

Stay calm, Romily told herself. *Don't panic.* Everything had slowed down and her mind, though working fast, seemed to be taking it step by step. Beneath her fear, she felt angry. *Not again! This is crazy!* 'We don't have any money,' she said curtly. 'The shop has already been turned over. There's nothing left. The register is empty – hell, the register has disappeared!'

'I don't care about that,' the boy said, waving the gun jerkily in her direction. 'I don't want that shit. Been through it already. There's nothing worth crap in there. Whatchu got?'

Romily stared at him. Muffy seemed to be frozen with fear.

The boy narrowed his eyes. 'Come on!' he shouted. 'I don't have no time to waste here! Gimme your stuff! I'm not afraid to shoot.'

At this Muffy appeared to come to life. She began to undo her watchstrap and take off her rings, her fingers clumsy with fright. 'Here you are, you can take this,' she jabbered. 'It's a Rolex. I got it for my twentieth. And these are real diamonds in this ring, you can have it . . .'

Romily turned to her. 'Muffy!'

'Shut your mouth!' The boy swung the squat nose of the gun back towards her. Romily felt nausea at the sight of its vacant black barrel. 'This lady wants to give me her stuff. Get yours off too. I can see some nice hardware on you.

And give me your purses. Now!'

'My purse is in the shop,' Romily said. 'Can I go and get it?'

'Get it, but don't try anything or you'll regret it.'

Romily edged towards the door. *This is my chance*. But her chance to do what? Call the police? The phone had been ripped out of its socket and there was no time to reconnect it. Hope that a customer would come in? What good would that do?

'Go on!' shouted the boy. 'Don't try and mess with me! I know how to use this thing and I'm not afraid to – I've used it before!'

Muffy was shaking hard, pushing her things at him. 'Take them, take them!' she said. 'Please, just let us go. Don't hurt us.'

The boy snatched the jewellery from her hand and stuffed it in his pocket. 'I want cash too,' he called out. 'And cards. Anything you got.'

Romily went slowly into the shop. Their bags were sitting neatly under the counter: her cherry-red Hermès Birkin alongside Muffy's neat Dior black purse. She picked them up and turned back to the stock room.

'Come on, come on,' yelled the boy. 'I don't want to hang around.' He saw Romily coming back with the bags and his face brightened. 'That's what I'm talking about. Open 'em up.'

Romily knelt down with them. She had been contemplating throwing them in his face to startle him and then trying to get the gun off him, but she put that idea out of her mind now. The boy was so tense he'd shoot them in an instant without even meaning to. And Muffy was shivering with fear, her teeth chattering. There was no way Romily could depend on her for anything. It was better to let this little criminal take their stuff.

'Open them,' ordered the boy. 'Nice and slow so I can see what you're taking out . . .'

Romily couldn't restrain herself from saying acidly, 'We don't have any guns, you know. We're not really like that.' She took out Muffy's lizard-skin wallet bursting with credit cards and tossed it towards him. It skittered across the floor and came to a halt at his feet. *Not bad. My old PE mistress would be most impressed.*

He picked it up greedily. 'Now the other one.'

She reached into her Birkin, feeling for her Gucci wallet, wishing she didn't have to hand it over. It wasn't so much the money and cards inside, though she hated to give her possessions to a criminal, it was the other things: her photos of her mother and father and brother; the picture taken in a passport booth of her, Imogen and Allegra playing up for the camera on a trip to London; the used tickets and receipts that she'd kept because they reminded her of special occasions. But she didn't have a choice.

'Here.' She took it out and threw it at his feet.

At that moment, the room was filled with a strange piercing beep. The boy, strung so tight with nerves, almost leapt into the air. The beep sounded again and now, with a startled yelp, he tightened his finger on the trigger.

Time wound down to the slowest motion possible. The beep echoed round and round the stock room. Romily saw the boy's hand swing higher, put up her own hand and shouted, 'No, it's a cellphone, it's a cellphone!' but her voice came out far too slowly to make a difference. The finger pressed inexorably down. There was a flash of fire from the snout of the gun, then another, then another. Three loud reports filled the room with thunder.

There was a terrible scream and Muffy wavered in mid-air then fell to the ground like a building being demolished, its lower strata vanishing, bringing everything down with it in graceful, inevitable collapse.

Chapter 25

Oxford

The room was filled with a menacing silence. The two proctors sat behind a long table, papers in front of them, making notes. They were wearing their official garb of black suits and academic gowns with fur-lined hoods.

It must be hot in that get up, thought Allegra. She held her hands tightly together in her lap and tried not to fidget.

One of them, a stiff-looking woman with short brown hair, looked up. 'So, Lady Allegra, we just want to go through events one more time. I'm sure you understand a serious allegation has been made. It's important that we are completely clear on what occurred.'

Allegra stiffened her spine and sat up even straighter, staring the proctor right in the eye. 'Certainly,' she said coolly.

'As you know, we have witnesses who state that on the morning you missed your first paper in the Honour Moderations, an undergraduate was seen going into your rooms. That undergraduate was wearing sub fusc and had in all likelihood been sitting an examination that morning. Our witness says that the undergraduate – a female – stayed about half an hour and then left. Not long afterwards, you yourself emerged, also in sub fusc, and made your way to Schools. There, you explained that you'd missed the examination due to ill health and asked to be allowed to sit it that afternoon. You undertook that you had seen no one in that time and certainly no other undergraduate who had taken the paper. Is that true?'

The proctors fixed her with their icy stares and waited for her reply.

Allegra remembered how she'd had no hesitation in lying to the officials and that, when they'd believed her story, she'd felt triumphant. It was a different matter altogether to sit here in complete sobriety, far from the drama and chemically induced emotions of that day, and repeat the lie.

The proctor turned over the sheet of paper in front of her. 'You see, Lady Allegra, your marks for the examinations were not at all distinguished. They were, one might say, bad. You would have failed, but for one thing. You scored highly enough on your translation paper to scrape over the pass mark. That Anglo-Saxon paper saved you. Now we have this allegation. When you claimed you had seen no one, you were given the benefit of the doubt. Were we right to do so?'

Tell them the same story, she urged herself. *Defend yourself! Lie to them!*

But she couldn't. She'd been brought up to be honest, and in this formal situation, with its trial-like atmosphere, she couldn't bring herself to do it. *Who saw Imogen?* she wondered. *And who the hell wanted to grass me up?* But she knew that there were plenty of people who envied or hated her, and would be glad of the chance to pull her down. She could only be grateful that whoever it was had not recognised Imogen.

She opened her mouth. Her university career trembled on the brink. Would she save it or let it go? The moment seemed to hover for a long time before she said, 'I did see another undergraduate that morning.'

'I see.' The proctor sat back with a satisfied smile, obviously pleased that she had trusted her instinct.

'An undergraduate who had sat the paper that morning?' asked the other, a man with small, close-set eyes and a beard.

Allegra looked at him, her head high. 'Yes.' She couldn't lie – dishonesty seemed impossible in this situation. She was far too proud to sit here making up falsehoods to protect herself; she'd screwed up and now she'd have to take whatever consequences were coming her way.

The proctors exchanged glances with each other, and the bearded man put his pen down on the table.

'Lady Allegra, you must be aware that the university takes the most serious view of cheating. If someone gave you an unfair advantage in this examination, it is cheating, pure and simple. Did this person alert you to the contents of the paper?'

Allegra stared back at him and breathed deeply. Then she said, 'I dispute that I had an unfair advantage over any other candidates. I wasn't at all well' – *The fact that it was self-inflicted is beside the point,* she told herself – 'and I could barely see straight or think coherently. But I still wanted to take the examinations if I possibly could, which is why I turned up, despite feeling so awful. I could hardly gather my thoughts in English, let alone Anglo-Saxon.'

'That is not relevant. Every other student went into that examination unaware of the contents of the paper. If you knew in advance what would be there, you had an unfair advantage, and that is cheating.'

Fury filled her. It wasn't as black and white as it seemed, she was sure of it, but she felt powerless to argue her case.

'I take your silence as acknowledgement of guilt,' said the proctor. 'This is very serious. I'm sure you're aware of the consequences of cheating in university examinations. We will need to consult your tutors and the Rector of your college. In some cases, however, we are able to issue fines and allow an undergraduate to resume their course. We would consider this option on condition that you give us the name of the undergraduate who told you the contents of the paper.'

Allegra straightened her shoulder and set her jaw. 'Absolutely not.'

'I see.' The female proctor raised her eyebrows. 'It will not help your case at all if you do not co-operate. You may face the severest penalty.'

'Do whatever you like,' she said haughtily. 'I'm not going to tell you who it was, so you might as well not bother asking me again.'

'I see. Thank you, Lady Allegra. That will be all.'

The wheels of Oxford justice turned slowly. Allegra went back to Foughton, unsure of what her future held. Then she was summoned back to Oxford, this time to her college and a meeting with the Rector and her tutors.

Xander insisted on coming with her. He drove her to Oxford from London in his battered MG convertible, swearing and cursing to himself all the way as they roared along the M40. 'I should never have let you come to the bloody Gaveston!' he shouted. 'That's what got you into this mess.'

Allegra ignored him, too low-spirited to bother shouting back above the noise of the engine, and stared at the golden and green fields spreading out lushly into the distance. But when they pulled up at the St Margaret Road house, she said, 'You can't organise my life for me, Xander. It was my decision to go to the Gav. And I even made Imogen come with me – she's the one you should feel sorry for. I nearly fucked up her chances as well. I'm just glad she was sensible enough to revise thoroughly beforehand.'

'You've got to stop leading her astray,' Xander said softly. 'She's not like us. She's a good kid with a decent future in front of her and we can't be responsible for wrecking it.'

'And I haven't got a decent future?' Allegra demanded, stung.

Xander sighed and ran his hands over the steering wheel. 'Of course you have. You're bright and beautiful, and you have just about every advantage it's possible to have. But I don't know . . .' He gazed over at her, his dark blue eyes sad. 'I worry about our family, that's all. Sometimes I think we're destined to be miserable, despite everything. At least, I am. I hope you manage to escape it.'

'But you've got everything as well!' Allegra said, reaching out and putting her hand on his arm.

Xander smiled at her, a sad yet sweet smile. 'I know. That's the bloody stupid thing.'

He drove her into town and waited as she made her way nervously to the Rector's House in her gown, clutching her mortar board.

Her brother was waiting for her in the quad as she emerged, white-faced, an hour later. He had his hands in pockets and was kicking small pebbles about the paving. When he saw her, he came hurrying over. 'Well? What did they say?'

'It's no good,' Allegra said in a voice that came out sounding strangled. 'I'm out. They've sent me down.'

A look of despair passed over Xander's face. 'No? Fuck! I can't believe it! Can you appeal?'

She shook her head, too numb to feel anything. 'That's it. It's been made quite clear. It's finished.'

'This is mad. You don't deserve this. If they're going to send anyone down, it should be me. I'm a waste of space, I never do any work . . . I wish they'd take me instead and let you stay.'

'It doesn't work like that,' Allegra said sadly.

'Shit.' He wrapped her in a tight hug. 'God, I'm so sorry.'

'That makes two of us.'

PART 3

Chapter 26

Scotland
Summer 2003

Imogen rang the great bell that hung next to the front door of Foughton Castle. She was nervous. Her mother had reported that Allegra had returned from her meeting with the Rector but there'd been no other indication of what had happened. It was bad enough that things had got to that stage. Imogen felt sick whenever she thought about it – it was her fault, after all. She had told Allegra what was in the Anglo-Saxon paper without being prompted. In doing so, she'd made cheats of both of them. But it had seemed the only hope at the time.

The maid who answered the door said that Lady Allegra was out on the terrace at the back of the house. Imogen made her way through the fusty darkness of the house and out through the drawing room. The terrace was bathed in summer sunshine, the loch glittering blue and silver beyond, while the sky had that peculiarly Scottish tinge of pale blue and violet. Allegra was sitting on one of the chairs, reading the paper, wearing frayed cotton shorts and a long navy jumper that was probably Xander's. Her eyes were concealed behind a pair of Rayban sunglasses.

'Hi,' Imogen said as she came out on to the terrace.

Allegra looked up, and smiled. 'Oh, hi. You've heard then.'

'I heard you were back so I came straight over – I hope you don't mind.'

'Are you on your own? Did you pass your test?'

Imogen nodded.

'Well done you! So you don't need to rely on your mum bringing you over all the time.'

'No. Freedom at last.' She sat down in the chair next to Allegra's. 'So . . . how did it go?'

Allegra sighed and took off her sunglasses. Her usually clear eyes were bloodshot and swollen. 'There's been a bit of a row here, I'm afraid. I got sent down.'

Imogen gasped, horrified. 'Oh, no! No! I can't believe it!' Tears of mortification sprang to her eyes. 'I'm so sorry. Oh, God, it's all my fault.'

'No, it's not. They were quite clear with me. Cheating – as they called it – was only part of the reason. I was on borrowed time anyway. My work record was abysmal. They said they'd sent people down for less. I'd only just scraped a pass in Mods, and if the Anglo-Saxon paper mark was discounted, then I'd failed very badly. It's not your fault. You did your best for me. I'm sorry I let you down.' Allegra put her sunglasses back on. 'I seem to have let everybody down. Mum's furious.'

Tears spilled out of Imogen's eyes and rolled down her cheeks. She sniffed.

'Oh, don't. You'll set me off again if you're not careful.'

'But I can't imagine Oxford without you . . .' She gulped back a sob, not wanting to break down completely.

'You'll probably do a lot better once I'm not there to distract you. You got a decent two:one in Mods, but we both know you can get a first if you put your mind to it, and you've got two years left to go for it.'

'I don't want to be there without you!' Imogen choked out. She felt desperate at the idea of facing Oxford without Allegra. 'I'll leave as well! It's horribly unfair. Why can't they give you another chance? It's not as though you're the worst offender – look at all those idiots and layabouts who manage to stay on. Why you?'

'I got caught. Everything went wrong. It's my own fault, Midge, I know that. I partied too hard, that's all. Everyone who does that has to be able to pull something out of the bag when the crunch comes, or risk being sent down. I lost that day after the Gaveston, and it cost me big time.' Allegra leaned over and took her friend's hand. 'I appreciate the sentiment, but if you dare leave Oxford because of me, I'll bloody kill you. Understand? Not another word about it. I'll think of something to do with myself, don't you worry.'

It's strange, thought Imogen, *but a load seems to have been lifted off Allegra's shoulders. It ought to be the other way around – after all, she's lost her chance of a degree and hasn't got a clue what she wants to do. But she seems a little less troubled. That's weird.*

But she didn't say anything. She felt the two of them growing closer again now that they were back in Scotland together, healing the rift that had grown between them during the last two terms. They had plenty of time now to relax and talk and learn to be their old selves again. Allegra was deeply in disgrace at home, and forbidden from enjoying herself during the summer holiday: no parties, no trips to London, no travelling abroad. She had to spend the summer at Foughton and think over her sins.

'It's ridiculous, really,' she said to Imogen as they lay in the garden sunbathing. 'I'm usually the good one, in comparison to Xander. They haven't the first clue about what he gets up to and now he's out in St Tropez, partying at Club 55, and I'm stuck here all on my own. Mum and Dad have gone away and there's no one here till the end of the summer when the shooting parties start.'

'Yes. It's very silly,' murmured Imogen from her place on the rug. Xander's name sent a quiver of excitement through her. She had been trying not to think yearningly of him, but it was hard. After the Gaveston, she'd longed to see and speak to him but it had been impossible: exams followed on immediately, and then it was the end of term.

The last time she had seen him was only a fleeting glimpse at the Magdalen College Commemoration Ball, held just before they'd all gone down for the long vacation. She went with Sam but had taken special care with her appearance in case she saw Xander, choosing a long gown of dark mossy green chiffon that flowed over a darker silk shell, with a high empire-line waist from which her bosom emerged, luscious and snowy. Allegra had lent her a pair of real emerald earrings that sparkled in her ears, and she'd gone to the ball looking like a ripe forest nymph and wishing, treacherously, that it was Xander instead of Sam who was taking her there.

Nevertheless, it had been a wonderful night, full of fun, enchantment and dancing, and just before dawn she saw Xander in his tail coat and the Commandoes bow tie of quartered black and red, wandering through the cloisters and smoking a cigarette, but he hadn't seen her. At seven a.m., she and Sam had gathered with the other ball survivors on a great stretch of grass for the early-morning photograph: hundreds of them in various states of dishevelment after the long night. Sam had put his arm around her and grinned broadly at the camera, while Imogen had been unable to stop herself from pulling away from him, scanning the crowd for the face she really wanted to see, but he'd been as elusive as a dream.

Perhaps I imagined what happened in the orchard, she thought, pressing her face into the rug and closing her eyes against the sun's glare. But she knew it had been real –

that extraordinary and tender moment when she'd offered herself to him to assuage his loneliness. None of her fantasies had been as amazing as the real thing.

Maybe Xander had forgotten what had happened that night in the soft summer darkness. Or, if he remembered, should she even expect him to care? She'd made no demands of him, simply given him what she could. He couldn't have the first idea that she loved him, or that she was willing to give him anything he wanted from her. If she could only see him again, she would know, but she had no idea when he'd be back from his glamorous jaunts.

Well, I'll just be grateful that I had that magic moment with him, a tiny slice of his life when he belonged entirely to me. I can live off that if I have to.

It was an unusually hot summer and Foughton sparkled with almost incandescent beauty against the blue sky and the sparkling loch. Imogen spent nearly every day there, arriving mid-morning to find Allegra lazing on the terrace over a pot of coffee and toast and honey. They revelled in having the place to themselves, with only the housekeeper there to provide meals and tidy up. Just as when they were girls, they read magazines, played music and chatted endlessly, though now their conversations were a little more grown up than before. They'd take picnics of wine and strawberries and wander off to find a warm, heathery spot where they could sunbathe and read; some afternoons they went boating on the loch or, if it was a really sunny day, they'd sit in the cool of the pink marble temple, smoking and talking endlessly about everything. Imogen would often end up staying for dinner and then the night, when it was too late and she'd had too much wine to drive back.

'We hardly ever see you,' complained her parents. 'Can't you stay home occasionally?'

So she did, but she always missed Foughton. It fed her romantic soul and felt more like her home than the place where she actually lived. Everything at the castle was dear to her, and sometimes she crept away and let herself into Xander's bedroom, so she could open his wardrobe and touch his clothes, lie on his bed and bury her nose in his pillow, trying to find some scent of him.

'Tell me about Sam,' Allegra said one day, as they lazed on the rug on the lawn. 'Isn't he coming up to see you?'

'Yes. Tomorrow.' Imogen shifted uncomfortably. It had been Sam's idea to come and visit; she'd tried to put him off. She'd managed to get away at the end of term without confronting the fact that she'd been unfaithful to him, and since then had put him almost completely out of her mind, as a problem to be considered at some later date. Far from Oxford, she felt far from him as well, and had been avoiding his calls and emails. She felt as though she had absolutely no need for him at the moment and wished he hadn't persisted in this trip up to see her. He was going to make her think about him, force her to admit to herself that she didn't love him, and that Xander had proved to her that it was just a sham relationship. She felt cross with him, all the more because she knew he was the innocent party and his only fault was to love her.

Allegra's curiosity was pricked by Imogen's reticence. She propped herself up on her elbows and observed Imogen over the top of her Raybans. 'Aren't you looking forward to it?'

'Um – not really. I'd much rather he stayed away, actually.' She spoke slowly, surprised to hear herself say it out loud.

'Oh?' Allegra raised her eyebrows. 'That doesn't sound very promising. Well, you hardly ever talk about him. Not really a sign of devouring love. What's the matter with him? He seems lovely. And he obviously thinks the world of you.

I saw him at the Magdalen Ball – he couldn't keep his eyes off you.'

'He's fine, it's just . . . I don't know.' Imogen rolled over, feeling helpless. 'I don't think it's right for the long term.' She wished she could confide in Allegra. She was dying to talk to someone about it all, but this was one thing she couldn't confide in her best friend.

'He doesn't light your fire, huh?' Allegra grinned. 'I understand. We'll have to find you someone else – devilishly handsome and a tiger in the sack. We need to get your loins really burning. I'll ask Xander. Maybe he's bringing someone back with him.'

'Oh – is Xander coming home?' Imogen tried to sound casual but at the mention of his name she felt her stomach turn in lazy excited loops, like the slow cycle of a washing machine.

'Today, apparently. He's been on yachts, off yachts, up and down the French coast and I don't know what. But he's coming back and bringing a couple of friends.'

'Girlfriends?' Imogen asked, a little too fast.

'Dunno. We'll have to wait and see. He should be back any minute. Depends if he comes straight back or goes out to Hopetoun for a bit. They're having a house party there, apparently, and he was at school with the boys.' Allegra turned her attention back to the magazine she was reading. 'Maybe you could bring Sam over here. There're bound to be some impromptu rave ups. But, of course, he might want to be on his own with you.'

'Maybe,' Imogen said, cursing Sam for turning up at just the wrong moment. She didn't want him here, she knew that: this was her place – hers and Allegra's and Xander's – and Sam's presence would only be jarring and wrong.

But she was on tenterhooks after that, knowing Xander was already close.

*

She was almost asleep on the rug, which was now in the welcome shade since the sun had moved behind the trees. Allegra had gone inside to get some drinks and Imogen felt peaceful and relaxed, thinking only about the buzzing of summer insects and the wind in the trees.

Suddenly she felt something pressed against her mouth. Her eyes flew open. For the first instant she saw only a shadow against the bright sky, then she realised that Xander's face was close to hers. He was crouching next to her and pressing a raspberry to her lips. She opened her mouth to gasp and he popped the soft red fruit inside. It burst with sweet deliciousness on her tongue.

'Hello,' he said, smiling at her, and sat down beside her on the rug.

All the breath felt knocked from her body. He looked unbearably handsome, with the sun he'd soaked into his golden-brown skin in St Tropez. His hair had lightened several shades and his blue eyes were darker than ever. She felt as if she were quivering all over and hoped he couldn't see the naked longing in her eyes.

'Hello,' she said, her voice sounding surprisingly normal considering her turmoil. 'Have you had a nice holiday?'

'Yeah. Wicked.'

'It's lovely to see you,' she said, trying not to sound too breathless.

He smiled at her. 'You too. How have you been?'

'Fine. Just chilling here with Allegra. We've had a wonderful time.' It all sounded so normal – just two old friends chatting – but inside she was crying, *Do you remember? Do you remember what happened between us?* She said casually, 'How's Temple?'

'Temple?' He was surprised. 'OK, I guess.'

'The last time I saw her, she was being taken away in an

ambulance.' Imogen watched him carefully. *When we were together at the Gaveston* . . . she added silently.

Xander looked amused. 'I forgot you didn't know what had happened. She was absolutely fine, but she broke her bloody leg. Not a serious break and she was damn' lucky to get off so lightly. But you'd think the world had come to a bloody end, the way she carried on, hobbling around on her stupid crutches and expecting everyone to be her sodding servant and complaining endlessly about her suffering.'

'So . . . are you back together?' She hoped her voice didn't sound too breathless but it felt as though everything was hanging on his reply.

'No. We're not. She gave me a short sharp lesson in how tiresome she is, and that was that.'

'Oh.' Relief rushed through her, as welcome as a cool drink. *He's single. As far as I know* . . . There were, after all, other girls in the world besides Temple: gorgeous, desirable creatures – and Xander could take his pick.

He put a hand on her arm, making her skin prickle where he touched it. She hoped he wouldn't notice that she was almost trembling. He said softly, 'You're looking delectable. Like a sunburnt summer maiden.' He reached out and tucked a loose strand of her hair back behind her ears. Being so close to him almost made her gasp out loud.

'Xander . . .' she began, but was interrupted by a shout.

'Hurray, you're home!' Allegra put down her tray of drinks and raced across the grass to the rug. She jumped into Xander's arms, knocking him into Imogen and pushing them both down so that, for a moment, the three of them lay together in a kind of embrace. Then Allegra sat up and said, 'So how was it, you lucky bastard?'

'Riotous.' Xander stayed lying on the rug, grinning up at his sister. 'Totally depraved, of course. I've brought Ollie and

Luca back. They're putting their stuff upstairs. I thought we could have a barbie tonight.'

Imogen lay beside him, unable to move, full of suppressed pleasure at being next to him.

'Great. Poor old Midge and I have been bored stiff on our own. We need some sexy men. Well, I do. You don't, do you, Midge? Her boyfriend is coming up tomorrow.'

Xander turned to her, raising his eyebrows. 'Your boyfriend? Imogen – you break my heart.'

Damn. Why did Allegra have to mention that? She nodded slowly.

'You'll just have to bring him over here so I can tell him to do the right thing by you.'

'You don't need to do that,' Allegra said. 'He's totally mushy over Midge. Worships the ground she walks on.'

'So he should,' Xander said with a grin. 'Now, ladies, shall we get some of that lovely lemonade you've brought out? I'm parched.'

It's the damn' flirting, Imogen told herself, as she got ready for dinner upstairs. *That's what makes it so difficult. He treats me like a little girl, but always with that edge, teasing me, pretending that he's interested . . . Does it mean anything or not? Does he remember what happened? God, it's so confusing.*

She examined her reflection, pleased that they'd been sunbathing so much recently. Her legs were a good colour, and she had sun-kissed arms and shoulders, and a pretty pink-brown tinge to her cheeks. She'd borrowed one of Allegra's loose summer dresses which was a little too long and too tight, but that's what came of being short and plump compared to her friend.

On the way down to the lawn, she looked out of one of the windows and saw some people gathering on the lawn, Xander among them, now in shorts and a canary-yellow polo shirt. He'd obviously taken control of the barbecue and was monitoring it carefully while his friends stood around, drinking beers, smoking and chatting.

Imogen was filled with a sense of happiness. Here she was: young and carefree, with a castle at her disposal, and the man she adored downstairs. They had a summer's evening ahead of them when anything might happen . . . What pleasure. She shivered with anticipation and went down to join them.

Xander's friends were like him: casual but entirely confident, with the easy manner that came from knowing the world well already, and from the vantage point of wealth and privilege. One, Luca, was an Italian who spoke perfect English. The other, Ollie, was an old school friend of Xander. Imogen took the glass of Pimm's that was offered to her and settled down to watch the men and listen to their conversation, which was full of gossip about their recent trip to the South of France. When Allegra joined them, she was keen to party, pouring herself a large glass of wine. 'It's been so dull here!' she declared. 'Just Midge and me – no one's come near the place for weeks and weeks!'

'Haven't we got a house party coming?' asked Xander, putting some steaks on to the grill.

'Yes – but that's not exactly going to make it party central round here, is it? A load of old fogies and their tweeds. Hopefully I'll have got away from here by the time they all arrive for the shooting.'

'Have you got plans?' Imogen said, surprised. Allegra hadn't said anything about going anywhere.

'I'm working on it. I've got to think about the future at any rate. I can't stay here for the rest of my life. But let's not talk about all that now.' She lifted her glass. 'Up your bums, everyone! Let's get pissed.'

Dinner was delicious: simple but just right. Xander

barbecued the steaks perfectly and served them with the housekeeper's buttery new potatoes and salads. Allegra kept their glasses topped up and the boys amused them with funny stories and gossip from the Mediterranean playground of the rich. The Scottish summer evening seemed to go on and on. It was not dark even at ten o'clock, though the sky was fading to lavender and there was a chill in the air after the warm day.

'Shall we add a little spice to this party?' asked Xander idly, and brought out a wrap. 'Anyone for a pick-me-up?'

'Yes, please,' said Allegra promptly. She seemed to be in high spirits, Imogen thought, and looked wonderful as usual. Like Xander's, her hair had taken on a lustrous golden sheen from the sun, and her floral mini dress looked effortlessly stylish and yet casual, teamed with pink flowery flip-flops. She had been flirting hard with Luca whose dark Italian looks, curly hair and strong jawline, had obviously taken her fancy.

Xander took a mat and opened his wrap out, pouring the powder on to the shiny surface. Everyone carried on chatting but Imogen watched as he chopped up the powder with a razorblade from his wallet, clearly well practised at it. When he'd refined it sufficiently, he divided it up into five neat lines, took out a silver straw and passed it first to Allegra.

'This is cute,' she said, holding the straw.

'Present from James,' replied Xander. 'He had it made 'specially.'

Allegra put the straw to her nostril and made short work of one of the lines. 'Mmmm,' she said, sniffing and putting her head back. 'That's good. Here you are, Midge.'

Imogen took it and followed suit. She hadn't had any cocaine since the days of the fiercest partying with Allegra before meeting Sam, but as soon as she'd inhaled it she remembered the numbness of her gums, the bitter taste at the back of her throat and the rush of confidence that followed. *I can see why Xander likes it.* She liked it too – but she also knew its power and had been careful not to acquire a taste for it.

Immediately they had taken the cocaine, the party seemed to shift into another gear. What had been a pleasant enough dinner with some wine and some friends, suddenly became something edgier. It was nearly dark. Candles were lit. Allegra began to flirt more blatantly with Luca. Xander cut more lines and passed the little mat round again. Allegra declared she wanted to dance and began to move around sensuously, humming to herself, while Luca watched her with appreciative eyes. After a while he got up and joined her, and before long they'd disappeared together into the darkness.

A few minutes later, laughter and shouts came from the perimeter of the lawn.

'What are those two up to?' Xander said, his face illuminated by the flickering golden light of the candles. 'Shall we go and see, Imogen?'

She got up at once, her heart beginning to race. 'Yes.'

'Oh, great, I'll just stay here like a bloody great gooseberry,' Ollie said crossly. 'Not enough women at your bloody parties, McCorquodale!'

Xander laughed and shrugged. He stood up and took Imogen's hand. 'Bad luck, mate. You should have tried harder with Allegra.'

The next moment, he and Imogen were wandering together, hand in hand, into the soft darkness.

This is perfect happiness, she thought, as they made their way across the lawn and into the heathery woodland beyond, smelling the warm grassy scents of the summer night. There was the subtle chirrup of crickets and soft fluttering as birds settled down for the night. *Walking with*

Xander, holding his hand, knowing that sooner or later he's going to kiss me . . .

He said nothing to her but the air was rich with tension. As her eyes grew accustomed to the darkness, she guessed where they were going, and a few minutes later they arrived at the pink marble temple that glowed white in the moonlight. There were distant shrieks and laughter. Allegra and Luca were far away, perhaps down by the water from the sound of it.

As soon as they were in the temple, Xander turned to Imogen and, without a word, seemed to fall upon her as though he wanted to devour her. His mouth was pressed to hers, his warm tongue pushing at her lips until her mouth opened, while his hands were tugging at her clothes, pulling down the straps of her dress, yanking at her zip, lifting the skirt and bunching it around her thighs, as though he wanted everything to happen at once and as fast as possible.

All she could do was help him: she wanted to surrender to him utterly, to demonstrate the extent of her passion for him by giving herself to him exactly as he wanted. She pulled her zip down and let her dress fall to the floor, then undid her bra so he could pull it off. With a smooth movement, she pulled down her knickers and stepped out of them, so she was completely naked in front of him.

Then he was pushing her down to the ground, taking her with him to the marble floor. She gasped as her bare skin touched the icy stone. He pulled off his polo shirt, put it under her back and lay down beside her, still kissing her as though she were offering him the breath of life. She put her arms round his warm body, glorying in the sensation of his smooth skin under her palms, and then moved her hand down to his shorts. His cock was rock hard against his fly. As she unbuttoned it, his penis seemed to leap free, eager to find her. He rolled over so that he was between her thighs and she pushed the shorts and his boxers down so he was entirely released.

'Christ . . .' he muttered. He dipped his head and buried his face in the tender part of her neck where it met her shoulder, kissing and nipping her in a way that was almost unbearable. She closed her eyes and put her head back, turning her consciousness inwards so that she concentrated only on what she could feel: his penis was pushing against her mound, its head occasionally pressing against the bud of her clitoris and sending a strong buzz of pleasure radiating through her whole body. He pulled back his hips and grasped his cock in his hand and directed it towards the entrance of her pussy. She was ready for him.

For a moment, his tip pushed at the tight hole, then he found the sweet spot and his cock moved freely, her juices making it easy for him to slide in, filling her up in the most delicious way. She made a sound like a kind of sob: an expression of the beauty of what she was experiencing. He seemed to be in the very heart of her, moving inside, while his mouth gnawed and pulled at her neck, nipping and sucking and driving her wild.

'Oh my God . . .' she gasped.

He began to breathe heavily as he picked up pace and moved inside her faster and faster. She threw her legs round his back, desperate to drive him deeper and deeper inside her. She wanted them to become one completely, to possess him as utterly as she could. Reaching down, she seized his buttocks and dug her nails into them, pulling him down into her core.

He changed position slightly, making her move one leg and interlock it with his, then he slowed his pace and began to thrust into her rhythmically and slowly.

She gasped again and opened her eyes, watching his face as he moved. The new position meant that as he pushed in to his deepest, he rubbed against her clitoris at its most sensitive point, sending shudders of pleasure through her that increased in intensity with every thrust.

'Yes,' she whispered. 'Yes . . .' It was all she could say.

'Is that right? Is that good?' murmured Xander.

'Yes!' It seemed so feeble but it was all she could do to say that, with the sensations that were beginning to overwhelm her. It was like nothing she had known before: it felt as though all control were being taken from her and all she could do was let it happen. *Oh my God, I'm going to come . . .* she thought, half astonished, half elated. She'd thought she'd had orgasms before: little tremulous things that Sam rubbed her to with his fingers. Never had she felt this extraordinary rush, never like this, with a cock plunging strong and hard inside her and the unbearable, unstoppable rubbing of Xander's body on her clit. *It's happening . . . I can't stop it, I have to come . . .*

She pulled him to her as her head went back, and she cried out with astonishment as the climax gripped her, shaking her from within through her whole body. Xander gasped and his back arched, he pushed hard into her and the waves broke over them both.

It was some moments before they came back to themselves and an awareness that they were lying on freezing stone.

'I wasn't expecting that,' Xander whispered, stroking her cheek. 'I often can't perform as completely as I'd like when a bit of charlie's been involved, if you see what I mean.'

'You didn't seem to have too much of a problem,' Imogen said, smiling, luxuriating in the wonderful post-orgasm feeling, and the intimacy she felt with him.

'Oh, dear.' He inspected her neck. 'I seem to have left my mark on you.'

Her hand went to it. It felt fine. 'What do you mean?'

'I've given you a love bite.' He grinned at her. 'What on earth is your boyfriend going to say?'

'Sam . . .' She'd forgotten all about him, as usual.

'You won't be able to hide that from him, will you?' He took hold of her hand and kissed it. 'So very sweet,' he murmured. 'Everything about you – so sweet. I want you to stop wasting yourself on men who aren't worthy of you. Do you promise?'

She nodded, not able to take her eyes off his mouth. Was there ever such a beautiful, well-formed mouth, such perfect lips? 'I'm going to tell him we have to break up.'

'Darling, I'd say it's non-negotiable. Now, you're shivering. Let's get you dressed and off this bloody cold floor.'

Chapter 27

Allegra rolled over and looked at Luca's handsome face as he slept beside her. They'd had fun last night, skinny dipping in the loch and fooling around on the shore. Then they'd come back to find Ollie had gone to bed and Xander and Imogen were nowhere to be seen, so they'd gone to Allegra's room.

He isn't bad, Allegra decided. She liked the patch of soft dark curls that spread out across his chest towards his dark brown nipples, and the caffe-latte colour of his skin. Those dark, heavy-boned looks were so different from her own blonde fairness, and she admired the contrast: soft white wrist against a brown one dusted with fine black hair.

What had the sex been like? *The same as always,* she decided. Whenever she had sex, the same thing happened every time. She would try to lose herself and enjoy it, but always there was that out-of-body sensation, as though she were floating up and observing what was happening from far above. Then the little voice would begin: she hated that little voice but nothing would make it be quiet. It insisted on making its running commentary on events, always with that edge of contempt in its tone: 'Look at you now, with your tits out. Are you really going to let him suck you like that? It doesn't feel very good, does it? It feels of nothing! What does he think he's doing? That's right, open your legs, just as you always do! Now, here it comes.

You'd better sigh or moan or he won't think you're enjoying it . . .'

But I could enjoy it, I know I could, if I could only be allowed, she thought furiously. *What the hell is wrong with me? I can't enjoy sex, I can't fall in love . . . I'm just not normal.* She knew what she was scared of: she was being punished for the bad things she'd done. For Sophie Harcourt. For that bad man in Paris who'd made her do those things with him. For not being good enough for everything she'd got.

Luca stirred and rolled towards her, his face innocent in sleep.

Could I fall in love with him? she wondered. *Can he break the spell?*

But she was already sure it was a waste of time. Hadn't the voice told her so even while she was pounding on top of him, urging him to his climax? *It's a waste of time!* it had said scornfully. And it was always right.

Allegra stormed out on to the terrace. 'Xander! Did you really shag Imogen last night? Ollie says you did!'

Her brother was reviving himself with black coffee and fruit salad while Ollie and Luca had gone down to the tennis court for a match, saying they wanted to sweat out the toxins.

He looked up, unperturbed. 'Morning. You haven't been listening to idle gossip again, have you? Besides, what's sauce for the goose is sauce for the gander. You shagged Luca.'

'That's different!' she said crossly, putting her hands on her hips.

'Why?'

'Imogen's my friend!'

'Luca's my friend.'

'It's not the same, and you know it's not. You've known

Midge for years. She's a friend of both of us. You can't just sleep with her!'

Xander remained irritatingly calm. 'It's fine, and it's none of your business. She knows how it is. She understands. It's just something very sweet and nice between two old friends.'

Allegra frowned. 'Are you sure she sees it that way? You know, she's always had a soft spot for you. If you start sleeping with her, she's bound to fall in love with you, and then you'll break her heart. You mustn't do it, you really mustn't.'

'All right then, if it bothers you so much, I won't.' Xander shrugged and took another sip of his coffee. 'Like I said, it's not a big deal.'

'You haven't led her on or anything, have you?' Allegra said warningly. 'You're the one who was telling me not to lead her astray!'

'Of course I haven't. I said some nice things to her – and I meant them. She's a lovely girl and I'm very fond of her. But I've never said anything more than that. I'm not going to lie to her. Like I said, she knows how it is.'

'Oh, God, I blame myself for this.' Allegra walked over to the edge of the terrace and stared out over the loch, which was covered in little white caps where the wind was whipping up the water. 'I told her to look out for you. I probably set the whole thing off. Oh, bugger . . .' She turned back to her brother with a warning expression. 'If you've done anything to hurt her, Xander, I'll be so furious with you! It's not fair to include her in your womanising ways.'

'If it matters that much to you, I won't go near her again,' he said in a bored voice. 'You're making way too much of this, Allegra.'

'Good. I think it's best if you don't. I couldn't bear it if you messed her up.'

'Quid pro quo, Allegra. Go easy on Luca.' Xander grinned.

'Ever spent any time with a broken-hearted Italian? It ain't easy. All those tragic arias.'

'Ha, ha.' She went back over to the table and sat down. 'Now can I please have some coffee? I've got a hell of hangover here.'

Allegra wasn't surprised when Imogen didn't call that day. Not only were they all wiped out after the impromptu party, but Sam was due.

Whenever she thought about Xander and Imogen, she felt a surge of protectiveness towards her friend. *I've been so stupid. Of course . . . she's not in love with Sam, and she's so romantic, she's bound to fall for someone like Xander – the charming but reckless womaniser who needs looking after. I was an idiot to put the idea into her head. I've got to warn her off before she starts getting some kind of serious crush on him. I'd be caught in the middle, she'd get hurt . . . it'd be awful.*

When Imogen did ring the next day and suggested coming over to Foughton, Allegra said that she was bored of hanging round at home, and what she actually needed was a trip out. Why didn't they to go to Edinburgh and do some shopping?

They met outside Jenners on Princes Street, just as they always had since they were schoolgirls, and wandered about, eventually finding a nice little tea room where they could take a break from the busy streets outside. The festival would be starting soon, and the city was filling up in preparation.

Allegra ordered a pot of Earl Grey and lit up a cigarette, while Imogen decided to have a banana milkshake.

'So – quite a night the other night!' Allegra said, with a mischievous grin, mentioning the subject for the first time. 'I suppose you know I pulled Luca?'

'Did you?' Imogen seemed very interested in stirring the

blob of ice cream that was melting on top of the yellow milk. 'I thought you might have.'

'Mmm.' Allegra nodded, holding a mouthful of smoke for a moment and then exhaling. 'It was a laugh, actually. We had a swim and then went back to my room and got serious.'

'What was he like?'

'Passionate.' Allegra nodded. 'He really put his back into it.' She laughed. 'I could hardly walk the next day.'

'Are you going to see him again?'

'Maybe. He's gone now. So has Ollie. Xander's still at home, but he wants to leave before the family start arriving. It's going to be grouse-shooting fever for the next few weeks and he isn't that keen.' Allegra looked carefully at Imogen who still appeared entirely unaffected by the subject matter, except for a slight pink stain on her cheeks. *Thank God for that!* 'So . . . how about you?'

'What about me?'

'A little bird told me that you and Xander got kind of close the other night.'

Imogen's face turned scarlet. 'Oh . . . well, yes . . . a bit . . .' She looked confused and stopped talking.

Allegra laughed. 'Well, we all got a bit carried away, I suppose. I had stern words with him.'

'Did he say anything about it?' Imogen said breathlessly, her grey eyes eager.

'Not really. Just that he thinks you're sweet.'

'Does he?' Her face lit up. 'Did he say that?'

Allegra leant towards her friend, her own eyes kind but serious. 'Midge, I don't want to be horrible but I've got to say it: please don't get het up over Xander. He's not a prospect. Really. He's far too flaky for you and he'd mess you about. You know what's he's like, he's an incorrigible womaniser. He loves them and leaves them all the time.

Steer well clear, that's my advice. You deserve someone much more reliable – like Sam.'

'That's all finished,' mumbled Imogen glancing away. Her hand went to her neck where she wore a scarf tightly knotted. 'We agreed it was best.'

'Oh, God, I'm sorry. Was it horrible?'

Imogen nodded, looking downcast. 'It was. He wasn't happy.'

Allegra put her hand on her friend's. 'I'm sorry, love. But you did say it was going to happen, so I suppose it can't be too upsetting for you. And you'll find someone else, I know you will.' She took her hand away and lifted up her china tea cup. 'Just make sure he's nothing like Xander, that's all.'

'All right,' Imogen said in a weak voice. 'It didn't mean anything, I suppose.'

'Exactly. I'm glad you see it that way. I think it's much the healthiest approach. Besides, you and Xander . . . well, it's a bit close for comfort, isn't it?' Allegra sipped her tea. *There. I think that's sorted it. Thank God I found out about it before any more damage was done.*

Chapter 28

Imogen sped along the road to Foughton, driving more recklessly than usual, shooting past slow lorries and overtaking cautious holiday drivers unaccustomed to the winding country roads. Adrenaline coursed through her.

I can't bear it another minute. I have to find out what he feels. Any moment he'll be off again and then it will be just like it was last time. He'll leave me hanging, not knowing what it all meant. But it's not like the Gaveston, he can't pretend it never happened. It was different! I know it was! People don't have magnificent sex like that for it to mean nothing.

The last few days had been full of emotion. After her night with Xander she'd gone home the next day feeling elated and excited but also guilty. Going over and over what had happened and thrilling to the memory, she knew that he'd told her to break up with Sam. *It's non-negotiable,* he'd said. Surely that meant that, after what had just happened between them, they were supposed to be together . . . And he'd told her how sweet she was. Why would he if he didn't feel something for her? Then there'd been the love bite on her neck, a livid red mark on her skin as though he'd branded her his personal property. How could it be a coincidence that he'd done that the night before Sam arrived?

It had been awful the next day. She'd felt nervous, tearful and cross as Sam's car had pulled into the drive. When he came inside, she turned her face so that his welcoming kiss, meant for her mouth, landed on her cheek. He was bright and cheerful, happy to see her, and she became colder.

At first, he'd tried to hide his hurt at her lack of pleasure in seeing him but eventually he'd asked if something was wrong.

Imogen had looked up at him, her eyes full of tears.

'Hey, you're crying! What is it?'

'Oh, Sam!' Her irritation with him suddenly melted away. She felt sorry for him, and for herself. He was a good man, really, and didn't deserve this. But what could she do? She was in love with someone else.

'Come on now, it's OK.' He took her in his arms and hugged her to him, rocking her gently and resting his cheek on her hair. 'What's the matter?'

She leaned into him for a moment, taking comfort from the solid warmth of his body, and sniffed. 'Allegra's been sent down,' she said quietly. 'She's not coming back to Oxford.'

He pulled back and looked at her, his hazel eyes surprised and sympathetic. 'Really? Poor kid. That's bad.'

'You don't care!' Imogen burst out. 'You're glad she's not coming back!'

'I'm not glad they've sent her down. But I think it might be a good thing for you. I know she's your best friend, but she's a crazy party animal and takes you along for the ride. I don't think you're really like that. Now you've got a chance to discover your own identity. Maybe you'll like it.'

'No, I won't,' cried Imogen stubbornly. 'I'll hate it without her. I might not go back myself.'

'That would be the stupidest thing you ever did,' Sam said, holding her hand. 'I know you're upset but you'll be surprised how quickly things there will seem normal. You'll make other friends.'

'That's so typical of you!' Anger coursed through her, and she was glad of it: it helped her find the courage she needed.

'You've always hated Allegra! You're jealous of her. Don't think I haven't noticed because I have.'

Sam frowned. 'What's that?'

'What?'

He was gazing at the flowery scarf she'd wrapped around her neck. 'That.' He reached out and pulled the floating chiffon away. Imogen gasped and put her hand up to her neck to cover the mark, but he grabbed her wrist and held it back. His expression changed, the warmth and concern flooding out of it. Now it was cold and grim. 'Is that what I think it is?'

'I . . . I . . . N-n-no,' Imogen stuttered.

'Yes, it is.' He dropped her hand as though it had suddenly burned him. 'What have you done, Imogen? Have you cheated on me? Have you slept with someone else?'

She stared at him, unable to think of a word to say, trying to think of an excuse but none came. There was no way she could explain that mark away: it told its own story. Her face flamed. She knew that guilt was written all over it.

'I see.' Sam seemed to wince as though some unseen force was causing him pain, and a look of hurt and bewilderment passed over his face. 'Shit . . . Shit! Why? Why did you do it?'

'I don't know,' she said helplessly. How could she begin to explain?

'Who is it? Are you in love with him?' Her gaze slid away from him and his expression changed. 'It's that tosser, isn't it? Allegra's brother. It's Xander fucking McCorquodale! The lord of the manor, conveniently just up the road. You've always been like a puppy round him, panting eagerly, hoping for a little pat and a bit of praise. You fucking idiot – did you really go and sleep with him?'

'Yes,' she said defiantly. 'I did!'

Sam groaned and rubbed his hand through his short

brown hair. He sat down in an armchair and for a long time stared at his hands. When he looked up, his eyes glistened with wetness. 'You've thrown us away, for that?'

She felt reckless. She was a woman caught in sin with her lover, a tragic heroine, an Anna Karenina. 'I love him,' she declared, stoutly.

Sam shook his head sadly; his anger seemed crushed by his sorrow. 'Oh, Imogen. You think this is the beginning of something beautiful, don't you? Can't you see what he's like, how he operates? He shags girls all the time! Do you think you're any different? I suppose you've got some crazy idea that he'll realise your devotion to him and that you're worth hundreds of those society girls he hangs out with, and miraculously fall in love with you . . .'

Imogen flinched. That was exactly how it was. It hurt to hear the scornful tone in Sam's voice as he casually laid bare her dearest wish.

'He's going to use you and throw you aside, just like all those others. And you're going to let him. Can't you see – if he loved you, he'd be with you by now? He obviously knows he can have you whenever he wants, on tap.' Sam put his face in his hands for a moment and breathed hard. 'But you've made your choice. I can see that. If you had any love or respect for me, you wouldn't have slept with him. It's obviously over between us.'

She said nothing but stared at him. He seemed deflated. His bright cheeriness was gone and his shoulders were slumped.

He seemed to be waiting for her to say something. When she remained silent, he said quietly, 'Well, I'm not going to embarrass us both by staying. I don't think there's anything more to say.'

'All right,' she replied in a small voice. She was desperate for him to go now, not wanting to hear any more he might want to say about her and Xander. He didn't understand how it was, that was all.

When her mother came into the sitting room five minutes later, she found Imogen sobbing on the rug.

'Oh,' she said, surprised. 'Has Sam left?'

Imogen had wrapped her arms round her knees and nodded, crying too hard to say anything, and her mother had known at once what had happened.

'There, there, darling.' She came over, knelt by Imogen and hugged her. 'What a rotter, coming all this way just to give you the elbow! You're better off without him.'

Now Imogen pulled the car to a halt on the sweep of gravel in front of Foughton Castle. She jumped out and skirted the side of the house, taking a short cut to the lawn and from there into the heathery wilderness where the little pink temple stood on its own.

Xander saw her approaching and stood up, waving. For the first time in ages, she didn't feel the usual tremulous excitement on seeing him but a fierce determination to make him talk to her and tell her what was going on. He owed her that now.

'Hello, sweetheart,' he said as she came up to him. 'Here I am, all present and correct, just as ordered.'

She sat down on the cold stone bench next to him, puffed from her run across the grass. 'Good,' she said. He was wearing sand shoes without laces, worn denim shorts and a vintage T-shirt, and looked adorably summery.

He leant forward and dropped a small kiss on her cheek. 'Lovely to see you. So . . . what is it you want to talk to me about?'

'Xander!' she said, exasperated, flushing. 'What do you think?'

He took out a packet of cigarettes, tucked one between

his lips and lit it. As he blew out a cloud of smoke, he said, 'About the other night, I suppose.' He glanced at her neck. 'Did your boyfriend find out?'

She put her hand to the place. 'It's nearly gone now, thank God. My mother was beginning to wonder why I keep wearing my scarf. And, yes, he did find out. We broke up.'

'Ah.' Xander narrowed his eyes and stared out across the heather. 'Well, I think that's probably for the best, don't you? You weren't exactly behaving like he was the love of your life.'

'No,' she said, thinking, *No, because you are!*

He said nothing, even though she longed for him to say something. In her wildest fantasies he cried out that now she could be his, and pulled her into his arms to kiss her. That seemed utterly stupid, sitting beside him while he remained silent.

'Aren't you going to say anything?' she said in a small voice. 'About what happened? I thought it was lovely . . .'

He turned to her swiftly. 'Hey, it *was* lovely.' He put a hand on hers, smooth and warm. 'I'm sorry, I should have said.'

She waited for more and, when it didn't come, said, 'Is that all? Isn't there anything else you want to say?'

'Well . . .' Xander blinked and thought hard. 'You are a lovely, sexy girl, and thank you for sharing that with me.'

She felt desperate. Was he being deliberately obtuse? 'You haven't even asked me if I'm on the Pill! You . . . finished . . . inside me. I might be pregnant for all you know.'

He looked startled, taking his hand off hers. 'Really?'

'Well . . . no. I am on the Pill as it happens, but that's not the point. You didn't ask me. You pretend these things – us being together – don't exist after they've happened. Sometimes I don't even know if you remember them! I just need you to tell me if . . . if . . . if it's going to happen again.'

She could hear the beseeching note in her own voice and knew she was looking at him with pleading eyes.

Xander's face softened. 'Of course I remember. We both know it was glorious. You're a very sexy, lovely girl . . . but you're far too good for me.'

'No, I'm not,' she protested. 'Not at all.'

His eyes became solemn. He tossed his cigarette to the floor, scrubbed it out under his shoe and then turned to face her. 'You are, I promise you. Listen, Imogen, if you're holding a torch for me, you'd better put it out right now. I'm telling you, it's really not worth it. *I'm* not worth it.' He reached for her hand again, taking it in his. 'You know that I'm half in love with you – because you're sweet and funny and good, you're something real and natural in my crazy world – but that doesn't mean it's enough.'

'But . . .' She was agonised. 'You wanted me to break up with Sam!'

'Only because I could see he's not right for you. It doesn't mean I'm the one who'll take his place. You do understand that, don't you?'

She kept her head bowed so that she was staring at his hand over hers. *Don't cry,* she told herself sternly, even though despair was coursing through her. *Why won't he even give me a chance?*

Xander's voice was light-hearted again. 'You're going to find a fantastic guy one of these days, I know it. And I shan't forget the lovely times we've spent together.'

She felt a sob rise in her throat and choked it back. Her shoulders shook with the effort.

'Hey.' He was tender, stroking his hand over hers. 'Don't cry. Please, Imogen. Like I said, I'm really not worth it.'

Oh, Xander, you are. But what can I do if you don't want me?

Chapter 29

Paris
Summer 2003

It was a great relief to be home, even if the circumstances of her return were not quite what she would have hoped.

In her daydreams, Romily had imagined Cherub becoming a successful chain of stores, with an outlet on all of the world's most exclusive shopping streets. That dream was well and truly shattered now. Cherub was over and, to be honest, she was glad to see the back of it.

Right from the start, the idea had been cursed. She dated the bad luck back to the opening night, when she'd seen that man being beaten up in the alley. From then on, things got worse and worse but the culmination was the robbery. It was lucky that the boy robbing them had been such a bad shot he had managed to sink all the bullets he fired into the wall of the stock room. Lucky for Muffy too that she had fainted: several entered the plaster at head-height, and she had been in line for one in the skull if she hadn't hit the floor first.

Romily had stayed amazingly calm: she didn't mean to be brave but something inside had taken over and she had remained mentally alert, able to dart forward, knock the gun out of the boy's hand and yank him by the coat. He'd stared up at her for a long moment, looking very young and very scared, before he'd shrugged the coat off and slipped from her grasp, running out of the door. He'd taken Muffy's wallet with him but left hers. It was small consolation.

Once Muffy had been taken away in an ambulance, Romily had locked the shop for the last time. *I never want to go there again!* she told herself, as the driver negotiated their way back to the Fifth Avenue apartment and civilisation. The whole thing was ruined for her. New York was ruined for her. She told the lawyers she was through with her shop and left it to them to deal with closing it down, tidying up the paperwork, settling any bills and getting it off her hands. She herself booked a flight back to Paris for as soon as she possibly could.

It stung to see how happy her mother was that she was back. Romily could tell that she was very satisfied with the way things had turned out, even if she was appalled at what the girls had gone through. It was clear that Athina de Lisle thought she had been very generous in allowing Romily to play at keeping shop and that everything had turned out just as she'd thought it would, although perhaps a little more violently. The shop was finished, Romily was bored with the notion of a career, and now they could go back to how things were supposed to be. In New York, Romily had refused to have a bodyguard. Well, there would be no more nonsense like that now . . .

'You've missed the best fashion shows,' her mother said happily, almost before Romily was back in the apartment. 'We'll have to ask for special viewings. I'm sure they'll do that for us. They know how we like to place our orders at this time of the year. There is so much to think about – the ball in Rome is in October and I haven't anything to wear, and nor have you! So we'd better get a move on.'

Romily surrendered to it all. She had failed at what she'd set out to do, and that was a bitter pill. But soon, she hoped, it would be forgotten about and she would be able to find something else to do with herself. She had a feeling that her mother was about to concentrate very seriously on potential matches for her; there was the definite sense in the air that a wedding was due, or at least a little bit of romance and courtship. When Athina de Lisle told her cheerfully that she had been married at Romily's age and already running a home, she knew her suspicions were correct.

It's another game she wants to play, she thought crossly. *I'm no more than a great big doll to her. She dresses me, orders my life, controls me . . . now she wants to marry me off. No doubt she's keen to pick my wedding dress and organise the party to end all parties.*

Well, she can dream all she likes. The last thing I'm going to do is get married.

'Hello, Imogen? It's Romily! How are you, darling?'

'Rom, how wonderful to hear from you. Where are you? In the States?'

'No, I'm back from there.' Now that she was home, she was beginning to remember her old life and the girls who'd been her dearest friends only a few short years ago. 'I had a lovely time in New York, but now I'm home. What's happening with you?'

'Oh, God! I'd love to see you.'

'Then come to Paris. You and Allegra. What's stopping you?'

There was a sigh down the telephone line. 'Allegra won't be allowed. She's been grounded since she was sent down—'

'Sent down?' Romily was shocked. 'When did this happen?'

'A few weeks ago. She's stuck at home for the foreseeable. Why don't you come here?'

'Scotland, darling? It's the back of beyond. And I won't

have time, I'm committed to so many things already. Why don't we compromise on London? Maybe Allegra will be allowed to see me there.'

'Well, I'll ask . . .'

'Good. We obviously have a lot to catch up on.'

After a few attempts to make arrangements, the London trip was abandoned. Allegra wasn't allowed, Imogen explained, and it was so near the beginning of term, she herself had a lot of reading to do before she returned to Oxford. But they would meet very soon, she promised. Perhaps when things were settled, Romily could come to Oxford and see the sights . . .

Romily was disappointed. She'd been looking forward to seeing her old friends and swapping all their news. There had obviously been developments while she'd been away, with Allegra's scandal and Imogen's break up. She had so many questions, but finding out what had gone on would have to wait another few weeks, she supposed.

But the long silence from Allegra bothered her. It had been almost a whole year since she'd heard anything, even though she'd sent her usual postcards, always remembering to add *MG4E*, to show that she hadn't forgotten their schoolgirl bond. Why on earth was she so distant? Imogen had spoken enigmatically of Allegra's party lifestyle – perhaps she'd simply become absorbed in the excitement of Oxford and the new people she was meeting. Yes, that must be it. It was easily done – after all, Romily herself had hardly given a thought to the other two when she was caught up in Cherub. A visit, and soon, would remedy all that, she was sure of it.

It was a rare get-together for several branches of the de Lisle family. These happened only occasionally because members were usually scattered around the globe, but the occasion was Charles de Lisle's sixtieth birthday and there was going to be a grand party at the Ritz to celebrate in appropriate style. But before that very extravagant occasion there was an intimate family dinner for twenty at Reynard on Ile-St-Louis.

'I've never heard of this place,' Romily said to Estelle, who was busy bustling about making sure that her chosen accessories for the evening were in immaculate condition. Romily picked up a chandelier earring and held it up against her ear. She frowned as she turned her head to see the effect. The diamonds glittered against her smooth brown skin. 'Usually I know all the best restaurants,' she continued, deciding to wear her emerald and platinum drops instead because they would contrast beautifully with the lavender silk of her Lanvin dress. 'Perhaps this is a new one.'

'I don't know, mam'selle,' Estelle said politely. 'Which shoes will you be wearing this evening?'

'With the Lanvin, it has to be either the lavender Blahniks or the dark green Prada,' Romily said. 'Bring me the Prada. I don't want to be too much of a symphony in purple.'

I'm sure this evening is going to be tedious beyond belief, she thought as she slipped the other earring into her lobe. *No men to flirt with.*

Her cousins were fine young men but there was no point in flirting with them. They were as familiar to her as brothers. Although she and Edouard had experimented a little together as teenagers during long hot summers on Chrypkos, there was no real spark there. She was feeling the lack of any romance in her life: it had been some time since she had had so much as a kiss on the cheek. Her sojourn in New York had been remarkable for the lack of any male attention – but then, she had been rather taken up by Cherub and her burgeoning business. Usually men buzzed around her, attracted by her elegance, good looks and, of course, the vast fortune of the de Lisle family, though most of them tried to hide their interest in that aspect. Her mother was fiercely protective of Romily, screening any young men in the vicinity and constantly trying to push candidates who came from her preferred background.

Money was important: Athina de Lisle felt that Romily would only be happy with a man who was independently successful and already comfortable in the world of the super-rich. It was not as though Romily needed anyone to support her, but a man rich in his own right could not possibly be fortune-hunting. Or at least that was the idea. The only poor man Athina de Lisle might be prepared to look on favourably would be one with royal blood, or blood so noble that his name would bring honour and prestige to the de Lisle family. There were a few of those knocking about: Bourbons with claims to the non-existent throne, or sons and grandsons of deposed kings and emperors. There were some Russian Grand Dukes, still hoping that the Romanovs would be restored, and while they were dirt poor, or at least in comparison to the de Lisles, Athina de Lisle would be prepared to overlook that for the sake of Romily becoming a Grand Duchess. A princess – a crown princess, in particular – would be even better, and she was always trying to find out when any eligible Danish or Spanish princes might be about, despite their irritating propensity for marrying Americans and Australians.

Romily didn't care either way: a prince was fine by her, as long as she was in love with him. As for sex, she would see if her marquis was in Paris and perhaps resume their sensual afternoons, although she had been hoping that by now there would be someone new on the scene.

She put on the Prada shoes that Estelle had brought over: they looked wonderful and she adored the contrast of the dark green with the lavender, and the way they picked up the glitter of her emeralds. 'Very nice,' she said. 'Which bag shall I take?'

'I thought the green Fendi,' Estelle said, producing it from its protective bag.

'Excellent.' Romily smiled, satisfied. 'Then if you could fetch my wrap, I'd better get downstairs.'

The Rolls Royce took them to Ile-St-Louis. At the restaurant, the maître d' greeted them with polite enthusiasm and led them to a private dining room on the first floor.

De Lisle relations were already gathered and there was a flurry of kisses and greetings before people took their places at the table.

'I've never been to Reynard before,' declared Charles de Lisle, 'but I've heard great things about it, so I'm very much looking forward to it.'

The food was indeed delicious. Accustomed as they were to fine dining and Michelin starred chefs, the de Lisles were favourably impressed by the cooking. It was traditional French food with a modern twist that caught their interest and gave their spoiled tastebuds something new to titillate them.

'Really very good,' was Charles's verdict as they moved to dessert, a frozen chocolate parfait with a warm vanilla froth. 'I must bring Albert here – he will appreciate this, I think.'

Romily took a tiny spoonful and let it melt in her mouth, savouring the sweetness on her tongue and the smooth seductiveness of the chocolate. She saw her mother shoot her a warning look that she knew was saying, *Romily, don't eat too much of that! I don't care,* she thought. *The only time I ever have something sweet is at times like this, and even then, I only ever eat half of it.* That was the rule: she could have dessert but only in minute amounts. It was the same with wine: she had one small glass of whatever was being served with the food, but drank only half of it. Her mother had impressed on her the fattening nature of alcohol – 'A glass of wine has the same calorie content as a glass of butter!' she would declare – and the fact that a woman drunk was one of the most vulgar sights in the world. The way English girls tucked away alcohol was an absolute scandal to her, and proof that the British had lost their standing in the world. Women should know about good wine, appreciate and savour it, but they were not to swig it back like men under any circumstances. This lesson had been stressed so strongly that Romily had entirely lost her taste for alcohol and often preferred to have a single glass of champagne and then drink water.

'And what have you been doing with yourself, my dear?' said a soft voice at her elbow. It was her aunt, who had been engaged in conversation with her other neighbour for most of the dinner.

'Oh, I've been away in New York,' she said. 'I decided to stay there for a while.'

'Didn't you know?' her mother said, leaning closer with a tinkling laugh. 'Romily decided to try her hand at playing shop! Her first and, I hope, only foray into being a career girl.'

'Oh.' Her aunt raised her eyebrows and smiled at Romily's mother. 'That doesn't sound like such a bad idea. I myself believe it is very good for everyone to work. I've always encouraged Edouard and François to take jobs and earn the money they need.'

'That's different,' declared Athina de Lisle. 'They're boys!'

'Why is it different?' asked Romily, feeling anger spark into life.

'Well . . . it's obvious. A man must go out into the world and do something – and succeed. It's vital for his self respect. Look at your father, he works very hard managing the family business.'

Romily bit her tongue to stop herself retorting that her

father's work there was largely a front. He had an office where he amused himself playing at being head of this and that, but not much was actually done except by the lawyers and accountants and managers who really looked after the vast de Lisle fortune. She said in a tight voice, 'And women don't need self-respect?'

'Don't be silly. Of course they do. But a woman's self-respect comes from knowing she's as beautiful and elegant as she can possibly be, and that she is a good wife and mother. Isn't that right, Régine?'

But Romily's aunt said quietly, 'I don't know if that is all they should do, if they are capable of more.'

'Exactly!' declared Romily. 'I know I can succeed in business if I want to, all I need to do is learn how.'

Athina de Lisle pulled a disbelieving expression. Then she laughed again. 'But look at your silly little shop! My darling, I don't want to hurt your feelings but it was a disaster! You chose the wrong location and didn't understand the first thing about how to sell. I saw it for myself. Were you selling clothes or lighting? Jewellery or cushions? It was impossible to tell. Such a mess. I'm not surprised it failed.'

Romily drew in a sharp breath, feeling hurt and angry. The whole table was now listening to Athina de Lisle's views on the role of women and everyone heard her dismissal of Cherub, her daughter's first business effort, as an unmitigated failure.

Romily jumped to her feet. 'I'm not staying here to listen to this rubbish!' she shouted. 'How dare you speak to me like this? At least I've tried to make something of myself! You'd be happiest if I spent all day beautifying myself and dressing myself and planning my social life. Well, don't you understand? I want to do something *more* than that! I refuse to let you imprison me like this. Ever since I got back, you won't let me move without a bodyguard . . .'

'Can you be surprised?' retorted her mother. 'When you nearly got yourself killed by a thug?'

'At least I had the courage to try and live on my own. When have you ever tried venturing out of your cosy little world and seeing how other people live?'

'Romily, sit down!' ordered her father sternly, taking his napkin from his lap and dropping it on the table. 'Don't speak to your mother like that.'

'You always take her side!' cried Romily, not caring that the whole family was staring at her, aghast at this public display of emotion, particularly on such an occasion. 'You don't care that she wants me to waste my life doing nothing, just like you!'

Her father gaped at her, looking outraged.

'Romily, you're disgracing yourself,' hissed her mother. 'I can see you're upset. Please, let us all calm down. I'm sure we all know you're very talented.' She smiled around the rest of the room as if to reassure them that Romily's tantrum was nothing to worry about.

This condescension only increased Romily's anger. Blood rushed to her face and fury made her hands tremble. She opened her mouth to speak but, in her rage, nothing came out. She could feel tears building behind her eyes and her lip begin to tremble. *I won't cry in front of them! I won't show them I care*. She turned on her heel and ran out of the room.

She clattered down the stairs in her high shoes, then out through the restaurant and on to the street. The car had left, and anyway she didn't want to go home. She needed somewhere private. Looking around her, she saw a side street, headed for it and found herself in a quiet area that led around the side of the restaurant. A line of bins showed it was the back entrance to the place they'd been eating at. Not caring anything for the beautiful lavender silk of her Lanvin dress, Romily sat down on the doorstep and began to cry.

It was pitch dark, she realised, and cold. She'd left her wrap behind in the restaurant cloakroom, though she'd had the presence of mind to pick up her bag. But there was no money in it. How would she get home? She would have to swallow her pride, go back inside and face the humiliation of asking if she might ride home in the car. This thought made her cry even harder. *They're right,* she thought with a sniff. *I am totally dependent on them. I'm utterly useless. I failed with Cherub, just as Mama said. I'm only good for wearing expensive clothes and going to parties.* She wrapped her arms round herself as protection from the chilly night air, and wept.

'*Bonjour. . .excusez-moi,*' said a voice with an execrable French accent. '*Parlez anglais?*'

Romily looked up. Standing by the restaurant bins was a chef in the traditional white jacket – though this one was stained with food, gravy and oil – and baggy kitchen trousers. 'Yes,' she said thickly. 'I speak English.'

'I don't like to interrupt a woman when she's getting something off her chest,' he said, 'but it looks to me like you need a cigarette.'

'Oh, I do!' Romily said emphatically. The chef held out his cigarette packet and she took one gratefully, leaning forward to light it from the flame he offered.

'Feel like telling me what's the matter?' he asked sympathetically as she took a long drag.

'Oh, my family!' she said. 'I hate them!'

'Ah, yes, the eternal problem. No one's parents understand them.' He smiled at her. 'And I mean that with total sincerity. Mine certainly didn't. My theory is that no one who has any success in life is really understood by their parents. You need to feel well and truly fucked off to make something of yourself.'

'You're American,' she said, interested.

He nodded. 'Yup. The traditional American in Paris. Are you French? You sure don't sound like it.'

'I speak English with a British accent thanks to years in a girls' boarding school. But actually I'm French.'

'You're not only French, you're cold.' The chef looked at the goose bumps standing out on her skin. 'Do you want to come inside?'

She shook her head. 'No. My whole family is in there, and I've just made a terrible scene and stormed out. I can't go back.'

'I doubt they'll be in the kitchen,' he said. 'But, on second thoughts, I won't take you in there. You'll distract everyone from their work.'

'Shouldn't you be working?'

He shrugged. 'I was covering for someone but he's just come back and told me he's fine to take over tonight. I think he was told Chef's looking for someone to fire and doesn't want it to be him, even if he has a temperature and ought to be in bed.' He dropped his cigarette butt to the pavement and ground it out. 'But I oughtn't to tell you that, especially if you had the fish. Now, what are you going to do?'

'I don't know,' Romily said helplessly. She took another drag on her cigarette and sighed. 'I'll walk home, I suppose. It can't be that far, can it?'

'Anywhere is far if you're wearing that get up.' He eyed her silk dress and towering heels. 'Listen, at the very least, put on my jacket and warm up.' He unbuttoned his chef's white tunic and took it off, revealing a clean white T-shirt underneath, stretched over an impressive chest. He wrapped it round Romily. Its warmth was delicious and she snuggled into it.

'But now *you're* cold,' she said.

'I can take it.' He smiled. 'Listen, why don't I walk you back to wherever you're living? I don't have anything else to do and I don't like to think of you out here on your own in the cold and dark.'

'Well, I don't know . . .' Years of being protected by bodyguards and treated like a precious possession in imminent danger of breaking had left her wary of strangers.

'Hey, I promise, I'm not a crazy. But I am a gentleman and I can't just leave a lady in your condition on her own.' He smiled. He had kind eyes, she noticed, dark brown like her own.

I trust him, she realised.

'And, this way, I can be sure I'll get my jacket back.'

'OK,' she said. 'I'd like that. Thanks.'

They walked back across the island and crossed the bridge over the Seine towards the Latin Quarter.

'Are we going the right way?' her companion asked. 'You haven't said where you live.'

'I don't care. I don't really want to go home,' Romily said mournfully. 'I'll only feel as though I'm sitting there, waiting for my parents to come back and give me a telling off.'

'OK,' said the chef affably. 'Then why don't we go and get a drink somewhere?'

'I don't have any money.'

'I guess I can stand you a glass of wine. Come on, I know a nice little place around here where they do a good *vin rouge.*'

They went down a few smaller streets, vibrant with Moroccan restaurants, bars and cafés. People swarmed around them: students, tourists, romantic couples, and the workers and local inhabitants of one of the most busy and popular areas of Paris.

'Here we are,' said Romily's escort suddenly, and showed her down an iron staircase to a basement doorway that led into a dingy bar. He found a table for them, pulled out a rickety chair for her, summoned a waiter and ordered a carafe of *rouge*.

'Now, this is better than walking the cold streets, isn't it?' He smiled at her. *He's very handsome,* she realised suddenly. She hadn't seen it until now, but the soft low light in the bar illuminated his features so that his good looks were unmissable. He had a firm, square chin and a strong nose, and under straight dark brows, those brown eyes were strikingly well-shaped and alluring.

'Yes, it is,' she said, embarrassed as she realised that she was staring at him. She looked away.

'Hey . . . wait a minute.'

She looked back at him. His smile had vanished and he was frowning, leaning towards her. 'What is it?' she asked.

'I know you, don't I?'

She shook her head. 'I don't think so.'

'Yes – yes, I do. I know your face! But . . .' He scrunched up his own, thinking hard. 'Where would it be from? You're really familiar, but it's like I've seen you in a dream or something.'

Romily laughed. It sounded like a silly line to her. Seen her in a dream? 'Perhaps it was a past life?' she suggested. 'Maybe I was Cleopatra and you were Mark Antony.'

'No, no . . . I know I sound dumb but it wasn't quite like that . . .' He bit his lip and frowned even more fiercely. 'Damn! This is going to drive me crazy.'

The waiter arrived, put down the carafe of wine and two bistro glasses, then left without a word. This was novel to Romily, who was used to plenty of attention in bars and restaurants.

The chef leant forward and poured out the wine. He passed a glass to her and took a healthy gulp of his own. 'Jeez, I just can't shift the thought that I know you . . .'

'I don't see how,' she said reasonably. 'Besides, I've only been back in Paris a week.'

'Back from where?'

'From New York.'

The man's expression changed, and he seemed to go several shades paler. 'Oh my God,' he whispered. 'I've got it. I know where it was. It was you!'

'What was me? I mean, who was me? I mean . . .' Romily stopped, confused. *What am I asking him?* Maybe going for a drink with this man had not been such a good idea. He seemed a bit mad.

He leant closer again, his expression earnest. 'One night in New York I had a really bad experience. I got on the wrong side of this guy and he ordered a couple of his heavies to take me out and teach me a lesson. They drove me to God knows where, threw me out of their car, dragged me into an alley and proceeded to beat the living crap out of me. It was not pretty. But the girl who found me was. And I think she was you.'

Romily gasped. She saw the whole thing in her mind instantly. But that poor man had been badly beaten – his face swollen, his eyes puffy slits, and all covered in blood. He'd been nothing like this extremely handsome man. 'That was *you*?' she said incredulously.

His face cleared and he smiled broadly. 'Sure was. Theodore Mitchell at your service. But you can call me Mitch.'

Chapter 30

Foughton Castle
Scotland

'Well, Allegra – what do you suggest you do with yourself now?' Her father leant back behind his desk and pressed his fingertips together while he glared at her.

Her heart had sunk when he'd summoned her into his study after dinner. It was like some kind of Victorian interview between the pater familias and the youngest son sent down from the 'Varsity in disgrace. And, by the looks of his bloodshot eyes, he'd already been at the brandy.

'I thought I'd move to London and find a job,' she said, trying not to show that she was nervous of him.

'Really?' His lip curled. 'As what?'

'I don't know. I'll find something.'

'I suppose you could be like Miranda and get yourself a shitty little job on a pointless society magazine, but I'd hoped for more from you.' He sighed. 'You've turned out as useless as the others.'

I won't cry, she told herself, clenching her teeth. *I won't let him upset me.*

'I suppose you'll want more money. What you were living on in Oxford won't be enough in London. You can stay at Onslow Square until you've sorted yourself out and I'll see about raising your allowance.'

'I don't need that,' she replied in a loud voice, almost to her own surprise.

'Don't you?' Her father raised his eyebrows. 'You think you'll get by without anything more, do you?'

'I can look after myself,' she said proudly. 'I don't need your money – any of it.'

An expression of irritation crossed his face. 'Well, you haven't done very well so far. And you've only got your A-levels now you've thrown away your chance of a degree, so God alone knows what kind of job you're going to get.' His eyes drifted down to her thighs, bare below her cut-off denim shorts. 'Or perhaps you think you're going to find a man to pay for you.'

Icy rage filled her breast. 'I don't need a man to look after me. And I don't need *you* either! You've never given a damn about me so I don't know how you dare be disappointed in me now!' She jumped to her feet. 'And you can keep your stupid allowance! I don't bloody well need it, any of it!'

Her father slammed his hand on the desk and roared, 'Piss off then, you ungrateful little bitch! And don't come back until you've learned a little humility.'

'Fine by me!' yelled Allegra, and marched out of the study, slamming the door behind her. Then she ran upstairs to her bedroom and sobbed into her pillow, half afraid that he would come after her, ready to deal out more of the blows he had distributed so readily in the past.

Just as London's high society was heading out of town for the last dusty days of the sweltering summer, Allegra was making her way there. It was the only place she could think of to go. She was furious with her father: as usual, he hadn't even tried to understand her. He had no sympathy for her over what had happened and she was full of resentment that he'd never so much as patted her on the shoulder for managing to get into Oxford in the first place. After all, Miranda hadn't even passed her A-levels without spending almost four years at a very expensive crammer. And while she nominally worked at a glossy magazine, it was actually only in the subscriptions department. Miranda's title guaranteed her a flashy social life and entrée to the best parties, but no one could pretend she was a go-getter. She was just waiting for the right husband to come along and provide her with the London flat, the country house and the cluster of children. Fine, if it made her happy.

That's all Dad thinks I'm good for, too. But I need more than that, I need to do something with my life. I hardly register on his radar – the youngest daughter in his enormous family. He probably doesn't even remember I exist half the time. Well, I'm damn' well going to make him notice me.

The problem was, what could she do? She hadn't been entirely sure what an English degree would equip her for in the first place, and now she didn't even have that. *Whatever I do, I need to be free,* she decided. *And I have to have a go at doing something amazing.*

She couldn't think of anywhere else so went to the Kensington house, which felt empty and unloved. Even the housekeeper was on her annual leave, so the fridge was unstocked and there was a thin coating of dust everywhere.

I can't stay here forever, she told herself. *I might as well live at home if I do that. And I'm going to prove I can make it on my own.*

The problem was, all her friends were still up at their universities. In two years' time, there'd be a rush of people flooding to London, looking for flatmates and places to live. Right now, she was on her own, living on the last of her allowance. At the end of the month, there'd be nothing. Her father had been true to his word and arranged to have it stopped.

I'll talk to Miranda, she decided, *see what she's got to say.*

*

She met her big sister for dinner in one of her favourite Chelsea hangouts.

Miranda really is the most roaring Sloane, thought Allegra as they ate the house burger with goose-fat chips.

It wasn't just that her sister naturally fitted the brief, it was that she actively tried to fulfil all the criteria. Apart from her long blonde hair, which she constantly flicked away from her face, her sunglasses and her Sloane wardrobe of jeans, frilly, flowery tops and boots, she also talked in an almost unintelligible drawl, chain smoked Silk Cut, and was preoccupied only by her social life: a round of lunches at fashionable restaurants near her office, and evenings at pubs in Fulham and Kensington, dinner parties in Belgravia flats, or dancing in Chelsea nightclubs. She managed to fit skiing and country-house weekends into this packed schedule, but all that left her with barely enough energy for the requisite amount of shopping and gossiping.

'It's just, like, soooo exhausting at the moment! I've got a fortnight with the Cable-Johnsons in Rock, then straight off for a weekend at home. I'm taking Mitty, Annabel and Pogo, then back here 'cos I couldn't get any more bloody holiday out of work – can you believe it? Absolutely everybody else is going to St Trop for another week as the Greens are having their party and it's going to be *crazy*. In September, I've got four weddings and only one in London . . .'

Allegra sat there and listened and wondered how Miranda was ever going to be able to help her. Eventually she managed to break in long enough to ask if there was any work going at the magazine, but her sister looked doubtful.

'I don't know, sweetie, it's really, really difficult to get in. People are *desperate* to work there, and you have to be so well connected it's unreal. I'll ask lovely Sue, my editor, but I can't promise anything, particularly when you've got no experience.'

'I don't mind doing anything – I'll man the phones.'

But Miranda just blinked at her.

'I'm desperate, Miranda, I don't have any money. I need a job.'

Her sister sipped at her Pinot Grigio and reached for another Silk Cut. 'I can't believe you had a row with Daddy,' she said. 'Darling, I wouldn't dare! I don't know what I'd do without my allowance. That's another reason not to come near the mag, it pays an absolute pittance! All the girls have private incomes, it's the only way we can manage.'

Allegra sighed. 'Can you think of anything else?' she asked at last. 'I really need to find somewhere to live and something to do. I'm getting desperate.'

'Look, darling, I'll ask at work. Someone might need a nanny or something. And as it happens, I've got some girlfriends who are looking for a flatmate,' Miranda said. 'It's just a box room so hardly anyone wants it. You might get it cheap if you offer to do the cleaning. Their Bulgarian girl's just buggered off home.'

'Where is it?'

'Outer reaches of Chelsea. Far end of the King's Road. Bit too close to the suburbs for me, but Susie seems to like it. I'll ask her about it, if you like.'

As autumn began to swirl about the streets of Kensington and Chelsea, Allegra tried not to think about the beauty of Oxford when the new term began. This year she had been going to live out of college in a Victorian terrace house on Divinity Road with a couple of other students from her year. Imogen's college offered accommodation in the second year, so she was moving into a set in Peckwater Quad, sharing a panelled sitting room with two tiny bedrooms leading off it. Allegra had been looking forward to experiencing digs instead of the slightly suffocating college buildings.

Fuck it, I don't care, she told herself firmly. *I'm going to have a great time. I mean, I'm in London, for God's sake! If I can't have a good time, here, I'm a miserable specimen of humanity.*

Her mother begged her to stay on in Onslow Square and live rent-free, but Allegra refused. Instead, she took the offer of Susie's boxroom, which came at a cut-price rent as long as Allegra tackled the cleaning twice a week – something she soon discovered was a mammoth job as neither Susie nor her flatmate Coco so much as lifted a finger to wash a cup. But then, like her, they'd never had to.

Cleaning the bathroom and washing the dishes came as quite a shock to Allegra but she soon found it almost therapeutic. It felt as though she was earning her own way at last. Every dish cleaned was another step away from her failure at Oxford and towards independence.

Susie and Coco didn't take much notice of Allegra: she was six years younger than they were and they were in the full flow of London life. They thought she was sweet-natured and pretty, and having a lodger-cum-cleaner with a title gave them a little added cachet, but apart from that, they left her alone. For the first time in a long while, Allegra was truly lonely. She kept getting invitations to parties in Oxford with people who were still there, and couldn't bring herself to accept. It was just too painful.

So she whiled her days away, wandering up and down the King's Road, reading in Chelsea Library, buying endless cups of coffee in cafés, or going to Peter Jones for tea and cake.

Is life passing me by? she wondered. *I'm only twenty. Can it really all be over?*

A casual recommendation by Susie brought her a job in a candle shop on Walton Street where she soon learnt to consider scented candles one of the most pointless inventions in the world. Still, it used up a few hours every day, earned her some cash and gave her plenty of dreaming time to wonder what on earth she was going to do with herself next.

A letter arrived, forwarded to her from Foughton Castle.

Allegra chérie,

How are you? It's been too long! I miss you! I've just had a lovely long email from Imogen, who filled me in on some of your news. I was so sorry to hear that you got sent down – what horrible bad luck. You're probably feeling a bit low after all that but, knowing you, you're raring to have a go at something else.

I was going to go to Oxford to see Midge but she's working too hard at the moment, she says. I think she's depressed about a boy – do you know anything about it?

If you're not busy, why don't you come and see me? I've just got back to Paris from New York and am having an amazing time. I'll tell you the whole story when I see you, but in a nutshell I've fallen madly, madly in love and he's wonderful! Come and meet him . . .

I don't know where you're living and Imogen didn't say, so I'm sending this to Foughton and hope it reaches you. You can get me on this number. Do you have the same mobile? Perhaps you didn't get my texts. Be in touch, I'd love to hear all your news.

Lots of love,

Romily x

P.S. I haven't forgotten . . . MG4E

Allegra finished reading the letter and dropped it on the kitchen table. She hadn't seen or been in touch with her friend now for over a year. Somehow, she couldn't bring herself to contact her. She knew it was stupid and irrational but whenever she thought of Romily, she remembered her trip to Paris, and the very thought of that made her palms clammy and her heart race.

I don't know why, she told herself. *It's not as if she did anything wrong.* Something shadowy flickered at the back of her mind, but she refused to look at it or think about it.

She's in love. The idea made Allegra feel simultaneously nauseated and depressed. She looked at the letter again. *Perhaps I'll call her. Maybe it would be fun to go to Paris.*

But she knew in her heart that she wouldn't go.

Chapter 31

Scotland
January 2004

Imogen returned from the first term of her second year feeling thoroughly disconsolate. Back in Oxford, she'd been told in no uncertain terms that she had to pull her socks up.

'It's been noted that you wasted your potential in the first year,' her tutor had said. Although he'd been perfectly friendly and had plied her with sherry as usual, he'd been quite clear about what the college expected from her. 'We know you're capable of more. I don't want to see you waste your time here, becoming some kind of social gadfly. There are too many people who take that path. Please don't be one of them.'

There wasn't much chance of that any more. Without Sam and Allegra, Imogen had lost her entire social circle; invitations to the smart set's parties dried up with startling speed, and without Allegra to manage things she no longer had entrée to Oxford's smartest clubs and houses. In fact, she had no one at all except for Nick, with whom she was sharing a set, who was still her tutorial partner.

'Ah, love,' he said sympathetically. 'No more tales of the high life from you! Don't worry, you've still got me.'

And, thank goodness, she did. Nick was always ready to listen, and always keen to pop open a bottle and sympathise while she talked about Xander, which she did a lot.

She simply couldn't help it. He was like an obsession with her. Although she was working hard at her second-year studies, she could think of little else when she wasn't deep in Chaucer or *Paradise Lost*.

'Do you think he's going to go out with me one day?' she would ask Nick, having gone through every facet of the relationship from beginning to end all over again.

'He might,' Nick would say, putting on another Kate Bush track. 'It's definitely possible. But I think you should wait for him to come after you. No bloke likes a sure thing – let him do some of the chasing. But, to be honest, from what you've said, it doesn't sound like he's going to.'

Imogen tried to listen to his wise words but the longing for Xander was overwhelming, despite what he'd said to her in the temple. Even though he'd told her he didn't think their liaison would ever go anywhere, she was powerless to resist his lure. She spent hours trailing round Oxford, from library to library, from pub to café to restaurant, hoping she might run into him by chance. On more than one occasion, she found herself walking past the St Margaret's Road house late at night, wondering if she dared knock on the door. Once, she even stood outside on the front step for five minutes before she quailed and hurried away. Every day she checked her pigeon hole, hoping that he would send her a note, an invitation, something . . . anything . . . but he never did.

What am I going to do? she agonised. *How can I see him again? I know if I did I could convince him to give us a chance.*

Allegra was her best hope, but she had no interest in coming back to Oxford. Imogen tried to invite her for a visit but she was resolute.

'No way,' she said firmly when Imogen phoned her and suggested it. 'I'm not going back, ever. You come to me if you want.'

But Imogen was working too hard to get away, and anyway, what was the point of that when Xander was here in Oxford? Unless, of course, he was in town. 'What's Xander up to?' she said casually, but Allegra guessed at once.

'Oh, no, honey, I'm not putting you two together again! I won't expose you to that. He's a menace, Midge. Honestly, I'm doing it for your own good. Xander's going off the rails these days and I don't want him to take you with him.'

If Allegra had been trying to stoke Imogen's obsession, she couldn't have done better. Now Imogen couldn't fight the powerful conviction that Xander needed her, depended on her, even if he didn't know it.

The Christmas holidays came and she went back to Scotland, feeling miserable. With Allegra in London, there was no reason to go to Foughton. Even her parents noticed how downcast Imogen was, and tried to cheer her up, but it was no good. She moped about, unable to focus on anything, losing weight through her lack of appetite, believing that for her life was over.

She was lying on her bed one afternoon reading, trying to quench her thirst for romance with her favourite Georgette Heyer novels instead of studying Shakespeare. The doorbell rang downstairs and she thought nothing of it until she heard her mother call for her.

She sighed, closed her novel and got up. At the bedroom door, she shouted, 'What?'

'There's someone here to see you,' called Jeannie.

'Who?'

'Come and see. A surprise.'

Xander? she thought at once, and her heart raced. *Don't be so silly,* she told herself. *Of course it won't be him.* She went down the stairs grumpily and into the sitting room.

She gasped. There, sitting on one of the armchairs and looking radiant, was Romily. 'Rom! Oh my God! What are you doing here?'

'Hello, Midge, my darling! It's been soooo long!' Romily jumped to her feet and rushed over, enveloping Imogen in a strong hug. Then she stood back and looked at her friend. 'You look different. Thinner! Are you OK?'

Imogen hugged her back, amazed and delighted by the unexpected appearance of her old friend. 'Yes, I'm fine. But you look incredible.'

Romily was wearing a beautiful grey checked dress, nipped in at the waist with a wide patent leather belt that showed her slender figure, a smart charcoal jacket and long black boots. Her brown hair was longer now and glossy with health and expensive low lights. More noticeable than that, though, was her aura of happiness and the sparkle in her brown eyes. Romily laughed. 'Yes, I'm feeling amazing at the moment.'

'It's wonderful to see you, but what are you doing here? I thought you were in Paris.'

'I was.' Romily laughed again, unable to disguise her happiness. 'But I've come to Scotland. Guess why?'

'To see Allegra?' Imogen hazarded. 'Is she back? Are they having a party or something?'

'No, it's not to see Allegra.' A shadow passed over Romily's face but cleared almost at once, her joyful smile restored. 'You'll never guess so I'll have to tell you.' She seized Imogen's hand and said excitedly, 'I'm getting married!'

Imogen's mouth dropped open. 'What?' she said at last, when she'd regained the power of speech. 'Married? Who to?'

'To the most marvellous man. Remember I told you I'd met someone?'

'Yes, yes . . .' Imogen shook her head and laughed. 'But that was only a few months ago. Are you really getting married?'

Romily nodded. 'He's just amazing. You'll love him. At least, I do . . .' She blushed prettily. 'I never imagined feeling this way. But I'm utterly, totally, head over heels in love – and it's incredible.'

Imogen squeezed her friend's hand, smiling: Romily's joy was infectious. 'A whirlwind romance . . . how amazing. Sit down and tell me absolutely everything.'

They sat together on the sofa as Imogen said eagerly, 'Well, where is he? Did you bring him here? I'm dying to meet him. Tell me all about him.'

'He's sorting out some of the finer details for the wedding,' Romily explained, her eyes softening as she spoke. 'I didn't want to spring us both on you at the same time.'

'You should bring him here right now,' declared Imogen. 'I'm dying of curiosity. But why on earth are you getting married in Scotland? I would have thought a grand affair in Paris or the Caribbean was more your style.'

'We're eloping. We're going to Gretna Green – so much more romantic than Vegas. Isn't it wonderful? At least, I think it is.' Romily sighed happily. 'You see, my parents wouldn't exactly be in favour. If they knew. Which they don't.'

Imogen laughed. 'Ah. Oh, dear. You're going to be in trouble.'

'Never mind about that, I don't. But I said to Mitch, as long as it's Scotland, then I must see Imogen.' Romily leaned forward, her brown eyes wide and beseeching. 'I've got a huge favour to ask you – will you be my bridesmaid? We need a witness. Mitch was going to ask anyone who was about on the day, but it would mean so much to me if someone I care about is with me when I get married. My mother won't be there naturally. You and Allegra are the closest I have to sisters. Would you think about it?'

'Are you crazy?' Imogen leaned over to embrace her. 'Of course I will! I wouldn't miss it for anything!'

The two friends laughed and hugged, excited and moved at the same time.

Imogen thought the story was an incredible one, from the dramatic first meeting between the lovers to their chance reunion on the steps of a Paris restaurant.

'No one could be more astonished than I am,' Romily confessed, shaking her head in surprise at her own tale. 'I mean, a chef! And not even a French one at that! But once we realised that we'd met that night in the dirty alley behind my poor little shop . . . well, it was as though we suddenly saw each other . . . *really* saw each other.' She sighed happily. 'He's gorgeous, Imogen. And as for the sex . . .' She flushed and gave a tiny shiver, as though she were recalling his touch. 'I never knew it was possible to experience anything like it.'

'So, you fell in love that same night you met again?'

Romily nodded. 'Yes. Nothing really happened. But somehow we both knew. He walked me home and we said goodbye and there was absolutely no reason for us to meet again. I couldn't sleep that night but I was certain I would see him again. Sure enough, the next day he came to the house and asked for me, and I was waiting. The minute I saw him – he was so handsome in his jeans and leather jacket – I knew we were going to fall in love that very day, that we were already half in love with each other.

We went for a long romantic walk in the Bois de Boulogne and within five minutes he was holding my hand. Half an hour later we were sitting in the grass, staring into each other's eyes. Within an hour, we were kissing wildly, as though no one could see us! That very night – I was supposed to be going to a cocktail party at the Hôtel de Vendôme but I didn't give it a thought – I went back with him to his tiny *chambre de bonne* in Pigalle and we made love on his very uncomfortable bed. Honestly, Imogen, I never knew such thin mattresses even existed! But it didn't matter a bit, it was so magical.'

Her eyes sparkled and her cheeks flushed at the memory. 'I'd never experienced anything like it in my life. It was as though he'd switched me on . . . or like I'd been sleeping for years and years and he woke me up. We knew within days that we were meant to be together. It was agony, though, finding times when we could meet. I didn't want to make my parents suspicious so I had to go through with my usual social engagements, find ways to get away from my guards, act as though nothing was happening, even though my life was transformed. Mitch's job as a chef means that he works very late so sometimes I would sneak out of the house at midnight and go to meet him in a bar near the restaurant, or else be waiting for him at the flat in Pigalle when he got back. Or he would get up early and spend the day with me, even though it meant he had only an hour or two of sleep before he had to be back on duty. He loves me, Imogen, he really loves me!'

'I can believe it,' she said, enthralled. 'And now you're getting married! It's perfect.'

Romily smiled. 'We both know it's the right thing to do. I've never been so sure of anything in my life.'

'But why are you eloping?' Imogen frowned. 'Surely your parents want to give you the biggest wedding they possibly could.'

Romily made a face. 'I don't think so. You don't know my mother. If she had an inkling what I was planning, she'd be furious and I know exactly what would happen then. She would fight me every step of the way, do her very best to persuade me it was a mistake, say the most terrible things about Mitch – and I just don't want to hear them. In the end, I would win, but it would take months of horrible fights and tears and recriminations until finally she would come to the wedding, and weep all the way through, and be too ashamed to ask any of her friends to be happy for me . . .' Romily jumped up and danced about the room, unable to contain her excitement. 'I don't want any of that, Imogen! I'm so happy, I don't want anything to ruin it! So we're going to elope and come back married, and then, when they've all come round to the idea, we'll have a big party.' She flopped down on the sofa and giggled. 'You see? I've got it all planned!'

'Are you sure this is the right way?' Imogen asked.

'Absolutely,' Romily said, her voice adamant. 'This is the only way. I know it.'

'Then I'm with you, every step of the way.'

Imogen was cross with both her parents. They couldn't see how romantic it was – the heiress and the chef, eloping to avoid her parents' wrath – and instead made worried noises about contacting the de Lisles and letting them know what was happening.

'Don't you dare!' she shouted, furious. 'Just because you're old and boring and your lives are over, it doesn't mean you have to spoil it for everyone else!'

Her mother gave her a hurt look and her father told her to behave herself, but they couldn't see how much she wanted to believe in the fairytale coming true, in the triumph of love over everything. If Romily could do it, then surely there was hope for her own dreams . . .

'She's nearly twenty-one and she can do what she likes,' Imogen pointed out. 'And I'm going with her.'

They couldn't stop her. The next day Imogen packed her bags and went to join Romily and Mitch at their hotel in Edinburgh.

'So you're Imogen,' Mitch said in his broad American accent, holding out his hand, his brown eyes twinkling. 'I've heard a lot about you.'

'Hi,' she said, taking his hand and shaking it firmly. 'I'm your bridesmaid! It's great to meet you.'

He laughed. 'Hi, Bridesmaid. Great to meet you too. Now I know you almost as long as I've known the bride.'

She warmed to him at once. He was as handsome as Romily had promised: tall and well-built, with a fine-formed face, soft brown eyes and dark hair that had an endearing wave to it.

He smiled. 'Sit down and let's have a drink to celebrate meeting at last.' They were in the small but elegant bar of the New Town boutique hotel where Romily and Mitch were staying. When they were settled, he said, 'Now, I hope you're going to behave yourself. Apparently you and Romily got into a lot of trouble when you were at school together!'

Imogen shot her a look, wondering if Mitch knew everything that had happened at Westfield, but Romily seemed oblivious. *I don't think she's told him. I'm sure she wouldn't.* 'Oh, we're good girls now,' Imogen said with a smile.

They drank champagne and talked. It was exciting just to be around them, sharing their fizz of happiness and excitement. Mitch evidently worshipped Romily: he could hardly keep his hands off her, and when he wasn't holding her hand or slipping an arm round her waist, he was gazing at her with frank adoration. Imogen's mind was quickly set at rest on the question of whether Romily had managed to fall into the clutches of a gold digger. Imogen was certain that

Mitch was no such thing; whatever he thought about falling in love with a rich woman, it was certainly not the reason for the wedding. If anything, from the way he talked, he saw Romily's wealthy family as a drag, an obstacle he would not have to overcome if she were from an ordinary background.

'But I guess her folks'll come round eventually,' he said confidently. 'When they see how much we love each other.'

Romily and Imogen went out shopping that afternoon for a bridesmaid's dress for her to wear for the ceremony, and then they stayed up late into the night, too excited to sleep, talking about the wedding, and Romily and Mitch's life together. The next day they set off for Gretna Green in their unremarkable hire car. Mitch didn't have much luggage, just a plain black suitcase, but Romily had two cases and numerous bags as well as a dress carrier. 'It's something I picked up in Paris before we left,' she confided to Imogen. 'You'll have to help me get into it!'

Gretna Green seemed quite an ordinary place when they arrived, a small Scottish town on the border with England, except for its historic role as a venue for young runaways wanting to get married without their parents' consent. Every guestroom and hotel was offering special packages and advertising the traditional 'over the anvil' wedding.

Romily didn't seem to mind the wintry grey weather or the drabness of the out-of-season town. Nothing could dampen her radiant happiness.

'When is the ceremony?' Imogen asked as they pulled up in their hotel car park.

'This afternoon,' Romily said dreamily. 'It's all booked.'

'I can't wait, baby,' Mitch said, smiling at his bride. 'Come on, let's get inside.'

They checked in, Mitch carrying the heavy luggage up to their first-floor rooms.

'I can't believe my wife-to-be has to travel with so much!' he said, puffing slightly under the weight of the cases. 'I thought eloping meant travelling light.'

'Oh, darling!' Romily laughed happily. 'This *is* light. I usually have at least four times as much!'

Imogen laughed at the look on Mitch's face. 'What time is the kick off?'

'At four o'clock. They said that January is usually one of their quieter months, so I could pick my time.' Romily grabbed Imogen's hand. 'We've only a couple of hours to get ready. Better get going.' She turned to her fiancé. 'We'll see you there.'

'You bet,' Mitch said. 'Just be on time. I won't be able to stand the wait.' He gathered her up in a hug, kissing her for so long and so hungrily that Imogen became quite uncomfortable. The happy couple pulled apart at last, sighing and smiling at each other. Mitch turned to Imogen then. 'You make sure she's there, OK?'

'I will,' she said fervently, like a Girl Guide promising to do her duty.

'Now let's get ready,' Romily said.

The hotel sent up some dry sandwiches for the girls to eat while they bathed and dressed. Romily had certainly come prepared with all her kit, from a professional-strength hairdryer to a box of cosmetics that would not have disgraced a make-up artist.

They spent a happy couple of hours primping and preening, rubbing in moisturisers, primers and foundations, painting shimmery colours on their lids, neatening brows, emphasising their eyes with liner and mascara, and applying lipstick. Imogen dried Romily's hair, pulling the long brown tresses over a metal and bristle brush until they billowed with life and gleamed chestnut.

'Now,' Romily said, 'the dress.' She went to the garment bag which had been carefully hung over a wardrobe door. Unzipping it, she brought out a dress in the purest ivory silk.

'Oh, Romily,' Imogen gasped. 'It's beautiful.'

'Wait until you see it on.'

She was right. Once the dress was on, it looked even more breathtaking. It was simple enough, and modest too: a long figure-hugging silk sheath that was so expertly constructed it seemed to flow effortlessly around Romily's body, despite the boning and corsetry concealed inside it. It was sleeveless but over it she wore a stunning antique-gold lace jacket covered with hundreds of tiny sequins in tarnished silver, bronze and old gold. It shimmered as she moved, a vision of winter glamour. The hand-stitched label inside showed it was Armani couture.

She slipped her feet into gold silk slippers and pinned her hair back with glittering gold and crystal combs. Then she turned to Imogen. 'Well?'

Imogen's eyes welled with tears. 'You look gorgeous,' she said in a choked voice. 'Just like a bride should look on her wedding day.' She felt simultaneously happy and sad: Romily shouldn't be here, on her own except for Imogen, with no one else to see and appreciate her bridal beauty. Where were her parents, her brother, her friends and relatives? Suddenly Imogen could see that, despite the whole thing being about the happy couple, without that precious audience, full of love and admiration and joy, it was only half a wedding.

'I haven't got any flowers,' Romily said, with the first touch of melancholy in her voice. 'I forgot to organise any. I won't have a bouquet.'

'Yes, you will,' declared Imogen. 'Even if I have to take some from a vase in the lobby.'

'Please don't,' her friend said with a laugh. 'I don't know if this dress will respond well to drips.'

'Actually,' Imogen said slowly, 'I think they're plastic . . .' They caught each other's eye and burst out laughing.

At half-past three they were ready to go. Imogen was wearing the outfit they'd chosen the day before in Edinburgh – a cap-sleeved, knee-length fitted dress in old gold satin that picked up the same antique colours in Romily's lace jacket, enlivened with the jaunty touch of a pair of leopard-print Gina heels borrowed from the bride.

The hotel had booked them a taxi, just a plain old grey Ford with a driver who had plainly seen too many brides to be excited by having another in his taxi. Imogen made him stop on the way when she saw a florist's shop and darted out to buy all the ivory roses they had in the shop, making them fashion a hasty wedding bouquet.

A few minutes later they were drawing up in front of the Blacksmith's Cottage, an old building of white render and black beams.

'I can't believe you're really about to get married!' Imogen breathed, her eyes wide. This was it: a wedding that felt as illicit as any that had been held in the forge over the centuries. Did the de Lisles have any idea what their precious daughter was about to do? There was no doubt they would be horrified if they did.

Inside, they were greeted by the owner and led to the room where the ceremony was going to be performed.

'The registrar is here, and so is the groom,' the woman said as she took them down a low, beamed corridor. 'It will be a short ceremony – only fifteen minutes or so.' She stopped outside an oak door with an old iron latch and glanced admiringly at Romily. 'And, if I may say so, you make a gorgeous bride. Your fiancé is inside.'

The door opened on to a small cosy room with tartan carpet and curtains and a coal fire burning in the fireplace.

As Romily walked in, Imogen suddenly had a glimpse of another life, where a majestic organ boomed out and Romily entered the portals of a magnificent cathedral, accompanied by her father and a host of bridesmaids, to a burst of joyous music. That was the wedding they'd all expected for her. There was no choir today, no gilt or marble or cloud of incense. Nevertheless, there was something infinitely touching about the way Romily walked gracefully into the room, keeping her eyes fixed on Mitch who stood by a blacksmith's anvil, handsome in a dark suit that showed his broad shoulders and narrow waist. Her eyes blazed with love and happiness. She clearly didn't miss the grandeur or ceremony for a moment: the sight of her beloved Mitch was enough for her.

Imogen found it hard to hold back her tears through the simple service. The registrar, standing behind the anvil, read out the legal definition of marriage, bringing a gentle poetry to the formal words with her soft Scottish accent. Then she asked the couple to make the declarations and repeat the vows after her. They were unadorned promises, plain and clear: they were free to marry each other; they would love and support each other all their lives, and they recognised the legal nature of their promises.

Romily and Mitch stared into each other's eyes, held hands and repeated the lines in voices tremulous with emotion.

Imogen gulped and felt hot tears run down her cheeks. She had never expected to find a wedding so moving, particularly one as simple as this. Perhaps it was because it was Romily, whom she'd known from a schoolgirl, now taking this hugely adult step. Perhaps it was because no one could fail to be moved by those life-changing promises, made with so much hope and love. Whatever, she couldn't help giving a huge sniff.

Romily turned to her, laughing, but her eyes also were bright with tears. 'Oh, Midge, you're setting me off!'

'Have a heart – I'm only just holding on here,' Mitch said with a grin.

'Sorry!' Imogen said, and sobbed, then laughed, then cried again. 'It's *so* beautiful!'

'Congratulations,' the registrar said, smiling. 'You are now husband and wife.'

Romily threw her arms around her new husband, her bridal bouquet pressed against his back, and shut her eyes tight, unable to say a word.

Chapter 32

She nuzzled into his neck, pushing her lips against his ear. A strand of her hair brushed against his cheek. 'Tomorrow we'll go to London,' she said, her breathy whisper sending electric pulses of excitement across his skin. 'I've booked the Royal Suite at Claridge's. Then the honeymoon can really begin.'

'I don't care where I am, as long as it's with you,' he replied huskily. 'Now, Mrs Mitchell, I believe it's traditional to carry the bride across the threshold on their first night as man and wife.'

They were standing outside their hotel room, a drab grey door with gold plastic numbers stuck on it. Romily giggled. She was definitely a little drunk after three glasses of the best champagne the hotel bar could offer, which they'd had with their wedding breakfast of steak and kidney pie and chips, followed by an extraordinary whisky and oat concoction called cranachan. Mitch could see now why Scottish cuisine hadn't caught on as a world favourite.

'I thought it was supposed to be the threshold of our first home!' protested Romily, as he swept her up in his arms. 'Oh! Mind the jacket, darling!' She giggled again.

Mitch pushed the door open with his foot and went inside, gazing into Romily's eyes as he carried her in. He put her down gently on the shabby carpet. 'Here you are. The bridal chamber.' He took her hand and looked down into her face, thinking that he'd never seen another person look so astonishingly beautiful. 'I can't believe it. You're my wife.'

'And you're my husband,' she said softly, staring back at him.

Is it possible to be any happier than this? he wondered. For months now, he'd been living in some charmed existence so far from his old one that he couldn't stop marvelling at it. Sometimes he was seized by panic at the thought of how nearly it had never happened. If Robert had not come back from his sickbed, and he had not been standing outside the restaurant . . . If Romily had not argued with her family . . . It all seemed so tenuous. His whole life had turned on these tiny events happening at exactly the right time. Without them, he'd still be slaving in the kitchen at Reynard, and Romily would be trotting about on her round of social engagements, perhaps flirting with someone, wondering who her destiny was.

Well, they knew the answer to that now. It was him. Theodore Mitchell. No man in the world could love her more than he did, he was sure of that.

'So, Mrs Mitchell . . .'

'Yes, Mr Mitchell?' Her brown eyes sparkled at him.

'Shall we retire from the exertions of our wedding day?'

'Oh, yes, please, Mr Mitchell, if you don't mind.' She looked up at him coyly from under her lashes.

They began to kiss and a wave of tenderness and passion crashed over him. What had he done to deserve this happiness? He'd never known anything as perfect as passion mixed with deep, all-encompassing love. Heroin had once made him feel blissed out but it had also made him feel like shit. But this . . . this extraordinary natural high only made him stronger, better, healthier . . . and unutterably happy.

The sequined jacket was abandoned on the floor, and he

pulled down the zip of the silk shift. Underneath, she was wearing a strapless bra of ivory silk that pushed her breasts up into soft mounds, wispy matching knickers tied with ribbons at the seams, and a creamy lace suspender belt attached to a pair of fine stockings. He murmured appreciatively when he saw her underwear – she knew how much he liked it. She began to undress him, pushing off his jacket, unfastening his trousers, ridding him of his clothes until he stood naked in front of her, his proud cock showing how much she excited him.

She pulled the ribbons at the sides of her knickers and the triangles of silk fell away, leaving her in only stockings, suspender belt and bra. Then she led him to the bed, made him lie down on his back and climbed on top of him, sinking her soft sweet mouth on to his. He could feel her breasts in their bra pressing against his chest, her mound with its strip of brown hair brushing his belly, and his prick against the sheerness of her stockings. He moaned with pleasure, lust burning through him. 'My gorgeous wife,' he muttered, leaning down to release her breasts from their cups and lick and suck them.

'I can't wait any longer,' she breathed, and straddled him. 'I've been desperate for you for hours.'

'Since the moment I saw you in that room . . .'

'I wanted to fuck you the minute we were married.'

'Oh, Christ . . .' He felt her lift herself up, position her pussy on the tip of his cock and then press down, engulfing him in the hot wetness, taking him in as far as she could and pressing down to rub herself against his pubic bone. He put his hands on her hips, huge against her soft slender body, and sighed as she began to move up and down, making the most delicious friction.

'Mitch,' she moaned. She sat up straight and threw back her head, rubbing her hands across her breasts and down across her belly, rubbing her clitoris and then reaching back to run her hand over his balls.

They moved together for long minutes, gazing into each other's eyes when they weren't closing them to concentrate on the sensations they were causing in each other.

This was his new beginning, he knew that. He'd thought it had been when he'd come to after that terrible beating and realised he had to change, when he'd decided to leave New York, break his heroin addiction and make something of his life. But that had just been the prologue to this, the real beginning of his life. From the moment he'd met Romily, he'd known she was his destiny. He longed to prove to her that he was worthy of her love, and had already decided that he was going to devote himself to making his dreams come true. He would go places. He would show everyone. They would think he had married her for money; he'd demonstrate to them all that they were wrong. He'd make a new fortune, one of his own. Then no one would doubt their love or that he was her equal.

He already had plans. He'd been set on his path even before he met Romily. After he met her, he was doubly determined to win through. And with his beautiful wife by his side, how could he go wrong? Her sharp intelligence and cool judgement impressed and excited him. Her understanding of the European mind and sensibility was invaluable. Her taste was exquisite, her style impeccable, and her knowledge of the finest luxuries the world could offer was unsurpassed . . .

He moaned. Oh, yes . . . and her hot pussy drove him wild. He was going to come any moment now, he knew that, and could see that she was close as well. Her eyes were glassy, her tongue darting out to lick her lips. She was breathing in short gasps. He couldn't bear it any longer. Pulling her down next to him, he rolled on top of her so he could feel her legs around his back, her hands on his buttocks urging him on, and so he could thrust hard into that delicious tightness until they both cried out, possessed by their shuddering climaxes.

'Oh, Mr Mitchell,' she said, sighing, as the crisis left them.

'Mrs Mitchell . . .' he said, grinning, his hair damp with sweat. 'The first fuck of the rest of our lives.'

'You know what? I don't think that's long enough for me,' she whispered, pulling his mouth back to hers for another kiss.

Chapter 33

Allegra was unpacking a box of vanilla-scented candles and feeling rather overcome by their sickly sweetness when she heard the door of the shop open and the ting-a-ling of the little bell that announced a customer.

'Just a moment, I'll be right with you!' she said from her position on the floor behind the counter.

The customer said nothing but she heard footsteps walking about as whoever it was inspected the wares on the shelves. She quickly pulled out the last dozen candles, folded up the box and stood up.

This customer was a man, which was surprising: men almost never came into this shop, with its candles, scented drawer liners, padded hangers and lavender bags, except for just before Mother's Day and Christmas, when there was an unseemly rush to buy gifts. The man was standing with his back to her, examining the liquorice and ginseng range, and wearing a rather gorgeous green tweed jacket over navy trousers and brown brogues polished to a conker shine.

Allegra was just frowning and thinking that the jaunty figure looked very familiar when it said sternly: 'I'm very, very angry with you, young lady!' The man turned round to face her. 'You've been in London for weeks and you haven't even let me know!'

'Uncle David!' she cried joyously.

'That's enough of the Uncle,' he said, trying to look strict but unable to keep the smile off his face. 'You're grown up now. It's time I was just David, I think.'

He came over and she dashed out from behind the counter to give him a hug. He kissed her on both cheeks, then pulled back and examined her. 'Hmm, you're looking rather radiant, considering you've just nabbed the post of official black sheep from your brother. Sent down from Oxford! What on earth did you have to do to get that dubious honour? Don't worry too much, I'm sure Xander will be stealing this particular tag back from you in no time.' David looked about the shop. 'What can you be doing in this place? I didn't expect to see you as a shop assistant. And how can you stand the *smell*? It's like being inside a giant pudding!'

'You get used to it,' Allegra said. 'I hardly notice it any more. I'm just passing the time until I work out what I want to do.'

'Passing time? At twenty? My dear girl, *never* simply pass time unless you are in a dentist's waiting room. You have to seize it while you can. Let's go out for lunch and you can tell me all about everything and then we'll work out something exciting for you to do.'

Allegra perked up. 'That sounds fun.'

'Yes. And you can explain to me exactly why you haven't been in touch with me before now. As you can imagine, I'm furious. Now let's go. We'll go and have oysters and a very crisp Sancerre downstairs at Bibendum.'

'I can't! I'm all on my own here. My lunch break isn't for another hour.'

'Whose shop is this?' David enquired, frowning.

'Jane Armstrong's.'

'Oh, dear Jane! Her cushion shop must have failed, I assume. Well, candles are the next most obvious step. Better luck this time round. She's a dear old friend. She won't mind if I explain to her that you absolutely had to go out. Come on!' David flicked the sign on the door round to Closed. 'Have you got a key? I don't suppose anyone will steal this lot, but we ought to play safe.'

Allegra giggled. Uncle David was irresistible. 'I'll get my jacket,' she said.

Twenty minutes later they were sitting in the cool, tiled oyster bar beneath Bibendum. A huge silver stand, packed with ice and heaving with crustaceans, had just been put in front of David, who tucked a napkin into his Turnbull & Asser shirt and eyed them greedily.

'My absolute favourite,' he breathed. 'Now, while I dig in, you tell me all about what happened at Oxford.'

Allegra peeled a langoustine and regaled her uncle with the whole story. He listened solemnly as he sprinkled shallot vinegar over his oysters and shook them out of their shells into his waiting mouth, swallowing them down with gusto. He nodded when she told him about the row with her father.

'I imagine that's shaken him up a bit,' David remarked. 'Your father's not used to people standing up to him. You must understand, Allegra, his entire family relies on him for money, and he likes to use that power over them. Our father used to do the same to us. You can imagine how much your grandfather thought of *my* career – interior designer, that's what I said I wanted to be! When I was supposed to go into the army, the Black Watch, like every other younger son in the family's history. But, of course, I refused. Can you imagine how I would have survived *that*? There was simply no way on earth. So he cut me off. "All right then, Pa, if that's the way you want it," I replied, and gallivanted straight off to London. I haven't looked back.'

'Is that when you started up the club?' Allegra asked, interested.

'Oh, well, no . . . not right away. I started out doing up people's houses – friends of the family at first. I loved it and found I had an eye for it. I spent my days with dowager marchionesses picking out fabrics for their drawing-room cushions, or choosing antiques with countesses, lampshades with duchesses . . . generally amusing myself hugely with society ladies. But come the evening it was a different story. There were deathly dull dinner parties, or else dancing to the house band at the Old Hundred or Les Ambassadeurs, in full evening dress. And that was it. Really, the social scene was awful, so antiquated and stuffy! We needed something a little more amusing and no one else was doing anything so I thought I would open a little nightclub and see how it went.'

'And that was Colette's?'

David nodded. 'Named after my favourite French novelist. It was really because a friend of mine, Eddie Frobisher, decided to open a casino. The gambling laws had just been relaxed and casinos were going to be the next big thing. He bought a house in Mayfair – a total wreck, so it was cheap, cheap, cheap! By Mayfair standards, anyway. And he brought me in to do the interiors. *Comfort* was the watchword. People had to feel utterly relaxed and yet cosseted in great luxury. It should be like a wonderful country house, full of muted grandeur, and yet as warm and comforting as a hug. We understood each other completely. I knew exactly what he wanted.

'Before long, I was restoring the very gracious Georgian interior with the help of some wonderful craftsmen and plasterers – and that was when I stumbled on the basement. It was dark, dingy and damp – usually the things that turn me off the most – and yet . . . there was something about the place. It breathed magic over me. It felt like somewhere things could happen: naughty, nefarious, delightful things.

And that's when I thought – I know, I can do something with this, if only Eddie will let me. And I remembered my old idea of opening a nightclub and was sure I'd found my ideal spot.'

'And he didn't mind?'

'Oh, no!' David swallowed the last of his oysters and put the shell back on to the ice, sighing with pleasure. 'Well, that was delicious.'

Allegra was fascinated. She wanted to hear more. 'So he said, go ahead?'

'He said more than that. He said, "What a bloody brilliant idea!" He was aiming his casino at the richest and most influential people in the land. They would gamble big money at his tables and then there would be a special added extra: an exclusive, members only nightclub where they could kick back, relax, enjoy the company of beautiful women – not whores but good pedigree girls who knew how to behave – and take a break from the intensity of the tables.'

'And was that what you wanted?'

'I wanted style,' David said simply. 'I wanted to create a beautiful, special place that belonged to me, that realised my vision. You see, I believe in the redeeming qualities of beauty, and the utterly worthwhile pursuit not just of luxury but the *discipline* of luxury. I aimed to create a place where everything was always perfect, from the table linen to the cocktails, from the bread rolls and butter curls to the way the towels in the lavatory hung over the rails. Somewhere you would always get the most sublime Martini, the best food, the most dedicated service. It would be a place that would never disappoint you. And where you would always be among friends.'

Allegra's eyes were wide. 'And you did it?'

'Of course.' David sipped his Sancerre. 'I can't pretend it

was easy. At times I felt hugely frustrated. And the actual construction was a nightmare. In order to get enough space for the club, we had to excavate down and out into the garden – an administrative and architectural ordeal. Sometimes, standing in the dark, dirty shell, surrounded by heaps of mud and the whole thing open to the elements, I thought it would never be finished, would never be worth all the pain and hard work. But, eventually, it was done. And then the fun could really begin.'

'What happened next?'

He eyed her with his piercing blue gaze. 'I created Colette's, of course.' He gazed at her thoughtfully for a minute. 'Would you like to go there?'

Allegra gasped. 'Are you kidding? Of course I would!'

'I know I've been promising you a trip there for years but I've never thought that the time was right. But now . . . now I think you're ready.' He leaned forward conspiratorially. 'I'm going to show you the magic first. Always see the play before you inspect the set and the props. Do you have anything suitable to wear? Imagine a chic cocktail party where you might conceivably bump into a duke.'

'Not really. All my best dresses are at home.' Allegra's face fell. 'I've got some clubbing stuff, but that's no good for somewhere smart. Oh, dear. I can't turn up looking like a scruff.'

David looked about for a waiter and motioned for the bill. 'I seem to recall that Chanel is just over the way. Let's go and see what we can find.'

They spent a very enjoyable couple of hours in the shop, and when they left Allegra was holding a large black stiff cardboard bag with the word 'Chanel' on it in white capital letters. It made her think of shopping with Romily, but she put that out of her mind.

'Go home and get ready,' her uncle said. 'I'll meet you at the club at nine. That will give us time to look around before it starts to get busy.'

'What's the address?' Allegra asked, enjoying the feeling of anticipation.

David looked surprised. ' Don't worry about that, darling! Just get into a cab and say you're going to Colette's. They'll know where to take you.'

Allegra savoured every moment of getting ready, from the washing and careful drying of her long blonde hair to the unwrapping of her gorgeous new dress from its protective tissue. It was black, of course. 'One of your most important colours,' David had told her solemnly. 'While you have that golden hair and pale skin, you'll always look striking in black.'

She slipped it on and looked at her reflection in the mirror bolted to the back of the door. Her box room was so small there was barely space to turn around in front of it, but even by the light of the 40-watt bulb and its dingy shade, she could tell she looked good. The dress was knee-length. It had a silky undershell and over that a black shift heavily embroidered with tiny, bright ebony beads, with a high but very wide neckline so that her shoulders emerged, creamy and eye-catching, from the sparkling dark material. She wound her long hair up into a high bun and tied a black velvet ribbon around it. She'd gone for a sixties look in her make-up: smoky dark eyes with swoops of black liner, and pastel-pink glossed lips. The effect was definitely soignée, a blonde Audrey Hepburn off to a nightclub. She put her feet into kitten heeled, pointy-toed satin slippers. That was it. She was ready to go.

Susie was in the kitchen making herself some supper when Allegra passed by. She looked up in surprise. 'Wow!

You look amazing. Off somewhere nice?'

'To Colette's,' Allegra said, and enjoyed seeing the impressed expression on Susie's face. 'Don't wait up.'

The taxi took her through London's most exclusive districts: purring up the King's Road, circling Sloane Square and then up past the embassies and great private houses of Belgravia. Along the roadside, the most expensive cars were parked, some with chauffeurs inside, idling away the time until their employer returned from the theatre, restaurant or dinner party.

London's so beautiful, she thought. It was all navy blue sky, orange street lamps and the white stone of monuments, hotels and houses as they passed Apsley House and sped up Park Lane, past the twinkling lights of the Dorchester. On the other side, Hyde Park stretched away. Xander had told her that the park was bigger than Monaco, which was probably more a comment on Monaco's smallness than Hyde Park's vastness, but still . . . how many other cities had a park bigger than an entire country? *I can't imagine living anywhere else. Between here and Foughton, there's nowhere else on earth I'd rather be.*

The taxi glided into Mayfair, passing red-brick houses with wrought-iron railings and vast chandeliers glimmering inside. They came to a large square, edged with office buildings, shops and private banks, all occupying what were once grand houses – but few people lived here now. In the middle of the square was a garden with benches and a statue in the centre.

'Here we are!' called the cabbie. He pulled to a stop in front of a grand, red-brick house with two sets of long sash windows to each side of its wide polished front door. An ornate iron arch spanned the steps leading to the front entrance, a large lantern hanging from its apex.

As the cab stopped, just to the left of the arch, a doorman uniformed in a dark blue jacket and trousers and matching cap, came forward to open its door. Allegra passed the cabbie a tenner and climbed out as elegantly as she could.

'Is this Colette's?' she asked the doorman, looking up at the grand house.

The doorman remained blank-faced. 'No, miss,' he said politely. 'That is Frobisher's. This is Colette's.' He gestured behind him and she saw that to the left of the front door of the main building was a gate in the railings that allowed access to the basement. The staircase down was roofed in grey lead, lined inside with striped fabric. It looked like the entrance to a smart marquee.

'Are you a member, miss?' enquired the doorman.

'No. But my uncle is David McCorquodale. I'm Allegra. He's expecting me.'

The doorman was clearly accustomed to keeping his expression neutral no matter how many society beauties, film stars or famous faces passed by, but even so Allegra detected a subtle change in it: an added sense of respect and deference. He stepped back and gestured down the stairs.

'Thank you,' she said, and began to walk carefully down them, not wanting to trip in her high heels.

The stairs descended to a level where there was a sharp left turn into the basement of the house above. Light came flooding out, as though beckoning her in, and Allegra walked straight into a long, narrow hallway through a pair of open saloon-style doors painted the same dull cream as the walls. A man in a smart suit stood by a reception-style window and nodded his head politely as she approached.

'Good evening, miss. Are you with a member?'

'No, no,' she said, looking around for David. 'I mean, yes. I'm Allegra McCorquodale. I'm meeting my uncle, David McCorquodale.'

'Of course.' The man smiled and gestured to a doorway behind her. 'Would you like to leave anything in the cloakroom?'

'No, thank you.'

'Then please follow me to the bar and I will find Mr Mac for you.' He turned and walked ahead of her down the corridor. They passed a sitting room off to the left, and then, just ahead, the corridor opened up. On one side was a bar area with tall stools around the polished wooden counter, and on the other was another large sitting-room area. The immediate impression was of somewhere that was cosy and welcoming.

'Where would you like to wait, miss?' asked the man.

'At the bar, please.'

He led her over and pulled out a stool for her. As she sat down, he said, 'What would you like to drink, miss?'

'May I have a white wine spritzer, please?' That sounded suitably grown up and sophisticated, she thought. It was the kind of drink Miranda had when she was lunching at Daphne's with her friends.

'Of course.' He nodded to the man behind the bar, who was wearing a pale grey jacket over a white shirt and black tie, and he immediately started preparing her drink. 'Now, if you'll excuse me, I'll fetch Mr Mac for you.'

She glanced around at the bar. She noticed now that its ceiling was vaulted and there were pillars running the length of the corridor, no doubt supporting the house above. Between the bar and the corridor, and the corridor and the sitting area, the pillars had been semi-filled with a low wall that created both a visual barrier and a handy place for people to sit when there were no chairs available. It was quiet at the moment: at the other end of the bar, a businessman was sitting alone with the *Evening Standard* and a glass of something strong on the rocks. In the sitting-room area, a middle-aged couple were turned to each other on the red-velvet banquette, talking and laughing. The things she noticed most were the pictures: the walls were covered in them. Above the bar hung racing oils and prints; on the walls around it there were Bateman cartoons and *Vanity Fair* caricatures.

The barman placed her drink in front of her. She thanked him. It looked very inviting, packed with ice cubes. She took a sip that bubbled lightly over her tongue.

A moment later, David was standing beside her. 'Hello, my darling. I was just in the office. What are you drinking? White wine spritzer? Oh, how vile. How is it?' He examined everything critically as he spoke while the barman looked on anxiously, obviously hoping that nothing would be found wanting.

'It's fine. Very good.' Allegra smiled at him. Her uncle looked very smart and Savile Row tonight, wearing a beautifully cut dark suit, a blue-and-silver striped silk tie and black Lobb shoes, his thick silver hair brushed back with a touch of the bouffant.

'You look utterly gorgeous. Stand up.' She did so and he looked her up and down with an expert eye. 'You really are a ravishing creature, Allegra. You were quite ordinary as a child, I thought, but look at you now! I'm so jealous, you must have a perfect queue of gorgeous men.'

Allegra smiled. It was certainly pleasing to be complimented by Uncle David, and as she knew he had wonderful taste, she was particularly happy. 'Thank you.'

'Bring your drink and I'll show you around. It's very quiet at the moment. We only open at eight o'clock and generally it's just a few members in the bar then, savouring the quiet before going home. Some people are in for an early dinner – there's usually an eight o'clock table or two – but things don't really start moving until ten, then take off at midnight.

We close at three. I've been a night owl for longer than you can believe – lucky that I don't need much sleep.' He led the way out of the bar. 'We'll have a spot of dinner ourselves once I've shown you around.'

Beyond the bar was a long vaulted room carpeted in rich, dark rugs and with columns running the length of both sides, no doubt structural, and a series of bays between these. Each bay was designed like a tiny private sitting room: a cosy sofa was piled with cushions, and to each side stood comfortable armchairs with smaller antique chairs and stools set in front of a low table. Every inch of space was occupied by something: on the walls hung gilt-framed paintings of all styles and periods – oils, watercolours, sketches and oriental silk prints all packed together; every surface held another gorgeous lamp with a classic pleated silk shade in dark red or old ivory, or a plant emerging from a Sèvres cache-pot, or a vase of creamy flowers, or a sweet statue of an eighteenth-century lady or bronze figure of a dog, or a row of gilded, leather-bound books propped up by bronze bookends. The fabrics used were all luxurious and the colours were rich: dark reds, forest greens, golds and purples. The lighting was kept discreet, with only the soft glow of lamps and tiny spotlights illuminating the pictures. The effect was warm and welcoming with so many tasteful little details that it seemed entirely idiosyncratic, not at all like the bland, corporate vision of modern restaurants and hotel chains.

'It's just like someone's home,' exclaimed Allegra, looking about her.

'Yes,' David said simply. 'My home. Come on, I'll show you the dining room.' The sitting rooms led into another vaulted chamber but this was opened out into one large room. Along the sides ran sage-green velvet banquettes with stiff square cushions in the same fabric. In front of them stood a row of tightly packed small tables, each covered with a thick cream linen tablecloth and dressed with napkins, wine glasses, silvery cutlery and a small square-based lamp with a square cream shade. The wood-panelled walls were hung with hundreds of cartoons from Hollywood's golden age.

Several of the tables were occupied and David cast his eagle eye over each of them. Then he went to the maître d', who stood so quietly and respectfully at the entrance to the room that Allegra hadn't even noticed him, and whispered quietly in his ear. The maître d' looked stricken but immediately summoned a waiter and conveyed David's orders in a low voice.

'David, hello!' called someone from the nearest table. A businessman in a dark suit was waving and smiling broadly. 'How are you?'

'Hello, my dear,' David said smoothly. 'How wonderful that you're here. How are you? Do you have everything you need?' He went over and spent a few minutes talking to the businessman and his guest, and then went to all the other tables in turn to ask if they had what they wanted and how things were, before expertly disengaging himself and returning to Allegra's side. Meanwhile, a waiter had arrived with fresh jug of water for one table while another refilled the wine glasses on a second.

'I like it done just so,' David muttered as he put an arm round her waist and guided her down the long room. 'I can't bear things not to be right. Now, there's also a private dining room that seats thirty just over there behind that door. And over here is another small bar and more seating. And that, of course, is the dance floor.'

They were now standing at the far end of the club. *It seems to go on for a long way, but really it's a very small space,* thought Allegra, glancing back towards the main part of the dining room. She turned to look at the dance floor once more which took up about a quarter of the dining room, with the DJ booth tucked in behind it. It was only about two metres by three and very dark, with a blue underlit floor flickering with hundreds of tiny star lights and more little lights shimmering in the ceiling above. More banquettes, this time in a black-and-white zebra print, were built into the wall so that tired dancers could rest for a moment before returning to the fray. Soft, innocuous melodies floated out of hidden speakers.

'This will be heaving later,' David said. 'But it's pretty much deserted early on. This discotheque bit was part of what made Colette's so special when we first opened. All the other clubs had live bands playing the hits of the day, like some sad, countrified wedding reception. But we had two turntables and a DJ playing records seamlessly. That's what brought the young crowd in. You wouldn't believe who I've seen dancing in here: everyone from royalty to pop stars. I gave a party for the Rolling Stones in the seventies. People are still talking about it.' He smiled down at her. 'Or so I like to think. Shall we go and sit down? I don't know about you but I'm famished.'

They went back into the main part of the dining room and David pulled out a chair at the table nearest to the door so that Allegra could sit down. 'Hope you don't mind if I take the banquette. It helps if I can see what's going on. Lots of owners take the best table in the house, but I prefer to take the least best. There is no bad table, but somehow everyone seems to consider this to be it. So I make everyone's life easier by taking it myself, and that seems to keep them all happy.'

A white-coated waiter appeared and handed them the menus: stiff cream card printed with dark green flowing script.

'Now, let's see. What do I feel like tonight?' David said

critically. 'The wood pigeon is very good . . . but perhaps I'll have the grouse. No, I shall ask Adrian to make up my favourite, a steak tartare. It's not on the menu today but he keeps some beautiful fillet just for me.'

Allegra cast her eyes over it: it was a very English and very traditional menu, featuring potted shrimps and roast game and rich nursery puddings. 'I'll have the chicken,' she said, noting that there were no prices on her menu.

'Oh, Allegra, if we were anywhere else I'd be very cross. Chicken is always for the faint of heart. But, luckily, you are in Colette's, where the chicken is spectacular. Adrian is under orders to make it so. Now, champagne, I think, if you're finished with that ghastly spritzer thing.'

The service was so discreet that Allegra hardly noticed her food and drink arriving, but suddenly there it was in front of her and it was delicious: everything tasted wonderfully of itself, without too much tinkering and fancification. Meanwhile David talked on, about the club and how he had come to create it.

'Just friends at first, and friends of friends. I had to raise rather a lot of money and naturally none of it was forthcoming from Papa. I'd burnt my boats there – so I got most of it from my rich pals, promising them founder membership of the place. I knew I had to make it three things: very expensive, very exclusive and very, very sexy. And it was – right from the start. It helped that the opening night was attended by Terence Stamp and Jean Shrimpton, two dukes and at least one royal princess, along with hundreds of others, and that the party went on until dawn.

'The nights we had! The *jeunesse dorée* all came: beautiful young debs in mini-skirts, louche young aristocrats just down from university and looking for fun, models, actors, artists . . . I devoted myself to making sure that they would all have the best time possible – the best food and wine, surrounded by luxury. I planned endless parties: carnivals, festivals, themed weeks. All I insisted on was perfection – and that's not so very much to ask, is it?

'Colette's quickly became my life and has stayed so ever since. I'm here every night, making sure that everything is as it should be. I also have my staff, who are all immensely loyal. I don't much care for change. I like things to stay exactly the same, and so do the members. That's why they keep coming back.' David relaxed in his seat and smiled. 'You know, the funny thing is – I only did it for the laughs. I never expected it to last. Even when we were the rage, the toast of the town, turning them away from the door, I always thought it would all blow over soon enough, and quieten down. But it never has.'

'How many members are there now?' asked Allegra, eating a wafer-thin slice of Scottish smoked salmon which had arrived with golden triangles of toast.

'About five thousand.' David smiled at her. 'Such a relief they don't all want to come at once!'

Allegra looked about her. The dining room was filling up a little more with dark-suited men and women in smart evening dresses. She hadn't seen anyone of her own age yet. 'It's very formal, isn't it?'

'Of course it is, darling!' Her uncle looked scandalised at the idea it could be anything else. 'The rules are: jacket and tie for men, and absolutely no jeans or trainers. Anyone who's inappropriately dressed is turned away, I don't care who they are. No exceptions. Cocktail dresses for women – and if they arrive wearing furs, so much the better.'

Allegra laughed. Her empty plate disappeared, and a moment later her chicken arrived as her champagne was topped up. 'It's not much like the kind of club Miranda goes to,' she said confidingly.

To her surprise, a look of hurt passed over David's face.

'Why ever not?' he demanded. 'She's very welcome to come. I like pretty women in here. She could bring lots of her friends, the ones she goes skiing with. I've noticed they all have very good legs.'

'She's down at those Chelsea places – you know, the kind with three dance floors, VIP areas, cocktails in goldfish bowls with a dozen straws, dry ice and dance music.'

David shuddered. 'How grim. Why on earth does she like those places?'

Allegra didn't know how to explain. Colette's was beautiful, she could see that, but it wasn't exactly hip and groovy. Most of the people she'd seen so far were in their forties and fifties, and the atmosphere, while expensive and luxurious, was sedate and calm. David had said the dance floor would be heaving later, but she hadn't yet seen any signs of it. Still, in nightclub terms it was still early. 'I suppose it's just what young people like,' she said at last.

'Why wouldn't young people like this?' her uncle demanded, and waved his hand to indicate the dining room.

'Perhaps it's just a little too quiet for some,' she said soothingly. 'But I love it! I think it's amazing.'

'It's not quiet,' he said grumpily. 'It'll be simply throbbing later. You'll see.'

Later, there were more people in the club, and a few younger ones at that, although Allegra was still struck by the lack of anyone like her own friends. The young people here looked just like the old ones in their dark suits and safe evening dresses. The DJ played the latest music, and a dozen figures bopped around the starlit floor, some more in control of their movements than others. Allegra was not tempted to join them. Instead, she enjoyed observing everything from the small bar where she and David sat and talked on. She told him all about what it had been like to be sent down, her desire to do something different, and her complete lack of ideas as to what that might be.

'Do you want to do something serious?' he asked. 'Study law, or medicine, or go into banking?'

'Not really.' Allegra shook her head. 'I know I've got talents, I'm just not sure what they are yet. And I don't want to commit myself to anything that demands three years of study without knowing if it's what I really want.'

'Mmm.' David sat back and stared at her. 'Tell me what you think of Colette's.'

She looked about. 'I think it's the most glamorous place I've ever been. I think it's amazingly enduring – I can hear all the echoes of the good times that have been had here. It's timeless and gorgeous.'

'But . . .' David raised an eyebrow. 'I can hear what your undertone is. It's not for you.'

'On special occasions!' she protested. 'I can imagine having a wonderful birthday party here, or getting engaged, or something like that. But not for every night.'

'I see. And Xander? Do you think he would come here?'

'Oh . . . well . . .' Allegra thought of Xander and James Barclay and Luca and all the other rich boys, with their drugs and their drinking and womanising. 'Perhaps. But I don't know if you would like having them very much.'

David seemed to think about this and then frowned. 'You know what, Allegra, I have an idea. I think it's rather brilliant myself. It's this: you must come and work for me. You might wonder what on earth needs doing in a club that's just a restaurant and bar, but you'd be surprised. It takes a lot of work and organisation to keep this going. And besides that, I'm considering a little bit of expansion. And I'm not stupid. I know this place will only survive if the fashionable young things want to come here. The original members are starting to fall off their perches. Plenty of people want to join, of course, that's not the point. Too many of them are corporate types, only wanting to wine and dine clients in impressive surroundings. I need to keep the genuine spirit of Colette's alive: the spirit of meeting friends, good times, love and laughter. And for that I need youth. I think you could help me to do that.'

Allegra stared at him, her mouth open.

'Well?' he prodded. 'What do you think?'

She blinked at him. A whole new life had suddenly opened up in front of her, entirely unexpectedly. And yet, as soon as she imagined it, she knew that it was exactly what she wanted.

'Oh my God! I think I'd like that. I think I'd like that very much.'

Chapter 34

Paris
Summer 2004

The lawyer watched the proceedings with interest. Emotions were flying high in the Paris boardroom, despite the efforts of all parties concerned to remain composed and business-like.

The young man – and he was still very young, despite the expensive suit he was wearing – was evidently furious. His jawline was set, showing clenched teeth, and his fists were balled so angrily that his knuckles gleamed white through his tanned skin. His brown eyes were hard as flint despite their soft shade. He leapt up and strode to the window, gazing down unseeingly on the rue du Faubourg St Honoré below.

'I think you'll find that this is a very reasonable request,' said the man sitting at the head of the table in an oversized green leather chair, designed to mark him out as the key figure in the room.

'Reasonable?' The younger man turned round, his face contorted with fury. 'I don't believe it! I can't believe I actually came here to listen to this shit. You have completely misunderstood me, sir.'

'Perhaps I have,' replied the other man smoothly. He ran a slender white hand over the polished mahogany of the boardroom table. The suited men around the table watched with silent deference, their Mont Blanc pens poised over their notepads, keeping track of proceedings.

I don't think this enterprise can succeed, the lawyer thought. *The young man is passionate, that is obvious. He is in love. Why would he listen to this? It's madness.*

'You certainly have.' The young man looked almost as puzzled as he was angry. 'You must think I'm so dumb. Do you really think I'm going to keep quiet and do what you ask? Do you honestly believe you can buy me off?'

The older man shrugged, a sardonic smile on his face. 'I simply wish us to find the easiest way out of this mess. You cannot blame me for beginning in the most straightforward way.'

'I'm afraid we disagree fundamentally. You see a mess where I do not.'

'From your point of view, I can easily see how this might be termed a success.'

'Ah!' The young man screwed up his face in frustration, obviously keeping his temper with difficulty and biting his tongue. Then he said, 'There you go again. You totally misunderstand me but, OK, I too can see why. You've spent her entire life protecting your daughter, probably fearing that she's the target of fortune hunters. Now it looks like your worst nightmare has come true. Some gigolo has come along, seduced her, convinced her he loves her and married her under your nose. He's stolen your precious prize purely because he wants to get his greedy, grasping hands on your family's money.' He gazed at the other man imploringly. 'But, sir, it's not like that at all. I had no idea who your daughter was when I fell in love with her.'

Charles de Lisle snorted.

'You've got to believe me. I married Romily for love, and no other reason.'

The older man's lips tightened and his eyes glittered

dangerously. 'If that is the case,' he said in a calm, cold voice, 'then why did you run away together like a pair of criminals? If your love was true and your intentions honourable, why act as if you wanted to steal our daughter away from us? Why marry before we could arrange some reasonable safeguards? If your heart is as pure and untouched by any desire for money as you say, then why not sign a prenuptial agreement? My lawyers could easily have drawn up a piece of paper that would have allowed you to demonstrate your motives by renouncing all claims to my daughter's substantial fortune. I note that this did not happen.' De Lisle shrugged lightly. 'And therefore I must draw my own conclusions.'

A good point, observed the lawyer. *This undermines the case for love somewhat.*

'Sir, I had no idea of the extent of Romily's wealth.' The young man came back to the table and leant on it, his eyes imploring.

'You saw where she lived. Hardly the kind of place you'd find a poor girl.'

'I'm an American, Mr de Lisle. All of Paris looks like it's pretty fancy as far as I'm concerned. I don't know where your rich people live or which are the exclusive districts. I only ever saw the outside of the place and, yeah, sure, I thought it looked like her folks were doing all right – but that didn't mean I had any idea what Romily was truly worth. To be honest, we never discussed it.' He seemed to be working hard to control himself but couldn't disguise the note of frustration in his voice. 'I never asked – because I wasn't goddamned interested!'

'Mmm.' The older man eyed him sceptically. 'And yet you ran away. You must admit that looks underhand? Deceiving, even. Guilty.'

'It was entirely Romily's idea. I didn't care when or how we got married. She convinced me that we should elope because she said otherwise her parents would stand in our way and she simply couldn't wait. I went along with it because I loved her, but it was all her idea.'

'Of course it was.' Monsieur de Lisle smiled thinly.

The funny thing is, I believe the young man, thought the lawyer. *He seems genuine. Or he is a fantastic actor? That cannot be ruled out, I suppose.*

'You are a chef,' Monsieur de Lisle said disdainfully. 'You have nothing. How did you expect to support your new wife?'

'I'm a chef right now,' Mitch said, evidently working hard to hang on to his patience. 'But I have big plans. I intend to open my own restaurant, here or in New York, and it will be a great success. The restaurant business is booming.'

'I see.' Monsieur de Lisle looked bored by the whole idea. 'But now we come to the heart of the matter. Your true motives come to light. You will need to finance this fantasy of yours, will you not?'

Mitch gritted his teeth and took a deep breath. Then he said, 'Yes, I'll need to find backers, that's true. It can't be done without an initial investment.'

'You *did* need to find backers. You will not now. Because you have very conveniently married one.' Monsieur de Lisle's voice had a triumphant ring.

And that is a good point, thought the lawyer, raising his eyebrows slightly and gazing over at the young man to see how he would defend himself against this accusation.

'I have no idea if Romily has any interest in backing my venture or not. I haven't mentioned it to her. And I don't have any idea how much money she has, believe it or not.'

'I *don't* believe it!' Charles de Lisle seemed to lose his temper then. He slammed his fist down on the table. 'Come on, Mr Mitchell! Do you seriously expect me to believe that you don't know what my daughter is worth? You could find out anywhere what her family owns, what she is due to inherit.'

He fixed the young man with a hard stare. 'You know that she owns several de Lisle paintings, surely. Just one of those could fund your restaurant several times over. Do you really think I could be so naive as to believe you had no idea of any of this? Please, Mr Mitchell, do not insult my intelligence.'

'It may surprise you, sir, but these thoughts never once crossed my mind. I'm in love. I've just got married. I'm enjoying this time in my life.'

Charles de Lisle gazed at Mitch's suit. 'And finding time for a little shopping, I see. Are you still working at the restaurant?'

'No, sir, I'm on an extended honeymoon, and Romily and I are still deciding our future.' Mitch paused and then said, 'Sir, it would make us both so happy if you and her mother could find it in your hearts to give our marriage a chance. Family is important to both of us.'

At this, Charles de Lisle's face burned with fury and he leapt to his feet. When he replied, his voice was trembling with rage. 'You are not part of my family and you never will be, do you understand me?'

'Very well.' Mitch stood up straight and squared his shoulders. 'If that's the way you want it. I have to warn you, sir, you cannot use money as a threat against Romily and me. We don't care if we have it or not.'

'Ha! Easy to say, less easy to live by. Do you imagine Romily will be happy being poor with you in a garret somewhere?'

'Yes, I do,' Mitch retorted.

'Then you're a fool!' spat Charles. 'You know nothing. She has lived all her life in luxury, surrounded by high society. She has never wanted for anything. She has no conception of what it means to live without money. The reality would amaze and appal her.'

'You said yourself, she owns valuable paintings. There is no need for her to go without if she doesn't want to.'

'Aha! Now we see. Now we see!' Charles de Lisle looked pleased, despite his palpable rage. 'You admit she has her own money? You're prepared for her to sell her birthright to maintain you both?'

'If that's what Romily wants to do, I'd never stop her.' Mitch spoke in a clipped manner as though still trying hard to remain reasonable while anger simmered within him.

'Of course you wouldn't.'

The young man added with a tone of finality, 'But I intend to earn my own money.'

'Very admirable,' hissed Charles. 'And very unlikely. You'd have to cook millions of meals just to buy Romily her winter wardrobe for one season.'

Mitch shrugged and smiled. 'I love her, sir. I do appreciate the generous amount of money you've offered me to divorce your daughter' – his voice held just a tinge of sarcasm now – 'but I don't intend to take you up on it. You won't be able to change my mind.'

De Lisle sat down slowly, averting his gaze for a while as though defeated. Then he lifted his eyes and stared Mitch full in the face, his expression ambiguous. 'If I cannot persuade you, perhaps my daughter can.'

'What?' Mitch frowned, a deep crease forming on his handsome brow.

'Please, sit down.'

What on earth is coming next? wondered the lawyer. He'd been impressed by the chef's tenacity and determination, and was privately convinced that he had married the girl for love and not money. Nonetheless, he could see it from the father's point of view. *The girl hasn't a clue what she's let herself in for. In a marriage of unequals like this, resentment comes creeping in before long. When the ecstasy has worn itself out, the recriminations begin.*

Mitch stared at his father-in-law for a long moment and

then sat down in a chair, muttering, 'I'm not going to change my mind.'

Charles de Lisle made a gesture to one of his flunkies who came forward and placed a small machine on the table next to de Lisle's place. 'Thank you.' He looked at Mitch. 'The very latest in technology,' he remarked. 'So clever. A remarkably discreet but very sensitive digital voice recorder.' He turned back to the assistant. 'Turn it on, please.'

The flunky pressed a button and the room instantly filled with sound. It was the background noise of a café or restaurant: tinkling glasses, the gentle clatter of cutlery on china, and the hum of conversation. Then a female voice asked, 'So what about this chef you've married?'

There was the sound of laughter and then Romily's voice said, 'It's such fun, darling. Do you know, the best thing about it is the way my parents have hit the roof? They've gone ballistic! All very satisfactory.'

'And do you love him?'

Romily's voice was playful and light-hearted. 'Huh, love! I don't think so! It's a game, isn't it? The sex is amazing. He'll make a very good first husband.'

'How long will you stay with him?'

'I don't know. While it's fun. No doubt we'll buy him off when the time comes.'

Charles de Lisle leant forward and clicked off the button. Silence filled the room.

The lawyer glanced quickly at Mitch and felt sorry for the poor young man. What they had just heard on the tape had turned everything he'd said into a ludicrous farce, humiliation on a grand scale. *What a tour de force,* he thought admiringly. *De Lisle lured him brilliantly all the way down the path and then – snap! The trap sprang shut.*

Mitch sat, white-faced and perfectly still. He stared at the table, his hands held tightly together to prevent any possibility of their trembling. Then he stood up and returned to his spot by the window, staring out on to the street below until Charles de Lisle broke the silence.

'Perhaps you would like a little time alone, to think over what you've heard?' he suggested almost gently.

Mitch spun round, his expression unreadable but everything in his face looking tight and ill. 'No need for that, sir. May I please borrow that thing?'

Charles shot a look at his assistant, who raised his eyebrows in return. 'Yes,' he said hesitantly. 'But you must know that we have many copies of this recording. You can't simply lose it or throw it into the Seine. Make it go away.'

'I have no intention of doing that. And, you can rest assured, I'll return your property within the day.'

'Very well.'

The young man came over, snatched up the player and stared at it.

'It's very straightforward, like any tape player,' said Charles helpfully. 'Look, rewind, and play.'

Mitch slipped it in his pocket, his gaze distracted as though he was only half seeing the room. 'I'll be back later. You'll have my answer then.' Then he strode out of the room, slamming the door behind him.

Charles de Lisle looked at his lawyers. 'So,' he said, satisfied. 'That seemed to go very well. I think we have achieved our objective, gentlemen. I'd be very surprised if things do not go our way after this.'

A triumph, agreed the lawyer silently. *And a surprise. I believed in that love story. Who would have thought the girl was a cynical little puss all along?*

Mitch strode through the streets of Paris, not seeing anyone or anything as he wove his way through the tourists on the broad avenues, intent only on getting back to the tiny flat in the Marais that he now shared with Romily. As he walked he heard those few lightly spoken sentences over and over again in his mind:

Huh, love! I don't think so! It's a game, isn't it?

He'll make a very good first husband.

No doubt we'll buy him off when the time comes.

Emotion choked him: fury, despair, shock, grief, and a horrible sense of sickness that made him fear he would have to stop and vomit in the street. He had felt nothing like it since he had put himself through cold turkey to break his heroin addiction. But he managed to contain it, determined only to get home to Romily and demand the truth from her.

The journey passed in a nightmarish swirl of faces and nausea, and then, suddenly, he was bounding up the steps to their apartment. He opened the door and burst into the tiny sitting room where Romily was on the sofa, her legs tucked beneath her while she talked on the telephone.

'Oh, hello, darling!' she said brightly, as he came in. 'That's Mitch,' she said into the receiver, 'he's just come home.'

He marched over, snatched the phone out of her hand, pressed it off and threw it on to the floor.

'What are you doing?' she asked, looking shocked.

'Get up,' he snapped.

'What?' she stammered. 'You're frightening me. Is something wrong?'

'Get the hell up!' He grabbed her arm and pulled her to her feet. 'Now. Listen.'

He took the machine out of his pocket, powered it on, pressed rewind and then play. The background noise of the café or wherever it was sounded loud in the quiet of the small flat. The voices began. *'So what about this chef you've married?'*

Mitch watched his wife closely as she listened. When she heard her own voice, her eye flickered wide open in surprise.

As her words echoed round the room, the colour drained from her face and she seemed stunned.

It was all over in just a few moments. He clicked off the tape and they stared at each other, seeing their own hurt and bewilderment reflected in each other's eyes.

'But, but . . . No, it's not true! It's not true!'

'Is that your voice?'

'Yes, yes . . . and it all sounds familiar. But I never said it like that!'

'Is it your voice?' Mitch asked again.

'Yes . . . it's me . . . but I don't understand.'

'Did you say, "He'll make a good first husband"?'

'Yes, but—'

'How could you, Romily?' he whispered. Pain clenched his guts.

She stared at him, frightened and desperate. 'I wasn't talking about you. Please, Mitch, you've got to believe me!' She put out her arms to hug him but he shook her off.

'How many husbands have you damn well got? I've been taken for a hell of ride,' he said hoarsely. 'I've just been put through the fucking wringer by your father, and I've sworn on my life that we're madly in love. Then I hear this. Is that all I am to you? A game? A bit of fun in your rich girl's life? You just like the way I screw you, huh? Well, now you've screwed me, real good.'

Romily began to sob. 'No, no! I love you, Mitch! I don't understand how this is happened.'

'Yeah, I guess you must be wondering who stung you. No one is as very, very sorry as the guy who gets caught.' He stared at her, seeing only guilt in her tears. 'I can't believe it. I thought we had it all. I thought no one could have anything better than us. Turns out I was just a sucker.' He went to the door. 'Goodbye, Romily.'

'Mitch, don't go!' she begged, her voice high and verging

on hysterical. 'Let me explain!' She ran to him but he was already out of the apartment, heading down the stairs. 'Mitch, don't go! Come back!'

The echoes of her cries followed him down and out on to the street, but he didn't turn back.

Romily sat on the sofa in the silent apartment. What had been a pleasant sunny morning in the home she adored sharing with her new husband had turned to ashes around her. She was shaking violently, her hands tightly clenched in her lap, tears rolling unstoppably down her cheeks even though she wasn't making a sound.

All she could do was replay in her mind the events that had destroyed her life and happiness: that click and the sound of voices filling the room, saying those dreadful things, those lies. It was her voice, she had said those words – she remembered saying them – but they hadn't come out in conversation like that. *He'll make a good first husband.* She *had* said it – but not about Mitch. They'd been talking about someone else entirely. *When the time comes, we'll buy him off.* She hadn't said that, she had said '*they'll* buy him off', while they had been discussing Annalisa dei Riacolta's latest romance with a bouffant-haired playboy who made his living ensnaring heiresses.

She'd been framed, of course. Someone had set a trap, that much was obvious. The fact that Mitch had believed in the fraud and let it override all his love and trust was what was killing her. How could he? Why wouldn't he let her explain? Surely he must realise that someone had doctored her voice, re-engineered it so that she was apparently saying those awful things? What kind of belief did he have in her if it shattered in the face of the first obstacle? She'd warned him that her parents would try and split them up and divide them. He'd gone to see Charles de Lisle that day perfectly prepared for the fact that he would be offered money. But he obviously hadn't been expecting them to play dirty.

He had no idea of the lengths her parents might go to, of how shattered Athina de Lisle had been by her daughter's marriage and what Charles was capable of when he saw his adored wife in pain. Romily could see how hard it was to explain away what sounded like a genuine recording. *But he didn't even let me try! Why wouldn't he listen? Was it because he wanted to divorce me all along . . .?*

Terrible thoughts began to race through her mind. *Maybe this is a stroke of luck for him. Maybe he's got what he wanted – the perfect excuse to play the wounded party and take whatever my father's offered him without losing face and admitting he married me for money all along.* All the implications of this, if it were true, began to sink in, making her skin crawl with horror. *It must have been his lucky day when he found me on the step outside that restaurant. I bet he couldn't believe his good fortune . . . and when it turned out I was the girl who'd helped him in the alley, it must have seemed like fate . . .*

'No!' she cried out loud. 'I can't believe it, I won't! He loved me, I know he did.' She began to sob. 'Oh, Mitch. What have you done? How can you let them win like this? I can't believe that was all it took to destroy us.'

But there was another worm of suspicion crawling in her heart. She knew exactly where that conversation had been recorded – it had been in the tea room of the Ritz in London. And there had been only one other person with her, so that person must have made the recording and given it to her father to doctor and use as evidence to Mitch.

And that person was Allegra.

PART 4
FOUR YEARS LATER

Chapter 35

London
2008

Allegra walked through Colette's, glancing keenly around her. The club was busy tonight: the bar was crowded and the dance floor packed with bodies.

She frowned as she saw Stav Starchios chatting up a bored-looking girl who was young enough to be his granddaughter. He was swaying slightly from the effects of too many Martinis and clearly didn't realise how ridiculous he looked, with his jutting belly, dyed black hair and gold jewellery, as he tried to persuade the razor-cheeked beauty to dance with him.

I must talk to him about it. He's got to stop acting like such a fool. Does he really want yet another wife to take yet another billion off him? And it's so off-putting for everyone else.

It was people like him that gave Colette's its reputation for being middle-aged, despite Allegra's best efforts to shake off this reputation over the last few years. She'd prefer it if drunken older members didn't paw the younger guests, and generally treat the place like a meat market.

She went up to Gennaro, standing at the reservations book in the dining room. 'Is everything all right?'

The club manager glanced up. 'Fine, Lady Allegra. Everything is under control.'

'I thought I'd slip away early tonight.'

'Of course.' Gennaro smiled, his strong, distinguished face softening. 'You deserve it, Lady Allegra. You spend far too much time here. You should enjoy yourself once in a while.'

'My thoughts exactly,' she said, returning his smile. 'I'll leave everything in your capable hands then. Good night.'

She walked back through the club to the front door, ran lightly up the stairs and said her farewells to the doormen. It was good to be out of there, she thought as she walked through the Mayfair square and round to the mews house that contained the office.

It had been her idea to move the administration of the club out of its former cramped premises in Colette's. Every scrap of storage space in the club was vital, and it was clearly impossible to run a complex operation from a room the size of a cupboard, especially when it could be put to much better use as an *actual* cupboard. When a building had come up for sale in the mews directly behind them, she had suggested to David that they buy it and transform it into the club's office. David was as resistant to change as always, arguing that he liked the dark little cubby hole with its ancient fax machine and manual typewriter on which he wrote his official correspondence, sending it out to agency secretaries to be professionally retyped.

'But, David,' she had said, infuriated, 'it's crazy! You come down to work in the club when the cleaners are here, tidying up after the previous night. The bell is going all day long with deliveries for the restaurant, and the kitchen staff are banging about, trying to restock, while you're slaving over the accounts! And when the place opens, you've already been there all bloody day and are feeling far from fresh. Let's move everything out. Modernise. We need a computer for a start. I'm not about to start typing in triplicate.'

David had finally seen sense, after much bullying and persuasion, and agreed to buy the mews house, despite its £5 million price tag. Mayfair property had never come cheap, after all, which was why Allegra was sure their investment would repay them very well in the end.

It had proved an excellent decision: 'Like all your decisions, darling,' David had conceded happily. He enjoyed having a new space to design and fill with beautiful furniture, but it never quite matched his vision of perfection because it was always full to overflowing with things from the club: boxes of bar supplies or cases of wine were often piled up in the hall; there were stacks of pictures everywhere that he had either bought for the club and was intending to hang or had moved out because he wanted to replace or sell them.

Allegra's own office, though, was always immaculate. She refused to have a single box or crate in there. 'Because I know what will happen next!' she declared. 'It'll be the thin end of the wedge. I'll end up clambering over mountains of Château Petrus just to get to my desk.'

She had even managed to convert her uncle to the wisdom of installing computers, though he himself still had no idea how to operate one or send an email. 'That's what you're for, my clever sweetheart,' he'd said fondly after he'd made her laugh one day by asking if he could send off any emails for her when he popped out to the post office.

Tyra, Allegra's assistant, a good-natured girl from Peckham who'd written a sweet letter asking for work experience and ended up staying on when Allegra had realised how invaluable she was, sat in her own smaller room and dealt with lots of the day-to-day admin, sending out club correspondence and fielding the many enquiries. It was all made very much easier when they finally had computers, access to the internet and the ability to communicate by email.

'Out of the dark ages at last! This is like Alexander Graham Bell demonstrating the telephone,' said Allegra with great excitement when her first email pinged through to Tyra's computer. She couldn't think how they'd ever coped without it.

The mews was dark now, Tyra long since gone home. Allegra went quickly up the stairs to her office and over to her desk. She took a small golden key from its hiding place under a marble paperweight and opened the bottom drawer. She removed what she was looking for – a mirror, a razor blade and some small paper wraps – and quickly arranged it so that there were two fat lines of white powder on the silvery surface. Taking a twenty-pound note from her wallet, she rolled it and snorted up the lines, then moistened the tip of her finger and picked up any stray grains which she rubbed over her gums.

God, I needed that, she thought, sitting back and sniffing. Then she got up and went over to the wardrobe. It had been designed to her specifications and opened out into a small dressing room, with one door concealing racks of shoes, bags and scarves and the other backed with a full-length mirror that folded away flat against a row of drawers with jewellery and make-up arranged within. She checked her reflection – the short stretch jersey Moschino dress in her trademark black did full justice to her figure – then brushed her hair and retouched her make-up, and she was ready.

There were lots of places she could go when she got the itch. She was well-known all over Mayfair and had automatic entry to dozens of private clubs and nightspots. But occasionally she felt like going somewhere she wasn't known and then she hailed a taxi and went to a different part of town.

Tonight, she asked the taxi to take her to Asylum, a small

and eccentric club near Baker Street. Even though it wasn't far from where she lived, she was anonymous there and its seedy atmosphere felt a world away from the polished ambiance of Colette's.

Her high had kicked in by the time the taxi arrived at the club. She got out, feeling deliciously confident and reckless, shook out her long blonde hair, and went in.

There were twenty or so people in the dark, intimate depths of the room and she moved through them to the bar. She ordered Grey Goose vodka on the rocks and sipped it as she looked around, identifying potential targets. She didn't have to wait long before someone tried to talk to her but she shook him off easily. He wasn't right, she knew that at once: he was too old and jaded and looked as though life had disappointed him too many times.

No. She'd spotted her prey. He'd been standing alone at the bar with a glass of whisky, watching the antics of the others in the club. Now, she was sure, he was watching her. She turned to look at him. He was tall – which was good considering that in her black leather Louboutin platforms she was over six foot herself – and slim, with a narrow face that managed to carry off its large aquiline nose thanks to a strong chin and high cheekbones. His coppery-brown hair was short but brushed forward slightly in the Roman fashion. In fact, he looked a little like she imagined Julius Caesar might, if he were living in modern London, in his late-twenties and wearing a dark suit: a bit beakish, but imposing and with intelligent, piercing hazel eyes under well-formed brows. *Yes. All in all, an attractive man.* She smiled at him coquettishly; the cocaine had hit her bloodstream and she was fizzing. *He's the one for tonight.*

Two hours later, they were in her flat, both naked and panting. He was sitting on a chair and she had rolled a condom down over his swollen cock and was now plunging up and down upon it, while he held her hips and watched her full breasts bouncing as she moved. He tried to reach for her head and pull her lips to his, but Allegra leaned away.

'No,' she gasped as he thrust into her again. 'No kissing. Not today.'

They fucked on the chair until he could stand it no more. Eventually he lifted her up and pushed her down on the floor where he could use the full force of his hips and thighs to thrust his cock home over and over.

When he'd come, she yawned and said, 'That was very nice, thank you. It was lovely to meet you.'

He lay next to her on the floor, hazel eyes glittering in the dimness of the sitting room. 'That's that, is it?' he said.

'Mmm. Yes. Like I said, thank you.' She wished he would go away. Her craving for excitement was satiated again. Now all she wanted was sleep.

'Can't I even know your name?' He sat up on the polished floorboards, resting his weight on his broad palms. He really was tall, she noticed, and under that conservative suit, surprisingly fit and toned.

'I don't think there's any point, darling.' She reached for her dress. 'Now, if you'll excuse me.'

'Interview over.' He sounded amused.

''Fraid so.' She sighed and yawned again.

'OK.' He picked up his clothes and started to put them on. 'Do you do this a lot?'

'I don't think that's any of your business,' she said frostily.

'It's not a criticism. I'm just interested.'

'Don't be.'

He said nothing more but got dressed and left. She shut the door behind him with relief. She was always glad when they had gone which was strange when she considered how badly she'd wanted them only a short time before, those nameless strangers she picked up in bars. Every time she went out to find them, it was to gain a little respite from the loneliness she felt late at night alone in the flat, and the terror of the dreams that came to find her when she slept. Only hours of empty sex kept them at bay.

Maybe it would help if she got what she wanted from sex: some kind of satisfaction, some fulfilment. But she was still tormented by that ugly little voice, mocking her, telling her how pointless it was, how she was wasting her time.

She padded back through the flat, picking up her discarded shoes and stockings and lacy pants. Then she saw it on the chair: a small rectangle of ivory card, engraved with grey capital letters that read 'Adam Hutton'. Below this was a mobile telephone number and an email address.

She let out a half laugh. This one was audacious. Then she threw the card down on a bookshelf and went to bed.

Chapter 36

London, Spitalfields

'Imogen, is this your box?' Fiona appeared in the doorway. 'It ended up in my room.'

Imogen looked up from where she was unpacking. She'd thought she had hardly any stuff, but there seemed to be mountains of it now. 'Oh, yes, that's mine. Thanks, Fi.'

'No problem.' Fi put it down and went back to her own unpacking. They'd been in the flat only a few hours and were both keen to get it sorted as quickly as possible, make it cosy and homelike. It was exciting – a first proper flat. No more rooms in shared houses or student digs. Life was going to be a bit more settled for a change. Imogen and Fiona, a sweet-natured Australian girl from Perth, had made friends at law school and now both had articles with Guthrie & Walsh, a high-flying City firm where they were now trainee lawyers, so it had made sense to get a place together near the office.

Her student days were behind Imogen. Now she had the business-like dark suits, the briefcase, the tiny laptop, the Blackberry, and all the other accoutrements of the young professional. She'd been with the firm for four months now, starting to move through the different departments, gaining experience in every area of their practice so that she could decide which she would specialise in.

Imogen got up and went over to the box that Fi had deposited by the door. She frowned. What was this? She couldn't remember seeing it earlier that day when they'd packed up the van. It looked older than the others, and dusty. She knelt down, pulled the tape off and opened it. Inside, she could see piles of papers, exercise books and photographs.

'Oh my God,' she whispered. She knew what this was now. Her keepsakes from Westfield. Her father must have brought this down by mistake when he drove down some of her other boxes from home. 'I haven't seen this lot of years.'

She sat down on the carpet next to the box and started leafing through its contents. 'Talk about Memory Lane,' she muttered as she pulled out a photograph of herself, Allegra and Romily, sitting on desks in their classroom and grinning broadly at the camera. On the back was scrawled: *'Midnight Girls 4 Ever!'*

It was odd to look at her younger self, with that long mousy hair she'd clearly grown in imitation of Allegra's, and those plump pink cheeks and wide, candid grey eyes.

She put a hand to her hair, which was now the colour known as 'blondette', a cross between blonde and brunette. A good hairdresser had taken her in hand and given her a flattering long bob with a loose fringe, adding light and bounce with some clever colouring. And she was a great deal thinner than the plump schoolgirl she'd once been. Had even discovered some cheekbones lurking below her puppy fat. She was never going to look like Allegra, who even at fifteen was clearly a beauty, but she made the most of what she had and tried to show herself off to her best advantage.

The biggest difference, though, she thought wryly, was that the innocence in those eyes had vanished. Imogen felt like she knew the big bad world pretty well these days.

And there was Romily, with all her sophisticated French

flair. What the hell was she doing now? It had been two years since Imogen had seen her last, since the whole notion of the Midnight Girls and their unbreakable bond had come to a shuddering, terrible end. She traced a fingertip over the outline of Romily's face, remembering what had happened on their last encounter and the choice Romily had asked her to make.

A letter had come just after Imogen had finished her finals – a mysterious and exciting invitation from Romily to visit her at Lake Como, but with no mention of Mitch or why she was in Italy.

Imogen had thought it would be a wonderful reunion; after all the romance and excitement of the wedding, they'd been close for a while. Imogen had sent her friend some photographs she'd taken of the day, and there'd been some happy telephone calls, and gushing postcards and letters raving about how happy she was, but then silence. It seemed as though marital bliss had swallowed her up entirely.

The trip had started well enough: arriving in Italy had been like stepping into a beautiful fairytale. Imogen left behind cold grey Scotland and arrived to balmy warm weather, with the sky a clear baby blue and the sun shining.

A driver met her at Milan airport and drove her out of the city and into the hills, along winding roads and through villages until they turned off down a long driveway. They were waved through electric gates by a guard, down a sun-dappled lane, and finally came to a halt in front of a large and beautiful villa. It was three storeys high and built of white stone, with swooping carved flourishes around the windows and ornate balconies. It was charming and graceful.

'What a gorgeous house,' Imogen breathed as she climbed out of the car.

The front door opened and Romily came dashing out. She

was simply dressed in a plain white shirt, black trousers and flat sandals, but Imogen knew that with her such simplicity was deceptive: nothing that Romily wore would be anything less than the best.

'Midge, Midge!' she called, and flung her arms around her old friend, kissing her cheek. 'I'm so glad you're here. How are you?'

'Hello! I'm great – but all the better for seeing you. You look wonderful. What are you doing here? Is Mitch with you?' Imogen glanced around for him.

'We can talk about all that later. Come in, come in!' She put her arm through Imogen's. 'I can't wait to hear all your news.'

They walked together into the hall. 'It's a Liberty-style villa from the turn of the last century,' Romily explained. 'Do you like it?'

'It's beautiful,' said Imogen sincerely. Inside, the floors were covered in intricate Art Nouveau mosaics of wide-petalled flowers and twirling vines in soft greens, oranges and yellows, and the walls were frescoed with more flowering plants and fruit.

'Wait until you see the back,' Romily said. 'This way.'

She led Imogen through the cool rooms and out on to a weathered stone balcony wreathed in ivy. They were high up and the rear aspect seemed to rise from the steep summit of the hillside, with the ground beyond plummeting away beneath them. 'What do you think of that?' With a wave of her hand Romily indicated Lake Como lying below them, a great dark body of water surrounded by mountains, stretching away in every direction. The view was stupendous.

'How amazing!' cried Imogen. She leant on the balcony and gazed out over the tranquil lake.

'We're on the western side,' Romily explained. 'I keep a mooring down by the water so we can get to Como quickly by motorboat. We'll go over later for dinner perhaps. Or tomorrow if you don't feel like going out. How was your flight?'

'It was fine. I was feeling tired when I got off, but this place has completely reinvigorated me.'

Romily smiled. She held Imogen's hand and said, 'It's so lovely to see you.'

'You too.' Imogen smiled back. 'Thank you for asking me.' Then she looked about. 'Is Mitch coming?'

'Oh, he's not here,' Romily said lightly. 'I'll tell you all about it later. For now, let's go to your room. I'm sure you'd like to get yourself together after your trip.'

In her bedroom, Imogen luxuriated in a feeling of comfort and ease. Her room had a magnificent high ceiling painted with frescoes of flowing drapery and cherubs proffering baskets of grapes. Tall shuttered windows looked out over the lake beneath. She had said that she was more than up to dinner in Como, so Romily had left her to take a long lazy bath in the pink marble bathroom that opened off her bedroom before she dressed for their outing.

An hour and a half later she ventured out, feeling refreshed and ready for a good gossip. She'd packed carefully, knowing that, with Romily, she'd need to keep up with a world-class wardrobe. She'd done her best, with a scallop-edged short skirt in pale pink organza that had the look of Chloé about it, even though she'd bought it in a chain store. With that she wore a loose dove-grey silk T-shirt with ruffles down the front, cinched in with a grey snakeskin belt. A row of enamelled bracelets in pastel colours ran up one arm, and she finished the outfit off with nude patent peep-toe heels it had taken her an age to find because she wanted the look of Louboutin without the price.

She'd pulled her honey-brown hair back from her face,

and emphasised her eyes with lots of mascara and her lips with shell-pink gloss.

'Oh, you look gorgeous!' Romily announced as Imogen joined her in the main sitting room, having found her way there with the help of directions from a housemaid. She herself was wearing an elegant black Prada shirtdress which she'd dressed up for the evening with a silver belt and platform heels. 'I love your outfit. That skirt could definitely be Chloé!'

'Do you think so?' Imogen said, pleased. After all, Romily really knew her designers and if she thought the skirt looked good, she must be right.

'Mmm. And all the lovely pastels . . . just right.' Romily looked quizzically at her. 'Imogen, what's happened to you? You've really blossomed! Last time we talked, I got the distinct impression you were nursing a broken heart.'

She flushed a little. 'Well . . . that was ages ago . . . I'm over it now.'

'Was it that boy you told me about? Sam?' Romily gestured to the place on the sofa next to her. 'Come and sit down.'

Imogen obeyed. It felt so lovely suddenly to be back with Romily, with her serenity and her poise and her attitude that everything could be worked out in the end. 'Actually,' she said, a little hesitantly, tracing her finger over the embroidery of a cushion, 'there was someone else. Someone I was crazy about. And we had a couple of passionate encounters but it didn't work out. He wasn't keen enough in the end. I offered him my heart and he said "Thanks, but no thanks".'

Romily leaned forward, her brown eyes full of sympathy. 'Oh, Midge, I'm sorry. He must have been an idiot.'

'I don't know. Maybe it was for the best. I moped around for a couple of terms, then decided . . . you know . . . sod him. I needed to get on with my life, so I had a bit of an image makeover and put him out of my mind. I've been out with plenty of guys since – no one special yet but I'm still hoping.'

'Of course you'll meet someone! Especially now you look so gorgeous. No man could resist you.' Romily put a hand on her arm and smiled encouragingly. 'And I think it's brilliant that you've moved on.'

'I have. Completely.' Though it wasn't entirely true, Imogen knew that. There was still a bit of her heart that belonged to Xander, and always would, no matter what.

'I want to hear more over dinner. We ought to go now. But I know what you need . . .' Romily jumped up. 'I won't be long,' she said, and dashed away. When she reappeared a few moments later, she was carrying a camel-coloured trench coat over one arm and, over the other, a grey leather tote with a gold chain and gold charms hanging off the strap. 'A coat for the boat!' she declared. 'It's cold on the water. And a Dior bag. I love my Diors and this will look just perfect with your outfit. It needs a tiny touch of gold to lift it.'

Imogen sighed over the beautiful bag. Romily was absolutely right, of course: the richness of the gold transformed her high-street outfit into something special. 'Never underestimate the power of accessories,' Romily said wisely. 'Now, shall we go?'

She pressed a buzzer to the side of the massive fireplace and, a moment later, a burly man came in, wearing jeans and a leather jacket. With his solemn expression and pumped up muscles, he could only be one thing.

'Carlo, we're leaving now,' she said, slipping on a white mackintosh. 'Carlo is my bodyguard,' she explained as they left the villa. 'It's a bore, but there it is. I've got so much security here, you wouldn't believe it. But I make them be as discreet as possible. I can't bear the thought of being surrounded and watched all the time – although I am. Once we get to town, you'll forget he's there.'

Imogen thought they'd be climbing into one of the expensive-looking cars parked in the driveway but instead they walked through the gardens and out of a small gate at the back, opened by a code taped into an electronic keypad.

'We're going to the water the quick way,' explained Romily, her eyes sparkling. 'You'll enjoy this.'

A few moments later they emerged by a cable-car station. A small red car was already waiting for them and they boarded.

'Come and see,' Romily said, indicating the window overlooking the descent. 'It's an amazing view as we go down.'

A moment later the engines began to grind and the cable car bumped into life, then they were descending the mountain face.

'Good thing I'm not afraid of heights,' said Imogen, seeing the great drop yawning below. 'Wow!'

Darkness was beginning to fall. The water of the lake was fading to black, the sky above to a misty charcoal. Along the shore, lights sparkled and twinkled in the exquisitely pretty little towns.

Romily said, 'We'll be in Argegno in four minutes. That's where the boat is.'

A few minutes later the cable car swung to a stop in the lakeside station and they disembarked, their burly escort keeping close by and evidently alert to everything around them. They walked down cobbled streets, stepping from stone to stone on tiptoes to save their heels, until they came to the water. There, a powerful motorboat with a handsome young driver was awaiting them.

'*Ciao, Marco. Come stai*?' called Romily cheerfully, and chattered away to him in a flood of Italian as they boarded.

They took their seats as he started up the engine. The next moment the boat was moving a trifle bumpily out of its mooring and towards the middle of the lake.

Romily was right, it's much colder down here, Imogen thought, grateful for the coat.

As soon as they were out on the open water, Marco opened the throttle and the boat zoomed off across the water, almost flying as it skimmed lightly over the surface and then took off again, throwing up spray. The feel of the cold wind whipping their skin and hair was exhilarating.

'I forgot we needed to wear headscarves!' Romily laughed above the roar of the engine. 'Never mind, I have a hairbrush!'

It was too noisy to talk much. Imogen watched the shoreline, the bright colours of the houses fading with the setting of the sun as they roared past over the water. Twenty minutes later they were approaching Como itself, a beautiful medieval town built around the bay at the south-westerly point of the lake. Semi-circles of tall pink, yellow and terracotta buildings were stepped against the dark green mountains behind, all dominated by the verdigris dome of the cathedral. In the marina, rows of white yachts were moored, masts flourished like a battalion of spears against the lake-front.

Marco steered the boat to a temporary mooring so they could disembark.

'*Può tornare alle dieci, per favore?*' Romily called and waved him off as he turned the boat round. They walked into the town with Carlo following at a discreet distance, now wearing a pair of mirrored aviator shades and looking exactly like a bodyguard.

'Don't you think he just draws attention to you?' Imogen asked, feeling self-conscious.

'I suppose so. But at least I'm not surrounded by eight man mountains like some of those pop divas – that's *really* attention-seeking. But I suppose they need protecting from their adoring public, whereas I need protecting from something altogether more sinister.' She shrugged. 'The downside of being rich, I guess. Carlo was trained by the best – the SAS. He knows exactly how to look out for me and he's got a very scary-looking gun in his armpit. Now, let's find the restaurant.'

They were dining in a simple, stylish restaurant where Romily appeared to be a regular. Carlos was shown to a separate table where he could keep them in his eyeline without overhearing their conversation.

'I love Italian food,' Romily confided as they sat down, spreading out the large linen napkins on their laps. 'I might learn to cook it one of these days.'

Imogen laughed. 'I seem to recall you used to have trouble working the toaster at Westfield!'

'It's true.' Romily giggled. 'I've never cooked so much as a boiled egg. In fact, I don't think I've been in a kitchen more than a few times. Silly, isn't it?'

'It's not exactly normal.' Imogen picked up her menu. 'Goodness, this looks amazing. Lobster risotto . . . how wonderful. I'm starving!'

When they'd ordered their food and each had a large glass of sparkling water, Imogen leant across the white tablecloth to ask the question that had been intriguing her since she'd arrived. 'So, where is Mitch? Is he away working or something?'

Romily's face grew serious. 'No.' She looked down at her water glass and turned it slowly on the tablecloth. 'I wasn't going to talk about this until tomorrow,' she said at last. 'I've got some other serious things I want to discuss with you then. But of course you want to know, it's only natural. After all, the last time you saw me, I was getting married and that was only last year. You must imagine I'm still living in love's young dream.'

Imogen watched her friend's eyes fill with sadness. *Oh, God,* she thought, panicked. *Mitch has died – he's been in a car crash or something. Poor Romily!* She put her hand out to cover her friend's.

Romily looked up and smiled wanly. 'When I talk about this, I feel such a fool. You see, it seems whatever I touch, I manage to mess it up badly. I wanted to start my own chain of shops and dreamed of having outlets all over the world – I couldn't manage even one. It failed miserably. Then I thought I'd found the love of my life. You saw us and what we were like. We were head over heels for each other . . .'

'I've never seen any two people more in love,' Imogen put in softly.

Romily gave her a grateful look. 'That's good to know. You were the only one who really knew me well enough to see that. I'm glad you did. But, as you can imagine, my parents were far from pleased. Mitch and I spent a glorious honeymoon in London, and then we had to go back and face the music. My mother virtually had a nervous breakdown and my father hit the roof. But Mitch and I weren't going to be deterred by that. I couldn't live my life in order to please my parents. They'd had their love story, so why couldn't I have mine? I couldn't understand why they wanted to me to marry a rich man. I've got more money than I can ever spend! I'm one of the few people in the world who never has to worry about that, so surely if anyone can marry for love, it's me! But they didn't see it that way. Not at all.'

Imogen had a feeling something awful lay unspoken and was almost relieved when the waiter arrived with their starters. But when he'd put the plates before them and gone, she said, 'So what happened?'

Romily picked up her fork and toyed with some rocket at the side of her plate, her mood sombre. 'We bought a little flat in the Marais, and I made it so cosy and comfortable. I loved it – so different from that grand house on the avenue Foch with all its gilt and mirrors and chandeliers. I was tired of all that. I wanted to be normal – to live an ordinary life with my husband. They said I'd be kidnapped or shot if I didn't live behind their iron gates and bullet-proof windows surrounded by guards, but I thought that I would be fine with Mitch to protect me. I didn't want to be the de Lisle heiress any more, just plain Mrs Romily Mitchell.'

Imogen smiled. 'I don't think you could ever be plain anything, Rom.'

'I can try, dammit!' she laughed. 'Maybe I wasn't going to give up my couture habit, but I was sure I could do without the gold-plated taps and the ridiculous cars.'

There was a pause before Imogen said quietly, 'And then?'

'Something terrible happened.' Romily pushed her plate away. 'My father got to Mitch. He offered him money to divorce me. And Mitch took it.'

Imogen gasped, shocked. 'No! I can't believe it!'

Romily looked sorrowful. 'It's true. He left me. We'd been married only six months.'

'But that's astonishing! I saw the two of you on your wedding day. I never would have imagined he would leave you so easily.'

'There's no accounting for men and their motives. Perhaps he was the most accomplished actor in the world. So . . .' Romily put down her fork. 'Having been a blushing, hopelessly smitten bride, I was suddenly an abandoned divorcee – in just over than six months.'

Imogen was flooded with sympathy for her friend, mixed with incredulity at Mitch's behaviour. She never would have believed it of him. *So much for my ability to judge character!* 'Oh, Rom . . . I'm so sorry! How could he? What an unbelievable shit.'

'The pain was . . . terrible. Still is. That's why I'm here. My parents got what they wanted: they destroyed the love between Mitch and me, poisoned it with their money. But they didn't realise that in doing so they would lose me forever. Outwardly I'm still the perfect daughter, dutiful and loving, and my father hasn't cut me off without a cent or whatever it is that angry fathers are supposed to do, but in reality I've gone far away from them. I couldn't stay in Paris, it was too painful and difficult, so I decided to move to Italy and spend some time alone to get over my grief. I came looking for somewhere I could lick my wounds, and when I found the villa, set high above the lake with those views . . . well, I knew at once that I could find some peace there.'

'Oh, Romily. You're here all alone?' Imogen could hardly bear the thought of it.

'For now. But even so, I'm always surrounded – the servants, the bodyguards. My little brother Louis comes to stay sometimes and so do a few friends, when they're passing through. I've found it a relief just to be still for a while.'

The girls sat in silence for a moment. *I have no idea what to say*, Imogen realised. *She's just like a young nun, shutting herself away from the world.* The waiter came and removed their plates, Romily's almost untouched, and they were both grateful for the interruption. After it, Romily said in a more cheerful voice, 'So that's why you won't see Mitch here. Just like you, I've put it all behind me and I'm moving on. I have a wonderful life otherwise so don't feel sorry for me. But what about you, Midge? Tell me about what you're doing. What are your plans now that you've finished at Oxford?'

Imogen realised she wanted to change the subject and obediently tried to move the conversation to happier matters, but all the time she felt the sadness that had enveloped her friend and wanted to weep for Romily's broken heart.

It wasn't until the next day that Romily dropped her bombshell.

They'd spent a happy day sightseeing and then lazing around the villa and were soaking up the warm afternoon sun on the terrace when she said casually, 'How is Allegra?'

'Fine, I think,' Imogen answered, enjoying the feeling of sunshine on her face. She looked over at Romily, who was in a loose linen top and casual slouchy trousers. Her eyes were hidden behind a large pair of Versace sunglasses. She said nothing. Imogen continued, 'I've hardly seen her over the last year. She's been in London and I've been slaving away in Oxford. We've swapped the odd email but that's about it. I hope we'll see more of each other when I get to law school.'

Romily nodded, her expression inscrutable. 'You know, I never understood why Allegra went cold on me. For ages she didn't reply to any letters or texts or emails, and I wondered what I'd done to offend her. Then, after I got married, Mitch and I went to London on honeymoon and I contacted her at Colette's. You told me she worked there, remember? We went out for tea together at the Ritz. That was the last time I saw her.'

'And how was it?' Imogen said cautiously, surprised. She had told Allegra all about the wedding, and often spoken about Romily to her after it, but Allegra had never mentioned their meeting at the Ritz. Romily was right: Allegra *had* gone cold on her, though she would never say why.

Romily said nothing while she poured out some tea. Imogen waited, sure that she was going to add something that would clear up the mystery of the coolness between her and Allegra.

'Do you remember school?' she said at last.

'Of course.'

'Our silly little club. The Midnight Girls. The three of us against everyone else.' Romily laughed with an edge of bitterness to her voice. 'I believed in that and everything we promised each other, just like I used to believe in love. Well, all that's been kicked out of me.'

'Has something happened between you and Allegra?' asked Imogen slowly.

Romily took off her sunglasses and fixed her with a serious stare. 'She betrayed me, Imogen. In a way I could never have believed her capable of.'

'What did she do?'

'She colluded with my father in persuading Mitch to divorce me.'

'What? No!' Imogen was amazed. She clutched the table. 'I don't believe it!'

'Yes.' Romily's face became stony and her voice cold. 'Mitch was played a recording in which I appeared to be saying that I didn't love him, had only married him for fun and that I would buy him off when I was tired of him. Of course, it was a fake. A perfectly innocent conversation had been recorded and then cleverly cut and edited. It was so well done it was almost impossible to tell that it was a forgery, but I managed to buy the original recording from my father's assistant, thanks to some bribery and very sweet talking. I gave it to a sound expert who analysed it and discovered exactly where my words had been pasted together.'

'Did you play that to Mitch? Tell him it was a set-up?'

Romily shook her head, and looked out over the lake for a moment. The late-afternoon sun caught the gold of her earrings and they sparkled. She turned back to Imogen. 'It was over by then. There was no way back. He hadn't trusted in me. Refused to listen when I tried to defend myself. That was enough for me. It showed he wasn't the man I thought he was. That he didn't truly love me.'

'But I don't understand,' Imogen said, confused. 'What does this have to do with Allegra?'

There was a pause and then Romily said clearly, 'She was the one who recorded me.'

Imogen's mouth dropped open and she could only stare at her friend, hardly able to take in what she had just heard.

'I know it without a doubt,' Romily continued. Her firm tone brooked no argument. 'There were two voices on the tape, mine and hers. There is no way anyone else was present or that we could have been recorded without her knowledge. We only decided on the Ritz at the last minute – we had been going to the Wolseley. No one else knew our plans. The conversation was recorded in such a way that whoever it was had to have been present the entire time.' Romily shrugged. 'It was her.'

'But why would she?' Baffled, Imogen stared at her fine china tea cup, not seeing what was in front of her as questions whirled round in her head.

'I don't know, Imogen, and if you can't tell me, then we're both in the dark.' Romily's eyes flashed and her face coloured with anger as she said bitterly, 'I've never been anything but a friend to her! She came to stay with me in Paris, we had a wonderful time and then . . . I never heard from her again. I was hurt but kept on trying because I treasured our friendship and meant to stand by our promises. When she agreed to see me after the wedding, I was elated because I thought that whatever it was had gone away and we were friends again. But she only did it in order to betray me . . . to ruin my life. It is beyond any doubt.' Her eyes glittered, although whether with tears or anger Imogen couldn't tell. 'I don't know why she wanted to destroy me, but I do know that I can never forgive her. And I also know that no friend of hers can be a friend of mine. That is why I had to see you, do you understand now? So, Imogen, who do you choose? Her or me?'

Chapter 37

Lake Como
2008

'Papa,' Romily said sulkily, 'I don't understand why I can't have a plane. Why can't I?'

'It's an added expense, my darling,' Charles de Lisle said from his office where the lighting was not exactly flattering. His face looked a little green over the web camera. 'We have two planes already, can't you use one of those?'

'I can't believe you're being so mean! What does the money matter?' Romily frowned into the web cam, pushed out her lower lip and made the face of a little girl deprived of the thing she wants. 'I only want a little one!'

'*Ma chérie*, you don't understand. It's not just the money – although planes don't come cheap, even the little ones – it's the logistics. Where will we keep it? Who will pilot it? How many staff will it require? When and where will maintenance be undertaken?' Charles shook his head. 'No, my darling, it's all far too much of a headache. Charter whatever you need if ours aren't available.'

'It's not fair!' cried Romily. 'I bet you get one for Louis!'

'Only if he can fly it himself.' Charles looked grieved, as he always did when Romily was upset. Ever since the end of her marriage, he'd granted most of her wishes, as though to make up for the great hurt and anguish he had caused her then.

'Huh!' Romily sighed heavily and looked away for a moment. Then she said, 'Well, I must go, Papa. I'm very busy, I'm afraid.'

Charles's expression was sad, his thin mouth turned down at the corners. He looked older these days, with his grey hair thinning and his wrinkles deepening. 'Very well, *ma chérie*. Will we see you soon?'

'I suppose so. I'll let you know. 'Bye, Papa.' She clicked off the connection and sat for a moment staring at the screen. What a shame. She had particularly been hoping for her own plane, which she'd already planned to kit out in white fur (fake, to please her vegetarian designer friend) and white leather (real, because there was only so much a vegetarian friend should expect) and platinum fittings. That would have set them all talking! But as it was, she was quite happy to turn her mind to some other delightful little schemes.

She opened her calfskin monogrammed diary and perused her engagements. In two weeks she had to be in London. The days she would be there were marked with heavy dark lines in pen. She was looking forward to it, anxious for it even, and the time was dragging. Until then, all she could do was plan her trip and prepare for it. There were always clothes to be bought, of course. A definite chill of autumn in the air meant it was time to think about berry-coloured crocodile-skin handbags, beautiful coats, fine buttery tweeds and oodles of cashmere. And, of course, shoes. She'd been drawn to the new shapes and colours like a bee to a lavender bush, and relished an afternoon trying out the latest styles in Milan.

Yes. That was how she would spend this afternoon. She picked up the house phone and her assistant, Monica, answered. '*Oui*, madame?'

Romily stood up and examined her reflection in the large

gilt mirror opposite as she talked. 'Call the car, please, Monica. I'm going to town today. Tell them five minutes. And please send an email to Countess Bianca to check she's coming for dinner tonight.'

'Of course. And, Madame . . . Vincente has telephoned five times already today.'

'Has he? How charming.' Romily watched her reflection smile wryly and thought how much she liked her new white shirt: chiffon with tiny velvet polka dots all over it. She ran one hand over the smooth grey skirt she was wearing. 'I'll call him from the car. I think he'll be with us for dinner tonight. Will you tell Cook please?'

'He wanted to confirm the menu with you—'

'I don't care about that,' Romily said. 'Whatever he thinks is best. He is the chef after all, not me.' She hung up, thinking of the afternoon that lay ahead of her, surrounded by the best shoes in the world. She would probably spend a lot of money . . . *a lot* of money. Well, if they wanted her to be a spoilt heiress, what on earth did they expect?

She got back from Milan laden down with bags from expensive shops and boutiques. Monica was waiting for her in the cool hall, clutching her notepad and looking serious as usual.

'Hello, madame,' she said as Romily put down her goodies. 'I'm leaving in a few minutes so I just wanted to update you . . .'

'Of course.' Romily patted her slightly windswept hair back into place.

'Countess Bianca is arriving at seven and bringing a friend. Vincente will be here in half an hour.'

'Thank you, Monica. I'll see you tomorrow,' Romily said with a nod. She watched as her assistant went back to her little ground-floor office to tidy up. An ironic smile played about her lips. *She probably thinks Bianca is my closest friend* . . . She caught a glimpse of herself in one of the gilt-framed mirrors and sighed. *Actually, she probably is, these days. Ever since . . .*

She thought of Imogen with sadness. When Romily had laid out the stark choice between allegiances, her friend hadn't been able to believe it. With tears in her eyes, she'd begged Romily not to ask her to make such a choice, but she'd held firm. It was impossible, she'd said, to remain loyal both to her and to Allegra, so which one was it to be?

When Imogen refused to make the choice, Romily had turned cold. She'd hoped so much that Imogen would choose to side with her, when she was so obviously the wronged party. Allegra had betrayed her, for God's sake, and ruined her marriage! How could Imogen decide to stand by her?

'Then you'd better leave,' she'd said coolly. 'I understand. I'm sorry it's come to this but you must see that I can't have anyone in my life who is in contact with that woman. I respect your loyalty, even though it's misplaced.' She'd held out her hand. 'And I wish you all the best, Imogen.'

'Romily!' her friend had cried, tears spilling over. 'Do you really mean it? You don't want to see me ever again either?'

'I'm afraid not. You remember what happened at school all those years ago, on that terrible night? You and I protected Allegra then but we both know the truth. She was the one responsible. We thought at the time it was an awful mistake, but now I know for sure that Allegra is rotten through and through. I just hope it's not you who suffers next. Now, I'll order the car for you.'

Imogen had left, miserable and weepy, unable to believe she was seeing Romily for possibly the last time. But Romily remained adamant: her life had to be cleansed of Allegra's poison.

*

The evening sunlight cast brilliant rays into the drawing room, and the balcony radiated the heat it had absorbed during the day. The scent of late-summer roses filled the air.

'Are you going to the Hennessy party in Cannes?' Bianca asked idly. She tossed back her long black hair and crossed her tanned legs, admiring the coral polish on her toe nails as she did so.

'I expect so,' Romily replied, her voice as careless as Bianca's. *We're far too worldly to care about yet another party,* they seemed to be saying to each other. But in reality, each party was another fabulous excuse to compete with their clothes, their make-up, their coverage in the press and their tally of famous friends. They were sitting in the drawing room, enjoying a drink before dinner. Bianca and Romily had taken their places on the vast cream sofas while Vincente was lounging in an artfully shabby Deco leather club chair. Bianca's date was still getting ready.

Romily sipped her champagne and said, 'Do you like these, Bianca? They're the latest range. I got them in Gucci this afternoon.'

'Darling, I *love* them,' purred Bianca, leaning forward to admire the high shoe boots, studded all over with tiny metal rings. 'They're so channelling the punk-Gothic feel I adore! I'm jealous you got them first.'

Romily smiled down at her beautiful and very expensive shoes. She'd teamed them with a silver chainmail mini-dress from a quirky boutique she'd seen in Como, and the effect was pleasingly metallic.

'Am I coming?' Vincente said in a mournful voice.

'What?' Romily looked over at him with a mildly irritated expression. He was half sitting, half lying in the armchair in his cream Armani suit and Dolce & Gabbana striped shirt.

He was a short man with blond hair and ginger stubble that had grown out to a little goatee on his chin.

'The Hennessy party. Am I coming with you?' He looked over with pleading eyes.

'Oh, I should think so. You usually come to these things with me, don't you?' Romily was fond of Vincente but his childishness sometimes annoyed her. He was always pretending he was helpless, just a boy with no idea of the way the world worked. She was sure it concealed a much sharper mind than he was letting on. But he was a genial man and, for the most part, good company, and he was useful for accompanying her to these endless parties and events. She hated walking down that red carpet on her own, with the bulbs flashing and the people staring. It was much better to have Vincente to hang on to, to deflect some of the attention. And he did so love it.

'Great!' he said, cheering up. 'How are we getting to Cannes? Will your family send the yacht?'

'I can ask them, I suppose.'

'Yes, please,' Vincente said happily. 'I like the yacht.'

Romily rolled her eyes at Bianca. 'It's because of the recording studio Papa had installed on *La Belle Dame.* So many of our musician friends came to the yacht and then complained that they'd been struck by inspiration in the night and had nowhere to work that he decided to help them. Vincente likes to pretend he's a pop star. When he's not lazing on deck or swimming in the pool.'

'Sounds charming,' Bianca said, tossing her hair again in her favourite gesture. She sipped her drink. 'Now, darling, we need to compare diaries. I'm going to be in London at the same time as you. We can go to all the parties together. Except. . .' Bianca frowned. 'You were at school in England, weren't you? You probably have your girlfriends there to see and spend time with.'

'Oh, no,' Romily replied lightly. 'I don't have any special friends in London. Just the usual crowd. You know them all, of course.'

Bianca's face cleared. 'Good. There are so many parties and I can't stand going to them without you, *cara*.'

The butler came in and announced that dinner was served.

'Thank you,' Romily said. 'Now where is your Rudy? He's so vain, that man. Still preening, I should think. Well, we'll start without him.'

Later that night, after they had dined and spent a quiet hour on the terrace talking, Romily had retired and was sitting at her dressing table in a silken robe, preparing her face for bedtime by removing every scrap of make-up, cleaning, toning and moisturising using her tailor-made skin system. There was a knock on her door.

'Who is it?' she called, smoothing rich cream into her eyelids.

'Me,' a voice announced.

She sighed and turned towards the door. 'Go away, Vincente!' She went back to her mirror, rubbing in the lotion with light circling movements.

'No,' came the muffled reply, and he knocked again, more loudly. 'Answer the door.'

Romily made a cross face at her reflection. Then she sighed again, got up and went to the door. Vincente was standing in the corridor outside looking sulky.

'What is it?' Romily asked, putting one hand on her hip and staring at him.

'I suppose you're not going to sleep with me,' he said dolefully. 'Again.'

Her voice was crisp. 'Correct.'

'Why do you never sleep with me?' he moaned. 'I'm very

good! All my girlfriends have been most impressed with my technique.'

'I'm sure you're an excellent lover, Vincente, but I don't want to. Thanks anyway.'

'You never want to. It's not normal. You must have a hormone deficiency,' he said frowning, his honey-brown eyes earnest. 'Perhaps you should see a doctor.'

'I'm perfectly well. Leave me alone and go to bed. Good night.' And she shut the door gently in his puzzled face, and returned to the dressing table thinking, *Thank God . . . London in only two weeks.*

Chapter 38

London

'Mr Mitchell, good afternoon. Please come in.'

The man in the elegant dark suit led the way into an office. It was situated above a busy and exclusive restaurant, the kind where there was usually at least one photographer loitering outside, camera ready to snap a celebrity coming or going. Mitch followed with Malik, his assistant, close on his heels. The two of them made an impressive pair, he knew that, with their superbly cut Savile Row suits – Huntsman for Mitch, Kilgour for Malik – both well-built, tanned and handsome. He spent a lot of time making sure that they projected the right image. They had to look like they meant business, like they knew what they were talking about. They needed to be taken seriously in a world where appearances and being able to fit in meant everything. So far, everyone had taken him at face value – if they guessed that he was just an ignorant chef from a small town, who'd spent most of his life stoned on dope, they'd think he wasn't worth the effort. They'd be wrong, of course, but there it was.

Their host took his place behind a large desk and gestured to them to take the seats in front of it. When he'd offered them drinks, which they refused, he sat back and said, 'Now, gentlemen. Let's talk about the reason for your visit.'

Mitch and Malik exchanged a quick look. There were times when Malik's Harvard and Stanford education meant it was best for him to do the talking, but in general it was Mitch who led the way.

He smiled pleasantly at the man behind the desk. 'Mr Evans, we've heard it on good authority that you're considering a sale of the Belgrave Restaurant Group.'

Evans looked surprised. 'Where on earth did you hear that?'

'Just a rumour. It's not widely known. . .' Mitch shrugged and smiled. He found that playing the American naïf could be an effective card. People often underestimated him as a result and were lulled into a false sense of security by his good-natured, smiling bonhomie.

'I should hope not,' Evans said with a look of indignation. 'It's not public knowledge at all.'

'So it's true?' Mitch pounced on the giveaway words.

Evans looked uncomfortable. He folded his arms and pursed his lips. 'Well . . . there have been discussions with my business partner, Alan Joliffe, but up until now it's been a private matter between us and some of our trusted advisors.'

'Those trusted advisors!' Mitch said jocularly. 'They're the worst. They're like sieves.' He glanced at Malik. 'Except for you, of course.'

'Goes without saying, Mr Mitchell,' Malik replied, his expression deadpan.

Evans stared at them both, clearly wondering if they were mocking him. Mitch instantly turned on his best professional manner: powerful, in control, smooth and, usually, irresistible.

'Mr Evans, I'll come straight to the point. I'm interested in buying the Belgrave Group.'

Evans raised his eyebrows. 'I'm sure a lot of people are.'

'OK,' Mitch said easily. 'But you're not going to sell it to them. You're going to sell it to me.'

'I'm impressed by your confidence, Mr Mitchell.' Evans appeared a little more comfortable now, as though he was back in control of the situation. He pressed his fingertips together and looked appraisingly at Mitch. 'But the Belgrave Group isn't simply about money. Alan and I put our life savings into creating La Joie. We'd both worked our way up in this mad business and knew what a risk it was. Nonetheless, we believed that our shared vision would make it a success.'

'And you were proved right,' Mitch replied, in a conciliatory tone. 'Everyone knows what a magnificent establishment it is. And two Michelin stars are not to be sniffed at.'

Evans sighed a little huffily and leant back in his red leather chair. The light from the diamond-paned windows flickered over his face as he moved, highlighting his long thin nose. 'I've never been bothered about that. The chef likes them. Our bank manager likes them. They are good for business, in a way. But my partner and I believe good dining is about more than just food. It is an *experience* . . . an enhancement of life. We treasure that.'

'Me too,' Mitch said with a smile. 'Now – are you going to sell to me?'

'What I'm trying to explain . . .' Evans said in a tone of infinite patience, as though he were talking to a child '. . . is that this is not simply about the money. Alan and I will only sell to the right person. And, of course, it's not only La Joie. It's The Old Print Works, Blowers and The Viennese Café as well.'

Malik tapped his fingers on the arm of his chair and interjected in a cold voice, 'We're well aware of the group's holdings.'

Mitch shot him a look and made a slight gesture with one hand. 'It's good to be clear. Thank you, Mr Evans.'

Evans frowned at Malik, but a little uneasily, as though he still couldn't quite evaluate the men sitting opposite. 'I'm trying to tell you that the personality of the buyer of our business is at least as important as the amount of money on the table.'

'Mmm,' Mitch said. He smiled again, and adjusted his green-and-gold checked Hermès tie. 'I understand. These places are your babies. You don't want to hand them over to just anyone.'

'Exactly.' Evans looked a little smug. 'It must be someone we can trust to care for our precious children.'

'Right.' Mitch's expression changed from genial to sharp. 'So what are we talking, Mr Evans? How much?'

'How much?' Evans seemed to suppress a shudder. 'Perhaps I haven't made myself plain. I would need to know a lot more about you and your business before I could even contemplate making a decision. I must be frank with you, Mr Mitchell . . . I've never heard of you and neither have any of my friends or associates. You appear to have come from nowhere.'

Fuckin' limeys looking down their noses, Mitch thought. *Who cares if he's heard of me or not? Asshole.* But he didn't show his feelings. He simply became very still and very focused, fixing Evans with his eyes and speaking quietly and clearly. 'I own four restaurants in Paris, all top-class names making money. Bought the first four years ago, and one a year since then. I've had your business valued – it's healthy, and it's bankable. It's worth around forty-nine million, with assets, profitability, liabilities, stock and so on. So here's the thing. I'm going to offer you sixty. Right now. But the catch is you only have twenty-four hours to decide.'

The blood seemed to drain from Evans's face. His mouth

dropped open. When he'd gulped for air, he said weakly, 'Sixty?'

Mitch nodded. 'Million. Cash.'

'Oh . . . oh, I see. Well, that's very interesting,' he stuttered, his pale skin flushing. 'Sixty, you say . . . well, I'll certainly talk to Alan . . .'

Mitch stood up and Malik followed suit. 'Great!' Mitch said, resuming his big, friendly American persona. 'Don't forget, twenty-four hours. There are some other investment opportunities I've got my eye on and I like to move fast.' He made for the door. 'Thanks for seeing me. I look forward to talking to you this time tomorrow at the latest.'

On the way out of the building, Malik laughed softly. 'The personality counts as much as the money!'

'Uh-huh,' Mitch said with a grin, putting his hands in his pockets. 'They like to think that. But the buck will always win the day. 'Specially when it's good old-fashioned hard cash. There seems to be a shortage of that these days, so no wonder he's excited. What do you say we hear before the day is out?'

'Maybe he'll leave it until tomorrow morning – to save a bit of face.' They walked towards the black Rolls Royce parked by the kerb, its number plate reading M1 TCH.

Mitch opened the door and swung himself down on to the buttermilk leather seat. 'Nope, I think today. He won't want to lose this deal.'

They were back in the house in Chelsea playing pool, Mitch bending over the table and shooting for the far pocket, when his business phone went off. He straightened up and grinned at Malik who was holding a cue and watching intently from the far side of the table. 'Fifty bucks says we're the owners of the Belgrave Group.'

'You know what, Mitch? I never want to bet against you,' Malik said, shaking his head.

'Hello?' Mitch put a hand in his pocket and strolled over to the window. 'Well, hey. It's great to hear from you. Yeah . . . yeah . . .'

He turned back to Malik and nodded slowly, a big smile spreading over his face.

Malik made a fist and shook it in triumph.

'Our lawyers will be in touch, Mr Evans. Thanks so much.' Mitch clicked off his mobile and stared at it for a moment. When he looked up at Malik, his eyes were burning with emotion. 'This will show that bitch,' he said, his voice suddenly icy. 'Now I own one of the swankiest restaurant empires there is, and I'm not going to stop there. I'm going to make sure everyone who ever underestimated me realises what a fuckin' mistake they made.'

'Yes, sir,' Malik breathed, eying his boss with admiration. He was a driven man, that was evident, though what it was that gave him that burning ambition wasn't. And Evans was right – no one knew where Mitch had come from, or where he got his seemingly bottomless resources. He had appeared on the scene just a few years before, gradually buying up four of the best restaurants in Paris, and now he had his sights set on London. All Malik knew was that he was glad he was on Mitch's side. He didn't care to imagine what it would be like to be his enemy.

Chapter 39

Allegra changed her Jimmy Choo pumps for Pedro Garcia Liberty sneakers in silver for the walk home from Mayfair.

She had bought a flat in an apartment building in Marylebone, just off the High Street, with all its desirable shops and restaurants. She liked being in the heart of London and there was still something of a village feel to Marylebone that appealed to her. It felt as though proper families with children lived in this area, with its playground, child-friendly cafés and glamorous young mothers pushing expensive Phil and Ted buggies as they roamed between Aveda, Agnes B and Brora or picked up some china in Emma Bridgewater's shop. Just to the north was Regent's Park where Allegra met her trainer at six-thirty every morning for a work out or a run, and where she often went for a peaceful stroll through the gardens when she needed to get her head together. To the south lay the madness of Oxford Street but, after crossing that and heading west, she'd find herself in the calm oasis of Mayfair, where very expensive shops and exclusive restaurants, gambling dens and grand gentlemen's clubs, rubbed shoulders with the few remaining private houses that hadn't yet been turned into those things.

The walk home was always a good time to ponder over her latest problems. She adored Colette's and never regretted for a moment taking the job David had offered her, but it had turned out to be a much bigger undertaking than she'd ever imagined. She'd envisaged taking on only whatever David was too busy for, but the truth was that very quickly she'd started to run the whole thing. Uncle David was getting old. She could hardly believe it because he seemed so youthful and vibrant still, but he was into his seventies and slowing down. He didn't have the energy to put in a full day at the office and then spend his evenings in the club, overseeing its smooth operation while acting as a genial, if eagle-eyed, host.

And the truth was, more and more of his days were spent going to the funerals and memorial services of his friends, which made him rather gloomy.

'My generation is dying off,' he said, 'and it's utterly miserable. They're falling like flies, darling. Cancer here, cancer there, cancer every bloody where.'

He was often fretful and melancholy, though he still retained his capacity for joy and amusement, and his insistence on perfection and routine was as strong as ever. Sinbad, the barman at Colette's, had invented a special Mac cocktail, named after David, and every Sunday morning he travelled from his home in north London to David's Knightsbridge home, an immaculate and gorgeous little house in a street tucked behind Harrods, and mixed him the perfect Bloody Mary, which he drank at exactly eleven-thirty.

Like all the staff, Sinbad held David in a reverence and awe that was close to worship. He was their captain, their boss, and the fount of all that was good and true. As a result, it had been very hard for Allegra to get them to obey her at first. They were all very polite and professional, but immediately she'd finished issuing her instructions they would trot off to find 'Mr Mac' and run it all past him. If he was happy, they were. In the end, it took a staff meeting and David laying down the law to convince them: 'Lady Allegra is my second-in-command. She has my complete faith and support. If she says to do something, you must do it. No more rushing off to find me and making sure I approve. I do. Understand?'

After that she had no more trouble, and when the staff began to understand that she shared her uncle's vision and didn't want to change Colette's radically and sack them all, they relaxed and began to hold her in the same esteem as they did David. The one who held out the longest against Allegra was Freda who had been the ladies' lavatory attendant since the club's opening night. She had seen all manner of stars, grand ladies, princesses and even crowned queens use the facilities. To Freda, the only thing that really mattered was if they washed their hands after the event, taking the fluffy white towel she held out to each lady as she exited the lavatory. If a princess didn't wash her hands, then in Freda's eyes she was no better than she ought to be. She was still scandalised by a Hollywood actress who'd sauntered out, leaving the seat a mess, loo paper scattered everywhere, and without washing. She had vowed never to see another of the woman's films because she wouldn't be able to look at her again without feeling ill.

Freda was not keen on Allegra and, although she said nothing overt, it was obvious she was spreading dissent among the others. There were mutterings about 'young things thinking we old ones are useless' and rumours about people being forcibly retired. Allegra guessed at once that anxiety lay at the heart of this campaign. She went to Selfridges and bought a big bottle of Freda's favourite scent. Then, as soon as the club opened, she went to the ladies and presented it to her.

'Very nice, I'm sure,' Freda said without a smile. 'Thank you, m'lady. Very kind.' She stared at it with suspicion, looking anything but pleased.

'I can see what you're thinking Freda.' Allegra settled herself down in one of the green-and-red-striped slipper chairs where ladies could rest and powder their noses. 'You're worried this is a sweetener. That I'm about to break some bad news. Well, you're right. I do have some bad news.'

'Oh?' The old lady's eyes turned flinty though her expression didn't change.

'Yes. I'm sure you're wishing that David and I would let you retire and get some well-earned rest after the years of service you've put in here. But the bad news is that we're not going to do that. I'm afraid we're going to ask you to stay on just as long as you can possibly manage. I hope you're not too angry with us.'

Freda's eyebrows went up as she absorbed this, and the next moment a big smile spread across her face. 'I think I can manage that, m'lady!' she announced. 'As long as you or Mr Mac need me, I'll be here. Don't you worry. Now, let me open this bottle and get a spray of it on. I do love this one.'

After that, Freda was Allegra's biggest fan, and Allegra dropped in almost every evening to spend half an hour gossiping in the ladies. Despite the fact that Freda seemed to spend all her time shut away in the cloakroom, she knew absolutely everything that was going on and was an invaluable source of information about the state of the kitchens, any squabbles or rivalries, and even what was going on in the private lives of the members.

'That cabinet minister was in again last night,' she'd say. 'He's having an affair with that blonde thing he brings. Scandalous. Still, this is the only place in London he could get away with it.'

Allegra knew that Freda never breathed a word outside the club and that the secrets of Colette's stayed safe inside its subterranean walls.

She could never have guessed how much time she would

spend managing her staff, but then, she hadn't realised the half of all the work that had to go on behind the scenes in the club. That first night in Colette's she'd dimly perceived it as a sort of grand restaurant, and of course she knew nothing about the restaurant trade. Now she knew that it was indeed the finest restaurant, turning out exquisite food that reflected David's individual taste and perpetual quest for perfection. Some dishes had been on the menu almost since opening night, such as the luxurious baked potato – golden, buttery mashed insides smothered in sour cream and a huge dollop of caviar – that was David's favourite comfort food. But he was fond of the best of everything: foie gras, lobster, caviar (Beluga or Oscietra), fillet steak, Pyrenean lamb, cream, truffles . . . all featured on the menu in one form or another.

Allegra didn't have to learn to cook, but she had to learn how a kitchen functioned and what she could request of it, how to oversee the orders and the purchasing, the delivery times and the planning of the menus. She considered Adrian, their head chef, a priceless treasure and a great talent. David had sent him not just all over London but all over the world to sample and learn dishes worth adding to their menu. If David found the perfect lobster bisque in Rome, Adrian would be on a plane within the day to taste and learn, and he never minded expanding his impressive repertoire. He had a wonderful team who could turn out an astonishing amount of excellent food from a tiny kitchen, and he knew how to handle David who had previously been prone to firing the entire cooking brigade if something displeased him or he considered the kitchen to be underperforming. Adrian could usually mollify him or else knew when to offer up a lesser member of the team as a sacrifice to his rage, while protecting the talented chefs he needed to keep.

But Colette's was more than simply a restaurant, of course. It was a place where people drank and danced and celebrated. It was a place some considered their second home and loved as passionately, or even more passionately, than their own house. They noted every little change: whether a painting was moved or replaced; if a new cocktail was added to the bar menu. And they expected that on any given night Colette's would always be perfect: the tables laid in precisely the same manner with the flower-patterned Limoges dinner service, starched linen napkins, Venetian glasses and small silver-and-glass dishes filled with crisp flakes of sea salt, the tiny silver spoon set at exactly two o'clock; everything must be clean and spotless, gleaming with love and care, the silver burnished, the brass polished, the picture frames free from dust and the glass shining.

All this took a lot of work, considering the battering the club took from the sheer volume of people who used it. It was a huge task to keep the whole place looking as comfortable and inviting as it did. Once a year they closed down for a thorough overhaul, with every socket and wire inspected, every carpet and rug cleaned, everything dismantled, checked, repaired, cleaned and reassembled, from the upholstery on the chairs to the silver and glass chandeliers in the private dining room. It was a mammoth task and it cost a fortune. Allegra likened it to renovating a National Trust property annually.

The crazy thing is how much I love this job! she thought as she strolled towards her flat. *It's like being part of a family, a really special little family, as well as an extended one that includes all the members and their families. It ought to be dull and repetitive but it's not. It's always changing and always challenging.*

But something was making her uneasy. David had hired her to refresh Colette's and bring in new blood, while covertly resisting any change she suggested every step of the way. She had won the battle over the mews house, but there were other, more important battles that he would not allow her to win. Her attempts to make the place more appealing to younger people had been knocked back, even though she had managed to increase membership.

One of her first successes had been to persuade her cousin Jemima Calthorpe to hold her birthday party in Colette's. Jemima, a hugely well connected and beautiful young viscountess, had brought a sparkling social mix into the club, and Allegra had put on a fantastic party for them. The guests had drunk champagne, feasted on lobster and then danced till dawn, before spilling out into the square to continue the party. It had made quite a splash and been written up in all the papers. Afterwards there had been lots of enquiries about membership from Jemima's sparkly young friends. A triumph, Allegra had assumed. A travesty, as far as David was concerned. To him, Colette's was about discreet style and privacy, not newspapers and celebs and drunken cavorting off the premises.

Allegra had now given up trying to alter the club in any radical way. She realised she'd have to think of an entirely new approach if she was ever to spread her wings.

She reached her mansion block and unlocked the front door. Stepping into the hallway, she was startled by a man who had been sitting at the foot of the stairs but now leapt to his feet.

'Oh my God! Xander! You startled me,' she laughed, panting a little in the aftermath of the surprise.

He stepped forward and wrapped his arms around her in a hug. 'Hello, darling. One of your neighbours let me in.'

'Why didn't you let me know you were coming?' They walked together up the broad staircase until they reached the third floor and Allegra's front door.

'I thought I'd surprise you.'

'You didn't know I'd be coming back. I might have been staying on at Colette's.'

'If you hadn't turned up, I'd have moseyed on down to see if you were there.'

Allegra looked at his jeans and open-necked shirt. 'I don't think Harry would have let you down the stairs in that get-up. Jacket and tie only.'

'Surely they'd make an exception for me . . .'

Allegra shook her head. 'No exceptions, Xander. Princes and pop stars have been turned away for not having a tie. But the manager has one you can borrow.'

'I'll bear that in mind.'

Allegra unlocked her front door and they went inside. Her flat was fresh and modern, the walls painted in soothing tones of mink and cappuccino, with bursts of light and colour in the fabrics and furniture, an eclectic mix of old and new, from the green clear plastic dining chairs to the antique ottoman and kilim rug.

'Would you like a drink?' Allegra asked, going through to her small kitchen. 'I'm drowning in champagne. A supplier has sent lots of bottles for me to taste – trying to convince me to change the producer of our house fizz, I think. Shall we open some?'

'Yes, please.' Xander came and leant against the door frame, watching her as she got glasses and a chilled bottle out of the fridge.

'So – to what do I owe this unexpected pleasure?' she asked as they went back through to the sitting room with the champagne.

'Just thought I'd come by and say hello,' he said casually. 'Do I need a reason to see my little sis?'

'No . . . but it's been a while, that's all. What have you been up to? Open this, will you?' She sat down on the sofa and gestured to the bottle.

'I've been staying with James in his place in the hills above Marbella. It's incredibly beautiful there, looking down off the mountains to the sea.'

'I thought you were browner than usual,' Allegra remarked. She watched as her brother picked up the bottle, tore the foil from the cork and began to unscrew the gold wire frame around it. Although Xander had a healthy brown glow, she noticed that he was looking thin. In fact, he'd lost a lot of weight; his cheeks had hollows below the bone and she could see that his arms were far more slender than they used to be. The rest of him was hidden by his clothes. Xander tried to manoeuvre the cork out of the bottle but gave up after a few minutes. 'Fuck it. This thing's impossible. You try.'

He handed it to Allegra, who pulled out the cork without much effort. She frowned as she poured the fizzing liquid into the glasses. 'Are you all right?'

Her brother leant back on the sofa. ''Course I am. I'm fine.'

'You seem a bit . . . I don't know . . . a bit under par.'

Xander shrugged. 'I have a fucking awful cold.' He gave a sniff as if to demonstrate it. 'Just can't seem to shake it off.'

Allegra noticed that his eyes had a yellowish, dull quality and that, beneath his tan, his skin looked lifeless. 'You don't look well. You're far too skinny.'

Xander laughed. 'You know me, weight falls off if I don't eat. It was so hot in Spain, I just didn't feel like it. I'm getting better now.'

Allegra picked up her glass of champagne and tasted it. She couldn't help evaluating it as she did so: *Not quite dry enough . . . the bubbles aren't crisp enough either . . . I can imagine what the members would say if I put this on the wine list . . .* Then she pulled herself back to the present and looked over at her brother. When she spoke it was slowly and carefully. 'I heard a rumour you were considering going into rehab.'

Xander shifted uncomfortably, his gaze dropping to the azure-and-purple striped cushions on the yellow sofa. 'No,' he said. 'I don't need that.'

'Really?' She glanced anxiously at his thin wrists.

Xander looked up, his blue eyes flashing. 'Really! I'm not a junkie, you know. I'm not an addict. I'm a recreational user, like all my friends are. We dabble, we have fun . . .'

'It's hardly dabbling,' said Allegra, then she sighed. 'Listen, I'm not out to get you. I'm no hypocrite, I still use myself occasionally' – she mentally crossed her fingers – 'a bit of charlie, some E. But if it's a problem for you, then you need help.'

'It's not,' Xander insisted. 'Anyway, I rehabbed in Marbella. We lived very simply, ate well, and just chilled in the sunshine. It was really peaceful. I feel like a new man.'

She put down her glass and leant towards him, her eyes anxious. 'You would tell me, Xander, wouldn't you? If you were ever in trouble? If you ever needed help?'

She watched as her brother stood up and began to pace about the sitting room, examining pictures and photographs. 'Yes,' he said, almost carelessly. 'Of course I would. But I'm fine, I'm in control. It's all fine.' He paused before an antique print of Foughton Castle and stared at it for a while. Then he turned to face her. 'Hey, whatever happened to that friend of yours . . . Imogen?'

Allegra looked over at him, surprised. 'Midge?' She wondered what had made him think of her. The castle? He certainly hadn't seen her for years. 'She's fine. She's started at her law firm and is quite the party girl these days. They work her hard so she likes to let her hair down at the end of the week. She comes to Colette's sometimes.'

'But she's happy?'

'Yes, I think so.' Allegra glanced at him quizzically, trying to work out why he was interested.

'Good,' Xander said, as if satisfied. 'I'm glad she's on the right path.'

Allegra stood up and went to join him in front of the picture of their childhood home. 'And what about you?' she asked quietly. 'Are you on the right path?' She took his hand in hers and squeezed it.

He smiled one of his wistful, little boy smiles. 'My life is fine. I like hanging out with James. I'm actually very fond of him, and I suppose his family billions do help things flow with a certain ease. I like this life. I belong in it. It's just a hassle that I can't afford it on my own account. Which brings me to a certain little matter I'd like to discuss . . .'

Allegra stared at him, her heart sinking. *So now we get to the point. I know what this is going to be.*

'The thing is, I'm a bit low on cash. I've spent all the old allowance for this month and the next. I wondered if you might have a bit you could lend me.'

'What do you need money for?' Allegra said, feeling depressed though she tried not to show it. She'd learnt that he didn't take kindly to people feeling sorry for him or trying to hector him into changing. But it looked liked Xander had only come here to ask for one of his never-to-be-repaid loans.

He shrugged. 'This and that,' he relied vaguely. 'My rent.'

'I thought you were staying in Onslow Square.'

'Oh, yeah – but I owe some back rent from my last place.'

'How much do you need?' She could never say no to him, even though she dreaded to think what he was spending the money on.

Xander sensed her weakening and said cheerfully, 'Not much. Say . . . five hundred?'

Allegra reached for her bag. 'OK. I'll write you a cheque.'

'Don't suppose it could be in cash, could it?' he said with a sheepish smile. 'Only I kind of need it right away.'

There was a pause and then she replied, 'All right. When we've had our drink, we can take a stroll to the cash point.'

'Thanks, sweetie,' he said with obvious relief. 'I owe you. Big time.'

I'm not going to get it back, she thought. *But I don't care about that. My real worry is what he needs that money for.*

Chapter 40

Imogen had been given membership of Colette's as a present by Allegra, though they'd kept it a secret from David, who never gave out free memberships.

Lucky, really, as I'd never have been able to afford it otherwise, she thought as she dressed up for a Friday evening visiting Allegra. *Even now I'm on a good salary, it's hard to justify spending a whole thousand pounds of it on joining a nightclub.*

Her flatmate poked her head round the door. 'You're back then. Thought they were working you hard tonight on the Fielding case?'

Imogen turned round to face Fi as she poked a dangly chandelier earring through a lobe. 'The client's called a halt to it. I'm home free for the *entire* weekend.'

'Lucky you,' Fi said enviously. 'I'm in tomorrow at the crack of dawn. A Saturday. That sucks, doesn't it? So I'm off for a run.'

'Have a good time,' Imogen said with a smile. She turned back to her reflection and continued getting ready.

'It's so wonderful you're here,' Allegra said, kissing Imogen on the cheek and giving her a big smile. 'I could do with a nice gossip. Sinbad, two of your best Cosmopolitans, please.'

'Of course, Lady Allegra.' The barman instantly began work, handling the tools of his trade with practised ease as he mixed their drinks.

The girls were in the bar. It was still early for Colette's, and there was plenty of room to sit down. 'Let's go over here,' Allegra said, leading the way across the comfortable seating area and going over to one of the velvet banquettes. She looked elegant in an understated way in her black Burberry shift, nipped in at the waist with a big silver leather belt, and effortlessly graceful on towering Rupert Sanderson heels. She was perfectly made up, her hair long and supermodel glossy, and looked slender and toned.

I'm never going to look like that in a million years, Imogen thought a little wistfully. Her own outfit – a Top Shop green and grey sequined cocktail dress which she'd teamed with high gladiator sandals that criss-crossed up her legs – had looked delightful and a little mermaidish in her bedroom, but somehow didn't match up to the expensive simplicity of Allegra's outfit. But she didn't have that kind of money – not yet, at least. *Give me time. Ten years and I'll be a partner and earning hundreds of thousands. Before bonuses.* 'You look great,' she said sincerely. 'I love that dress.'

'Thanks.' Allegra smiled. 'It's part of the job, really. I have to project the Colette's style all the time. It is expensive but David gives me a dress and grooming allowance to make sure I'm always perfectly turned out – it's the kind of thing that matters to him.'

'Do you mind spending your free time here as well?' Imogen looked about her at the alcove they were sitting in. A vase of white peonies stood next to a brass lamp with a scarlet shade. Its soft golden light illuminated pictures hung frame to frame – portraits of dogs in this particular alcove. She took a sip of her drink, enjoying the tart taste of cranberry and lime with the slight burn of vodka underneath.

'Not really,' replied Allegra. 'I spend most of my time in the office rather than the club, and anyway, if I didn't want to spend my evenings here, I could hardly expect the members to.'

'It's so gloriously glamorous,' Imogen sighed. 'Why on earth does it feel so special?'

'That's what I'm trying to discover,' Allegra said, sipping her drink. 'I'm working out just what the secret is.'

'Really?' Imogen gave her a sideways glance. 'That sounds intriguing . . .'

Allegra laughed. 'The astute lawyer! I should have known you'd pounce on that.' She raised an eyebrow at Imogen. 'I'll tell you over dinner.'

'Oh, yes, please. And I'm starving, so the sooner the better.'

'So . . .' Imogen said, when they were tucked away in the dark dining room at Allegra's special table, lit only by small tea lights flickering in the Venetian glass holders. 'Do you have something up your sleeve you haven't told me?'

Allegra was staring at the wine list. The candlelight played on her hair, illuminating the golden strands. 'Would you like red or white?' she asked evasively. 'You can even go off-menu if you like. We have cases of wildly expensive vintages that aren't on the list, kept exclusively for our most discerning guests. We can't advertise them or we'd run out. In fact, we have the last bottles in the world of some vintages. Last week, we had a large family in to celebrate a birthday with a magnum of Château Haut Brion 1875. Seventeen thousand pounds a bottle! They got a taste for it and ordered another, which was our last, so then they moved on to the 1955 vintage, which is legendary, like liquid gold. Six thousand a bottle. They all got completely sloshed on fantastic wine. With the couple of magnums of champagne they ordered as well, the bar bill was ninety thousand pounds. Quite a tab, even for Colette's.'

Imogen gaped at her. *Ninety thousand pounds?* 'I wouldn't like to wake up with a hangover like that,' she said weakly. 'I was going to say red, but now I think I'll just have water.'

'The house red is perfectly delicious and only thirty-five pounds a bottle. We'll have that.' Allegra put down the wine list.

Imogen perused her menu and said carelessly, 'Now, did I miss something or did you just cunningly change the subject?'

Allegra gave her a conspiratorial look and leant across the white tablecloth towards her. 'I'll tell you when we've ordered,' she murmured.

Imogen ordered lobster croquettes followed by steak Diane. When she was tucking into her croquettes, she said, 'So . . . what's going on? I know you. Something's on your mind.'

Allegra gave her an amused look as she broke off a piece of bread and spread some butter on it. 'God, you're good. OK, I've got a plan.' She looked around the dark room, filling up now with members and their guests, and dropped her voice. 'I want to expand.'

'What? Colette's?' Imogen glanced about, wondering how the small space could be used any more effectively than it already was.

Allegra shook her head. 'No. I've realised now that David is never going to be able to alter this place – and, in many ways, he shouldn't. It's an institution. Perfect as it is. But I've got a hankering to try something new, and I think I'll be able to persuade him to invest in my plan.' She smiled and her eyes sparkled with excitement. 'A new club. One aimed at a different market from Colette's but that will still offer the high-quality glamour this place is associated with: wonderful service, exquisite food, comfort and privacy – plus a bit of youth and modernity.'

Imogen was impressed. 'Sounds like a wonderful idea,' she said enthusiastically. 'I'd join.'

'It's early days,' Allegra said quickly, 'and I haven't yet sorted out all my ideas, but I really think I could be on to something. I'm sure David will be interested.'

Imogen frowned as she mopped up the sauce with her last exquisite morsel of lobster croquette. 'Isn't it a bad time to expand? Economically, I mean.'

'It might be the best time,' Allegra said quickly. 'We're in good shape, and we've got some cash to invest. And property is cheaper than it used to be.'

'Well, I'm sure you know what you're doing.' Imogen's grasp of economics was hazy but the main thing, she was sure, was for Allegra to find the money. If David had it and therefore didn't need to borrow it, and if they were confident about the new venture, then that was fine, wasn't it? Except that she'd always heard that the restaurant business was notoriously difficult and quick to fold when times were tough . . .

They finished their main courses and Imogen ordered the amazing dark chocolate and ginger ice cream.

'It's one of Colette's signature dishes,' Allegra said approvingly. 'Much imitated and never bettered. Here, let me have a taste.'

'Get your own!' Imogen said with a laugh, batting away Allegra's spoon with her own. 'What did Romily always say? A moment on the lips, a lifetime on the hips.'

There was a sudden and awkward pause. Her name was rarely mentioned between them.

'Do you know how she is?' Allegra said abruptly, staring down at the table. Her hands had clenched almost involuntarily and the tops of her knuckles were white.

'No,' Imogen replied quietly. 'We're not in touch any more. I . . . suppose . . . we've all just drifted apart, haven't we? I mean, she lives abroad, she's got that glamorous heiress lifestyle, always in the papers, muse to a designer, all that nonsense . . . I think our worlds have become too different.'

'Mmm.' Allegra picked up her wine glass and took a long gulp of red wine. Imogen watched her, feeling sad as she always did when she remembered the way their girlhood friendship had disintegrated. She'd made it plain to Romily that she wouldn't be forced to choose between her two dearest friends, and her subsequent rejection had meant that Imogen's loyalty was now all to Allegra. But she'd agonised over what she'd been told. Had Allegra really done that terrible thing and deliberately set out to destroy Romily's marriage? It was unforgivable if so. Imogen couldn't bring herself to believe it – there had to be some kind of misunderstanding – but she also couldn't bring herself to ask Allegra about it. So she let it lie between them, the unspoken question, burning a hole in their friendship that only she could see. Was this a chance to find out what had mystified and bothered her friend for so long? Imogen took a deep breath and looked over at Allegra, hoping her face didn't give away her sudden nervousness. 'Well, you know she got married . . .'

'Yes, of course. You told me all about it and then I saw her when she was over in London. She was all of a flutter, very much love's young dream. We had tea at the Ritz.'

'Did you? You never said.' *Is she about to confess? To tell me what she did?*

But Allegra remained clear-faced, calm and innocent. She shrugged. 'Didn't I?'

'Did you know she got divorced after only six months of marriage?' Imogen watched her carefully, staring into those navy blue eyes.

Allegra looked startled. 'No, I had no idea. But why?'

'He got the idea that Romily didn't love him,' Imogen said abruptly.

'Really?' Allegra appeared genuinely surprised. 'I got the impression she was completely mad about him.'

I don't understand, Imogen thought, baffled. *She's so plausible, there's not a trace of guilt about her. But Romily was convinced Allegra was the one who recorded her. Could she have made a mistake?* She said sadly, 'Well, he turned out to be more interested in money after all.'

There was a flicker of something like relief in Allegra's eyes but she said nothing, only took another long sip of wine.

A pause settled between them and then Imogen said quietly, 'I never understood why it went wrong between us. We swore we'd always be friends.'

Allegra looked up at her, a flash of steel in her dark blue gaze. 'Yes, we swore we'd always be there for each other. Well . . . I wasn't the first to break that promise.'

'What?' Imogen shook her head in amazement. 'What do you mean? What did Romily do?'

'Nothing, nothing.' Allegra looked suddenly very sad. She gazed down at the snowy white tablecloth and her hand curled into a tight fist. 'She did absolutely nothing.'

Chapter 41

Romily flew on the family jet to Heathrow with only twenty-seven pieces of luggage and Carlo, her bodyguard. The British driver met her off the plane in the Mercedes and drove her to the family house in London, a beautiful seven-bedroomed white stucco mansion in Chester Square, Belgravia. It was smaller than most of the family houses but one of Romily's favourites because of the beautiful garden it overlooked.

Once she'd arrived, she summoned her London beauty therapist and masseuse for a full treatment to help her recover from her journey. When she was feeling relaxed and revitalised, she set up her office in a small room leading off the first-floor drawing room that had a charming view over the garden square, and worked on the details of her stay.

Here, there was no Monica to oversee her diary and field calls, but in many ways that made things a great deal easier. Such privacy was useful when it came to conducting the business she kept concealed from everyone closest to her.

She spent her first afternoon working, using the internet to check on progress, emailing her closest contacts and making all the necessary arrangements. There was a lot to catch up on and she felt energised and raring to tackle it all. The most important email she sent simply read, *I'm here*.

When she was satisfied with what she'd achieved, she shut down her computer and went to bed for an early night.

*

Bianca came over the next day. She'd arrived a few days earlier and was staying at the Dorchester.

'Such a bore,' she said as she arrived wearing tight black leggings, stiletto boots and a mustard yellow tunic layered with grey and black knits. 'Mariah Carey's staying in the hotel. The noise is dreadful.'

'She's not that bad a singer,' Romily joked, leading her through to the drawing room.

Bianca blinked, puzzled. 'No, I mean from her fans. What a fuss. They scream every time she leaves the hotel.'

'Of course.' Romily's mouth twitched at one corner.

Bianca shook out her hair and walked up to a mirror on the wall, gazing seriously at her reflection. 'This party tonight, at the Joshis' house in Kensington Palace Gardens . . . you're coming, aren't you?'

'Oh, yes . . .' Romily looked as though she wasn't bothered much one way or the other. 'I'll drop in for a while anyway. I won't stay late. I'm so tired.'

'Did you bring your pink leopard-print Jimmy Choo clutch?' enquired Bianca, tearing herself away from her reflection.

'I think so.' Romily frowned trying to remember. 'Would you like to borrow it? I'll go and see if it's been unpacked. The maid did most of it yesterday.'

She left Bianca in the drawing room and went quickly upstairs where she found the evening bag sitting neatly on its shelf in her dressing room. She took it back to the drawing room and was surprised to find that her friend had disappeared.

'Bianca?' she called, frowning, looking around the room. There was nowhere for her to hide – it was a simple square room in tones of white, off-white and oatmeal: cool and serene.

'In here,' came the reply, and Romily realised that Bianca was in the anteroom that led off the drawing room, the one she had chosen for her study. She gasped and sprinted across to the doorway, seeing Bianca inside bending over the desk with its open laptop and neat piles of papers.

'What the hell are you doing?' barked Romily, her face burning. 'Get away from there!'

Bianca jumped and looked up, startled. 'Sorry, darling, I just wanted to check something on the Chanel website . . .'

'Get away!' Romily dashed over and pushed her aside, slamming the laptop shut and gathering up the papers around it. 'This is private.'

Bianca blinked at her in her usual bemused way and shrugged, unruffled. 'Sorry, sweetie, didn't realise.' Then she saw that Romily was holding the pink leopard-print clutch and her face lightened. 'Oh, wonderful! You've got the bag. That's great.'

She took it from her trembling hand and wandered back with it into the drawing room, leaving Romily panting and shaking behind her.

The Kensington Palace Gardens house glittered with beautiful lights: crystal chandeliers hung in shimmering tiers from brass chains, exquisite lamps burned in alcoves and niches, and twisting silver candelabra held up their shining wax offerings on every other surface.

Beautiful women and distinguished men moved through the huge rooms, stopping to greet each other or gathering in small circles to talk as they sipped the ice-cold Bollinger offered to them by waiters or plucked delicious morsels from the trays carried by waitresses.

Romily moved through them, drawing admiring glances as she passed. She was wearing a deep midnight-blue gown, tightly wrapped round her body, emphasising her tiny waist and rounded hips, before flaring out to the ground. The satin glowed against her warm olive skin and her long dark brown hair fell in glossy waves over her shoulders as she made her way through the room.

'Ah, *ma belle*! How wonderful to see you, I had no idea you were in London!' An older woman in bright purple silk, her dark tan sunk deep into her pores from years of sunbathing, stepped into her path and offered her pursed, coral-coloured lips for an air kiss.

Romily stopped reluctantly. 'Francesca, hello.' She turned her head politely for the pretend embrace. 'I can't stay, I'm looking for Bianca . . .' She glanced about the room, looking for the familiar dark hair being tossed over one shoulder.

Francesca gestured towards a doorway. 'She's in the other salon, talking to some ambassador or other – someone with a big ribbon and medals anyway.'

'If you'll excuse me, then . . .'

'Come back later, do you hear? I want to find out all your news! And ask about your dear mother, whom I've not seen for an age.'

'Yes, yes, of course. Until then.' Romily smiled firmly and walked purposefully away. *That's the trouble with these parties. There's no one I want to talk to.* It crossed her mind for a moment how much more fun it would have been to be here with Imogen or Allegra, able to giggle at the pomposity all around as well as to enjoy the luxury. But she pushed that thought away. *That's all over now.*

She found Bianca in the red salon and drifted up to join her circle, greeting everyone with the usual kisses. A waiter brought her a glass of champagne and she sipped it as she listened to the conversation. Bianca had managed to extricate herself from the attentions of the ambassador and was complimenting Romily on her gown when she suddenly gave her a fierce nudge. 'Do you know who that is?' she hissed in a loud whisper, gazing across the throng.

'Who?' Romily asked, following the direction of her gaze. It was hard to make out anyone in particular in the ranks of dark-jacketed backs and vibrant silks and satins.

'That devastatingly handsome man over there!' Bianca said. 'Next to Kevin Tong.'

Romily saw who she was talking about and immediately her insides seemed to turn to water. She felt as breathless as if she'd been running a mile. The tall man in the Gieves and Hawkes bespoke dinner jacket and sober black silk tie was none other than Mitch. He was talking to a younger man who looked Indian, and an elegant Chinese man sporting velvet evening slippers where most of the men were wearing patent leather shoes.

'That's Ted Mitchell, the mystery billionaire,' Bianca said excitedly. 'I saw him in the Dorchester last night – he was dining with Kevin then. I bet they're talking about business . . . He's American, and apparently he's buying up the most glamorous clubs and restaurants in London. Maybe he wants to buy Kevin's place.' She sighed happily. 'So rich and so good-looking. I just have to meet him!' She pulled at Romily's arm. 'Come on, let's go over, Kevin will introduce us.'

'No, no,' Romily protested weakly. She was still so stunned by the sight of Mitch that all the strength seemed to have left her body.

'Come on,' insisted Bianca, pulling her across the room. At that moment the men they were discussing seemed to feel their presence because Kevin turned round, saw Bianca and gave a broad smile.

'The exquisite Countess Bianca! What joy. Come and talk to us, dear. And Romily de Lisle . . . I haven't seen you in age, sweet thing!' Kevin put out a hand to her and the next moment she was standing in their circle, only aware, as Kevin kissed her cheek, of Mitch just a foot or so away. She was blinded by confusion, unable to look up, seeing only dinner suits and the vibrant green of Bianca's split-skirt Versace dress.

'Now,' Kevin said brightly, still holding her hand, 'Romily, have you met Ted Mitchell? He's the newest addition to the London scene and making rather a mark by buying up all our favourite watering holes!'

There was a pause where Romily was duly expected to smile and glitter, to say hello and how lovely to meet you and tell me all about it, but she couldn't. As she fought her churning emotions, the pause lengthened into an awkward silence.

'Well, I'm *dying* to meet you,' gushed Bianca. 'I've heard so much about you. Are you enjoying London?'

There was another pause as everyone waited for Mitch to answer. Kevin shifted uncomfortably.

'I *was* enjoying it,' Mitch said in an icy voice.

At the sound of it, a whirl of emotions rushed through Romily. That voice . . . how much it had meant to her! Oh God . . . she still remembered so much . . . a moment from their wedding day sprang into her mind and she heard his voice murmuring his vows.

'Romily and I have met before, haven't we?' he said. She managed to look up and saw the cold smile that didn't touch his brown eyes. She nodded and said nothing. The others swapped glances – the chilly, almost venomous atmosphere was unmistakable, though they clearly had no idea why it was so. 'Oh, yes,' he said harshly. 'We're old, old friends.' Then Mitch glanced at the others in the circle. 'I'm sorry, would you excuse me? I really must find our host. He's expecting me in the library in five minutes.'

'What was *that* all about?' hissed Bianca, appalled and

intrigued at the same time, as they made their way to the supper room quarter of an hour later.

'I don't know what you're talking about, darling.' Romily had recovered herself by now and spoke in an easy tone. She flicked a tiny piece of her satin gown between her fingers.

'You and Ted Mitchell! How come you know each other?'

'Oh, we don't really, I don't know why he said that.' Romily shrugged carelessly and then allowed herself a tiny smile as she said, 'I think he's an old friend of my father. That must be it.'

She made her excuses as soon as she could, and summoned the Mercedes to the front of the house.

As the car glided away down the private road, she said to the driver, 'We're not going home, Walter. I have another appointment to go to first.'

Then she sat back on the seat and watched London sailing past, dark and shadowy in the autumn night.

The evening isn't over quite yet . . .

Chapter 42

Allegra looked up from her desk as Tyra put her head round the door.

'Your visitor is here, Allegra.'

'Yes, thank you, show him in,' she said, not looking up from her screen where she was typing up an email to the company accountant. It was another PR visit. They came to call every now and again, persistent men who wouldn't go away until she'd had a face-to-face meeting with them. Who was the latest? She flicked her gaze over to the note on her pad. Oh, yes. Hutton Productions. Well, she would spare their representative twenty minutes, listen politely and then send him on his way.

There was a gentle knock on the door and a figure appeared at the door to her office. Allegra looked up and froze in horror. The man in the doorway did the same, but recovered his self-possession after a moment.

'Lady Allegra McCorquodale?' he said, advancing into the room.

'Yes.' She stood up, her face flaming.

'Adam Hutton.' His coppery-brown eyes were friendly and a smile played about the corners of his mouth. He held out his hand to her. 'I think we may have had the pleasure of meeting before.'

She took his hand and shook it, simultaneously having a flashback to him sitting naked on her dining chair while she pumped herself up and down on his cock. 'Yes, yes,' she said, looking at her desk, then at her screen, and anywhere else she could avoid his gaze. 'Hello. Well. This is a coincidence.' *Adam Hutton.* The name came back to her now. But she hadn't given it a thought since she'd tossed that business card away weeks ago. 'Please. Sit down.'

She sat in her chair, a beautiful Frank Lloyd Wright barrel design in honey-coloured wood with a mint-green leather seat, and gestured to him to take the one opposite.

'Thank you.' He gazed at her, his expression amused and almost kindly.

'Now . . . why are you here?' she asked, fighting to regain her self-possession. She set her shoulders straight and lifted her chin. When she spoke again, she sounded cool and controlled. 'I'm happy to hear your spiel but I never use promotional companies. Colette's avoids all aspects of PR.'

Adam Hutton settled into the chair and smiled again, friendly and confident. 'Of course. That is part of Colette's undeniable charm. Everyone appreciates that it operates on different terms from most nightclubs. Discretion is the better part of its particular valour.'

'If you understand that,' Allegra said slowly, 'then what is the point of this visit exactly?'

These PR men were always the same: they tried to convince her that she needed to drum up interest in Colette's with stories in the press, start holding promotional nights and invite young celebrities with big breasts and short dresses, create customer databases and send the members streams of emails imploring them to come to the club with 'special offers' and 'two for one' deals. It was laughable. All that was a world away from Colette's usual style and what its members expected or wanted.

But Adam Hutton didn't look like a typical PR man in an open-necked shirt, badly fitting jacket and jeans, mobile phone practically glued to one ear and hair that had the best part of a bottle of gel on it. Instead he wore a crisp shirt in tiny blue-and-white check with a navy silk Hermès tie, and a suit in dark charcoal that she was sure was Ralph Lauren. And she remembered his aquiline good looks very well now; his tall, well-honed body. She remembered him thrusting into her . . . and quickly pushed the memory away before she could lose her composure again.

'I'm in complete awe of Colette's,' Adam Hutton said smoothly. 'I've been there a few times and have never experienced anything less than perfection. It's a hub of mature luxury in a world that seems increasingly obsessed with drunk teenagers.'

'Thanks to you – or people like you,' Allegra said pointedly. 'In my experience, PR companies are only interested in the kind of people who feature on the front of cheap magazines on a weekly basis. Soap stars and glamour models.'

Adam nodded and gave a wry smile. 'That may not be entirely fair. It's a chicken and egg situation. Do we create people's desires or respond to them? It's a mixture of the two, of course. If it's any comfort, I don't actually deal with that kind of client. Hutton Productions is strictly upmarket. We prefer to attract high-end celebrities to our clients' clubs and restaurants.'

Allegra frowned. She crossed one long leg over another, admiring her Christian Louboutin shoes as she did so. They were black leather on wooden platforms with towering five-inch heels that gave her sober Aquascutum office suit a sexy twist. Even though the last thing she wanted was to see one of her one-night stands again, she couldn't help being glad she looked good today. *And he is rather attractive,* she thought, casting a glance at him from under her lashes. *Better than I remembered.* 'But I don't understand why high-end restaurants need to use promoters at all. Don't they get enough customers as it is?'

'No one can afford to rest on their laurels. Even somewhere like the Ivy – not that different from Colette's in terms of its high-quality, desirable status and exclusive nature, not to mention its venerable years. It still needs to keep the stars coming in and maintain its reputation. Another fashionable place can open, the in crowd can flock there, and the next thing you know . . . you're empty. There's no shortage of contenders vying for the crown.'

Allegra rested back in her chair and fixed him with a steady, confident gaze. She felt in charge again. 'It's not like that at Colette's, and I can't imagine it ever will be. We have a waiting list to join, you know. It can be up to five years before people get membership, and then only after the committee has scrutinised their applications very carefully.'

'If you don't mind my asking, how much are your membership fees?'

'I don't mind at all. There's a two hundred and fifty pound joining fee, and after that, subscription is a thousand pounds a year.'

Adam raised his eyebrows. 'A thousand pounds?'

'Seven hundred and fifty for under-twenty-fives,' Allegra added.

'Mmm. A bargain.' She stared at him, unsure if he was being sarcastic, but his expression was innocent. He went on: 'And you've got . . . how many members?'

'Five thousand.'

He did some quick mental arithmetic. 'So you have an income of around five million pounds a year, and that's before you factor in the profit you make from the food and drink you sell, the parties you host and so on. And I seem to remember from my visit to Colette's that it's not particularly cheap. I bought a round of drinks for some friends and it cost me over a hundred pounds. You must be doing very well.'

Allegra nodded. 'Yes, we are. But it's not all profit. We have vast overheads: taxes and other charges, utilities, maintenance, staff wages, administration . . . It all costs money, a great deal of it.' She gestured to the room around them. David had decorated it in cool colours, whites and pale greens, and it was hung with paintings of bright, hot scenes. 'To keep your spirits up on rainy London afternoons,' he'd said.

Adam looked about him at the office, nodding thoughtfully. 'Yes. And I suppose your members don't flinch at a thousand pounds a year for the privilege of spending yet more money here.'

'Of course not. In fact, it's a simple way of keeping the club the way the members like it.'

'Reserved for the rich.'

Allegra raised her eyebrows, but Adam's expression was still innocent and his tone neutral, as though he was not implying any criticism of Colette's. 'It all depends how one wants to spend one's money, I suppose,' she said a little icily. 'There's no requirement to be rich in order to join.'

'But it helps. Anyway, that's the spirit of Colette's, isn't it? Luxury is always expensive, and that's what makes it worth having.'

'Exactly.' Allegra smiled, mollified. 'Now, you haven't explained exactly why you want to see me. I think I've made it clear that I'm not looking for any promotion for the club.'

'I don't just offer promotion,' Adam said smoothly. 'If I did, I'd call the company Hutton Promotions. What we do is wider than that. We offer a consulting service as well.'

Allegra burst out laughing. 'You want to offer consultancy to us! We're the oldest, most respected club in London. Dozens of people have tried to emulate Colette's, and none have succeeded in getting our recipe just right. I'm beginning to think you might be some kind of corporate spy, trying to weasel in and find out the secret of our success.'

Adam smiled broadly and his face lit up, making him look quite different. He laughed too, a surprisingly deep sound. 'I can see it seems a bit ridiculous when you put it like that. But you need to watch out that success doesn't make you complacent. Have you got a website, for example?'

'No. I don't think we need one.' Allegra sounded insouciant, but the truth was that David was resisting her ideas for a website as hard as he could. He thought they were vulgar, and a way for nosy people to get a glimpse inside the club.

Adam shrugged and she noticed his broad shoulders, remembering what he looked like underneath the crisp cotton of his shirt. He had a smooth chest with only a few small curls of hair in the middle . . .

He said, 'It's the kind of service your members will expect. Top-level businessmen are always at the forefront of technology. They live all over the world, travel widely. They don't want a newsletter posted to them, they want to be able to access club information quickly and easily, get their secretaries to book tables online . . . all sorts of things. We could do that for you. All you'd need to do is brief me on what you want, and I could liaise with designers and website builders.'

'OK.' Allegra nodded. 'Is that all?' She was still sceptical about this. *Honestly, I think I could manage to get a website going on my own.*

'No.' Adam leant back in his chair and fixed her with a steady gaze. 'I was wondering about the average profile of your members. It occurred to me that it probably swings towards the ageing, wealthy businessman who brings his clients to Colette's to show them a bit of London's famous high life.'

Allegra kept her expression neutral, staring at him across the desk. She rolled her tortoiseshell Mont Blanc between her fingers. Then she said, 'We have plenty of female members and lots of family events are celebrated in the club. We have engagements practically every week – getting engaged in Colette's over a bottle of club champagne is virtually de rigueur. There are wedding receptions, private dinners, birthday parties. Our members often give memberships as gifts to their children for their eighteenth birthday.'

'That's interesting,' said Adam. 'And how many of those children actually come here? My guess is they don't exactly flock here. They're at Mahiki and Boujis and Whisky Mist.'

'Maybe they are,' she said carelessly. 'But we don't intend to become that kind of establishment.'

'So once all the wealthy ageing businessmen are too old to come out, or retired, or dead, who is going to take their place?'

'I told you, we have a waiting list. Plenty of people wish to be members.'

'But I'd make a bet that almost all the people on your waiting list are more of the same: middle-aged chaps who've made their pile and like the upper-crust coddling that Colette's offers: it's quiet, it's comfortable, it's reliable.'

Allegra said nothing. *I know what you're saying. But I've already got plans . . .*

'I think I've made my point anyway,' Adam said quietly after a moment. 'You want to know what I can offer and I'm showing you that I've got a perspective on your problems – problems you might not even know you've got – and perhaps some solutions. There was one other thing . . .'

'Yes, Mr Hutton?' Allegra tried to sound polite but couldn't help an edge creeping into her voice. She didn't like hearing any implied criticism of Colette's, even if she secretly agreed with it. He didn't realise that there was no way David would ever allow his club to change.

'Please – call me Adam.' He looked down at his leather-bound notebook for a second and then fixed Allegra with his clear, perceptive gaze. 'I've heard you're looking around for another property. You're perhaps thinking of expansion. Is that right?'

Allegra gasped. 'How on earth did you hear about that?'

He smiled. 'It's my job to know what's going on.'

'But . . . but . . .' She was astonished. She had discussed her plans with David and they had viewed two likely sites, but without telling anyone else what they were up to.

'I'm interested,' he said bluntly. 'Is this going to be along the same lines as Colette's – or something new?'

Allegra gaped at him then said, 'I'm sorry, but I really don't intend to discuss any of this with you.'

'Very well. That, of course, is entirely your privilege.' He stood up. 'But please think about it, that's all I ask. You have an amazing brand in the Colette's name and image. I think expansion is a wonderful idea, and you've got every chance of making a new club really appealing to the younger market. I'd love to help you, and contribute to your success.'

Allegra stood up as well. 'Thank you for coming by, Mr Hutton. I appreciate your comments and I have your details. I'll be in touch if ever I think I need your help.' She held out her hand.

Hutton's eyes sparkled and he laughed lightly as he shook it. 'You're thinking it will be a cold day in hell before that happens, aren't you? But don't give up on me. And call any time. And, may I say, this meeting was almost as enjoyable as our first.'

'Tyra will show you out,' Allegra said crisply, and watched thoughtfully as he strode out of her office.

Chapter 43

London
2008

Romily thoroughly enjoyed the day, from the moment the team arrived at the Chester Square house: the make-up artist, hairdresser, stylist, photographer, lighting technician and, of course, the journalist. They came early to survey the house and discuss locations and set up shots. It was important to select the rooms where Romily would be looking casual, in Marni trousers and a Rochas silk tunic blouse, or Theory two-tone tank dress with a Matthew Williamson knit over the top, and those where she would be in glamorous cocktail dresses and evening gowns.

While these important decisions were being made, Romily was interviewed. As the hairdresser worked her magic and the make-up artist selected the colours and brands she wanted from her vast trunk, the journalist sat on the bed and asked questions, recording Romily's every word.

'Is it true that you're Sebastian LeFarge's muse?' the young reporter asked, looking impressed despite herself.

'Oh, yes,' Romily said, watching her in the mirror as the hairdresser brushed her hair out into glossy straightness. 'Dear Sebastian. I spend a week a year with him on Capri, helping him sort out his latest ideas. And we always have at least another week on his yacht . . . such a dear little thing, almost a toy. From that, he seems to get an awful lot of inspiration.' She added hastily, 'And, of course, I adore his clothes.'

'Is your life busy?' The reporter was scribbling notes despite the tape recorder.

'*So* busy . . . you can imagine, with all my travelling.'

'Many other women in your position feel a calling to some kind of work,' the journalist said almost shyly. She really was very young, Romily noticed. 'Do you ever feel that?'

'My position is a demanding one,' Romily replied solemnly. 'I'm well aware of that. I feel that I can lead by example, showing women that it is possible to be elegant and lady-like. I like to think I can inspire *grace*. That's really my life's work.'

'I see.' The journalist gave her a sycophantic smile. 'How wonderful.' This kind of interview was not exactly hard-hitting – nothing Romily said would be challenged, she knew that. It was why she had picked this magazine. Who wanted to be ripped to shreds, after all?

When the interview was finally concluded, the reporter told her that it would be in the following week's issue.

'Oh, good,' Romily said happily. 'The sooner the better.'

Imogen saw it at the news-stand as she walked to work. She stopped dead on the pavement, forcing a man behind her to sidestep quickly, and stared at it as he muttered a curse at her.

The glossy image and text seemed to shout at her: there was Romily in an exquisite grey tulle gown standing in a luxurious white drawing room. *Heiress Romily de Lisle invites us into her stunning home and tells us about her glamorous life.*

'I'll take this, please,' she said politely to the vendor, fishing in her coat pocket for some money.

She didn't look at it until she got to work, then she pored

over it, turning the slippery pages quickly until she found what she was looking for. It was the main feature, spread over several pages, with a long interview. She read it once, then she read it again, and then she lingered over every picture, drinking in every detail, until her senior lawyer came in and she hustled it under the desk.

From the sound of it, Romily couldn't be happier: travelling the world, socialising and buying clothes. Imogen never would have thought it, but apparently Romily had no desire to do anything else with her life but 'inspire grace'. Imogen shook her head in disbelief. There was no mention of Mitch but a coy reference to someone called Vincente di Auguro, who was apparently her boyfriend. She looked stunning in every photograph, her skin impossibly smooth, her hair glossy, her figure perfect. And the clothes were a dream: haute couture evening gowns and designer pieces.

But it was painful to see her. It brought back memories of their happy times together and a painful recollection of their rift. *It wasn't supposed to be like this,* Imogen thought. *We were supposed to be friends for ever. I wasn't supposed to learn about her life from the pages of a magazine . . .*

She couldn't help yearning for the days when the three of them faced the world together.

Malik brought a copy of the magazine into Mitch's office where his boss was sitting behind his desk, staring intently at a screen. A frown creased his brow and his mouth was set in a line that showed his concentration.

'Sorry to interrupt you, Mitch, but I thought you might like to see this.' Malik put the magazine on the leather desktop, pushing it gently across as though it might explode.

'Huh?' Mitch looked confused and then, as he clocked the cover, his expression changed, first to surprise and then, for a fleeting moment, to something like tenderness, followed immediately by sardonic amusement. 'What the fuck has she done this for?'

He looked up at Malik. 'I think she may be reminding me of her existence.' He picked up the magazine unopened and threw it in the rubbish bin. 'Well, she's wasting her time. As if I could ever forget.'

Chapter 44

Allegra unfurled the architect's drawings and spread them out across the table in the dining room of David's Knightsbridge house.

'This is what I thought we could do to the interior. We need to provide different spaces for different moods and activities. See? On the top floor, a restaurant with a retractable ceiling. This not only gives a lovely outside space in good weather, but also gets around the smoking ban. People will be able to enjoy their cigarettes at their tables without bothering other diners.'

'Yes, that's civilised,' David said, bending over the polished wood to inspect the plans. He loathed the smoking ban and, after a lifetime of abstinence, had even taken up puffing away on small cigars after dinner to show his disgust. The ban had meant that they'd had to open up a small outside space on the other side of the dance floor in Colette's so that members did not have to ascend to street level in order to enjoy the expensive contents of the club humidor. David railed against the indignity of this, and the inconvenience to those dancing, but the law was the law.

Allegra was bursting with enthusiasm as she pointed out the design features. 'After midnight it will become a dance floor and people can get late night meals in the restaurant downstairs. The kind of stuff you want to eat when you've been drinking: bacon and eggs, hamburgers and chips, chilli con carne . . . comfort food.'

David peered at the plans. 'But what on earth is this?' He tapped them with a bony finger.

'A private viewing room – you know, like a small cinema.'

'What!' He looked outraged. 'What on earth do people want with a private cinema? Are you going to show dirty films?'

Allegra laughed. 'No, of course not. Members might very well work in film or television or advertising, and want a place where they can show off what they've done.'

David harrumphed and stroked the head of his black Labrador, Caius, who sat beside him. 'I don't understand,' he grumbled. 'That sounds like work, not like fun.'

'People mix the two nowadays,' Allegra said reasonably.

'Not at Colette's.'

'Oh, come on, David, they do it all the time! Half the members use the club for corporate entertaining, you know they do! And you can hardly blame them, with our kind of cachet. It's impressive to bring your clients to Colette's for the evening, isn't it?'

David frowned, not wanting to concede the point, then he said, 'Perhaps. But it's subtle. They're not getting out their flipcharts and black pens and giving a bloody lecture.'

Allegra sat down on one of the Regency spoon-backed dining chairs. Like every room in David's Knightsbridge house, this one reflected the same taste that gave Colette's its country-house chic: a muted Colefax & Fowler striped wallpaper covered with good pictures, prints and etchings; solid furniture, mostly Queen Anne or Georgian; lots of lamps and flowers. The whole house was done in the same perfectionist style, right down to the custom-built circular wardrobe that revolved so David could move effortlessly from his silk and linen summer suits to his tweed and wool winter ones. His handmade shoes were stored in polished mahogany lockers, a pigeon hole for each pair, sorted by style.

Allegra stared at the architect's drawings and sighed. This was going to be a very difficult task, she could see that. David was determined to thwart her at every step, or at least make her life very hard. *Is it just me or has he got worse lately?* she wondered.

'We've said that Colette's itself will remain the same,' she reminded her uncle, 'but that the new club would be aimed specifically at a market we're not reaching at present. The children and grandchildren of our members don't come to the club. They will in time, particularly if they're already members of the new club, but we need to offer them what they want in this day and age: casual restaurants as well as more formal ones. Colette's is a true nightclub – it opens at eight and closes at three. But in the new place, we'll open at seven in the morning and offer much, much more. A gym in the basement, so people can exercise before work. Breakfast and lunch – food all day long, whenever it's wanted. Access to rooms where members can work, hold meetings, entertain, whatever they need. Bedrooms for people who want to stay over. Wifi and internet access, of course, and the private cinema. It's got to appeal to young people. That's the kind of place they want, I promise.'

'It all sounds rather . . .' David wrinkled his nose '. . . *vulgar*. Bedrooms? It'll be a knocking shop.'

'Oh, David. The world can't stand still.'

'I'm well aware of that, darling.' He coughed, the spasms getting stronger until he gestured for a glass of water, which Allegra passed him. When he'd recovered, he said, 'If I could have stopped the whole thing in 1975, I probably would have. Life was much nicer then.'

'For some people,' she said with a laugh. 'It's much better for most people now.'

'Mmm. Women have more rights, I believe,' he said vaguely, 'which I suppose they enjoy.'

Allegra laughed again. 'You're a wicked old tease. You know perfectly well what's going on, and you also know perfectly well that it's a very good idea to expand. You'll let me do what I want in the end, I know you will. But, gosh, you're making me fight for it!'

'I had to fight to create Colette's,' he said, waving a finger at her. 'No doubt it all seems like a sure thing to you now, but it wasn't at the time. I had to beg for backing. No reason why you shouldn't have to prove yourself like I did, and convince me with your passion. How much is all this going to cost?'

'Well, first the freehold of the house. It's in Soho.'

'What?' David looked scandalised. 'Among all the pimps and prostitutes? It's full of red-light dives and topless bars!'

'You know very well it's not like that any more. Just because it's out of your beloved Mayfair . . . Soho is very smart now, as I'm sure you're aware.'

'Hmmm, I suppose I have to believe you. So – how much?'

'The house will cost several million. Then there's the development cost – at least several million more. If the house is listed or has any protection orders, costs will rise, of course. I think we need to budget at twenty-five million with another seven for contingency.'

David leaned back, patting Caius on the head again as he often did when he needed to feel calmer. 'That's a lot of money, Allegra. Do you have profit forecasts for how we'll make this all back?'

'Of course.' She smiled at him, trying to convey how important this was to her. It was so obviously the right thing to do.

'Good. I shall need to be convinced – wholly convinced – before I allow that kind of investment. We'll be very exposed if anything goes wrong.'

'Trust me, David. It's absolutely the right thing to do.'

Allegra came out on to the busy Knightsbridge streets, full of their usual odd mixture of rich residents and trainer-and-backpack-wearing tourists, and sighed deeply to release the frustration she was feeling.

She stood for a moment, looking down the road towards Harrods with its long frontage and dark green awnings. Then she pulled her mobile phone out of her bag and dialled a number on her contacts list.

'Hello, is that Adam Hutton . . .? Hi, Adam. It's Allegra McCorquodale. I was wondering if we could meet.'

An hour later she was walking into a Mayfair pub. Inside it was far removed from the traditional old public house with bare floors and scrubbed wooden tables and chairs. Although the pine floorboards were original, they still seemed modern and attractive. The room was a tasteful fusion of old and new, with expensive touches.

'Hi, it's great to see you.' Adam greeted her with a kiss on her cheek and held out a chair for her. He was looking casual but groomed in a Gucci linen suit and open-necked shirt. 'I hope you don't mind us roughing it here. It's not quite Colette's, I'm afraid.'

'Of course I don't mind.' Allegra was glad she was dressed fairly casually in her Seven For All Mankind jeans, a Daphne Guinness white shirt from Comme des Garçons and her favourite Tod's loafers. She put her tan leather Mulberry Bayswater on the chair next to her. 'I'm not always in cocktail dresses and quaffing champagne, you know. I do exist outside Colette's.'

'I know.' Adam raised his eyebrows and shot her an intense look.

She flushed but maintained her cool. *I don't want to think about that.* As far as she was concerned, Adam was now part of her business life. The other side of her existence – the secret nights with strangers, the little stash of drugs in her locked drawer – was none of his concern. She didn't care if he was handsome – and every time she saw him, she was impressed again by his fine-boned features and broad, slim frame. She liked that soft reddish-brown hair, almost fox-coloured, and the faint dusting of freckles over his nose . . . Mentally she shook herself. *Stop it. Business, that's all.*

Adam went on smoothly, 'I thought you might like to see this place. You'll notice it looks quite ordinary – pleasant enough but ordinary. The prices aren't ordinary, though. I know there's such a thing as Mayfair prices but here it's twenty-five quid for a plate of shepherd's pie.'

'Is that expensive?' asked Allegra, frowning.

He laughed. 'You've been spending too much time in Colette's. Yes, it is expensive, for a pub lunch. Maybe if it was cooked by a Michelin-starred chef it would be reasonable. But it isn't.'

'So?'

He leant towards her and lowered his voice. 'This place was just a normal pub, and a pretty empty one at that, until one day a fancy Hollywood film actor and his mate decided to buy it and have a bit of fun owning their own place. They stripped out the interior, gave it an overhaul, and started hanging out here with their celebrity mates. They were papped coming out at two in the morning after a lock-in. They held their birthday parties here. The place became associated with them, and started drawing in the crowds. Young kids wanted to come here and happily spent far too much on basic pub grub because, that way, they were kind of cool, like the owner. They started a little members club upstairs so that their VIP pals wouldn't be bothered by the plebs while they were enjoying a pint and talking about their latest films.'

'That's clever,' Allegra said, interested. 'So they turned a basic pub into a desirable restaurant?'

'And made a mint.' Adam's brown eyes glinted as he smiled at her.

The waitress came up to take their order.

'The shepherd's pie, please.' Allegra shot a look at Adam. 'And some water. Thanks.'

'Sounds good. I'll have the same – but make my water a bottle of Beck's, please.' Adam handed the menu back to the waitress. When she'd gone, he leant back in his chair and said to her, 'Have you heard of someone called Theodore Mitchell?'

Allegra frowned and shook her head. 'Should I have?'

'I'm not altogether sure. I'm keeping my eye on him. He's an American businessman who's suddenly appeared and is buying up some of the best and most exclusive bars, clubs and restaurants in London. Just recently he's made some big purchases and it seems that his pockets are deep. He's just acquired the Belgrave Group, and that means he's now got five Michelin-starred restaurants in his portfolio, including La Joie, Alfred's and Numo, that Japanese place all the stars go to.'

'Oh.' Allegra raised her eyebrows. 'Should I be interested in all this?'

'I don't know.' Adam leant closer confidingly and she caught the tang of a citrussy cologne. 'The rumour is he's just in the process of buying this joint off the film-star owner. Seems he's looking away from straight restaurants and more towards the new hybrid club/restaurant. He doesn't seem keen on the clubs that are all about drinking and the youth market – places like Boujis. The profile is more sophisticated.'

'And . . .?'

'And Colette's fits the bill. In fact, it's precisely the kind of place he'd be very, very attracted to.'

'Well, if he is, he hasn't got a hope,' she said vehemently. 'David will never sell, I'm completely sure of it. Colette's is precious to him. He'd rather die than see some American take it over.'

Adam laughed. 'I see. Well, as David's company is privately owned, I guess he's the one who makes the decisions.' He glanced over at Allegra, as if waiting for her to add anything to this, but she said nothing. He continued, 'Now . . . to what do I owe the pleasure of this invitation to meet you?'

Over the pricy but admittedly delicious shepherd's pie, she told him about her plans for the new club. 'It's going to plug all the gaps,' she said, 'and get the young people in. I listened to what you said, and you were right. Our membership is mature. But there's no point in trying to change Colette's to bring in young people. We'd simply destroy the magic and lose the members we do have, who pay us so handsomely to come to us. And could I reproduce the Colette's ambiance in another building? I don't know. Its underground intimacy is so integral to it. But what I can do is take the ethos behind Colette's – comfort, luxury, perfect service – and make it the driving force behind a new venture. We'll reel in members in their twenties, and when they've had enough of the new place, and want a bit more pampering and can afford our food and drink, they'll move on to Colette's.'

Adam put down his fork and smiled at her. 'That's brilliant. I think you're doing absolutely the right thing.'

'You do?'

'Yep. It's exciting. It meets a need. There's nothing else like it in the market. There are clubs that are media hang outs and clubs that are dance venues. You'll be combining the two plus adding the kind of luxurious extras that will make the place a real home from home: the gym, the members' bedrooms, the breakfast opening . . . It's inspired.'

She felt a surge of pleasure at his praise. Adam was the first person she'd ever shared her business ideas with. It had taken a while before she'd had the confidence to trust in herself. Had she learned enough at Colette's to make a whole new venture work? Adam's response seemed to show she had – and his opinion was surely worth something. According to his company website, he'd worked with some of the best in the industry.

He pushed away his empty plate and said, 'But why are you sharing all this with me now? I got the impression last time we met you didn't see the point of me, to be blunt.'

Allegra put down her fork. 'I'll come straight to the point. I want you to help me. My uncle is the driving force behind Colette's and the man with the money. But he's finding it hard to share my vision and think outside what he already does. I don't want to take on a project like this alone because I don't know the market as well as you may expect. My years in Colette's have blinkered my vision somewhat. I don't find paying forty or even fifty pounds for a main course unusual any more. I don't blink at bottles of wine costing five thousand. I need someone who's got a foot in the real world. And I think that could be you.'

Adam looked pleased. 'That's interesting,' he said at last. 'Very interesting. The truth is I'm pretty busy right now – I've got quite a lot of projects on. I'm working with a bunch of guys who are creating an elite concierge service and it's absolutely massive.'

'Oh! But . . .' She couldn't conceal her disappointment.

She'd expected Adam to accept immediately and with alacrity, considering he'd come to her in the first instance.

He burst out laughing. 'Don't look so miserable! I'm flattered you're so keen to involve me and I wouldn't miss out on this for the world. I'm in. And after lunch we can go back to my offices and discuss terms, if you like. No harm in getting started right away.'

Chapter 45

London
January 2009

Imogen looked up from the legal document she was checking and stared out at the offices and skyscrapers of London, standing grey against an even greyer sky. It might be miserable and wintry outside but she was elated to be back in the groove, back in London, back at her job and partying again.

She'd spent a lazy Christmas in Scotland, eating far too much, sleeping as many hours as she could, and generally recovering from her very demanding life at Guthrie & Walsh. Her parents had spoiled her, delighted to have her back home with them again, and she'd barely stirred out of the front door. It had been lovely being looked after: all her meals cooked, her laundry done, her bed made . . . Even her New Year's Eve had been cosily middle-aged, sitting with her parents in front of the television and toasting in the year with a wee dram.

But by the end of the holidays she'd been champing at the bit, keen to get back to her life in the big city. Her job was intense but stimulating and exciting, even if her trainee status meant she was given the boring jobs to do. She was hungry for knowledge and keen to get on.

'What do you say we go out clubbing tonight?' Fiona had

said as they'd walked through Spitalfields on the way to work. 'It's Friday. I feel like dancing.'

'I'm on for it,' Imogen said. 'I'll need to cut loose after today.'

'Good. So we're on.'

Now all she had to do was get through the next few hours and then she'd be free for some fun . . .

They both managed to get away from work before seven, and after a dash home and a quickfire change, were on their way north by eight. In Camden they met up with some friends in a pub and settled down for some drinking, chatting and food before they went to the club at ten.

Once they'd queued, paid, got rid of their coats and made their way inside, Imogen was ready to party. She was feeling pleasantly high after a few drinks in the pub and was eager to dance. She was wearing her favourite party dress: a blue Hervé Léger-style body-con bandage dress that she'd found in Reiss. The music was pumping out, the lights were flashing and she was keen to get moving.

'I'm going to dance!' she shouted to Fi over the noise.

'OK! Do you want a drink? We're going to the bar!' Fi gestured over at the crowd buying drinks.

Imogen shook her head and pushed her way through the onlookers and on to the dance floor. The beat was pounding out and one of her favourite songs was playing. She found herself a space and started dancing, not caring that she was alone. Life was good at the moment: it felt like she had a purpose and a future, and she was young, single, solvent and looking for fun.

How long was she dancing before it happened? Perhaps twenty minutes. Perhaps longer. But, suddenly, in the middle of swaying to a sexy disco tune, she looked up and there he was.

At first, she couldn't believe it. *I know him,* she thought, confused, as she gazed into those blue eyes. *Who is he?* Then it came to her in a burst: *Xander!* But all she could say was, 'You!' while her stomach somersaulted with excitement, just as it always used to.

He smiled at her, that gorgeous lopsided smile she'd once loved so much, and nodded. He looked the same: shorter hair and thinner, but still that same handsome face and those dark blue eyes that always seemed amused and faintly flirtatious. He took her hand, and the next moment he'd pulled her to him and was kissing her.

The touch of his lips sent her whirling back through the years to that hot summer night in the Oxfordshire orchard, and the ecstasy she'd felt on the chilly floor of the temple. Just as before, she felt their mouths fit together, two halves of a whole, and the next moment she was sinking into the kiss, revelling in it, and nothing else around her existed. As they kissed, she felt his body against hers and she closed her arms around his neck, pulling him even closer, savouring the sweet smell of him and the warmth of his body.

Xander, she thought, and a wave of deep but thrilling calm washed over her. *It's like being where I belong. Oh, Xander . . .*

When he broke the kiss, she blinked at him, surprised. *Is this all real?* She smiled at him and clutched his hand. He cocked his head towards the doorway and she nodded eagerly, Fiona and her other friends forgotten. She'd found him – or rather, he'd found her – and she couldn't lose him now. She held his hand tightly as they made their way through the crowd and out of the club.

Outside the club, they stopped on the pavement, taking no notice of the people milling about them.

'It's been a long time,' he said, smiling, still holding her hand.

'I can't believe it's you!' she said breathlessly. 'What are you doing here?'

He said slowly, 'I guess I was supposed to find you . . . I always had a feeling I would, you know.' Then he kissed her again, wrapping her tightly in his arms as though he was worried she would float away if he let her go.

They took a taxi back to Imogen's flat. On the way, she texted Fi to let her know she'd left.

She felt shivery with excitement one moment, and perfectly content the next. It was bizarre and yet it seemed completely normal that Xander should be sitting with her in the back of a black cab, heading back to her place, just as it been astonishing and yet natural for him to kiss her in the club. He had said that dramatic, almost unbearably exciting thing – 'I was supposed to find you' – and now he was asking her what she was doing these days, just as an old friend would.

'Clever you,' he said, when she'd told him. 'I always knew you'd do well. You're very sensible and sane.' He grinned at her. 'Unlike me.'

'What are you up to?' she asked. Allegra had said only that he still hung round with his old university crowd, and as far as she knew had no direction in his life.

'Not much. I'm not as busy as Allegra is, that's for sure. I saw her in Soho today and she was directing hundreds of builders, looking at curtain fabrics and deciding where to put steam rooms. She's quite the entrepreneur these days.'

'Yes. Her new club.' Allegra had bought some premises the preceding autumn and now building work was beginning. 'She's doing amazingly well.'

'Who's this Adam?' Xander asked. 'He seemed to be hanging around a lot. A boyfriend?'

'No . . . just a friend, I think. As far as I know.' Imogen

smiled at him, feeling shy again.

'It's lovely to see you, little Imogen,' Xander said with the old tenderness in his voice.

'You too.' She smiled at him. *I'm over you,* she wanted to say. *Your spell was broken years ago.* But as soon as he'd kissed her, the enchantment had returned, as strong as ever. *But why did he kiss me? What does it mean?*

Then she thought, *I'm not going to question it. I'm just going to go with it and see what happens . . .*

Back at the flat, they opened a bottle of wine, sat down on the sofa and talked. Imogen told him about law school, about Fiona and the flat and her new life. Xander told her about a film he'd seen that day and loved. She listened and laughed, observing him while he talked, and remembering.

'You're such a good listener, you know?' he said at last, when they had drained the bottle. 'That's what I always loved about you. You're so easy to talk to. You make me feel calm. Not like most girls. They make me nervous.'

'Do they?' Imogen found that hard to believe: he had always seemed to attract women effortlessly. She longed to ask him if had a girlfriend at the moment, but it seemed too leading a question.

Xander nodded. 'I'm surrounded by James's harem all the time. The Anxious Annies, I call them. Anxious because they're worried one of them will snare James and marry him, get all the money and take him off the market. So they're all busy trying to outwit each other in charming him. Naturally he loves it. He's permanently in Switzerland for tax purposes these days, so I'm not living with him at the moment. I camp out in Onslow Square when I'm in Dad's good books, and sleep on friends' sofas when I'm not.'

'Are you working?'

Xander laughed and pulled a face. 'No. Who would hire

me? I can hardly tie my own shoelaces. I scraped a third from Oxford and I've done nothing since. I'm not proud of it. It's just the way things have turned out.' He leant forward and took her hand, gazing into her eyes. 'That's what I meant all those years ago . . . you always were too good for me. I'm just a wastrel.'

She blinked at him. He was right, in a way. He'd left Oxford five years ago and had nothing to show for that time. But that didn't mean there was no hope. 'Xander . . .' she whispered.

He looked at her intently. 'Would it be terribly inconvenient . . . I mean . . . would you mind . . . if I kiss you again?'

'Come here,' she said, and pulled him even closer.

'There's a bloke asleep in our sitting room,' Fiona said, as she came into the kitchen in her dressing gown the next morning. 'Anyone I know?'

'It's an old friend of mine. I met him in the club last night and we came back here to talk.'

'Ooh!' Fiona made a saucy face and raised her eyebrows. 'He's good-looking, I can tell. So . . . nothing happened?'

Imogen shook her head as she poured hot water over a teabag in a mug. They had kissed, tenderly and gently for a long time, until Xander had pulled away and said apologetically, 'This is no reflection on your charms, Midge, but I'm absolutely bushed. Do you mind if I sleep?' And then yawned hugely.

She'd laughed because it was not the end to the evening she'd envisaged, but then, Xander always had excelled at not fulfilling her romantic dreams. She'd gone to find him a rug and, by the time she'd got back, he was sound asleep on the sofa, so she had tucked him up and left him there.

'I'm heading out for a run,' her flatmate said, appearing

a few minutes later in her kit.

'Not *another* run? You never stop,' teased Imogen.

'Got to keep my endorphins up.' Fi grinned and hurried off.

Imogen sat on the chair opposite the sofa, drank her tea and read the paper until Xander woke up, deliciously dishevelled and bleary-eyed.

'Oh, good,' he said with a smile when he saw her. 'I was worried I'd dreamt you.'

'Morning,' she said. 'Would you like some coffee?'

'You angel. I would. But a shower first, if that's all right . . .'

After Xander's shower they breakfasted together, both in high spirits. *I still can't believe he's here,* Imogen thought wonderingly as she watched him butter his toast or reach for the jam. *It's wonderfully normal.* They were so relaxed, so comfortable together, as though they'd spent hundreds of mornings like this.

'What are you doing today?' he said, as they finished up their breakfast.

'It's Saturday. I don't have anything particular planned . . . maybe some shopping.' Imogen spoke casually but was terrified he would say he had to go now and slip out of her life again, lost for the third time.

'Then why don't we spend the day together?'

Her heart contracted with joy and she felt a smile cover her face. 'I'd love to.'

'Good. I have to set off for a party later but I'm yours until then.'

They spent a blissful day together, walking down to the river, across Tower Bridge and along the South Bank to Borough Market, where they wandered among the food stalls, tasting delicious morsels, and then bought tortilla wraps filled with spicy chicken and rocket and ate them in the garden of Southwark Cathedral, the sound of the choir singing an anthem drifting towards them as they sat on the low stone wall. Then they walked on, past the Globe Theatre and towards the towering chimney of Tate Modern, St Paul's Cathedral sitting stately and imposing on the opposite bank. Xander said they should go and improve their minds with art so they went in and explored, talking and giggling together in a happy conspiracy of laughter while they admired the art.

They were sitting in the café having afternoon tea, enjoying the splendid view of the gun-metal grey Thames and the magnificent domed cathedral that sat across it, when Xander looked at his watch. 'Shit! I have to go.'

'What?' Imogen said, disappointment crashing through her. She stared down at the dirty cups and crumb-filled plates, trying to hide it.

'I've got to get back to Onslow Square for my stuff and then it's a drive out of London.' He made a cross face. 'I'd much rather stay with you.'

'Me too,' she said weakly. She'd been imagining that their day would morph seamlessly into the evening, and they would go out to dinner together, and it would turn into something even more wonderfully romantic than their time so far had been.

'I promised Piers, that's the thing.' Xander frowned and thought for a moment. Then he said, 'Tell you what . . . why don't you come too? It's going to be a bit wild but you won't mind that, will you?'

'Go with you?' She brightened, remembering the parties she'd once gone to with Allegra and Xander. Would it be like those raucous, glamorous nights?

'Sure. Come along. I'm sure Piers won't mind. The more the merrier. I'll call him to let him know there'll be one extra.'

'OK. I'll come.' *What else was I ever going to do? When have I ever said no to Xander?*

'Just one condition. You have to wear black.'

She went to the flat to locate a black cocktail dress and get ready while Xander made his way back to Onslow Square to change into his dinner jacket. He arrived at the flat in his battered MG, clean, freshly shaven, and looking devastatingly attractive in his DJ and black bow tie.

'You look gorgeous, Midge,' he said appreciatively when he saw her. 'We're going to make a pitstop on the way, I hope that's all right.'

'Of course,' she said, climbing in, and the next minute they were roaring through the London streets on their way east.

They hadn't been going long and had just passed through Whitechapel when Xander pulled off the main road and took a few turns until they were in a shabby street of down-at-heel Victorian terraces that had been turned into flats.

'Won't be a minute,' he said with a charming smile. 'You don't mind waiting, do you? It's not worth coming in.'

She barely had a chance to speak before he'd disappeared. Imogen sat nervously in the dark car, wondering if anyone on the outside could see her sitting there alone. But, as he'd promised, Xander was back very soon.

'All done and dusted,' he said, starting up the car. The engine roared into life and he pulled away from the kerb. 'Now it's a bit of a drive, but worth it . . . you'll see.'

After fighting their way through the traffic and buses, they finally joined one of the artery roads out of the city and then the M1. As the motorway rolled away under their wheels, Imogen was overcome with tiredness, her head flopped back and she slept. When she woke, it was late evening.

She yawned loudly.

'Hello, sleepy head,' Xander said, looking over at her. 'You're just in time. We're nearly there.'

She looked around, trying to work out where they were. They were travelling down the kind of English country lanes that could be anywhere.

'We're in Northamptonshire,' he said, as if reading her mind. 'And here we are!'

They drove through a pair of enormous wrought iron gates and up a long driveway lined with lime trees before coming to a halt on a semi-circular gravelled carriage turn in front of a spectacular Jacobean mansion.

'This is it.' Xander turned off the engine. 'Get ready to leave your inhibitions outside, Imogen. This kind of party requires a broad mind.'

'I'm sure I can handle it,' she said with a smile as she checked her make-up in the tiny visor mirror.

'Good. Come on then. Let's party!'

The great arched oak door was opened by a man in black tie, with sandy thinning hair and sharp, pale blue eyes.

'Ah, Xander!' he cried as he saw them. 'Well done, old chap. You'll get the party started.' He turned to Imogen.

'This is Imogen,' Xander introduced her. 'Imogen – Piers.'

'Delighted,' purred his friend. 'Any friend of Xander . . . as the saying goes. Please come in. Everything's warming up nicely in the library.'

He led them down the stone-floored hallway, on and on, past many rooms, until finally he opened a door and a burst of laughter and chatter greeted them.

The bookshelves were filled with leather-bound volumes shut away behind wire screens; the remaining walls hung with large gilt-framed oil paintings and a collection of antique swords. Several people lounged about on sofas and armchairs, equally divided between men and women, the men in black tie and the girls in black dresses. They all looked very sophisticated and glamorous.

Imogen looked about her, interested. The copious amounts of booze and drugs on display gave her a hint as to what Xander had meant about her needing to be broad-minded. On a polished walnut table was a huge silver tureen full of crushed ice in which a dozen bottles were chilling, with another dozen ready on the table. Across the room on another table was a selection of other mood enhancers: a bowl of tablets, tiny tabs of acid laid out on leather writing folder, and other pharmaceuticals she didn't recognise. The guests at this party were evidently intent on losing all constraints and letting rip.

'I think you'll see the theme emerging,' murmured Xander in her ear. Her skin prickled pleasantly at the feel of his breath on her neck. 'Even the hors d'oeuvres stay true to the colour scheme.' He gestured at a large bowl of ice holding a crystal dish piled high with caviar, the black eggs moist and gleaming.

'Xander, my man!' roared another of the guests, a fleshy-faced man with pink cheeks and small round spectacles. 'Wonderful to see you. Would you like a drink?'

'Hello, Gawain. I certainly would. This is Imogen.' Xander propelled her smoothly forward.

'Gawain Tudor-Jones. How d'ye do?' He bowed, offered Imogen his arm and led her towards the drinks table. 'A drink for you too, dear Imogen?'

'Yes, please,' she said, smiling. Perhaps this was going to be fun. The public school crowd Xander ran with might have its faults but they always had good manners – at least, at first.

Gawain gestured over at the table. 'I've had quite a time finding champagne in a black bottle so we compromised on the Dom Pérignon OEnothèque 1995 – the bottle is actually a very, very dark green, but it's got a black label and black foil, so we think it counts.' He turned and called, 'Robin, we're ready for another bottle!'

Yet another young man in black tie came forward, carrying a sword taken from the display on the wall. He went over to the silver tureen and pulled out a bottle. Holding it out wide by the base, he put the blade against the neck for a second, then took back his sword arm and with one strong stroke sliced through the bottle, decapitating it neatly at the neck and leaving a clean, diagonal edge. White foam fizzed up through the gap as Gawain darted forward with a pair of flutes.

'Nice cutting,' he said admiringly.

'Thanks,' Robin said, 'I'm getting my eye in now.' He poured the champagne into the waiting glasses.

Imogen laughed. 'Isn't that rather a dangerous way of getting bottles open?'

'Tonight *is* dangerous,' Gawain said, handing a foaming glass to her. His eyes glittered. 'And drama is everything.' He took a sip from his own glass, then ran his gaze appreciatively over her low-cut dress and high heels. 'You look very sexy, my dear, but somehow a little too *pure* to be Xander's usual type.'

She took a sip of champagne, enjoying the sensation of the bubbles fizzing on her tongue and the dry, biscuity taste. *Perhaps I'm going to be naughty tonight. Perhaps I'm going to get very drunk and stoned and do outrageous things . . .* 'We're old friends.'

Gawain raised his eyebrows and smirked. 'You must be a very understanding old friend.' Then a lecherous expression crossed his face. 'And I hope you'll be a good friend of mine before the night is out.'

Imogen raised her eyebrows flirtatiously and said, 'We'll see, Gawain, we'll see.'

'What are you saying, Gawain, you old fraud?' Xander said, coming up to them. 'Have you got that drink for me?'

Imogen gazed at him fondly. He looked unutterably beautiful in evening dress, his dark blond hair spiky and his cheekbones even sharper than they used to be. They shared a conspiratorial smile as Gawain filled another glass and handed it to Xander. Just then Piers came into the library carrying a large bowl of black powder.

'Ah!' cried Gawain, his face lighting up. 'Treats!'

'I thought tonight we could rechristen this "gunpowder",' Piers declared loudly as the assembled crowd buzzed with appreciation at the sight. 'Don't ask me how I managed to make it black – I'll just admit that it was bloody difficult. But . . . a theme is a theme.' He sat down on the sofa and pulled a small card table towards him with a grey marble slab set ready on its top. Then he spooned out some powder and began preparing it to hand round to his guests.

Black cocaine, Imogen thought. *It seems even more decadent than the usual white stuff. It certainly looks more sinister.*

Piers handed the slab to the girls next to him, who took some proffered cut-off black straws and inhaled the lines eagerly.

'Us next,' murmured Xander into her ear. Gawain had wandered off and was chatting happily to a redheaded girl by the window.

When the slab came to Imogen, she took a straw and snorted up her line along with all the others. *What the hell?* she thought recklessly. *I'm a grown up. Why shouldn't I have some fun too?* A few moments after taking it, she felt the pleasurable rush. She knew she would never do this in her ordinary life – the life of a respectable trainee lawyer who might party at weekends but who didn't mess with Class-A substances. But there was something about being with Xander that made her live in the moment, heedless of the consequences. She felt capable of anything and ready for excitement and risk. Picking up her glass of champagne, she took a large swig.

'Would you like to see the orangery?' Xander whispered in her ear.

'Yes, please,' she said, hungry to spend some time alone with him, and followed him as he wandered out of the French windows and down on to a soft green lawn. Behind the house, the lawn stretched away, sloping gently down to a wood at the bottom.

'You mustn't mind Gawain,' Xander said, as they walked towards a long honey-coloured stone building with arched windows that stretched from just above the ground almost as high as the roof along its whole length. 'He gets a little carried away.' He lit a cigarette. 'But he's harmless, really. Just tell him to piss off.'

They walked into the orangery which was warm from the trapped heat and the micro-climate created by a lavish assembly of trees, bushes and shrubs in all kinds of pots, from tiny to gigantic, scattered about seemingly at random. It was very quiet inside. They wandered over to a wrought-iron bench and sat down together, clutching their champagne glasses.

'It feels like this is gearing up to be quite a party,' Imogen remarked. 'That's a lot of booze and drugs waiting for us all in there.'

Xander nodded. 'I'm holding back for a while. Don't want to get too out of it, too soon. Besides, I'm starving and I know Piers has arranged a dinner. If I get stoned now, I'll lose my appetite for a while and that's no good. My bloody doctor says I'm too thin.'

'Your doctor?' Imogen asked with concern. 'Are you OK?'

'I'm fine.' He took another sip of his drink.

'Do you party like this a lot?' she asked gently. The iron

bench felt cold under her thin dress. The dense aroma of tropical plants in a confined warm space filled the air. It was almost stifling.

'There's no denying it, Midge, I party like this all the time. It's pretty much all I do with my life.' He grinned, half apologetically. 'Doesn't everyone want to live like this, if they can? All my rich friends could do anything with their lives, and you know what they *want* to do? This.' He shrugged. 'So I guess I must have the perfect life.'

There was a pause and then she said in a small voice, 'But where will it all lead to? Where will it end?'

'Well, there's the rub. It's self-perpetuating. Just goes on and on until, I guess, even partying starts to be boring. That's when I'll find something more serious to do. Maybe I'll get married then and do the family thing. I'd like a load of kids someday – I like kids.'

'But . . . don't you ever feel like you're wasting your life?' she enquired tentatively. She didn't want him to think she was criticising him.

He laughed and fixed her with a gaze that was both tender and amused. 'Of course I am! That's partly the point. It feels so ridiculously luxurious to waste a life. It's the ultimate way to show how free you are: just letting the years dissolve away in the pursuit of pleasure.'

Imogen put her hand on his arm and said earnestly, 'You could do so much more. You're not like these other guys. You've got talent, you're clever and funny . . .'

'And I'm not really all that rich, so I'd better get myself sorted out, right?' Xander smiled. 'You've always wanted to look after me, haven't you? I can feel your desperation for me to get myself straight – it's reaching out to me.'

'It's not that I disapprove . . .' she began quickly, but he interrupted.

'I know.' His expression changed. He stared down at his

glass, frowning and nervously toying with the base. 'Actually . . . you're right. I do want to change. I have had enough.' He stared straight up at her, his eyes serious. 'The drink and drugs and wasted sex . . . they're tiring me out. I want to feel good again. It's so long since I've felt *really* good, you know? Happy and healthy and raring to go. Christ, I'm only twenty-six.' His gaze softened and the corner of his mouth twisted up in that lopsided smile of his. 'You used to be in love with me, didn't you, little Imogen?'

She flushed. 'I . . . I suppose I was. Once.'

He reached over and put his hand on hers. 'I told you I was half in love with you too, remember? I know you would have been terribly, terribly good for me. Maybe you could even have given me a purpose in life. Led me out of this crazy world.'

A rush of hope filled her as a new future suddenly opened up in front of her. 'There's time,' she said breathlessly. 'I still could – if you'll give me a chance.'

'Really?' He looked at her almost imploringly. 'You still feel like that? I thought you would have grown out of your schoolgirl crush years ago.'

She stared at him, trying to drink in everything about him: his casual grace, the intensity of his dark blue eyes with their sweep of dark lashes, the size of his hands holding the glass. Was he really asking her if they could be together, if they had a chance? 'I've never stopped loving you, not really,' she whispered, half stumbling over the words, her heart racing. 'I wanted to – but I couldn't.'

His eyes softened and he reached out his hand, touching her bare shoulder. 'Is that true?'

Her skin seemed to burn where he touched it. She nodded, yearning for him to embrace her again and this time tell her what she'd waited so long to hear: that he loved her too, and wanted to be with her.

A loud clanging interrupted them. The dinner gong was being banged loudly in the house. For a long moment they stared at each other in the prickly warmth, not sure who would reach for who first. Then Xander smiled at her and squeezed her hand.

'Let's go in,' he said, standing up. 'I'm starving.'

Dinner was served in an enormous ballroom with one long table arranged in the middle. The room was dark, lit only by the candles from two vast candelabra on the table. The candlelight revealed a scene like that from a Dutch eighteenth-century still-life. Along the black tablecloth dark-skinned fruit and vegetables were piled: aubergines, black grapes and apples painted black. Decanters of rich red wine were dark as blackened blood in the dim light. Everything was twined with black silk ribbon and ivy spray-painted black.

Beside each plate was a gift wrapped in black crêpe paper and tied with silk ribbon. The others had taken their places by the time Xander and Imogen came in.

'Imogen, sit here by me.' Piers patted the place next to him. Xander sauntered over to his seat between two girls, a beautiful blonde and a gorgeous brunette, who both greeted him enthusiastically. 'I think we should open our gifts.'

Imogen took hers from beside her plate and opened it. Under the crêpe paper was a box and in that was a small packet of black Sobranie cigarettes, a pill, a black bottle of fluid marked 'Deliciously warming, tingling and easing oil for a lady's hot cunt', a small black vibrating dildo and three black condoms.

Oh, God, she thought, staring at the contents. She wanted to giggle. So now it was absolutely plain what sort of a party this was.

There was much laughing and exclaiming over the gifts.

The boys had bottles marked 'A libidinous, enlivening lotion for the rearing tool of a gentleman' and a cock ring with a vibrating clitoral stimulator.

What are the rules? she wondered. Then rebuked herself. *Don't be an idiot. There won't be any.* Already energised by champagne and coke, she was tickled and a little excited at the thought of what lay in store. *As long as it's Xander, I'm happy.* She looked over to where he was sitting. The blonde next to him was cooing over his cock ring, and saying how much she loved the little buzzing device, while the brunette on his other side was making much of downing her pill with a gulp of Dom Pérignon.

He looked over at her and raised one eyebrow, a smile playing about his lips. *Isn't this an amusing game?* he seemed to be saying. *But I'd rather be with you . . .*

It was no surprise that the whole dinner followed the black theme: black-clad waiters brought in a black soup, melba toast and more caviar. The main course had been doctored with food colouring and in the dim candlelight it was very hard to see what anything was, but Imogen thought she detected mashed potato and some kind of roast bird as well as vegetables. Pudding was a magnificent black pavlova, the whipped cream like a dark silk pillow on the crisp base, decorated with blackberries.

After pudding, coffee and dark chocolate were brought round, and finally the port was passed along with black-rinded cheeses and charcoal biscuits. The liberal amounts of wine, cocaine and pills had their effect throughout the meal. The conversation was loud and manic, punctuated with roars of laughter. Imogen talked to Piers on one side of her and to Robin who was on her other, and they kept her amused. She kept one eye on Xander all the time, though, feeling ripples of jealousy whenever he talked to the beauties on either side of him. *I'm not letting anyone else have him,* she told herself firmly. *He's mine tonight.*

'And now!' Piers roared suddenly. He pushed away his coffee cup and wine glasses, clearing a space in front of him. 'Let's get the party started!'

Someone must have been listening for this cue. The room suddenly filled with pounding rock music, thudding and urgent. Piers climbed up on his chair and then on to the table as the other diners whooped, cheered and clapped. Dancing clumsily in time to the music, he took off his dinner jacket and threw it to the floor, then undid his bow tie, whipped it round a few times and tossed it to one of the women.

Imogen stared up at the gyrating Piers, laughing and clapping. *Oh my God, he's going to strip!*

But then he unbuttoned his shirt, opened it, and revealed not his naked skin but a black corset laced tightly up his back so that little folds of fat had gathered at the front that looked like tiny breasts with a mass of curly hair between them. As the room full of people screamed with delight, he dropped his trousers; underneath he was wearing black silk knickers which bulged outwards and his corset was attached by ribbons to a pair of fishnet tights that showed off his surprisingly shapely legs. He'd already taken his shoes off, so now he stepped easily out of his trousers, kicked them away and began to do a kind of pole-dance routine, writhing and rubbing himself all over.

'Hello, darling,' said Robin, on Imogen's other side. He leant over and kissed her on the lips, pushing his tongue between them and rolling it inside her mouth before she'd realised what was going on. She pulled away and said lightly, 'Hello, yourself.'

All round the table, people had obviously taken Piers' routine as the signal to get going: some neighbours were kissing passionately; one man leant back and looked on appreciatively as the girls to either side of him started snogging fiercely, flicking their tongues in and out of each other's mouths so that their observer could see precisely what they were doing. One of the girls next to Xander was plucking at his buttons, undoing his shirt, while murmuring appreciatively.

It was as though some extraordinary spirit of indiscriminate lust had possessed everyone instantly and they were powerless to resist it. A girl was already almost naked, two men stripping her off hungrily as she giggled and pushed her breasts together and rubbing them sensuously with her hands.

'You're gorgeous,' breathed Robin, his eyes glassy with lust. He put his hand on Imogen's breast and dipped a finger into her bodice, tweaking a nipple. 'I want to suck your tits . . .'

'You'll have to get in line, Robin,' drawled Xander, suddenly appearing next to him and taking his hand firmly out of the front of Imogen's dress. 'But why not go and see Bebe and Josephine? They want to play.' He gestured over at the girls he had been sitting next to. Robin got up happily and went to join them.

Imogen glanced up at him, her eyes sparkling. She stood up as he took her hand. 'I thought you'd never get here.'

'Unavoidably detained.' He grinned, looking down at his unbuttoned shirt, then pulled her close to him. She savoured his scent, inhaling it and trembling with desire for him.

'I don't think I'm all that keen on having sex with Robin,' she whispered.

'I'd be very offended if you did,' said Xander with a laugh. 'I want you all to myself.' He put his arms round her and kissed her, pressing her lips open with his until they were kissing properly. Then he pulled away, leaving her breathless and dizzy. 'Shall we go somewhere a little more private?' he said, his eyes glittering.

She nodded. All around them was movement and activity. Some people had moved over to the cushions laid out on the floor. Robin was already lying there, his face slack with lust as Xander's brunette pulled out his cock and began to lick and suck it. Another man was already pushing the dildo up under the skirt and between the legs of a woman who held the vibrating toy to her nipples, watching as they stiffened under its touch.

The two men had finished stripping the girl naked and had laid her out on the dining room table, her legs splayed over the edge. One had already buried his face in her mound while the other was kissing her and caressing her breasts.

Everywhere Imogen looked people were kissing and licking and stroking, in all combinations and in various states of undress. Their lack of inhibition was liberating; she felt bubbles of lust climbing inside her. 'Let's go somewhere, quickly,' she said, fired up, desperate to have Xander.

He understood, took her hand and led her through a pair of double doors into a smaller room, also covered in cushions. He shut the doors behind them, closing them off from the dining room and plunging them into darkness.

'Imogen,' he said, his voice hoarse and cracked with desire. He pulled her into his arms and they kissed hungrily, as though they couldn't get enough of each other. Then they were stripping each other's clothes off as quickly as they could, fired up by the sight of the activity in the dining room. She pushed off her dress and stepped out of it, her breathing short and her pulse racing. Xander took her right nipple into his mouth, pulling and tickling it with his tongue as he pushed her down on to the floor. He was naked now, pressing his body against hers, murmuring softly as his hands ran over her hips and stomach.

She lay back, arching her neck as he moved down her

body, kissing and licking her stomach, till he reached her knickers. He pushed his face into the soft silk, inhaling her as he caressed her thighs, and then he gently pulled them off, pushing them down her legs and exposing her small dark bush. He breathed lightly on it, tickling it unbearably and making her gasp. Every nerve ending was straining; she longed to feel him touch her but he made her wait, as her pussy throbbed and ached. Then, he dropped his mouth to her and began to lick and nip at its soft folds and the bud that was already stiff and proud. The sensation was almost unbearable: smooth waves of delicious pleasure mixed with the tingle of electricity as his soft tongue touched her most sensitive place.

'Please . . . let me . . .' she gasped, desperate to touch him, to return some of the exquisite feelings he was giving her. He understood, and shifted so that she could reach for his prick. She seized its shaft, hot and hard in her hand, and flicked her tongue over it. Then she took it in, rolling the tip of his smooth penis round her mouth, moving up and down the shaft and tickling the end with her tongue as she played with his balls, stroking and moving them in their sac.

They spent long minutes sucking and teasing each other, drawing out the pleasure, making their nerves taut and responsive to every touch. She ran a fingernail around the sensitive area behind his balls and then up to the tight hole of his bum, which made him quiver and moan. As he took the whole of her clitoris into his mouth, sweeping his tongue around it, sweetly and deftly, he pushed a finger up inside her, then two, moving them hard, though all she wanted was for him to go faster and harder, and she lifted her hips to meet his hand.

She gasped, taking her mouth away from his cock, feeling it hot and hard against her cheek. The next moment, he'd turned round, pushed her thighs apart and was plunging down, ramming it into her. She spread herself as open as she could, revelling in the feeling of his penis hard in her depths. They fucked fast for several minutes before he pulled out of her. She turned round and raised herself up on all fours so that he could re-enter her, this time from behind. He knelt there, one arm round her belly, his fingers deep in her bush, twiddling with her maddened clit, while he stroked his cock in and out, forcing a gasp from her every time he hit home, ramming the head of his prick against her womb.

When she could bear the excitement no longer, she pulled free, turned round and lay back for him to enter her from the front again. Now he knew what she wanted, grinding his pubic bone against her, pushing her ever closer to her climax as he thrust in and out.

'Oh, Xander,' she cried, digging her nails into his back as the waves of pleasure began to radiate out from her hot and swollen pussy. 'Oh, Xander . . .'

'Come on, come for me,' he murmured, thrusting harder.

She began to cry out as the orgasm possessed her, racked her with shudders of pleasure and then gushed out of her. Just as her cries subsided, his began, and he bucked and arched on top of her as he climaxed deep inside, spurting out his own orgasm to meet hers.

Then they collapsed together, panting and laughing.

'Better than a stupid old orgy any day,' Imogen said with a giggle, wrapping her arms around him.

'Fuck, yes,' Xander said. He kissed her.

She yawned. 'I'm so tired now.' She smiled at him and sighed happily. 'In a good way.'

'Come on, then. There's a lovely cosy bed upstairs just for us. Let's snuggle up there and go to sleep.' He kissed her again. 'Thank you, Imogen.'

'What for?' she asked, luxuriating in her post-coital bliss.

'For everything.'

*

When she woke up, it was just after dawn and the bedroom was cold and grey. She was alone in the bed.

'Xander?' she asked, sitting up and looking about. They had sneaked through the dining room with its mass of writhing bodies and found this room the night before. They had fallen asleep wrapped in each other's arms but now Imogen was on her own. She got out of bed, feeling woozy with her nascent hangover, and pulled on her dress. Outside the sky was a translucent pale blue and the golden morning sunshine burned down. The garden was deserted but some abandoned clothes showed that fun had recently been had there. She blinked against the light, deciding to go barefoot rather than wear her heels.

She padded out of the room, went down the hall and knocked at the bathroom door. 'Xander? Are you in there?' There was no answer, so she opened the door. It was empty.

She went on down the hall, calling softly for Xander. No one was stirring. The whole house had an exhausted air, blown out by the frantic scenes of the night before.

Imogen went down the huge staircase. Perhaps Xander had gone to the kitchen to get a drink. She certainly needed some water: her mouth was fluffy and dry and she craved cool liquid. Would she be able to find the kitchen? It must be towards the back of the house.

She set off down a long, picture-lined corridor and began to recognise it from the night before. She passed the door to the ballroom, and then came to the door to the library, paused and opened it.

Inside the room smelt stale and smoky. Someone had enjoyed a cigar in here at some point in the last few hours. The sword lay abandoned on the floor, surrounded by bottles and their severed tops. The silver tureen was full of tepid water and the crystal caviar bowl upturned in a pile of dirty slush. Everything seemed drained and empty.

She was about to leave when she noticed that, in the gloom at the far end of the room, someone sat hunched over a desk, asleep, a dark green rug draped over their shoulders. She began to move towards the figure. In front of it, the surface of the desk was covered in paraphernalia: a spoon, a syringe, needles, swabs, tin foil, a pair of scissors, some tubing and a pipe. Bags and wraps with traces of powder lay scattered about.

She approached quietly although she was sure they wouldn't wake. The whole house felt as though it was under Sleeping Beauty's spell, with everyone in it slumbering deeply.

As she drew closer, she realised it was a man, and that some soft dark blond hair was emerging from the top of the rug.

'Xander?' She plucked off the rug.

He sat slumped forward, his cheek resting on the desk top. She knew at once that something was dreadfully wrong. His face was grey and the muscles beneath his skin didn't seem right, as though they'd slipped. Dark red blood had streamed from his nose and mouth on to the desk, though the flow had stopped and was now thick and sticky. No warmth came from him.

'Xander! Xander, wake up!' she called frantically, shaking him as hard as he could. He was cool to her touch. 'Xander, can you hear me? Talk to me! Wake up! Please, Xander, please . . . wake up, wake up, wake up . . .'

Then she began to cry, horrible, broken, harsh sobs, because she knew that he would never wake up.

Chapter 46

Lake Como
January 2009

Romily loved breakfasting on the terrace, even in the winter. It was a sun trap, and it only took a little sunshine to make it into a warm bower where she could look out at the massy mountains opposite and the gleaming blue jewel of Lake Como beneath.

She was sipping her coffee as she read a book when the maid came out and said, 'Marco to see you, madame.'

'Thank you, Gina. Send him out.'

The maid nodded and stepped back into the house. A moment later, the curly-headed Marco appeared, looking uncharacteristically bashful and clutching his battered white cotton hat in his hand.

'Good morning, Marco.' Romily smiled at him and gestured for him to take a seat opposite her. 'Would you like some coffee?'

'No, thank you all the same,' he said, sitting down.

'You look very strange out of that boat and off the water,' she said.

'I haven't been in the house before.' He looked about. 'It's very grand here. I'm not used to it. I'm more at home on the lake, that's for sure.'

'Well, I won't keep you away from it for long. I just

wanted to tell you that we are having a staff change soon.'

'Yes?' Marco frowned anxiously.

'Don't worry, I don't mean you. Carlo is leaving us for a while. I've got a new bodyguard coming. His name is Rocco – he's Carlo's cousin and comes highly recommended. I'm sure you'll like him. He's arriving this afternoon and will come down and introduce himself to you. He's going to be with Carlo for a few days while he learns the ropes and our security routines. I wanted to let you know.'

'That's very good of you, *signora*.' Marco still looked worried, his knee jiggling.

Romily laughed. 'You'd better go. You clearly don't like my house!'

He looked stricken. 'Oh, no, your house is very nice . . .'

'I know, I know. You want to get back. That's fine. I'll see you later, Marco. I want to go to Como this afternoon to do some shopping.'

He got up, clearly relieved to be on his way. '*Ciao, signora*. Till then.'

She sipped her coffee and watched him go: a lithe figure in jeans and a fleecey top, his skin tanned dark brown from his outside life despite the season. He was just a boy but in a man's body – and a rather fabulous one at that. Romily couldn't help appreciating his broad shoulders and long back. In the summer he often went shirtless and she had idly wondered what it would be like to feel that smooth skin under her hands . . . perhaps to urge that back on as it bucked on top of her.

After all, it had been a long time.

No, Romily. Don't go there. It's not time for that quite yet. She sighed. *But I'm still so young! Too young to live like a nun, that's for sure.*

The maid came out with the usual selection of the day's papers from across the world. She turned first to the British papers, which she always enjoyed reading the most. Some political issue took up the front page of the *Daily Telegraph* so she turned it idly. The second page had a big photograph taking up almost half: it showed a handsome, smiling young man who looked vaguely familiar to her.

EARL'S SON IN MYSTERIOUS OVERDOSE DEATH read the headline, and underneath: 'Suicide ruled out in tragic death of Hon. Alexander McCorquodale'.

Romily gasped, putting her hand to her mouth. *That's Xander!* She read on quickly. The article reported that he had been found dead the morning after a raucous house party:

> . . . where evidence of illegal drug taking and free-ranging sexual behaviour was rife. The body of Mr McCorquodale was discovered by his friend, Miss Imogen Heath, who called the emergency services immediately. Nothing further could be done, however, and he was reported dead on arrival at the hospital. A post-mortem examination found 10 ml. of cocaine in his body – just 1 ml. is enough to bring on a heart attack. At the inquest, Miss Heath said that she could think of no reason why Mr McCorquodale would want to kill himself, but that he had expressed dissatisfaction with the direction of his life. She said that he had seemed eager for a fresh start and not in a suicidal frame of mind. Other witnesses expressed the same opinion. The coroner said that he accepted suicide was not a factor in this case, and recorded a verdict of death by non-dependent abuse of drugs. Mr Piers Twistleton, owner of Thurston House where the death occurred, is currently under investigation for the possession and supply of Class A drugs and is helping police with their enquiries.

Romily dropped the paper, blinking as she absorbed the news. Imogen found his body? How extraordinary. What were they doing together? She was caught between conflicting emotions: on the one hand, she was desperately sad that *Xander* had died. *Poor Allegra – what must she be feeling? She loved him so much. No matter what she did to me, I wouldn't wish that on her, or anyone.* And, on the other hand, she was curious to know more. What exactly were the circumstances of Xander's death, and why had Imogen been with him?

She picked up her cup absent-mindedly and took another sip of coffee. Well, Allegra always was recklessly destructive, and it seemed her brother had been too. The whole McCorquodale clan was tainted with poison, and now Imogen was caught up in their vileness. The poor girl – what she must have been through. Romily couldn't help feeling sorry for her, even if she had chosen to take Allegra's side.

She got up and went through the cool terracotta-floored sitting room to her private study. Sitting at her desk, she picked up the telephone receiver and pressed a speed-dial button. It connected her at once, and the ringing tone was answered within a couple of seconds.

'Hello,' Romily said. 'I've just read the paper. About McCorquodale's death.'

She listened to the person on the other end of the line.

'Well, I want to know exactly what happened,' she said. 'Can you organise that? I'd like a report on exactly what took place – and I mean the truth, do you understand?'

She nodded, apparently satisfied with the reply. 'Good. Yes, everything here is fine. I'm watching your progress with a great deal of pleasure. It's all very impressive. I'm looking forward to further updates.'

A moment later she put the receiver down and sat back in her chair. Then she fired up her desk-top computer. She would see what she could find online, she decided.

Poor Xander. What an end. He had everything, and yet . . . it just wasn't enough.

Chapter 47

Scotland

Xander's funeral took place the week after the inquest.

Allegra couldn't remember much about the first week or two after he died. She had been relaxing at home on a sunny Sunday morning, looking forward to some calm, quiet hours away from the Soho building site. Every day was taken up with the minutiae of the build and the design, the problems and snags they had to cope with, and the management of a large team of workmen. The club had to be absolutely right, she knew that. If she'd learned anything from David it was that the pursuit of perfection was everything. She refused to compromise on anything when it came to her vision and that meant her workers simultaneously detested and respected her. She was sure they were cursing her behind her back when she insisted on a light fitting being moved two inches to the left or a wall being repainted for the third time. But who cared about being liked? The club was more important than that.

It was strange how many problems they were running into. Neighbours had unexpectedly objected to their licence application, planning had come down hard on them, even the first building contractor she'd hired had suddenly pulled out of the job which meant she'd had to tackle a long and difficult search for another. Nothing went smoothly. Every day the whole project felt as if it was threatened with total failure.

Then the phone call came.

Imogen had been half hysterical. At first Allegra couldn't understand what she was saying. When she realised it was all about Xander and that he was in a Northampton hospital, she knew she had to get there right away. Picking up her keys on the way out, she realised that her hands were shaking violently and her mind racing with panic. *Oh, fuck, I can't drive. I mustn't.* Her hands were trembling almost too hard for her to dial the number on her phone, but all she could think of was to call Adam. He'd been her right hand man now for weeks. She'd grown to trust him and to make the most of his confident, can-do attitude.

'Allegra, what can I do for you?' he asked, not sounding at all surprised to hear from her on a Sunday morning.

'Are you busy?' she said breathlessly. 'Can you drive me to Northamptonshire? I have to get there right away. My brother's in hospital. I think it could be serious.'

'I can do better than that,' he said, grasping the situation at once. She had told him some of her concerns about Xander before now – somehow it was easier to talk about her brother's problems than her own. She could confide her fears over Xander's drug use but said nothing of her own, or the lonely searches for anonymous sex, or the nightmares that still plagued her. 'Stay where you are. I'll call you back in two minutes.'

She paced about the flat, desperate to be doing something. Should she call her parents? Miranda? David? But she knew nothing about her brother's condition beyond what Imogen had stuttered out: Xander in a coma, taken to hospital. What could she tell them? She would only worry them all. She would wait until she knew more and could calm their fears.

Her phone buzzed and she picked it up.

'I'm coming to get you,' Adam said. 'Then we're taking my friend Ben's helicopter. He's a qualified pilot. He's meeting us at his helipad in the City. Keep calm. I'll be with you as soon as I can.'

Adam must have driven very fast because he was with her in about fifteen minutes, despite the distance from his North London home to Marylebone.

'I was lucky with the lights,' he said smoothly. 'Let's go.'

Within the hour, they were soaring above London and heading out over the countryside.

In normal circumstances she would have enjoyed the flight and the beauty of the landscape beneath them. As it was, she could only watch the fields and towns disappear and silently urge the little aircraft on.

Adam sat beside her, casual in his jeans and T-shirt, deftly using his iPhone to make all the arrangements, locating a place to land near the hospital and arranging permission, while Ben sat at the controls, guiding them towards Northampton.

When she arrived at the hospital, the first person she saw was Imogen, wearing a black cocktail dress and high heels with Xander's dinner jacket over the top. She looked distraught, her hair unkempt and last night's smudged make-up on her face. 'They won't tell me anything!' she stammered. 'They're waiting for you!'

She should have known at once from Imogen's face that she already knew the truth. She should have known from the way they ushered her into a private room, with solemn eyes and no sense of haste, but somehow she didn't. All she wanted was to get Xander out of here and home.

That's it. He has to go into rehab. We can't take any more of this. It's too serious now. We'll take him back to Scotland, take him home. We'll make him better, we've got to . . .

But it was all too late for that. They told her he was dead.

He had died sometime during the previous night of a suspected overdose. There had been nothing they could do for him.

She had been floored by shock. *No, not Xander! He can't be dead. It must be a mistake. How can Xander be dead*?

They'd made a terrible mix-up, she was sure of it, and any minute she'd see him, smiling his lopsided smile and saying, 'Sorry to give you such a fright. I've been an idiot again.' But then they took her to identify the body, and there was no mistake.

She looked down into his face, pale and still, the dark blue eyes she knew so well closed, and knew he was no longer there: it was serene but empty, a shell that looked like Xander. Whatever it was that was him had gone. She said nothing but a wail began in her head: *My brother . . . my Xander . . . where are you? Where have you gone? Why, Xander, why?*

She couldn't believe she would never see his smile or hear his voice again.

Adam got her and Imogen back to London. The girls huddled close together in the back of the helicopter, sobbing, grateful for the noise of the helicopter that drowned out the sounds of their grief.

Back in London, he arranged for Imogen to be taken home. He drove Allegra back to the flat himself and stayed with her that whole first terrible night and the next day, which was almost worse. She woke having forgotten, for one blissful moment, what had happened. When it all came back it was with a sickening punch of recollection. It felt as though there would never be another happy carefree day in her life again. She was drenched in sorrow, and horrified by the pointlessness of such a death. More than anything, she felt lonely to the depths of her soul.

Adam was her rock. Through it all he stayed at her side, arranging things, supporting her, listening to her, giving her drinks when she requested them and gently removing the bottle when she'd had enough.

Late at night, in her sitting room, she said in a low voice, 'Thank you so much. You've been wonderful to me. This is more than I deserve.'

'It's the least you deserve,' he said seriously. 'Besides, I know what it's like to lose someone you love. These days are the worst. But, I promise, you'll learn how to cope with this. You need only put your faith in time, which will heal you.'

'I miss him so much . . . I don't know how I'm going to get through a week, let alone a lifetime without him.' Allegra's head drooped and she covered her face with her hands, wondering how long she could bear these terrible feelings.

He put his hand on her back and rubbed it gently. 'You can do it. You have to.'

Adam insisted that she didn't return to work, even though she wanted to get back to the new club as soon as she could. He would cover everything, and David and Tyra could cope with Colette's in the meantime, he told her.

David was very shaken up by the news. When he came round to see her, his eyes were reddened. 'It's wrong,' he said, 'young Xander is gone and I'm still here. I'd trade places with him in a second if I could. I've had my life and he'd done nothing.'

The news soon leaked out to the press, and the minute that happened, Adam insisted that Allegra should go back to Scotland.

'Go and be with your parents,' he said. 'You all need to be together at a time like this.'

Perhaps he'd known that the press would soon be

wondering exactly how Xander had died. Suspicions of suicide began to be raised, along with plenty of juicy features on the wealthy upper-class set and their decadent parties. One of the girls from the Black Party sold her story to a tabloid, and each spicy instalment was accompanied by that smiling picture of Xander they all used. When a photographer started loitering outside her flat, Allegra knew it was time to go home. Besides, she would feel closer to her brother there.

Her parents were utterly shattered by their loss, and the shared grief bound them all together: the row between Allegra and her father faded to nothing in the face of something that mattered so much more. The great house seemed heavy with sadness; no one had been untouched by Xander's charm and charisma, and so no one was untouched by his death.

They went to Northampton for the inquest. In the Coroner's Court, Allegra saw Imogen for the first time since that ghastly day in the hospital. She looked thin and pale, dressed in a simple black suit for her appearance in the witness box.

Allegra watched, feeling a strange sense of distance between her and her old friend. She listened to Imogen recount the events of the night, and felt only coldness and the stirring of anger. As the coroner listed the drugs found in Xander's blood – cocaine, heroin, amphetamines and ecstasy – she closed her eyes and clenched her teeth, thinking, *You bloody fool, you bloody fool. How could you not know that would kill you?* And she fought back hot despairing tears.

Afterwards, Imogen came to find her. 'Allegra?' she asked, her eyes beseeching. 'Are you all right? Are you coping?'

'How do you think I'm coping?' she retorted. She was tense and exhausted, plagued by her frightful nightmares more than ever. 'I'm a fucking mess, of course.'

'I've wanted to come and see you . . .' Imogen stopped talking and stared at the floor. She looked drained and ill. Her face was gaunt, eyes red and tired, the skin around them grey.

'Then why didn't you?' Allegra snapped.

'I . . . I don't know. I don't know anything at the moment. It's all so terrible.' She wrapped her arms around herself and looked up beseechingly as if hoping for some kind word. Allegra said nothing and she felt nothing except for a cold, hard emptiness. Imogen looked away from her piercing gaze, then said quietly, 'When's the funeral?'

Allegra realised that her hands were balled into tight fists and her shoulders were tense. *Of course she'll come to the funeral. She has to, I suppose.* She said, 'The coroner is releasing Xander's body now and the funeral is next week, in Scotland.'

Imogen's eyes filled with tears. 'Will you send me the details?'

'Yes.' Allegra glanced over her shoulder and saw her parents standing at the door to the court, talking to an official. 'I have to go now.'

'Allegra . . .' Imogen breathed nervously and bit her lip. 'I'm . . . I'm sorry.'

'I'll see you at the funeral,' she said brusquely, and hurried off.

Allegra had no idea how she survived it.

She'd never been to the funeral of a young person before, and there was no feeling of celebration or completion. Here, the church was filled with the weight of their despair at the senselessness of a life cut short for no reason.

The whole congregation felt it, and the service was almost unbearable. The hymns could hardly be sung, except in cracked and broken voices, the readings were delivered by people choked with tears. The address, given by their father, was punctuated by sobs from the congregation.

Allegra sat or stood through it all, unable to sing a note. She could only listen, fighting the chaos that was battling inside her. She felt as though it was boiling up, building up a head of steam, and was frightened of what might happen when it decided to burst out of her.

At the graveside their mother collapsed, howling, on to her husband and had to be led away. Allegra stepped forward and threw a small bunch of heather from the garden at Foughton on to the coffin. She stared at it, the rough stalks with their miniature bell flowers on the smooth pine box, unable to believe that Xander was inside it, and that in a few minutes he'd be consigned to the cold underground darkness forever. For a moment she trembled on the edge of panic and hysteria.

He's not there, she reminded herself, fighting for control. *He's gone.*

If she didn't believe that, how could she cope?

She saw Imogen step out from the mourners and toss in her own tribute: a beautiful white rose in full bloom.

'Goodbye,' she said. 'Goodbye, Xander.' She looked up and locked gazes with Allegra. Imogen's eyes were swimming with tears and her lip was trembling. For a moment they stared at each other over the open grave. Then Imogen turned away, covering her face with her hands, her shoulders shaking.

The wake was held at the castle. The weather was still fine, so they were out of doors, on the lawn. It was as though no one wanted to be shut up in the gloomy interior of the house: they wanted to be outside where they could breathe and see the sun.

Allegra talked politely to relatives and staff, but it was difficult. The atmosphere of overwhelming misery was oppressive and the social chatter felt pointless in the light of the terrible thing that had happened. Couldn't they all understand that it was over? There wasn't any point any more. She reached into her handbag for her cigarettes – she'd been smoking far too much recently, she knew that – and wandered away from the main gathering, grateful for the small comfort of a lungful of smoke. She walked further and further away, seeking some peace, until she found that she'd reached the pink marble temple where she and Xander had spent so much time together as children. Here they'd lain on rugs, read books and munched apples and biscuits; later they'd smoked cigarettes and shared nips of the spirits stolen from the drinks table in the library.

Perhaps I'll put something here, she thought, *something to remember him by.* She sat down on the cold stone bench and imagined a small plaque or inscription, something that commemorated him in a private way. What could it be? As a boy, he'd memorised some of his favourite poems and had loved Lear and Belloc. She'd look through the books and find something. She began to remember some lines from 'The Owl and the Pussycat'.

'Allegra?'

She looked up. Imogen was standing at the entrance to the little temple, a mournful figure all in black, her hair tucked up inside a beret and her grey eyes huge in her wan face.

'I wasn't following you,' she said quickly. 'I came here to remember Xander.'

Allegra stared at her and took a drag on her cigarette, releasing the smoke in a long, slow stream. 'So did I,' she said. As soon as she saw Imogen, it was like a cold metal shutter had slammed down inside her. *Go away,* she thought, *you have no right to be here. Leave me alone with Xander*.

Imogen walked slowly in the temple, her boots tapping on the stone floor. She sat down on the bench next to Allegra and looked at her, but Allegra kept her gaze fixed straight ahead, out between the marble columns of the little temple and over the bleak Scottish countryside.

'Allegra . . .' Imogen's voice was quiet, barely more than a whisper. 'I know how you must feel . . .'

'I don't think so,' she managed to say through gritted teeth. 'I don't think you do.' The anger inside her was swirling round, getting faster, like a whirlpool gathering strength.

'I loved him too.' The words were breathed rather than spoken, to be picked up and carried away on the winter breeze.

Allegra whirled round on her, her eyes blazing. 'If you loved him,' she shouted, 'then why did you let him die?'

Imogen recoiled in shock, her mouth falling open, her eyes appalled. '*What*?'

'You heard me!' The words came out now in a fierce torrent. She was saying things she didn't even know she'd been thinking. 'What were you doing with him that night anyway? How could you have let this happen? You, of all people! You owe our family for everything you've got – everything! He trusted you and you let him kill himself in this stupid, stupid way!'

'No, no . . .' Imogen shook her head. Her voice was agonised. 'You can't blame me for this.'

'Who else is there?' cried Allegra. 'You could have helped him! You let him die!'

'How can you say that?' Imogen's face contorted at the

awfulness of Allegra's words. She clutched the edge of the bench, her knuckles white. 'I loved him! For half my life I adored him.'

Allegra jumped to her feet and walked to the entrance to the temple. She spun round and said, almost imploringly, 'Then how could it have happened, Imogen? How?'

'I don't know.' Her voice cracked and she closed her eyes. 'He did it to himself. I'll never know why.'

'I'm so angry!' cried Allegra. Her mouth trembled, then distorted, and she hit the marble column with her fist as tears began to pour down her face. 'I'm so angry – with death, and with Xander, and with everything!'

'I've got to live with it too, you know!' Imogen shouted, standing up, her hands shaking and her face pale. 'Every day, I wonder if I could have stopped him. Every day, I feel guilty that I didn't wake up and find him before it was too late. I can't stop remembering what it was like to find him . . . to know he'd gone, that he was dead. You're not the only one to suffer!' She began to cry, sitting back down on the bench, her shoulders slumping.

Allegra stared at her, wiping away her tears with the back of her hand. She took a deep breath. 'No. You're right,' she said, calmer now she had said the thing that had been poisoning her for days. Now it had been released, it had lost some of its power and her cold anger began to melt away leaving only the despair. 'You didn't let him die. We all did. None of us stopped him when there was still time.' She stared down at her tear-streaked hands. 'But that's what my life is like, you see. I never manage to do the right thing until it's too late. I kill everything. Xander . . . my friendship with Romily . . .' She gazed down at Imogen, her eyes dark with sorrow. 'Sophie.'

'No.' Imogen shook her head. 'No. You didn't kill Sophie.'

'It's all my fault.' Allegra bowed her head.

'It isn't. It's not your fault, or my fault . . . none of us is responsible for what someone else chooses to do!' Imogen stood up and walked towards her.

'My life is horrible,' Allegra whispered. 'It always has been. Ever since Sophie died . . . even before . . . Only Xander knew what it was like, because only he had been through the same. He was the only one who understood. And now he's left me.' She stared down at her friend, tears welling up and sliding down her face. 'What am I going to do?' Her voice shook. 'How can I go on?'

'You've got me . . . you've still got me,' Imogen said, and threw her arms around Allegra, who remained stiff and unbending. 'Please, Allegra . . .'

Allegra felt the weight of her sorrow crushing her down. She put her head on her friend's shoulder, her arms round the other girl, and cried, huge, shuddering sobs, until there didn't seem to be any more tears left inside her.

When the storm of crying was over, she was left drained and calm.

'I'm sorry,' she said, lifting her head at last. 'I shouldn't have said those awful things.'

Imogen led her back to the bench to sit down again. She took a tissue out of her pocket and gave it to Allegra, who blew her nose and wiped her eyes. 'He didn't mean to kill himself, I know that. And I would never have hurt him. I meant it when I said I loved him.'

'I know you did. He was like a brother to you as well.'

'No.' Imogen shook her head. She gazed steadily at Allegra. 'I really loved him. Properly. I had for years. I thought it was hopeless, but that last night we spent together . . . for a moment there seemed a possibility we might be together. I was so happy – and he was too. I just know it.'

Allegra stared back, absorbing Imogen's words. 'Did he

feel the same? Were you going to make a go of it?' she asked wonderingly.

Imogen said, 'I can never be sure. But I hope that he might have given us a chance.' Her voice trembled. 'That's why it's so hard to live with. It seems so horribly cruel, to give him to me and then take him away like that, so soon.'

Allegra put her hand out to her friend. 'I'm so sorry, Midge. I didn't realise.'

Imogen took it and they held hands, taking comfort from each other. Then Allegra spoke in a quiet voice.

'I'm glad that you were there with him. Fate must have made you bump into each other that day, so you could go with him to that awful party. He spent his last night with someone who truly loved him – and who was his friend. That makes me happier. It's one crumb of comfort in this terrible mess.'

'There is something else.' Imogen took a deep breath then said, 'I'm pregnant. And the baby is Xander's.'

PART 5

Chapter 48

London
September 2009

Oscar's was lit up, every room blazing with light. The front door was open and burly security guards stood to each side of the entrance. On the pavement people had stopped to stare, held back by velvet ropes, as the glamorous guests arrived in their smart cars and taxis.

Inside they were greeted by waitresses holding trays of Krug, and then directed up the main staircase and into the club.

Allegra and Adam had arranged the guest list between them: a thousand people had been invited to become founder members of Oscar's, and almost everyone had accepted. Now they were arriving to celebrate the club's inception and satisfy their curiosity. What did this new place have to offer? After all, there were plenty of other clubs in London to join, according to your taste. What was so special about this one?

The answer was apparent from the first moment they came into the house: just like Colette's, Oscar's was built around luxury and comfort. The whole place felt like a home rather than a commercial space. The walls were papered and covered in proper paintings, mostly twentieth-century, from great abstract oils to quirky modern prints. Sculpture and ornaments were displayed everywhere, along with the vast amounts of flowers that were a feature of Colette's, too. Sofas, chairs and banquettes were luxuriously and expensively upholstered, and piled with soft cushions.

But where Colette's style was graceful English country house, Oscar's felt like something altogether more modern. Its design, colour choice and decor were all more contemporary, as though these premises belonged to a fashionable, rich art collector with an eye for interior design. The first floor contained the restaurants – there were two, one informal and the other more grand – the luxurious rest rooms, and the bar and sitting rooms, where members could relax with their guests and enjoy some excellent cocktails or fine wines. Colette's specialised in French wines – classic Bordeaux was a particular favourite among the members – but here the wine list was more varied and suited to people who'd grown up happily quaffing Californian, Australian and New Zealand wines, and had no problems with a decent Chilean Merlot.

On the next floor was the private screening room, and a function room that could be used for private dinners, cocktail parties, or even (though no one dared admit it to David) business meetings. On this floor too were the library and study area, expanded from the original plans as Allegra realised how many writers and journalists were going to be on the membership list. All of those people would appreciate a quiet place to work. On the floor above was the restaurant with the retractable roof that became a dance floor at midnight. The plans had been adjusted to include a terrace area that would become the smokers' refuge when the weather was too bad to open the roof.

On the ground floor was the reception area, cloakroom and club offices, and storage area. In the basement were the gym and eight luxurious bedroom suites for members who were up in town for the evening, or for those who found themselves a little too tired to make it home. They could only be booked for the entire night; Allegra had wanted to make them available in two-hour chunks so that women members could have somewhere nice and private to get ready for their night out, but Adam had pointed out the potential for abuse.

'We don't want people bringing prostitutes here – or treating the place like a knocking shop. That's a reputation we *don't* need. Decent rooms at a high enough price will discourage it, I think.'

Allegra could see he was right.

Tonight, all their hard work had finally paid off. The club was finished and it looked amazing. The place was thronged with new members. Allegra and Adam had picked carefully: there were some celebrity faces in the crowd, but also a lot of influential people who weren't as famous as the stars but well-known in their fields: musicians, writers, scientists, producers, architects, designers . . . Above all, the crowd felt youthful and vibrant. The dress code was so relaxed as to be non-existent, but tonight everyone had made an effort: boys in sharp, sixties-style suits mingled with girls in gorgeous party dresses with killer make-up and shoes.

Allegra herself had made a special effort with a petrol-blue asymmetric mini-dress by Preen. A wide strap came over one shoulder to join the bodice, which was pleated in a bandage effect, while the thigh-skimming skirt was layered, with a bubble skirt over a body-contour underskirt. She teamed this with Stella McCartney high sandals in a nude mesh and the look showcased her magnificent legs. A row of chunky golden bracelets ornamented one arm almost to the elbow, and a gold slave collar was wrapped round her neck. She looked different now that she'd had her long blonde hair cut down to a choppy bob that ended just below her chin: she had done it soon after Xander's death and it seemed to symbolise the fact that she had grown up.

'You look amazing,' Adam murmured as he brought her a glass of champagne.

'Thank you. You look pretty good yourself,' she said with a smile, admiring the handmade suit by Armani and Paul Smith shirt. He looked handsome tonight, she thought. *I've never noticed how long his eyelashes are* . . . She glanced at her glass. 'I mustn't drink too much of this. I need to stay on the ball. We've got so many journalists here covering the party and I need to sweet talk all of them.'

'You're already doing a magnificent job. I saw you bowling over that hairy little man from *The Times*.'

'He was raving about the canapés. Said they were the best he'd ever had.'

'I should think so – we never settle for less.'

They smiled at each other. They'd agonised over every detail of this night and had worked tirelessly together to get it completely right.

'Of course, you know that this is just the beginning, don't you?' Allegra said, making a face. 'We've proved we can do it best – and now we've got to keep doing it. Our standards have to be this high *every night*. That's what we already do at Colette's, and that's what we have to do here. I can tell you, it's very hard work.'

'I'm up for it,' Adam said, raising his eyebrows. Then he caught sight of someone coming in and said, 'See you later. Got to go and be nice to someone important.'

Allegra watched him go. The two of them had grown very close over the last few months. They'd always worked well together – she appreciated his calm approach and habit of doing immediately what he'd said he would do – but the trauma of Xander's death had brought them closer. She felt that now they really were friends. She'd always respected his professional abilities and the way he understood the world of clubs; now she found she was looking forward to seeing him every day, and that often their late nights meant they would have dinner together, chatting over their meal and a glass of wine. They never referred to their previous encounter in her flat, and it should have been long forgotten, but lately she'd begun to find that it played through her mind more and more.

She shook the memory away. She had achieved her aims and Adam had helped her. Now they ought to part ways, but somehow she couldn't bring herself to think about it.

There's the new project anyway, she told herself firmly. *I'll need his help for that. I don't want to do Astor House on my own.* Astor House was her next venture. She had secured a Palladian-style property in Hampshire and her plan was to transform it into a luxurious hotel and spa, the perfect retreat for members craving some country quiet.

'Allegra, Allegra!' David was pushing his way through the crowd towards her. He was perfectly turned out as usual in a loud double-breasted pinstripe suit in dark blue with big lapels. With his bright red tie and red silk handkerchief, he was obviously channelling the eighties in some way.

'David!' Allegra kissed him as he drew level with her. 'Are you having a good time? Do you like the club?"

'Taste this!' he said furiously and handed her his cocktail glass.

She sipped it. It tasted like a perfectly fine gin Martini to her – Tanqueray gin, she suspected. 'What's wrong with it?'

'What's wrong? It tastes bloody filthy, that's what!' David looked angry, his cheeks high with colour. 'That's what happens when you don't have Sinbad here. Call that a vodka Martini? I don't think so! You must sack the barman at once.'

'It's gin, isn't it?' asked Allegra, frowning.

'Is it?' David looked confused. 'No . . . no . . . it's vodka.'

Allegra sipped again. 'Definitely gin. He's made a mistake. I'll get you another one.'

'Oh, don't worry,' her uncle said sulkily. 'I can't be bothered now. I'll have a glass of champagne, I suppose.'

Allegra beckoned over a waitress, put the rejected Martini on her tray and took a glass of Krug for David.

'How do you like the club?'

He glanced about. 'You've made it look very nice – but it's so bloody big! It's not like Colette's, where you feel like you're at a wonderful and very exclusive party.'

'No – but this isn't Colette's. Nothing else ever could be,' Allegra said reasonably. 'We're attracting a different crowd.'

'I'll say.' David looked about, a little snootily. 'I don't recognise anyone in here at all, and that is quite unusual for me.'

'No one?' Allegra said surprised. Among the crowd were quite a few society figures whose parents had surely known David in his time, and who must have visited Colette's.

'No. Except . . .' he scrunched up his face in distaste '. . . some *celebrities*. I don't like it, Allegra, I really don't. And photographers outside! And journalists in here! I've seen them, poking around nosily with their horrid little pads, taking notes. I don't like it at all.'

'We've been through this before. You know that this is the way the world works now . . .'

'Doesn't mean I have to damn' well like it!' David said, and marched off, leaving Allegra sighing behind him.

The party was a great success. Dozens of bottles of champagne were drunk along with hundreds of cocktails, delicious canapés were hoovered up, and the dance floor throbbed with people; although it was a cool autumn evening the roof was open so that they were dancing under the stars. It was closed at one a.m., in accordance with the noise restrictions placed on them, but the party went on.

At four o'clock, Allegra saw that only stragglers were left. She caught a glimpse of herself in a mirror as she passed. Her eyes were still smoky and well defined, her cheeks sparkled with glittery pale blusher, and her lips were dark pink now that her red lipstick had faded a little. *I don't look that bad, considering,* she told herself. *What a night!*

Adam was in the main bar, helping one of the staff clear up. 'There you are,' he said with a smile when he saw her come in. 'I wondered if you'd gone.'

'Just about to. Nasser says he's going to lock up for us.' Nasser was the club's manager, lured away from the Groucho to join their team. Allegra and Adam had gone on a manhunt, pinpointing the best staff at the very best places in town, and then luring them to Oscar's. Very few people had been able to resist them, and their team was already highly effective and brilliantly professional. She sighed. 'I could do with going home.'

'Me too. Let's go together. We'll have to take a taxi, I can't drive for another few hours. I can drop you off on my way.'

'All right.'

They went down the stairs and out on to the street. A black cab with a glowing yellow light soon came past. They hailed it then collapsed on to the wide leather seat. They turned to one another as they both sank back, exhausted.

'We did it,' she said softly.

'We did,' he answered, and they stared at each other. Instantly the atmosphere in the cab was transformed: crackling with tension. The next moment Adam reached for her and they were kissing passionately.

When it happened Allegra felt no surprise. *Yes, this was supposed to happen. This is what I want.* His kiss sent thrills through her body. She couldn't think of anything but the delicious taste of him and that she wanted as much of him as possible.

A moment later he pulled away and stared at her. 'Allegra,' he said in a soft voice.

'Shhhh.' She put a finger to his lips. 'Let's not talk about it. Not yet.' She pulled his head back to hers and kissed him again. He responded fiercely

The taxi driver discreetly ignored them until he came to a halt outside the house. Allegra had moved over the summer from her beloved Marylebone flat to a large Georgian double-fronted mansion on the edge of Regent's Park. The taxi stood outside for quite a while before the driver said, 'S'cuse me, mate, we're at your address!'

Adam pulled reluctantly away from Allegra, brushing her hair down with a gentle hand. 'Shall I come in?' he asked breathlessly.

'No,' she said. 'Imogen's asleep inside. I don't want to wake her.' There was a pause. 'Can I come to your place?'

He laughed with relief. 'Of course you can!'

They sat in silence as the taxi headed north towards Kentish Town. The early-morning buses were already starting their routes, the delivery trucks were taking the city's supplies to its clubs, restaurants, hotels, schools and hospitals. The night was almost over but Allegra sensed that the most important part of it for her was yet to come. She felt oddly calm but very happy with Adam's hand wrapped tightly around hers.

Less than ten minutes later the cab drew up in front of a large mansion block. Adam led her in through the front door and up to his second-floor flat. The minute they were through the door, he was pressing her up against the wall as he kissed her. She reached for his jacket, pushing it over his shoulders and forcing it off, then started unbuttoning his shirt. He had one arm round her slender waist, pulling her close to him, as he ran his other hand over her body.

He pulled away from her mouth and panted, 'How do you undo this dress?'

Allegra laughed and said, 'You'd better let me do it.'

She stepped away from him and, in the dim light of the hall, unzipped the side fastening of her dress, slipped off the shoulder strap and let it fall to the floor, so that she was standing there in her pale pink bra, tiny lacy pants and high-heeled shoes.

'Christ,' said Adam hoarsely. 'You're so beautiful. I can't believe it.'

She moved towards him, walking like a catwalk model, swinging her hips. She felt suddenly amazingly sexy, overcome with lust for him. She hadn't ever felt like that about someone she'd already slept with. He could only stare at her in wonder as she snaked her arms round his neck and pulled him close, pushing her tongue into his mouth and kissing him deeply. He hastily finished unbuttoning his shirt, then she pushed it back off his shoulders, revealing his firm, toned chest and stomach, and it fell to the floor as well. As they kissed, she undid his trousers deftly and then slid his boxer shorts down, putting her hands on his round, hard buttocks. He pushed in towards her and she felt the hot iron rod of his prick pressing against the scratchy lace of her pants.

'I want you, Allegra,' he said, kissing her neck, her ears, her chin. 'You've been driving me mad for so long . . . Do you know how difficult it's been working with you, knowing what you look like naked, what you feel like, what you taste like?' He pulled back and stared into her eyes. 'You do want me too?' he asked quietly.

'Yes,' she said, almost as a sigh. She buried her fingers in his hair and pulled him close to her so that they could devour each other's mouths again. He lifted her up, she wrapped her legs round his waist, and he carried her into the bedroom, laying her down on the soft smooth silk blanket. He lay down beside her, stroking her body continuously as he kissed her, as though unable to keep his hands off the beauty of her shoulders, breasts, belly and thighs.

She wondered when the little voice was going to come and spoil everything. She waited for it as she and Adam kissed, rolling round the bed. When she slid her lacy knickers down her thighs and off, she expected to hear it mocking her, as usual, even while Adam drew in his breath in excitement as he saw her bush of light blonde hair, and the coral lips of her pussy. She listened for it as he pushed his cock into her and they moved sweetly together.

But it didn't come. There was no little voice, it was silenced.

Oh my God, am I finally free? she wondered as he moved deep inside her and she wrapped her arms around him, tightening her thighs round his waist. *Am I allowed to enjoy this?* She felt a rush of joy and moaned with pleasure as he stiffened and arched back, his eyes closed tightly as he rushed to his orgasm. Then he fell back on the pillow beside her.

'Did you come?' he asked anxiously. 'I wasn't sure, I tried to wait.'

'No,' she said, 'but believe me, I had a wonderful time.'

'Really?' He looked doubtful. He wrapped his arms round her.

'I mean it.' She ran a finger down his face, smiling at the look in his eyes. 'I'm glad you care. I'll tell you more another time.'

'All right.' He dropped a kiss on the end of her nose. 'I'll never rush you. Whenever you're ready. Are you sure I can't do something?' He brushed a hand lightly over her bush.

'Not now, darling.' She sighed happily. 'There's plenty of

time for all that. I'm sleepy.' She rolled into his chest, nestling close to him. 'Night-night.'

'Good night.' He rested his head on top of hers and the next moment they were both asleep.

She woke to a delicious sensation, warm waves of pleasure rolling out from her pussy. She groaned almost without knowing why and put her hand down to her groin. Adam's hand was already there, his index and middle finger rubbing gently over her clitoris, sometimes dipping down to her pussy to stroke the entrance to her hole, smoothing her juices back up to her clit so that he could carry on rolling smoothly over it, pushing its small hood back and pressing on its sensitive tip.

She gasped, almost unable to bear the electric sensation, the extraordinary tingling in her entire groin that was verging on painful.

He pushed into her neck, kissing her softly and nuzzling her, moving towards her mouth. The combined sensation of his mouth on her neck and his fingers twirling and twirling over her clit was extraordinary. The feeling built and built until she wondered what on earth could happen next, and then she felt a rush of pleasure as though she were taking off; she grabbed him, digging her nails into his arm as she convulsed, the orgasm taking hold of her and keeping her in its grip for what felt like minutes.

When she fell back on the pillow, her breathless panting turned to laughter.

'What?' he asked with a gentle smile. 'Was that funny?'

'No . . . no . . . it was lovely. I've never been woken up like that before.' She gazed into his eyes. 'Thank you. That was . . . gorgeous.'

'Was it?'

'Yes. More than you know.'

Chapter 49

London
September 2009

'Mum, I don't need you yet, honestly,' Imogen said into the telephone, jigging up and down. 'Now I've got to go . . . really, I must. I'm desperate for the loo. The baby's pressing right on my bladder.'

This was enough to get her mother off the phone and she dashed to the lavatory, as fast she could with an enormous bump to carry with her. She was vast now and constantly floored by tiredness. She hadn't been able to go to the party at Oscar's the previous night because she felt like an elephant and couldn't keep her eyes open after eight p.m.

She went downstairs, slow and ponderous, and into the kitchen. There was no sign of Allegra but that was not surprising: it had probably been a late one last night and she was no doubt exhausted after all the hard work of getting Oscar's launch party ready. It was extraordinary how, on top of that workload, she'd also found time to locate and buy Astor House, and start planning all that as well.

Who would have thought that flighty, lazy, feckless Allegra, who had so loved scandalous partying, would now be carving out a career for herself in the world of exclusive nightclubs? Everyone would have marked out Imogen as the career girl, and Allegra as no more than a wastrel.

But look at me now! I'm the one who's abandoned my promising career: pregnant, single and no way of looking after myself. Well, thank God for friends, that's all. It had been Allegra's idea that Imogen should share her large Regent's Park house, where there was plenty of room for two women and a baby.

She made herself a cup of tea and then waddled back out into the hall with it. She would take it up to bed and try to relax for a little longer. The door, she noticed, had not been chained. Even though it was dead bolted in three places, Allegra always liked to put the chain on the door when she came in. And there was no sign of her coat, bag or shoes. Usually, when she came in after a late night, she would drop her things on the floor and kick off her heels, leaving them where they lay.

Imogen frowned. *That's odd. I don't think she's come back.*

Well, Allegra was a big girl and could no doubt look after herself. And she deserved to let her hair down after the stress of the launch night. Perhaps she was still out, partying somewhere.

Just then, Imogen felt a little shimmer in her belly and put her hand on it. It was hugely distended and very firm to the touch, a smooth tight drum of a stomach. Until recently, she'd felt lots of kicking but lately it had calmed down. 'The baby's engaged,' the midwife had told her, 'and it's a tight fit in there now. Not much room for kicking any more.'

But her due date had come and gone and no sign of an arrival yet. She was getting tired of the discomfort and eager to meet her baby, but wanting didn't seem to have any effect. *I think I'm always going to be pregnant,* she thought, *I'll be a freak of nature who just goes on getting bigger and bigger . . .*

As she climbed back into bed, she felt another movement in her stomach, but this was a little different. It was a short, sharp clench, not painful but definitely not something she could recognise. She waited for a while but there was nothing else so she took up her book and sipped at her tea. Then the pain came again. She looked at the clock. Ten minutes since the first one. It might be a false labour. Some practice contractions, perhaps. But ten minutes later, another one came, and then another, a little firmer and stronger.

She sat there, smiling, clutching her huge stomach. 'You're coming at last, baby,' she said to it. 'At last.'

Allegra arrived at lunchtime, still in her beautiful Preen cocktail dress, but barefoot, her mesh sandals over one hand. She came into the kitchen, eyes sparkling, hair ruffled and messy, looking joyful.

'How did it go?' Imogen was sitting at the kitchen table, eating soup. A big piece of fruit cake sat on a plate next to her. 'You look very happy.'

'I am, I am.' Allegra slid into the seat next to her. 'It went wonderfully. I'm going in tonight to make sure that everything is ready for the official opening tomorrow. We left quite a mess behind but I'm sure Nasser can deal with everything. He's great.'

'So tell me all about it!' urged Imogen eagerly, sipping her soup.

Allegra had begun to recount the events of the party when Imogen suddenly clutched her stomach and groaned, her face scrunching up. A few seconds later, completely recovered, she picked up a pen, looked at a piece of paper next to her and said, 'Five minutes since the last one.' She noted down the time and wrote *5 mins* next to it.

Allegra gaped at her. 'Are you in labour?' she demanded.

Imogen smiled, her eyes bright. 'I think so. I think this is it.'

'Oh, Midge!' Allegra stared at her with a mixture of fear

and happiness. 'How is it? What's happening?'

'I'm sure there're hours to go. It's been three or four already and I'm only at five minutes apart. The pain isn't too bad. It started off just like little period pains but now it's growing and getting stronger . . . much more like I'm wearing a corset and someone is pulling it really, really tight and then letting it go.'

'Should we go to the hospital?' demanded Allegra, getting up. 'I'll get changed. Is your bag all ready? We'd better leave at once.' She had booked Imogen into the exclusive and expensive private Portland Hospital months ago.

'No, no,' Imogen said calmly. 'We don't have to think about leaving until the contractions are about three minutes apart. And I haven't had any show of blood or fluid. It's a first labour. I'll probably be like this for days. That's why I'm eating this lentil soup and fruit cake – lots of slow-release energy.'

'So there's time for me to have a shower?'

'Oh, yes, loads of time.'

Allegra smiled at her, her eyes gentle. 'I can't believe it's really happening. You're going to give birth. You're so brave.' She hugged her friend.

'I don't know if I'm brave,' Imogen replied, laughing. 'There's not a lot I can do about it now!' Then she stiffened, held her breath and her face contorted with pain. When it disappeared, she said breathlessly, 'That was definitely stronger than the last one. And four and half minutes since the last one. Perhaps you'd better hurry up with that shower after all.'

When Allegra emerged, washed and dressed in jeans and a Marc Jacobs floaty black top, Imogen was still in the kitchen. Her soup and fruitcake had been abandoned and her notepaper and pen discarded. She was white-faced and panting, kneeling against one of the kitchen chairs, clutching its seat.

'Are you OK?' Allegra rushed to her side, her eyes anxious.

Imogen groaned as another spasm gripped her, her whole body shaking with the force of the contraction. It seemed to go on for long minutes. When it had passed, she looked drained and scared. 'It's happened so suddenly,' she panted to Allegra. 'One moment it was all lovely and calm, and the next . . . They're coming so fast, only a minute or two apart! And it's so painful, I think I'm going to be sick. Can this be right? It's awful! How am I going to stand it?'

'I'll ring the hospital,' Allegra said, panicking and looking for the phone. 'Then I'll call an ambulance.'

'No, no, that will take too long. It will be quicker if you drive me.' Imogen looked up with terrified eyes. 'Can you do that?'

'Of course I can. I'll get your bag.'

'Oh, God, it's coming again . . . Oh no, no, I don't like it . . .' Imogen let out a huge moan of pain as she was gripped again by a fierce contraction.

Allegra ran upstairs, fighting to keep calm and rebuking herself for not insisting they should go to the hospital as soon as she returned. What if Imogen had her baby in the car? What if she, Allegra, had to deliver it? She'd gone to some of Imogen's ante-natal classes but she was definitely not prepared to be a midwife. She rushed to her friend's room and picked up the bag that was waiting by the window.

Downstairs, Imogen was doubled up over the chair again, groaning with agony.

'Can you make it to the car?' Allegra asked urgently, trying to hide her anxiety.

'When this one's gone,' panted Imogen. A moment later her face cleared and she said, 'OK, it's gone.'

Allegra helped her up and they went as fast as they could to the front door, down the front steps to her car.

'Shit!' Allegra said crossly. 'It's just not designed for a pregnant person.' There was no way Imogen was going to squeeze into the front seat of the sleek but small Jaguar convertible. 'You'll have to lie on the back seat.'

Imogen clambered in just in time for the next contraction. Her face contorted and she moaned loudly.

'Are you sure we shouldn't call an ambulance?' cried Allegra, panicking again.

'Just get me to the hospital!' Imogen groaned. 'Please, Allegra, I've got to get there . . . right now!'

The journey to the Portland was mercifully quick. The hospital was only on the other side of Regent's Park and they pulled up in less than ten minutes. To Allegra's huge relief, Imogen was soon in the care of nurses and on her way to one of the delivery suites where a midwife was waiting.

'Are you going in? Are you her birth partner?' the receptionist asked, after Allegra had given all the necessary details.

She nodded. 'Yes, I'll go in. She needs me. There isn't anyone else.'

The midwife told Allegra afterwards that Imogen's delivery had been very trouble-free and extremely fast. Allegra thought that a quick and easy delivery seemed bad enough: for three hours Imogen was shaken by contractions every minute. She sucked at the gas-and-air the midwife offered, but it didn't seem to make any difference to the pain that gripped her. Allegra tried to help as best she could but, beyond offering Imogen cups of sweet cordial to drink, there was nothing she could do. Her friend seemed to have retreated to another place, and she didn't want to be spoken to or touched.

The midwife was calm and cheerful, encouraging her and checking the baby's heartbeat every few minutes. Then Imogen entered a quiet period when labour seemed to ease off and she appeared to be asleep.

Then it started again, now with an elemental, animal quality as her belly seemed to take control and move visibly, pressing down with each great contraction.

'I have to push!' roared Imogen. She was kneeling on the floor in her green hospital gown, where she seemed to be most comfortable, resting her upper body against a chair.

The midwife checked her. 'Yes, you're fully dilated. It's time. Now, with each contraction, you must push down as hard as you can!'

Imogen turned to Allegra. Her face was grey and sweaty, her eyes exhausted. 'I don't know if I can do it,' she whispered.

Allegra knelt beside her. 'Of course you can! The midwife says this is the last stage. You're nearly there! You're going to push out the baby.'

'The baby?' Imogen licked her dry lips and her eyes flickered with interest, as though she'd forgotten about the baby altogether in the last few hours. Another contraction gripped her. She put out her hand to Allegra, who took it between both of hers.

'Push, Imogen!' shouted the midwife. 'Use the contraction . . . push down into it!'

'You're doing brilliantly, you're amazing! You can do it,' urged Allegra, holding her hand tightly. Imogen squeezed back forcefully, her eyes screwed shut and her teeth gritted as she pushed down hard, growling with the effort.

'I can see the baby's head!' announced the midwife. 'This

little one is going to be born very soon. Just a few more pushes, Imogen.'

This promise seemed to galvanise her and, when the next contraction came, she pushed down with all her might.

'Nearly there!' cried the midwife.

'Well done, Midge, you're nearly done,' Allegra whispered, clutching her hand.

With the next push, the midwife cried, 'The head is out! Keep pushing, Imogen. On the next push, the shoulders will turn and the baby will be free. Come on, you're almost finished!'

With a great cry, Imogen squeezed Allegra's hand, gave one final push, and the next moment the midwife was holding a tiny slippery body in her hands, bluish-grey and red, the little face scrunched into an extraordinary frown.

'You've done it!' cried Allegra, overcome. 'The baby's here.'

Imogen turned round and the midwife held the baby close to her. 'It's a boy,' Imogen said in a weak, wondering voice. 'A little boy. Hello, my darling. Is he all right?'

'He looks completely fine,' the midwife replied with a smile.

A few moments later, the midwife had dealt with the cord, got Imogen on to her bed and put the baby on her chest. 'We'll check him in a moment and then you can start to feed. And I'm going to give you an injection to release the placenta, if that's all right with you. Well done, young lady.'

'You did it,' Allegra said, awed by what she'd just witnessed. 'He's beautiful, Midge! Your son.'

'Your nephew,' Imogen said with a smile, and they looked at each other with tears in their eyes.

Chapter 50

'Adam?'

'Hi.' His voice was low and sweet. 'I'm so glad you called me. I was just about to ring you.'

'You'll never guess what's happened since I left you.'

'What?'

'I'm an aunt! It happened this afternoon.'

'Oh, God, that's fantastic! Is everything OK? Is Imogen all right?'

'She's fine. She's coming home tomorrow morning after she's had a chance to recover but it was all very straightforward. He's a little boy – Alexander after his father. We'll call him Alex, I think. There couldn't be another Xander.'

'That's wonderful. I'm so happy for you.' There was a pause. 'So – will I see you tonight?'

'Well, I'm kind of tired. It's not every day I help out at a birth.'

'But the house is empty, right? After tomorrow, there'll be Imogen and the baby there. Let me come and see you. I can't think about anything else except how desperate I am to touch you again.'

Her stomach filled with delightful butterfly sensations. 'Me too. OK, come round. Come and see me.'

When Adam arrived an hour later, she'd changed into a Missoni stretch mini-dress in zigzag stripes. *Nothing too formal. But I want to look my best* . . . She couldn't help the delicious sense of excitement that was giving an extra sparkle to her eyes and a flush to her cheeks.

'You look gorgeous,' he said appreciatively as he kissed her. Her pulse raced at the sight of him, lean and handsome in his dark suit and open-necked shirt.

'Thank you. I've got us some supper. Are you hungry? Because I'm starving!'

Allegra led the way to the kitchen. She'd had the house redesigned so that she had a large eat-in kitchen in minimalist white, with a long table by the glass extension where a meal had been laid out.

'You cooked this?' he said admiringly, looking at the food beautifully arranged on white crockery.

'Um, no.' Allegra laughed. 'Cooking is a skill I have yet to acquire. I had the chef at Colette's send it round. It seemed like a day to celebrate and be a little indulgent.'

'And I've brought champagne.' Adam put a bottle of chilled Tattinger on the table. 'To wet the baby's head.'

It doesn't feel as though anything has changed, Allegra thought with relief. She'd worried they would be awkward with each other, unable to face each other as freely as before now that their relationship had moved on to something different, but it didn't feel like that at all. Adam still seemed to be what he'd been before: her best friend. Any change in that was for the good: a delightful undercurrent of anticipation of what would happen after they'd eaten.

'So Imogen is going to live here with the baby for the foreseeable future?' he asked, as they sat down to their food. The chef had sent Allegra's favourite black cod glazed in honey and ginger with a miso and soy dressing and crushed peas. 'This is delicious, by the way.'

Allegra nodded. 'She's on maternity leave but she didn't want to go back to Scotland and live with her parents, so I decided that she would move in with me. This house is plenty big enough for both of us and we've got a gorgeous little nursery all ready upstairs.'

'It sounds like a wonderful arrangement.'

'We've always been best friends. Now we're family as well. Little Alex is my nephew. He's all we've got left of Xander. He's the most precious thing in the world to both of us.'

After they'd finished their dinner, they went through to the drawing room where a Mozart piano concerto played on the sound system and a fire glowed in the grate of the marble fireplace. Instead of the raging passion of the night before, they moved almost unbearably slowly, kissing for minutes on end before undressing each other. They lay down together in front of the fire. Allegra kissed Adam's chest, moving down his body until she took his cock in her mouth, licking and sucking it as she caressed his balls, until he could bear it no more. Then she slid upwards and lowered herself back down on the stiff rod of his penis, sighing with pleasure as he pushed inside her. She rode him like that for a long time, sometimes slowing down and nipping his cock with her inner muscles, sometimes sliding right to his tip and then engulfing him again with exquisite patience. Then she let him grasp her hips and thrust hard into her, when he couldn't restrain himself any longer.

No voice! she thought joyfully. *I'm free, for the first time in my life. It's . . . it's just beautiful!*

Adam put an arm round her waist, rolled her over and began to push hard inside her. 'Oh, fuck,' he gasped, 'I can't take this. You're so beautiful, your pussy is the most incredible thing in the world, I can't stop myself . . .'

She surrendered to the pressure of his body on her mound, opening up to him, urging him forward with the movement of her hips. When he gasped and reared back as his orgasm gripped him, she felt a great surge of excitement and release, as though she'd just been whisked on to an amazing helter-skelter, and, to her astonishment, a fierce climax possessed her: her limbs stiffened and her head thrashed as she cried out, and she and Adam came together in a rush of pleasure.

Afterwards she lay in his arms, kissing his shoulder and chest as he stroked her hair.

'That's never happened to me before,' she said at last, savouring the warmth of their naked bodies pressed together.

'It's not exactly an everyday occurrence for me either,' he said with a laugh, and looked into her eyes. 'We've got something special here, Allegra. You're the most amazing thing there's ever been in my life.'

'I feel it too,' she said softly, put her cheek against his chest and sighed contentedly.

Imogen came home the next day, still a little fragile and tired but happy. In his new car seat was baby Alex, now pink and sleeping peacefully, wrapped in a baby-blue cashmere blanket that was a present from his aunt Allegra.

They cooed over him together, settling him into his nursery although he'd be sleeping in a Moses basket next to Imogen's bed for the time being. Bouquets, presents and cards were already arriving, and Imogen's parents were on their way down to stay for a few days until she had settled, grown used to her baby and learnt to feed him.

'It's not as easy as I thought,' she said, sitting in the large and very comfortable feeding chair, a present from the Earl and Countess of Crachmore. She stroked the baby's soft downy head; a light blond fuzz covered the tiny skull. 'But I expect we'll both get used to it, won't we, little man?'

'You'll make a brilliant mother,' Allegra said, watching as little Alex's jaws moved rhythmically with his sucking. 'You're a natural.'

She felt a rush of pure joy at the sight. For the first time since Xander's death, Allegra knew what it was like to feel happy. She loved the baby with a fierceness that was rivalled only by Imogen's adoration of her son. She was also falling in love with Adam, and her body seemed to glow with the rapture of the sexual pleasure they were sharing. Oscar's was buzzing with new members and more people were clamouring to join: features on the most glamorous club in London were in every paper and magazine, and Allegra herself had been profiled in *Vogue* and asked if she would do a *Tatler* cover. She'd been listed as one of the most influential women in London and there was talk of her being nominated for the Veuve Clicquot Businesswoman of the Year Award. Colette's was still running as smoothly as ever. It felt as though the dark days were behind them now. At last, she could begin to enjoy some happiness.

Chapter 51

Colette's
November 2009

This might be the best Martini I ever tasted, Mitch thought as he sat at the bar in Colette's. The rotund barman in the dove-grey jacket had mixed it for him in a few seconds and yet it was sublime. *It's got to be up there, anyway.*

He looked around discreetly at the comfortable room behind him; the line of racing prints on the wall above the well-polished bar. He'd come here twice over the last year, visiting under his pseudonym, wearing unremarkable suits and dark glasses and keeping a low profile. It had taken a few pulled strings and favours called in, but he had managed to get a membership arranged, that meant he could scout out this, the glittering prize of London's nightclubs, and he'd loved it immediately and passionately. He wanted it to be his, he hungered for it. He would have it, he'd promised himself that. And he would do anything it took to get it. *I have a few tricks up my sleeve after all,* he thought wryly. *I just hope no one recognises me.*

A beautiful girl came striding towards him , elegant in a black cocktail dress and towering heels. Her golden hair fell about her face in a long bob and she had striking dark blue eyes and red-glossed lips. *A real looker,* Mitch thought. *You can see the breeding, I guess. I've not seen cheekbones like those for a while.*

'Mr Mitchell?' Her voice was cool, in that clipped, drawling and very sexy British upper-class accent. 'I'm Allegra. How do you do?'

'Lady Allegra.' He smiled at her, took her outstretched hand and bowed over it. 'Pleased to meet you.' When he looked up again, she was smiling with a touch of amusement at his old-fashioned courtesy.

'Plain Allegra is fine, thanks.' She noted his glass. 'You have a drink, I see. Shall we sit here or would you like to go straight through for dinner?'

'Let's go through. And you can call me Ted, by the way.'

She inclined her head in a half nod, and then led him to the dining room. There was a mildly anxious moment as the maître d' scrutinised him as they passed, and Mitch thought he caught the faintest flicker of a frown, but nothing was said.

When they'd settled at one of the tables, Allegra said, 'You're not at all what I expected.'

'Oh?' He gave her his most charming smile.

She raised an eyebrow at him. 'I thought you'd be older. A man with your business portfolio.'

'I guess I'm a bit of a prodigy,' he drawled in his best corn-fed American Boy accent. 'Let's get our order out of the way, Allegra, and then we can talk.'

When the waiter had taken it, Mitch glanced around the room, admiring the cunning use of space which maximised the number of tables and the opulence of the decor which was luxurious without being gaudy or cluttered. 'This is everything I'd hoped, I must say. The atmosphere here is something special. Why should that be?'

'It's thanks to my Uncle David,' Allegra said with a smile that showed her perfect teeth and heightened her beauty.

'His personality and taste are stamped everywhere. That's why this nightclub has something nowhere else can match. They might attempt to define luxury but something will always let them down – there'll always be something mediocre about the spirit of the place. Here, you can never be let down.'

Mitch nodded. She had put her finger on it. It sounded easy and yet he knew from experience how difficult it was to achieve and easy to lose. 'I see that.'

'Your wine, sir.' The waiter produced the bottle of Château Mouton Rothschild 1996 that Mitch had ordered.

'Your list here is superb,' he said in heartfelt appreciation when the wine had been tasted, approved and poured out. 'Some of the best wines in the world are on that list.'

'We've been collecting for forty years,' Allegra explained. As their food arrived, she told him about the sommelier at Colette's who was the son of the original sommelier David had hired back when the club first opened. 'That tells you more about this place than I ever could. It's a family concern. Even the staff pass their jobs down.'

'Are you quietly telling me to get lost?' Mitch said with a smile.

'It depends.' Allegra took a sip from her glass. 'Are you asking me anything I need to say get lost to?'

He laughed. 'You assume I'm about to tell you that I want to buy Colette's, right?'

She raised an eyebrow. *God, she's a cool customer.* He appreciated that self-possession and confidence, though. They made Allegra formidable despite her relative youth. *I could use someone like her. I could harness that ambition.* 'What else am I supposed to think?' she asked him. 'You have a reputation for buying up the most exclusive places in London.'

'Not just London,' he said, with a shrug. He took another

sip of the blackberry-rich wine. 'Across the world. I'm investing heavily in Monte Carlo at the moment, and I've bought stakes in the most luxurious hotels in Dubai.' He told her about the extraordinary amounts of money and the eye-widening glitz of the seven-star hotels there as they finished their starters and the main courses arrived.

Allegra listened with interest and then said, 'But is it wise to invest in Dubai? I've heard things are going very flat there. The property market has ground to a halt and the luxury market is apparently suffering from its worst downturn in many years with the current financial climate.'

'It doesn't seem to be bothering you,' Mitch said with a smile. 'You're expanding, aren't you? I've heard great things about Oscar's. Everyone is clamouring to join. You must be doing well.'

She nodded, her golden hair shimmering in the candlelight. 'I believe our brand is solid enough to weather any recession. People will always want to come here. We don't depend on silly money. Just real money.'

'But you've borrowed a lot. You're very exposed.'

'We can easily keep up repayments on our loans. Our parent company is in good health and the assets remain strong. We've got a couple of million sitting in our wine cellar, as it happens. More on the walls of the clubs. David's eye for art and furniture has always been superb and those markets will remain strong in the downturn because interest rates are so low. People are looking to invest in solid assets at the moment.'

'You're right. And I happen to believe that there will always be millionaires who want to show how big their dicks are by throwing their cash around.' Mitch was impressed, both by her acumen and her positive approach. It was refreshing at a time when so many business people were full of gloom and negativity.

When their main courses arrived, Allegra said, 'You're a player, that's for sure. I've seen some of your recent acquisitions. You're spending money at a time when hardly anyone else is.' She leant across the table and fixed her blue eyes on him. 'Where does your cash come from?'

He burst out laughing, amused by her chutzpah. 'Very few people dare to ask me that! They all wonder, but no one says it. OK . . . the truth is, I have a kind of godfather figure in America who is also my backer. He has great faith in me and likes the way I think, the way I operate. He also likes the percentage I return on his investments.'

'A godfather?' Allegra smiled. 'I see. How handy.'

'I started in Paris, but in the end decided I didn't like it all that much. So I came to London, and realised that here were the places I found the most alluring. I love the old world heritage, the sense of privilege – and anyone can have that if it's on offer in a restaurant. Anyone can be included, if they want to be and if they work hard enough. That appeals to me.'

Allegra nodded slowly and took another bite of her salad of monkfish tails and bacon. 'I see.'

He tried his fillet steak. 'This is good. Seriously.'

'Why don't you get to the point, Mr Mitchell?'

He coughed lightly. 'Would you mind if we wait till coffee? Only, I'm really enjoying myself here, and I don't want you to throw me out before dessert.'

'That bad, is it?' Allegra laughed.

'I don't think so. But you might.'

Over pudding, he said, 'It won't surprise you to learn that I want to buy Colette's, along with Oscar's and Astor House.' He smiled winningly. 'I love them all. They showcase great talent. You've clearly inherited whatever it is your uncle has. And I want them. It needn't be the end of your association with them. You could come and work for me.'

'I'm terribly sorry, Mr Mitchell, but you can't have them – or me,' Allegra said smoothly. 'Now, we both knew I was going to say that, so it can't have come as a surprise.'

He continued smiling good-humouredly. 'You're right. It hasn't.' He took a scoop of the dark chocolate and ginger ice cream and let it melt across his tongue. 'Oh, wow. That's great. An epic dessert. I heard it was famous in London, and I'm not surprised. Boy, I would love to own that ice cream!'

'Consider the whole bowl a present,' she retorted.

He laughed, tickled by her spirit. 'Thanks, ma'am. I will. But what I really want to know is whether you can ever imagine selling your group in the future?'

'No.' Allegra remained emphatic. 'It's not only that I would never hear of it. My uncle would rather die than let anyone else own his beloved Colette's. And he has the final say.'

'Does he? I guess that's blown my plans out of the water, huh?'

The girl pulled a helpless expression. 'I'm afraid so.'

'But no hard feelings, huh?'

'Certainly. None on my part.'

'I've had a wonderful dinner with a beautiful dining companion, so I have no complaints.' Mitch raised his glass to her. 'Your very good health, my lady.'

Allegra raised hers back. 'Yours too, Mr Mitchell.'

He watched her as she drank, thinking, *Unfortunately, my lady, this is one battle you are going to lose.*

Chapter 52

La Belle Dame

Romily came up on deck and looked out over the sparkling waters of the Mediterranean. It was still early-autumn but the weather was gorgeous, almost warm enough to sunbathe – certainly warm enough for her to wear her very pretty Bottega Veneta jersey dress in honey-coloured silk. Her shoulders and upper arms peeked through the slit sleeves, and her huge sunglasses protected her from the glare of the sun off the sea.

'Would you like something, madam?' asked one of the stewards with a bow.

'Yes, some water, please,' she replied. 'And a black coffee. Strong.'

She walked along the lower deck to the seating area at the stern and leant against the railings for a while, watching the rippling waves that followed in their wake.

I should enjoy this. It could be my last bit of solitude for a while.

Once she got to Chrypkos, she would be surrounded by family. But it was time to go back. Her mother had sounded so anxious to see her, and when she had offered to send the yacht to meet her in Naples after a shopping trip in Rome, Romily had decided to accept. She'd been working very hard and it was almost time to return to London anyway.

It's nearly time to start making things happen. Everything is almost in place.

The small motor-boat moored at the jetty on Chrypkos and she disembarked, pulling on a broad-brimmed white hat and leaving her luggage to be brought on after her. Rocco, her guard, would follow later. His duties were less onerous now that she was on the island – not only was there already excellent security provision here but no one could land on Chrypkos without the family's permission. It had always been the place where they felt the safest. A small white jeep was waiting to drive her the half-mile or so to the main house. It had been a while since she'd been on the island and she'd forgotten how beautiful and peaceful it was, covered in woodland and olive trees, with several white, flat-roofed houses hidden about the groves. The main house dominated the south side of the island. Near it were a handful of smaller lodges for guests to stay in, and a private chapel.

A moment later the jeep pulled up in front of a two-storey white villa built in traditional Greek style. It looked simple enough from the outside but inside it was supremely comfortable and spacious, expanding into two wings that encompassed a vast garden and swimming pool.

Athina de Lisle came rushing out to envelop her daughter in a great hug. 'My darling, you're here! We're so happy . . . so happy! Come with me.'

They went through to a large sitting room. It was full of ancient Greek artefacts – beautiful urns, statuary, plates in terracotta and black – decorated with pictures of the gods. They had been collected by Isabelle's father, a Greek shipping billionaire with a passion for his country's cultural heritage. His accumulation of ancient treasures was second only to the world's best museums. This house was a showcase for his collection and as such was dressed very simply, with terracotta floors, elegant but plain furniture, white linen and muted blue fabrics, so that the splendour of, say, the *kouros*, a statue of a boy carved in 530 BC that stood in the wide entrance hall, might be appreciated in all its glory.

Athina de Lisle summoned drinks with a wave of her hand, and sat down next to Romily.

'You look well,' she said. 'And that dress is beautiful. Only you youngsters can carry off such unstructured pieces. I'm confined to tailoring for the rest of my life, so enjoy it while you can, darling. How was the trip?'

'Very good.'

'Did you see your papa had *La Belle Dame* redecorated? Dear Nicky did it – he's made it delightful, hasn't he? I love my new marble bathroom.'

'I hadn't noticed . . .'

'Well, you haven't been aboard for a long time. I think we should take a trip this summer, just the two of us. We've got so much to catch up on.' She reached out and took her daughter's hand, stroking it fondly. 'Oh, did I say? I've invited Gabriella Viney for next week with her two sons. The older one is at business school in America but is going to be running the family company in no time. Apparently he's a wonderful young man. You must meet him.'

'Next week?' Romily looked regretful. 'I'm leaving before then, I'm afraid.'

'Leaving? But why?' cried her mother, dismayed. 'I thought you were staying here the whole month with us?'

'No. I'm going to London.'

'For a party?'

'No. I haven't been there for a long while and I have business there.'

'What kind of business? I don't understand how you can have business! What business?'

'Things I must do, that's all,' Romily said vaguely. 'Small

projects. You wouldn't be interested at the moment, but I'll tell you all about it when the time comes.'

'And this is why you must go to London?'

'Yes. I'm afraid so.' Romily stood up. 'But now, Mama, I'm going for a swim. I really must stretch a little and get some exercise.' She left her mother gazing mutely after her.

She must know that she's powerless to stop me now. I'm not a little girl to be ordered about any longer. I intend to live exactly as I want from now on.

The mood in the house was upbeat. Romily's parents were glad to have her with them for however short a time and Louis was there too, back from his job in Los Angeles where he was making his first bid to be a film producer by staking some of the family money on projects that he liked. They enjoyed a happy family dinner together, dining on the traditional Greek food they all loved so much: grilled lamb shish kebabs, roasted peppers and courgettes in fragrant spicy olive oil, and marinated barbecued baby octopus. Afterwards they ate rich honey baklava and drank strong sweet coffee, and talked about the old days on Chrypkos when the children had been small and the holidays endless.

Later, in her room, Romily changed into her silk camisole and knickers to sleep, then sat on her bed and made a call on her phone.

'It's all arranged,' she said when the call was answered. 'I'm coming to London. Papa has said I can use the plane – it's at Athens airport at the moment. A helicopter will come for me the day after tomorrow to take me there. But I don't want to stay at the family house in London, it's too ostentatious. So I need you to find me somewhere else.'

She listened to what the person on the other end of the line said and then laughed. 'Wouldn't that be funny? Well, we'll see. Perhaps I'll find time to dine somewhere special.'

She listened again and then said, 'That will be fine. I'll leave all the arrangements to you. I'll see you in London. Yes, I'm looking forward to it too.' She clicked the phone off and gazed thoughtfully at the ceiling, thinking over her plans for the future.

The next day she took a long walk around the island with her brother, relishing the peace and quiet and her freedom. She wondered if she'd made the right decision, leaving Chrypkos so soon. It was so lovely not to be tailed by guards wherever she went. But she had made her plans and it was important that she be on the spot from now on. Things were promising to hot up nicely over the next few weeks and she wanted to be able to witness it all close up.

When she got back to the house, she summoned her guard, Rocco to see her in the drawing room.

'We're leaving for England tomorrow,' she said, 'so please prepare whatever's necessary. The helicopter will take us off the island at three p.m.'

He looked annoyed, a frown on his broad face. 'Very well, *signora*. But it would help if you would give me more advance notice of your plans.'

'Why?' Romily raised her eyebrows at him.

'Because I need to make the necessary security arrangements. I'll need to know the times of your flights, and how you intend to travel between them. I may need back-up if we are in very exposed areas. And what address will we be at in England? A hotel?'

Romily sighed wearily. 'God, this is all such a bore. I can't think why I have to put up with all this, no one is in the least interested in me. I'm staying in a private house – a flat in Notting Hill probably.'

'I will need to examine it or send colleagues to check it out,' Rocco insisted.

'This is stupid! No one else knows where I'm going to be.'

'Someone will know, believe me. I must insist, *signora*, or I'm not doing my job.'

Romily stared at him but could see by the stubborn set of his jawline that he was going to be obstinate about all this. 'All right. As soon as I have the address, I'll give it to you. Satisfied? Now go and enjoy some beers or whatever you like. Tomorrow, work begins again.'

Chapter 53

London

Allegra inhaled the scent of the ravishing peonies that sat in a Herend vase on her desk.

'Those are beautiful,' Tyra said admiringly, as she put the last things into her boss's in-tray. 'Are they from Mr Hutton?'

Allegra nodded happily. 'Yes. It's very generous of him.' She tried to hide the flush creeping over her cheeks. 'I'm meeting him tonight, actually. We're dining at Colette's.'

'Yes, it's in the diary and booked. Gennaro has reserved the usual table for you.' Tyra picked up the new photograph frame that Allegra had put on her desk that day. 'Oh, I haven't seen this! Is it little Alex? He's gorgeous!'

A fat-faced, blue-eyed baby gazed out of the photograph, his hair a blond fuzz and his smile giving him pouched cheeks. Allegra's eyes softened as she looked at it. 'Yes, isn't he? He's nearly three months old now and a total angel. The love of my life.'

'Except for Mr Hutton,' Tyra said mischievously. 'I'm off home now, is that OK?'

'Of course. See you tomorrow.'

When Tyra had left, Allegra spent a little longer going through some design specs that had come through for Astor House. The designer had given her two looks for the main drawing room, one casual and one formal, and she was trying to decide which one she liked the most. One idea she had been toying with was creating much more of a Colette's feel at Astor House by painting the walls the same pumpkin yellow as the main bar of the club, and using the same jewel-coloured velvets and striped silks in the upholstery. But was that wasting an opportunity to do something new?

At eight o'clock she tore herself away from her work and got changed into one of the selection of evening dresses and accessories she kept in the wardrobe in her office. Tonight she selected a black Roberto Cavalli dress with a plunging V-neck and three-quarter-length sleeves, ruched just below the bust. The effect was subtle but very stylish. When she dined at either of the clubs she avoided her more attention-grabbing clothes, such as her favourite crazily coloured Matthew Williamson sequined mini-dresses. The look then had to be more discreet, to remind everyone that she was working when she was on the premises and not partying. Nevertheless she enjoyed dressing up and wanted to reflect the spirit of Colette's, so she only wore the very best. She looked at her reflection in the glass, then added a turquoise and gold medallion necklace by Alex Monroe and slipped on her Christian Louboutin champagne satin sling-back sandals.

She took one last turn in front of the mirror, satisfied. She was ready.

She left the offices and took the short walk into the square. The doormen were waiting as usual at the entrance, ready to scrutinise everyone who wanted to come into the club and to open the doors of the expensive cars that pulled up. They touched their dark blue caps as Allegra approached, and she said her usual good evening to them, passing a few minutes by asking after their families. Then she went downstairs. The club was still quite empty which gave her time to say hello to the staff and check on preparations for the evening. It all looked wonderful, as usual. Sinbad, in his dove-grey bar uniform, was keeping an eye on his two young assistants and checking on the liquor stocks in the recessed cupboards to each side of the bar, disguised as mirrors with Lalique clouded glass in scallop-edged surrounds.

She was chatting to him while he mixed a Colette's cocktail for her, a delicious blend of vodka, Benedictine, dry Martini and lemon, when Gennaro, the club manager, came out of the restaurant looking upset.

'Lady Allegra, may I have a word with you, please?' he said quietly.

'Of course, Gennaro. What is it?'

'In private, please,' he murmured.

They went through to the private dining room which was not being used that evening. It was a small but lavish room, dominated by a huge Sargent oil on one wall and by rows and rows of bottles on the other three. A large Baccarat crystal chandelier hung from the ceiling, and vintage Tiffany silver candelabra were arranged on the table beneath.

'What's wrong, Gennaro?' Allegra asked, concerned. The manager was usually completely unflappable and capable. He understood the Colette's way and managed the staff with a firm but fair hand.

'It's Mr Mac,' Gennaro said, looking worried. 'He came in here earlier, before we opened. He said he wanted to check that all was well but he was acting very strange . . . very angry with everyone. Well, he thought that the cutlery was dirty . . . but it wasn't! I wouldn't allow such a thing, Lady Allegra. He insisted that every fork and knife in the place was tarnished and insisted we begin to re-polish before we opened. So I sat down all the staff and we began to polish the cutlery on all the tables. He seemed happier then, and a few minutes later he left. So I stopped the polishing and sent everyone back to their usual jobs.' He looked at her anxiously. 'I thought I should let you know.'

'Thank you, Gennaro. It was the right thing to do.'

The club manager went out and Allegra sat on a dining chair, thinking hard. This wasn't the first instance of David acting erratically. It was worrying. He was still officially in control of the clubs even if she was the managing director. What he said, went. If his eye for perfection were finally deserting him . . . what then? What did that mean for the future of Colette's, Oscar's and Astor House?

She looked at her watch. Adam would be here any minute. She hurried back to the bar to be ready to greet him.

Allegra woke up with a small cry, reaching out for someone, trying to hold on as hard as she could. Her eyes were terrified and unseeing, her face and body clammy with panic, and she was breathless.

Under her urgent, grasping hands was a firm, solid arm. Next to her in the bed, the duvet rumpled over him, Adam lay staring at her, concerned, calming her down with his gentle voice, saying, 'It's OK, it's OK, it was just a dream. I'm here . . .'

She blinked at him, coming back to reality. It had been the usual dream: she'd been reliving those last few seconds of Sophie's life, trying desperately this time to hold on to her, to alter the frightful outcome, but no matter how hard she tried, she never could. The cold horror of it was hard to shake off but she smiled weakly. 'A nightmare,' she explained.

'I guessed.' He looked worried. 'Was it the same one?'

Allegra was wary. 'How do you know?'

'Just the way it always unfolds. You get so frantic, reaching out, trying to hold on.'

'Do I say anything?' she asked. *So many years keeping my secret. It would be ironic if I gave it away in my sleep.*

Adam stared at her for a long while, then he reached out for her and kissed her tenderly, wrapping her in his strong arms. 'No,' he whispered into her ear. 'You never say anything. And you're always safe with me, do you understand?'

She nodded, relaxing against the warm security of his body, feeling the fear flow out of her and away.

Chapter 54

Imogen saw the small brass plate on the office door, engraved with the words 'David McCorquodale Group'.

Alex was strapped to her chest in a sling and she ran one hand over his small head in its soft woollen hat. It had been a lovely walk down from Regent's Park, breathing in the autumn air and relishing being out and about. Motherhood had been a shock: she'd had no idea how far a baby would subsume her existence. Every hour of every day had been about Alex since the moment she'd arrived home: his feeding, his sleeping, his playing, gurgling and smiling. She was utterly in love with him, though, from his bright button eyes to his adorable curling little toes.

The strange thing was how much he resembled Xander. When Allegra played with Alex, the McCorquodale resemblance was so strong he could be her son rather than Imogen's. Seeing those navy blue eyes and the expressions that reminded her so vividly of Xander was a bittersweet sensation: Alex brought Imogen great joy and comfort and was the most precious thing in her life. But she also recalled every day what she had lost, and what Xander had lost too.

Sometimes she stood over her baby's cot, gazing down at him and saying softly, 'Your daddy would have adored you, darling. It breaks my heart that he's not here to love you like I do.'

The hole in both their lives where Xander should have

been could never be filled. They would both miss him forever.

But I can do it on my own, she told herself resolutely. *I've got lots of support. My parents dote on Alex. I can always turn to them to share all those special moments: the first birthday, first word, first step . . .*

And she could turn to Allegra, of course. On the spur of the moment she had decided to call in at the club offices and say hello.

She pressed the doorbell and immediately an answering buzz and click told her the door was open. She went up the small staircase to where a friendly-faced girl was waiting for her at the top.

'Hello, I'm Imogen, you must be Tyra.'

'Yes, I am,' she said. 'And this little sweetheart must be Alex! Can I see him?'

They went into Tyra's office where Imogen unstrapped Alex who blinked sleepily and then grinned at the women who cooed over him for a while.

'He's gorgeous!' Tyra said, melting at the sight of him. 'I'd love a little baby.'

'Hmm. He's gorgeous right now, but you might think differently at two in the morning,' Imogen said with a smile. She looked about. 'Is Allegra here?'

'No.' Tyra shook her head. 'She's gone down to Astor House for the next couple of days to oversee the work.'

Imogen groaned. 'I'm an idiot! Of course she has. I completely forgot – she told me at breakfast. That's what having a baby does to you, Tyra.' She sighed and said to Alex, 'Back home for us, wee man.' She glanced back at Tyra. 'Would you mind if I give him a feed first?'

'Go right ahead. Use Allegra's office, if you like. I'll bring you some water.'

'Thanks.'

Imogen settled down in Allegra's chair and latched Alex on to her breast with a muslin at the ready to catch any spills, then sat back to enjoy the calming sensation of the baby suckling. Humming to herself and rocking gently, she fell into a dreamy state that was hardly surprising when she'd only managed four hours sleep the night before. Vaguely she was aware of hearing the door below open and then close. Then she realised there was someone standing in the doorway, staring at her.

'Who the hell are you?' barked a voice.

She jumped, startled, and Alex popped off her breast, leaving one milky nipple exposed. She realised it was David McCorquodale.

'I said, who are you?' he said again, in a querulous voice.

'It's me, Imogen.' She was afraid. *How stupid – it's only David. There's no reason to be scared.* Perhaps he was confused by the sight of her breastfeeding. 'I just came in to feed the baby.'

'Imogen?' He looked her up and down, frowning. 'Who's Imogen?'

'Allegra's friend . . . Alex's mother . . .' Her voice faded. How could he not recognise her? She'd seen him only recently when he'd come over to spoil Alex and give him a basketful of beautiful presents including an Asprey's silver rattle.

His face cleared suddenly and he smiled. 'Oh, yes, of course! Imogen! How are you? And how is that gorgeous great-nephew of mine? I just came in to drop off some papers. Now, I'm going to the club to talk to the manager. If you've finished there, would you like to come?'

'Yes,' she said, relieved that he seemed his normal self. 'That would be lovely. I've not been in Colette's for ages.'

Together they walked round the corner to the club, Alex back in his sling on Imogen's chest. Inside it was buzzing with activity as the staff worked busily, clearing up from the night before and preparing for another.

'Ah, here's Gennaro!' called David as the club manager approached them. 'Have you met the lovely Imogen?'

An Italian man with grey-flecked black hair came forward, a smile on his face. He looked kind and capable. 'No, I haven't. How do you, madam?'

'Imogen's almost family, you know, Gennaro,' David said. 'Her little boy is my great-nephew.'

Gennaro looked down at Alex's head and the tiny fist curled round Imogen's finger. The baby had gone back to sleep after his feed. 'How wonderful,' he said tenderly. 'I love little babies. I'm sure he's beautiful.'

Imogen caught a glimpse of a young man leaving the bar behind Gennaro and going into the restaurant beyond. He looked familiar. *How funny . . . do I know him?* 'Who's that?' she asked. 'One of the waiters here already?'

Gennaro glanced over his shoulder and said, 'Oh, no. My young nephew, visiting from Italy. He wants to see if he can get some DJ work in London and Mr Mac kindly said he can use the decks here and, if he's any good, perhaps do a session.'

'Yes, and now Mr Mac wants to have a word with you,' said David impatiently. 'Excuse us, Imogen. It was lovely to see you and Alex, but we must get on.'

'I ought to get this one home,' she said. ''Bye, David. It was lovely to see you. Come and visit us soon, won't you?'

She walked across the square towards Oxford Street where she would pick up a bus to Regent's Park, by far the quickest and easiest way to get home. She was standing on the edge of Oxford Circus, waiting to cross the road, when a large sleek car came past, crawling along in the flow of traffic. Imogen looked at it idly, wondering where such a smart vehicle was going. Then she glanced inside, and gasped.

She stood frozen as it drove past, unable to decide whether to wave or cry out. Then it was too late. The traffic cleared, the car gathered speed, and the next moment it had pulled smoothly away.

But Imogen knew without a doubt that the passenger sitting on the pale leather back seat, alone and elegant, was Romily.

Chapter 55

Whenever he entered one of his own restaurants or clubs, Mitch was reminded of Mr Panciello. When his old boss had come into the establishment there'd always been a frisson, a little rush of fear and excitement, and everybody had raised their game, whether they were likely to cross his path or not.

Mitch felt the same atmosphere now when he came into Alfred's, his high-class Italian restaurant just off Piccadilly. There was a sense of bustle just out of sight as everyone made sure that things were looking right in case he happened to glance in their direction.

'Good morning, sir,' said Tony, the maître d', 'everything is prepared for your lunch.'

'Am I in the private room?'

'Yes, sir, the small one, as you requested.'

'OK. I'm gonna check that everything is perfect.'

'Very well, sir. Let me lead the way.'

Mitch followed the back of Tony's well-tailored suit as he led the way through the elegant main dining room, up some carpeted stairs and into a small hexagonal room built into the tower, designed by a previous eccentric owner of the building when it was still a private house. Mitch looked about.

'That vase of flowers is wrong,' he said brusquely. 'It's too small and stingy. I want something richer. Colette's always has wonderful, generous arrangements, and certainly nothing with freesias in it. Change it.'

'Absolutely,' Tony said with a nod of the head, and gestured to a nervous waiter who removed the offending vase at once.

Mitch inspected the rest of the room which was set out carefully with the best china, cutlery and glassware. 'Let's hope this satisfies the old man,' he muttered. Then he sat down to wait.

At precisely one p.m., David was shown into the private room. Mitch got to his feet, and welcomed him with a warm handshake.

'It's an honour to have you here, Mr McCorquodale. A great honour. You're a pioneer in your field, a true master.' He stood back so his guest could sit down.

'Very sweet of you to say so, dear boy, if a trifle over-exaggerated. It's true I did blaze a bit of a trail in my time but I'm sure I was only one of many who saw that our generation craved youthful vigour and not the stuffy old ways.' David took his place at the table, his eagle eyes glancing quickly over it, taking in every detail.

The old man is quite a dandy, thought Mitch. David was dressed in lime-green corduroy trousers, a violet velvet jacket and a black and white checked shirt. On his feet were perfectly polished Gucci loafers.

Mitch joined him at the table. At once a waiter appeared to pour chilled water into their glasses. A second later he was back to offer four varieties of bread baked that morning in the restaurant kitchen.

'Rosemary foccacia . . . how delicious,' David said as he took some. 'And I see you use proper sea salt. Very good. Who do you get your balsamic vinegar from?'

'Er, I'm not absolutely sure,' Mitch said, wishing he'd thought to check. It was always the tiny details that mattered most.

David dipped his bread in the oil and vinegar and said, 'My particular favourite is from the Saggio family. They boil the grape juice in an open pot on a fire for well over a day, then age it in their vats. The best has been aged for fifty years. Giuseppe Saggio is only a little older than his choicest vinegar. Such fun, don't you think? I love to go to Italy on my buying tours, sampling the best oils – my favourite thing is tasting the new pressing, so strong and peppery, over hot bruschetta. This one you're serving is very good: dense and fruity. From Ornellaia, isn't it?'

'You know your business, Mr McCorquodale,' Mitch said, smiling, as he followed suit, dipping his foccacia into the balsamic vinegar and oil. 'And you obviously love it as well.'

'Of course. I couldn't devote my life to it if I didn't love it.'

'Let's order. I'm hungry.'

David started with grilled polenta served with mushrooms and thyme, while Mitch had pea and prosciutto soup. Then they each had a small amount of fresh tagliatelle, dressed very simply with truffle oil and well-aged Parmesan.

'Delicious!' pronounced David. 'I really am impressed. Your chef is good. I must think about stealing him for Colette's.'

'Please don't,' Mitch said with a smile.

They talked about food, restaurants and the industry, all very cordial and always avoiding any mention of themselves, over pan-roasted pigeon stuffed with cotechino sausage for David and simple grilled sea bass with fennel for Mitch.

'No, no pudding, thank you. Well, that was an excellent meal,' David said happily as their plates were removed. 'I do feel so *glad* when that happens. It's one of life's ineffable pleasures. I love parties, and I love good food and wine. How lucky that I've been able to turn those things into my living.'

'And still do.'

'Still do.' David sighed slightly. 'Up to a point. I expect you're wondering why I asked to meet you.'

'I *was* a little curious,' Mitch replied. *Now we get to the heart of the matter. I bet you didn't come just to sample my balsamic vinegar* . . . 'I supposed you wanted to tell me to my face what your niece said to me the other night.'

David frowned. 'What? What did she say? Allegra met you?'

'Well, yes. I would have thought you'd know about it.'

'No.' The old man's expression turned icy. 'I didn't.' He clenched his fists and his knuckles turned white. 'It seems I don't know much these days.'

'I offered to buy Colette's and the other clubs,' Mitch said easily, watching the other man's expression with interest. 'But, of course, she turned me down.'

'Did she? On whose authority, I wonder?'

'She was sure it was what you'd want, sir.' Mitch spoke carefully. He wasn't sure where this was going. Why was the old man so angry with his niece?

'So sure she didn't need even to consult me!' David's face had flushed dark pink. He leant towards Mitch, his eyes flashing with anger. '*This* is what I have to put up with! I'm undermined at every step! And those dens of smut she's opening . . .'

Mitch raised his eyebrows, astonished though he didn't show it. He'd assumed that the old man wanted to turn him down to his face. But if what he was saying was true, then this could be just the opportunity he'd been looking for . . . 'I thought Oscar's was a fine and innovative place. Something you could be very proud of.'

'But it's nothing like what I dreamed of! It's full of celebrities, the members are obsessed by the famous, and they're letting in anyone who wants to join! It's not true to my ethos . . . my vision. For me, my clubs are places for friends to gather, to be among like-minded people. Not tacky pick-up joints for actors and actresses, or footballers and pop stars.'

How ironic, Mitch thought. *Allegra's only doing what David himself did all those years ago, when he broke new ground and turned away from the older generation and towards the younger. But he can't see it. He's a fool. She's his only hope.*

'No!' The old man's eyes bulged with fury. 'She's betraying me and destroying my company. I should never have asked her to join me. And here's the thing . . . If this is the way things are going, I would rather no McCorquodale be associated with Colette's ever again! I would rather a complete stranger had it than that one of my family should bastardise it.'

There was a pause while Mitch absorbed the inference behind David's words. Then he said quietly, 'Are you saying you're willing to sell the clubs to me?'

His guest said shortly, 'Perhaps. I'm considering it, let's put it that way. What's your offer?'

Mitch said, 'What's your price?'

'A hundred million. For all three. With Astor House completed.'

Mitch whistled lightly. 'That's quite a price.'

'And there's a condition. You must promise to keep Colette's just as I have made it, and to bring Oscar's and Astor House into line with my vision. Would you do that?'

Mitch fought to control himself. Elation was coursing through him. He wanted to punch the air in triumph. *Yes! I can't believe it! It's fallen into my lap!* His mouth twitched with the effort of keeping a broad smile from appearing. 'Sir, I can assure you that I would maintain everything you created in just the way you'd want it maintained.'

David fixed him with a steely glare. 'I think you would. I

believe I can trust you. Allegra is trying to oust me, to take over my most precious possessions. She must learn that what I have given, I can easily take away.'

'Sir,' Mitch said, a gleam in his eye, 'that is quite a harsh lesson.'

'Well, I haven't made up my mind yet. I'm still thinking about it. Send me whatever you think will convince me.'

The minute David had left, after promises to meet again soon, Mitch was on the phone to his lawyer. 'I need you to draft documentation to buy the David McCorquodale Group. He's asking for a hundred million so I want you to start work right away on due diligence and valuing the assets, OK? I want to know everything about the clubs, right down to the cost of the mustard pots. But I'll tell you this: he could ask two hundred million and get it, if that's what it takes. This is sweet, my man, very, very sweet.'

When he'd finished that call he took his phone outside and made another, where he could be absolutely sure of not being heard.

'Listen, it has to be done as soon as possible. The time is right. Go now. It will never be better than this.'

Chapter 56

The house just off Green Park was lit by thousands of candelabra, which was perhaps a little dangerous considering the amount of silk wafting about, but plenty of staff were on hand to make sure that the flickering candle flames were kept well out of the way of swishing skirts. The party, given by an ambassador to celebrate one of his country's important anniversaries, was in full swing.

It was already late when Romily arrived so there was no one to make a fuss of her, which was exactly how she'd planned it. She checked her reflection in a full-length mirror in the marble hall. This dress was one of her particular favourites of the season. Marchesa always made gowns she loved, and this was no exception: a dream of crimson silk chiffon, halter-necked with a ruffled collar, a plunging V-neck and a waterfall of ruffles running down the front. It floated around her, making her feel feather light as she walked through the black-and-white marble entrance hall, greeting friends and nodding to acquaintances. The party was full of familiar faces – friends from all over Europe – but she didn't want to stop. She knew exactly where she was going.

She walked easily through the large rooms with their polished parquet floors and huge windows. Most of the furniture had been removed, with only spindly gilt chairs lining the walls, so that the rooms were left airy and spacious. Later an orchestra was going to play and there would be dancing, but for now people were still emerging from the dining room.

Romily stopped to talk to her hostess, who was dripping with diamonds and dressed from head to foot in Christian Dior couture, then made her excuses and carried on her walk through the house, the crimson silk floating lightly with every step. Back in the hall she ascended the great curving staircase, greeting people as she went and murmuring, 'Would you excuse me?' as she pressed on, determined.

At last she came to a long, quiet corridor and went quickly along it, counting the doors as she went. When she reached the sixth she stopped, looked briefly back the way she had come, then opened it and stepped inside into the darkness, closing the door behind her.

Blinking, she waited for her eyes to become accustomed to the darkness but even then could make out nothing but shadows and dark shapes. She put her hands out in front of her and took a step forward, and the next moment she gasped in surprise as someone grabbed her wrist. 'Hush, now,' a man's voice whispered close to her ear. 'We don't want anyone to know you're here, do we? It's better not to talk at all.'

Her heart began to race. The man pushed her gently back against the wall and turned her round so that she was facing what she thought must be bookshelves. He came up close behind her, pressing against her without using any force. Then he put his hands around her waist, running them up and over her breasts. After a few moments, he reached down and gathered up her silk skirts, pushing them up around her waist and revealing her bare bottom underneath, which he ran his hand over with a low moan of pleasure. He put his trousered leg between her bare thighs and prised them part.

She tried to control her breathing as he deftly dealt with his fly, and the next moment felt the head of his cock pushing against her, searching for her entrance. She was tight after so long, though she'd been smooth with juices of arousal since the moment she'd entered the room. The tip of his penis rammed against her until she felt herself slide over its head and he was in. With a hard thrust, the man went deep into her, almost lifting her off her feet. He grasped her round the waist and thrust again and then again.

She shuddered and cried out. It was so deep within her, she seemed to feel it in her belly. The man fucking her grunted with excitement, increasing the strong rhythm of his movement. She never wanted it to stop, thrilling to the sensation of him pounding up inside her. She slid a hand down to her mound, pressing down where the delicious tingling was begging her to rub and play with herself. Then, with a muffled shout, the man thrust hard and climaxed. They stood together as they were for a moment, her pussy still gripping his cock, and then he pulled gently free.

'Thank you. That was beautiful,' murmured her lover. She felt her skirts float back down around her legs and the warm trickle of his spending slide down her inner thigh. Then she heard his footsteps, there was a flash of light as the door opened, and the next moment she was alone in the darkness.

The driver opened the door for her and Romily climbed inside. She'd left the party as swiftly as she'd arrived, dying to get home. She was knotted inside with frustration. The experience in the darkened room had been wildly exciting, but it had left her desperate for more, eager to release the spring of lust coiled tightly inside her.

As the driver shut the car door, returned to his place and began to steer the car smoothly towards the west, she rested her head against the cool window pane, wondering how she could dampen down the heat inside her. It was all she could do not to lift her skirts right there on the back seat and bring herself to another shuddering climax.

Rocco, her bodyguard, sat in the front seat beside the driver and she glanced at his broad back, wondering for a moment if she dared ask him to perform quite another kind of service for her. She needed a man, and she needed one soon.

Damn this frustration! It's killing me!

Back at the Notting Hill apartment she went quickly up the steps, Rocco following her as usual while the driver took the car away.

Inside, she brushed away enquiries from the housekeeper as to whether she needed anything. 'No, no, I'm fine. I need to be alone.' She hurried to her bedroom and from there to her bathroom, turning on the bath taps and letting the hot water gush out at full speed. She added a splash of costly bath oil and then got out of her dress, abandoning thousands of pounds worth of silk chiffon in a heap on the floor.

She unclipped her bra and tossed it on to the bed, then stood in front of her full-length chiffonier glass wearing only her silver high-heeled Jimmy Choo sandals, staring at her naked body. She ran her hand over her small, dark-rose-nippled breasts and then down to the strip of brown fur between her legs. She ran her fingers through its softness for a moment or two, then shivered and sighed, wishing she had the man from the party here with her now.

Not much longer, she reminded herself. Things were going well – damn it, they were going brilliantly! Everything was in place. Her business today had gone exactly as she'd hoped . . .

She went through to the bathroom. Perhaps a hot bath would help to douse her lust.

When she emerged an hour later, wrapped in a fluffy towel, she felt better: the fire had burned down to a kind of languour. She rubbed at her damp hair and wondered if she felt like something to eat.

Just then there was a knock at the door. She opened it to see her housekeeper outside, holding a large brown envelope.

'Yes?' Romily said.

'This was just delivered for you, madam.' The housekeeper held out the envelope, looking worried. 'The courier said I was to hand it to you without delay.'

Romily took it. 'Thank you. Oh, and could you send supper to my room, please? Something light.'

'Yes, madam.'

Romily took the envelope over to her bed and sat down. She opened it and pulled out a clear case full of photographs, large black and white prints like something taken for a newspaper. The first showed her walking through Heathrow as she had done only recently, dark glasses on, her luggage being pushed on a trolley beside her, Rocco at her side.

The next showed her getting into her car at the airport. She flicked faster and faster. Each photograph showed her in the recent past: coming and going from the apartment, entering shops, getting into the car or out of it. The last thing in the file was a piece of paper with printed letters in a large font that read: YOU ARE BEING WATCHED. BEWARE.

Romily felt herself turn cold all over, the warmth of the bath quite gone. *Oh, God,* she thought. *What the hell is this?*

Ten minutes later she came out of her room, dressed in jeans, a white shirt and navy cashmere jumper, and a pair of

Prada patent boots. With her, she had a small overnight bag and a briefcase. She had packed as quickly as possible; she had to get away, then she would make contact. As she dashed out, she almost collided with her housekeeper who was carrying a tray with a dish of smoked haddock and poached egg arranged on it.

'Madam!' gasped the housekeeper, keeping her balance with difficulty. 'What is it?'

'Get my guard for me,' Romily ordered abruptly. 'Tell him to be up and ready to leave immediately. And call the car.'

'Your supper . . .?'

'Don't worry about that now. Just do as I say.'

She went into the sitting room and over to the sash window. She looked down at the Notting Hill street, quiet in this area at this time of night, only the odd figure passing by, illuminated by the nearest streetlight. *Is he out there right now, with his camera trained on my house? What the hell does he want with me, whoever he is?*

A moment later Rocco came bursting into the room, pulling on a sweater over his T-shirt. 'What is it, madam? You want to leave?'

'Yes, Rocco. Look at these.' She pulled the photographs out of her bag and thrust them at him. 'I'm being watched. Stalked.'

He flicked through them quickly, taking in every detail. 'Yes,' he said roughly. 'Your every move for the last week is here. They must be expert at remaining hidden.'

'We're leaving right away.'

The guard frowned. 'Where are we going?'

'Somewhere safe. I can't stay here, you must see that. We've got to get away as soon as we can. I know where we can go.'

'But where?'

'I don't want to say,' Romily said quietly. 'But we'll be welcome there.'

The bodyguard looked agitated. 'For your own safety, you must keep me informed, *signora*. I can't do my job if you don't.'

'Just get your things – and don't forget your passport. We'll be safe soon enough.'

Rocco went out as ordered, as the housekeeper came back in. 'I've summoned the driver,' she said. 'He's bringing the car round now.'

'Good.' Romily went back to her vigil at the window.

Moments later she was climbing into the car, Rocco on high alert, his hand hovering near the gun in his armpit, his gaze flicking about, looking for trouble.

'We're going to Chelsea,' she instructed the driver. 'I'll tell you exactly where when we're closer.' Once she was in and the car was pulling away, she sighed with relief. Taking out her phone she tapped out a text: *I'm on my way to see you. Will explain when I arrive.* Then she leant back and watched the night-time city glide past the window.

Romily didn't know London well but she knew enough to be sure that they weren't heading for Chelsea as she'd instructed. From Notting Hill it was a quick journey down towards High Street Kensington and from there into the heart of Chelsea. Twenty minutes, perhaps, if the traffic was average. A little more if they were unlucky and caught all the red lights. But before long, she was sure that they'd veered off somehow and the next minute they were crossing one of the bridges and heading south.

She pressed the button that allowed her to communicate with the driver. 'Where are we going? This isn't Chelsea. We've crossed the river.'

Rocco's voice came back. 'I think we're being followed, *signora*. Trust me, we're taking a long route to lose them.'

She looked out of the back window: some cars and

motorbikes were behind them but she couldn't see anyone specifically tailing them. *That's because I'm not SAS-trained, I suppose, and Rocco is.* But as they went ever further south without turning back for Chelsea, she became anxious.

'I want to go back,' she commanded. 'I don't care if we are being followed. They'll give up when they realise where we're going.'

'Very well,' Rocco said in reply. 'We'll turn around now.'

The car pulled smoothly to a halt at the side of the road and he got out. Romily turned to watch him, wondering what he was doing. He opened her door and climbed quickly in next to her. Just as she was opening her mouth to speak, he pulled a cloth out his pocket and pressed it over her face in one rapid movement. She tried to scream and struggle but it was impossible to make a sound with his hand pushing her face into the suffocating cloth. She couldn't help it: she had to take a breath. Then another. As soon as she did, she felt herself begin to float away. She felt her eyes rolling back and, even though she fought it, unconsciousness possessed her.

Chapter 57

Driving back to London along the M3, Allegra felt happy with progress at Astor House.

Fuck it, I'm more than happy. I'm totally bloody ecstatic! It's slow but it's just right. There's no point in hurrying and getting it wrong. We're still on course to open next Easter, when the countryside will look fantastic.

She and Adam had spent a happy two days at the site. The house was now completely gutted, stripped back to bare brick in places, and they were conserving and repairing the original features, including intricate plasterwork.

'I never realised there was so much to know about bloody plaster,' Allegra had said, her yellow hard hat on. 'But this place has it all: egg and dart cornicing with columns, fluted this, drop-swagged that, and don't get me started on ceiling roses, corbels and panel mouldings.'

'The perils of Grade One listing.' Adam smiled at her.

'The bloody *price* of Grade One listing,' she grumbled, pushing her hands in the pockets of her protective overcoat. 'English Heritage seem to think we're made of money and have nothing better to do than source original roof tiles of the precise size, age and colour of the ones on the roof already.'

'David would approve.'

'Oh my God, he would!' Allegra laughed. 'He's such a perfectionist, he'd get on really well with the Heritage guy.

But he's going to be *so* excited when he sees this place. When it's nearly finished, I'm looking forward to going on a fantastic shopping trip with him, sourcing some magnificent Regency antiques for the hotel.'

Adam looked round. 'I can see it now. It's going to be an amazing blend of old and new: the speed and convenience of modern life, and the comfort and luxury of days gone by.'

'Exactly.' Allegra nodded. 'And service . . . that's the key. Such wonderful, personal service you'll feel utterly cosseted and cared for. Along with the finest of everything, from the bed linen to the water glasses. Come on, let's go and look at the spa.'

They went out to the old coach house that was being converted into the health and beauty area.

'Did I tell you I've decided to franchise this out?' she said. 'My cousin Jemima runs a perfume house with her sisters and they've recently developed a range of fantastic spa and beauty treatments. In fact, she's opened a very successful spa at her own house in Dorset. I went to see it recently. Jemima says she'd love to take over here, stock it with Trevellyan products and offer their treatments.'

'It's not like you to hand over control to someone else,' remarked Adam, studying the old building with its sagging beams and dirty floor.

'I trust her and her brand,' Allegra said with a smile. 'It fits with the McCorquodale ethos of quality and luxury, the best of the best.'

'I'd like to meet her.'

'I'm sure you will. Now, let's visit the vegetable garden. It's going to supply the hotel and maybe even the London clubs if I can get enough production going here. Come on.'

She was pleased that Adam seemed so impressed with the progress so far. It was important that he respected her business ability as well as her body – though she didn't mind him showing his appreciation of that as well . . . She'd left him on-site to oversee some work and liaise with the site manager while she headed back to London. As she was driving back in on the M3, her phone went. She switched on her hands-free.

'It's your uncle,' Tyra said when she'd answered the call. 'He's asked if you can go straight round to see him at home.'

'Did he say why?'

'No. Just that he'd like you to get there as soon as you can.'

'OK. Can you ring him and tell him I'm just approaching Richmond? I'll be there in about forty-five minutes.'

'Will do,' Tyra said, and rang off.

Odd, thought Allegra as she drove on. *I wonder why he didn't call me himself.*

The traffic wasn't too heavy. Within thirty-five minutes she was heading up Kensington High Street towards Knightsbridge. She parked outside David's house and ran up the steps to the front door. His housekeeper answered and showed her in to the drawing room.

She wandered about, looking at David's pictures. She never grew tired of the many and varied paintings he had hung close together all over the walls. Her favourite was a portrait of an aristocratic young man with a lazy yet wicked glint in his eye.

There was a sound behind her. She turned to see her uncle coming in through the door, his face serious, a pile of papers clamped under his arm.

'Hello, David,' she said cheerfully. 'How are you?'

'I'm well, very well. Sit down, Allegra, please.'

She sat down, telling him about her latest trip to Astor House while he settled himself opposite, spreading out some of the papers he'd been carrying on the low table. He seemed to be listening with only half an ear, grunting a response from time to time.

'Now,' he said suddenly, cutting her off, 'I went round to the office today and collected the details of last night's takings. And the night before's. In fact, I got the whole week's worth.'

'Yes?' Allegra sat forward to see what was on the papers, but he snatched them away from her.

'I'm very concerned,' he said, fixing her with a cold gaze.

'Why? Is something wrong?'

'Yes, I believe it is. I believe there are significant sums missing. There seems to be a shortfall amounting to almost two hundred thousand pounds.'

'What?' cried Allegra, dismayed. 'Where? How?'

'That's what I'm hoping you can tell me.'

'Well, I've no idea.' She was baffled. She kept a tight rein on the accounts. There was no way such a large amount could vanish without her noticing. 'I'm sure I would have noticed a sum like that disappearing. After all, it's almost a quarter of our profits on sales for last year.'

'I've asked my own man to look into it. I also want some explanation of the spending on Astor House. It's astronomical.' He gave her a cold look. 'Don't you understand the climate we're all working in?'

'Of course I do, but we both agreed we couldn't stop trying to expand just because times are hard. We need to make sure we're prepared for a better future. We agreed that.' She was bewildered by his hostility. Why was he being like this? She'd always been careful to get his agreement to anything she did.

'Still doesn't explain *this*,' David said, gesturing to the papers. 'Where is this missing money?'

'I've truly no idea. I keep a firm grip on the accounts but I'll need to go back to the accountant and go through everything with him . . .'

'Was it for your car?' her uncle asked abruptly. 'You've

been driving something fancy lately. Did you decide to give yourself a little cash advance to go and get it?'

Allegra was astonished. 'My car? It's about five years old. You've seen me driving in it for ages.'

'No, I haven't,' he snapped. 'I've never seen it before.'

She stared at him, appalled. How could he say that? He'd seen it, and often. Was he pretending or could he honestly not remember? *Is he trying to accuse me of stealing? That's ridiculous, David could never think that. It must be some kind of misunderstanding, surely* . . . But her spirits sank as she realised that this was just the latest manifestation of his odd behaviour and memory lapses. She said gently, 'David, are you all right? You haven't been yourself lately. Do you think you should see a doctor?'

'Why do you say that?' he said in an ominously quiet voice.

'Because you really haven't been yourself for ages. I noticed it a while ago. You've been acting oddly, making mistakes, forgetting things. Tyra's noticed it too. It's not like you, it really isn't. I wish you'd see somebody about it, get yourself thoroughly checked out.'

'Oh, you'd like me to see doctors, would you? Kindly friends of yours who'll certify me as not of sound mind?' He suddenly swept all the papers off the table and on to the floor, roaring, 'I see your game and it's bloody filthy!' Then he leapt to his feet and went to the door. 'Rosa!' he called, as he opened it. 'Send them in here.'

Allegra stood up, confused. 'Do you already have a doctor?' she asked.

'Oh, no, my dear, I do not.' He stood back and the next moment a troop of men in sober suits came into the room carrying briefcases. David went to his desk by the window and sat on the leather-seated chair. 'Gentlemen, I am ready to sign.'

'Sign what?' Anxiety was making Allegra's skin prickle. 'What are you going to sign, David?'

'These gentlemen are lawyers,' he said, almost kindly. 'Mine are from Baxter and Harvill, the family's legal advisors. And the others are from some whizz-bang City outfit. Their client has already signed the contract.'

The lawyers opened their cases and began to bring out documents. One of the men laid a thick pile of papers, stapled in the left-hand corner, in front of David and offered him a pen.

'Thank you, I prefer to use my Cartier,' he said, flicking through the document.

'David, what are you going to sign?' Allegra repeated, trying to get near him so she could read the print, but the lawyers seemed to be blocking her, trying to keep her away.

'I'm going to sell the David McCorquodale Group, of course. I've been offered a price that's more than fair. And do you know what? It's time I had a rest. I've been slaving away at Colette's for almost half a century and I fancy a cruise. I think a hundred million pounds should buy me rather a nice one.'

'David, no!' Allegra shrieked. She reached out her hand towards him. With a few strokes of his pen, he was going to bring down everything they'd worked so hard for. Oscar's, Astor House – in just a second it would all be gone, along with her beloved Colette's. 'It's Mitchell, isn't it? He's got to you! He's persuaded you to sell to him . . . Why, David, why?'

Her uncle's face contorted as though some malevolent spirit had possessed him. 'Because you *know* what you are!' he hissed. 'You stole my money! And you're wrong. I'm not selling to Mitchell. I'm selling to Romily de Lisle.'

Allegra paled. All the strength seemed to leave her. 'What?' she whispered. She could hardly take it in. Romily?

But how? Through blurred vision she could see David poise his pen above the contract. 'No.' Her voice came out hoarse, barely audible. 'Please, I'm begging you . . .'

'Beg all you like,' he said tartly. And signed his name with a flourish.

Chapter 58

Romily woke up with a thudding headache and a dry mouth. She tried to lick her lips and realised that she couldn't because a thick gag was wrapped tightly around her mouth. Trying to move, she discovered that her hands were bound together, as were her feet. She was lying on a filthy sofa in a large room that looked as though it might be in a warehouse: at least, there were rows of industrial-style windows running along the highest point of the walls, where no ordinary house would have windows. It was daylight outside, but the grey patch of sky visible gave no indication what time it was.

What happened? she thought blearily. *Where am I?*

Then she was drenched in cold horror as she recalled the previous evening. *I've been kidnapped!*

All her life she'd been aware of the threats that surrounded her and the entire family: kidnap, extortion, murder. She'd heard the story of the little Lindbergh baby, kidnapped, killed and buried before his parents could pay a ransom; she'd read about Patty Hearst, abducted for her family's wealth and turned into a gun-toting criminal; and she knew of the Getty boy who'd had his ear cut off by his captors. She'd always been promised that this would never happen to her – it was one of the reasons she'd accepted the restriction of having bodyguards and security all her life. Everyone knew the de Lisles were worth billions. Romily and her brother had grown up two of the most closely guarded children in Europe.

But it had all been for nothing.

She was cold and stiff. She tried to stretch out but it was difficult without the use of her hands to push herself out of the well of badly sprung seat cushions.

Oh, God, what's going to happen to me?

She felt herself tremble on the brink of hysteria. If she were able to open her mouth, she feared she'd start screaming and not be able to stop. She began to breathe fast, sucking in air through the gag and her nose, on the point of hyperventilating with panic.

No, stay calm, she told herself. She forced herself to breathe slowly through her nose, pulling as much air as she could into her lungs and holding it in a few seconds before exhaling. It helped. *My only hope is to stay completely aware of everything that's happening. Now – what can I see exactly?*

She turned her head and strained to observe everything she could. A pair of wide double doors were tightly shut but she could see a bar of light coming from underneath. If her kidnappers were still around, they must be through there. She was sure she was alone in this big, chilly room. Thank God she'd put on her cashmere jumper before she'd left. Imagine if she were still in her red dress . . .

She tried to think back over the evening's events. *It was Rocco,* she thought dully. *He stifled me with that handkerchief. He must be in on this plot somehow.*

Remembering the packet of photographs that had arrived that evening, she recalled his agitation. *He didn't know someone else had me in their sights. He must have guessed I was changing my plans unexpectedly, going somewhere that meant he wouldn't be able to do whatever it was he had planned. So he's brought everything forward.*

That, she realised with a cold thud in her stomach, could

prove dangerous for her. A kidnap planned and executed on the hoof would mean edgy, panicky captors. She would have to be careful not to shock or frighten them.

Whatever happens, keep calm, be friendly, remind them you're a human being. Then . . . perhaps they won't kill you.

Allegra pulled to a halt in front of Adam's mansion block. She was damn' lucky she hadn't been stopped by the police on her careering journey across town from Knightsbridge to North London, her vision sometimes blinded by tears, but she'd wiped them away angrily and carried on.

Only Adam would understand. Only he knew what it had been like over the last year or so. And to have it all taken away like this!

Why? Why did you do it, David?

She jumped out of the car and buzzed Adam's apartment. There was no answer. She'd thought that he was heading back here this evening. She pulled out her telephone and rang him, but it went straight through to his voicemail. *Where are you?*

She stood forlornly on the doorstep, wondering what to do next, then the door unexpectedly opened and one of the inhabitants of the building came out. As the woman left Allegra stepped behind her and stopped the front door from closing. She slipped in and hurried up the stairs to Adam's flat. Outside his flat was a fire extinguisher cupboard and she knew he kept a spare key stuck to the underside of the cupboard top, out of sight.

I'll go in and wait for him. He'll be back soon.

She found the key easily enough, opened the door and went inside. She'd spent many nights in the flat since she and Adam had been together, but had never been here on her own. It was clean, modern and decorated in a plain style, monochrome with the odd flash of colour. Adam liked his gadgets all right – he had a huge plasma screen HD television with cinema-quality sound and plenty of other toys to amuse himself.

What am I going to do? He'll be devastated, she thought, wandering desolately through the flat. *All our work together . . . how am I going to tell him?*

She went into his bedroom. She wanted to lie down on the bed, curl up and go to sleep. Perhaps when she woke up, all this would be just a nasty dream and everything would have gone back to the way it was before.

She shivered, feeling cold. The heating hadn't come on in the flat and the evening chill was beginning to permeate it. *I'll wear one of Adam's jumpers.*

She went over to the long line of built-in wardrobes where he stored all his clothes and opened it. The wardrobe ran the length of the room and inside was divided up into more cupboards, shelves and drawers. Pulling out some of the drawers, she looked for something suitable. Everything was neatly folded and arranged in colour-coded stacks. She found a grey V-neck lambswool jumper, took it out and slipped it over her silk blouse. It warmed her immediately. Being among Adam's clothes gave her some comfort, and the neatness of the cupboards and drawers made her smile: it was so like Adam. He liked everything nice and neat. She pulled open another cupboard and stood there, blinking in confusion.

Unlike the other parts of the wardrobe this cupboard was a mess, or at least a muddle of things. No clothes hung from the rail, but some necklaces and rosaries did. On the back wall of the cupboard pictures and newspaper articles were stuck all over, some annotated and highlighted. On the shelf above the drawers were a large framed photograph, some trinkets, and two candles in silver sticks, half burned down, their wicks black and curled.

She frowned and shook her head, unable to take in what

she was seeing. Everything looked so familiar and yet so odd. The framed photograph was a face she knew almost as well as her own, even though she hadn't seen it for years – at least, not in reality. She'd seen it in her dreams many times but not alive since that dreadful night ten years ago at Westfield Boarding School for Girls.

It was Sophie Harcourt.

Chapter 59

Imogen stood in the kitchen, watching Alex as he lay on his back on the rug, kicking hard, and listening to the ringing tone. After a minute or so Tyra picked up.

'Allegra McCorquodale's office.'

'Tyra, it's Imogen. Wasn't Allegra due back from Astor House this afternoon? She said she was coming straight home but she hasn't turned up and her mobile's off.'

'Yes,' Tyra said, 'but she's going directly to David's house. He wants to see her about something. I should think she's nearly finished, that was a while ago now.'

'OK. Well, if she calls, tell her to let me know when she's going to be back, will you?'

'Sure.'

When Imogen hung up, she looked at the clock again. It was getting on for five o'clock and Allegra liked to be back for Alex's bedtime as often as she could. It was strange not to hear from her . . . She went over to the rug and picked him up, dropping a kiss on his satin-smooth cheek. He gurgled at her.

'That's my favourite noise in the whole world,' she said, smiling at him, and he grinned gummily back, kicking even harder.

The doorbell buzzed. She put Alex down on the rug and went over to the intercom. 'Yes?'

'Delivery for Allegra McCorquodale.'

'Okay, I'll come and get it.' She went up the stairs to the hallway and along to the front door open it. Then, in a flurry of bewildering movement, she was being pushed backwards. A huge man was grabbing her arms, forcing them behind her back and wrestling her against the staircase. He was hissing in her ear, 'Where the *fuck* is she? What have you done with her?'

Imogen couldn't speak, almost blinded by shock. Panic rushed through her. All she could think was, *My baby! My baby's downstairs. Don't hurt me!*

'Come on, tell me! What have you bitches done to her?'

She realised that the man holding her down had a strong American accent. His face, red with rage, was inches from hers, and she could feel his spittle as he ground out his words. She managed to pull herself together enough to stammer out, 'I don't know what you're talking about!'

'Don't fuck with me!' yelled the man. He grabbed her shirt and shook her like a rag doll. 'I wanna know where she is and you're going to tell me, or you'll be so fucking sorry you won't know if you'll ever make it better.'

'I don't know what you're talking about!' she shrieked again. 'Are you robbing me? Do you want money? My purse is over there!'

'I don't want money.' He pulled back, looking at her contemptuously. For the first time she got a look at his face and gasped, unable to believe it. 'Listen,' he went on, 'you oughta know that I have extremely good connections. If you don't give her back to me, you are going to regret it.'

'Mitch . . . is that you?'

He stared at her, his eyes hard. 'Yeah, it's me.'

'But Mitch . . . it's me, Imogen! Romily's friend. I was at your wedding.'

'Yeah, I know.' He curled his lip scornfully. 'I know who you are. I know pretty much everything except why you are dumb enough to take me on.' He took his hands off her and ran one through his hair, looking exhausted. 'Fuck! This is crazy.'

Imogen tried to keep her shock and fear under control. *Surely Mitch won't hurt me.* She had to understand what was going on so said, calmly and clearly, 'Mitch, you've got to believe me, I don't know what you're talking about. Who do you think I've got?'

'Romily, of course,' he growled. 'I guess you two have found a way to get back at me.'

Imogen's mouth fell open and she shook her head slowly. When she found her voice, she said, 'Romily? Why would we do anything to Romily?'

'To hurt me, of course! Allegra must know by now that her uncle has sold the business to us and she's hit back, very quickly and very cleverly. I don't know how she did it, I'll give her that. It must be that freaky boyfriend of hers.'

'David's sold the business?' Imogen couldn't take it all in.

Mitch nodded. 'If everything went according to plan, it went under the hammer this afternoon. I've been up all night and most of the morning, locked in talks with the lawyers, thrashing out the final contract. Our drafts were signed yesterday. I expected David McCorquodale to sign his this afternoon. I'm just waiting for the call.'

Imogen put her hands to her mouth in horror. 'Oh, no . . . no . . . poor Allegra!'

'She doesn't know?'

Imogen shook her head, numb with shock. 'I don't think so. She went to see David this afternoon but she hasn't called and I'm sure she'd tell me first, as soon as she knew. Oh my God, I can't believe it! Why would David do it? She's done everything for him!'

'Fuck that. I need to know where Romily is.'

'But why would *we* know?' Imogen closed her eyes, trying

to understand everything. 'I know she's in London, I saw her in a car just a few days ago. I've been wondering about trying to contact her, but we parted in such an awful way . . .'

Mitch seemed to fill up with anger again. 'Don't play the innocent with me!' he roared. 'It has to be you two . . . it must be! You've got the motive and you've got the money. I don't know how you've done it but I want her back, *now*! Understand?'

'But . . . but . . .' Imogen shook her head in confusion. 'You two are divorced. You broke up. That was the whole reason Romily decided she hated Allegra.'

'Yeah. Sure it was,' Mitch said softly. He took a deep breath and shut his eyes. He appeared to be thinking hard for a moment then opened his eyes again and fixed her with a steely gaze. 'We didn't break up. We may be divorced but we're still together. We only split for a couple of weeks but officially we've stayed apart ever since because it was the best way to get what we wanted.'

Imogen stared back. 'What you wanted? Colette's? The clubs?'

Mitch nodded. 'I was always going to build my restaurant empire, and it was kind of convenient that we could, in the process, take Allegra's away.'

'So your reason for buying Colette's is to punish Allegra for what she did?'

'If you want to put it that way.' He shrugged. 'It was kinda useful that she turned out to be so good at building up nice little businesses as well. But I can't pretend it isn't sweet to take everything away from her. That's what we wanted most.'

'And you're using Romily's money to do it?'

'My money, Romily's money – it's more or less one and the same thing. I bankrolled my first purchase thanks to the money her daddy paid me to get lost. After that, Romily was my partner and, I have to admit, her ready cash made it easier to go shopping for more but my business interests have been extremely lucrative.'

'I just can't believe it,' Imogen said softly. 'All this . . . this huge vendetta . . . over a simple misunderstanding?'

'Allegra turned on Romily,' Mitch said gruffly. 'Sold her out and tried to ruin her life. Where's the misunderstanding?'

'I don't know,' Imogen said helplessly. 'But I know it's there somewhere.'

'Look, I haven't got time to waste. So you don't know where Romily is – let's say I believe you – but that still doesn't rule out Allegra. Where is she?'

'The last I heard she was going to David's . . . but there's been no word from her.' Imogen glanced anxiously towards the kitchen. 'I must go back to Alex.'

Mitch's phone beeped and he answered it as he followed her downstairs. Alex was still happily kicking on the rug, murmuring to himself, and Imogen rushed over to him as Mitch talked curtly, listening for most of the time.

He finished his call and looked at her. 'OK. Allegra was there when David signed the papers. She was cut up and left soon afterwards. About an hour ago. You oughta hear from her soon, I'd say.' His phone beeped again and he consulted it, reading an email. 'My people are on the case, searching for Romily. Goddamnit!' He clenched his fists with frustration. 'She was on her way to me. If I'd been at home . . . if I hadn't been called out to the lawyers for the whole goddamned night . . . she's been gone for hours and I've only just found out. And if it's not you and Allegra playing stupid games, then it's something much, much worse.' He stared at her and she could see fear in his eyes.

Imogen stood up, Alex in her arms, and took a deep breath. 'I want to help you find her, Mitch, you must believe me. But Allegra and I don't have her, I can promise you that.

For one thing, Allegra has barely mentioned Romily's name to me in years. She doesn't have any idea you are the man who was once married to Rom, I'm absolutely certain of it. I had no inkling myself that you're Ted Mitchell. I'm going to find Allegra to make sure. Besides, I have to know how she is now the clubs are gone.'

'Imogen!' He grasped her hand, his voice agonised, his face fearful. 'Do you think we're going to find Rom? What if she's . . . if they've done something to her!'

'Wait. I know what we can do.' She went to her handbag and found her battered old address book. She leafed through it with one hand, looking for a number. 'Here it is.' She picked up the phone and dialled as Mitch hovered anxiously nearby.

The phone was scooped up on the first ring with an anxious, '*Oui*?'

'Madame de Lisle? It's Imogen Heath here. Romily's friend from school.'

There was a pause and then Athina de Lisle said in a strangled voice, 'Romily isn't here at the moment, my dear. I'm so sorry. Goodbye.'

'Wait, wait!' cried Imogen. 'Don't hang up. It's important! I think something's happened to her.'

There was a pause and then the other woman whispered, 'What do you know about that? They said no one else knows!'

'So it's true . . . she's been kidnapped?'

'How do you know this?' Athina de Lisle's voice rose to a shriek. 'How do you know? They will kill her, they will kill her . . .'

The phone was snatched away abruptly and another voice said, 'Who is this? What do you know about Romily?'

'Monsieur de Lisle? This is Imogen Heath, Romily's schoolfriend. I believe she's missing. I was expecting to see her this morning but she hasn't arrived, no one at her house knows where she is and her phone's not being answered. Is everything all right?'

'We cannot speak about this. We must remain absolutely silent. Any hint that the police are involved and . . .' He broke off with a gulp.

'You have my word, monsieur, I won't go to the police. But it's possible that I can help you. After all, I'm on the spot here in London and I have connections.' She glanced over at Mitch who stood watching her, his jaw set with worry. He nodded emphatically. 'Just tell me everything you know.'

Monsieur de Lisle appeared to think for a moment and then said, 'I don't know whether I can trust you. I don't know on whose behalf you are calling or working. You say you're Romily's friend but I have only your word for that.'

'I understand. Please, just tell me one thing then. I believe she has been kidnapped. Is that true? If I'm somehow in league with her enemies, it won't hurt to tell me what I already know. But I'm not, I swear to you. I'm one of her oldest friends and I'm desperate with worry.'

There was another pause before Monsieur de Lisle said in a low voice, 'Yes. She has been taken. And the ransom is twenty million dollars.'

Chapter 60

Romily was on her own for at least two hours after she woke before anyone came in, though it was hard to tell exactly without being able to look at her watch.

She was wondering if she would simply be left there to die when one of the double doors behind her opened and someone came towards her, approaching carefully so that they couldn't be seen. The sound of footsteps coming across the concrete floor towards her was so chilling that she began to tremble. A moment later, something dark descended on her eyes and then she was being pulled up and round to a sitting position. The dark thing round her eyes was tightened at the back of her head into a blindfold, then she was ungagged. A glass of water was held to her lips and she gulped at it gratefully, desperate for liquid in her dry mouth.

'Come on,' a voice said in accented English, and she was pulled to her feet and made to walk. It was horribly disorienting, walking blind, being pushed from behind with no sense of where she was or where she was going.

A moment later, she was thrust into a tiny space as the blindfold was removed. She blinked, confused, and then realised she was in a lavatory. She'd been given a loo break.

'Two minutes!' snarled the voice.

She was sure it was less than that when the door was pulled open and she was jerked out by the arm, the blindfold wrapped around her head again before she had the chance to see anything bar a blur of grey-white walls and dirty floors.

'Back!'

She was marched again across the concrete floor and pushed back down on to the sofa. She felt the person near her preparing to leave. 'Can I have something to eat?' she asked, panicked that she was going to be left alone for hours.

There was no reply and a moment later the footsteps left the room.

She curled up on herself again. *What are they going to do to me?*

She longed to sleep but was too alert, despite her fatigue. Any sound sent her senses spinning and her brain working furiously to decode it. The possibilities for her immediate future whirled around in her head: *They'll kill me. The police are coming. They'll dump me on the side of the road somewhere. Where's the money? Will my parents pay the ransom?*

She couldn't imagine that they wouldn't. They'd do all in their power to save her life, she was utterly convinced of it. But would they know what to do? Her ignorance of her own situation was frustrating and exhausting.

The door of the room she was in opened again and she heard footsteps approaching. They were very quiet but she could tell they were those of someone she had not yet been in contact with. They seemed heavy and graceless. They also seemed oddly familiar.

The person approached her slowly and stopped when they were standing beside the sofa. She could feel warmth coming off a body, hear breathing and smell the tang of an aftershave she knew.

'*Signora*?' whispered a voice. 'Are you OK?'

She drew in her breath sharply. 'Carlo? Carlo, is that you? What are you doing here?'

'I'm here to help you,' he said in a low voice.

Her heart started racing. 'How did you find me? How did you know I was here? It's Rocco . . . he's taken me. Wants money for me, I heard him say so. Quick, we must get away as soon as possible!' Hot relief ran through her. 'Carlo, I'm so happy you're here . . .'

'You, *signora*, are a fucking idiot,' he said in a rasping voice, and then laughed nastily.

Her head whirled as she realised he'd been taunting her. He was one of them.

'Here.' He pushed a dry sandwich into her hand. 'You think I'd be here if I wasn't involved? That I'd just walk in and rescue you?'

Her stomach spun with sick fear. 'Carlo,' she whispered. 'How can you do this? I was always good to you, wasn't I?'

'Here, eat your food,' he said scornfully. 'I hate wasting it on a piece of shit like you, but I need you alive.'

'Why do you hate me?' she asked through dry lips.

'I hate everything about you, and your family, and its stinking privilege. I'm engaged in a little bit of wealth redistribution, that's all. And if you think I like you, you are very wrong, understand? Now shut the fuck up, or it will be my pleasure to beat some respect into you.'

His footsteps marched away over the echoing concrete, leaving Romily cowering on the sofa, the sandwich forgotten in her shaking hand.

Chapter 61

Allegra's phone chirruped with news of an incoming text. She jumped violently and pulled it out of her bag with clumsy hands. She clicked on it. It was from Adam.

I'm coming. Stay where you are.

'Oh shit,' she breathed. 'Oh, holy fuck. I told him where I am! He must be worried that I'll find this.' She put one trembling hand to her forehead. *What am I going to do? What does all this mean?*

She'd been staring for what felt like hours at the bizarre shrine. The cut-out newspaper reports of Sophie Harcourt's death were illustrated with views of Westfield School, snatched shots of girls sobbing and hugging in the forecourt, photos of the Headmistress looking solemn and capable. The headlines still screamed out, after all this time:

GIRL AT £10K PER YEAR PRIVATE SCHOOL IN DEATH PLUNGE

SUICIDE AT TOP GIRLS' PUBLIC SCHOOL

MYSTERIOUS DEATH OF PUPIL

Words and lines had been highlighted in the reports: 'she was not considered suicidal by pupils and teachers'; 'instances of bullying had been reported, according to sources at the school'; 'no one knows who was the last person to see Sophie Harcourt alive'.

Other newspaper cuttings reported the inquest and

funeral. One showed the grieving family standing behind the coffin. The young lad with his hands clenched together before his sober black suit, his head bowed and his brow furrowed with sorrow, was, according to the caption, Adam Harcourt, the girl's brother.

'Adam, no!' she whispered as she realised what it meant. 'Why didn't you tell me?'

Sophie's face gazed out at her from the silver frame, smiling, her hair neat and tidy, her school tie perfectly straight, ever and always fifteen years old and full of promise. Allegra could hardly bear to meet the candid stare of the girl in the picture, now just dust. It reminded her of the nightmares that still haunted her.

The other cuttings were all about Allegra herself. She'd often featured on society pages, photographed at parties or openings or launches. Her appointment to Colette's had also been extensively covered in the press. There was a collage of her press appearances on one wall of the cupboard. The most recent cutting was from the *Daily Telegraph* birth announcements. It read:

McCORQUODALE: To the late The Hon. Alexander McCorquodale and Imogen Heath, a son, Alexander Ivo Dunstan McCorquodale.

She felt a shiver of fear. Why was Adam interested in Alex? 'Oh my God,' she whispered. 'What does it all mean?'

His text galvanised her into action. She'd been in a state of near paralysis since she'd opened that cupboard. Now she began to move, frantically. She flew through the flat, picking up her things as she went, then slammed the front door behind her. As soon as it was shut, she remembered with horror that she'd left the cupboard door open, revealing the shrine within, and that the spare key must still be on the coffee table where she'd left it.

Too late now. She had to get away. She needed to get home, to think. *Adam was Sophie Harcourt's brother!* The man she'd fallen in love with, the man who'd banished the terrible voice, the man who'd been her rock since Xander's death . . . *Sophie Harcourt's brother.*

Why does he have those cuttings? Does he want to hurt me?

In the car, she pulled away at speed while dialling her mobile with the other hand. She pushed it into the hands-free cradle and activated the speaker as she turned the car towards central London.

Imogen picked up within a few seconds. 'Allegra, thank God!'

'Midge, where are you? Where's Alex?' she shouted.

'I'm at home. Alex is asleep. Where are you? You've been gone for hours!'

'Get Alex and get out of the house, right now! I'll meet you out the front.'

'Alex? What are you talking about? He's fine. He's fast asleep.'

'I'm serious!' Allegra yelled. 'Pack his things. I'm coming to get you. Be ready for me.' She pressed End and cut the call before Imogen could ask anything else.

When her Jaguar screeched to a halt in front of the Regent's Park house, Imogen was ready for her. It was dark. In other circumstances, Allegra would have wanted nothing more than to go inside the cosy house, have some dinner and chat with Imogen about the business of the day. But today was far from normal. Today was the day she'd lost everything she'd worked so hard for. Today was the day she'd discovered that she knew nothing about her boyfriend except that he must believe she'd had something to do with his sister's death . . . Her only thought was to get herself, Imogen and Alex somewhere safe, somewhere Adam couldn't find them. She needed to think everything through, understand it . . .

She jumped out of the car as Imogen came down the front steps with Alex slumbering in his car seat, warmly tucked in, oblivious of all the fuss.

'I'll put him in. You put the bags in the boot.' Allegra wedged the seat into the back and began to thread the seatbelt through it as Imogen stowed the large amount of luggage that Alex needed, no matter how short the journey.

When they were all safely in the car, she turned to Allegra and said breathlessly, 'What's all this about?'

'I'll tell you when we get there,' she said grimly, and the car pulled away from the kerb with a squeal of tyres on asphalt.

The Jaguar wove through the late-evening London traffic, down past Regent's Park, along the Marylebone Road then over to Marble Arch where they headed south down Park Lane, flying round Hyde Park Corner to head west on the lower side of the park.

'We'll go to Onslow Square,' Allegra said. 'As far as I remember, Adam doesn't know about it.'

'Adam?' Imogen looked confused. 'I thought this must be about Romily.'

'Romily?' Allegra threw her a startled look. Was Imogen talking about the sale of the clubs? 'How do you know about Romily?'

'Mitch told me,' Imogen stuttered. 'But I didn't realise you knew. I was going to tell you when you'd stopped driving.'

'What the hell are we talking about?' shouted Allegra, bewildered.

'Please, let's just get to the house,' Imogen begged, throwing a glance over her shoulder to the back seat where her son was sleeping peacefully. 'We can talk about it all there.'

A few minutes later they screeched to a halt in front of the Onslow Square house. Allegra had not been there for years. She'd shaken its dust from her feet, feeling it represented everything in her life that was holding her back. Perhaps she'd been right.

She pressed the bell. *Please, God, don't let my parents be there!*

There was no answer for a long while.

'Fuck, fuck, fuck!' she swore, pressing down with her thumb on the bell while Imogen stood, white-faced and anxious, holding the car seat over one arm.

At last, the front door opened and the housekeeper stood there in her dressing gown. 'Lady Allegra!' she gasped when she realised who she was looking at. 'I wasn't expecting anyone tonight. I was in the mews house at the back when the buzzer sounded.'

'Hi, Julie. Sorry to spoil your evening. We're staying here tonight. This is Imogen and this is her baby, Alex, Xander's son. I'm sure you know about him.' Allegra pushed past her into the hallway.

'Of course, her ladyship showed me the pictures. Ooh, what a lovely baby!' crooned the housekeeper.

Imogen proudly turned the seat to display Alex to best advantage. 'He's nearly three months old!'

'Can we do all the cooing and cuddling when we're safely inside, please?' Allegra demanded brusquely. 'Shut the door, for God's sake.'

Twenty minutes later, Alex had been transferred to a bed, bolstered in by pillows so he couldn't roll off, although he usually lay unmoving in his sleeping bag all night long. He was fast asleep.

Imogen and Allegra were in the drawing room, sitting with cups of hot sweet tea and a plate of sandwiches and biscuits in front of them. Julie had retired to her mews flat once she was sure that they were well looked after and had all the towels and fresh bedding they needed.

'This may be the second worst day of my life,' Allegra said. She looked grey and drawn, nothing like her usual glamorous self. 'The day Xander died was the worst. But this is close.' She looked up at Imogen with tragic eyes. 'We've lost the clubs.'

'I know,' Imogen replied in a soft voice. 'I can't believe David would do such a thing.'

'He's ill,' Allegra declared emphatically, wrapping her fingers round her tea cup as if seeking comfort from its warmth. 'I'm sure of it. He's been strange for months. Forgetting things, getting stuff wrong that is basic for him. I should have taken more notice, made the connections. Today he . . .' Her face contorted at the memory. 'He accused me of stealing money.'

Imogen gasped. 'Oh my God, that's terrible! How could he? You're right, he must be ill. But . . . I don't understand. What's Adam got to do with all this?'

'Oh my God . . . Adam!' Allegra put her head in her hands, chilled suddenly, remembering the shrine in the flat. 'Midge, it's terrible. Adam is Sophie Harcourt's brother.'

Imogen drew her breath in sharply. '*What?*'

Allegra nodded. 'I found out when I was in his flat this afternoon. What's even worse, it looks like he's been stalking me for years and years.' She shut her eyes, pain on her face. 'I don't understand, Midge. I love him and I thought he loved me. It must all have been a lie! Oh, God, do you think he blames me for Sophie's death?' She shuddered.

Imogen sat bolt upright. 'No. I can't believe that. I've seen you together. He loves you, I'd swear on my life.'

'But, Midge . . . he's Sophie's brother.' Her voice was tight. 'How can he love me?'

'But he can't possibly know what happened. None of us have ever told. We were never linked to Sophie's death.'

'I know, that's what's freaking me out. *Why*? Somehow, he's made the connection.' Nausea bubbled in Allegra's stomach and she held on to the sofa, swaying slightly. 'God knows what conclusions he's drawn.'

'Do you think he wants to hurt you? To hurt us?' Imogen asked, her face frightened. 'Is that why you wanted to get us out of the house?'

'I just don't know,' Allegra cried. 'I can't believe he's capable of hurting me – or why wouldn't he have done it months ago? He's had every opportunity!' She had a sudden flashback to her first encounter with Adam, when she'd picked him up in that bar. If he had wanted to, he could have killed her then. No one would ever have known they'd met. But he didn't. 'No . . .' She frowned. 'I don't think he's going to hurt us. But I wanted to get us both away from the house until I can get my head sorted out.'

'So you don't think he could have been involved in what's happened to Romily?' Imogen asked in a quiet voice.

Allegra looked at her, her face apprehensive. 'What's happened to her?'

There was a mixture of fear and disbelief on Imogen's face. 'Oh, Allegra – Rom's been kidnapped! Mitch came to the house today and told me everything. Ted Mitchell is Mitch, her husband. Their divorce was a sham, they're still in league with each other . . . they bought the clubs together. I think she's been funding his business empire all along. Whoever's taken her wants twenty million dollars – or they'll kill her.'

Chapter 62

Imogen took some persuading to leave Alex behind, but after the long-suffering housekeeper had been woken up again and asked to sleep in the same room as the baby, with the security system in place and the phone by her bed, she finally agreed.

'We needn't be long. You've *got* to come with me,' Allegra said to her. 'There have been too many misunderstandings and mistakes. We need to stand together now.'

The drive from Onslow Square to Mitch's Chelsea house was not a long one. Imogen had already called to say they were coming.

'You're only just in time,' he'd told her. 'I'm leaving in a few hours.'

'Where are you going?'

'Not on the phone. I'll explain when you get here.'

They pulled up in front of a white-rendered, low-built house. They rang the doorbell and a tired-looking maid answered and led them through the ground floor. It was contemporary in style and ostentatiously expensive, with black marble floors, white columns and halogen spotlights everywhere. The chairs and sofas were upholstered in either white or black leather and the tables were of glass, marble or chrome.

'Very fancy,' murmured Allegra, as they followed the maid to a closed door. When she knocked, a voice inside called,

'Come in!' and the maid opened the door and stood back to let them pass.

The room was a large study, dominated by a vast and extraordinary desk covered in cream crocodile skin. Men in suits stood about it and sitting in the chair behind the desk was Mitch, looking tired and anxious, the least formal of them in a black crew-neck sweater and Armani jeans. He got up when he saw them and walked over. He stopped a few paces away and waited apprehensively as Allegra strode towards him.

She stood facing him, proud and beautiful. She looked him up and down very slowly, and then said in a voice dripping with disdain, 'So, Mitchell, you bastard, you stole my clubs after all.'

Mitch's eyebrows flickered in a barely discernible frown. Then he replied in a lazy drawl, 'Well, I guess you're the bitch who wrecked my marriage.'

They stood there, facing each other off, antagonism crackling between them.

'This isn't going to help anyone,' Imogen said in a pleading voice. 'We're here to help Romily, not have a fight. We can worry about the other stuff when she's safe.'

There was a pause while Mitch and Allegra still eyed each other suspiciously, then he turned to Imogen. 'OK,' he said reluctantly. 'I'm willing to button my mouth for the time being. Why are you guys here? What have you got for me?'

'How good of you,' Allegra retorted coolly. 'I don't know if I'm feeling quite as magnanimous, if I'm honest.' Just then her phone beeped. She looked at it and her expression changed. She held it out to Imogen. 'It's from Adam.'

' "You're not at my place. You're not at your place. Where are you?"' Imogen read out in a faltering voice. 'Do you think he knows that you've found out?'

'He must by now,' Allegra said. 'I left the cupboard door open. He'll know what I saw.'

'What's this about?' Mitch said impatiently. He gestured round at the men standing silently by. 'We have work to get on with.'

'I have a possible lead, someone who might be connected to Romily. I've discovered my boyfriend is someone from our shared past.' Allegra hesitated before saying slowly, 'Does the name Sophie Harcourt mean anything to you?'

Mitch gazed back at her and then nodded. 'Sure. I know about what happened. Romily told me.'

Allegra took a deep breath. 'I've just found out that my boyfriend Adam is Sophie's brother. And he's been following my every move for years.'

Mitch whistled lightly. 'OK. I can see that's serious. It goes beyond your average coincidence.' He thought fast, frowning. 'You think this guy might have kidnapped Romily?'

Allegra put a hand on her hip and stuck out her chin. 'I don't know. But it's possible. All three of us are connected to his sister. I thought I should let you know, just in case.'

Mitch turned to a young Indian man and they stood aside for a brief, muttered conversation. The young man then directed Mitch's entourage back to work at a line of computer screens further down the office. Mitch himself approached Imogen and Allegra.

'OK,' he said, 'your theory is that this guy may be out to seek revenge on you for his sister's death. I agree he might be best avoided from now on, but I don't believe he's taken Romily.'

'Why not?' Allegra asked, a flicker of relief in her eyes.

Mitch shook his head. 'Where's her car? Her driver and her guard? Those things can't all just disappear thanks to one weedy English guy.'

'He could have help?' Imogen suggested.

Mitch nodded slowly. 'It's possible. But snatching one of the richest heiresses in Europe is not something an amateur can pull off; he'd need professional help. And if he's got that, I'm going to find out about it. That's why I'm leaving here. I need to see a friend of mine. Time to wheel out the big guns.'

'Where are you going?' Allegra asked.

'To New York. I'm going in an hour and I'll be there late-morning New York time. I'll be back as soon as I can. Meanwhile I'm going to get my team here on to this Adam guy – if there's anything to find out about him, they'll know it in a few hours. We'll find out the truth, don't you worry.' He addressed Imogen. 'Here's what I want you to do. Stay here where it's safe and keep in touch with Romily's parents. It's important that they don't break and go to the police yet; they must play for time, give the kidnappers the impression they're collecting the ransom. Whatever happens, they mustn't pay any money, not yet. I think that would be a death sentence for Romily.' A spasm of emotion passed over his face as he said the words, but he fought for control.

There was silence while they all absorbed this awful thought.

'We'll do what you think is right,' Allegra said at last. 'Whatever it takes to stop Adam.'

Mitch nodded. 'I appreciate that.' He stared at her hard. 'I'd hate to think I got you wrong, you know.'

'I think there are plenty of wrongs to put right,' she said softly.

Imogen reached for her friend's hand, and Allegra squeezed it in return.

Chapter 63

Another text arrived on Allegra's phone. *I know what you found. Let's talk about it.* She shuddered and passed it to Imogen, who gasped.

'This is really frightening!' she said, her voice tremulous. 'I want to be with Alex.' She looked upset. 'I can't believe I'm not with him.'

'He'll be perfectly safe,' Allegra said, trying to soothe her.

'I want him with me,' Imogen cried, her eyes filling with tears. 'I'm going to get him! He'll be safer here. There are hundreds of heavies to look out for us. Besides, he'll wake up for a feed soon.'

They were still at Mitch's house, in one of the black-and-white sitting rooms, huddled together on a leather sofa. He'd left half an hour previously to go to the airport. In his study, his associates were on phones and computers, following up leads and now working over everything there was to find out about Adam Hutton or Harcourt, whoever he was. Mitch had told them to make themselves at home, to sleep if they wanted, but they were both feeling too wired for that.

'Don't be silly, I'm sure he's fine,' Allegra said, trying to soothe her friend, but Imogen was too fraught.

'I'll take your car,' she said, looking for her coat. 'I can be there and back in twenty minutes.'

'No, I'll go,' Allegra said. 'You're too wound up. I'll go and get Alex. You wait here.'

Imogen sank down into an armchair. 'OK,' she said gratefully. 'I just want to be with him.'

'Of course you do. I won't be long.'

Allegra slipped out of the front door and headed for her car.

Imogen curled up on the white leather sofa, feeling much happier. Now that Allegra was fetching Alex, she could begin to relax. She couldn't wait to see him.

It was late – two o'clock in the morning. Time had flown since she got that phone call from Allegra telling her to get herself and the baby ready to leave. It had been a struggle to grasp all the links in the chain and see how they fitted together. Adam had seemed so nice and normal, so completely professional and utterly dedicated to Allegra: could he really be obsessed with seeking some kind of revenge? She couldn't believe he was involved in Romily's kidnap, but what he had in mind for Allegra was a different matter.

She shuddered. They might have known that things they'd considered long buried and forgotten would not stay that way forever.

And now here she was in a house in Chelsea, all alone except for some strange men who looked like they were on intimate terms with the shadowy world of crime and violence.

Mitch was no longer a poor chef but a rich man with a string of restaurants to his name – and now the owner, with Romily, of Colette's, Oscar's and Astor House. God alone knew what that would mean for Allegra's future. Her career had been wiped out at a stroke.

And all this time, he'd still been with Romily! That story she had told Imogen at Lake Como had been true – but only up to a point. Someone – Allegra perhaps, the de Lisles definitely – had tried to break up the marriage and appeared to have succeeded. And yet all along they had simply hidden their alliance, so that their plan for revenge could be undertaken in secret.

Imogen shifted on the leather sofa. She recalled Romily, her eyes candid, her expression sincere, telling her that her marriage was over and appearing heartbroken. That had been a lie. Her whole social gadfly routine, too, had been an act, so that she could hide her real role as an empire builder in partnership with Mitch. She must have been kept very busy, in the quiet beauty of Lake Como, acquiring that portfolio of international businesses, running things from behind the scenes.

An image popped into Imogen's mind. She and Romily were on the boat, skimming the surface of the water, on their way to Como. She was happy, Romily seemed happy – it had been a marvellous moment. But something was nagging her. There was someone else in the picture, someone she needed to remember . . . Oh, yes, that was right. Marco . . . Romily's handsome young boatman.

Her eyes flew open. *I saw Marco in Colette's! It was him, I know it was. Gennaro's nephew who wants to be a DJ . . . I knew he looked familiar.* She gasped as a thought occurred to her. *Perhaps he knows something. I should tell Allegra, we could find him and ask him.*

She looked at her watch. It was just after two in the morning. Colette's was still open. Gennaro would be there and would know where Marco could be found. She must go there right away.

She jumped up, invigorated by the surge of adrenaline that rushed through her veins. Allegra would be back in about twenty minutes, but that might mean it was too late to get to Colette's in time to catch Gennaro.

She ran to Mitch's study and flung open the door. The buzz of low conversation in the room stopped abruptly and the men inside turned to look at her, instantly alert in case she proved a threat to them. 'I need someone to drive me to Mayfair!' she said breathlessly. 'Right now!'

It took some persuading to find a volunteer prepared to leave the post that Mitch had assigned to him, but when Imogen said desperately that it might be the key to finding Romily, one of the men had stood up and said, 'I'll take you.'

A few minutes later they were in his standard-issue black Audi, pulling out of the Chelsea street and heading towards Mayfair.

'My name's Malik,' he explained as they flew through the near-deserted streets.

'Are you Mitch's assistant?' Imogen asked.

He grinned, showing a row of perfect teeth. 'Yeah. Kind of. I studied law at Harvard, then went to Stanford and got myself a business degree. Now I'm Mitch's right-hand man.' His smile faded and he shook his head. 'I've never seen him so shaken up as he is right now. When we found out his girl had been snatched . . . it's been all hands on deck ever since.' He stole a quick glance at her before turning his gaze back to the road. 'If you've got the breakthrough, I'm the guy who wants to be in on it. It would be the greatest thing in the world if I could help the boss.'

'I hope I'm right,' Imogen said, pulling out her mobile. She would text Allegra and let her know where she was going. No point in ringing – it would be sod's law that the phone would go off just when she was picking up the sleeping Alex. *Have gone to Colette's to see Gennaro. Think he might have a clue re Rom. Look after Alex and see you back at Mitch's house.* X She pressed Send and went back to watching the city as they steered through the back streets towards Colette's.

*

Allegra opened the bedroom door as quietly as possible. The room inside was dark, the only sound the deep breathing of Julie. She had not needed to wake the housekeeper this time, having picked up a spare key on her way out.

She wedged the door open so that light from the hall illuminated the bedroom enough for her to see what she was doing. Inside, Alex was fast asleep on the bed; he hadn't moved since they'd laid him there, still on his back and cosy inside his sleeping bag. His mouth was slightly open, his rosebud lips parted, and his long fair lashes curled down on to his plump cheeks. She couldn't help smiling at the sight of him. *He's so delicious*.

She gathered his things together, then picked him up and sat him in his car seat. His head lolled a little but he stayed asleep as she strapped him in. She looked over at Julie, who was in the other bed and still undisturbed. Allegra went over and shook her gently. The housekeeper opened her eyes.

'Julie,' she whispered, 'I'm taking Alex, OK?'

'Mmm, all right,' muttered Julie, and rolled over straight back to sleep.

Allegra put the handles of the bag over one arm and picked up the car seat in the other. She went carefully down to the front door, trying not to jerk the seat. At the door, she put down the bag and turned the latch. Immediately it had gone back into the lock, the door was pushed open from the other side and she was sent staggering backwards, trying to regain her balance.

'Allegra, I found you!' Adam panted. 'God, at last.' He stared at her, his brown eyes frantic and his body tense.

She gasped, terrified. Her first instinct was to push the car seat behind her so that Alex couldn't be seen but it was far too big and she fumbled awkwardly with it. 'Adam . . . what the hell are you doing frightening me like this?' she demanded angrily, trying to take control.

'You haven't replied to my messages,' he said, his breath still short. 'It's driving me mad. I have to talk to you!'

He was wearing the same suit he'd had on when she'd left him at Astor House the previous morning. *God, it feels like a lifetime ago*. He looked scruffy and stubbly, though, a long way from his usual immaculate appearance.

'What messages?' she bluffed. 'I've lost my phone.'

An agonised look passed over his face and he closed his eyes for a moment. He took in a shuddering breath and said, 'No, you haven't. Listen, whatever you're thinking . . . you're wrong.'

She blinked hard, trying to take in what he was saying. He looked so unlike her usual calm, dependable, loving Adam that it was like seeing a stranger. He seemed wound as tight as a spring, trembling and frightened. Managing to find her voice, she said, 'How did you know I was here?'

He smiled, almost sadly. 'You didn't think I knew about this place, did you? But I know everything about you. I've known for ages that the McCorquodales use this place as their London base, even if you don't. It was an obvious place for you to come once it was clear you weren't in a hurry to go home.'

'So you've been watching the house?'

He nodded. 'For about an hour now.'

'Why?' Her mask of cool fell away for a moment and she stared at him with beseeching eyes. 'Adam – why? Why all of this? You know what I found!'

'Yes.' He looked away, unable to meet her eyes for a moment. Then he gazed at her imploringly. 'That's why we need to talk. Please, Allegra, let me explain!'

She struggled with herself. She was desperate to know the truth, but this new Adam, shaking and wild-eyed, frightened her and she felt a strong urge to get away from him. And she still had Alex to think of . . . 'No, no. I have to go. I've got to be somewhere.' She made to push past him towards the front door, but he put one hand on her shoulder and stopped her with surprising strength. She gasped and looked up at him. 'Let me go, Adam.'

'No,' he said, his voice stronger. 'I can't let you go. I have to talk to you first. I have to tell you about Sophie.'

Malik brought the car to a stop outside Colette's and Imogen was out before Billy the doorman could get to the door.

'I'll park just up there,' said Malik, pointing to the top of the square.

'OK.' Imogen turned to the doorman. 'Billy, let Malik in, please. I'll tell Paul downstairs.'

The club was in party mode, though members and their guests were beginning to stumble out of the bar and up to the cool evening air, to catch one of the line of taxis waiting to pick up lucrative fares or to meet their drivers in the many Rolls Royces, Bentleys and Mercedes parked around the square.

Paul the greeter, who also made sure that anyone who tried to enter the club was either a member or a guest, looked surprised to see Imogen appear at that time of night.

'Paul, someone is with me, his name is Malik. Please let him in when he comes down.'

'Yes, madam.' Paul looked unruffled – a speciality of any member of Colette's staff.

'Is Gennaro here?'

'I'm not sure, madam. I think he said he might leave early tonight.'

'Oh, no,' Imogen gasped, and headed off down the corridor towards the bar and restaurant. She glanced around the bar, where some fat, rich old men were being amused by some very young and beautiful girls, but Gennaro wasn't there, so she went into the restaurant. Only a few tables were occupied now by diners finishing their meals and the room was resonating with music from the dance floor where about twenty people were bobbing and dancing. It was dark, the only light coming from the lamps on the tables and the lights on the dance floor. It was hard to see who was present.

She grabbed one of the waiters. 'Where's Gennaro?' she demanded.

He shrugged. 'Haven't seen him.'

'*Fuck*!' she swore. The waiter raised his eyebrows and hurried off.

Malik appeared beside her. 'Success?'

She shook her head. 'Come on, this way.' She went to the back of the club where the wine was stored. Flinging open the door, she almost screamed with relief when Gennaro turned round from inspecting a crate full of empty bottles.

'Yes?' He came towards her, frowning. 'Is something wrong?' He looked suspiciously at Malik.

'Don't worry about him, he's a friend. It's about your nephew . . . Marco.'

Gennaro looked grim. 'Oh. Marco. I *knew* he was in trouble. He told me he was mixed up in something and wanted to get out of it. What's the boy done?'

'I don't know but I think he might be able to help us. We need to talk to him.'

'Is it very serious?' Worry clouded the manager's face.

'I just don't know, Gennaro, and I can't tell you any more right now.' Imogen tried to control the nervousness and urgency in her voice. 'Where is he? Please tell me.'

Gennaro looked past her towards the restaurant. 'He's through there, in the DJ's box. He's doing the music tonight. I promised that he could.'

Imogen and Malik turned to stare at each other, then rushed back to the dance floor as fast as they could.

Chapter 64

Adam seemed to notice Alex for the first time. 'What's he doing here?' He took the car seat from her and pushed her ahead of him into the drawing room.

'I have to get him to Imogen,' Allegra said quickly. 'She'll be desperate.' Just then her phone beeped with an incoming text.

'Who's that?' Adam said nervously. 'Open it.'

She reached for her phone. 'It's from Imogen.'

'Show me.'

She handed it over and he read it, frowning. '*Clue re Rom*? What's she talking about?'

'Don't you know?' She watched him carefully as he shook his head, looking blank, searching for any indication that Adam knew what Romily's situation was.

'Should I?' If he was faking ignorance, he was doing it brilliantly. There was not a flicker of reaction in his eyes.

'You don't know why we should be interested in Rom?' she said slowly.

His face suddenly cleared. 'Oh, Rom. Romily. Your old school pal. But you haven't been in touch with her for years.'

She felt a chill shiver down her spine. 'Is there anything you don't know about me?'

A muscle twitched in his cheek and he blinked. 'Not much,' he admitted with a hollow laugh. 'Sit down.'

Allegra watched him put Alex's car seat on the hearth rug

as she sank on to the canary-yellow seat of the sofa. *I think Mitch is right. I don't think Adam is involved in Rom's kidnap. So what does he want?* She tried to stay calm and alert. He was obviously in a highly agitated state. He didn't appear to have a weapon but that didn't mean there wasn't something concealed on him.

'I need a drink,' he said, glancing about. He went over to the drinks table and poured himself a large whisky. 'Want one?' he asked, turning to Allegra.

She shook her head.

Adam stayed standing with his back to her and said in a high, tense voice, 'It really wasn't supposed to turn out this way, you know.'

'Wasn't it? What exactly did you want to happen?'

'That's the crazy thing.' He turned back to face her, his lips twitching. 'I don't know. Every step of the way, what I've wanted has changed. Except for one thing. I've always wanted to know the truth about how my sister died. You know she's my sister now, of course, since you found my memorabilia.' A despairing expression passed over his face. 'I was stupid to leave it there for you to find.'

'Maybe you wanted me to,' she suggested quietly.

He stared back at her, his eyes burning. 'Maybe. Because I want you to tell me . . . I've always wanted you to tell me . . . the *truth*. Those nights when I held you while you screamed and reached for me . . . I knew the truth was locked up there in your head.' His voice hardened. 'Sometimes I imagined ripping you open to get it out . . .' Then he laughed. 'Which makes me sound like a nutter, I suppose. Your worst nightmare.'

'But . . .' She tried to stop the fear that had rippled through her from showing on her face. 'But why would I know the truth about your sister?'

'Come on, Allegra.' He gave her a look that was almost

pitying, and took a big gulp of neat whisky. 'Because you were there.'

The office seemed almost eerily quiet after the thudding music of the dance floor. Marco sat on his chair looking very young and scared. Gennaro stood next to him, translating Imogen's questions, and Malik looked on, listening carefully.

'Did you come to London with Romily?' Imogen asked.

Gennaro relayed the question, and Marco shook his head.

'Then why are you here?'

When Marco replied, Gennaro looked over at Imogen with a worried expression. 'He's just said that he came to London to visit me, his uncle. But that's wrong. I had no idea he was coming and had the impression that he was surprised to be in London.'

He turned back to his nephew and the two of them talked in rapid Italian, Gennaro looking impatient and Marco round-eyed and frightened, his tone defensive and scared.

'Please, please, tell me what you're saying!' Imogen begged, unable to stand the wait.

Gennaro turned back to her and Malik. 'He says that he came over with two men but won't say who they are. They told him he could make some easy money and he was interested, but when he found out that they intended to kidnap his old boss, he didn't want anything more to do with the plan and ran off.'

Marco looked about, his eyes terrified, and released a stream of panicky Italian.

'He says that he tried to warn the boss,' Gennaro said. 'Sent her some pictures the men had taken, with a note. He says it's not his fault, there was nothing he could do.'

'What was the plan?' demanded Malik roughly.

'He doesn't know,' Gennaro said, looking helpless. 'They

planned to take her somewhere beginning with B. That's all he knows. He wasn't even sure if they were going to go through with it. He says he didn't know she'd been taken.'

'Beginning with B . . . In London? Bermondsey? Borough?' Imogen hazarded. 'Or further away? Bromley? Brighton?'

'No, no,' Marco said, shaking his head. He looked very young and very scared.

'OK.' Malik sounded impatient. 'I've had enough of all this. Tell your nephew he'd better co-operate. That lady is the wife of your new boss and it's very much in Marco's interests to tell us everything he knows.'

'Is this true?' Gennaro asked Imogen, looking shocked.

'Yes, I'm afraid it is,' she said sadly.

He straightened up proudly. 'We will help you because these men are bad and dangerous, not because we are frightened of our new boss, whoever he is. Marco knows very little – he ran away from these men and is very afraid of them.'

'He knows who they are,' Malik said curtly. 'We need to know that.'

'He won't tell – they will kill him if he does, he says.'

Malik looked grim. 'He might find the alternative just as bad. Now listen, we're all going back to the house, understand? We need to go through every aspect of this story and check it all out. Also, we will persuade Marco to give us the names of the men he came here with. He has nothing to be afraid of if he helps us. OK?'

Gennaro looked over at Imogen who said, 'Please, Gennaro. He must help us.'

'Very well, we will come.' Gennaro turned to Marco and talked to him in Italian.

Malik said, 'A wise decision, my friend. A very wise decision. You can be sure we're going to find the men responsible for this, and it will go very much in your favour if you help us. Now let's go.'

'How did you know I was there?' Allegra whispered. She was still sitting on the yellow sofa, and Adam was opposite her in an armchair. Outwardly, a civilised scene.

He sighed. 'When Sophie died, people said it was suicide. They said she'd killed herself even though the coroner didn't give that verdict. I knew she would never have done that. Became obsessed with knowing the truth. I spent my teenage years poring over it, trying to figure it out. There was a mystery there, I just knew it.'

Allegra said nothing but concentrated on keeping her breathing under control while she thought, *None of us ever told . . . except . . . Romily told Mitch. Is that where the leak happened?*

'I did a lot of research and there was something I kept coming back to. Who was this guy who found Sophie's body? A security guard, they said. Well, what was he doing there anyway? How many boarding schools have guards like that? I discovered eventually that he was a private guard, paid for by the de Lisle family to protect their precious little daughter. I devoted a few years to tracking him down and, when I did, he had some interesting things to tell me about your little gang.' Adam's dark hazel eyes searched her face. 'How you went up to that attic to smoke your cigarettes. The attic just above the spot where Sophie was found. He saw her . . . and he saw you . . . both of you at the window, struggling.'

Allegra gasped and leapt to her feet. 'Oh, God!' She saw it again, as plain as day, and the familiar terrified sickness coiled in her belly. She stared at Adam with wild eyes. 'It was an accident, you have to believe me!' She was back there on that terrible night, could feel the full force of

Sophie's weight as the other girl pushed and pushed . . . and then the surreal lightness as she disappeared through the open window. She still remembered the stark terror in Sophie's eyes in the split second before she fell. Eyes that were the image of Adam's. Why on earth hadn't she noticed it before? She'd seen those eyes so often in her nightmares.

She panted out, 'We were in the attic, where it was strictly forbidden to go. We had a stupid argument and got carried away. Sophie and I ended up . . .' Her voice cracked but she carried on. '. . . we ended up tussling, fighting . . . she tried to push me but I fought back and in the struggle by some awful chance, Sophie slipped and fell.' She gave a half sob. 'It was an accident, Adam, you have to believe me!'

He blinked at her for a moment. 'I believe you,' he said in a quiet voice. 'But why didn't you tell anyone? Why did you lie?'

Allegra dropped to her knees, wrapping her arms around herself. 'We should have,' she said in a broken voice. 'It was the worst mistake of my life. We didn't tell, and then we were caught in our silence. We couldn't tell.' She gazed up at him, agonised. 'It's haunted me all my life. You know . . . you've seen the nightmares! Maybe I was lots of things – stuck up, silly, naughty, hot-tempered, I don't know – but I never wished harm on anyone. What happened to Sophie . . . Adam, it ruined my life!'

He gazed at her, calmer now as he watched her emotional outburst, and then said in a cold voice, 'Yes. But at least *you* are still alive.'

The car was distinctly more crowded on the journey back, with two extra passengers. Gennaro and Marco sat in the back, muted and worried, as Malik drove them through Mayfair and towards Chelsea. It was now after three in the morning and the roads were quiet.

'What are you going to do?' Imogen asked in a low voice, turning her head towards Malik so he could hear her but those in the back couldn't.

'We'll find out everything he knows,' Malik replied, taking the car up a gear and increasing his speed.

'You're not going to hurt him, are you? He's just a boy.'

Malik stared straight ahead and shrugged lightly. 'That all depends. My hunch is he'll co-operate. If he doesn't, we'll use any means necessary. If he's telling the truth and tried to warn her, that will stand him in good stead.' He slid his gaze towards Imogen for a moment. 'Romily's life is at stake here. We've got to make him help us.'

Imogen nodded, letting out a slow stream of breath. She'd had a brief glimpse into a different world, one far removed from her own comfortable safe upbringing but existing alongside it. There were different rules in this parallel world. She shivered.

They arrived back at the Chelsea house and, before they were out of the car, Malik had his phone clamped to his ear and was murmuring urgently into it. The front door opened and they were all ushered inside by Mitch's staff. Gennaro and Marco were instantly whisked away down the hall, accompanied by three tough-looking men.

'Where's Allegra? Is she here?' Imogen asked, as another dark suited, broad-shouldered man strode past her. He shot her a glance and shrugged. She turned to Malik. 'Can you find out where she is?'

'Sure.' He walked off towards Mitch's office and returned a few moments later, looking worried. 'She's not here. She didn't come back.'

Imogen felt her stomach plummet. She gasped, 'But she was due back an hour ago at least! She only went to pick up Alex . . .' She ran to Malik and grabbed his arm. 'We have to go and find them!'

He stared back at her for a moment, his brown eyes unreadable, then he nodded. 'OK. I'm not supposed to leave here without permission and you're making me head out a second time, but I owe you for Marco. Gee, this is turning into a crazy night! Let's go.'

'Do you believe me?' Allegra asked in a small voice. She sat hunched on the carpet, her knees tucked under her. She watched Alex's peaceful sleeping face, envying his innocence and serenity, the clean slate of his life.

Adam looked down at her. He nodded and said slowly, 'Yes, I do. It was all I wanted. The truth. I knew you could tell me, I was waiting for it. There was never any need for you to know that I was Sophie's brother.' He laughed joylessly. 'But maybe you're right. Maybe I did want you to find out. I didn't want to live a lie, and conceal myself from the woman I love.'

She raised her head, gazing up at him. 'You love me?'

'Of course.' He rubbed one hand through his short coppery hair and took another slug of whisky. 'I can see how it looks . . . all those pictures of you. I found the first one of you in Sophie's school photograph in her bedroom. I think I fell in love with you from that moment.' He gave her a sad smile. 'You were the most beautiful girl I'd ever seen in my life. My dream girl. After that, I learnt all I could about your family. The handy thing about aristocrats is how interested everyone is in their lives. You were often in the papers, anything you did made some gossip column or other. "Earl's daughter buys clothes"; "Socialite goes to party". I half expected to read "Allegra McCorquodale breathes air, eats food".' He shrugged. 'The nonsense people like to read about.'

'I totally agree with you,' she said in a heartfelt voice.

'I read that you'd joined your uncle, running Colette's. By

then I'd discovered that you were probably with Sophie the night she died. It felt like fate somehow. I already worked in that world myself. I followed you. Learnt about your propensity for visiting those seedy clubs and bars and taking some lucky guy home with you.' He gave her a look that was half amused, half sad. 'I realised then how I would get to meet you. And you were everything I'd ever dreamt of.' He smiled softly, and for the first time that evening, she glimpsed the Adam she'd known so well and loved so much. A stab of bitter pain and regret pierced her. *Yesterday morning, I stared into those eyes as he made love to me*, she thought. *How has it all changed like this?*

'How has this happened, Adam? How has it come to this? We were so happy,' she said quietly.

He stood up, looking pained. 'I didn't want this! Yes, I wanted to know what had happened that night, but the longer we were together, the more I loved you.' He turned to her, his eyes burning. 'I mean it, Allegra. I love you. You know it's true. I never wanted to hurt you.'

She nodded. She believed him. 'I know,' she whispered.

'Tell me it's not over for us,' he begged. He sat back on the sofa and buried his head in his hands. 'I can't bear it if it's finished,' he said in a broken voice. 'I've got nothing without you. You've been my world for so long.' He gazed up at her. 'Please, don't leave me. Tell me we're still together.'

She stood up slowly, taking a deep breath. 'I can't say that. I don't know. I need time to think about it.'

'If I've lost you as well as Sophie, then my life is completely pointless.' He looked up at her desperately. 'I don't know what I'd do.'

She froze, absorbing the words, suddenly frightened again. *Is he threatening me?* 'You said you'd never hurt me,' she reminded him in a quiet voice.

'I know.' He stared back down at his feet. Then his

shoulders shook and his voice came out high, jagged with tears. 'But I need you, Allegra. And I can't bear to think of you living without me.'

'I love you too,' she said gently, intent on calming him down. 'But this is all a huge shock, you must see that.'

He nodded, sniffing.

'If you hurt me,' she said slowly, 'it would make everything a million times worse . . . you know that, don't you?'

'I'll never hurt you, I promise.' He looked up, his cheeks wet. Then he stood up and held out his arms. 'If you love me . . . come to me. Kiss me.' He took a step towards her and she flinched. 'See? You don't even want me near you! I've lost you already, I can see that.'

'You haven't lost me,' she said, filled with a rush of pity and tenderness for him.

'Haven't I?' He stared at her beseechingly. 'Then do it . . . kiss me.' He walked towards her.

She felt the nearness of him and suddenly yearned for his embrace and the comfort of his kiss. She truly did love him. He had given her a peace she'd never found anywhere else in her entire life. She lifted her face to his and he wrapped his arms around her, taking her against the security of his body and kissing her passionately. *Yes,* she thought. *It feels right. Even after everything that's happened. This is where I'm supposed to be.*

Then there was a strange cracking sound at the window followed instantaneously by a high whizzing sounds and the next moment Adam had jerked, staggered, thrown up his arms, his face utterly astonished, and then collapsed to the floor as though his legs had been kicked away from under him.

As Allegra stared, frozen in shock, she saw a stain of dark blood pool out across his thighs.

Chapter 65

As the private plane soared across the Atlantic, Mitch stayed in constant contact with his London operation. Every contact possible had been used in the underworld. Someone, somewhere, must know who had pulled off Romily's kidnap and where she was.

He waved away the attentions of the cabin crew with their offers of champagne and smoked salmon, accepting only a steady supply of black coffee to keep him going.

It was hard to bear the sensations of constant fear and panic that resolved themselves into an overpowering feeling of angry impotence. He and Romily had become so engrossed in their own machinations, the expansion of their empire and her secret participation, that they'd taken their eyes off the ball. They'd forgotten that her existence was hardly a secret and that her immense wealth was an irresistible lure to criminals. Her security was supposed to be rock solid but somewhere it had failed. The guard was gone too – either overpowered and now dead or else part of the whole operation.

He didn't buy for a moment this crazy guy Allegra was jabbering on about. One lone British man against an SAS-trained guard, a driver and a custom-built, top-of-the-range, armoured Mercedes? Uh-uh. Couldn't happen. No way.

The gorgeous cabin attendant came up with another pot of fresh coffee and he accepted a top up. *Jesus, I'll be buzzing like a fucking bee if I carry on like this.*

He lay back in his chair, watching through the porthole as they flew into the day ahead. Allegra drifted into his mind. She was a fascinating girl, there was no doubt about it. She was a heady mix of hot sexiness and aristocratic froideur, and if he wasn't already very much in love with Romily he'd have a hard on for her, absolutely. But he and Romily had sworn they'd bring her down for what she'd done to them, taking away what she prized most and in the most painful way – becoming her competitors, buying the business out from under her, trampling on her dreams.

And yet, on the very day she lost everything, she decided to help him.

Why?

His Blackberry went again and he picked up another message, listing contacts now doing investigative work throughout the world. Still nothing. He swore under his breath.

He tried to transmit his love and strength to Romily, wherever she was. *I'm coming for you, baby. I owe you everything. I can't live without you. I'm not going to let anybody hurt you.*

He'd kill with his bare hands anyone who'd touched her.

They landed at JFK in good time, the day already well advanced, bright and clear. A car was waiting to whisk Mitch away from the airport and into Manhattan.

He'd left a poor chef, with three hundred dollars to his name and a couple of black eyes. Now he was coming back, rich, successful and important. He'd left the city by bus for his economy flight. He returned in a private jet with his chauffeur-driven limo waiting.

And all to see the guy who'd given him those black eyes.

*

This is one hell of a trip down Memory Lane! thought Mitch, as he strode into the Greywell Brasserie. His associate-cum-bodyguard followed a few paces behind, on full alert, casing the restaurant as they went in. He remembered the guy he'd once been: a two-bit chef doped out on heroin half the time, cooking like a demon the rest of it – when he wasn't fucking waitresses. *A loser.*

Mitch approached the back table respectfully. As he neared it, the man sitting there flanked by two heavies stood up to greet him. He'd aged, Mitch noted, a trifle more stooped, the hair slightly more grey, the face more deeply wrinkled. But then, it was some years since they'd last met.

'Mr Panciello,' he said, holding out his hand. 'Thank you for agreeing to see me.'

Panciello stared at him for a moment with cold eyes. Then a smile spread across his face and he held open his arms. 'Come here!' he said. Mitch went to him and the older man embraced him, kissing him on both cheeks. 'Now sit down,' he ordered, and they all took their places at the table.

Mitch felt emboldened by this affectionate greeting. He hadn't expected it. 'Sir,' he said, 'I don't want to waste your time. I'll say what I've got to say and leave you to enjoy your lunch. I've come here for two reasons. The first is to thank you. Six years ago, you taught me a lesson that turned out to be the most valuable of my life.' He grinned at the old man. 'Not that I exactly thought so at the time!'

Everyone chuckled, and Mitch continued talking.

'But you taught me that I should always be aware of what is going on and keep in mind who the powerful, important people are. Remaining ignorant of that is total foolishness. *I* was a total fool. More than that, you taught me that the only kind of person to be is exactly that: powerful and important. You said "Be an owner" – and now I am. So I most sincerely want to thank you for that, sir.'

Panciello gazed back at him, nodding. 'Yes,' he said, his voice hoarser with age now. 'You're right. And you know what, kid, I knew this would happen. That one day you'd come back and show me what you'd done with your life. I had every faith.' His eyes twinkled. 'That's why I told my boys not to rough you up too bad. You still had to be able to go out there and make your mark on the world.'

They all laughed. Panciello said, 'Seriously – you were fucking up. Wasting your life. You were going to smoke yourself to death with that shit, or step on the toes of someone less merciful than myself. Then you'd wind up dead, that talent of yours screwed up and tossed away. So I tried to teach you the right way.'

'And you did, sir,' Mitch said earnestly. He folded his hands together on the table in front of him. 'But I have something else to be grateful for. You, Mr Panciello, are also responsible for my meeting my wife. The night I was . . . taught my lesson . . . I wound up in the alley behind her place, and she came to my rescue. Later, we met again, fell in love and got married. With her support, I've become the man I am today, with my own restaurant empire, just as I'd always planned.'

'And kept well away from mine!' quipped Mr Panciello. His associates laughed again, keen to show their appreciation of their boss's wit.

'And now, despite how much I owe you, I've come to ask a great favour.' Mitch grew serious and the mood around the table sobered. 'My wife has been kidnapped. A huge ransom is being demanded or she will be killed. I believe the people holding her are renegades, stupid amateurs in a world they don't understand. I also believe that someone connected knows something. They've had professional help from somewhere.' Mitch bent forward across the snowy tablecloth, his eyes pleading. 'Sir, your contacts are second to none. You know everything that is going on around the globe. Your influence is a thousand times greater than mine. If word gets out that you are against these people, they will be denounced and I will be able to deal with them and bring my wife home where she belongs. But time is running out. I desperately need your help, sir. Will you help me one more time? I'll be forever in your debt.'

Panciello stared back across the table, his liver-spotted hands clutching the cloth. He took a long slow drink of water from the glass in front of him. At last he opened his mouth.

'Go back to London,' he said hoarsely. 'Go back. If I can help, you'll find what you want waiting for you there.'

Elation surged through Mitch. 'Thank you, sir!' he said. 'My God, thank you!' He leapt to his feet.

A shadowy smile crossed Panciello's face. 'Well, having gone to the trouble of finding you a wife, I can hardly let her be taken away, now can I?' He nodded to the door. 'Now go. And remember me, like I'll remember you.'

'Yes, sir.' Mitch turned and left as quickly as he could.

Romily could sense that the people guarding her were becoming increasingly fearful.

How long have I been here?

It was hard to know now that she was blindfolded. The hours passed by, each as black as the next, with no clue as to what time it was. She'd been taken to the loo three more times, and been given water and sandwiches twice. Did that mean she'd been gone twenty-four hours? Or longer?

On one of her journeys to the loo, she had heard Carlo arguing with someone, perhaps Rocco. It made her feel sick to think that these men, who knew her so intimately, had betrayed her like this.

But they don't know about Mitch, she reminded herself.

Their meetings had been conducted away from the eyes of the guards. *Like the last time I was with him.* She remembered that secret rendezvous in the library at the ambassador's party when they'd coupled so quickly and beautifully. It had been like that for so long now. They'd both been living for the time when they'd be able to be free and open about their relationship, could live together like any normal couple.

But will that ever happen? she wondered, agonised. Perhaps the guards had forgotten she spoke fluent Italian – or maybe they no longer cared what she knew, because they were going to kill her whatever. Carlo had been spitting with rage that there was no sign of the money, that her parents seemed to be prevaricating.

'How can these rich people pretend they don't have money?' he'd raged. 'They must have twenty million in the safe at their house, for fuck's sake! At least!'

Rocco had been trying to calm him down. 'It's only been one day. They're probably getting their funds together as we speak. I don't believe they've gone to the police. My girl in the house says there's been no one visiting, no detectives.'

'If I hear of one policeman walking through that door, she's dead!' cried Carlo.

'And with her, any hope of getting the money. Come on, Carlo, we always knew this would be the tough part. We must keep our nerve, get the cash, and then . . .'

She'd heard no more, hustled away and back into wherever they were keeping her.

Oh my God! Someone is spying on my parents! Five minutes before, Romily had been praying for them to get the police and anyone else involved. Now she realised with sick horror that it would be her execution warrant if they did.

And if the money didn't come soon, she'd die anyway, she was sure of it.

*

Back on her uncomfortable couch, Romily rolled up into a foetal shape. She longed to sleep and find oblivion, wake up back at home in her own bed.

Was it really so little time since she'd been taken captive? Only the day before yesterday she'd walked into David McCorquodale's exquisite Knightsbridge house, perfectly dressed in a Louis Vuitton suit, ready to convince him to sign on the dotted line and surrender his business empire to her. He'd been charmed by her elegance and when he'd agreed to sell, she'd been full of triumph, a conqueror, her revenge on Allegra complete at last. How silly and hollow that all seemed now, her obsessive pursuit of Allegra's possessions a meaningless and empty waste of time. *If I get out of here,* she vowed to herself, *I'll learn how to live again.*

But now I know who they are, will they have to kill me? she wondered. The very word 'kill' no longer had the power to shock her, she discovered. *I'm getting accustomed to the idea of my own imminent death.* The thought frightened her to the core.

Mitch! Where are you? Come and find me, please! I don't know how much more I can stand.

Chapter 66

As the day advanced, the mood in the Chelsea house grew more and more grim. There were still no leads and no word from Mitch.

Allegra was sitting with Adam, who lay on a bed in a spare room, his thigh heavily bandaged and his leg raised. He'd been shot in the thigh and the bullet was probably lodged in the bone. The bleeding was heavy but he'd been lucky the bullet had missed an artery.

The moment after he'd been shot, there'd been fierce knocking at the front door and she'd opened it to find Imogen and a strange man holding a revolver. They'd dashed inside and the man had immediately dropped to the floor beside Adam, assessing his condition. Imogen ran straight to Alex, who was howling, unclipped him from his car seat and pulled him into her arms to comfort him.

'What the hell is happening?' Allegra screamed at Malik, as Adam writhed in pain. 'Why did you shoot him?'

'He was trying to hurt you, wasn't he?' the young man retorted. 'I acted to protect you.'

'He was kissing me, you fucking idiot!' she yelled. 'Oh my God, is he going to be all right?'

Malik had turned back to Adam, his expression sheepish. 'Yeah, but we need to get him seen to as soon as possible.'

'I'll call an ambulance,' Imogen volunteered.

'No,' Malik said sharply, pulling out his mobile. 'I'll call the boys. We don't involve any outside agencies, understand? You' – he looked at Allegra – 'get me a sheet or something.'

She raced to the linen cupboard, astonished that Julie was still sleeping soundly in the spare room despite all the drama. All she could think of was whether Adam was going to be all right. *That fucking arsehole, shooting him like that!* she thought, fiercely protective. *Oh, God – perhaps I really do love him after all . . .*

They'd bound Adam's leg with a sheet. He'd regained consciousness and groaned with the pain, but had been docile enough when forced to hobble to the car, one arm over Malik's shoulders. Once they were safely stowed, they'd returned to the Chelsea house. Adam had been taken away, his leg seen to by someone with medical training. He'd also been given a hefty dose of morphine for the pain.

'What's going to happen to him?' Allegra said anxiously, as he was taken to a bedroom. 'Shouldn't he go to hospital?'

'He will be seen professionally,' Malik said. 'But not right now. It's not time for clean-up yet. We're still mid-operation and casualties will have to wait until we know the full situation.'

'OK,' she said uncertainly. 'Well, I'll stay with him for a bit.'

Now she sat by Adam's side, watching as he drifted in and out of a morphine-induced sleep, wondering how on earth it had come to this.

They slept as the day went by. Food appeared, brought from the kitchen by several maids and placed on the coffee tables: sandwiches, sushi, salads and muffins.

'You should go home,' Allegra said to Imogen. 'You don't have to stay any more now that they've got Marco. I'm going to stay with Adam.'

'So he wasn't going to hurt you?' Imogen asked.

Allegra shook her head. 'It's so complicated, Midge. I don't know what to think yet. But in some ways, nothing has changed between us. And I don't want to lose him, if I can help it.'

'Don't throw happiness away,' Imogen said softly. 'It's very precious, you know. Not as easy to find as people think.'

Allegra went back to check on Adam and Imogen went down to the kitchen to beg milk, water and some baby-friendly food for Alex. Now he was awake, he was in a cheerful mood, intrigued by his surroundings and softening even the toughest of Mitch's assistants with his gurgling and kicking.

'Hey, he's so cute,' Malik said. He sat down to join Imogen and Alex, playing together on a white fluffy rug. He held out a coloured block from the bag Imogen had brought with her. 'Here, kid, here you are.' Alex took it with a long coo and an interested look, then carefully brought it to his mouth and started chewing it. Malik smiled at him and looked at Imogen. 'Isn't his dad gonna be worried about where you guys are?'

Imogen shook her head, not taking her eyes off her son. It was amazing how she could spend long hours just staring at him, marvelling at how beautiful and clever he was. 'No.'

'Ah.' Malik nodded. 'You two split, huh?'

'No. He's dead.'

'Oh.' Malik looked embarrassed. 'Hey, I'm sorry.'

'That's OK. He died before Alex was born.'

'Gee, that's sad. He never saw this little fella?' Malik put out a finger to Alex, who clutched it and shook Malik's hand up and down. 'Poor guy. He missed out.'

'Any news from Mitch?' Imogen asked, after a moment.

'Yeah.' Malik seemed relieved by her deft subject change. 'He's on his way home right now.'

'That was a quick visit. How can you get to New York and back so fast?'

'He was only in Manhattan for an hour. And having your own plane helps the whole thing along. He'll be back in a couple of hours.'

There was a sudden flurry of activity; men began running about and shouting. Malik stood up, instantly alert, and listened.

'What is it?' Imogen asked, standing up too.

He turned to her, his eyes shining. 'A name,' he said. 'The kid's broken. He's given us a name. Now we're getting somewhere.'

Mitch's car, long, sleek and elegant, with blacked-out windows, sped back into town from Heathrow. It was almost dark. A whole day had gone by and he'd seen only an hour or two of it outside the confines of an airplane.

During the return flight, he'd received an unexpected message from London. His boys had found a source and, after interrogation, that source had provided vital information. He'd instantly transmitted it to Panciello's people to help their investigations. Then it was back to waiting.

Every few minutes he checked his email and made sure that he hadn't missed a call. There was nothing.

Have faith, he told himself. *The old man will come through for us.*

But he had gnawing doubts. And what if they were too late, after all this? He caught a glimpse of his reflection in the mirror above the passenger door. He looked ten years older: grey and haggard.

I'm on my way, Romily. Hold on, baby, hold on.

They were coming into central London when his phone buzzed. He pulled it to his ear in one smooth movement. 'Mitchell,' he said.

'Mitch, I've got the information you need.' He recognised that hoarse voice.

His heart thudded and his palms became clammy. 'Yes, sir?'

'The address where you can find your property will be sent to your company email address. It will be marked for your attention. It will also be encrypted. Your guys will know what to do with it. They should look now.'

'Thank you, sir. Thank you.'

'You're welcome.' The line went dead.

He stared at his phone for a long moment, unable to function now that he had the precious information they needed. Then he put through a call to his chief technician who was sitting in the operations room of the Chelsea house, monitoring all data traffic.

'Sir?' came the alert response to his call.

'Arthur, check my company email account – the holding company. There should be something there. It will be encrypted. Get the address and research it. Pass it to Clarke for evaluation. The property we're looking for is there. Understand?'

'You bet.'

'Good.' Mitch cut the call. He leant back on the leather seat and sighed. The car moved slowly through the evening traffic. *Relax,* he told himself. *You'll need all your strength in a little while. The best people are working on it right now. You've done what you needed to do.*

Romily could hear voices, raised and angry. Someone had left the doors open again.

She was thirsty and her stomach growled painfully, even though she didn't feel hungry. More than anything, she longed for a hot bath or a powerful shower, to blast the dirt of all of this away. Her hair felt lank and oily, and her skin was in desperate need of moisturiser. She had never gone for so long without being able to care for herself, pamper herself and make herself beautiful.

I don't care about that now, as long as I can live. I just want to see Mitch again.

She had tried to pass the hours by thinking about him, replaying all their times together, from their crazy wedding in a blacksmith's cottage in Scotland to the last time they'd spoken: she'd called him in high excitement after her meeting with David McCorquodale.

'I told him,' she'd said. 'I'm sure he'll sell to us now. He took it all in. There's no way he'll let Allegra keep the company.'

'This is it, honey,' he'd cried. 'This time next week, you'll be walking into Colette's and it will be yours.'

'Ours,' she'd said, thrilled.

All that effort and money and time and planning . . . and for what? Now she was going to die here alone, condemned to death by the same money that had given her everything she wanted.

I just want to live.

Remember when you nearly lost Mitch? she asked herself. *He believed that tape recording. If you hadn't managed to prove to him that it was a forgery, you'd have lost him for good.*

She remembered the sweetness of that reconciliation, when they'd lain together in each other's arms in the little Marais flat, laughing with joy and relief. He'd admitted that he'd already been on the point of returning to her. That he simply couldn't live without her. 'I realised I'd rather be with you as your plaything than not at all,' he'd said. They'd giggled over his melodramatic demand to her father: *How much will you pay me to divorce your daughter*? And then they'd begun to wonder . . . and been tickled by the idea of Charles de Lisle giving Mitch the funds to start the business that would make him rich. So they'd cooked up a plan that would give them revenge on everyone: taking away Charles's money and Allegra's prized possession – Colette's. They'd divorced, so that it would look absolutely convincing and so that they could marry again, properly. 'You are going to have an amazing second wedding,' Mitch had told her. 'Forget three people in a cottage in Scotland. We're gonna do it properly next time.'

Hot tears escaped from Romily's eyes and soaked her blindfold. She sniffed. *I want that wedding. I want to get married.* She passed the long hours, dreaming up every detail of how it would be, trying to fight against the conviction growing in her heart that she would never see Mitch again.

It must be night again. She could smell food cooking. Eventually someone came, untied her and pushed something into her hand. It was greasy and hot. She tasted it: a samosa full of spicy meat and vegetables. The oil coated her lips but it was delicious and she ate it quickly. A glass of water was given to her and she gulped that down eagerly. There was nothing else. Her hands were retied.

She lay back and tried not to think about how much she wanted more food: a crisp salad with fragrant lemon and thyme chicken, new potatoes in butter . . . that would be perfect.

If I get out of here, I'm going to eat as much as I can! she told herself. *I want to feel alive.*

After another hour or so, she was hauled to her feet and taken for another bathroom break. As she went out of the room where she was kept, she listened out eagerly but heard nothing. She knew, though, by some other sense, that people were watching her as she walked past and this frightened her horribly. Why were they staring? She felt like a prisoner being taken from the dock to be hanged.

She spent as long as she dared on the loo before the door was rapped upon and then opened, and she was pulled out while still fumbling with her jeans.

Then she heard it again, more crazed shouting, worse than ever this time. She could make out distinct words. 'Not waiting any longer . . .' '. . . we mean business . . .' '. . . tell them thirty more minutes then she's dead' . . .

Her skin crawled with horror. *Thirty minutes? Do I have only thirty minutes to live?*

But why hadn't her parents paid up? She had been certain they would. She'd thought that she would die not because of lack of money but because she knew too much about her kidnappers and their plans. She already knew they planned to travel to South America with their new riches, and vanish there into a life of secret luxury.

Then heavy footsteps came rushing towards her and she was pulled off the sofa and thrown to the ground.

'Where's your money?' hissed a voice in her ear.

'Carlo? Is that you?' she asked, trying to make her voice sound strong. She ignored the pain where she'd hit the hard concrete of the floor.

'Doesn't matter who the fuck I am, you whore!' The man pulled her up on to her knees. 'Your daddy isn't going to pay. So here's what we'll do. Do you have money at home?'

'Yes,' she stammered. *Is this in my interests or not? What should I tell them?* 'But in my bag is a card. You can use it to take out cash. I'll give you the number. You can buy things with it as well.'

She gasped as she took a heavy blow round the head that left her ears ringing.

'How stupid do you think we are?' jeered the voice. 'Your account might be watched. And we didn't risk all this for five hundred stinking Euros or whatever your cash machine will give us. We want cash . . . jewels. Have you got that?'

'Yes, yes,' she said, fighting the dizziness that was overwhelming her. 'Cash – about ten thousand Euros and five thousand pounds. And the jewellery I'm travelling with, along with my Rolex – that must come to over one hundred thousand Euros.'

There was a pause and then another voice said in a scornful tone, 'All this for a hundred thousand Euros, Carlo? This is a fucking disaster.'

'Fuck you!' roared Carlo. 'We're not going to get the twenty million. They would have given it to us by now.'

Just then, a phone rang. Someone answered it hastily, speaking in a language Romily didn't understand. Then they said, 'Call the parents. They have the money. Call them now, they want to pay.'

Romily didn't know whether this was good news or bad. She carried on kneeling, her head bowed, trying to keep quiet and not be noticed.

Carlo strode away, not bothering to close the door behind him. She heard him growl in French but couldn't make out what was said. Then he returned, marching up to her. He pulled off her blindfold and she was staring up into his face, the face she had once trusted implicitly.

'Hah!' he sneered. 'Seems you're worth something after all. Mummy and Daddy have found our twenty million. They're following the delivery instructions right now. If the drop is made successfully, our courier will call us. If the drop is a trap, he won't. Either way, we'll know in twenty minutes.'

Romily closed her eyes. Blindness seemed preferable to seeing that contemptuous face in front of her.

Twenty minutes. She began to send last thoughts out to everyone: her parents, friends, brother, and Mitch. *I'm so sorry, darling. I wish this hadn't happened. We were going to be so happy. I'll always love you . . . always.*

She thought of her death. *Will it hurt? Will it be quick? I hope it's quick. I don't want pain.* She began to feel faint but steeled herself. *I can stand it They mustn't see I'm scared.*

Carlo came close to her. She could feel his body heat radiating through his clothes; smell the bitter cumin-flavoured tang of his sweat. It repelled her. She turned her head and opened her eyes to look at him, hoping that with her gaze she was reminding him that she was a woman he knew, a human being, and she asked him with her eyes how he could contemplate killing her for money.

He stared back but his own eyes were cold and full of hatred. It was as though he didn't really see her at all.

Then he pulled a gun out of his pocket and pushed the barrel against her head, the cold dark O of the barrel pressing into her temple. In the other hand, he held his telephone. 'Five more minutes,' he said in a harsh whisper. 'Five more minutes for you.'

I will be strong, she told herself. *I won't let them see that I'm afraid, or that I want to live.* She stiffened her spine and straightened her shoulders.

'It will be my pleasure,' Carlo said, 'to rid the world of another parasite like you.'

She breathed out slowly and refused to speak, sensing that in the room there was fear and dread to balance out Carlo's rage-fuelled bloodlust. Someone watching did not like what was going on at all. *Help me,* she prayed.

'Carlo, do we have to kill her?' It was Rocco, sounding calm and reasonable. 'Worse for us if we are caught. If we get the money, let's just leave her here.'

'She knows us!' snarled Carlo.

'They'll already guess I'm involved. And that idiot Marco is bound to blab at some point. Everyone will know we did it. But once we're away, they won't be able to find us.'

'I'm going to find Marco and kill him, believe me,' Carlo

said. 'And if all that ties me to this is you . . . well . . .'

The gun was taken from her head and the next moment there was a loud explosion. A heavy body hit the ground next to her. Romily opened her eyes and looked down. It was Rocco, blasted through the chest, a huge hole in his back, his face twisted. Blood was rushing from the gaping wound, streaming out all over floor.

'Now you,' Carlo said brusquely. The barrel came back to her head. He cocked the gun. She closed her eyes and waited for the explosion. And then it came.

The room erupted in a tornado of sound. She collapsed to the floor, into the warm stickiness of Rocco's blood. *Am I dead? What's happening*? she thought, confused. She'd always imagined that when she was shot, the world would turn off instantly, like a radio. But the noise, the raging gunfire, was going on forever. On and on: blasting, shouting, thudding. And then . . . quiet fell. A couple of muted voices was all she could hear.

Footsteps came running across the concrete floor beside her. Then she was being lifted up in strong arms and held close to a warm body.

'Romily! Romily, it's me. Are you OK? Are you OK, baby?'

She opened her eyes to the most beautiful sight she'd ever seen. Mitch was looking down into her eyes, his face grey with anxiety, his chin covered in stubble. *If that's how he looks, I must look terrible!* she thought. And then she laughed at the stupidity of the thought, though it came out a weak, small sound.

'My darling,' she said in a croak. 'You came for me. I'm not dead.'

'But you're hurt. You're covered in blood!' he said in panic.

'Not mine. Rocco's.' She looked to where her guard lay on the warehouse floor. She could see Carlo's body a few feet away, also blood-soaked from many wounds.

'You're safe, my love.' Mitch pulled her close to him and wrapped his arms around her, sinking his face into her hair. 'I've found you. I'm never letting you go again.'

Malik answered the telephone call, then he came dashing out to find Allegra and Imogen, who were waiting in the sitting room, both tense and nervous. They'd seen Mitch and his boys leave in three huge Land Rovers and had known that they were going to get Romily.

'They've got her! She's fine, she's fine. They found her in a warehouse in Brixton.'

Imogen and Allegra hugged each other, laughing and crying at the same time.

'Can we see her?' asked Allegra, when they were able to speak again.

Malik shook his head. 'I don't think so. It's time for clean-up.'

'Clean-up? What's that?'

'After an operation like this, we have to clean-up, of course. The police were not involved and we've got to make sure that there's no reason for them to be. There are . . . things to be disposed of. I think you girls should go home and try to act as normal as possible.'

Allegra looked at Imogen and they exchanged glances. Normal? How could they feel normal after all this? They'd been in Mitch's house for almost twenty-four hours, waiting, wound up to a fever pitch. Life couldn't just go back to normal, could it?

'What about Adam?' asked Allegra. He was still lying sedated in the spare room.

'He's part of the clean-up, I'm afraid. We're going to get him to a surgeon tonight or tomorrow, to get his leg seen to. Then he'll have it explained to him that it's in his best interests to forget he was ever here or ever shot.'

'Will you tell me where he is? I want to be with him if I can,' Allegra said anxiously.

Malik looked at her sympathetically. 'Maybe I can stretch the rules, just this once.'

'It's the least you can do,' she replied sardonically, 'considering you shot him for absolutely no reason.'

Malik shrugged. 'I was protecting you, in case you've forgotten.' He looked over at Imogen. 'How about you? Any requests?'

She smiled back and shook her head. 'Actually I can't wait to get home. But please – when you see her, give Romily our love. Tell her we want to see her as soon as she's up to it.'

'You bet. It'll be my pleasure.' Malik looked at his watch. 'Now if you'll excuse me, ladies, I need to get clean-up underway. And that includes getting a glazier out to your house, Allegra, to deal with the bullet hole in the front window, so if you wouldn't mind warning your housekeeper – and making sure she's going to be discreet – that would be great.'

Allegra raised her eyebrows. 'I'm impressed.'

'It's the little details that count. See you guys soon, I hope. And give Alex a block to chew from me.' Malik grinned at Imogen, and headed out of the room.

Chapter 67

Two Weeks Later

Allegra walked along the hall to the impressive rosewood and brass double doors of the Davies Penthouse in Claridge's. She buzzed and a moment later a uniformed butler opened the door.

She tucked her Hermès Kelly bag back under her elbow and smiled. 'Lady Allegra McCorquodale here for Miss de Lisle.'

The butler stood aside to let her in and then led her through a magnificent black-and-white hallway to an oak-floored sitting room with French doors leading on to a terrace. The room was a subtle mix of Claridge's signature Art Deco look and a classic Victorian feel.

The butler announced her in a ringing voice, and then withdrew.

Romily was standing at the black-framed window, looking out on to the terrace. When she heard the announcement of Allegra's arrival, she turned round. She was wearing a beautiful navy blue dress with white piping around its square neckline. It was body-hugging, emphasising her waist and hips, and she wore white strappy sandals in a thirties style, round-toed with four slender white buckled straps across each foot. Her dark hair was freshly styled into a choppy bob, a fringe ruffled across her forehead, and she wore pearl and diamond earrings that glowed richly against her colouring.

Allegra stood very still. For a long minute, they stared at each other. Then Romily held out her arms and, after a moment's hesitation, Allegra went over to her and they embraced.

They pulled back and looked at each other. Then Romily said slowly, 'Imogen isn't coming for another thirty minutes. I thought perhaps we needed to have some time alone first.'

'Yes. I think that's a good idea.' Allegra smoothed down her Lagerfeld pencil skirt, moved gracefully to an armchair and sat down.

'Wilson will bring us some tea,' Romily said, taking her place on a small carved sofa next to her. She looked at Allegra and smiled. 'How are you?'

'How are *you*?' Allegra rejoined. 'After all, you were the one who was kidnapped!'

'I'm remarkably well,' Romily said. 'I feel safe here, right at the top of Claridge's. I didn't want to go back to my flat after what happened, and I'm just not very keen on Mitch's place.'

'I know what you mean,' Allegra said jokily. 'It's like being stuck inside a leather chess set. And all those down-lighters give me a headache.'

'I'm sure we'll find something much nicer,' Romily said. 'I shouldn't have let him go and pick something on his own.'

There was a brief silence. Allegra looked down at the carpet.

Romily began speaking in a gentle voice. 'First, Allegra, I want to say thank you – because you tried to help Mitch find me.'

'My help was kind of useless – he would have found you with or without me,' she said frankly. 'It was Imogen who provided the real breakthrough when she remembered Marco.'

'Maybe. But you tried to help. On the very day we bought you out and destroyed your dream.'

'Mmm.' Allegra shifted uncomfortably. At last she said, 'Some things are more important than business.'

Romily leant forward, looking earnest. 'But for years I've been tormented by a question. I've asked myself over and over again – why did Allegra betray me? Why did she want to destroy my marriage? Try as I might, I could never think of an answer. After all, we had promised to stick together, no matter what.'

The butler came in with the tea: he placed the pot, teacups, milk jug and sugar carefully on the table between them, followed by the large cake-stand, covered in sandwiches, scones and tiny, perfect cakes.

When he'd gone, Allegra looked up. Her expression was solemn, almost nervous. 'I've never told anyone about this,' she said at last, in a small voice. 'But you remember when I came to stay with you in Paris, before I went to Oxford?'

Romily nodded. 'Of course. It was the last time we were really friends.'

Allegra nodded too. 'And remember that man . . . Monsieur Antoine? He was a friend of your parents.'

Romily frowned and then said, 'Oh, of course. That fat little man. Yes, I remember him. He took you to the Musée d'Orsay.'

'He didn't just take me to the museum,' Allegra said slowly. 'He took me back to his apartment and . . . he forced me to have sex with him.'

Romily gasped, her hands flying to her mouth, her eyes horrified. 'Oh, Allegra, no! No!'

She nodded, her face grim. 'Yes.'

'Why didn't you tell me? You said nothing!'

Allegra looked away. 'I couldn't. You see, he was very clever. He manipulated things in such a way that I felt completely to blame. I couldn't tell *anyone*. I never have until now.' She looked back, her expression tortured now. 'But I blamed you for it – because you were ill and couldn't come to the damn' museum! I know it was stupid and unfair, but I transferred all the anger I felt towards that horrible little man on to you. I couldn't bear to think about you, or Paris. It all came to mean the same to me: that terrible afternoon.'

Romily closed her eyes. When she opened them, they glittered with tears. 'That's how all this started? Oh my God, Allegra – that's too sad. Too awful. You were raped!' She began to sob. 'And I never noticed, I never even knew! You were our guest and we let that happen to you. No wonder you hated me.'

Allegra reached out a hand to her, her own eyes stinging with tears. 'No. It wasn't your fault either. It was that dreadful man's. I made a mistake. I should have told you – and I should never have blamed you.'

'And that's why you let yourself be used to record our conversation . . .' Romily said wonderingly.

Allegra looked shame-faced. She ran her fingers through her blonde hair. 'I should never have done that. But your mother rang me . . . said you'd been charmed by a hopeless gigolo who was only after your money. Of course, I knew you were madly in love but I let myself be persuaded that I was doing the right thing by taping our tea at the Ritz. And at the end of the conversation, I felt sure that I couldn't really cause any trouble – you were so obviously utterly sincere in your love and you believed in Mitch completely. You convinced me.' She looked at her friend beseechingly. 'I had no idea what your parents would do to the recording. Imogen told me how they manipulated it. I'm sorry, Romily, I really am.'

Romily stared at her for a moment, then her eyes softened and she laughed. 'You know, it's so silly. Their plan backfired – Mitch and I grew stronger than ever. Perhaps we wouldn't even be together now if it hadn't been for that. So maybe I should thank you.' She poured out the tea. 'What is that saying? To understand all is to forgive all. It seems it's true. Now we both know everything, we no longer need to hate each other. And . . . I'm sorry about Xander too.'

'Thank you,' Allegra said quietly.

The doorbell buzzed again and a few moments later the butler announced, 'Miss Imogen Heath.'

Imogen came in, looking apprehensive, but when she saw the other two sitting by the window, she smiled, evidently relieved.

'Romily!' She ran over to her friend and threw her arms around her. 'I'm so glad you're safe. What a horrible, horrible ordeal you've been through.'

Romily hugged her back. 'It wasn't great,' she admitted. As Imogen kissed Allegra hello and settled herself down, Romily poured her out some tea and said, 'The strange thing is that now it's happened, I feel wonderfully, marvellously free. All my life, this threat has been hanging over me, hemming me in, making me afraid. Now I feel as though I've faced it down, and it's gone. Of course, I know it hasn't completely. There's no reason why someone won't try again at some point – but now I've actually been there and come back, I know I can survive something like this. It's made me feel very strong. And I've learnt how little actually matters in the world. Love, family and friends' – she looked at the other two girls, smiling – 'those are the only things you care about in the end, it turns out.' She shot them a mischievous look as she helped herself from the cake-stand. 'Along with Claridge's apple scones, of course.'

'So, everything is all right?' Imogen said tentatively, looking between the two of them.

Allegra nodded. 'Yes. Some old misunderstandings have been cleared up.'

'That's fantastic,' Imogen declared, obviously relieved, and leant forward eagerly. 'That's made my appetite come right back. I'm afraid I have to claim this wonderful-looking éclair immediately.'

They talked on for two hours, just as they had when they were schoolgirls, chattering rapidly, flying from one subject to the next, catching up on all the news they had missed.

'What's happened to Adam, Allegra?' Imogen asked, licking the cream from her fingers. 'Do you know?'

She nodded. 'He's gone home to recuperate. I think we both need some time apart to think things over. But after that . . . who knows? I still think there's a chance for us. I do love him, despite everything.'

Romily looked sombre. 'I feel sorry for him. He lost his sister in those awful circumstances.'

'In a way, that links us together. We've both suffered by Sophie's death. And we both know what it's like to lose a sibling in a stupid, wasteful way. We've both been through it.' She gazed down at the table for a moment and then looked up again, her face strangely happy. 'He brought me back to life, taught me how to love. I'll always be grateful to him for that, no matter what.'

They were all quiet for a moment, remembering Sophie Harcourt. Those days were so far away they could finally look back and acknowledge all that had happened. It seemed far more serious and solemn now than it had at the time: that poor girl had died while they had gone on, to learn all about life and love and the world. Sophie had never had that chance.

Romily broke the gravity of the mood. 'Imogen,' she cried, 'where is your little boy? I'm dying to meet him.'

'He's at home with the nanny. You must come and meet him soon.'

'I'd love to,' she replied warmly. 'And if I don't meet him before, then I hope you'll bring him to the wedding.'

The other two looked at her questioningly. Romily laughed and held out her hand to display a large baguette white diamond with two yellow diamonds flanking it. 'I'm getting married, next month, here in London. Mitch and I always thought we'd go crazy when we did it again, but after what's happened we want a quiet affair, with just family and close friends. So I hope you'll come.'

Imogen shot a glance at Allegra. Reconciling with Romily was one thing – but with Mitch? The man who'd stolen the things she cared most for in the world? Maybe that was too much to ask. But Allegra said in a heartfelt tone, 'I'd love to come, Rom. Wouldn't miss it.'

'Can you imagine?' she laughed. 'Married twice before I'm thirty! I guess it's not so bad if it's to the same man.' She turned to Imogen then. 'How about you, Midge? I hope you're coming to the wedding.' She added in a naughty voice, 'Malik mentioned he'd like to see you again. He's going to be Mitch's best man, by the way.'

Imogen blushed scarlet, then laughed. 'I'd better find something extra special to wear then,' she said.

'I've got something you can borrow, if you like,' Romily offered. 'We'll have a look through the wardrobe in a minute.'

'We're going to look at Romily's clothes?' Allegra cried. 'Now I know everything's back to how it was!'

They all looked at each other, laughing. The Midnight Girls were reunited at last.

Chapter 68

The Lechlade Private Hospital
London
Three weeks later

'You'd better come quickly,' the voice had said. 'He's asking for you. And I think time may be short.'

So Allegra had gone at once to the private hospital in Kensington and been taken to the white room where David lay in bed, connected to all manner of flashing machines and drips.

As they walked down the quiet corridors, she said, 'I had no idea . . . no idea at all.'

The nurse looked at her sympathetically. 'He refused to tell anyone,' she said. 'We urged him to, but he wouldn't. He used our support nurses here a little, but that was all. I don't think he realised how quickly time would run out for him. His brain tumour was only diagnosed eight months ago.'

'There was nothing to be done?'

The nurse shook her head. 'It's inoperable. The only thing that might have helped was intensive radiotherapy, and he refused that. And in some ways it was a good thing – intensive radiotherapy is only recommended for someone who is fit and in good health, or it can make things much worse for the patient. David knew that with prolonged radiotherapy he'd spend the rest of his life in hospital feeling very ill, and that it was unlikely to do much to change his situation, so he had a short course to slow the growth, and now we're concentrating on palliative care. All we've been able to do is make him more comfortable.'

Allegra's eyes filled with tears. 'I can't believe it. Not David.' She turned to the nurse. 'He doesn't want to see anyone else? I could call my father.'

The nurse shook her head. 'No. Only a few friends. He specified no family – except for you.'

David was hooked up to a drip and had a drain in his head to remove excess fluid that might cause pain and swelling. Allegra bit her lip when she saw him, even though the nurse had assured her he was comfortable.

'Hello, David.' She went over to him, sat next to the bed and took his hand in hers. 'It's Allegra.'

His face had changed in only the few weeks since she'd seen him last: it was very pale and the cheeks were sunken. When he heard her voice, his eyelids flickered and he let out a long, low sigh. Then, slowly, he opened his eyes and moved his head just a little so he could see her.

''Legra,' he said in a low whisper, the last syllable of her name coming out like a breath.

'Yes, David, I'm here.' Tears blurred her vision. 'Why didn't you tell me you were ill?'

He raised his eyebrows a little. 'So . . . *boring*. Illness. Nothing to be done anyway.'

'But I could have been with you, helped you . . .' A tear spilt out and ran down her cheek. 'I hate to think of you going through this alone.'

'No different from my life. Always alone, anyway.' He sucked in a breath and let it go in a rasping exhalation. 'Don't cry. Really . . . no point.'

She wiped away her tears and sniffed. 'You are a stubborn

old thing, aren't you? You won't let people love you.'

He made a strange huffing sound and she realised he was laughing. 'True! Love makes life so . . . difficult. I learnt that a long time ago.' He looked at her again. His usually fierce blue eyes looked tired and watery. 'I asked you here . . . because I need to say . . .'

'You don't have to say anything,' she said, squeezing his hand gently. 'I understand.'

'No . . . no . . .' He frowned. 'Must say it. 'Legra, I'm sorry. You didn't take any money, I know that now. I don't understand why I thought you did.'

'It was your illness,' she said. 'It's perfectly clear. You weren't yourself. I should have spotted it ages ago. You don't have to apologise.'

'I . . . want to,' he said firmly. 'Not just the money. I sold the clubs . . . took them away from you. I didn't want you to have them – I don't know why.'

'They were yours.' She put out a hand and stroked his hair. 'You could do what you liked with them. I always knew that they were yours.'

He blinked at her slowly and tried to smile. 'So sweet of you. I know you loved them. Should have left them for you . . . don't know why I didn't.' His eyes clouded. 'She paid me a lot of money. Lots and lots. But I did something else . . .'

She waited.

'I . . . I . . .' He closed his eyes and breathed another long, slow breath, as if gathering his strength. Then he opened them and gazed at her, a deep melancholy on his face. 'I made a new will. I cut you out. Too late to change it . . .' He scrabbled for her with his other hand, putting it on top of hers. 'I'm so sorry. You worked so hard. You'll have nothing to show for it.'

'That's all right, David.'

'Please . . . don't hate me for it.' His eyes were pleading.

'I don't hate you.' She smiled at him. 'You silly thing, I love you! I don't care about the money, I never have. I'd spend all I have in an instant to make you better.'

He closed his eyes and a tear leaked out from under his lids. 'I'm a . . . stupid old man. You were my pearl. Best thing in my life. So sorry . . .'

'Shhh. Don't give it another thought,' she soothed. 'It doesn't matter a bit. Just sleep and get your strength back.'

He sighed, and slipped into sleep as though his confession had sapped his strength. She sat with him, watching his chest rise and fall and his lips tremble with the effort of drawing in breath. All she could do now was be with him, and she did that right through the night until the day was breaking and, slowly, his breaths became longer and shallower until they rattled in his throat. The pauses between them lengthened and then, as light broke over London, he took his final breath, releasing it with a long, childlike sigh and letting himself go with it.

Allegra whispered, 'Goodbye, David.' Then she bent over his hand, still clasped in hers, and wept.

It was a grey wintery morning as she walked slowly down the hospital steps. People were bustling around, hurrying on their way to offices, meetings, appointments, or wherever their busy lives were taking them.

Allegra moved among them, tall, calm and pale, carrying her sorrow with a kind of grace that made passers-by look at her as they walked past. Who was that beautiful girl in the long black coat who looked like a queen in a solemn procession?

Allegra didn't notice them. Instead, she walked on, not really knowing where she was going. It was as though she'd only just realised what had happened to her in the last few weeks: she had lost her work, her lover, and now her uncle and mentor, the man who'd taught her so much.

And the money?

David had got one hundred million for the clubs, money he would never have made if she hadn't recreated Colette's and added Oscar's and Astor House to his portfolio. Now, not only was she penniless but she had no job. She'd gone into the office to clear her desk before Christmas, and hadn't been back since.

That doesn't matter, she thought. *I'll start all over again. I'll have to work a while to make some money, get some capital together, but I can do it. This will be my greatest challenge yet.*

Watch out, world. Here I come.

She walked to a park bench in a city square. A man was waiting for her there, bundled up in a long dark coat. He stood when he saw her, rising with difficulty on a weakened leg. He held out his arms and she went into them, shaking her head.

'Oh, Adam, he's gone,' she sobbed.

He kissed the top of her head and hugged her as though he would never let her go.

Chapter 69

Farm Street Church in Mayfair echoed to the sounds of the choir as they sang the triumphant recessional, a sparkling piece of Handel. The bride and groom were leaving the church, radiant with happiness.

As Romily went past her two friends, she winked at them both.

'Thank God she didn't make us bridesmaids,' Allegra murmured as they turned to watch the happy couple leave.

'She knows us too well to put us in matching purple satin,' Imogen replied with a grin. She bounced Alex on her knee. He chortled and said, 'Da, da, da!' 'See? Alex agrees.' Imogen sighed with pleasure. 'She looked beautiful, didn't she?'

'Amazing dress.'

'Thirteen fittings! It's Valentino couture. That lace is incredible.'

'I expected no less. Come on. Let's take Little Lord Fauntleroy there and get to Claridge's for the reception.'

The bride and groom had already left in a cream Daimler to be driven the short distance to the hotel. The rest of the congregation walked: a stylish procession of men in morning coats and dark striped trousers and women in the most beautiful couture, silk heels and feathered fascinators.

Allegra was in Chanel: a classic two-piece suit in hot pink, with a daringly short skirt that showed off her long legs. She wore Fendi heels in pale grey suede, with grosgrain ribbon trim, and carried a Marc Jacobs quilted shoulder purse in hot pink satin for a touch of rock and roll. Her hair was up in a loose pony-tail and she'd used an antique Victorian cameo brooch in black and white as a hair pin.

Imogen had chosen a beautiful silk jersey dress by Temperley, its black flutter-cap sleeves and skirt offset by a white bodice in the same fabric, ruched around the breasts with a silken white flower in the middle, with a draped panel of white silk down the front. She wore it with a pair of Jimmy Choo slingbacks in champagne-pink satin and carried a white quilted Chanel bag.

'My perfect accessory, of course, is a pushchair,' she said brightly as she pushed Alex through the Mayfair streets in his apple-green Bugaboo. It was a beautiful spring day and the blossom was out.

'It suits you wonderfully.'

'Well, the nanny's coming to take him away in an hour or so, and then I'll be able to let my hair down. We're going to Colette's later, aren't we?'

Allegra nodded. 'The party continues there after the reception.'

'You will come, won't you?' Imogen said, giving her friend an anxious look.

'Yes. It will be hard – but I'll go.'

The reception was small by the standards that might be expected of a rich and well-connected bride like Romily: two hundred people had come to see the happy couple wed and then toast them with glasses of the bride's favourite vintage Bollinger.

The wedding breakfast was elegant and delicious, the speeches all the more moving for the fact that the couple were marrying for the second time. Very few of the guests knew of Romily's ordeal, but they could see how overwhelmed with joy she was, along with her family, who appeared delighted with their son-in-law.

'I think Mitch has won the de Lisles over,' Allegra murmured as she watched Athina de Lisle fawning over him.

'Do you think it's his incredible success as a businessman or his brave rescue of Romily that did it?' Imogen asked with an ironic laugh.

'Ooh, that's a tough one. But, I must say, he looks pretty irresistible in that suit. Savile Row's finest, Romily told me.' Allegra gave Imogen a sideways look. 'And Malik has scrubbed up pretty well too.'

Imogen flushed and glanced away.

'Just teasing. I bet he's nervous about his best man's speech. He'd better not make any jokes about Mitch's underworld connections or he might be sleeping with the fishes by nightfall!' Allegra laughed at her own joke.

Imogen rolled her eyes. 'Some things it's better not to joke about. I'm sure there are a couple of distinctly *Sopranos*-style blokes hanging around.' She let one of the waiting staff refill her glass with champagne. 'And who is that funny-looking guy over there with the goatee?'

'Oh, that's Vincente, Romily's one-time boyfriend. Bet he's pissed off he's lost her to Mitch.'

Imogen laughed. 'It's a bit late now to put up a fight!'

After the meal, the toasts and the speeches, most of the guests headed back to their own homes or hotels, or to fly off somewhere glamorous. A select forty went to Colette's, to carry on celebrating in the most magical nightclub in the world.

It was a strange feeling for Allegra as she went down the staircase into the place that was so familiar. She couldn't help thinking of David almost constantly: his presence was still so strongly felt in the club. Mitch had kept it exactly as it had been, so David's exquisite taste was still in evidence everywhere. The staff were delighted to see her, each one coming up to greet her and ask how she was. She was pleased to see that no one had been laid off and that they were all happy with the new management.

'Some things have changed,' Freda said frankly when Allegra went into the ladies to see her. 'There are a lot more girls who are no better than they ought to be – teenage things from Russia and wherever. And some nights there are queues outside to get in! Can you imagine? Queues outside Colette's, like some second-rate cocktail place. I'm no fan of the new music either. Too bumpy and spiky. They don't play my favourite Sinatra numbers any more.'

'I'm just glad you're still here,' Allegra said, giving her a hug. 'I can't imagine Colette's without you.'

When she came out of the ladies, she found Mitch waiting for her outside in the corridor.

'Ah, Allegra, I've been looking for you. Would you mind coming with me, please?'

She raised her eyebrows. 'Of course. It's been a beautiful day, Mitch.'

'It has, hasn't it?' He grinned at her. 'This way.'

He led her to the private dining room. Inside, a bottle of champagne was chilling on the table in a solid silver ice bucket. Romily and Imogen were already waiting there, Imogen looking as surprised as Allegra felt. Romily had changed from her wedding dress into a stunning Marchesa coffee-cream lace dress that set off her smooth brown shoulders beautifully.

'Please, do sit down.' Mitch gestured to the chairs. 'This won't take long, but I did want us all to be able to talk in private.'

They took their places and waited for him to enlighten them. He reached into his jacket pocket and brought out a long, thick white envelope, put it on the table then slid it across in Allegra's direction. 'This is for you.'

She stared at it, but didn't touch it. 'What is it?'

Mitch looked a little shamefaced. Romily touched his arm, encouraging him to continue. He said gruffly, 'I'm aware that mistakes have been made in the past. Misunderstandings led to things happening that maybe should not have happened. You lost your stake in these clubs through no fault of your own, and I want to show my appreciation for the help you offered me when things were tough. I also now know that your uncle's state of mind contributed to his decision to sell. So I want to give back some of what was taken from you. I'd like to return a third share in the David McCorquodale Group to you.'

Allegra stared at the envelope for a moment, then looked up at Mitch with a big smile. 'That's very kind of you, Mitch, but no.'

'No?' He looked astonished and glanced over at Romily.

Her expression was concerned. 'Why not?' she asked.

'I can't take this as a gift. I just can't.' Allegra shook her head. 'It wouldn't be right, no matter how much both of us might want it. The only way I can consider this is if I buy it from you.'

'Buy it?' Mitch sounded dubious. They all knew that Allegra had been cut out of her uncle's will. He'd left the bulk of his fortune – the proceeds from the sale of his clubs, plus his properties and furniture – in trust for baby Alex.

'How can you do that?' Imogen said. Alex's money could not be touched, so they couldn't possibly use it, no matter how tempting it was.

Allegra looked at them each in turn and smiled. 'Because David forgot to cut Xander out of his will. He left money to

Xander's estate and heirs. And Xander's heir is . . . me.' She laughed at the looks on all their faces. 'He didn't know he was going to have a baby or he would certainly have changed his will, but as it is, I don't think Alex is going to miss it from his fortune. So I'd like to use that money to buy back in.' Her expression became serious. 'With certain conditions, of course.'

'What are those?' Mitch said, raising his eyebrows.

'I want a share of Oscar's and Astor House only, and I want to control and run those two places myself – and have Imogen on my team as my in-house lawyer. If she wants to join me.'

Imogen looked delighted. 'You bet I want to! I wouldn't miss it for anything!'

'Sounds very reasonable.' Mitch frowned. 'But you don't want a share of Colette's?'

Allegra shook her head. 'No. It's time to leave Colette's. This was David's baby, not mine, and I can't imagine going on here without him. I'm prepared to let it go. After tonight, I don't think I'll ever come back here.' She looked melancholy for a moment, then her eyes flashed. 'But I want to put my heart and soul into the clubs *I* created. I know I can make them special.'

'I believe you,' Mitch said softly. 'And I'd be crazy to pass up the chance to have your talent on board.'

'Then perhaps,' Romily said thoughtfully, '*I* will take on Colette's. I think I would enjoy running this place.'

'Oh my God!' Mitch laughed and threw up his hands. 'I'm gonna be overwhelmed by you three! But you know what? I might just like it.' He reached for the champagne. 'Do we have a deal? We'll thrash out the details in due course, but I'm more than happy with the idea.'

An expression of relief and happiness transformed Allegra's face. 'Are you sure?' Mitch nodded. 'That's fantastic.'

'I consider myself the lucky one,' he said. 'The more I've seen of what you've achieved with Oscar's, the more talented I think you are. I'm delighted you'll be joining me. I've got plenty of other ideas for where to use you as well.'

'One step at a time,' laughed Allegra.

'One step at a time,' Romily said, still looking radiant. 'But together all the way.'

Mitch popped the cork of the champagne, filled each flute with sparkling liquid, then they raised their glasses to each other.

'Here's to the success that's waiting for us in the future,' he said.

'Here's to all of us,' Imogen said. 'Health, happiness . . .'

'Family and friends,' said Romily.

Allegra smiled. 'Forgiveness and understanding.'

They all drank to their toasts.

'Mmm,' Romily said thoughtfully. 'I wonder what the woman who runs Colette's ought to wear. Vintage Dior? Pucci? Something a little bit seventies – Diane von Furstenberg, perhaps . . .'

'Honey, are we talking about clothes again?' Mitch grinned and took his wife's hand in his.

She smiled back at him, then looked round at the circle of bright faces. 'We've all had our tragedies. I think our greatest triumphs are yet to come.'

'You bet they are,' Allegra said, with feeling. 'I'm only just getting started.'

Imogen smiled at her friends. 'It's exciting! So full of possibilities. Let's toast the Midnight Girls – more midnight than ever now, with the clubs. Now we're together again, we can't fail.'

They lifted their glasses and clinked once more. Allegra lifted her eyes to the oil sketch of her uncle that hung on the wall, and smiled, sending him a silent message of thanks.

Acknowledgements

Thank you to everyone at Random House, particularly my editor Emma Rose who worked wonders and gave me terrific encouragement, Kate Elton, Louisa Gibbs, Claire Round, Amelia Harvell, Caroline Sloan and the superb sales team for their support.

Thank you to Lynn Curtis for her brilliant work on the text.

Special thanks to my splendid agent, Lizzy Kremer, who is amazingly patient, unceasingly supportive and very clever, and to wonderful Laura West at David Higham Associates.

Thank you to Emily for helping me with my research – it was hard work, going to exclusive nightclubs, but it simply had to be done.

Thank you to my family for helping so much during the months of writing, and to my friends, especially Fiona and Claire, who were so kind and generous when I needed those precious hours.

ALSO AVAILABLE IN ARROW

Heiresses

Lulu Taylor

They were born to the scent of success. Now they stand to lose it all . . .

Fame, fashion and scandal, the Trevellyan heiresses are the height of success, glamour and style.

But when it comes to . . .

. . . WEALTH: Jemima's indulgent lifestyle knows no limits; Tara's one purpose in life, no matter the sacrifice, is to be financially independent of her family and husband; and Poppy wants to escape its trappings without losing the comfort their family money brings.

. . . LUST: Jemima's obsession relieves the boredom of her marriage; while Tara's seemingly 'perfect' life doesn't allow for such indulgences; and Poppy, spoiled by attention and love throughout her life, has yet to expose herself to the thrill of really living and loving dangerously.

. . . FAMILY: it's all they've ever known, and now the legacy of their parents, a vast and ailing perfume empire, has been left in their trust. But will they be able to turn their passion into profit? And in making a fresh start, can they face their family's past?

ALSO AVAILABLE IN ARROW

The Popularity Rules

Abby McDonald

Rule 1: All's fair in love, war and popularity . . .

Kat Elliott has spent her life rebelling against phony schmoozing – and it's led her nowhere. Just as she's ready to give up her dreams and admit defeat, in steps Lauren Anderville. One-time allies and outcasts at school, Lauren and Kat had been inseparable. Then one year Lauren returned from summer camp, blonde, bubbly and suddenly popular, and Kat was left to face the world alone.

Ten years later, Lauren's back. She wants to make amends by teaching Kat the secret to her success: The Popularity Rules. A decades-old rulebook, its secrets transformed Lauren that fateful summer. And so, tempted by Lauren's promises of glitzy parties and the job she's always dreamed about, Kat reluctantly submits to a total makeover – and finds that life with the in-crowd might have something going for it after all.

But while Lauren has sacrificed everything to get ahead, is Kat really ready to accept that popularity is the only prize that counts?

'A brilliantly written story full of humour, heartbreak and attitude – you'll love it.' *Closer*

'A funny, true-to-life tale about a woman who ditches her laid-back, anti-schmoozing lifestyle for glitzy parties, buzzing contacts and popularity.'
heat

arrow books

ALSO AVAILABLE IN ARROW

Friends, Lovers and Other Indiscretions

Fiona Neill

From the author of *The Secret Life of a Slummy Mummy*

It's 2008 and the credit crunch is starting to bite. Sam and Laura Diamond and their friends are approaching forty and feeling a lot less certain about life. Laura dreams of having a third child, while Sam longs to give up his job and have a vasectomy. Wild child turned corporate lawyer Janey Dart finds herself unexpectedly pregnant and married to a wealthy hedge fund manager who loathes her friends. While Sam's oldest friend, restaurant-owner Jonathan Sleet, can't control his roving eye, so it's no surprise that back on his organic farm in Suffolk his wife Hannah is finding distractions of her own.

When they all come together for a holiday, things get really interesting, because six friends, two decades of tangled fortunes and a complicated secret from the past make for an explosive combination . . .

'Funny, and packed with observations of wince-making accuracy . . . Superb entertainment' *The Times*

'Neill's characters are so cleverly depicted, you feel as if you've met at least one of them before' *Vogue*

arrow books